D1715432

The Byrdwhistle Option

ALTERNATIVE LIFE-STYLE NOVELS
BY ROBERT H. RIMMER

The Rebellion of Yale Marratt
The Harrad Experiment
Proposition Thirty-one
Thursday, My Love
The Premar Experiments
Come Live My Life
Love Me Tomorrow
The Love Explosion

OTHER NOVELS

The Girl from Boston, A Sex-with-Laughter Novel
The Gold Lovers (formerly titled *The Zolotov Affair*),
  Destruction of the Gold Myth

NONFICTION

The Harrad Letters
You and I Searching for Tomorrow
Adventures in Loving
The Love Adventurers
The Harrad Game
Sexmaking on Television

The Byrdwhistle Option

by
Robert H. Rimmer

ℙℬ Prometheus Books
Buffalo, N.Y. 14215

Published 1982 by Prometheus Books
700 East Amherst Street, Buffalo, N.Y. 14215

Copyright 1982 by Robert H. Rimmer
All Rights Reserved

Library of Congress Catalog Number: 82-081709
ISBN: 0-87975-184-3

Printed in the United States of America

PRELUDE

Man is a wanting animal — as soon as one of his needs is satisfied, another appears in its place. The process is unending. It continues from birth to death. Man continuously puts forth effort — works, if you please — to satisfy his needs.

Douglas McGregor
Theory X: The Traditional Way

The Byrdwhistle Option

1

Squeezing efficiently past the full planeload of passengers who had just arrived with him on the late Sunday afternoon U.S. Air flight from Buffalo to Boston, Ronald Coldaxe recovered his suitcases from the baggage carousel and was the first outside the terminal to commandeer a taxi.

He slumped wearily on the back seat and told the driver to take him to the Ritz-Carlton. He would finish his current three-week junket no later than Wednesday afternoon. Probe for dope on potential acquisitions, and then hope, was what it really amounted to. With a little bit of luck, he could gather the facts and a total picture of the Byrdwhistle Corporation and be home in Santa Monica Thursday night—Friday at the latest.

Ronald was convinced that Byrdwhistle was not a good potential for W.I.N. Incorporated. Even though it was one of the largest mail-order businesses in the country and even though he knew that Ralph Thiemost, Chairman of the Board of W.I.N., was intrigued by their supposed high profits, the truth was that Byrdwhistle didn't fit into the W.I.N. management structure, which was largely oriented to heavy industry and electronics.

But, for the moment, Ronald couldn't concentrate on business problems. After one month of no sex—at least one week of which he knew was his own fault—he hoped that his wife, M'mm, would be understanding and that, when he finally got home, they would get to bed quickly, before they got involved in one of their interminable arguments. M'mm never really made an issue of what she called his "incessant pursuit of success and never-ending search for power" unless he complained about what he called her "unsavory, anti-establishment, counterculture friends."

"Grey-haired, sagging-breasted, and pot-bellied radicals are ridiculous," he often told her. "Rebellion was dead and buried in the late nineteen-sixties. Why won't you quit? We're living in the age of narcissism now. No one gives a damn anymore."

At forty-seven, with two teen-age children, Tina, eighteen, and Mitchell, sixteen, Ronald couldn't understand why M'mm wouldn't grow up and stop championing lost causes. If she wasn't trying to get propositions on the California ballot to eliminate the construction of nuclear power plants, she was championing Jerry Brown's latest insanity, like putting an amendment on the Constitution to control federal spending, or worse, she was trying to legalize prostitution, or group marriage, or make it possible for everyone to swim bare-ass on all the beaches in California.

"You knew the kind of person I was twenty years ago when you married me, Ronnie," she responded blithely to his complaints. "I still love you. Occasionally I even like you — especially when you aren't being the prickish vice president in charge of acquisitions of the Washington International Numerator Corporation."

"We changed the name to W.I.N. Incorporated last year," Ronald reminded her sarcastically. He knew damn well she knew it.

Her response was a grim shake of her head. "Don't keep reminding me. Now we're all supposed to be relatives in Ralph Thiemost's family of Winners. In case you are unaware of it, at the Christmas party last year your egotistical chairman of the board reminded me, not too subtly, that I wasn't his idea of the proper wife for a rising middle-aged executive." M'mm shrugged, "Your boss thinks that wives of top brass should be good hostesses and be completely oblivious to economics and politics and that they should give men like Ralph the feeling they might be willing to jump in the sack with them sometime between lunch and dinner if it would advance their husband's career."

Before she left Ronald at the airport three weeks earlier, M'mm told him: "The basic problem with our marriage, Ron, is that years ago we were both certain that we could use our attraction for each other's bodies as a lever. Eventually, somehow, we thought we could reform each other. So far, we haven't succeeded." Then she added, pointedly, "Maybe, since we sleep in the same bed only about twenty-six weeks a year, I should take a lover." She was grinning when she said it, but it made Ronald feel uneasy. "Don't worry, it won't be Ralph Thiemost. I refuse to be acquired by *him,* or you!" She kissed Ronald affectionately, "Maybe on this trip you'll find a winner. Then you can get rid of your losing wife."

If there had been time, Ronald would have tried to convince her that they could reserve a room at the airport motel for an hour or two. It wasn't a good time to be leaving for a three-week business trip, not after their mutual unresolved hostility during the past week had given him eight sexless nights. But M'mm was more pragmatic about screwing than he was. While he was pretty sure that she hadn't wandered from their marital bed, it irked him when she laughed and told him, "Never mind, it'll keep." Her words didn't sound like the hot little sex-pot she had been when they had lived together at Berkeley. Then she told him that women with high I.Q.'s weren't afraid to admit that they enjoyed screwing. Ronald reminded her that she had once even confessed that "to stay calm and keep my head on straight, I need to make love at least once a day," but her chuckling answer as she kissed him goodbye was: "Who said I was calm, or had my head on straight?"

Ronald prided himself on his ability to compartmentalize the various unrelated phases of his life, but sex wasn't one of them. When he arrived in Buffalo on his second week to survey the Sunwarm Corporation, he had closed the doors of his mind temporarily on Big Byte, the Chicago-based corporation he had explored the week before. Big Byte was a natural fit. The specialized computer peripherals that they manufactured tied in closely with the data-processing equipment manufactured by one of the major subsidiaries of W.I.N.

That wasn't true of Sunwarm. This final afternoon, when he had agreed to visit Niagara Falls, which he had never seen, with George and Betsy Winston, the plain truth was that he was feeling so sexually deprived and crawly that he had a difficult time keeping his eyes off Betsy's behind and the curvature of her mound, a fetching green triangle, molded by the tight pantsuit she was wearing. It didn't help, either, that in a very obvious way Betsy was trying to establish a special rapport with him. When the *Maid of the Mist* was making the turn at the bottom of the Horseshoe Falls, George had disappeared somewhere below deck. Betsy had leaned against him beguilingly and told him that, with the spray from the falls dripping down his bald crown, he looked like a reincarnation of one of the early Norse explorers who was discovering Niagara Falls for the first time. And she adored balding men. They looked so powerful!

"I have a bachelor's degree in business administration, you know," she continued, trying to drown him in her brown eyes, which were liquid with loving appreciation of his acumen. "George is a genius in the laboratory and the Sunwarm solar panels wouldn't exist without him, but you and I have much more in common. We know the hard-headed reality of the world."

Ronald was rather certain that she was implying sexual reality as well as their common need for money and power, but for a moment he wished that M'mm was more like Betsy—a woman who had worked shoulder to shoulder with her husband to make the Sunwarm dream possible. A quick vision of himself and Betsy spending the rest of the afternoon in a loving encounter and discussing Sunwarm, from a somewhat different perspective than he had with George, flashed through his mind. But then

George returned and, although he was sure Betsy had implied that she would have been agreeable, it would have been quite insane to get sexually involved. Ridiculous, too, because after twenty years of marriage to M'mm he wasn't at all sure he'd know how to act with another woman.

At lunch in the revolving restaurant in the Skylon Tower on the Canadian side of the falls, he tried to make it clear to both of them that this was not a W.I.N.–Sunwarm honeymoon.

"Ninety-eight percent of our probes eliminate any further hope that a particular company will fit into the W.I.N. family structure," he told them. Ronald accentuated the word *family.* Like Ralph Thiemost, who had built the company from scratch, acquiring over thirty-three subsidiaries within the past ten years, Ronald avoided the dirty word *conglomerate.* Wall Street speculators insisted that even with two-and-a-half billion dollars in annual sales, W.I.N. had been erected on sandy foundations; but top W.I.N. executives ignored the pundits who said, "The W.I.N. family better pray together, or they may not stay together."

"You have to understand," he told the Winstons—he was trying not to notice the deep cleavage that Betsy's blouse and bra gave her breasts, making him want to plunge his hand into the soft, warm fleshy tunnel— "I personally feel that Sunwarm might be a good prospect for the W.I.N. family. Considering the financial growing-pains that you've had, your twenty-million annual sales is an amazing achievement; but whether we proceed any further is up to our Acquisition Committee—and, of course, Ralph Thiemost himself. Ralph is a genius at projecting return on investment. He devised the formulas for diversification that has made W.I.N. so successful.

"Whatever happens," he told George, who was probably well aware that without W.I.N. Sunwarm's future was dubious, "I'm glad Betsy is watching the day-to-day finances for you. If a deal is consummated, be sure to keep her in the front office. Then you'd have time, George, to concentrate on research and development."

Betsy showed her gratitude at the airport with an unnecessary and slightly embarrassing goodbye kiss. "Please make it happen, and come back," she whispered huskily in his ear. George didn't hear her, but Ronald suspected that her words implied a trade-off, involving more than stocks or dollars.

But, despite a potentially interesting sub-rosa merger with the distaff side of Sunwarm, Ronald hadn't told the Winstons the whole truth about the W.I.N. decision-making process. They didn't know that, guided by Ron's final analysis, Ralph Thiemost would have to make a crucial decision. The problem was more than a simple exchange of stock. After a sharp drop in earnings in the past fiscal year, W.I.N. might not be able to afford the additional investment in Sunwarm that Ronald's report would assure Thiemost was absolutely necessary. Sunwarm needed at least five million dollars to increase plant efficiency and to build up a more aggressive group of eastern distributors and contractors to promote the unique Sunwarm holistic operating principles. Even if the Winstons gave their stock to W.I.N., Ronald wasn't convinced that the five million dollars would be a worthwhile investment.

Glancing at his watch as the driver slowly edged through the Sunday evening traffic in the Sumner Tunnel, Ronald confirmed that it was only six-thirty. The coach flight from Buffalo had taken an hour and fifteen minutes. He reminded himself that it wouldn't have been worth the extra cost to travel first class. While he didn't like having to be aware of his expense account, it was closely related to his upward mobility in the W.I.N. structure. Thus it was a compartment in his brain that refused to stay closed.

He had certainly forged ahead at W.I.N., and in his opinion he was at least partially responsible for its spectacular growth. But his office was still a few floors below the top-executive suite on the fifty-fifth floor of the W.I.N. building in Los Angeles. As one of the highest paid executives — $85,000 a year, with bonuses — Ronald felt that in his case Ralph should have waived his coach travel edict. Especially since Ralph Thiemost's "onward and upward" policy was in large part due to the accounting wizardry that had been made possible by more than one profitable acquisition that he, Ronald Coldaxe, had unearthed and guided to completion.

A year earlier, when Ralph had announced at one of his budget meetings that first-class travel for all executives would be eliminated, Ronald had been enthusiastic. Of course he had little choice, Tom Hudnut, the beady-eyed puffy-faced president of W.I.N. was watching to see that all upper-echelon executives were applauding the idea. It was a good publicity move. Too many of the young turks in the 88,000-employee W.I.N. family were living higher on the hog than their capacities warranted. After all, W.I.N. was a publicly owned company. Last year, when earnings suddenly dropped to three percent before taxes — forcing dividends to be cut in half — putting the brakes on expense accounts was one of the numerous economy moves designed to mollify stockholders. It also proved that although Ralph Thiemost was sixty-six years old, he still hadn't lost his grip on the huge enterprise that he had personally created.

But it was interesting that one of the two eight-million-dollar W.I.N. corporate jets had survived the cutbacks. Ronald was well aware that Thiemost and Hudnut never moved their asses more than two hundred and fifty miles in any direction unless they had the comfort and privacy of one of these planes. Thiemost took great pride in showing lesser executives his two private bedrooms, where he, or Tom, could get a few hours sleep on a cross-country junket. And he was especially proud of his own private lavatory.

Of course Ronald could have paid the extra few hundred dollars and traveled first-class on this current three-week trip. It would have been quite simple to juggle his traveling expenses to cover the extra cost. But fifteen years ago, when he had been in the accounting department of W.I.N., Ronald had won his first brownie points by tightening up on every kind of expense account. In addition, he had established, both with his business associates and with M'mm and the kids, that he was not the kind of man who indulged himself—particularly at his own expense. The extra cost of first-class travel would have deprived his family of a few thousand dollars a year—and God knew they were having problems enough living on his fifty-nine-thousand-dollar after-taxes income.

While he was paying the taxicab driver, who had pulled up in front of the Ritz, and the doorman was calling a bellboy to take his suitcase, it occurred to Ronald that he could telephone Elmer Byrd. He had intended to call him from Buffalo but had been diverted by Betsy Winston. According to Elmer's secretary, who had acknowledged his appointment, if he arrived earlier than he anticipated, Elmer could be reached at his apartment on Lewis Wharf on the Boston waterfront. Elmer had written that he would be happy to take him to dinner with H. H. Youman, their executive vice president.

It irritated Ronald that he had been able to dredge up so little information on the privately owned Byrdwhistle Corporation. All he knew was that its two hundred million dollars in annual sales made it one of the largest companies in the mail-order business. He hadn't discovered Byrdwhistle himself, and he suspected that Ralph Thiemost knew more about the company than he had admitted.

Actually, until Thiemost had summoned Ronald into his penthouse office, which was furnished like a French country estate, giving no hint that business was ever transacted within its walls, and handed him a photocopy of the Byrdwhistle operating statement, Ronald had never heard of the company. Thiemost had just returned from a business trip to Europe, and somewhere along the line he had met Thornton Byrd, the seventy-six-year-old founder and majority stockholder of the Byrdwhistle Corporation. Ralph had cruised from Cannes to Southern Portugal in Thornton's yacht, *Love Byrd,* and then flown from Lisbon back to New York and then to California in the W.I.N. jet.

"Thornton is still chairman of the board of the company," Thiemost told him, "but he rarely comes back to their headquarters, which is in a town called Everett, a few miles from downtown Boston. Thorny meanders around the Mediterranean from port to port like a modern Ulysses. The *Love Byrd* is one hundred and twenty feet long, and, at today's prices, must be worth at least ten million dollars. Old Thorny keeps it well stocked with expensive wine and women. Young and old, they wander around the decks barebreasted and practically bare-assed. At night, Thorny always has some female flesh—thirty to forty years younger than his own—to snuggle against. I even heard on good authority that the horny old bastard can get it up, not just once, but twice a night. According to him, Byrdwhistle donates a few hundred thousand dollars a year to some research organization that is determined to discover the key to human aging and produce an ageless human being before the year 2000."

Thiemost chuckled, "You won't believe this, Ron, but Thorny tells everyone that the Byrdwhistle theory is not based on drinking fairy-tale C-98 water from Russia that Irving Wallace wrote about a few years ago, but on happy fucking—at least once a day from age seventeen until you die blissfully in the saddle.

"I haven't met his son Elmer," Thiemost continued, although disconcerted at not receiving a more enthusiastic reaction from Ronald, "But I would guess the old man is pretty annoyed with him. Except for sex, Elmer's not a chip off the old block. Never really buckled down to business. Byrdwhistle doesn't manufacture anything. According to Thornton, the company runs itself; but there's some guy in Boston named H. H. Youman, their executive vice president, who makes sure the store is open. Thornton thinks Youman is getting senile. Youman is sixty-one. He tells everyone that he doesn't believe in competition."

Thiemost grinned. "But that's all right, neither do I. The only sane thing to do with competitors is to drive them out of business. Anyway, Thornton thinks that H. H. Youman and his son Elmer are in cahoots against him. Thornton controls sixty percent of the stock. Elmer has thirty percent. There are no young male Byrds, so the company is up for grabs. Thornton thinks that he's an astute businessman, but the truth is that he's not a winner. He's just one of those lucky guys who got rich playing on a winning team. Thornton gave me his five-year operating figures. That's all he gets from Youman—quarterly profit-and-loss statements. Can you imagine that? No balance sheets. Something very weird is going on at the crossroads. But, up to now, and ever since his retirement five years ago, Thorny's evidently trusted his son to watch out for things. Take a look at these figures, Ron, they'll make your mouth water."

Ronald could absorb accounting reports almost at a glance. For the past four years, the Byrdwhistle Corporation had consistently earned close to fifteen percent, after taxes, on sales that increased from eighty million to two hundred million in four years. In the past three years, Byrdwhistle had a total profit, after taxes, of over eighty-six million dollars. Ronald knew what Thiemost was thinking. If, by some miracle, Byrdwhistle could be purchased cheaply, with an exchange of W.I.N. stock for Byrdwhistle stock, for example, and only a small cash sweetener for the owners, Byrdwhistle's earnings could help improve W.I.N.'s paltry one hundred forty-six million profits. Properly handled, the Byrdwhistle acquisition could push W.I.N.'s profit up a percentage or two.

2

Two weeks later, the day before he left for Chicago, Thiemost suddenly broke precedence and appeared personally in Ronald's office, demanding to know what additional information Ronald had managed to uncover on Byrdwhistle. Ronald tried to conceal his annoyance. "It's not like a public company, Mr. Thiemost. Whoever issues their corporate information to Dun's and other sources has been very cozy. They have a "1" capital rating, but since they provide no balance sheets or operating statements to any of the credit companies, whether they are AAA-1, or way down the letter-rating alphabet is unknown. However, suppliers report very slow payments. They evidently make no attempt to discount their bills."

Ronald handed Thiemost a D & B report. "Their headquarters are located in a five-story mill building in Everett, Massachusetts. It was built just after the Civil War and is owned by the corporation. Evidently it has been extensively remodeled, but for some reason credit investigators have never penetrated the upper floors or the executive offices. Each floor is fifty thousand square feet. The building apparently functions as the Byrdwhistle warehouse as well as its headquarters. They also list fifteen active subsidiaries who deal in everything from books to vitamins. Most of the subsidiaries are located in other states, but only city addresses are given. We tried to contact them, but none of them have phone numbers."

Ronald held up a sixty-page, four-color catalogue with "The Byrdcage" emblazoned on the cover. "My wife is on their mailing list," he told Thiemost disgustedly. "Women go for this kind of crap." To his knowledge, M'mm had never dared to order anything from Byrdwhistle. Ronald hoped he had convinced her that all mail-order operators were fast-buck hustlers who loaded their mailbox with junk mail and sold overpriced garbage that the average retailer wouldn't handle. Just before Thiemost arrived, Ron had skimmed rapidly through the Byrdwhistle catalogue and had been turned off by its whimsicality.

"It's full of crazy gimmicks," he told Thiemost. "As you can see, they are mostly gadgets designed to catch the female trade. All the items are catalogued under various kinds of birds with a play on the Byrd name. There's a Sleepy Byrd gadget that you keep near your bed. It plays the sound of ocean waves, or pattering rain, or summer breezes, and helps you go to sleep. There are Dreamy Byrds, weird stuff like astral soundtapes that help you project yourself out of your body; there're Bright Byrds and Happy Byrds—apple-peelers, vegetable-cutters, Bowie-knife steak sets; there're Byrdies—junk you can't live without—like home blood-pressure machines and digital gadgets like biorhythm calculators and I Ching predictors. There're Byrds-in-the-Hand video-tape recorders and video-tape movies. There're Byrd Baths—machines that turn your bathtub into a sexy whirlpool. The bathroom section has vibrators, personalized towels, and soap made from some crap called "loofa," a cucumber that grows in Korea."

Ronald scowled at Thiemost, who was turning the pages with a bemused expression. "There's no end to the kind of Byrds they've cooked up," he continued. "There're Daddy Byrds, Mommy Byrds, Byrd's Eggs, Byrds of Paradise, Love Byrds, Byrds in the Bush, Byrds on the Wing, even Byrds of Prey—sexy clothing for men and women. They even offer Thornton and Elmer Byrd dolls."

Thiemost shrugged and handed the catalogue and the Byrdwhistle file back to Ronald. "Mail-order sales in the United States are running thirty-six billion dollars a year. It's a growth industry, Coldaxe. The world is changing. Working wives don't have the time to shop in stores. For the price of a stamp, or a phone call, you can shop by mail. It saves gasoline. It has occurred to me that mail order might prove a profitable avenue of sales for some of our companies. That plastics company we acquired last year, Lovett Corporation," Thiemost stared coldly at Ronald for a moment, "you led us astray on that one, Ron." He scowled. "Anyway, Lovett might benefit from a little mail-order know-how."

Lovett is better off selling direct." Ronald was quite emphatic. "They did over fifty million last year. They're giving Tupperware a run for their money." Ronald was certain that Lovett's home-party system, into which even M'mm had been conned—returning one evening with a pile of plastic dishes that a friend of a friend had convinced her she couldn't live without—was a more effective distribution system than mail-order selling.

Thiemost frowned. He presumably encouraged opposing points of view, but not when they involved his own opinions. "You've got to admit, Ronnie, that you took us down the rosie path on Lovett. You should have told us to pull the plug on Hugh Lovett and to get rid of him before he sank another five million into that asshole division. Marsha Lovett Cosmestics. Trying to compete with Mary Kay and Avon, he created a disaster. Lovett only turned in five percent after taxes. It's not helping our return on investment. Maybe we could spin off the cosmetics division into Byrdwhistle and sell cosmetics by mail. It could open up a whole new approach."

It was on the tip of Ronald's tongue to tell Ralph that years ago when M'mm had used cosmetics she had often made her own. He was sure that, like many of their friends, Thiemost would be sure that M'mm's blunt "Crisco, with a little home-made perfume added, is just as good a cleansing cream as anything sold by Elizabeth Arden, or Avon, and it will keep you as young looking as Olay," was just one more instance of

M'mm's continuous anti-establishment rebellion. Ralph would be convinced that anyone who didn't support the ten-billion-dollar cosmetics industry was in the same bailiwick as the nuclear power plant protestors. Anyway, he knew that if Ralph mulled over his own insanities long enough, he eventually attributed them to someone else and rejected them.

With his feet perched on Ronald's desk, Thiemost revealed that he had more inside information on Byrdwhistle than Ronald had managed to acquire. "Thornton told me a little of the Byrdwhistle history. He started the company forty years ago with another man, Fred Entwistle. Thornton eventually bought out Entwistle, but they were known as Byrd and Entwistle until Byrd hired H. H. Youman. That was about thirty years ago. Youman was teaching philosophy at Boston University and living the genteel life of a starving professor. He had married a woman a few years older than he was. Adele, Youman's wife, was making quite a bit of money as a courtroom illustrator for a local television station and doing portraits of proper Bostonians on the side. Just after they were married, she was painting a portrait of Thornton Byrd. She suggested that he hire her husband. That was right after World War II, when MBA's weren't available for a dime a dozen."

Thiemost grinned at Ronald's grim expression. "Not all of us have been as fortunate as you, Ronnie. I only finished the sixth grade." Ronald knew Ralph enjoyed needling his subordinates who had master's degrees in business. As Thiemost continued, he was certain that Ralph wasn't telling him everything that had happened on his cruise with Thornton Byrd.

"Adele Youman is quite a woman," Thiemost was continuing with a faraway expression on his face. "She's got a lot of imagination, but she seems to be on her own trip. Anyway, years ago, when Thorny hired Youman, Byrd and Entwistle were doing four million dollars in annual sales, selling Christmas cards by mail and all kinds of useless junk like toilet-bowl cleaners and praying hands that light up at night, and Christmas tree ornaments and address labels—a lot of crap all priced for five dollars or less. Evidently Youman changed all that. According to Thornton, Youman's greatest contribution to the company was to convince him to change the name to Byrdwhistle Corporation and upgrade the line. In the intervening years, Youman, who is evidently somewhat of an eccentric, has developed into a sharp mail-order operator. It was Youman's idea to give anyone who ordered anything from their catalogue a free bird whistle."

Ronald looked at Thiemost with raised eyebrows. "A bird whistle? What the hell does anyone do with a bird whistle? Everyone lives in highrises. Who ever sees a bird?"

Thiemost scowled and thumped his fist on the Byrdwhistle catalogue. "Evidently, Coldaxe, you haven't read *The Byrdcage* carefully. Byrdwhistles are fully described on page two. You blow the damned things!" He tossed a white plastic tube with tiny holes in it on Ronald's desk. "If you practice, you can imitate bird-calls. Thornton has a boatload of them. He gives them to everyone he meets. Tells them it will help them make friends with the birds."

Thiemost patted Ronald on the shoulder. "The trouble with you, Coldaxe, is that you haven't learned that 'shit for the birds' is part of the ecology movement. You'd better get with it. If you can put together a few deals like Byrdwhistle, I can assure you, you'll be in the top-executive suite before you're fifty. Bill Bishop has only a few years to go. Eventually, we've got to stop expanding the W.I.N. family and consolidate. We're going to need a go-getter executive vice president in charge of operations. I don't know what other situations you are looking into on this trip, but when you get to Boston I want you to upgrade your accommodations. No Howard Johnsons or Holiday Inns. Take a suite at the Ritz. Get acquainted with Elmer Byrd. Take him out on the town. He's the man we have to convince. It's time he relaxed like his old man and enjoyed life."

"How important is H. H. Youman?" Ronald was growing more certain that Thiemost was omitting some important details about Byrdwhistle.

Thiemost shrugged. "I'm sure that one of our people could manage Byrdwhistle if it were necessary." He pointed to the Dun report. "The reason the company makes so damned much money is probably because it's in the right business at the right time. They employ only about four hundred people, and there's probably no god-damned union. As you can see, there's only one other vice president, Margaret Slick. She functions as controller. She's fifty-two. We'll probably need her. There shouldn't be any problem with Youman. Take him to dinner with you, and on the town, too, if he's the type. If we agree to a marriage, even before the wedding we've got to know whether we want Youman to join the W.I.N. family. Temporarily, of course. A contract for a couple of years should do it. That should make Youman feel pretty good. I know for a fact that his wife would like him to retire and live in Europe with her. They have a villa in Portugal, in Albufeira, an artist's colony on the South Atlantic side. It looks a lot like St. Tropez. Youman owns ten percent of the Byrdwhistle stock. He could end up with a few thousand shares of W.I.N. stock. Then he'd have something he could sell for a change. After all, who'd ever want a minority interest in a privately held company like Byrdwhistle?"

Ronald wasn't too sure about that. If Byrdwhistle declared dividends, they would provide a much healthier return on investment than W.I.N. dividends ever had. In the past two years, W.I.N. stock had plummeted from a high of $62 a share to $19.50. But there was nothing on the Byrdwhistle operating statement to indicate that dividends had ever been paid. Of course, that would be logical. There was a Massachusetts tax on dividends, so why pay state taxes when the money could be taken out in salaries? Still the report indicated that total officers' salaries were under two million dollars. Bonuses to employees were an extraordinary million dollars. But, even after that, there was still that amazing profit. Unfortunately, what was happening to the money could only be determined from the balance sheets, and neither he nor Thiemost had them.

3

Unpacking his suitcase and glancing out the window, Ronald was deliberating about whether he should telephone Elmer Byrd or simply eat dinner and relax. The sensible thing would be to forget business for a while and take a walk through the Boston Common and try to enjoy the warm summer evening without the benefit of female companionship. On the other hand, if he got in touch with Elmer tonight, he might pick up a lot of details that would save him time in the coming week. According to the Dun report on Byrdwhistle Corporation, Elmer was fifty-six. He had graduated from the New England Conservatory of Music, and then, evidently under pressure from his father, had changed directions and earned a bachelor's degree in business administration from Boston University. Ralph Thiemost was sure that Elmer wasn't a winner. Thorny had told him that his son had illusions about Hollywood. Elmer thought he should have been a writer or an actor. A few years ago, Elmer had presumably written a musical called *Rum Ho!* about rum-running in 1923 in Provincetown. But Broadway's producers thought it was too old-fashioned, and would be too costly to produce anyway. The only other thing that Ronald knew about Elmer was that he had been married twice and was a bachelor again. Since he had an apartment, on what Ronald had been told was Boston's swinging waterfront, Elmer might know an adventurous female who would enjoy an evening in the sack with the vice president of one of America's largest industrial conglomerates.

But Ronald resisted this thought. Until he knew Elmer Byrd and the Byrdwhistle situation better, and even afterwards, he should keep them at arm's length. Tomorrow would be soon enough to meet Elmer. Anyway, after so many sedentary days, he needed exercise. Eating a lonely dinner in the Ritz dining room, he tried to ignore the whisperings in his mind, that if nothing else was available there were probably still a few strip-joints on lower Washington Street. If he couldn't touch female flesh, at least he could look and daydream.

Walking across the Common, half-angry, half-loving thoughts of M'mm kept weaving through his mind. Her forty-five-year-old body, all one hundred and eighteen pounds of it, was still very attractive to him, but, damn it all, in any marriage there had to be a president and vice president. M'mm wasn't like Betsy Winston or a lot of her own friends. M'mm couldn't run things herself. She needed to be led. It would make their marriage a hell of a lot more pleasant if she would only acknowledge that.

As he watched women walking together and sitting on park benches, it occurred to Ronald that, although he had never done such a thing in his life, a little discreet inquiry might produce a woman who would take care of his sexual uneasiness. In Los Angeles, San Francisco, and New York, newspapers carried prostitutes' advertisements with photographs and telephone numbers. For sixty-five dollars an hour, and up, they would serve traveling executives in their hotel rooms. Unfortunately, the Boston censors didn't believe in sound business methods. Boston newspapers didn't carry massage-parlor or hooker advertisements. Unless you had a connection, you had to rely on a woman soliciting you personally.

Ronald had been amazed to learn from other W.I.N. executives that many prostitutes accepted credit cards. Although Ralph Thiemost sanctimoniously extolled God and family in his public utterances, he had been divorced twice, with four sons and two daughters by his previous wives, as well as numerous grandchildren. Ralph was lenient about extracurricular sex-account "perks" for members of the executive suite. He privately admitted that the need for sex and the need for power were opposite sides of the same coin. Unverified rumors abounded that at sixty-six Ralph was still a mighty cocksman and especially enjoyed friendly bondage orgies, where he was the master and various younger women played the willing role of slaves.

The thought of paying for a woman's body was abhorrent to Ronald. After all these years of marriage, and despite continuous variations of undeclared and cold wars with M'mm, he had not screwed with another woman since they had been married. Actually, although he wasn't very happy with her sexual performance recently, M'mm had never refused him in bed. He really had no excuse to wander. But it was true that in the past few years M'mm had become more and more casual. When he complained that she seemed only to be going through the motions and asked where her mind was, she just hugged him and laughed. "You get what you give, honey. I have a feeling sometimes when you're screwing with me you're fantasizing about someone else. Who is she? A female version of Ralph Thiemost?"

After such a remark, M'mm would become scientific and move her ass very determinedly, asking him all the while if that felt better. It did, but then the whole business became too damned mechanical and it was over too quickly and M'mm hadn't been affectionate, at least not the way he wanted and not the way she had been in the days when she told him that the best thing about him was his gluttony for loving and that with him she could have her cake and eat it—literally. Now she had become a time-study woman. Since they couldn't agree on most subjects for more than a half-hour at a time, M'mm seemed to operate on the theory that it was better to get sex over with quickly, before they lost all two-way communication.

And she knew the damnable truth. While Ronald was very commanding in the business world, he was unsure of himself with most women. He really didn't know how to go about being unfaithful.

It wasn't that the thought hadn't often crossed his mind; especially in the past few years when his feuds with M'mm had grown in intensity. Occasionally at parties, after a few drinks he would suddenly feel an intense attraction to some friend of M'mm's. If M'mm was aware of it, as she often was, she would coolly defuse him. Whispering in his ear, she'd ask him if he were horny and if he were being led around by his prick. If he was, she'd take care of him later. Not quite blushing, he knew that she had guessed what he was thinking. It might be nice to explore the body of a more complacent woman. But the few times he had made the overtures to some of their women friends, he had been rejected. "Oh Ronald," one of them told him. "How could you do that to M'mm? She loves you." Another had responded, "Ronald, I'd really like to, but M'mm is my best friend." When he propositioned Beth Tolman, who had been recently divorced and who he knew was occasionally sleeping with the husbands of some of their friends, she grinned at him and thanked him for the compliment. "I'd enjoy it, Ron," she told him, "But you'd feel guilty as hell afterwards."

Lost in his thoughts, Ronald suddenly realized that he was on Boylston Street in what remained of the old Boston "Combat Zone." A dingy-looking blonde woman smiled beguilingly at him and told him that if he had the time she had the place. Finally, the only way he could escape her was by buying a ticket for an X-rated movie called *Mom's Afternoon Orgy*. After thirty minutes of watching a very sexy-looking woman in her late thirties kiss her husband goodbye, drive her children to school in the necessary ranch wagon, and then return home to welcome sundry salesmen and peddlers into her bed for sexual dalliance—which included detailed closeups of the actress's vagina being penetrated by the largest penises he'd ever seen, followed by even more lascivious shots of Mom with her open mouth sliding up and down these huge phalluses—Ronald hastily left the theater and hurried back to his hotel room.

Examining himself naked in the mirror he was aware that his penis wasn't very happy with him. It needed to be in Santa Monica safely ensconced in M'mm's vagina. Ronald tried to get his mind off the growing feeling that the only solution was to masturbate and get it over with so that he could concentrate on more important things. The movie had raised uneasy thoughts in his mind about M'mm. How did she control her sex urges when he was away on these trips? In the past few years, her complacent but detached accommodation of him in bed had worried him. M'mm might try to convince him that it was simply the result of middle age and years of familiarity, but he really did wonder if she had a lover. He looked at his watch. It was only nine o'clock—six P.M. in L.A. He'd wait until ten before he called M'mm. Actually, he was tempted to telephone her later in the evening—around eleven, but that would mean staying awake until one. Of course he knew he was being ridiculous. M'mm would never carry on an affair in her own house. How could she with Tina and Mitch underfoot and in a bedroom next to theirs?

Trying to keep his mind off a vague but insistent sexual crawling that was making it difficult for him to concentrate, he got into bed with his *Wall Street Journal*. Maybe tonight, with luck, he'd have a wet dream. Ronald's wet dreams were usually more creative and interesting than any waking fantasy.

When he read the *Journal*, Ronald often timed himself. He would read the weekly columns devoted to taxes or labor or the Washington front and general economic surveys first. Then he skimmed the front-page news summaries. He followed that by a swift reading of the articles on international and business problems that appeared on the right and left columns. This took approximately fifteen minutes. The article that appeared in the center column was often devoted to some frivolous aspect of business, and he skimmed this quickly since it occasionally provided the grease for business luncheons.

Ronald looked forward to at least another quarter-century of productive business life, but almost always the first item he looked at in the *Journal* was the final sentence in the third column from the left, which reported the death of important businessmen and world and entertainment leaders. Thus he learned which celebrities had departed from the planet the previous day. While he had never confided the thought to M'mm—why did they have so many areas of noncommunication?—he had often envisioned his own obituary notice in the *Journal*: "Ronald A. Coldaxe, 78, formerly president and then chairman of W.I.N. Inc. for three years before his retirement, died today in Palm Springs." The *Journal* never went into much detail or provided gory details. Thirty-one years from now, with all his goals achieved, Ronald imagined that he would still be trim and dynamic and still playing golf and would drop dead of a heart attack a few minutes after making a two-hundred-yard drive at the Country Club in Palm Springs. M'mm, who of course would survive him, would be a lovely old lady standing bravely at his grave with their children and grandchildren while an Episcopalian minister gave the eulogy.

But before that final day, a lot of water would flow under the bridge, and there was much fish to fry. He felt better as he skimmed through the inside pages of the *Journal,* reading in detail the business acquisitions news and the inevitable stories about former trusted business leaders who had moved too fast in pursuing their corporate grow-or-die philosophies, and those who had flaked out and left the United States with a few million dollars of corporate funds safely stashed away in strategic foreign banks, and about those who, through forces of circumstances usually not beyond their control, had been forced into the inevitable Chapter 11 bankruptcies or, through sheer inability, had finally gone down the drain in a Chapter 10 bankruptcy. He let go of his semi-erect penis and repressed his sexual urges.

He prided himself on his encyclopedic knowledge of what corporations owned other corporations, as well as on his knowledge of the ins and outs of business malfeasance in general. It was useful information for a man who must carry an invisible machete in one hand as he slashed his way through the corporate jungle. Anyone involved in the buying and selling of corporations was well aware that ulterior motivations for the sale of a particular company often weren't revealed until long after the final purchase and sale agreements were completed.

In addition to the *Wall Street Journal* and innumerable trade journals dealing with areas germane to W.I.N.'s many subsidiary companies, Ronald also read *Business Week, Time,* and at least two best-selling novels a year. Although he rarely had time to watch sports events on television, he made it a point to be able to converse knowledgeably on the strengths and pecadillos of the teams and players in most major sports. M'mm had told him, disparagingly, that he was a businessman's businessman. The perfect square peg in a square hole. M'mm didn't realize that was an ultimate compliment. There were too many men in the business world who didn't know their ass from a hole in the ground. Scanning through the editorial page, Ronald remembered that this was one page in the *Journal* that fascinated M'mm. She was intrigued by the essays and editorials that, according to her, proved conclusively that capitalism was dead. Most major economists and politicians couldn't agree on how to stop inflation and, at the same time, prevent depressions. None of them knew where the money was going to come from to rebuild factories and replace outmoded and worn-out equipment. The only answer they all could agree on was to increase productivity. According to M'mm, that was simply a variation on an old story: "How to Squeeze One More Drop of Blood Out of the Poor Working Man."

LUDAMUS I

If the male genitals remain vigorous and produce their internal secretions freely and abundantly, then youth is prolonged far beyond the usual duration. Said Serge Voronoff, "Men thus fortunately endowed reach advanced ages. Possession of active genital glands constitutes the best possible assurance of long life.

John Langone
Long Life

4

Sunday night, while Ronald Coldaxe was waiting to telephone M'mm from Boston, Thornton Byrd was lying in his bed in the master stateroom of the *Love Byrd* watching a digital clock on his dresser impassively flicking off the passing minutes. It was 5:32 A.M. Anchored in the harbor at Pireaus, the one-hundred-and-forty-foot yacht rocked gently on the currents. The pink-shafted, gray morning light assured Thornton that the cool, early morning air would gradually shift into another warm, timeless Grecian day. Thornton was happy to be back in Athens. He had often stood on the Acropolis pretending he was Pericles. The eroding monuments of past centuries, cohabiting with modern buildings and the frenetic activity of the city, not only put man's striving in perspective but gave Thornton a sense of immortality.

And, in her way, so did Adele Youman, who continued to sleep blissfully beside him. Her head was snuggled against his chest. Her feather-cut hair was stark white against his leathery, tanned flesh, and falling over her still, perfectly chiseled profile it gave her a vulnerable, childlike appearance. Thornton wondered if she whitened her hair to enhance her dark complexion and her gamin look. Fifteen years ago, at the age of fifty, somehow or other Adele had become ageless. As Thornton was well aware, her big questioning brown eyes and high cheekbones and her well-preserved body made her sexually interesting to men of all ages. Most of them, including her husband, H. H. Youman, were much younger than he. Youman let his wife roam around the world and never seemed to worry about her infidelities, a word that evidently wasn't in the lexicon of either of the Youmans.

Thornton no longer required eight hours of continuous sleep. He slept when he needed to, like an old dog—fitfully—ready to spring awake at a moment's notice, bright-eyed and tail wagging. Now, amazingly, after last night, his penis, which Adele had lightly cupped along with his balls in her long fingers, was once again nodding in the direction of her vagina. In its first fifty-three years of activity, his penis may not have explored as many vaginas as Thornton might have wished, but in the past six years he had vastly improved his average. Less than five hours ago, after nearly three hours of continuous lovemaking, Adele, panting a little herself, had laughingly complimented him on his staying power.

"I reached an orgasm worthy of a twenty-year-old," he told her, while he lay lightly sprawled across her body, still big enough to remain inside her.

Adele hugged him. "You're delightful, Thorny, a living Mendes." She explained that Mendes was an ancient sex God resembling a goat. But she assured him, "You aren't quite an old goat. You're my loving friend and mentor. Maybe I love you because you remind me of my father."

Thornton grunted. "I'm only ten years older than you are, but I have to admit that when you're making love to me, you look twenty-six not sixty-six."

"That's because you make me feel protected," she grinned at him. "You really do remind me of Papa. Maybe that's why I love you. I always wanted to go to bed with him. Anyway, Thorny, don't get a big head just because you have a big prick. Victor Hugo recorded in his diary at 83 that during the previous year he had been to bed with at least eight women, and Thomas Parr was found guilty of adultery at 100. Cary Grant is still going strong at 75 and is even handsomer than you are, and Picasso had a woman in her fifties living with him when he was ninety and spent all his time drawing erotic pictures."

Sleepily caressing Adele's rounded behind, Thornton had to admit that whatever else H. H. Youman may have done with Byrdwhistle Corporation money, he had never objected to their annual quarter-million-dollar contribution to Dr. Alexi Ivanowsky's Center for Ageless Humans. Actually he, Adele, and H.H. were living proof of H.H.'s theories. Gently exploring a woman's cleft while she responded with a happy little sigh and slid her fingers across his stomach, as Adele was doing now, feathering the hair around his penis and then scissoring it horizontally between her legs while she quietly slept on, was a more valid mutual enjoyment than buying and selling things.

Until Adele had telephoned him from Paris four weeks ago, asking if she could bring Ralph Thiemost, Chief Executive Officer of W.I.N., Incorporated, to Cannes for a little cruise, Thornton hadn't been to bed with Adele for six months. Now he realized that he had missed her. At sixty-six, Adele was in nearly as good shape as the day he had first made love to her twenty-seven years ago. Her breasts, never too large, with aureolae the circumference of silver dollars, were not quite so pert as they had been then, but her stomach was only slightly curved. No one seeing her naked body could have guessed that she was the mother of a doctor, an engineer, and a concert pianist, not to mention having six grandchildren. And her vagina still became naturally moist within a few seconds of loving, which she never hesitated to initiate. And she could squeeze the walls of her still small and firm tunnel with a gentle sucking motion that was even more pleasurable than her mouth. It was a skill that most younger women couldn't emulate.

Thornton could attest to that. During the past six years he had discovered that younger bed-companions were easier to come by than women in his own peer group, who for the most part had long ago given up what Martha, his deceased wife, had referred to as "that silly business" but she had reluctantly told him, "If you must, I suppose you must." And Thornton had to admit that Adele was right about another thing. In her words: "You can't duplicate me, Thorny. The reason that I'm more fun is because I'm an old friend. Only with an old lover can you be yourself."

True as that was, before this day was over Thornton knew he had to make a decision. He must come to grips with Adele's arguments and her almost indisputable proof about Byrdwhistle. He had studied the auditor's reports on Byrdwhistle, certified by Marpeat, Young & Codbrand, which Adele had filched from H.H.'s attaché case. It seemed obvious that H.H., aided and abetted by his son Elmer, was playing fast and loose with his company. If he believed the auditors and Adele's incredible stories about H.H.'s juggling Byrdwhistle money, then he should have immediately done one of two things—or both. Ten days ago, when they had all cruised down to Faro in the *Love Byrd,* and Thiemost couldn't get a plane reservation back to Lisbon, he should have driven back with him in the Mercedes that Thiemost hired. Then he could have flown back to Boston via Lisbon in the W.I.N. corporate plane and tossed H.H. out on his ass. At the same time, he could have demoted Elmer to vice president and recaptured the reins of the company.

Instead, he had vacillated. He told Adele, who kept urging him to drive back to Lisbon with her and Thiemost, that he had to go to Yugoslavia. H.H. had more then ten thousand Love Rocks on the beach at Sveti Stefan waiting for the *Love Byrd* to arrive. All of the beaches in southern Yugoslavia were covered with these almost-round white rocks. H.H.'s plan was to sell them in the Byrdwhistle catalogue as potent love charms for ten dollars apiece. Adele might think the plan was ridiculous, but the fat was in the fire. In less than two months they would be advertised in more than a million Byrdwhistle catalogues.

So Adele had been trapped. Convinced that Thorny would certainly fly back to New York with Ralph Thiemost, she had agreed to drive back to Lisbon with them, and Thiemost had assumed that she was rejoining her sister in Paris for a week. "You'll be sorry," she told Thornton. "I'm only going back with him to Lisbon to save your skin. If Ralph asks me to be his third wife, I might take him up on the offer, but only if he agrees to take over Byrdwhistle and toss both you and Elmer, as well as Heman, out on your asses."

Yesterday, when she finally rejoined the *Love Byrd* in Pireaus, she was in a happier mood. "You knew the point of our cruise to Portugal wasn't for me to end up on a hundred-and-eighty-mile joyride to Lisbon with Ralph Thiemost, but you're lucky I took the trip. Ralph is still looking for acquisitions," Adele had smiled archly at him, "female as well as corporate. Anyway, I was careful not to tell him the whole lurid story about Byrdwhistle, and he is very impressed with the profit figures."

"I still don't know what the hell to do," Thornton told her, "or why you're so interested in having me sell the company."

Adele shrugged. "It may be the only way I can keep Heman out of jail. He'll never retire. I don't think he really gives a damn about Byrdwhistle. The real problem is that he thinks he's a reincarnation of King Gillette. You really should read Gillette's book, *World Corporation.*"

"Gillette died fifty or more years ago. What's he got to do with Byrdwhistle?" Thornton demanded.

Adele grinned, "Gillette had this mad idea that he could turn the world into one giant corporation. You've forgotten that my husband was a philosopher before he became a mail-order whiz-kid. *World Corporation* is Gillette's legacy to him. Heman is certain that he can use Byrdwhistle as a lever to change the world. If you don't interfere, he's going to do it at your expense." Adele put down the martini she was drinking and snuggled against Thornton's neck. I'm sure that if you sell Byrdwhistle to Ralph Thiemost, he'll fire Heman and then he'd have to retire and forget the whole insane business—which is what I'm convinced he should do before you're forced to put both him and Elmer in jail."

Of course Adele wasn't facing reality. If he fired H.H., and Thiemost didn't buy Byrdwhistle Corporation, then, unless he could find a new manager, he'd have to run the damned place again himself. He certainly couldn't rely on Elmer. Thornton had no qualms about his own ability to run the company. After all, despite H.H.'s profit-making record, H.H. hadn't built the company from scratch. Byrd and Entwistle were making money when Heman was still playing in his sandbox. The real question was whether he wanted to bother with all the nitty-gritty problems of running a business again.

"Don't forget, Adele, it's really your fault," he told her. "You're the one who forced your crazy husband on me. If I hadn't agreed to talk with him twenty-five years ago, when he was on his uppers, a second-string doctor of philosophy with no tenure, then I never would have become involved with him." By this time Thornton had his hands between Adele's legs and was delighted to discover that she was wearing no panties. "If you had been willing, I might have divorced Martha and

married you. Heman Hyman Youman. God! How could you marry a
man with a name like that? I'm like Dr. Frankenstein, I created my own
monster."

Adele laughed. "But Frankenstein's monster didn't have such a nice
fuckable wife."

Thornton could agree with that. For many years, while he had been
sleeping with Adele, H.H. had become like the second son that Martha
and he had wanted. In those years, even though both he and Adele knew
that H.H. was a free-wheeling, egotistical maniac, they both looked
upon him as "their big boy." When he told them, "What Heman Hyman
loves, everybody loves," how could they deny it? From the very beginning, hundreds of thousands of Americans sent Heman Hyman their
hard-earned dollars in exchange for the nutty things he dreamed up.
Thornton had even admitted to Ralph Thiemost that, without H.H.,
Byrdwhistle wouldn't be where it was. Elmer was a good boy, but he
didn't have a head for business. Even now, no matter what monkey business H.H. was up to, Thornton agreed with him that sixty was too young
to retire. Adele was wrong about that. And what's more, she wasn't facing reality. If she clipped H.H.'s wings and tried to incarcerate him in
Albuferia, together they would create a prison that would be worse than
any old-age home. Thornton was sure that the Youman marriage had
survived because they had given each other an unwritten, foot-loose and
fancy-free contract that had even survived the human need to meander in
different vineyards.

Thornton knew that he should be honest with himself. At seventy-six,
he was too old to get up every morning and go to work in that damned
mail-order business. He had served his time—nearly forty years of it. To
tell the truth, whenever he read the various Byrdwhistle catalogues that
Elmer sent him, he couldn't believe that anyone would ever buy such useless crap, or how H.H. managed to sell two hundred million dollars
worth of it annually.

On the other hand, if he wanted to strike a deal with Thiemost, without going through the proverbial meat-grinder, it wasn't going to be easy.
Right now, in all probability, one of the top W.I.N. executives was in
Boston giving Byrdwhistle a thorough going-over. Ralph was going to be
pretty damned startled when he got his hands on copies of the financial
reports that Adele had brought with her, and which neither of them had
shown to Thiemost during their short cruise to Portugal.

After Adele had left Villamoura to drive to Lisbon with Thiemost, he
had telephoned H.H. and told him that he was exploring the possible sale
of Byrdwhistle to W.I.N. Incorporated. H.H. had taken it very coolly.
Three thousand miles away, Thornton could hear him chuckle. "Don't
do it, Thorny. You don't have to sell Byrdwhistle. Try Zen Buddhism.
All you need to do is relax and flow with the current. If you do, you'll not

only live to be one hundred, but eventually *you'll* own W.I.N. and half the world besides!"

A few days later, Thornton received a video-tape by air mail. Speaking to him from the *Love Byrd*'s almost life-size television screen, H.H. and Elmer insisted, without providing much evidence, that he'd not only lose power and prestige if he sold Byrdwhistle but he'd end up "a washed-out old nebbish." What's more, wasn't Byrdwhistle supporting him in a style equivalent to that of a Greek shipping tycoon?

H.H. had made the tapes in his office, with Elmer sitting near his desk. He shook his head vigorously at Thornton and looked as if he might actually pop out of the television screen and jab the finger he was pointing into Thornton's flesh. "Hi, you crazy old bastard," H.H. said. "You're lucky that Elmer and I are running things for you. We've done a fast check on W.I.N. Corporation. This Thiemost character is a corporate shark. He swallows little fishes and silly old birds like you and digests them in his corporate stomach without even chewing them. If you exchange Byrdwhistle stock with him for W.I.N. stock, Byrdwhistle will be nothing but a burp. In a few years, all you'll be able to do with the W.I.N. stock is wipe your ass with it." H.H. had grinned. "You know damned well that stock certificates are printed on fancy one-hundred-percent rag paper. They won't do a thing for your hemorrhoids."

Elmer, smiling a sickly grin, agreed. "H.H. is right, Pop, and you can stop worrying about World Corporation. The accountants are wrong. World Corporation now owns Byrdwhistle, but you and I and H.H. control World Corporation." Elmer was mumbling a little as usual, and looked a little glazed, as if H.H. might have hypnotized him.

"You're not only going to be rich, but you're going to be famous," H.H. said. Staring persuasively out of the television screen he almost convinced Thornton. "Don't worry about W.I.N. If this character Thiemost sends anyone here, we'll cure him with a little acupuncture. We might even brainwash him. Just keep one thing in mind, Thorny. Anyone who is after Byrdwhistle doesn't really want the company, they just want to get their hands in the till." H.H. changed the subject by reminding Thornton that he'd better not forget those Love Rocks. He had to get them off the beach in Yugoslavia before Tito and the Yugoslavian government decided they were worth more than ten cents each.

Although Elmer had been promising for nearly a year to send him a tape showing the extensive remodeling of the old Byrdwhistle headquarters building, it was not included on this one. Instead, H.H. told him that the next two hours of the video-tape were devoted to a company production of Elmer's musical *Rum Ho!* and that he should watch it carefully because Elmer had put his hand on a money faucet.

Thornton listened to the opening bars of the musical being sung by a chorus of Byrdwhistle employees. "Keep mum—there's rum. Be frisky—

there's whiskey. Out on the limit—the twelve-mile limit—there's no limit." Then he flipped off the set with a grimace.

Neither H.H. nor Elmer had responded to his question, or Marpeat, Young & Codbrand's allegation that Byrdwhistle had a negative net worth, particularly if certain dubious assets like the investment in Elmer's musical were eliminated from the balance sheet. On the other hand, even Marpeat couldn't deny that last year's net profit, after taxes, was nothing short of phenomenal. But what was Heman Hyman Youman doing with the money? Byrdwhistle was becoming his own private charity organization. The solution was obvious. H.H. had been in power too long. Every ten years, any company or organization needed a thorough shaking up. No business or country survived or prospered when the same person sat on the throne too long.

But, basically, Adele was right. At his age, although he knew he was going to live until he was at least ninety, he really should get his monetary affairs in order. Before that crazy ass Heman Hyman had donated all his money to charity, Thornton was sure that he had at least fifteen sexually active years ahead of him. He could even start a new family if he wanted to. Obviously, he would need a younger woman than Adele, but that was no problem. The Byrds had good genes. His family was from the old South. He could trace his ancestry back to A.D. 900. If he were an egotist, he could have his sperm frozen, or, since he couldn't count on Elmer, he could even investigate cloning to perpetuate the Byrd traditions. But there was no damned sense in that. A vision of himself, the multimillionaire Thornton Byrd, with his toddling two-year-old son and his twenty-eight-year-old wife, enjoying the races at some track in England almost made him giggle. If nothing else, that was one way to shock the shit out of Heman and Elmer—not to mention Adele! But it was a pleasant fantasy that he would only act on if all else failed. In the meantime, he knew that the *Love Byrd* and his Sybaritic way of life required a lot of money. Operating the *Love Byrd* alone cost well over two hundred thousand dollars a year. Even though he envisioned himself as a modern Ulysses, he was damned sure that Heman Hyman was no Penelope, patiently weaving a rug, waiting for Thornton to return with a new heir.

Thornton decided that, when Adele finally woke up and they had made idle love for an hour or two, he'd tell her the truth. Even before she had returned from Lisbon, he had telephoned Thiemost in Los Angeles and set the wheels in motion. If, as he suspected, Elmer tried to use the proxies that Thornton had signed over to him and vote his stock to prevent the deal, then by God he would take the whole sorry business to court. Neither Elmer nor he had been in their right minds. No stockholders without undue influence would let the Byrdwhistle assets be used for the mad shenanigans of Heman Hyman Youman. If necessary, he might even prove that H.H. had tried to fleece them by rendering them temporarily insane. But over and above worrying about the financial aspects of the damned company and what action he should take, Thornton was uneasy on two other accounts. After all these years, even though Adele still "belonged" to Heman, she still managed to assert a proprietary attitude toward him.

"Martha often told me before she died," Adele insisted, "that I was your best friend and that if anything happened to her I should look after you."

But Thornton wasn't sure that Adele's motives were entirely altruistic. She was obviously a woman who enjoyed controlling the studs whom she admitted to her stable. Which was all right some of the time, and perhaps it was warranted by the fact that she was his oldest living bed companion, both in age and duration. Still, trying to peer into an uncertain future, he was afraid that if he returned to Boston, or settled down somewhere with Adele, he would have to be careful not to get involved in a corporate mess. He wasn't going to end up like some of those odd-ball characters, like J. C. Penney and H. H. Hunt, who went to their offices every day until they were finally carried out on a stretcher. If he died in the saddle, it was going to be a soft, creamy bucking saddle. A much more fitting end than slumping down dead in an executive chair covered with the skin of a long dead cow.

Moreover, even if Adele persuaded H.H. to retire and "enjoy a quiet creative life" writing a book about his damned Theory Z method of management, while she painted pictures of the fishermen and natives in Albufeira, Thornton didn't plan to spend his remaining years in the company of plump, widowed Boston matrons—they might want a male live-in companion, but not a sex addict like him. Most women in their sixties gave up sex for "higher" things. If he wasn't careful, the *Love Byrd* could end up rusty and unused in some Boston yacht-basin while he wasted away in a nursing home dreaming of all the lovely young and slightly older cunt from Faro to Cairo that he had yet to savor.

Amazingly, since Martha died, his plucky penis hadn't let him down yet. In fact, with constant use, it had regained most of its youthful vigor. The old boy between his legs thrived on the changing scenery. From the top of his head to the tip of his toes, Thornton knew that he was hooked on sex. But it didn't frighten him. He was delighted with his female awareness. It was a hell of a lot better than being a drug addict or an alcoholic or a vegetable in an old man's home who couldn't even use his poor withered tool to piss through without a catheter. Anyway, he wasn't a self-centered libertine. Most women, aside from the luxurious surroundings he provided them, enjoyed his reverent explorations of the lovely crisp forests growing between their legs. Older women were still God's best creation. But, alas, too damned many of them had let their playthings dry up and atrophy from disuse.

As for Adele, in many ways she was an enigma. She told him that she had stayed married to H.H. because she was fascinated by power-oriented men. According to her, he and H.H. and Ralph Thiemost, and God knew how many others she had bedded with, were all formed in the same mold. They fascinated her because, basically, if you traced their need for power to its roots, it originated in a kind of masochism, which carried to its extreme ultimately convinced them that they were in the service of God. Power-hungry leaders who managed to carry their schemes to fruition often become tyrants, like Hitler and Stalin and Napoleon. Like thousands of others before and after them, they were convinced that they were the saviors of mankind. "Masochists drive themselves unceasingly," she told Thornton. "They have to overcome their early failures and humiliations. Somehow or other, they must become heroes and be praised by everyone." On the other hand, Adele wasn't at all sure that Heman was a masochist. He certainly didn't believe in suffering.

Thornton suspected this kind of philosophizing did not come from the real Adele but were theories acquired by osmosis from living with H. H. Youman. Before Martha died, only dimly aware that he had been in bed with Adele at least once a week throughout the last years of their marriage, Adele had seemed to be a much simpler woman. She was then totally absorbed by her art and photography. It was during those years, too, that Elmer, probably egged on by H.H., got up his courage and told Thornton that it was time that he passed on the reins to the younger generation—which, in truth, was no longer young. Elmer was forty-four at the time and H.H. was fifty-six.

When Thornton finally agreed, he told Adele that this was her second and last chance. If she'd divorce H.H. and marry him, they could spend the rest of their lives cruising around the world on the *Love Byrd*. Elmer and H.H. had promised him a yacht as a retirement present, providing he would help make it tax-deductible. At first he hadn't believed that the I.R.S. would let him enjoy the six-million-dollar gift tax free; but so far H.H. had been right. Once a year, while Thornton moved into a hotel in Athens or Hong Kong or in some location where the Byrdwhistle loot was, the *Love Byrd* doubled as a freighter. Piloted by Pinky Fresser and Captain Jack Sludge, a cockney who had escaped from a London jail, the *Love Byrd* returned to Boston or Los Angeles loaded with imported items that H.H. had "discovered" in one country or another and which he believed could be sold in one of the Byrdwhistle catalogues.

Adele's response to Thornton's marriage proposal, then and now, was that she didn't have to divorce Heman to have sex with Thornton or any other man. As Thornton was well aware from the beginning, H.H. wasn't just a far-out philosopher, he was a person who lived his beliefs. She often told Thornton that she was sure H.H. was just a few steps ahead of the men in the white coats. One day they would hog-tie him and toss him into the loony-bin. Nevertheless, she loved Heman Hyman You-man. The reason she, as a young mother with two children, had gone to bed with Thornton the first time, nearly thirty-two years ago, wasn't only because she thought she could paint a better portrait of Thornton if she knew him better, but because she wanted to pry H.H. out of the academic world. She wanted to free him of all the nay-sayers in the world and give him a chance to fly. What better arrangement than to grab on to a loving Byrd? And right from the start hadn't H.H. given Byrdwhistle an Arabian Nights quality? The reason he was so successful was because he made customers feel like Aladdin with his magic lamp, or Ali Baba and the forty thieves.

Adele never kept any secrets from Heman. She had told him the first time she had been to bed with Thornton. They had both agreed that since Heman had done her the favor of marrying her when she was over the hill—she was damned near thirty, and Heman was twenty-four at the time—he might want to enjoy some other, younger females, and he might not want to have children. It was all right with her. She was marrying a younger man with her fingers crossed. She'd always been attracted to older men and she had paid the penalty. If they were any good, they were already married, Thornton included. She would never admit whether Thornton was the father of her third child, Yovela. It really didn't matter. Over the years, Thorny had been a surrogate father to all of them.

The last week in July, before Adele telephoned from Paris, Thornton had told Jack Sludge and Pinky Fresser that they should mosey up to Cannes and see what was happening at the film festival. Jack Sludge had transferred Adele's call from the bridge to the master bedroom of the *Love Byrd*. "Thorny, at last I've found you!" Adele still had a vestige of a French accent. "Where the hell have you been? Elmer and Heman thought you were in Athens. What are you doing in Cannes?"

"Luxuriating," Thornton grinned at Carla Minelli, who was sitting naked on his stomach when he received the call. Carla was brushing her breasts across his face and purposely giggling as close to the mouthpiece as she could as he was trying to respond to Adele.

"You're supposed to be on your way to Dubrovnik and Sveti Stefan," she told him. "Heman said that you had to pick up those damned Love Rocks of his before the end of August."

"Don't worry," Thornton was trying to divert Carla, who had now disengaged herself from him and was mounting an oral attack on his doughty weapon. "Pinky and Jack and I will get the Love Rocks back to Boston before the fall catalogue comes out."

"I miss you, Thorny. We haven't been to bed together since February in Majorca, and I don't give a damn about that silly woman who's giggling into the telephone and who is probably in the sack with you right now. She hasn't your best interests at heart as I have. Among other things, I'm sure that you're not aware that just two months ago Heman and Elmer acquired three nine-story apartment hotels for Byrdwhistle. They're practically on the beach in Portamaio."

"Where in hell is Portamaio?"

"It's on the Algarve in Portugal. Portamaio is a big sardine-fishing village—really a small city. Only a few miles away, there are lovely beaches. I tried to convince Heman to buy a retirement villa in Albuferia, which is only a few kilometers from Portamaio. He was intrigued with Portugal, but I never thought he'd spend all his time fucking around with realtors. I just discovered that he convinced Elmer that Byrdwhistle should go into the hotel business in Portugal. Anyway, that's only a minor part of the insane story I have to tell you when I see you. Right now, I'm planning to spend August in Albuferia. Heman wouldn't come with me. He loves Byrdwhistle better than me."

Thornton had ignored Portugal in his meanderings. He had been too busy exploring all the ports on Ulysses' route. As far as he was concerned, Portugal was in a mess. The country hadn't settled down sufficiently to really encourage capitalist investment. It was quite possible that it would revert to socialism—or worse, go communist.

"For Christ's sake," he demanded, grabbing Carla by the hair before she made it impossible for him to communicate further. "Why are we buying hotels in Portugal? The only good yacht-basin on the Algarve is at Villamoura. I never cruise in that direction."

"That's one of the reasons I've been trying to find you, Thorny," Adele said. "I told you last February you should fly home and find out what was happening with your company. If you really knew what was going on, you would blow the whistle on my husband and your son. I love you. I love Heman. But the latest Marpeat, Young & Codbrand report, which I'm sure you haven't seen, proves conclusively that Heman's gears are slipping." Thornton could hear Adele giggle. Maybe you won't believe it, but what's happened to Heman fits the male power-syndrome I have been exploring for the past year. I've nearly got enough material about power-mad men to complete my book, complete with drawings and photographs from life. Last week I added another power-seeker to my collection— Ralph Thiemost, the chief executive officer of W.I.N. Incorporated.

While Thornton was wrestling with Carla and holding her in a bear hug, Adele rambled on about the joys of people-watching, especially people of the other sex. As far as she was concerned, classifying and collecting examples of power-driven men was a lot more interesting, in one's old age, than becoming a bird-watcher. She couldn't understand why thousands of people gathered on Northeastern beaches every year hoping to see a Ross Gull from Antarctica that had occasionally been sighted there. The only bird she enjoyed observing was Thornton Byrd.

Trying to divert Carla from his genitals, Thornton hadn't been listening attentively, but Adele finally got back to the point. "Ralph is more famous than Jimmy Ling," she told him. "He built W.I.N. from scratch in twelve years. It's one of the biggest conglomerates in the United States. Anyway, right now, Ralph is in Europe for a few weeks. He's visiting his subsidiaries and investigating prospective mergers."

"Good," Thornton told her. "When your friend Thiemost goes home, meet me in Dubrovnik. We'll go to Sveti Stefan together and get Heman's Love Rocks.

"Damn you, Thorny," Adele was yelling. "Push that stray bitch on the floor and listen to me." Then she carefully explained her conviction that Ralph Thiemost could save Thorny's financial life and the Byrdwhistle Corporation from inevitable bankruptcy.

"Are you sleeping with Thiemost?" Thornton demanded.

There was a long silence, and then Adele said, "I have a couple of times. He's really not my type, Thorny. He's only sixty-six, but he's not like you. He has trouble keeping it up. He's an in and out man. Afterwards we don't have much to talk about except his achievements. Anyway, I haven't given him any of the grim details on Byrdwhistle. You can make that decision after you see the Marpeat accounting figures.

Adele arrived in Cannes a few days later with Thiemost. In addition to Carla Minelli, a lush Italian woman, Thornton had several other women on board—Gretchen Johannsson, a Swedish actress in her early thirties, Thori Sundelin, a film-maker, and two other women. Thornton introduced them all as cruising companions, and, while Ralph was talking to Thori, Adele spoke to Thornton, "Since you have either Carla or Gretchen, or both, for bedmates, I think I should bunk with Ralph. And, for heaven's sakes, let's not reminisce about us or Heman. Ralph just divorced his second wife but sexually he's the sneaky type. I told him that I had gone to bed with you years ago but that it was an ancient romance." Adele had slipped a thick envelope into Thornton's hands. "If you're agreeable, Ralph would enjoy cruising to Villamoura. It's not far from Faro and he can fly from there to Lisbon, where his W.I.N. jet will be waiting. W.I.N. imports a lot of Portuguese cork for one of their plants. A group of Portuguese businessmen are interested in having Ralph set up a subsidiary company. In the meantime, you'll have four or five days to get acquainted. If you play it cool, and don't let any of the madness that Heman has been up to hang out, I'm sure that Ralph will be interested in Byrdwhistle. I haven't told him anything except that Byrdwhistle might be for sale and that I thought it was very profitable.

5

While Thornton couldn't say that he liked or disliked Thiemost, he agreed with his philosophy. "You and I are winners," Ralph told him after he had toured the yacht. "Adele tells me that she's making a study of men like you and me and our need for power. According to her, Stage I power-needs are oral and have a mystic aura. You're still in Stage II, which is anal compulsive. I'm passing through Stage III, which, according to her, is phallic; that's the Don Juan acquisitive stage. She thinks her husband, who evidently runs your company, is moving into Stage IV, which is genital." Thiemost grinned at Thornton. "I can't quite figure out what Stage IV is all about, but evidently when you arrive there you are so powerful that you actually love everybody."

Thornton really didn't give a damn what stage he was in. He'd heard all this power bullshit from Adele before, and she had told him that he was oral, while she sat on his prick and leaned over him so that he could suck her tits. Actually, Thiemost finally did seem a little phallic to him. Every day while they were cruising, he would appear at the ship's pool on the afterdeck in a bikini so small that his developing paunch hung over it, but not enough to conceal a perpetual erection when Adele was fawning over him. The genius who could build the largest industrial company in the United States from a tiny computer peripheral operation in his garage was controlled by his penis — just as every man is.

But, according to Adele, who tried to perform a surreptitious juggling act during the five days they were together — soothing Thornton and telling him that he was still the greatest, while she slept with Thiemost and generally gave him the impression that he was Superman incarnate, all the while insisting, "I'm only doing it for you, Thorny, and my power book. I'd much rather be with you alone, but you don't have to worry about Ralph. He has a hard time getting it up, and then he has to rush like hell before it disappears on him. When that happens, Cleopatra herself couldn't bring him to life again. Don't tell anybody, but in bed Ralph is a loser." Adele scowled at Carla, who was trying to hear what she was saying. "But you're not, Thorny. I have to hand it to you. I don't know how you keep a sexpot like Carla satisfied."

Before Adele rejoined the *Love Byrd* in Piraeus and a few days after he arrived back in Los Angeles, Ralph telephoned Thornton. He quickly covered the amenities. "It was a great cruise, Thorny. I enjoyed it. Seeing Carla and Gretchen and those two other gals, Sally and Mimi, flipping around all day bare-ass made me want to announce my retirement and join you. As for your friend Adele, she's really a great female. You should have driven back to Lisbon with us. We stayed overnight in Evora at a former convent built in the sixteenth century. The Portuguese government has turned it into an inn—a pousada. Delightful. Adele is a charming, fun-loving woman. When you see her again, give her my best." While listening to Thiemost's enthusiastic reaction, Thornton grew more confident. Adele had obviously kept her promise, she hadn't revealed that he too was one of her current bedmates. More important, she hadn't given Thiemost any detailed information on Byrdwhistle.

"Our acquisitions vice president will be in Boston next week." Thiemost was finally getting to the point of his transatlantic telephone call. "But even before he reports to me. I have a good feeling about Byrdwhistle. If our investigation bears out what I've seen so far, then just for feelers I would say that a nice round sum for your company would be about one hundred and twenty-five million."

Thornton couldn't help smiling, but he didn't respond one way or the other and Thiemost continued. "Keep in mind, it would be a stock swap. We could base it on a selling price a few points lower than the current market price of W.I.N. Eventually it would give you a nice capital gain, because W.I.N. stock is selling much too low. It's going up and up. Of course on a merger like this, there would be no tax pay-out for you. In a few years, if you wanted to, you could diversify out of W.I.N. stock. The way I figure it, Thorny, it would put you and Elmer on easy street. You personally would receive W.I.N. dividends of five hundred thousand or more a year. What's more, I know the *Love Byrd* is important to you. Since it can't be a company charge-off for W.I.N., we'll toss it into the deal."

Thornton knew damned well that in the past year, if he included maintenance and the salaries of Fresser and Sludge, expenses for the *Love Byrd* had exceeded two hundred thousand dollars, which he charged off to Byrdwhistle, but while Thiemost was talking, excerpts from Marpeat's annual report kept filtering through his mind: "While Byrdwhistle has maintained a remarkable earning position," the Marpeat accountant had written, "for the past five years, the cash position of the company continues close to the wind. Not only does the management continue to maintain the heavy expenses of the company-owned yacht, *Love Byrd,* which is used to transport items for its catalogues—particularly its *Treasures of Croesus* catalogue, but the company is also involved in as yet unproved investments in Portugal. The Everett building reconstruction, the Grumman II company jet, the money expended on the Byrdwhistle national profiles, and two million dollars being held in escrow to produce Elmer Byrd's musical productions, plus numerous other smaller transactions, make a profitable cash flow from new items crucial for day-to-day operations. In addition, the relationship between Byrdwhistle and World Corporation, in our opinion, could endanger the future of Byrdwhistle. For reasons that Elmer Byrd, President, has not explained fully, the stock of Byrdwhistle has been exchanged for World Corporation, a holding company created by H. H. Youman and Elmer Byrd, who function as its sole officers. The stock of Byrdwhistle has paid substantial dividends to World Corporation in the past two years. With this income, and another five million dollars received from numerous small investors, World Corporation, as shown on these reports, now has assets of eighty-five million dollars, which has been invested in a wide portfolio of stocks in many American companies. It would seem that World Corporation is being maintained as some kind of private mutual fund for some as yet undetermined corporate purpose."

Thornton was pretty sure that when Thiemost telephoned he still hadn't seen the Marpeat reports. But actually what did it matter? Byrdwhistle was a good acquisition for W.I.N., but only if it could maintain future earnings equal to the past. All W.I.N. had to do was acquire World Corporation and dissolve it, and there were bound to be plenty of solid balance-sheet values left. With these thoughts rocketing through his brain, Thornton knew the only sensible way to respond to Thiemost was to hedge. "One hundred and fifty million would seem closer to reality," he told him. "But let's see what the next few weeks bring forth."

When he had told Adele about Thiemost's "feeler," her response had been that he should take one hundred and twenty-five million and run. "I don't think you've read all the stuff I gave you, Thorny."

The previous night, before they were actually making love, she lay naked in bed with him and told him as much as she could understand about H.H.'s Theory Z. "Based on Heman's new employment rules, no one can work for Byrdwhistle unless they are married," she explained to Thorny. "In addition, both husband and wife must pass a crazy examination before they're accepted for employment. Then Byrdwhistle pays them both equally—the median family wage—so that together, in most cases, they can earn more working for Byrdwhistle than they could anywhere else. That may be a good idea, but before you're hired you're told that Byrdwhistle believes that love is free and as necessary as the air you breathe. Everybody in the damned place screws around with each other. You know Heman's theories about love and sex. Byrdwhistle has become a joyous fuck factory. Wait until Ralph Thiemost reads this in the new Byrdwhistle employee manual."

Propped against a pillow, Adele flipped the pages of a booklet she had brought to bed with them. "I won't read it all, it would take all night, but listen to this, Thorny. This is what you get if you pass the entrance examination: 'Welcome to Byrdwhistle. You are reading this pamphlet only because you and your spouse have passed our employee qualification study of both of you and the kind of people you are. We are seeking fundamentally healthy people—being-cognizers. On the basis of your success with our examination, we believe that you have what Abraham Maslow referred to as "B-value Cognition," instead of a deficiency value cognition and a consequent poor relationship to your environment. The forty characteristics of B-value motivated people are listed at the end of this pamphlet.'" Adele turned to the back of the pamphlet and read them to a bemused Thornton. Then she continued. "'While you personally may not conform to all of these values, in the majority they represent your approach to life. With these innate qualities, working for Byrdwhistle as a husband and wife team you will not only earn a good living and participate in our bonus plan, but you will be participating in what we call Theory Z management. In addition, you will be involved in an ongoing experiment and a new approach to society and corporations that was originally proposed by King Gillette. Assimilating the unique growth process that your employment with Byrdwhistle will give you, we believe that you are capable of moving into a new hierarchy of values that will not only make you "transcenders" but eventually the new leaders of America. The key to . . .'"

"The hell with that crap," Thornton bellowed. He grabbed the pamphlet out of Adele's hands and threw it across the room. "You've convinced me. I'll phone Thiemost tomorrow and tell him to draw up the merger papers. It looks to me as if I should put all my cards face-up on the table before the man he sends to Boston screws up the whole deal." Thornton shook his head gloomily, "I don't know what the hell is motivating H.H., but if I were Ralph Thiemost and heard the inside story on Byrdwhistle, without a little encouragement from the actual owner I'd be scared shitless."

Adele laughed. "You don't have to rush, Thorny. Two weeks ago when you finally talked me into driving to Lisbon with Ralph I sacrificed myself for you. I always told you I had your best interests at heart. Ralph really likes me. He's helping me study the male power-syndrome." She leaned over and kissed Thornton on his nose and then slowly kissed her way down his chest and stomach. Taking a quick lollypop lap of his penis, she held onto it and looked at him with a pixie expression in her brown eyes. "If you'll come to the Acropolis with me tomorrow and stay until sundown while I take pictures of you at the temple of Athena for my book, I'll show you something very interesting."

Thornton grinned at her. "Sometimes I think you're not only as crazy as H.H. but that you're even more persistent. You've been harping on that subject ever since you arrived. I'll go with you, but why do I have to pose naked?"

"Because I have a theory that, when a power-obsessed male poses naked near a famous public monument, it creates an instant eroticism for him."

"You mean that I'd get a better erection than I have now?"

Adele shrugged. "Maybe it won't be a pointing-to-the-sky one, like

Heman had a year ago when I convinced him to pose for me in Pompeii; but I expect it will be more interesting, because it will be induced by history and not me."

Thornton guffawed. "You mean H.H. actually took his clothes off? Dammit, I'd like to see those pictures."

"I haven't got them with me," Adele grinned at him provocatively, "but I've got the picture of Ralph Thiemost I took the night we stayed at Evora."

Thornton was astonished, "You mean that Thiemost actually posed naked for you?"

"Well, he really didn't intend to, but Ralph can't resist a challenge. We were staying in the Pousada des Lois. After dinner, with a bottle of wine on top of the two scotches we had earlier, Ralph finished off with a couple of brandies. The pousada was a convent in the sixteenth century. Our bedroom was a former nun's cell. It got us talking about sex and how anyone could give it up for a lifetime. Then, after dinner, feeling very mellow, we walked around the temple of Diana, which is just outside the pousada, and overlooks a formal garden high above the city proper. The ruins of the temple and its ancient fluted Doric columns were lighted dramatically. Walking up the rough steps, I told Ralph that eighteen hundred years ago, when the temple was probably built, and the roof was still on it, it was used for the worship of Diana. This involved ritual intercourse between the local priest, who played the role of Vemi, King of the Wood, and local young maidens who symbolized Diana, Goddess of Fertility. Their sexual joining was supposed to make the earth gay with blossoms of spring and assure the autumn harvest."

Adele paused. Knowing she had captured Thorny's attention, she got out of bed and handed him a half-dozen eight-by-ten prints that had been in her shoulder bag. In the moonlight, totally naked, wearing no shoes, with one hand raised toward the columns that towered over him, Adele had photographed Ralph Thiemost on an angle that made him look like an ancient priest. There was a proud grin on his face, and the bastard had a huge erection. "When I suggested the idea," Adele ignored Thornton's scowl of jealousy, "I could tell that Ralph was really intrigued. The place was deserted, but he was afraid of getting caught by the local police." Adele laughed. "For a little while, I didn't think I was going to convince him, but then when he got in bed and didn't have an erection anyway, I suggested we could sneak around through the back courtyard of the pousada. We wrapped ourselves in blankets so we wouldn't have to get dressed."

"You said 'we,'" Thornton shuffled through the pictures, "I don't see any of you. Were you naked, too?"

"Of course I was, how else could I have convinced him? But when he finally got out there, and there wasn't a soul around, he was so pleased with himself—naked King Nemi, waiting to penetrate Diana—his power needs took over, as I guessed they would."

Thornton grabbed her and stared at her fiercely. "You're just one of those female bitches trying to prove men are no damned good."

"They aren't!" Adele couldn't stop laughing. "And you know it."

"If I agree to go to the Parthenon with you to do any such insane thing, I insist on taking pictures of you naked first."

"Then you'll most certainly have an erection." Adele frowned, "Look at what's happened to you now, just having the thought. That won't prove my point."

"I don't know what in hell your point is."

"It's quite simple. Like military uniforms, powerful environments make men feel powerful."

6

Half a world away, a few hours before Thornton finally agreed to take a taxi to the Parthenon, Meredith Matthews Coldaxe, known to her husband, her children, and a few friends as M'mm, was waiting for Ralph Thiemost's chauffeur to pick her up at her home in Santa Monica and bring her to what she thought was a pool party at his estate in Beverly Hills. Thiemost had telephoned personally yesterday. "It's been a long time since I talked with you, Mrs. Coldaxe," he said, and he sounded very genial on the telephone. M'mm remembered the last time very well. She had danced with Thiemost at the annual top-echelon husband-and-wife Christmas party. It was held every year at Thiemost's golfing home in Palm Springs in the second week of December. She remembered listening to Ralph elaborating his "winner" philosophy to a group of executives and their wives who hung on his words as if he were Jesus Christ himself. "Not to put down Jesus," he told them, "but He nearly led the world astray. It shouldn't be 'Blessed are the meek,' it should be 'Blessed are the aggressors,' without them the meek would have died of starvation. The world would be up to its ass in its own excrement. Sure the aggressors have started a few wars, and thus eliminated some of the surplus population; but, if it hadn't been for them, more people would have been wiped out by plagues and mosquitoes. The meek are the losers. Without realizing it, we condition our children from an early age to be winners and losers. I was one of the lucky ones. I had a tough old-man. He never made much money, but he lived by the philosophy of one of our great presidents, Richard Nixon. It can be summed up in one sentence, 'You're only defeated when you quit!' That's the philosophy of all winners."

To M'mm's disgust, Ron had agreed simperingly. "That's why that movie *Rocky* was so popular a few years ago," he responded to Thiemost. "The guy who wrote it, Sylvester Stallone, had the right idea."

Thiemost nodded his approbation enthusiastically. "You're exactly right. Rocky won the big fight, even though he actually lost it. And that's the reason that W.I.N. has become one of America's top companies. I never gave up. People laugh at that old saying, 'When the going gets tough, the tough get going,' but that's the way we function at W.I.N. And one of the reasons that I'm a winner is that I've always surrounded myself with winners like you gentlemen and your charming wives. Together, we're a family of winners!"

M'mm couldn't help herself. To Ron's shock, she challenged God. "You're lucky that there are losers," she said, ignoring the low gasps of surprise from the W.I.N. family. "Or else how would you know?"

"Know what, Mrs. Coldaxe?" Thiemost's voice was stern.

"Who the winners are," she replied. "Most psychologists believe that people grow and become more loving because they learn from their failures."

Not surprisingly, Thiemost wasn't thrown off balance. "You're exactly right, Mrs. Coldaxe. Too many people drown themselves in self-pity because they think they are failures. Failure is only a rubber rung on the ladder that you bounce on to get to the next one, before you get to the top and win. Even when your feet seem to be giving out from under you, you've got to keep climbing."

Then, graciously taking her arm, Thiemost edged her away from the group so that he could talk to her alone. Smiling coolly at her, he quickly revealed that the W.I.N. system of collecting information on its employees had more tentacles than an octopus. "Any W.I.N. wife who is as lovely as you are, Mrs. Coldaxe, with a husband going places, as your husband is, should shake herself loose from the failures in this world. I hope that the few days you spent in jail in Seabrook, New Hampshire, a while back have convinced you that winners can't make out behind bars."

M'mm had grinned at him mischievously, "You should come to one of our anti-nuke demonstrations, Mr. Thiemost. With everyone in blue jeans and long hair, the fuzz in New Hampshire couldn't tell the boys from the girls. They put the male and female losers in the same cells. Losers became instant winners."

Later, when she told Ronald about that conversation, he shook his head angrily. "A smart wife never challenges her husband's boss."

But M'mm just laughed. "When Ralph was dancing with me, he told me that subduing an aggressive woman like me was just as exciting as acquiring a new corporation."

She didn't tell Ronald that Ralph had actually proposed the time and place for his acquisition—the week after New Year's, on his yacht at the marina in San Pedro. Instead, M'mm had hugged him, "What you never understood, Ronnie, is that a smart woman may seem to be a loser, but if she grits her teeth and plays the male game, she can usually win—balls and all; and then, if the need arises, she can cut them off and hang them in her trophy room!"

Now, while she was remembering her last encounter with Ron's hero and mentor, Ralph Thiemost was telling her, on the telephone, that her husband was doing a very good job. "He's already uncovered one very good prospective acquisition in Chicago. Today, he's arriving in Boston to examine Byrdwhistle, a company that I personally am very interested in." Thiemost laughed. "While Ron isn't aware of it yet, I think I've practically wrapped up the financial details with Thornton Byrd, the old guy who owns most of the stock."

"Ron doesn't have much faith in the mail-order business," M'mm told him. "Before he left, he told me that Byrdwhistle is really too far afield, even for a conglomerate like W.I.N."

Ralph was silent a moment, and though M'mm couldn't see his face, she suspected he was frowning. "Ron shouldn't make prejudgments. They obscure his usually clear vision. Of course I don't have to remind you that W.I.N. is a family." His voice was suddenly less grim and sounded almost lascivious, "A loving family, I hope."

M'mm was wondering when Ralph would get to the point. She had a nervous premonition that now, after an eight-month interlude, in which he had been busy with other projects, Ralph Thiemost was finally getting ready to try to acquire Meredith Coldaxe. He was a dangerous opponent, and she didn't know how to refuse him. Actually, she didn't dare to refuse him.

"It's just an informal Sunday afternoon get-together," Thiemost told her. "But I really would like to continue the interesting discussion we had last December at Palm Springs. A lot of water has flowed under the bridge since then. We'll have a nice talk. Bring your bikini, we have a lovely pool."

M'mm wondered about the "we." Neither she nor Ron had ever been invited to the Thiemost home in Beverly Hills, but she presumed that Peggy Thiemost, Ralph's second wife, who he had divorced a year ago, no longer lived there. Maybe some of his children did. Waiting for Thiemost's chauffeur, M'mm made ham and cheese sandwiches for Mitch, who was going to the beach with his friends. She told him and his sister, who was floating vacantly through the kitchen waiting for her current boyfriend to arrive, that she would be home before eight. "I want you both to be here tonight, because Daddy might call from Boston."

"Daddy called from Buffalo last week, and you had an argument." Tina looked at her accusingly, "You hung up on him."

"Your father and I disagree about a lot of things," M'mm said calmly, "But most of the time we do love each other. Anyway, let Daddy and I be a good lesson for both of you. Marriage isn't all sweetness and light. And you remember what I told you, Tina. If you decide to go to bed with David, it's okay with me, but you don't have to make an issue of it in front of your father. My feeling is that if you're going to make love with a boy, you might as well do it in your own house, in your own bedroom. We both know that your father wouldn't approve of that either, but he didn't object to sleeping with me for more than a year before we were married. Of course I was someone else's daughter and not his."

"Are you going to bed with that fruitcake?" Mitch asked his sister. Both he and Tina were well aware that M'mm wasn't afraid of open sexual discussions with her children, even if their father was.

"It's none of your business," Tina told him. "David's not sex-mad like you. All you think about is getting into Alice's pants." Tina stuck her tongue out at her brother. "It's true, Alice told me."

Mitch scowled at her. "I don't care what crap Alice told you about me. I'm not like you. I've never even done it yet."

M'mm smiled at him approvingly. "You've got plenty of time, honey. If you and Alice go too far and you find yourself panting for her body, let her play with your jigger while you kiss her from head to toe. Actually, you both may find it's a lot more fun than a quick shove in her vagina." M'mm ruffled his hair. "And keep one other thing in mind— Alice, and probably most of your girlfriends, don't have such open communication with their mothers. Alice probably doesn't even know how to protect herself from getting pregnant. I know you've probably read those condom advertisements in Playboy, but no matter what your friends tell you, Mitch, whether they come in assorted colors, or they are all covered with little bumps—a stupid male idea that's supposed to make the female more excited—'safes' are only safe if you put them on right away and don't go poking around inside a female afterwards."

"David and I have already agreed not to become sex addicts," Tina said airily. With M'mm's guidance, she already had both the pill and a diaphragm, but M'mm had warned her that pills really weren't for young people. "So you don't have to worry, Mother," Tina continued, "I told David that sex is nice, and I like him, and he thinks he loves me; but he's only in his second year at the university, and I'm just starting in the fall."

M'mm hugged her. "Good girl. I love you. Dave is really a nice boy, but you both need plenty of time before you decide whether you want to imitate your mother and father. When you get married, like it or not, you'll be owned by the system."

"Is that why you're going to Mr. Thiemost's house?" Mitch asked. "Because you're owned by the system, and you're afraid not to because Mr. Thiemost is Daddy's boss?"

M'mm looked at him, startled. It wasn't quite true, but if she had refused and Ralph's invitation was really strictly business—which she doubted—it certainly wouldn't have helped Ron's prestige with Thiemost. She could hear Ron telling her, "As usual M'mm you're making waves over the wrong things."

"I'm not afraid of Ralph Thiemost, or any man," M'mm told Mitch, but as she said it she was wondering how far she would go to stay on Ralph's winning team. Then an excuse for accepting Ralph's invitation flashed through her mind. "Your father is meeting with Elmer Byrd tomorrow. If it weren't for that damned company, he would have been home tonight. He's still wondering why Ralph is so interested in the Byrdwhistle Corporation. Maybe if I ask Ralph point-blank, he'll tell me."

A half-hour later, with Mitch and Tina's enthusiastic "Wow! Look at that!" ringing in her ears, she walked out the door of their Santa Monica home. At the end of the walk, while a liveried chauffeur held the door open, she got into the back seat of one of Ralph Thiemost's Rolls Royces. Even before the car drove up in front of the house, she had tried to convince her children that his kind of conspicuous consumption really didn't impress her. Not when most of the people in the world had to buy smaller and smaller cars so they could afford to pay the high price of gasoline to make them go.

M'mm tried to shake off a feeling of hopelessness as the chauffeur maneuvered the Rolls into one of the stately, palm-lined roads in Beverly Hills and past stone pillars into a nearly quarter-mile driveway lined with carefully manicured flowers and green lawns to the entrance of the white Georgian mansion. No matter how much she protested, money *was* power! She was merely a serf responding to a command to appear before Ron's master and hers. Long Live the King! King Ralph, the Winner!

He greeted her at the front door, chunky, but physically trim, wearing tennis shorts that were cut high on his brown, tapered legs. Ralph was a heavy man, but there was no fat on his body. Guiding her into the house, he told her, "I'm delighted that you've come. There are cabanas out back near the pool. You can change into your bikini, or you can omit the bathing suit, as you please." He chuckled, "Like everyone else in Southern California, I am aware that you've been active on the various nude-beaches committees."

To M'mm's surprise, when he led her over the oriental rugs to the back patio, instead of a gathering of early afternoon guests, drinking and chattering banally with each other, the huge, kidney-shaped swimming pool, sparkling green in the afternoon sunlight, was completely deserted. Nor was anyone sitting in the fifty or more luxurious poolside lounging chairs. Except for a male servant, who followed them at a respectful distance, they were alone.

"I thought you were having a cocktail party," M'mm suddenly realized that she was a mouse who hadn't brains enough to stay out of the lion's den.

"It's early yet. A few friends will be dropping in later on this evening," Ralph smiled reassuringly. "Actually, although I wasn't able to entice you to spend an afternoon on my yacht, I think it's time we got better acquainted. Tell Chan what you'll have to drink."

M'mm shrugged at the Chinese butler who had followed them to a group of lounging chairs shaded by an umbrella. "Vodka and tonic will be fine, Mr. Thiemost."

"I think we can be a little more friendly, Meredith. You can call me Ralph. I believe that Ron calls you M'mm." He grinned at her surprise. "It sounds like an in-bed name. You are very m'mmy, but that can't be your real name."

M'mm shrugged. "My maiden name was Meredith Meta Matthews. The kids used to call me 3M, or M and M's. Years ago, long before I met Ron, a boyfriend dubbed me M'mm. I've been stuck with it ever since." She didn't tell Ralph that, when they first met, Ron had tried to call her Merry. But how could she be Merry when most of the time she was just damned mad, she had asked Ron. The United States was going to hell. Practically every red-blooded American male, and a lot of females, were just going to college to get their degrees in business administration. After that they joined the system and, when they weren't working their asses off for companies like W.I.N. to help make their bottom-line profits even better, they lived totally boring pseudo-lives glued to their television sets, or they joined all the other buying idiots in the shopping plazas. They all knew if they didn't get behind it the whole damned capitalistic system would collapse, and none of them cared what kind of denuded, polluted world their children would have to live in. So she didn't want to be called Merry!

But right now Ralph was telling her that he liked the name Meredith. "It has a sound of class to it," he smiled, raised his drink, and told Chan to bring them a second round. "Despite your letters to the *Times,* deep down, Meredith, you're my kind of woman. I like fighters. But unfortunately you persist in biting the hand that feeds you."

Sipping her too strong drink, M'mm could feel the alcohol coursing through her veins. Suddenly she remembered one reason that Thiemost might have summoned her. He had read her long and angry letter about China that had been published in the *Los Angeles Times* the previous Sunday. But what did it matter to him?

She listened, while Ralph, like a benign father, elucidated, "Once again, Meredith, you're on the wrong track. The best thing that can happen to China, and to the United States, is for us to help China make its great leap forward, not just into the twentieth century, but into the twenty-first century. Unfortunately, you gave the impression in your letter that the Chinese are better off living on the edge of starvation. I'm sure that if you were a Chinese woman struggling for your education, in a country that hasn't even enough universities to provide a college education for a tiny fraction of the millions who want one, or the teachers to teach them, you wouldn't fight the kind of system that eventually could provide it. I'm sure that even the most ideological, brain-washed Chinese citizen would be happy to change places with you and be delighted to have your home in Santa Monica, and your automobiles and television sets, and your clothes and books, and all the luxuries you take for granted."

Meredith was disconcerted, "All that I wrote was that the Chinese leaders shouldn't be corrupted by American materialism." She scowled, "I read that Pierre Cardin had been hired to revise Chinese tastes in clothing. If the Chinese ever have two billion automobiles, superhighways littered with beer cans and empty bottles, and hundreds of fast-food franchises, it won't make the individual Chinese any happier than most Americans are. Fifty years from now, instead of people enjoying each other in the simple happiness of communal work, and living close to the earth and loving one another, we'll not only have helped to create a billion alienated human beings, but we will have stripped the planet clean."

"But we will have saved ourselves," Ralph said. "What you don't seem to understand, Meredith, is that China is an inexhaustible gold mine. Helping the Chinese to achieve even a fraction of our affluence is equivalent to pumping continuous new blood into the industrial system of this country. In the coming years, the more that Americans can produce, the more certain we will be that we can keep employment up and reduce inflation."

"Doesn't it matter to you," Meredith said angrily, "that this earth can't support another billion people trying to live as high on the hog as most Americans do?" M'mm knew that Ralph was getting exasperated with her.

"Pardon the expression, Meredith, but that's bullshit. You've been conned into the scarcity, think-small syndrome." Chan reappeared, and Ralph told him to bring Meredith a third drink. Then he smiled, "It's too nice an afternoon to worry about economics and the future of the world. You can be sure that it will be here and thriving after we've both gone. But there is one thing you should understand. Our company, your family and mine, is involved in various negotiations with Chinese officials that could result in more than a billion dollars in sales for W.I.N." Ralph leaned over and patted Meredith's leg. "Come in, let's take a swim. I'm sure that, like Ron, you really know what side your bread is buttered on."

To her amazement, Ralph stood up, shucked off his tennis shoes, unbuckled his tennis shorts and stood before her, a tanned, hairy, beaming, naked gorilla. He grinned at her, "Okay, let's see if you dare to really put your money where your mouth is, sweetie." He dove in the pool and came up spouting water. "I agree with you on one thing—the only way to swim is naked. But not in front of thousands of voyeurs."

Bewildered, but knowing she had no choice except to rise to his challenge—if she didn't, she would make the man her husband depended on look ridiculous—M'mm slowly unzipped her yellow pantsuit and slipped off her jacket and blouse. Before she took off her bra and panties, she finished her drink and was dismayed to see Chan, apparently unperturbed by female flesh, replace it with another. Diving into the pool, she surfaced in Ralph's arms and his hands slid appreciatively over her body. "You're in great shape, Meredith. One of these days, if everything goes well, I want you to meet a friend of mine, Adele Youman. She's sixty-six and looks almost as young as you do. She claims that happy sex at least once a day is the key to staying young." Ralph looked at M'mm speculatively, "Ron's been away for about three weeks. Poor you! You've been neglected."

M'mm could feel Ralph's penis pressing against her stomach. The slimy bastard was not only trying to convince her that she'd better hop on the W.I.N. bandwagon—straighten up and fly right—but he was obviously sure that eventually she'd realize that when winners like Ralph decided to fuck you it was an honor. The female didn't protest, at least not too much.

"Just to set your mind at ease," he told her, "there's no one else coming this afternoon. Chan and Lily, my cook, and Billy, my chauffeur, are the only people here today. I can assure you they are very discreet. Lily has prepared lunch—baked lobsters flown in from New England. After that, we can relax." While Ralph was talking and treading water, one of his hands had slid over her behind and was poking gently at her vagina. At the same time, with his head under water, he had managed to nibble at both of her breasts.

When he no longer could continue his underwater explorations and had come up gasping for air, M'mm grinned at him. "Really, Ralph, fucking me isn't going to subdue me, or make you a winner. The truth is, even though I'm smiling at you, I'm so damned mad at you I'd like to scratch your eyes out. I'd even de-ball you if I got the chance."

No longer grinning at her lustfully, Ralph hastily backed away. "You might as well know it, Meredith," he said coldly. "It's not only your China attitude that aggravates me, but your anti-nuclear efforts aren't helping W.I.N., either. I haven't made it an issue with your husband yet, but he knows damned well that we sell millions of dollars worth of steam generators to nuclear plants. When the wife of one of W.I.N.'s top executives campaigns for stupidities like Proposition 15 and tries to stop construction of all nuclear power plants, and when she farts around the country picketing nuclear plants under construction, it isn't good for business."

"Neither are your steam generators." M'mm lifted herself up backward and sat on the edge of the pool. Ralph was staring angrily between her legs. "You know damned well, Ralph Thiemost, that corrosion, cracks, dents, and leaks have occurred in all of the steam generators, even those that W.I.N. manufactures. More than half of the nuclear plants in the United States have to be shut down every year for repairs. You may not give a damn about your kids, but I don't want to wake up one day and discover that millions of people are dying from radiation poisoning. Already everybody's forgotten what happened at Three Mile Island. What's more, those generator leaks probably endanger the safety systems of the plants. Even worse, no one knows what would happen if a reactor experienced an earthquake." M'mm frowned at him. "I'll make a deal with you. If you really want to go to bed with me, and you'll admit publicly that what I'm saying is true, then I might even consider it."

Ralph grabbed her arm and yanked her back into the pool. "Don't test my patience, young lady. Even if I did agree with you, I'd never admit it to the press." Ralph had one hand on her throat and was pushing her against the edge of the pool. He kissed her roughly, and then pushed her head under the water and held her for a second before he let her surface. "I think I'd be doing Ron a favor if I drowned you," he snarled at her.

Swooning a little in his arms, M'mm was glad to feel her feet touch bottom at the shallow end of the pool. Then she suddenly retaliated and grabbed his stubby, erect penis. "If you try that again," she said laughing, but not letting go, "You'll be dead at the bottom of the pool, along with me."

7

M'mm got home just as the telephone rang, and Tina was answering it. "Mother went to a party at Mr. Thiemost's house," Tina was saying. "She just came home."

Ron sounded both surprised and a little dubious. "What in hell were you doing at Ralph's house?" Sacrificing myself to Molloch for your sake, she wanted to tell him, but she breezed over it lightly. "Ralph knew that you would be away for another week," she told him. "He thought that I was probably lonely. He invited me to a big, noisy cocktail party. It really wasn't very much fun."

M'mm wondered how she managed to escape, especially after Ralph forced her to let go of him by the simple device of twisting her arm behind her back and pushing her up the stairs of the pool as Chan arrived with a platter of two five-pound Maine lobsters.

"You're not the winner yet," he had told her grimly. "It's two falls out of three. We'll continue the action after lunch."

M'mm had been certain that, if she didn't stop challenging Ralph, she would be carried screaming to some room in the house that was outfitted with whips and chains and especially designed to subdue women like her. Her only hope was to switch roles. When Chan had stopped hovering over them and had finally served the lunch, cracking a claw of her lobster she began extolling marriage, the family, and lifelong fidelity. "I know that you think I'm pretty far out, Ralph," she had tried to look tremulous. "But sexually, I'm pretty square, really. I've been a faithful wife for twenty years."

Scarily, Ralph quickly responded to her subdued, tearful expression. "I'm not really angry with you, Meredith," he said smiling and patting her hand. "I like women who challenge me. I'm confident that if you and I work together we can gradually re-focus your thinking. I'm sure that, at the very least, you'll let me give you some realistic facts about China and nuclear power that affect your future and Ron's as well as mine and W.I.N.'s. I want to be your friend. Deep down, we probably are twin personalities."

As he was talking to her, Ralph had slid his chair closer to hers and once again his hand was between her thighs. But somehow during the rest of the afternoon, before she told him that she had to leave early because Ron had promised to telephone from Boston, she managed to divert Ralph from sex to nuclear waste. But only after she had intimated that, if he really liked her and took it slow and easy with her, this could be the beginning of a beautiful relationship. "Winners like you always catch the brass ring," she told him in a purposefully suggestive tone as she bid him goodbye. She didn't tell Ralph of her real thoughts. While he was reaching for the brass ring, she'd like to shove the filthy bastard off the merry-go-round and laugh when he went sprawling on his face.

But now Ron sounded especially pleased when she told him that, although the party hadn't been much fun without him, she did have a nice discussion with Ralph about nuclear power plant problems.

"I even let him convince me," she told Ronald with a minimum of sarcasm, "that the fifty thousand tons of radioactive material that will have been accumulated by the year 2000 is really no problem. He assured me that W.I.N. engineers are working on a vitrification process. They will be able to bury all our nuclear waste in Carlsbad, New Mexico, with no danger of escaping radiation."

"Great," Ronald told her enthusiastically. "I'm glad you're on the right track for a change, M'mm. I wish I were home with you right now, snuggling on your tits."

M'mm grimaced into the phone. She didn't tell Ron that before she had managed to get dressed, and before Billy arrived to chauffeur her home, Ralph had managed to crush her in his arms, push his tongue down her throat, and force her hand once again to hold his penis, which felt as hard and thick as a fire hose. Actually, she was wondering why Ron always managed to sound more loving when he was miles away than when they were together, her breasts and vagina were readily available, and she wanted him, especially on those nights that he didn't begin things with an inevitable discussion of her weird behavior as a corporation wife.

"I told you that you should have let me come with you," she said. "We could be in bed together right now."

"Honey, you'd have been bored to death. I couldn't take you to these companies that I've been checking out. You would have had to hang around all day in hotel rooms in Chicago, Buffalo, and Boston." Trying to divert her, he told her about his final days with the Winstons. "Betsy is a real business woman. She said she'd like to meet you."

"I wouldn't like to meet her," M'mm told him coldly. "I hope you had a nice honeymoon at Niagara Falls. I've never been there."

"Believe me, it was strictly business. Betsy just came along to be sociable. Did Ralph tell you anything about Byrdwhistle?"

"Only that Adele Youman, who is married to one of their executives, is a sixty-six-year-old sex maniac."

"Damn." M'mm could hear Ronald groan. "I have a premonition that Byrdwhistle and W.I.N. have nothing in common. They'll never fly together. There's some fatal flaw in the Byrdwhistle set-up, and Ralph knows it but he's letting me find it out for myself. I hate like hell to walk into a situation where I have so little background information."

"Have them check their files," M'mm laughed for the first time. She wanted to tell Ron before he had left about the Byrdwhistle question-naire. But that would have only piled one more argument on top of those they had already had. "They have a detailed Byrdwhistle profile on the Coldaxe family."

"What the hell are you trying to tell me?" Ronald yelled, forcing M'mm to hold the phone away from her ear. "Has Elmer Byrd been trying to investigate me?"

M'mm couldn't help giggling, "It has nothing to do with you or me personally. The questionnaire is a gimmick. If you hadn't been so uptight about me buying things by mail, I'd have told you about it."

"You mean you actually bought something from them?" Ronald's voice was frigid. He was the executive about to hand his employee a pink slip for not obeying instructions.

"It was that Scrooge bath towel I gave you last Christmas. The one that had 'Bah! Humbug!' written all over it. The kids loved it, and after a while even you thought it was funny."

"You bought that damned thing from Byrdwhistle?"

"It was illustrated in the catalogue I gave you. It was priced at eighteen dollars. But Byrdwhistle was offering a twenty percent discount on anything in the catalogue if you'd fill out the Byrdwhistle Eupsychian customer profile. It's really a cute idea. In case you don't know it, Eupsychian is an idea dreamed up by Abraham Maslow. It's a culture that would be generated by one thousand self-actualizing people if they were confined on a sheltered desert island and weren't interfered with."

"What the hell are self-actualizing people?"

"Oh, damn, you've forgotten, Ronnie, I told you years ago that you should read Maslow. You've got possibilities, but you aren't self-actualizing yet."

"Never mind. Tell me what was in the questionnaire." Ron could hear M'mm giggling.

"Everything. There were more than one hundred and fifty questions about the respondents' marital likes and dislikes. Most of them revolved around one's sex life. You and I were supposed to fill out the two sets of questions separately and then compare answers. If we had, we might have discovered each other for the first time. Actually, if you're honest about answering some of the questions, it makes you feel quite sexy." M'mm sighed, "But I knew you wouldn't fill yours out, so I did it for you."

Ronald groaned. "Why in the hell would you do something like that? Go blatting our personal lives to strangers? Sometimes I think you need a custodian."

"I did it to save three dollars and sixty cents, silly. You're always telling me that my time isn't worth anything, but I do save coupons, and I got your Christmas towel for fourteen forty, delivered."

"I hope you didn't sign that questionnaire."

"Of course I signed it." M'mm was shouting and her voice rose an octave higher when she got angry. "Byrdwhistle is going to publish the results of their survey. If you're willing to sign the questionnaire, they'll send you the book at a discount when it's published."

Ronald wanted to tell her how damned angry he was. Sometimes M'mm acted like an irresponsible child. But what was the use? Especially when she was three thousand miles away and he needed her vagina so pressingly. "If I weren't sure, I am now,' he said coldly, "any company that goes to such extremes to analyze its customers is wasting the stockholder's money. Byrdwhistle is never going to fit into the W.I.N. family."

"I don't give a shit about Byrdwhistle," M'mm said. "You're just peeved with me because I bought that towel by mail. The only thing you care about in this world is your fucking W.I.N. family." Despite her words, M'mm's voice had become calm and well modulated. "If you really want to know what happened this afternoon, I'll tell you. Your egotistical boss tried to fuck me in his swimming pool, and he made it quite clear that you are simply his prat boy. He told me that he had practically bought the Byrdwhistle Company from Thornton Byrd last Wednesday." M'mm chuckled at Ron's shocked silence. "You and Ralph are both full of shit. You'd sell your wives into white slavery and toss in your mothers and grandmothers to close the deal."

"M'mm, calm down. I think you are becoming menopausal. Ralph doesn't have to chase after the forty-five-year-old wives of his employees. He can have the pick of the crop." Ronald didn't believe her outburst about Thiemost. Ralph was probably just being friendly, as he was with all women. What Ron wanted to explore was whether there was some truth in M'mm's revelation about Thiemost and Thornton; but his last statement to M'mm had blown sane conversation to the wind.

"I may not be the pick of *your* crop," M'mm told him angrily, "but old bastards like Thiemost prefer mature women who know what to do with their asses besides tease him with them."

"I'm twenty years younger than Ralph, and I'd like to know!"

"Damn you! If you had let me come with you, you could be finding out right now. You knew I wouldn't just be hanging around. I've got lots of friends in Chicago and Boston."

Ronald knew who those friends were—bearded rebels picketing anything or anyone who worked for a living. "You didn't have a babysitter."

"You're just being devious," M'mm replied. "Tina could have taken care of herself, and she would have kept Mitch in line. Mother would have come over every day and checked on both of them. The truth is that you didn't want me to come. You were afraid that I might get in touch with Jeff Staller and the Clamshell Alliance."

"Really, M'mm, that's a dead issue. The Seabrook plant is never going to be finished and you know it." Tears of frustration were gathering in M'mm's eyes. Pretty soon Ron would be reminding her that, at forty-five, she had to stop acting like a rebellious college girl.

"Okay, maybe you're right. I'm a loser," she said, repressing a sob before she hung up. "Honestly, Ron, you frighten me. Someday you're going to wake up in the morning and stare at me in complete disbelief. You'll sight the enemy and, lo and behold, you will have been living with her for twenty years—it's your wife!"

8

Thrashing in an early morning R.E.M. dream, Ronald watched Ralph Thiemost chasing M'mm. Ralph's naked penis was bouncing, like a monstrous salami, from side to side against his knees. As he chased her, he kept grunting at Ronald that M'mm was a loser whom they both could share.

About the same time—five A.M.—in what Elmer Byrd would have freely admitted was just as far a call from reality as Ronald's dream, Elmer was waving a forlorn goodbye to H. H. Youman before he slammed the door of the Byrdwhistle's Grumman II. Sitting in the co-pilot's seat beside Nick Ricci, they taxied out on the runway for a take-off for Athens.

Aboard the plane was Nick's wife, Maria, with whom Elmer had slept occasionally, and Marvy Upjohn. Although Elmer had met Marvy only twenty minutes earlier, she had already stripped off her dress and, stretched out on one of the lower berths of the plane, she told Maria that H. H. Youman must have cast a spell on her. "Less than twelve hours ago, I was flying from London to Boston," Marvy grinned. "Now, according to H.H., I'm on the Byrdwhistle payroll. It's a lark, really. I do love Elmer Byrd's music. H.H. thinks that I'd be perfect for the lead part of Francis Hardworthy—Elmer's old-maid schoolteacher." Marvy sighed. "My agent thinks I'm crazy. I haven't even read the book for *Rum Ho!* Songs are one thing, but the story could be a turkey."

Three hours earlier, when his telephone rang, Elmer had been sleeping. He was partially blanketed by Marge Slick, vice president and controller of Byrdwhistle, who was sprawling across his naked body. "If it's one of your former wives," Marge muttered, "tell her that you're thoroughly occupied with the male-order business." Marge had spent the past ten hours—all day Sunday—with Elmer in a warehouse in Beverly, Massachusetts, where the set designers were trying to convince him that his second act switch-back in *Rum Ho!* would be a terrible problem even for a conventional stage, and an impossibility for a circular one. It called for a shift from Freeman Pierre's rum-running schooner to a whorehouse in Nassau, and then back to the schooner as it was sailing from right to left instead of left to right. So was the final scene, where the ship flounders on the rocks off Race Point in Provincetown. But Elmer had been adamant. After hours of juggling with pulleys, with assistance from a willing team of fledgling actors, he had proved the scene changes could be made in less than fifteen seconds. But, when he got back to his apartment, he was so exhausted that he had fallen asleep on Marge's breast. Grinning at her, he told her that he was so pooped they'd have to wait until morning. After a night with him, she'd appreciate her husband even more.

Dimly aware that Marge's full breasts were dangling near his face, Elmer had answered the telephone and had been greeted by Adele Youman. She was reversing the charges from Athens. The connection was clear enough, but Elmer, his libido suddenly restored by the sight of Marge's erect nipples, was tweaking them absent-mindedly with his tongue and found it difficult to assimilate what he was hearing.

"Really, Elmer," Adele was losing her patience. "I can't repeat myself endlessly. This call is costing you money. A big, fat-ass Greek Achilles is standing right next to me. All I'm wearing is a bedsheet. The bastards won't give us back our clothes. If this Achilles wasn't wearing his heel between his legs, I'd stomp on it. It's still in his pants, but it's pointing right in my direction. If you and Heman don't get your father and me the hell out of here, I may be forced to poke Achilles right in his weak spot."

"I'm sorry, Adele," Elmer told her, "I'm not awake yet. It's two A.M. I'm a little befuddled. Will you start from the beginning?

"Elmer, dear, please pay attention." Adele was pleading. "I'll start from the beginning. Your father and I are in a rat-infested Greek jail. The damned-fool police arrested us this morning at the Acropolis. All we did was stay a few minutes beyond closing time so that we could take photographs of each other. They herded us into a van, and refused to let us get dressed. They drove us, stark naked, through the streets of Athens to this stinking jail."

"You mean they stripped you? Were you carrying grass? Or smoking it?"

"*They* didn't strip us," Adele sounded like a mother patiently explaining the obvious to her son. "I told you the Acropolis was deserted. Everyone had left. I had taken all the pictures I wanted, but then your father got this crazy idea that he wanted a picture of himself standing on the Erectheum next to one of the Caryatids. He was playing one-upmanship on a new friend of his, Ralph Thiemost."

"Jesus Christ! Don't tell me that Ralph Thiemost is with you." Elmer was fully awake now. "What the hell were you all doing naked in the Acropolis?"

Adele sighed, "The ancient Greeks thought nothing of it. You don't understand. It's a long story. Anyway, Ralph isn't with us. He flew back to California two weeks ago, but he's sending a man to look over Byrdwhistle. Your father is going to sell the company."

"Why didn't you call H.H.?"

"I didn't think Heman would be too happy with me. You seem to forget, Elmer, that Thorny is your father. You can't let your father down."

"I still don't understand why they took your clothes."

Adele sighed. "Elmer, they didn't take the clothes off our backs. Except for sneakers, we were already naked."

Sure that she wouldn't believe him, Elmer was holding the phone so

Marge could listen. "The Greek police caught Adele and Thorny fucking in the Acropolis," he whispered to Marge.

Adele heard him. "Elmer, we weren't fucking!" she screamed.

"Did you have any marijuana?"

"Oh, there was an ounce or two in my pocketbook, but we weren't smoking it. Thorny brought along a pint of ouzo. He likes that better. Please, Elmer, you've got to help us. They not only refuse to give us our clothing back, but they won't let us go. We tried to reach Pinky Fresser and Jack Sludge, but Thorny gave them a few days leave. A Greek maid and the butler are the only ones aboard. These bastards don't even believe that Thorny owns the *Love Byrd*."

Suddenly, over Adele's voice, Elmer heard an angry male grunt "Give me that god-damned phone. Let me talk with him." It was Thornton. "I don't give a shit if it *is* only two A.M. You listen to me carefully, son. I want you to telephone H.H. and then call Nick Ricci. All of you get your asses down to Logan Airport. I presume that we still own the Grumman. You can be here in eight hours. After you've identified us and bailed us out if necessary, I want to have a long talk with both you and H.H. and find out what the hell is going on with my company. And don't give me any god-damned back-talk. If you both aren't here by five P.M. Greek time, it'll be your asses." Thornton banged the phone down.

Elmer immediately telephoned H.H. and delivered his father's message. Although H.H. sounded calm, Elmer could tell that he had lost his Zen grasp of things and wasn't flowing with the tide. "You should have told Thorny that all he had to do was telephone the American Embassy," H.H. laughed. "I'm sure we have some exchange agreement for captured espionage agents. Never mind, I'll do it when I get to the office." Then H.H. changed the subject. "I've got good news for you. Last week, I told you that when I saw her in London I thought Marvy Upjohn was a natural for *Rum Ho!* She flew in early yesterday, mainly to talk with you about it. Where the hell have you been? I tried to reach you all day."

Momentarily, Elmer forgot about his father. Marvy was an American actress who had been around for a long time and had had only minor successes before taking a singing part in a London musical, *Edward and Wally*. She had become an instant star. But now, after nearly three years of playing Wally in London and on Broadway, she was weary of the part. Elmer had never met her, but even if he had he knew that he would never have had the nerve to approach her. He was an unknown writer of a musical that had been rejected by Broadway's top producers.

"Where is she now?" he asked.

"She's in bed with me," H.H. said.

"Jesus! You told me last week that you only talked with her for twenty minutes in London. How did you manage that?"

"Every woman has a responsive, loving chord," H.H. said, and Elmer recognized the smile in H.H.'s voice. "As a musician, you should be able to strike a particular one, even better than I. When I was driving her to the Copley Plaza, Marvy told me that she'd grown up in a big family in a big old house in Saybrook, Connecticut. I knew then that she'd be happier here with our little communal love group than rattling around an impersonal hotel room with no bedfriends, so I brought her to Merry Mount." H.H. chuckled. "As a matter of fact, we just got to sleep. We've been talking all night. I think I've convinced her not to listen to her agent. She loves the idea of the series of really American musicals that you have in mind. There's been nothing like them since *Oklahoma!* and *Music Man.*"

Elmer suddenly remembered the reason for his call. "If Thorny sells Byrdwhistle, there won't be any musical," he said gloomily. "Thorny doesn't sound very happy. He insists on seeing both of us tomorrow."

"Elmer, try to look on the bright side for a change. For once the gods are on our side. Your father and my wife have been caught with their pants down. It was Adele's doing, you can be sure of that. Damn, I just remembered. Erectheus, after whom the Erectheum was named, had the head of a Greek god and the body of a snake. He was Athena's consort. I hope the phallic symbolism doesn't escape you. To top it off, one of Erectheus' daughters was Pandora. The one who opened the box, and let all hell loose. Very appropriate."

"I still think we'd better both hop over to Athens."

H.H. was silent for a moment, then he exploded in a great gust of laughter. "It's really too early in the morning to be thinking creatively, Elmer, but I just had a great idea. You know that I can't go. Someone has got to stay here to take the wind out of W.I.N.'s sails. You told me Friday that their man Coldaxe — is that the bastard's name? — is due here Monday. Really, Elmer, it would be better if you weren't here at all. Just leave this character to me and Marge Slick. As executive vice president, I have a better grip on vice than you have. We'll cold cock Coldaxe. Right now, I'm going to call Nick Ricci, and Marvy and I will meet you at Logan in two hours. Marvy will fly to Greece with you. Your gold piano is still on board. She still hasn't read *Rum Ho!* You can play it for her, and you can go over the story-line together. If you're lucky and strike the right chord, Marvy may play spoons with you. She's really a warm, snuggly kitten."

H.H. hung up, but not before Elmer heard a woman's voice saying, "Heman Hyman Youman, I won't! I won't fly the Atlantic again so soon." And he heard H.H. responding, "Sweetie, this plane has beds. You can fly to Athens on your back. If you feel in the mood, you can even spend a blissful few hours with Elmer and join the Five-Mile-High Club."

Elmer found H.H. in the operations office at Logan, where Nick was filing their flight plan. The August morning was humid and the sun still hadn't found its way into the Western sky. H.H. was wearing bell-bottomed blue jeans and a white tee-shirt. His thick, pure-white hair, which hadn't receded even a quarter of an inch, was combed Caesar style over his forehead, and he seemed even taller than his six-foot height. He was calmer than Elmer, who had arrived without Marge. She had insisted that, H.H. to the contrary, Elmer wasn't taking advantage of a Byrd-whistle employee by sleeping with her, or with any other Byrdwhistle female who made the overtures to him, not if she had her husband's permission as she most certainly did. Fred Slick was at their Atlanta warehouse this week, and she had told Fred before she left that Elmer was feeling moody and really needed to be cheered up by a good bed companion.

"Byrdwhistle is really a family, for God's sake!" Marge had told him as she guided Elmer into her body and sat on his stomach grinning at him. "That's how H.H. has organized the company—the way John Humphrey Noyes formed the Oneida Community. On the other hand, Big John didn't want to know everything his children were doing at night. He left it up to them." Marge hugged Elmer before he left for the airport. "You're better than Thorny in bed, and equal to H.H. anytime. Be careful, honey, take care of yourself. We all need you, and don't worry about Ronald Coldaxe. H.H. and I will send him back to California with his tail tucked between his legs."

H.H. now introduced Marvy to Elmer. Behind huge glasses that made her look both prim and childlike at the same time, she smiled wide-eyed at him. "Isn't she lovely, Elmer? Your old high school English teacher born again! Only this time she'll not only tell you that you have extraordinary talent. When she reads *Rum Ho!* and you tell her about *Let Us Go, Brothers, Go!* and your third musical, *Miami,* Marvy will agree with me. The two of you are going to make musical history together."

Marvy grinned sleepily at Elmer. "Hi, Elmer Byrd. I think I met you years ago on Sesame Street."

Elmer grimaced. "I finally went into the mail-order business. Quite a few years before you were born, I'm afraid. I'm fifty-six."

"I'm thirty-eight," she smiled at him mischievously. "I hope your wings aren't clipped yet."

"He's sprouting new ones," H.H. said. "Now, come hell or high water, he's going to try them before old Thorny pushes us both out of the nest."

"I still think you should come with us," Elmer told H.H. as they walked out to the plane. "Thorny knows that I'm your patsy, and that I haven't got a mind of my own."

"Ridiculous," H.H. put his arm around Elmer. "Just remind him that last year we sold four hundred thousand copies of your book, *Adopt an Ancestor.* Before we're through, Elmer, we'll turn it into a television series. We'll make *Roots* look like small change. Believe me, it's going to sell five million paperbacks. And that's only a beginning." H.H. squeezed Elmer's arm affectionately. "I know it hasn't been easy, but I hope that you're gradually learning to live in a continuous state of mobile mental mania, balanced by daily maithuna. I assure you, when you have mastered the four M's, you'll not only extend your life span, but you'll achieve your Buddhahood." H.H. snuggled Elmer's face and kissed Marvy's lips. "Take good care of him, sweetie, he has the key to Fort Knox, and doesn't know it."

Maria, Nick Ricci's wife, was already aboard the plane. "She asked Elmer if he would co-pilot the plane with her husband. "I don't know about you, Marvy, but I absolutely have to get a few more hours sleep. The beds are ready and waiting. I'm usually Nick's co-pilot. Give me an hour or two in the sack and I'll be good as new. Then I'll take over for Elmer and he can enjoy you."

Before H.H. left, Maria asked him, "I wonder if it's okay if I drop off at Rome and visit my mother for a few days?"

H.H. had scowled at her. "Not en route. On the way back. Then you can all take a holiday. But until your total mission is accomplished, I want you all to stay together. After you get Adele and Thorny out of the pokey, then I want you to make sure that Thorny takes the *Love Byrd* up to Yugoslavia and picks up the Love Rocks. It's just a short cruise from Athens. You'll love Sveti Stefan. It's a former monastery, about 100 miles south of Dubrovnik. It was turned into a jet-set hide-away, a few years ago. The former monk's sanctuaries are connected by stone pathways which wander around the different levels like a maze," H.H. grinned. "If I weren't forced to stay here and divert the corporate sharks that Thorny has unleashed on us, I'd come with you. At night, we could play hide and seek, and when I caught you, or Marvy, we'd make love in the moonlight near the chapel that overlooks the Adriatic."

Maria laughed at him. "Sorry, H.H., five's a crowd. You'd have to find a Yugoslavian maiden. Anyway, don't worry, the four of us will do all right."

Two hours after Nick and Elmer took off from Logan, they were flying in the clear morning sunlight over a soft, continuous blanket of glistening clouds. Elmer was suddenly aware that Maria was standing behind him in the cockpit. Barechested, she was wearing only a skirt. "I like to fly naked," she grinned. "It gives Nicky and me something to do when we put the plane on automatic pilot." She brushed her breasts across Elmer's face as he surrendered his seat to her.

"How's Marvy doing?" Elmer asked.

"She stopped telling me that H. H. Youman had Svengalied her and that she wasn't going to sleep with you even though H.H. insisted that you were like his younger brother, only nicer. Right now, she's sound asleep on one of the lower berths. Wake her up and play *Rum Ho!* for us. She'll love the songs. Especially *I'll Paint My Dream* and *Song of the Rose.*

Elmer found Marvy, curled foetus-style, sleeping in her bra and panties, a sheet partially over her. The curve of her buttocks flowing into her thighs and legs, nature's perfect curve, invited his touch, but he resisted. Then, suddenly aware of him, she opened her eyes. "Tell me the truth," she sighed, "I'm really the Queen of Hearts. I'm not really flying to Greece. I'm playing games with a bunch of loonies." She grinned at him and pointed to the bed across the aisle of the cabin. "I suppose you could sleep over there, but according to H.H.'s philosophy that would be unfriendly." For a moment she looked at him speculatively, and then said, "Oh well, if you must, take off your pants and lie down with me. I never played spoonsies with a stranger until last night. If you do it H.H.-style, it'll be kind of relaxing."

Beside her in the narrow berth, not knowing who should hold whom, Marvy made the decision and put her arms around Elmer. "If you don't want to talk," she said, "then sleep, we can talk later."

"You really do look like Frances Hardworthy," Elmer said.

"Was that your schoolteacher's name?"

Elmer shook his head, "No, but when I visualize a female character, I always visualize someone I'm in love with, then the male counterpart— the hero—is easy."

"Why?"

"Because it's me. I'm not a very real person. Often, I can't distinguish my dreams from reality. I don't know who the hell I am."

Marvy laughed. "You're Elmer Byrd, and you know damned well that you just slipped your fingers into my panties."

"I'm afraid to ask you if it's all right."

Marvy kissed his nose. "I haven't screamed, have I? But I am embarrassed."

"Why?"

"Because, believe it or not, I'm not usually very promiscuous." Marvy grinned sheepishly. "It sounds silly, but I don't do this with every man I meet. Despite your Heman Hyman Youman, I'm not convinced that his 'mental mobile mania, balanced by maithuna,' is the best way of life, or that instant intimacy like this necessarily produces deep friendships."

"Did you make love with H.H. last night?"

"You mean before you telephoned?" Marvy giggled. "Remember, I arrived from London about noon yesterday. It was a short night." She was silent a moment. "It's strange. I was married for twelve years, but finally got divorced a few years ago. After *Edward and Wally,* my husband couldn't live with my success and his continuing failure. Then I went from being practically a married virgin to going to bed with half a dozen or so different men in the past few years." Marvy sighed. "But the truth is that until the fifteen hours or so that I spent in bed with Heman Hyman in London and Boston, I never experienced such easy intimacy with any man in my life."

"I don't flow with the tide as easily as H.H. does," Elmer said, a little morosely, "but we do agree that we will always love the women we have made love with."

Marvy pursed her lips. "Elmer, that sounds silly. Even your past wives? Did you divorce them or did they divorce you?"

Elmer smiled. "They divorced me. But that has nothing to do with it. Loving is the key to longevity. It's your personal pact with the universe. If you learn to flow with another person's mind and genitals, you participate in the lovely, endless current of life. If one or both of us fail momentarily to grasp the continuous existence of opposites, and we try to make our loving conform to one narrow channel, it wouldn't mean that I had stopped loving you. I still love Bridget and Trudi." Elmer paused; a quick smile flashed across his face. "They were my former wives. I even love Frances Hardworthy, my high school English teacher. Of course, Frances Hardworthy isn't her real name."

"Did you go to bed with her?"

"I was sixteen. She was twenty-eight or twenty-nine. I realized much later that she must have been a virgin. As an only child, she was forced to take care of her old daddy. One day while he was snoring in his wheelchair downstairs in the front room, she took me upstairs to read a story I had written. Instead, she undressed me and took me to bed, and we taught each other how to make love."

"What happened to her?"

"She died."

"And you wrote a musical about her."

Elmer laughed. "Not really. That would be a sad story. Sad men — Minniver Cheevys like me — assail the seasons, but we act the clowns and always write happy endings. I turned her into Frances Hardworthy, whose father had just died when *Rum Ho!* begins. Her former high school student, Norman Lovded, the town undertaker of Jedford, Massachusetts, had just buried him, and they have returned from the cemetary and she is weeping in the basement of Norman's funeral home. The time is 1923. Prohibition of alcohol has become the law of the land. But fifty miles from Jedford, Provincetown has become a wild gathering place for Yankee puritans, Portuguese fishermen, rum-runners, the Mafia, the Coast Guard, bootleggers, and a hideout for jazz-age flappers from Greenwich Village. Frances inherits a summer home in Provincetown, which belonged to her family but hasn't been used for several years because her father refused to visit this latter-day Sodom. He is also estranged from his brother Joshua, who lives in Provincetown. Although Joshua is a pillar of the church, he has been trafficking with the rum-runners. The musical opens with Freeman Pierre, a wealthy, upper-class businessman whose liquor importing business has been ruined by prohibition. He is telling his bootlegger, One-Eyed Jack, that he isn't interested in using his schooner to run booze from Nassau and then selling it on Rum Row, twelve miles out to sea. Pierre is planning to sell his schooner and has rented a house in Provincetown. It's the unused Hardworthy summer home. He's planning to relax there for the summer, and take up painting, like a modern Picasso."

Elmer suddenly kissed Marvy's erect nipples, and then continued his story. "After her father's funeral, in the basement of the funeral home, Norman Lovded gets his former high school teacher drunk, hoping to go to bed with her. But after two or three drinks, Frances is so far gone that she isn't a very appetizing bed partner, so he drives her to Provincetown in his hearse. In the first act, which all takes place in the summer home of the Hardworthys, Freeman Pierre arrives believing it's his house for the summer, but the basement is filled with booze that Joshua has brought in to Provincetown in his fishing boats and is waiting to be trucked up to Boston. Frances tries to evict them all from her house, and ends up being kidnapped by a Portuguese fisherman, King Rose, and One-Eyed Jack, who commandeer Freeman Pierre's schooner. In the second act they are on their way to Nassau in the schooner to load it with scotch from England to bring back to Provincetown." Elmer shrugged, and this time tentatively kissed Marvy's belly and pubic hair and was happy to find that he wasn't rejected.

"I love the songs," Marvy said. "Does Frances lose her virginity to Norman?"

"No. To Freeman Pierre."

"Is Freeman Pierre you, too?"

Elmer laughed. "Of course he is. And you're Frances." Elmer was aware that while he was telling Marvy about *Rum Ho!* her fingers were lightly exploring his stomach and testicles, and were now tentatively holding his penis. "Do you want me to come inside you?"

Marvy burst into a gale of laughter. "Oh, my God! Dear, dear Elmer." She was half laughing and half crying. "Up until last night, I never had a man ask me. Usually they just plunge in whether I'm ready or not."

While she was talking to Elmer, he straddled her and opened her legs. Moving his tongue gently over her labia for a few minutes, he informed her, "Physically you're ready." Then once again he lay beside her. "Tell me when you're ready mentally."

"Is this maithuna?"

"It's the beginning. Once our bodies are joined, the trick is to stay joined and experience bliss together for an hour or more."

Marvy leaned over him. "Damn it, Elmer, sometimes you sound like a duplicate of H. H. Youman. I think you're more dominated by him than by your father."

"Perhaps," Elmer suddenly seemed remote. "Keep in mind, though, that H.H. is a Zen Buddhist. The meaning of Buddhism is an awakening from sleep. An awakening to an acceptance of the opposites in the world that are both valid ways of being. Only humans distinguish good from bad, and reason from emotion. Those who are awakened have no need to dominate another person. H.H. will tell you that your mind should be like "a drawn bow." It is perceiving, but there is no content to the perceiving other than the act of perception itself."

Marvy shook her head. "It sounds to me that in addition to being in the mail-order business, Byrdwhistle is some kind of crazy sex club. H.H. gave me the impression that you all make love with each other every day."

Elmer couldn't help grinning at Marvy's skeptical expression. "We're supposed to. The theory we're exploring is that the best stress-reducer for human beings is sexual loving and sexual blending. Medical research is gradually proving that severe or prolonged stress—not physical stress, but mental stress—makes the body more vulnerable to ailments ranging from skin rashes, headaches, and migraines to the common cold, heart attacks, and cancer. So, ever since we got Thorny out of the company, H.H. and I have tried to create an entirely new kind of working environment, based on laughter and the joy of personal creativity. All Byrdwhistlers are "drawn bows." We are mobilely mental and happily manic. The key stress-reducer is maithuna—which is a nice form of exercise, incidentally, in addition to being a great deal of continuous, noncompetitive body movement. Every Byrdwhistler is taught the joy of movement. On top of this, we are supposed to follow a sound diet that excludes all meat but not fish or fowl, and if one does use escape inducers like alcohol, which sometimes help release stress, they should be counteracted with milk. H.H. has projected a ratio of one quart of milk to six ounces of booze. While he has investigated the greater longevity of many alcoholics who follow this regime, he still hasn't convinced Serge Ivanowski, who runs the Center for Ageless Humans. Incidentally, the center is subsidized by Byrdwhistle."

"My God," Marvy shivered as Elmer's finger traced her pubic mound and passed like a warm breeze over her clitoris. "I'm beyond readiness. Come inside me! I'm bursting." Then she grinned at him. "But I don't want to live forever. Not if I can die like this."

Enjoying the warmth of her vagina and their flesh pulsating together from the vibration of the aircraft, Elmer told her, "Neither does H.H. Actually, the secret he's looking for is not only to live life like a drawn bow but to die like the never-released arrow. Death, the arrow's release, will be at a time of his own choosing. That will be the day his bow begins to slacken."

Marvy couldn't help herself. She was suddenly crying. "Oh, Elmer, if your musical is as loving as you are, the whole audience will have an orgasm while they are listening to it." She moved her buttocks in very slow exquisite circular motion while at the same time her vagina nursed his penis. "Tell me more about your musical," she whispered to him, "and after we climax, you can sing it to me!"

LUDAMUS II

My faith is in man, and in the belief that every soul finds time for true expression when the weary money-maker rests.

King C. Gillette
World Corporation

What is crucially important is the fact itself that there are many other kinds of pay than money pay. I have been collecting advertisements for sometime in which the attractions set forth to lure the applicant are not only money but also higher need gratifications. Of course, a large portion of self-actualizing people have probably fused work and play anyway, i.e. they love their work.

Abraham Maslow
Theory Z

9

Having survived the night in the Ritz-Carlton without giving in to his need for self-love, Ronald Coldaxe managed to shower in the morning without undue soaping of his neglected penis. He dawdled over breakfast Monday morning with the current *Wall Street Journal,* which he had picked up in the hotel lobby. Finally, allowing time for Elmer Byrd to arrive at his office, read his mail, and have his morning bowel movement, if that was his custom, Ronald asked the doorman to hail a taxi for him.

He gave the driver an address in Everett and, settling back, opened his attaché case for one more glance through the meager information that he had accumulated on the Byrdwhistle Corporation.

"I hear rumors that the Byrdwhistle offices make the old Playboy Club look like a monastery," the driver told him as he weaved through the early-morning traffic toward the Mystic River Bridge.

Ronald looked at him blankly. He didn't enjoy small talk with cabdrivers. "Byrdwhistle is a mail-order firm," he said coldly.

"Maybe it is," the driver laughed, "but from what I've heard, you've got to be a firm male to work there."

Ronald didn't answer, but the driver continued, "Of course, it's all rumors. Everybody is pretty close-mouthed about what goes on in the offices on the floors they built on top of the Byrdwhistle building a couple of years ago."

Unable to engage his passenger in conversation, the cabdriver slouched in morose silence. Twenty minutes later, he stopped on a quiet street next to a hundred-foot-long red-brick building. Green Boston ivy vines were growing high above the windows on the first floor. "You're here, Mister. The entire building on your left is Byrdwhistle." The driver's lascivious grin, coupled with a sly, "Have a good day," turned into a grumbly "Aw, shit, can you spare it?" when Ronald handed him a dollar tip on the fifteen-dollar cab fare.

A massive iron-strapped door on the far corner of the building gave Ronald the happy impression of New England solidity. On the windowless door was a brass plaque with the words "Byrdwhistle Corporation, Subsidiary of World Corporation" engraved on it. The entrance to the building gave the appearance of a turn-of-the-century craftsman's guild, or perhaps a private club. Unostentatious, it exuded a subdued New England touch of class. But what was World Corporation? Ralph Thiemost hadn't mentioned that Byrdwhistle was a subsidiary of another company. World Corporation wasn't referred to in any of the financial information that Ronald had acquired on the company. Ronald scowled. He didn't like last-minute surprises.

Beneath the plaque was a smaller one, also brass and engraved, saying, "To enter, ring bell." Evidently Byrdwhistle wasn't overwhelmed with salesmen and suppliers' representatives, who arrived like a small army at most corporate headquarters by 9:30 in the morning. When he pushed the button, instead of opening inward, the door slid to the right, revealing that its Gothic-arch appearance was created by the stone entrance itself, not by the door.

Inside, in a small pine-paneled reception room, he was greeted by a young woman seated behind a telephone and a control panel. She was wearing a thin, flower-print blouse that revealed her naked breasts. Trying not to stare and, at the same time, to repress his suddenly awakened penis, Ronald handed her his business card, and while she read silently— "Ronald Coldaxe, Vice President, W.I.N. Corporation"—he told her that he had an appointment with Elmer Byrd.

"I'm sorry, Mr. Coldaxe," she smiled at him, "But Elmer won't be in today. He was called away unexpectedly. But H. H. Youman is expecting you. I'll ring and tell him that you're here." Pressing a button on a console that was already alive with flashing red and white lights, she smiled at him. "I'm Nina Kingsley. This is my once-a-year week as receptionist."

Wondering grimly if he had come all the way to Boston to go through a let's-pretend-we're-not-interested rigamarole with Elmer Byrd, and hoping that he didn't have to suffer the first day with second-string players who would try to give him the build-up on whatever price the Byrds might be asking for the company, Ronald noted several parchment scrolls hanging on the reception-room walls. Waiting for Nina to reach H. H. Youman, he read one with a growing feeling of incredulity.

Declaration of Principles of Corporate Party

I Am a Corporationist

I BELIEVE in "World Corporation," by the People — for the People, as opposed to corporations by Individuals for Individuals.

I BELIEVE in International Corporation with all nations, All nations with each other for the accomplishment of Universal Peace through "World Corporation."

I BELIEVE in the corporate acquisition and final ownership of all property, and control of all industry by the people.

I BELIEVE in the elimination of lines of demarcation between nations and people, and the establishment of equity between individuals throughout the world on the basis of intelligence.

On the opposite walls there were architectural illustrations of Utopian cities and a pyramid design entitled "Symbol of World Corporation," which rose from a base labeled "Preparatory Education" to "Education and Industry," to "Skilled Labor," "Superintendants," "Managers," "Technical Experts," "Specialists," "Administration," and culminated at the peak with the words "World Corporate Congress."

Balanced between the scrolls on the far wall was a large oil painting of a friendly, familiar-looking nineteenth-century gentleman wearing a moustache and a pointed, starched collar. Ronald wondered for a moment if it might be Elmer Byrd's grandfather. Nina anticipated his question. "That's King Gillette," she told him. "He not only invented the safety razor but created World Corporation. Isn't he handsome? We all think H.H. looks a lot like him." She paused, listening to a response on her telephone. "H.H. is in a sales conference," she smiled at Ronald. "But his secretary expects he'll be out of the hot-tub in about twenty minutes. In the meantime, would you please sign our security clearance? You can take the elevator to the solarium just as soon as his secretary signals that he is ready for you."

She handed Ronald a paper, and he glanced at it suspiciously. Even in Los Angeles, top executives didn't sit in hot-tubs at ten o'clock in the morning. "I don't want to go to the solarium. I want your executive offices."

"The solarium is our executive offices," Nina explained patiently.

"What's all this security clearance about?" Ronald demanded. "Does Byrdwhistle have a government contract for secret weapons?" Actually, he was just as curious to know why the painting of the long-dead inventor of the safety razor hung in the reception-room of Byrdwhistle. Gillette's World Corporation sounded like some kind of Karl Marx-Communist daydream. Control of all industry by the people. Jesus Christ! That was madness. But somewhere in the recesses of his mind he could hear M'mm chuckling. M'mm told all their friends that she believed in total monetary equality for everybody. But, as he constantly pointed out to her, she managed to spend three times as much money as most median-income families, and she never seemed interested in economizing. He often told M'mm that the radical opinions she voiced in letters to the newspapers and her eagerness to picket organizations she thought were against the common man were motivated by her guilt. He accused her of being an upper-class do-gooder who had never earned a dime and hadn't learned that there was no such thing as a free lunch.

"Our security clearance is self-explanatory," Nina told Ronald as he read the paper she handed him with growing disbelief. "The Byrdwhistle Corporation is experimenting with a new kind of management-employee association. We are synthesizing the theories of Zen, developed by Alfred Low in his book *Zen and Creative Management,* and the principles of Eupsychian Management, expounded by Abraham Maslow in his book by that name, with the theories of the Oneida Community. Because our approaches may prove startling to the uninitiated, and because the success of the experiments depend on maintaining a low profile (consistent with the nature of the mail-order business), we don't permit visitors to our upstairs office without prior arrangement. If you are reading this clearance sheet, you already have an appointment, otherwise you would have been received by a Byrdwhistle executive in one of the interviewing offices downstairs next to the reception room. We feel sure that, as a guest of Byrdwhistle's inner-management team, you'll agree to sign the security clearance."

Shaking his head and grimacing, Ronald read on:

1. The undersigned agrees not to discuss or reveal in any form to any free-lance writers or any representatives of the media, including newspapers, magazines, television, radio, any details of the unique interpersonal working

environment with which Byrdwhistle is experimenting. Nor will the undersigned aid or abet any rumors concerning the activities of Byrdwhistle
employees and management.

2. The undersigned agrees to leave any cameras or recording equipment
with the receptionist, where they may be reclaimed on departure.

3. The undersigned is aware that he/she will be under constant surveillance by video cameras, and Byrdwhistle reserves the right to video tape the
undersigned during his/her stay here, with the understanding that the video
tapes will never be used except on the premises of Byrdwhistle for instruc-
tional purposes.

"This is ridiculous," Ronald said coldly. "What if I refuse to sign?"

Nina shrugged. "I'm afraid that you won't be allowed beyond this
area. H.H. has refused to admit quite a few people, including the Governor of Massachusetts and representatives from various government
agencies who refused to sign the clearance." She chuckled, "But I'm sure
he'll talk with you down here if you prefer. So far, no one has arrived
with a search warrant. H.H. assures us that we pay all the corporate
taxes we have to. So Internal Revenue hasn't bothered us yet."

"My appointment is with Elmer Byrd. How can I reach him?"

"I'm afraid you can't, Mr. Coldaxe. Elmer flew to Greece last night."

"Greece?" Ronald exploded. "Dammit, why didn't he contact my
headquarters? I had a definite appointment with him today."

"Actually, I don't know whether it's for publication," Nina said conspiratorially, "but Elmer Byrd isn't very important around here. H.H.
seems to run everything."

Reluctantly, Ronald opened his attaché case and handed Nina a small
Sony tape-recorder. "I'm sure that after I talk with your Mr. Youman he'll
get this back to me immediately. I need it to take notes." For a moment he
stared angrily at the clearance sheet and then brusquely signed it.

"Be sure to write in your company name and address," Nina told him
sweetly. "H.H. says that he's expecting a telephone call from Athens.
Elmer is supposed to check in by eleven P.M. our time. I think that after
that H.H. will be free."

Ronald stared at her in exasperation. He couldn't bring himself to
remind her that she had told him that H. H. Youman was in the hot-tub.
"I thought you said that Mr. Youman was in a sales conference."

"He is, but when Elmer calls he'll take the call there. He suggested
that while you were waiting you might like to skim through our new Lov-
n-Learn editions of King Gillette's *World Corporation* and *Human Drift,*
Byrdwhistle reprinted them this spring. They are selling very, very well."
Nina pointed to a pile of books on a table. "You can take your own personal copy, compliments of Byrdwhistle. Mr. Youman is really sorry to
keep you waiting. Just as soon as he signals, I'll clear you and you can
take our guest elevator to the Solarium."

Scowling at her, and more than a little angry at the thought of wasting his time with a second-string stockholder in a company that he was already convinced was being run by incompetents, it occurred to Ronald that all he had to do was ignore Nina Kingsley, summon the elevator, and demand an immediate audience with this H. H. Youman character. All this business about security was nonsense. "What would happen if someone walked in here and pointed a gun at you?" He leaned toward Nina, getting a better view of her breasts, "What would you do then?"

"I'd scream," Nina grinned provocatively at him. "But you'd never get upstairs. The elevator door is controlled from a console on the fifth floor. You couldn't get out through the front door either, because you'd never figure out what combination of buttons to push here. Of course you could shoot me, but then you'd be trapped in here." Laughing, she pointed at the oil portrait, "What's more, King Gillette is watching us. There's a television eye in his stickpin."

Grimly, Ronald sat down in one of the red leather chairs and picked up a copy of *World Corporation*. Flipping the pages, he read: "As soon as practicable, after the World Corporation has reduced its possession and control of all agencies for production and distribution throughout the world, it will redeem all of its stock, after which time, the assets of the World Corporation *shall be the joint property, in equal shares, of all the peoples of the earth.*

Ronald shrugged impatiently. After three weeks on the road, he was in no mood to read such Utopian nonsense. But he tucked the book in his attaché case. He'd bring it home to M'mm. It proved what he'd always told her. Only millionaires with diamond stickpins, fat asses, and full bellies could afford to be idealists.

10

Finally, after his third request that she check out what was delaying Mr. Youman, Nina Kingsley smiled brightly at Ronald and told him that H.H. had cleared him to the solarium. In the elevator he grimly anticipated a wasted morning with an antidiluvian character. Anyone who believed King Gillette's theory that the only way to solve the problem of capitalism was to create an ultimate monopoly called World Corporation was either a fanatic, a wide-eyed believer in Utopias, or a typical upper-echelon executive, who, following Parkinson's law, had risen to the level of his incompetence and had become entrenched there. No wonder

Thornton Byrd wanted to sell his company. It was probably the only way he could get rid of H. H. Youman.

But when the elevator door slowly opened, instead of being met by the stoop-shouldered, doddering old man he expected, a totally naked woman in her late thirties — coolly ignoring his gasp of astonishment — extended her hand.

"Good morning, Mr. Coldaxe, welcome to Byrdwhistle. I'm Lois Rather." Despite her smile and the vulnerability of her nakedness, Ronald had a distinct feeling that she was hostile. "I'm manager of our Catalogue Art Department."

Behind her a naked young man on a diving board plunged into an oval pool, which seemed to be the terminus of a kidney-shaped swimming pool. He surfaced in the midst of several naked young women and waved at Ronald. Then, laughing together, they all swam around a curve formed by an interior wall of the building. Before they disappeared, Ronald heard one of them say: "That's the man from W.I.N.!"

Ronald was having difficulty averting his eyes from Lois's full breasts and the triangle of wet brown hair growing lushly below the soft curve of her stomach. Instead of the typical sleekly anonymous, fluorescent-lighted, broadloom-carpeted administrative office he had been expecting, the top floor of Byrdwhistle Corporation was covered by a huge glass bubble. Above it, the sky was a blend of late summer sun and frothy white clouds. The temperature was tropical, but in some way the direct heat of the sun was deflected and, despite the swimming pool, there was no humidity.

Trying to assimilate this strange environment, Ronald heard Lois telling him that Elmer Byrd hadn't telephoned H.H. yet and that he was probably still en route to Greece. She said that H.H. was also unsuccessful in trying to contact Thornton Byrd. Ronald was fighting to control his anger. This was the first time in any of his more than three hundred acquisition probes that lower-level management seemed to be fully aware of the purpose of his visit.

"I'm under the impression," he told Lois, "that Mr. Youman is purposely delaying seeing me. In any case, my appointment was with Elmer Byrd. Since he isn't here, I'm probably wasting my time."

Lois shrugged. "To be quite honest, Mr. Coldaxe, H.H. has briefed all employees on the purpose of your visit. None of us feel that a merger with your company is compatible with our individual futures or the larger experiment that is going on here." She smiled at him coolly. "H.H. expected that Elmer would be here, and he had a meeting scheduled for this morning that he had to attend. Actually, he suggested that, if you wished, you could join him. He's in the hot-tub on the floor below with Marge Slick and some of our key accounting people. They're going over profit and inventory projections for the spring edition of our *U-Can-*

Do-It Catalogue." Lois pointed to a door in a tiled partition opposite the swimming pool. "That's our guest locker-room, Mr. Coldaxe. You can leave your clothes there. Please take a shower before you enter the pool."

Ronald tried not to show the lurid thoughts battering against his skull. Employees swimming naked in a company swimming pool, business conferences in a hot tub, television surveillance and video-taping of visitors—Jesus Christ, what next?

"If you prefer, Mr. Coldaxe, while we're waiting we can take a swim through the main office. We're very proud of our pool. You can only see a small portion of it from here. Actually, it's a huge reverse S. It curves from one end of the building to the other and, except at the ends, it's ten feet wide and about one hundred fifty feet long. Company regulations are that all employees must swim the full length and back at least once a day. H.H. believes that most office and administrative workers don't get enough on-the-job exercise. At the other end, there's a wading pool. The company provides full day-care and kindergarten for all children of the Byrdwhistle family. After a child goes to school, or if the children are already in school, we have work schedules that parallel the children's school hours so that either the father or mother will be home when school is over. As you will discover, the family concept at Byrdwhistle has evolved much farther than the window-dressing of companies like W.I.N. who use the word *family* very loosely."

"You seem to be quite familiar with W.I.N."

"We've been under takeover sieges before, Mr. Coldaxe," Lois smiled briefly. "Whenever Thornton Byrd gets angry with his son or H.H. he threatens to sell the company. Fortunately, our profitability has not received wide publicity. But, as you will discover, H.H. believes that the only way to defeat potential corporate grabbers is to learn where your enemy is most vulnerable." Realizing that Ronald was trying to maintain eye-contact with her and not look at her body, Lois decided to challenge him. "Since you obviously don't wish to join H.H. in the tub, I'll be happy to take you on a tour of the building. At the same time I can give you some background of Byrdwhistle that you seem to be missing. Do you want to take off your clothes?"

"To tell you the truth, Ms. Rather," Ronald tried not to show his anger, "I'm not very happy with this insanity. It's obvious that I'm not going to see Elmer Byrd and I really have very little to discuss with Mr. Youman."

Although Ronald had never been naked with any woman besides M'mm, and only peripherally with men in the locker-room of tennis and golf clubs, he was quite certain that a naked "creative director," as an acquisitions vice president is often called, shouldn't try "to pick plums" in his birthday suit. His hairy, too-white paunchiness and his ineffective-looking penis—except when it was ready for action—would most certainly

dilute the necessary sense of power that was part and parcel of any preliminary takeover negotiations. Anyway, he was already convinced that
Byrdwhistle was no "sleeping beauty." From what he had seen thus far it
was a rotten plum. He looked impatiently at his watch. It was eleven
o'clock. "I'll give Youman another fifteen minutes."

As he spoke, he suddenly noticed a television camera high on an
opposite wall panning the area where they were standing. "And if you
don't mind, Ms. Rather, I'll keep my clothes on."

Lois followed his glance. "You don't have to worry. The video tapes
that we make of ourselves and visitors never leave the building. Really,
Mr. Coldaxe, I have a feeling that you're embarrassed by a naked
woman. Anyway, there's no place out here to relax comfortably with
clothes on. Why don't you follow me back to my office? I'll slip on a
dress and give you a company tour. Byrdwhistle is really quite unique.
H.H. can reach us anywhere in the building when he's ready to see you."

Reluctantly, trying not to gaze at her swaying behind, Ronald followed her along the inside curve of the glass-walled pool. He noticed that
there were various exits and entrances en route. At numerous points in
the building, if an employee felt like taking a swim, the meandering pool
was readily accessible. To Ronald's amazement most of the men and
many of the women were working at their desks naked to the waist, and
others were circulating through the offices completely naked. Evidently,
whether or not one wore clothes was a matter of personal preference.

"H.H. told me that in all probability you haven't seen the Byrdwhistle
employment manual and guidebook," Lois said. "You really must read
the pages called "Twenty-six Oneida Golden Nuggets"* which H.H. culled
from the Oneida Community circulars. Are you familiar with Oneida?"

Ronald vaguely remembered the name. "Wasn't that the communal
group in upstate New York who shared their wives?"

Lois laughed. "Actually you might have said the wives shared their
husbands. Oneida was founded by a minister, John Humphrey Noyes.
The community lasted nearly seventy years. They were very successful
financially. Among other things they manufactured bear traps, satchels,
thread, and finally silverware. But you are right. They didn't believe in
monogamous marriage. If you wanted to sleep with one of their community members, you asked him or her, just like at Byrdwhistle. But keep in
mind that Byrdwhistle is only partially communal. As you are well
aware, at the moment Byrdwhistle employees don't own the company.
H.H. says that until World Corporation becomes a total reality we are in

---

*"Twenty-six Oneida Golden Nuggets" culled from Oneida publications by H. H. Youman
are included in the last section of this book, together with an annotated bibliography of
books for readers who may be interested in more details of H. H. Youman's Theory Z syn-
thesis and the Byrdwhistle approach to corporate management.

an advanced transitional stage. While we don't merge our total lives, many Byrdwhistle employees—on their own option, of course—blend their sexual lives at work and enjoy occasional 'rest' periods in our Love Rooms."

Lois grinned at her euphemism, but it evidently went over Ronald's head. "Six years ago," she continued, "when Thornton Byrd finally retired, H.H. convinced Elmer that, with a new hiring policy and his evolving Theory Z approach to management, profits could be increased substantially, especially if we offered a new kind of family employment. H.H. proposed to Elmer that, if he were right, a portion of the increased earnings should be used for 'fun projects.'" Lois smiled. "H.H. believes there isn't enough fun in work. While Thornton has given Elmer the legal right to vote his stock in the event he is unable to attend particular directors meetings, lately it seems that Thornton isn't too happy with some of these fun projects." Lois shook her head sadly. "Of course, that is probably the reason that you are here."

She stopped at one of the offices they were passing and fondly rubbed the shoulders of a heavy-set, hairy-chested man, who was naked except for a pair of bikini shorts. He grinned at her and quickly brushed his face across her breasts. Then, smiling at Ronald, he asked, "Have you noticed that Lois has very expressive tits? They seem to carry on a conversation with you." Lois kissed his cheek. "Bill, behave yourself. This is Mr. Cold-axe from W.I.N. I'm going to give him the grand tour. Bill is in marketing," she explained to Ronald. "He's my primary love-ass."

Chuckling at Ronald's shocked expression, Bill responded, "Obviously, Lois is trying to get *your* ass. She probably hasn't told you that all Byrdwhistle employees, like Lois and I, are working husbands and wives. Only H.H. and Elmer aren't married to someone who works for the company. Altogether, including our branch warehouses and subsidiaries, we are approximately four hundred people, but we are also two hundred married couples. H.H. calls us all love associates—hence, love-asses. It's H.H.'s theory that pair-bonds, like Lois and I, working together every day on common projects can share happier lives." Bill patted Lois's buttocks affectionately. "How could anyone disagree with him? More than fifty percent of the women working in the United States today are working wives—not because they want to, but in many cases because they have to. H.H. has reversed most company hiring policies. Byrdwhistle will only hire married couples who have passed the Byrdwhistle entrance examination." Bill laughed. "Without much difficulty, H.H. has proved that one of Oneida's discoveries: that any kind of work can be accomplished much faster when it's done by an equal number of both sexes working together."

Ronald tried valiantly to stop scowling. "Byrdwhistle sounds like a sexual circus to me. If you don't mind my asking, what's the purpose of the entrance examination?" He was suddenly wishing that he had his tape recorder. Ralph Thiemost would be more impressed if he could hear these insane responses verbatim.

"I'm afraid you haven't grasped the total picture," Bill said. "It's an honor to work here. Byrdwhistle has thousands of applicants, but most of them can't pass that examination."

"It is designed to determine whether you have Theory Z potential," Lois interjected, "whether you can go one step beyond self-actualization to transcendentalism. H.H. is writing a book about it. Theory Z was originated by Abraham Maslow. It's a further development of Theory Y management techniques, which were originally proposed by James MacGregor. I'm sure that you're familiar with Theory X and Theory Y, Mr. Coldaxe."

Ronald nodded. He remembered vaguely from his days at graduate school that Theory X was the old-style autocratic form of employment management, where each employee's job was completely structured by the work itself and the particular rules governing the job. Theory Y was freer and called for more participative management. An employee had some say on how he or she would do a particular job. The end result, and not the means of doing it, was the criterion. From what Ronald had seen thus far Theory Z was not only the end of the alphabet, it was the end of sane management. It occurred to him that M'mm would be right at home here. Once she heard about Byrdwhistle, she'd be fighting for nude offices as well as nude beaches.

"I know all about Theory Z," he said grimly. "According to William Ouchi, who wrote the book, the Japanese are more productive and work harder than we do because they have lifetime jobs and their management is more concerned about their employees' welfare than our corporate managers are." Ronald shrugged. Although he didn't say so, he was damned sure that Japanese workers didn't run around their workplaces bare-assed. "Like Byrdwhistle, the Japs have been conned into thinking they're part of one big family."

Bill laughed, "We're not a W.I.N.-style family, and that's for sure. I'm sure that H. H. Youman will tell you that Ouchi's Theory Z is not Abe Maslow's. Maslow proposed a Theory Z style of management many years before Ouchi, and even before we were aware of what was happening in Japan. Unlike the Japanese, Byrdwhistlers are transcenders. We have a new approach to work. We play! One of the reasons for our entrance exams is to weed out certain kinds of married couples who probably could never learn how to play with each other and their friends."

"Bill is trying to tell you," Lois said, "that a strictly monogamous couple might be very uncomfortable at Byrdwhistle. Oneida had a system called Complex Marriage. Byrdwhistle has Love Associates, or 'love-asses.' It's comparable in a way to Oneida. H.H. believes that men and women who fully incorporate sex and loving into their total lives, and even express themselves sexually, if the need arises, during working hours, can substantially reduce their cellular aging. One of our fun projects is a continuous funding of research on sex and aging." Lois couldn't help smiling at Ronald's apparent disbelief. "It's not for publication, of course—that's why you were asked to sign our security clearance—but Byrdwhistle provides an environment where employees, if they wish, can enjoy several hours of loving every day."

"Not necessarily with one's original marriage partner," Bill obviously was enjoying Ronald's disgust. "I'm sure that Lois will show you the Love Rooms on the fourth floor. There are a dozen of them. Of course, if we use a room with a love-ass other than our primary spouse, we must get each other's permission."

Laughing, and telling Bill that she would see him later, Lois led Ronald to her cubicle, where she quickly snapped a skirt around her waist and buttoned a thin blouse over her breasts. Ronald wanted to ask her how "love-asses"—God, wait until M'mm heard that one!—obtained each other's permission for extracurricular loving, but outside her office, which had an entrance on the snakelike swimming pool, a man in his late fifties had just swum around the curve and was lifting himself out of the water. Waving at Lois and indicating that he wanted to talk with her, he stroked the water from his naked body and quickly dried himself with a towel that hung near the sliding glass-door exit.

While Ronald was wondering when in hell these people got any work done—he didn't know how women reacted to naked men, but he knew damned well that watching Lois's naked body prevented his concentrating on anything—Lois introduced the naked swimmer. "This is Bruce Maitlin, Mr. Coldaxe. Next to H.H., he is the best copywriter in the business. If H.H. would let him, he could write copy that would convince Aunt Emma in Sweetwater, Ohio, to invest her entire life-savings in World Corporation today and he could convince you that the collected works of Charles Dickens were the sexiest books ever written." She grimaced at Ronald. "I have a feeling that Mr. Coldaxe is quite turned off by Byrdwhistle."

Bruce laughed, "No offense, my friend, but I hope so. We're getting along very well without winners from W.I.N." Bruce didn't seem concerned that his penis was brushing the top of Lois's desk. "I'm sorry to bother you, Lo-Lo, but I wanted to know how you felt about my new copy for the copulating-deer layouts. They're ready for a third hearing, and I hope last, at the Symp meeting this afternoon."

Lois squeezed his arm affectionately, "They're great. I'm sure you've got it this time. We'll see you at Symp this afternoon." Lois held up an intricate carving of brown wood. "As you can see, Mr. Coldaxe, the female deer has a warm, loving expression on her face. She's even lifted her haunches to give the male full penetration. We import these hand-carvings from Bali. At $85.00 apiece we expect to sell fifty thousand of them in our Dreamy Byrd catalogue. We call them our friendly fucking deers."

"Maybe H.H. will bring Mr. Coldaxe along to the Symp meeting," Bruce said. "We have a Speak Your Mind Participation every Monday and Thursday afternoon. We cover the gamut. Anyone can blow off steam about whatever they like, from corporate-takeover artists like you, to some unique ideas on how Byrdwhistle should be run, to defending our choice of catalogue items, and to getting approval of new copy and new layouts. But the real fun begins when we criticize each other personally or try to decide whether Theory Z and Byrdwhistle is a crock of shit." Before he walked away to return to his office, Bill smiled at Ronald. "Nothing personal, Mr. Coldaxe, but I'm sure that W.I.N. would only lose if they acquired Byrdwhistle."

Lois explained to Ronald that Symps were patterned after the Oneida Community criticism technique. "But I'm sure that H.H. will tell you about them. For the past six months, Bruce and I have been making love on the premises once a week. Bill gave me permission. Bruce is married to Dottie. She's manager of the accounting department this year. Bruce is twenty-two years older than I am. He's fifty-eight. H.H.'s theory is that sexual age-gaps shouldn't exist. When men and women get to a certain chronological age, it gives them a new lease on life if they can discover that their sexual attractiveness hasn't waned and that a younger person can find them exciting and interesting both mentally and physically. I keep asking Bruce, 'How am I different in the sack from Dottie?' but he doesn't go into details. He tells me that I'm actually not so orgasmic as Dottie is, but my mind makes him more erotic than hers does, probably because he hasn't known me so long and I'm not so predictable."

Ronald knew that Lois was enjoying his amazement at this kind of uncensored conversation. "Does everybody go to bed with everybody else in this damned place?" he demanded. He had made up his mind that no matter what the financial figures revealed Byrdwhistle wasn't a business but a swingers' club that made money by sheer accident.

"If you asked me if I'd like to make love with you, and if your wife worked here and had already given you permission," Lois grinned, "I might tell you, 'No, I'm sorry, I'm already too occupied.' But, if I were intrigued, I might indicate that perhaps in two or three months it would be okay. If I were agreeable, I'd tell you first that I would have to clear it with Bill. A company rule is that a turndown is in no way to be construed as a personal rejection, and a 'No, but thank you,' answer is never to be questioned. Lois stared at him with raised eyebrows. "While I would hazard a guess that your wife might give you permission, I'm afraid that if you asked me my answer would be 'No thanks.'"

"How the hell do you know whether I've got a wife or not?" Ronald asked her.

For a second, Lois looked confused. She was about to tell him that she had seen video-tapes of Meredith Coldaxe, but then she decided against it. That was H.H.'s problem. "I was just guessing," she said, and then she changed the subject. "Actually, you should understand that the friendly sexual exchanges that occur among Byrdwhistle employees provide an intimacy—you might say a grease—that helps the larger concept work. Byrdwhistle is an experiment in turning a business organization into a limited form of an extended family. One of the Oneida Nuggets in their circular of August 1854 says, 'Let every distinct form of business which employs and supports a number of workmen be the gathering point of a *family* sufficient to man the business . . . Let the employer, whatever his line of business, live with his men.'"

Lois was leading him through the key administrative areas on the fifth floor and introducing him to various people in accounting, data processing, marketing, and catalogue preparation. From the tone of their greetings, Ronald began to feel more and more like a lone soldier walking through an enemy mine-field.

But having shed most of her rancor, Lois was now trying to indoctrinate him. "John Noyes was one of the first Americans to recognize that human sexuality has two aspects," she said. "He called them the amative and propagative. At Oneida, for many years while they were struggling, they couldn't afford to be overburdened with children. Oneida was a microcosm of the world today," Lois laughed. "H.H. believes that if Noyes were alive today he'd be working for Planned Parenthood. At Oneida, the male was responsible for birth control. Noyes called it 'male continence.' It simply meant that the male did not ejaculate when he had intercourse. With modern birth-control methods, I'm sure that Noyes would have approved of H. H. Youman's adaptation of Theory Z. H.H. believes that extended lovemaking is a way to transcend one's ego and that everyone should enjoy total sexual and mental intimacy with more than one person in a lifetime."

In the catalogue preparation department, Lois pointed out that fulfillment—actual mailing of the merchandise—with the exception of items from the Byrdcage catalogue was all handled directly from various subsidiary Byrdwhistle warehouses throughout the country. "Each separate catalogue division has its own warehouse shipping area," she told him. "We have a home-office rotation policy so that the two hundred or so love-asses who are employed in various other parts of the country can come to Boston with their kids—at least one month every year. They switch homes or apartments with the Boston people. Our subsidiary warehouses don't have the amenities we have here. So coming to Boston becomes a nice additional paid-vacation. On the other hand, many of the other Byrdwhistle warehouses are more strategically located. Three are in Florida, three in California, one near Lake Tahoe, one near Aspen, one in Vermont, and three in the New York City area. So we all look forward to the change of scenery made possible by rotation. In addition, every Byrdwhistle employee has his or her personal-decision month's vacation."

Ronald shook his head hopelessly. "How do you prevent everyone from taking a vacation in June, July, or August?"

"Oh, that's not the personal decision. Actual vacation time is based on seniority," Lois smiled. "The personal decision is whether we individually believe that we have actually earned our month's vacation. But before you can appreciate that you have to understand our salary arrangements. Everyone who works at Byrdwhistle is paid an identical wage. It goes up or down semiannually, based on the median family income figures published by the Department of Labor."

"You mean that no matter what anyone does here—they are paid approximately $22,000 annually?" Ronald knew what the median income was in that area.

"Actually, many of the Byrdwhistle people are worth much more," Lois said. One hundred thirty Byrdwhistle employees have their doctorate degrees, eighty have their masters, and most of the rest have a bachelor's or some kind of vocational degree. My husband Bill could get a job in the high twenties, but here we *each* earn $22,000—plus bonuses. Whether we do routine jobs or highly specialized jobs is immaterial. Every job is rotated. Even though my basic skills are in art and layout, next year I will be in marketing, and after that in accounting. A condition of employment is that we must learn other job skills. One of the Oneida Golden Nuggets discusses the advantages of job rotation, which eliminates work boredom. As for the routine jobs, like shipping of Byrdcage items from our inventory, which can't be automated, we do them together communally two afternoons a week. This follows the 'working bee' principle of Oneida. They made the discovery that routine work, when it is done with an intermingling of the sexes, instead of being boring can be a lot of fun. If you are still here tomorrow afternoon, you should join us on the shipping floors. In the summer, even on those floors, which don't have direct natural light, practically everybody runs around naked."

Ronald had moved beyond astonishment. "You haven't told me how an employee makes a personal decision about whether he or she is entitled to a month's vacation."

"We must make it in writing," Lois smiled. "Every three months we must submit a detailed analysis of our personal contribution to Byrdwhistle. It's partially based on total hours worked. Of course there are no timeclocks, but most of us average around fifty hours a week on the premises. We also have to evaluate our personal contribution to profits and, ultimately, to our bonuses and whether on the current workload our area will function smoothly during the month that we want to take off. There can't be any bullshit in the personal analysis because they're read at Symp meetings and are subject to very blunt criticism. Anyway, we don't build our lives around our next vacation. Most of us discover that when we are away from the Byrdwhistle family we miss our love-ass friends."

Lois had led Ronald to an elevator on the opposite side of the building. Waiting for it, she told him: "Our hot-tubs, the child-care area, two indoor tennis courts, our Love Rooms, and a lunchroom serving free breakfast and lunch are all on the fourth floor. If we want to eat meat, we have to bring it ourselves. H.H. is a vegetarian. The lunchroom only serves yogurt, fresh vegetables, and fruit. Also, on the fourth floor, we have an expandable theater that can seat up to seven hundred people. We use it for our Symp sessions and for various fun projects conceived by Elmer Byrd.

"This whole damned business seems to be a 'fun project,'" Ronald said sarcastically.

Lois shrugged. "I'm sure that H.H. will discuss the purposes of business organizations with you. H.H. believes that basically, after making enough money to finance ourselves and pay our couple-based salaries, the whole purpose of a business organization is to create an environment for fun, play, and self-realization. Elmer Byrd is a good example. I'm sure that H.H. will tell you about him. He never wanted to be president of Byrdwhistle. He wanted to be a musician or write musical comedies, or both. His father wouldn't encourage him, but H.H. has. Elmer has completed a musical called *Rum Ho!* Now he's working on a new one called *Let Us Go, Brothers, Go!* That was the rallying song of the Oneida Community and Elmer has assigned all rights on *Rum Ho!* and all future musicals that he writes to Byrdwhistle. A month ago, we produced an uncostumed version of *Rum Ho!* complete with thirty-two Byrdwhistle employees as actors and a Byrdwhistle orchestra of ten instruments." Lois was amused by Ronald's hopeless shrug. "No one took Elmer very seriously until we began to rehearse the musical. But it's really quite good—and very funny. Now, we're all sure that Elmer is going to make a lot of money for Byrdwhistle."

When the automatic elevator door opened, a woman of about forty-five got off and greeted them, "Good timing." She extended her hand to Ronald. "H.H. just left the tub. I'm Marge Slick. I'll take you to his office."

Trying to keep his eyes off her breasts and delta, Ronald had the impression that she had sparkling blue eyes, natural blonde hair, and was only five inches shorter than his five-foot eleven. She probably weighed a lush one hundred and fifty pounds.

"I hope you don't think that I've been too antagonistic," Lois smiled fleetingly as Marge led Ronald to another part of the building. "It was really nothing personal, Mr. Coldaxe. But I wouldn't buy Byrdwhistle if I were you. If Thornton Byrd is so senile that he actually wants to sell his company to W.I.N., you'll never be able to run it profitably — not without H. H. Youman and Theory Z."

11

Even as he was trying to shift his prior mental image of H. H. Youman, who he had thought would either be a jowly, endomorphic version of Ralph Thiemost, or an obnoxious, loud-mouthed, blue-eyed New York executive type, Ronald realized that his first words to Youman were somewhat pettish; but he couldn't help himself. He needed to make his growing dismay quite apparent. "I don't approve of video watching of employees," he told Youman indignantly. But then, as he said the words, he had difficulty suppressing the look of astonishment that he knew must have flashed across his face.

A little over six feet tall, H. H. Youman was lean and tanned. His full head of white hair looked like that of a poet or a musician, unclipped over his ears. He was grinning at Ronald, and his wide-apart brown eyes were both sparkling and quizzical. Nothing about his physical appearance showed the signs of hard-driving acquisitiveness that made most *Fortune*-style executives look like overcultivated frozen peas. Youman's square-jawed face, showing few wrinkles, except crinkly laugh-lines around his eyes, made him look like a Hollywood actor who had matured from romantic love parts to his real identity as a lovable conman. His sinewy, well-muscled arms and legs (Youman was naked except for a pair of brief white tennis shorts) made Ronald wonder if he was really past sixty.

Youman offered his hand, which Ronald took suspiciously. "You really don't have to worry, Mr. Coldaxe. No one looks at our video-tapes except the Byrdwhistle family; and then we do it together at our twice-a-week Symps. Actually, most of the time our video system isn't running." Youman smiled, but even though he was laughing there was a slight edge to his words. "We turned the cameras on today so that we could add to our growing dossier on W.I.N. and its vice president in charge of acquisitions."

They were still standing at the door of Youman's office. Marge started to edge away. "I'll leave you two alone, so that you can discuss Byrdwhistle."

"Actually, Marge," Youman put his hand affectionately on her shoulder, "if you don't mind, I'd prefer that you stay with us. Since Mr. Coldaxe objects to our video-taping, I'll turn the camera off in my office. At the next Symp meeting, you can function as interpreter for our family." Youman noted that Ronald seemed unable to withdraw his eyes from Marge's mature but seductive body. "I think your breasts and vulva are making it difficult for Mr. Coldaxe to concentrate. There's a terrycloth robe in my closet. Perhaps he'd be more comfortable if you wrapped yourself in it."

Laughing, Marge ignored Youman's suggestion. She flopped on a helter-skelter pile of multicolored cushions that were piled high against a twenty-foot wall of books. Ronald shrugged as she calmly raised her legs over her head and, for a moment, vigorously rode a bicycle. "Ms. Slick's nakedness doesn't bother me," he said nervously, trying not to concentrate on the unusual view. "Thus far, I've always managed to separate business from pleasure." Ronald knew that wasn't quite true, but happily his unfulfilled penis was momentarily disgusted and was ignoring the scenery.

Youman waved Ronald to a leather chair next to a square, well-worn mahogany desk that was covered with books and papers. Slouching in a chair behind it, he put one bare foot across the papers and pointed his toe in the direction of Ronald's head. "Here at Byrdwhistle," he said genially, "we don't believe in the Puritan work-ethic. Hopefully, before you leave, we may corrupt you a little." He pointed to a television camera in a corner of the ceiling that was pointing at Ronald's chair. Then he flipped a switch on his desk. "Now you can relax. You're not on 'Candid Camera'!"

Ronald tried to force a smile. Listening to Youman apologize for the delay in receiving him, he tried to grasp the fact that a company as relatively small as Byrdwhistle had a Grumman II corporate jet, and, right now, according to Youman, Elmer and the company pilot were flying it across the Atlantic nonstop to Athens. "Quite frankly," Youman said, "the purpose of Elmer's trip is to make contact with his father, Thornton Byrd, and dissuade him from any potential merger with W.I.N., Incorporated."

As he tried to absorb Youman's words, Ronald was aware that Marge was now sitting with her hands clasped around her knees, and was revealing her female parts in a way that he had never seen even M'mm do. Catching his astonished expression, Marge grinned at him but made no attempt to close her knees. Ronald abruptly looked away and stared out of the window.

Unlike the rest of the top floor with its curved glass roof, Youman's office had a conventional enclosed ceiling. The approximate twenty-by-twenty-foot office looked out through a sliding window wall onto a private patio that was shared on a right angle with another office. Below and across the skyline of Everett, Ronald could see the profiles and the roof-tops of industrial buildings. He was dimly aware that in the distance a liquified natural gas tanker was in the harbor. It was unloading the gas into the storage tanks he could see a few miles from the Byrdwhistle building. On a tripod in front of the window was a powerful telescope. Evidently, among other nonwork things, Youman maintained a private surveillance of the general area.

"The abutting office that you can see through the window belongs to Elmer Byrd," Youman said, noticing his glance.

But now Ronald's attention had shifted, and he tried to contain an audible gasp. He was suddenly aware that on the wall opposite the book-shelves there was a framed four-by-five-foot chalk-drawing of a naked gray-haired woman. She was lying on her back, her eyes closed, and she was obviously in a state of momentary sexual bliss. She was lying on an angle that revealed her parted legs, her slack breasts with hard nipples, and the shadow of a man hovering over her and about to enter her.

Youman grinned at Ronald's pursed lips. "That's my wife, Adele. It's a self-portrait. She drew it for me last year on her sixty-fifth birthday. The gentleman about to join her is presumably me, but it could be Thornton Byrd, or one of her artist friends, or one of her numerous admirers—including your boss, Ralph Thiemost, with whom we just dis-covered Adele spent her sixty-sixth birthday." Youman laughed, and Ronald had a feeling that he was laughing at his shocked expression. "My wife is a very loving woman."

It suddenly occurred to Ronald that Ralph Thiemost probably knew Youman's wife a great deal better than he had intimated nearly a month ago in Los Angeles. Angrily, he wondered what else Thiemost hadn't told him about his cruise with Thornton Byrd.

"You might as well know, Mr. Coldaxe, that my wife is on your side," Youman said. "She's determined to get me to retire from Byrdwhistle. Unfortunately, while she doesn't know all the 'ifs' and 'ands' about this company, I can assure you that at heart she's a true Byrdwhistler."

"Your wife certainly doesn't look sixty-six," Ronald couldn't repress swiftly passing his hand over his partially bald head. He could hear M'mm telling him, "Sometimes, Ronald, the way your hair grows around the rim of your head, it looks as though you're wearing a horseshoe. It irked him that H. H. Youman, who was nearly twenty years older than he was, had as much hair as a teen-ager. While flattery was not Ronald's style, he couldn't help adding, "As a matter of fact, Mr. Youman, though our information says you are nearly sixty-two, you certainly don't look your age either. Perhaps it has something to do with your project on aging that Ms. Rather told me about."

Youman shrugged. "Dr. Ivanowsky of the Center for Ageless Humans insists that I will never be able to establish a direct correlation, but both

Adele and I believe that a life of continuous romance—not as illusion, but as reality that culminates daily in the joining of penis and vagina— is the key to longevity as well as to preventing cellular aging." Laughing at Coldaxe's raised eyebrows, sure that Coldaxe's weak point was his puritanical W.I.N. conditioning, Youman twisted the knife in what he was now sure was a vulnerable spot. "Bald-headed men are supposed to be very virile—or, as they used to say, 'Grass doesn't grow on a busy street.'" Youman paused, "Actually, if you'd have a hair implant, you'd look younger and less formidable. It really could be a new psychological beginning for you, Coldaxe, your first step toward becoming ageless." Despite Ronald's obvious discomfort, Youman continued, "Marge and her husband have an M.D. friend whom I'm sure she'll be very happy to recommend to you. He's made a couple of professional ball-players and golfers look like young teen-agers."

Marge grinned at Ronald seductively. "If Mr. Coldaxe was my friend, I'd try to convince him to shave it all off like Yul Brynner or Telly Savalas. Even Marlon Brando looked better bald, and look what a completely bald head did for Mussolini! It made a midget into a dictator. Sam Gregory, in data processing, keeps himself completely bald. The only hair on his body is around his genitals and under his arms. More than one female Byrdwhistler has told him that it makes him appear sexually powerful."

"There you are," Youman beamed at Ronald's growing irritation. "Fred, Marge's husband, is in Atlanta this week. If I were you, I'd let her experiment with you. If you're not busy tonight, I'm sure she'd be delighted to turn you into Mr. Clean. Who knows? She might erase the intervening years and help you get a new grip on your childhood sense of wonder." Youman was now grinning delightedly. He was fully aware that Ronald didn't approve of the unprofessional drift of the conversation. "If you were totally bald," he continued, "you might even fit your name better. It could accentuate your image as a ruthless hatchet-man."

"I presume all this is very amusing to you," Ronald replied coldly. "Just for the record, my grandfather's name was Kaltaxt. When he immigrated to this country in the early 1900s, he anglicized it. He was unaware of the strange connotations his new name might have." Ronald shrugged. "In any event, Mr. Youman, my visit here is purely exploratory. In the unlikely event that W.I.N. acquired Byrdwhistle Corporation, I can assure you that we would try to continue successful management approaches. We would disrupt the present management as little as possible. Our usual policy is to send in one or two people to head up a new acquisition and align it with our overall objectives. This is not my function. I'm vice president in charge of acquisitions. Managing W.I.N.'s subsidiary companies is not my specialty." Ronald smiled frigidly. "Whoever the actual cold axe might be, I can assure you that it won't be me."

Youman seemed to relax, but Ronald had the feeling he was playing chess with a master. "At least we should try to be a little more informal," Youman said. "If you don't mind I'll call you Ronnie. Most of the Byrd-whistle family call me H.H. Some of my friends, depending on whether they are Wasp or Jewish, call me Heman or Hy—my middle name is Hyman, which means 'life.' With your Germanic background, you'll probably prefer Heman to Hy." H.H. grinned, "While it is spelled He-man the pronounciation is Hay-mahn. It was my grandfather's name. It's a favorite old New England name that also has Hebraic origins. It means 'faithful.'"

"H.H. is fine with me," Ronald said ignoring the sarcasm. He was glad that Youman couldn't see the sudden picture flickering across his mind. M'mm was sitting on him naked, whispering "Ronnie, Ronnie, relax, I love to ride you. I won't break it off . . . I love you, Ronnie!" No one called him Ronnie but M'mm. Grimacing, he shook the mental picture of his exasperating wife out of focus. "I can assure you, H.H., that W.I.N. is not a Wasp organization. We have many Jews in top positions among our eighty-eight thousand employees. The only problem you and I have at the moment is that you are obviously a minority stockholder. You can't speak for the Byrds."

Youman was staring at Ronald's face as if he were either trying to hypnotize him or trying to penetrate his brain with a laser beam. "I really am sorry that Elmer isn't here," he said finally. "We're not sure, Ronnie, but we probably know a little more about what is motivating Thornton Byrd than you or Ralph Thiemost do. We discovered about a month ago that my wife, Adele, was cruising with Byrd and Thiemost. Actually, Adele still is with Thorny." H.H. grinned, "As a matter of fact Elmer has flown to Greece to rescue them from a little predicament they got themselves into yesterday. But, before that, Thorny told us about Thiemost via a VCT—that's our video communication tape system. We use it to keep the Byrdwhistle family and our major stockholder informed about what is going on at headquarters. Even so, in the past few years Thorny has been enjoying his retirement so much that he is a little out of touch. Later, if you'd like to see it, I'll run Thorny's tape for you, but the essence of the matter is that he seems quite determined to sell the company. Quite frankly, I'm not happy about that."

Youman took his foot off the desk and leaned closer to Ronald, "Nor is Elmer Byrd very happy, for reasons that eventually will become apparent. In any event, until I was able to inject Theory Z, an entirely new philosophy of management, into Byrdwhistle, Thornton ran this company on the Blake-Mouton Management Grid system—somewhere between one-one—'Impoverished Management'—the exertion of a minimum effort to get required work done, and nine-one—an 'Authority Obedience Syndrome,' where efficiency in operations result from arranging conditions of work in such a way that human elements interfere to a

minimum degree." Youman shrugged. "From what information we have
been able to gather on W.I.N., although your management gives lip service to the nine-zero, the 'Blake-Mouton Team Management' approach,
which is similar to Theory Y, in all probability both W.I.N. and its subsidiaries are run on a five-five basis, which is a bureaucratic balancing
act, or the art of gamesmanship at all levels. In our opinion that kind of
management puts the lid on the kind of creativity that has made Byrdwhistle so successful."

Trying to avoid Youman's penetrating stare, Ronald was perspiring a
little. "I'm not so familiar with various theories of management as you
seem to be, Mr. Youman. Basically, W.I.N. believes that management-by-
objectives, with carefully spelled out directions, is the best way to achieve
bottom-line results. Quite honestly, while I plan to bring back as impersonal and comprehensive an analysis of Byrdwhistle as possible for careful
review at our headquarters, nothing I have seen thus far would lead me to
believe that Byrdwhistle could ever fit into the W.I.N. corporate picture."

"I'm glad that you feel that way," H.H. was smiling again. "But you
must realize that, being a target for potential acquisition by an organization we believe would terminate the employment of many of us, we
would naturally try to investigate you and the W.I.N. organization as
thoroughly as possible."

Grinning sardonically, he picked up a sheaf of papers from his desk.
"In your case, we've been particularly fortunate. Just a week ago it
dawned on Jeff O'Hara, who is in charge of one of our ongoing national
customer-relationship studies, that perhaps the Coldaxe family, which is
on our mailing list, has been one of our customers. We immediately
struck gold. We found that you and your wife had actually filled out and
signed one of our questionnaires, in exchange for which you were able to
purchase one of our "Bah, Humbug" towels at discount. As you may
remember, we promised that just as soon as it is available we will send
you a preview of the results of the largest cross-sectional study of the
American public's sexual and interpersonal attitudes ever completed. I'm
really very pleased that you are so interested, Ronnie."

"I've never seen your questionnaires," Ronald said stiffly. "My wife
must have filled them out without my advice or consent. He wondered
grimly what in hell M'mm had revealed about their marital life. "Frankly,
I consider questionnaires like these an unnecessary invasion of privacy—
equivalent to this continuous video-taping that you seem obsessed with
and which so far as I can see has nothing to do with running a successful
business operation."

"If you will read Peter Drucker's book *Management,* which incidentally is required reading for all Byrdwhistlers"—H.H. was trying not to
be pontifical, but humorless people like Ronald Coldaxe irritated him—
"you will discover in Drucker's words 'there is only one valid definition

of "business purpose," that is, *to create a customer.*' Whether you realize it or not, Ron, that is the purpose of this questionnaire, and of our video-taping as well as many other Byrdwhistle approaches. We are continuously studying the art of creating customers. When a Byrdwhistle customer returns our questionnaire, he or she automatically becomes a member of our huge national extended family."

H.H. was flipping through several booklets that he had taken from a file on his desk, but he wasn't looking at them. Then he suddenly tossed them to Ronald. "You see, we are creating exciting new kinds of customers, like your wife. She knows that Byrdwhistle loves her. She sounds like a fascinating woman. I'm sure you'll enjoy reading the answers she gave for herself and for you. Someday I'd like to meet her."

Seeing the color rise in Ronald's face, Marge intervened. "Actually, Ronnie, our questionnaires not only help our customers identify with the Byrdwhistle family, but they can be a very enjoyable, revealing experience for couples who fill them out together. If you'd like to have a blank questionnaire to fill in with your own answers, I'll be happy to give you one. In addition to using them to throw light on our marketing procedures, we are analyzing them in depth. In the past twelve months, we have collected a complete national family sexual profile, from more than a million of our customers. Most of them are married, or have been. So far as I'm concerned, it will be the most thorough, up-to-date analysis of American sexual mores since the Kinsey report. We plan to distribute the book through our Love-n-Learn Book Club. Even now, the material is a valuable asset. We carry the preliminary work on our balance sheet at a million-dollar valuation. I think—"

H.H. waived Marge into silence. They watched Ronald turning the pages of the questionnaire with an incredulous expression. "As you can see, Ronnie," H.H. was smiling, "our questionnaire is designed so that husband and wife can each answer all one hundred sixty questions separately. The questionnaire is based on a relationship study done by Arlene Rubin. We don't require that respondents sign the questionnaires. But, interestingly, more than half of them do."

Ronald wasn't listening to H.H. He was trying to digest some of M'mm's answers. To Question 31, "Is your relationship marked by frequent differences of opinion?" M'mm had checked, "Almost always." Question 98, "Do you confide in your mate?" was answered, "Occasionally." Question 112, "When your partner is away, how concerned are you about his or her becoming involved with some member of the opposite sex?" M'mm had answered, "Never concerned."

Damn her! Ronald wondered how she had responded for him on those questions. But much as he wanted to stop all conversation with Youman and carefully read M'mm's answers for herself as well as for him, he knew that was impossible. He saw one final question as he closed the booklet. To Question 129, "Do you share your sexual fantasies with your partner." M'mm had answered, "Never."

While he had never really shared any of his sexual fantasies with M'mm either, for some reason M'mm's answer made him even angrier. Shaking a little, he folded the booklets and put them in his pocket. "Obviously my wife, or anyone else who would answer this kind of crap, is being conned into a written striptease." Ronald wanted to say "was a mental idiot" but he constrained himself. "I find the whole approach quite disgusting."

H.H. shrugged. "The truth about marital relationships is often shocking. But I can assure you that when *The Byrdwhistle Marital Profiles* is published next year, it will be more reliable than Kinsey or any of his latter-day followers like Shere Hite and Arthur Pietropinto." H.H. paused, wondering whether he should give Ronnie the knockout blow. Why not? Inevitably, Ronnie would attend a Symp meeting. Before Coldaxe left Everett, he'd discover that, not only had all Byrdwhistle employees read the Coldaxe questionnaires, but they had all seen a video interview with Coldaxe's wife in which she had revealed that her husband didn't fully approve of her constant meddling in what she referred to as "provocative social problems."

"Before I turn you over to Marge, who, in accordance with Thornton Byrd's wishes, will give you access to any information, financial or otherwise, that you may require, I think I should mention that, about three weeks after your secretary's phone call advising us that you would be visiting us, Cathy and Steve Milner, who are in charge of our Club Wholesome subsidiary in Los Angeles, conducted a video street interview with your wife. She assumed that they were preparing material for a local television show." H.H. smiled at Ronald's dismayed look. "Marge will run the tape for you if you wish. I suspect that, if we had met under other circumstances and if your wife lived in this area, she would enjoy working at Byrdwhistle."

He pointed out of the window at the huge natural-gas storage-tanks several miles away near the harbor. If your wife were aware of the dangers of liquified natural gas and its storage in highly populated areas, I'm sure she would be just as agitated as she is by the threat of nuclear power plants." H.H. smiled benignly at Ronald. "Marge, make a note for me and I'll send her a copy of *Time Bomb,* a book that tells all about it."

12

"Among other things," Marge told Ronald as they continued the tour of Byrdwhistle, "H.H. is experimenting with Freud's pleasure principle versus his reality principle, which presumably govern man's behavior. Freud was convinced that such a thing as a nonrepressive developing civilization was impossible." She grinned at Ronald, well aware that he had been staring at her naked rump and was now unable to keep his eyes off her breasts, which were swaying ever so slightly—a provocative invitation to touch or kiss. "If you prefer," she said, "we can stop at my office and I'll put on a dress."

Ronald shook his head weakly. The angry response that he had restrained at H.H.'s cool putdown of W.I.N. had turned into a nasty bubbling in his guts, and he wondered if he could surreptitiously slip a Rolaid tablet into his mouth. "No, no. People"—he meant M'mm—"who have been to nudist camps or to nude beaches assure me that you get used to it."

Marge laughed, "That's just what you shouldn't do, Ron. Being continuously aware of human flesh, and in a subconscious way of the absolute miracle of a naked human being, makes you nicer to be with. Your stress would change to laughter and you would learn to accept the vagaries of human loving and of each person's vulnerability and transience. Freud believed that civilization advanced because man learned to control his sexual and erotic impulses. According to him, the Eros instinct has been deflected by the Oedipus compulsion. The patriarchal male prevented his male offspring from possessing his mother. When the young male finally killed his father so that he could fuck his mother, he was overcome with guilt. The necessity to repress guilt became a way of life for all men. Gradually, the patriarchal father-figure lost power and was replaced by the Protestant and Jewish work ethic and by the capitalistic system, which fertilized it. Then man's alienation was complete. He started living a joyless life and rejected his basic instincts, and in the process began to believe that suffering instead of the pleasure principle was the path to heaven. Natural genital joy and living in playful unrepressed receptiveness with one's own mind and body—as well as the bodies of friends—was labeled sinful and dirty. Unable to communicate their need to please one another, men and women became distrustful. People discovered it was easier to hate each other than to love each other, because by hating you could fortify your petty ego and not be forced to surrender it."

Trying to absorb what he considered this insanity, Ronald was reminded of M'mm, who, he was sure, could spout a similar philosophy if he ever gave her the provocation. "I find most psychological theories are full of wishful thinking," he said coldly. He was about to say "crap" but checked himself.

The elevator took them down to the first floor, where Marge explained that they could work their way back to the fourth and then have lunch in the cafeteria. "Approximately half of this floor is devoted to shipping Byrdcage items," she told him, "Imprinted items that we manufacture in our Byrd Track division are produced on the other half of this floor, or in about 50,000 square feet. As you can see, there are only a few people in the shipping area today. Most of the year, we ship on Tuesdays and Fridays. Of course, in late October and November and in the first two weeks of December, we ship every day. Even in the rush months, shipping is organized into "working bees." Byrdwhistlers drop all other work on shipping days. During pre-Christmas season, even Elmer and H.H. often help us out. Our shipping warehouses in other cities follow the same principle."

Ronald silently surveyed the floor and noted that the conveyor belts and slides could move items in and out of the floor above, which obviously housed the inventory for some of the catalogue items.

Determined to jar him, Marge continued her indoctrination. "To really understand Byrdwhistle," she rattled on, "you must be aware of H.H.'s underlying philosophy. He is convinced that Freud's reality principle, with its reliance on delayed satisfaction and unnecessary restraint of human pleasure and play, combined with a life of unremitting toil and the pressures for increased productivity and personal security, does not have to be the guiding force in human lives. Byrdwhistlers reject the Judeo-Christian work-ethic and its morality. We believe a total emphasis on making money and earning one's bread might have been necessary in the beginnings of human development, but the philosophy and psychology that dominated early civilizations woven into a Christian and Jewish theology and Freudian thinking is no longer viable. Unfortunately, they have been embedded in the human psyche. H.H. is determined to prove that giving full rein to man's basic loving nature and a philosophy based on the pleasure principle cannot only eliminate the anxiety, neurosis, and insecurity that plagues most of mankind but can prod the human donkey much better than guilt, suffering, and a success-work ethic based on the reality principle."

An electronically controlled fire-door opened as they approached it. "This is the Byrd Track manufacturing area," Marge waved her hand at about fifty people, all of whom were in various stages of undress. Some were running small printing presses that stamped gold-leaf monograms on belts, ties, towels, and various other items, and some were hand-lettering and painting buckles, keychains, room-markers, metal identification-plates, and an endless array of what Ronald was convinced was totally useless junk. As they walked through the area, Marge handed him a Byrd Track catalogue. "We have more than four hundred items that we personalize," she smiled. "It's an interesting commentary on human needs that many individuals are compelled to establish the reality of their existence. Of course, in the case of some of the more expensive items we offer, such as personal stationery, monogrammed crystal matchboxes, wastebaskets, nameplates, luggage tags, family crests, etcetera, the need is coupled with a need to express one's difference from everyone else. H.H. firmly believes that catering to the growing cult of individuality and human narcissism can make one very rich. At some of the Symp meetings, we have been kicking around H.H.'s belief that there's no reason that, for a relatively small sum, we couldn't guarantee anyone total fame and national and international recognition for one day in his or her life. Just think, Ron, if we could plot it, all you would have to do is to send your check to Byrdwhistle and within a few weeks you would become an instant celebrity. You'd be on national television. You'd appear in all the newspapers and magazines for your Once-in-a-Lifetime Day, courtesy of Byrdwhistle.

"You may think it's a crazy idea, but last year we sold nearly half a million picture-frames in which anyone can insert an eight-by-ten photograph of themselves and be instantly acclaimed by friends and relatives in a simulated newsmagazine format as Man or Woman of the Year. H.H. believes that we'll find the answer in our tape and video disc division, which we started two years ago in New York City—but I'll tell you about that later."

Only half hearing Marge, Ronald was trying not to stare at the male and female employees, a few of whom, as she was, were totally naked and wearing only sandals; the majority wore towels of various colors snapped around their waists. A few of the women had tied strips of cloth around their breasts and genitals, not to conceal them but to seductively emphasize them.

One man introduced himself. "Hi, Mr. Coldaxe, I'm Sam Rushton. Welcome to the world of smiling love-asses. Has Marge's bottom hypnotized you yet? I never realized that the female pelvis rotated in approximately an inch wider radius than the male's until I came to work at Byrdwhistle. It's a built-in, uncontrollable, erotic female feature that's very pleasant to watch."

A brown-eyed, smiling woman of about twenty-five who was bent over a small printing-press and presented anyone who was watching her with a clear view of her rosy anus, straightened up as they passed by and grinned at Ronald. "I was watching you through my intestines, Mr. Coldaxe, hope you don't mind." She noticed Ronald's consternation. "God, Marge, you'd better tell Mr. Coldaxe to relax. He looks as if he's going to need Ex-Lax tonight."

Marge laughed boisterously at Ronald's confusion and obvious contempt. "Modesty is not a way of life at Byrdwhistle," she told him, "but being dressed or undressed is a very practical matter. If you return in October or during the winter, you'll find Lottie and the whole department wearing thermal underwear, which, incidentally, we sell quite a lot of from our Dreamy Byrd catalogue."

At one bench, several woman were painting names on two-inch wooden cutouts that Ronald recognized as a silhouette of a dog. Marge introduced him. "This is Rose Shannon." Ronald noted that Rose's breasts, heavy with milk, were supported by a half-bra. "Her son Gary was born last week. He's in day-care on the fourth floor. When does he get fed, Rose?"

"Pretty soon. As you can see, I'm bursting and beginning to dribble. Ted is spending an hour with him this morning. Someone would have paged me on the speakers if Gary was fussy."

Marge called Ronald's attention to the music being played through the factory speaker-system. "It's a Mozart concerto. His eighteenth," she told him. "Byrdwhistlers on every floor plan their own musical and talk programs. Classical music is alternated with fifteen minutes of capsule information on just about every subject under the sun. We're even tied into a medical-news station that broadcasts only for doctors. Afternoons, African music or disco, or even faster, foot-thumping music, is popular. We also have a variety of video programs that can be run from cassettes on television in the cafeteria from noon to two P.M. Our own Love Byrd tapes—I'll tell you about them later—are very popular. Most of the programs, audio or video, are what H.H. calls 'mind expanders,' and that's a way of life at Byrdwhistle."

Before they moved on, Rose held up a six-by-twelve-inch square of prepainted Masonite. Glued to it was a picture of the entrance, in wooden relief, to a building labeled "Dog House." Inside the dog house and along side it were six hooks. Above the hooks, Rose had painted in white letters, on a deep background "Coldaxe Family." A wooden dog was lettered with the name "Ronald" and another with the name "M'mm." "H.H. sent down a message," Rose grinned at them. "He told us to prepare a Byrdwhistle dog house for your wife. To finish it we need to know your children's names and any pets you have—like a cat or dog."

"Kids love our dog houses." Marge was enjoying Ronald's astonishment, "When they put dogs with their parents' names on them in the dog house, it gives them a sense of power."

Reluctantly, Ronald mumbled, "Mitch and Tina," and Rose forced him to spell the names out. He finally admitted that the Coldaxes had a cat called Miss Cotton Fluff. "My children are in their late teens," he told Rose frigidly. "It's a nice gesture, but I really doubt that they will be captivated with your dog houses."

Marge chuckled, "We sold two hundred and fifty thousand of them last year at six dollars apiece. Your wife ordered our Scrooge towel. I'm sure that she must have a sense of humor. She may even enjoy hanging you in the Coldaxe dog house occasionally. How long have you been married?"

"I thought that H.H. had a complete dossier on the Coldaxe family," Ronald's voice was heavy with sarcasm as they moved away from the dog-house assemblies.

"We don't know everything," Marge said blithely. "Your wife's questionnaire indicated that you seldom make love more than once a week, but we don't know why." She grinned provocatively into Ronald's flushed face, pleased that she had momentarily ruptured his overwhelming smugness. "Actually, Ronnie, when you relax and smile, you look more lovable. You should give up frowning and try smiling as a way of life."

On the second floor, which was geared to a rubber-escalator freight-receiving system leading from the ground-floor docks, Marge led him rapidly up and down several miles of aisles loaded with inventory. "Keep in mind," she told him, "that this is the summer buildup. We're getting ready for the fall selling season. Of course we only inventory items here in Everett that are advertised in the Byrdcage or the Byrd Track catalogue. More than twenty-five percent of all illustrated items are drop-shipped by manufacturers with whom we have special arrangements. Inventory items for our other specific catalogues are carried in similar warehouse areas throughout the country. But, as you will discover when we get to the third floor, we maintain complete inventory control on the entire Byrdwhistle operation here at headquarters. Our computers are on line with theirs. Within twenty-four hours, we have complete ordering, shipping, and financial information from all locations. In addition, we have video-telephone interconnection with all of the warehouses so that we keep completely coordinated with each other."

Passing by one of the receiving escalators, Ronald noted about twenty cases of wine lying on their sides, labeled "Mouton Rothschild, 1945." "I presume that's pretty expensive wine," he said. "Do you sell that?"

Marge shook her head. "No, H.H. uses it for personal entertaining. They just arrived yesterday. They're destined for H.H.'s wine cellar in Louisburg Square, on Beacon Hill. I'm sure if he invites you to his home he'll open a few bottles of it for you."

"How much is a bottle of it worth?" Ronald would have guessed about twenty to thirty dollars. He restrained a gasp when Marge told him "H.H. paid three hundred and fifty dollars a bottle for that shipment. Today it's worth at least four hundred and fifty." She laughed. "H.H. doesn't stint himself on the finer things of life. We also have a company wine-cellar in the basement with several thousand bottles of fine California and French wines. Good wine is a fringe benefit of working at Byrdwhistle. About a month ago, H.H. bought a magnum of 1864 Lafite Rothschild. He keeps telling Elmer that they 'should crack it' after they've cooled Thornton down." Marge shrugged. "It's still unopened, but H.H. brought the subject up again before you arrived. This time he said, 'Maybe I'll do it when we get rid of Ronald Coldaxe and Ralph Thiemost.'"

"It would be too expensive a celebration for my blood," Ronald said. "I don't think I'd enjoy drinking wine that cost three hundred and fifty dollars a bottle."

Marge grinned. "The magnum of Lafite Rothschild wasn't three hundred and fifty dollars a bottle. It was three thousand nine hundred and fifty for one bottle. It's an 1864 bottling, which H.H. assures me he could sell for five thousand dollars."

Trying to digest the information that H.H. not only ran Byrdwhistle like a continuous saturnalia but personally lived like a Roman emperor, Ronald followed Marge through the extensive computer department on the third floor. She introduced him to various people who nodded at him curtly. Ronald had finally managed to stop staring at the sexual attractions of female Byrdwhistlers. Marge forced him to agree that the Byrdwhistle computing department was equal in sophistication to anything they had at W.I.N.

"H.H. is very sensitive to money, and to Byrdwhistle's finances," she told him. "His theory is that while the world is at the present stage of development we can play the Eros game and get away with it only if we are totally independent of the establishment—particularly bankers. Byrdwhistle has never had to borrow a cent."

In the elevator that took them to the fourth floor, Marge leaned seductively against the corner and thrust her hips forward, giving Ronald a very tantalizing view of her pubic mound. He had to restrain himself from grabbing this devilish, impious woman by her cunt and fucking her on the spot.

Well aware that she was inflaming him, Marge coolly continued her analysis of H.H.'s philosophy. "Freud believed," she said, smiling at him beguilingly, "that the reality principle, which is based on restraint and renunciation and which you are practicing with me now, safeguards the pleasure principle. Man strives for what is useful. Scarcity of the basic necessities for survival create what Freud called 'the eternal primordial struggle for existence.' He said, 'In the process, it teaches men that they cannot freely gratify their instinctual impulses and they cannot live under the pleasure principle.'"

"Amen," Ronald agreed fervently as the elevator door finally opened and saved him from himself. Marge, seemingly oblivious to his growing need to possess her body, led him into the day-care area, and Ronald tried to ignore the continuous sexual invitation in her twinkling blue eyes. It bothered him that at fifty-two, unlike many of his and M'mm's female friends, Marge was still very sexually attractive. She was a living, naked rebuttal of Freudian philosophy—and she knew it.

"I hope that you are becoming fully aware," she sounded serious, but he guessed that she was still teasing him, "that Byrdwhistle is a great deal more than a working environment designed to sell two hundred million dollars of *things* annually. We all agree that they are things that anyone could probably live just as well without, but H.H. calls Byrdwhistle a shadow cast by the inevitable future, a world where men and women really play together in a new kind of working relationship. If you stop to analyze the more than five thousand items in the Byrdwhistle catalogues, you'll discover that they all cater to the one basic human necessity of our times—a means, temporary, to be sure, to escape from one's domination by the reality principle."

"A principle which you are deliberately trying to breach with me," Ronald told her a little angrily. "I'm sorry, Marge, but I'm well aware that you are trying to turn me into a drooling idiot. But, if you wanted to be raped in the elevator, you picked the wrong customer."

Marge grinned at him with a quizzical expression on her face, "Don't be too sure. Thank God they don't give Ph.D.'s in business administration. It's difficult enough for a female to break through the built-in fortifications and conceit of the average Master of Business Administration." She laughed. "Whether I succeed or not, it's worth a try. Someday some female will drive you right out of your mind, Ronald Coldaxe, or into a monastery. The only way you can save yourself is to read Herbert Marcuse—and believe! Particularly his *Eros and Civilization*. It's required reading for all Byrdwhistlers. Marcuse shows that in the long course of human history, man prefers Eros and the pleasure principle. Ultimately, if he's prevented from living by the saner promptings of his basically loving nature, he'll end up in the loony-bin or spend his life like the Hitlers of the world, destroying instead of creating."

In the day-care area, Ronald watched a naked pregnant woman sitting on a thick-carpeted floor. She was playing with five two-to-three-year-old children who tumbled around her and were tentatively exploring her big belly. Two other children under a year old were sleeping in cribs, and in another area a bearded young man was reading stories and dramatizing them with growls and gestures for a group of young people listening with rapt attention.

"Day-care is rotated weekly," Marge told him. "Within any one year, about half the Byrdwhistle family gets a shot at it. H.H. reserves the right to come down here any time the mood seizes him and play with the children. He often takes the older of those who haven't started school yet on expeditions to the aquarium, or to the swan boats on the Common, or to the Children's or the Science museum. When Adele is out of town, he has eight kids ranging from two years to the late teens living in the twenty-room commune he supports at Merry Mount. H.H. insists that a key to maintaining one's creativity into old age is to have constant association with children and the younger generation. He tells everyone that the ancient theory of gerocomy is a two-way street that has wider connotations than anyone has ever dreamed and should be thoroughly explored."

"What the hell is gerocomy?" Ronald demanded.

"A belief that the breath and body of a young woman could revive older men and restore their youth." Marge couldn't help a burst of laughter at the look of disapproval on Ronald's face. "H.H. is not really a dirty old man. Every young female in the Merry Mount commune, including my daughter, loves to go to bed with him."

Ronald looked at her with raised eyebrows but refused to explore the ramifications of that statement. "Does your daughter work here, too?"

"No, Sylvia's a dancer, but she makes a living as a social worker. No one in the Merry Mount commune works at Byrdwhistle. Half of them are in the theater, or are working for publishing companies, or are writers or painters."

Marge led him across the hundred-thousand-square-foot floor toward the cafeteria and pointed out different areas that could be quickly divided off with sliding walls. One such space, of about five thousand square feet, was lined with aisles of shelving filled with books. "This is our library area," she told him. "Continuous reading is basic to keeping your job at Byrdwhistle. We subscribe to more than two hundred magazines and newspapers, and we purchase a thousand or more books a year. After two months Byrdwhistlers can take home the magazines, and after two years they can take the books. But the key to continuous employment here is an 'awareness program.' Working for Byrdwhistle is a never-ending educational process. Our entrance examination is only the beginning."

"Ms. Rather told me about the examination, I'd be interested in seeing it."

Marge grinned. "I'd take odds, Ron, that you couldn't pass it," she said. And then, seeing that Ronald looked disconcerted, she continued: "All it really amounts to is a test to discover whether you are the kind of person who could function in this environment, but our annual 'Be with It' examinations are much tougher. H.H. insists that all Byrdwhistlers must maintain a continuously creative outlook on life. It's the real key to delaying physical as well as mental aging. Most people grow old because they stop learning. What was good enough for Daddy is good enough for them. The so-called generation gap is self-inflicted. People let their brains die before someone has the good grace to bury the still surviving body. The purpose of our 'Be with It' examination is to eliminate Byrdwhistlers who can't, or won't, keep learning and exposing their minds to continuous change. Being aware of future shock, so that it isn't shocking but becomes an affirmation of what you know is inevitably going to happen, adds to the joy of living."

"I'm sure of one thing," Ronald told her. "Marge Slick is thoroughly brainwashed. From what I've seen so far, Byrdwhistlers sound as out of this world as the Moonies or the Hare Krishnas." He shrugged, "I'll concede that your annual examination may have some merit. Doctors, lawyers, and accountants are forced to keep up with their profession. Why not the businessman? But here you're dealing with the hoi polloi. You are ignoring the inevitable. Some must lead, but most must be led."

Marge laughed. "Byrdwhistlers are all leaders, that's why we're so successful. But once you've passed our initial examination it doesn't mean that you can play here or, as you call it, work here, until you're ninety or a hundred. Management insists that you prove that even though your body may be deteriorating your brain isn't. Being with It requires that Byrdwhistlers develop into generalists. Every employee must monitor the changing world. They must know what is happening in Zimbabwe and Lebanon and Peking and Israel. If you work here, you must know who has recently written something giving new insights into man. You must be aware of what is going on in just about every area of human knowledge, but at the same time you must never try to retreat into an intellectual haven where you don't understand, or no longer comprehend, human motivations. If that happens, you will be retired immediately. On the other hand, if you are over sixty, you will continue to be paid the average median wage until your relatives bury you." Marge paused, "If you wish to understand H.H., you've got to understand the King Gillette syndrome that motivates him. He believes not only that Byrdwhistle, and every other organization in the world of people who come together to produce a product or sell a service, including your W.I.N. Incorporated, can function as a total corporation owned by the people but that the people themselves must create a working environment based on a new kind of responsible play-ethic. Imagine a world where work is play, and all age groups, and particular employees of particular companies, are interrelated for a lifetime of two-way responsibility."

Marge pointed to a fifty-foot-long stage that they were passing. "When we remodeled this area, we created an instant theater. It can be used for Symp meetings or expanded to seat seven hundred people for the various dramatic presentations we put on to please ourselves and friends who we wish to invite. When the theater isn't being used, the walls are left open, as they are now, and the seats, as you can see, can be raised to the ceiling. Last March, thirty Byrdwhistlers staged Elmer's musical *Rum Ho!* A new group is working on his *Let Us Go, Brothers, Go!,* which takes place in the Oneida Community in the late 1900s. Although we're far from professional, our live performances help Elmer revise his music and story lines until they become quite hypnotic."

Passing through the cafeteria, Marge pointed out that all foods served were natural foods. Knowing that M'mm would be applauding if she could see him, Ronald chose yogurt and fresh fruit. He was relieved to discover that he was no longer staring avidly at the breasts of the partially naked women who, along with the men, were serving the various dishes in the cafeteria. But he couldn't help grimacing at the occasional sight of a dangling naked penis.

13

The strange unhurried ambience of the dining area, where men and women seemed in no obvious hurry to return to whatever work they were doing, shocked him. By contrast, in the cafeterias of W.I.N. subsidiaries, lunch was a half-hour of quickly bolted junk-food, often accompanied by reminder bells that time for eating was nearly over and time for earning one's bread would begin again. Here the atmosphere was more like the top-executive dining-rooms at W.I.N. headquarters, or, some of the more fashionable restaurants in every American city where businessmen and a scattering of businesswomen savored their luncheons and booze in the companionship of their peers, while they presumably discussed business problems or conned potential customers and clients as they pontificated on problems of national and international importance. Such dining was usually followed by a light-hearted discussion of whose expense account the repast should be charged to.

While Ronald tried to listen with one ear to fragments of conversation at nearby tables, which seemed to range all the way from what was happening in Mideast politics to the inability of the Federal Reserve to control the money supply, to a product that could be sprayed in a bedroom—a pheromone exaltaloid—which presumably enhanced sex, and which the speaker at the Symp meeting that afternoon was going to recommend be offered in the fall Dreamy Byrd catalogue. Marge was continuing to proselytize the merits of Byrdwhistle. He had noticed that she picked up a copy of *Eros and Civilization* when they passed through the library area. Now she told him that it was his to take home. "In the unhappy event that W.I.N. takes over this company, I think you should be forearmed, Ron." He knew from her expression that she was continuing to try to jar his seeming aplomb. "W.I.N. and Byrdwhistle could never function together," she said, "unless your management understands the Byrdwhistle basics. Noyes, Maslow, Low, Zen, and Marcuse— they hold the key to the future of man and his work. You're still a young man, Mr. Coldaxe. If you'd open your mind and broaden your understanding, you could become a leader instead of a follower."

Ronald nodded agreeably. He was determined not to be coaxed out on a limb. "How come I'm suddenly Mr. Coldaxe?" he asked. "I thought we agreed to be less formal, Marge. Really, I only *seem* to be an ogre. While I'm convinced that Byrdwhistle and W.I.N. absolutely have no future together, I'm open-minded. What's this book all about?"

Marge flipped it open. "All right, Ron, try to absorb this. Marcuse points out that Plato's *Symposium* contains the clearest celebration of the sexual origin and substance of spiritual relationships; 'According to Diotima.' And these are Plato's words." Marge read to him from Marcuse: " 'Eros drives the desire for one beautiful body to another, and finally to all beautiful bodies, for the beauty of one body is akin to the beauty of another, and it would be foolish not to recognize that the beauty of every body is one and the same.' "

Marge beamed at Ronald's puzzled expression. "Present company excepted," he smiled at her. "I mean me, not you, Marge. I don't consider my body beautiful. Although I'll admit that most of your employees seem above average in physical appearance, the truth is that most human bodies aren't beautiful. They're ugly. That's why people began to dress in the first place."

Marge shook her head. "You're wrong. Men and women don't wear clothes to cover their nakedness. They wear them to accentuate their sexual attractiveness. But that's beside the point. Why do you think your body is ugly?"

Ronald scowled. "As you already noted I'm prematurely bald and I have a little paunch."

"Believe me, Ron, you're not being honest. No matter how out of shape you may be, when you look at yourself naked you love yourself and you love your body. You have to. Everyone has to. Your body is you. It's the only image of yourself—whatever that self may really be— that you have as a clue to your existence. You have to love your body. Otherwise you can't be sure that you exist at all." Marge grinned at Ronald's bewilderment. "Anyway, just so long as your body keeps the *you* of you together, whether it's too fleshy, too skinny, or too old, or even too decrepit, it's not only beautiful to you, it's beautiful to me. It's profoundly amazing, and the amazement and wonder at life are the fundamentals— the sine qua nons of a true Byrdwhistler."

Marge continued reading from Marcuse's book. "Listen to this: 'Love, and the enduring responsible relations which it demands, are founded on a union of sexuality with "affection." This union is the long cruel process of domestication, in which the instinct's legitimate manifestation is made supreme, and its component parts are arrested in their development . . . The full force of civilized morality was mobilized against the use of the body as mere object, means, and as an instrument of pleasure.

" 'But,' " Marge continued, accentuating the words as she read them, " 'with the emergence of a nonrepressive reality principle, this process can be reversed. Freed of alienating labor, the body would be resexualized . . . this spread of libido would first manifest itself in a reactivation of all erotogenic zones and, consequently, in a resurgence of pregenital polymorphous sexuality and in a decline in genital supremacy, the body in its entirety would become an object of cathexis, a thing to be enjoyed—an instrument of pleasure.' "

Marge grinned. "To get Marcuse's meaning you've got to read him several times, but he points out that this change in value and scope of libidinal relationships will lead to a disintegration of the institutions in which the private interpersonal relations have been organized." She repeated the last sentence, but realized that she had passed beyond Ronald's comprehension. She patted his hand gently. "I'm afraid you don't understand, Ronnie. What Marcuse is saying is that not only is your way of life, which is based on the male-dominated family and a loving, monogamous wife, coming to an end but so are companies like W.I.N. Incorporated, which follow the same outmoded organizational structure. Companies like W.I.N., based on Freud's patriarchal-style reality principle, have served their purpose. Say hello to the future, Ron, Byrdwhistle is built on the pleasure principle!"

After they deposited their dishes in a cart destined for the dishwasher, Marge told him that she would now prove it to him, and she led him down a lushly carpeted corridor on the opposite side of the building. They passed by several closed doors with signs reading "Occupied" in black letters on a white panel that evidently were controlled from the inside. "Ah, here's a room," Marge pointed to one whose sign read "Unoccupied."

She opened the door and turned a circular metal sign from the inside. "Now it reads Occupied." She smiled warmly at him. "There are no locks on any Love Room doors. No Byrdwhistler would ever invade another's privacy."

Ronald stared uneasily around the small room. Several framed erotic drawings hung on the walls. The only furniture was a king-sized air-mattress covered with a sheet and numerous snowy-white pillows. The air mattress rested on a platform only a few inches high. Adjoining this room was a slightly smaller one with a toilet and a sunken tub that was capable of comfortably accommodating two people.

Marge pointed to the floor drain and a shower with a long cord. "Undress," she told him. "After we wash each other, we can fill the tub and sit together, or we can just lie down on the bed and talk."

Ronald knew his penis had hardened and was pressing against his pants. He was sure that during the entire tour of Byrdwhistle Marge had been not only trying to seduce him but had planned to end the tour in one of the Love Rooms. To his amazement, when he didn't immediately answer, she flopped on the air mattress. Her slightly flexed thighs were completely relaxed and constituted a spread-eagle invitation to the hairy delight between them. Her soft, pouting labia seemed to be saying "Touch me" or better still, "Taste me." All he had to do was shed his clothes and take a shower, and in a very few moments his poor neglected, swollen prick would be anointed with the warm fluid balm of Marge's vagina.

"I'm sorry," he told her uneasily, well aware that his fists were tightly clenched. "As tempting as your offer is, I'm not screwing with the vice president and controller of Byrdwhistle. What's more, I can't believe that any woman would lower herself to such an obvious attempt to discredit me."

Marge shook her head sadly and smiled at him. "Even with your trousers on, Ron, it's obvious that your penis is discrediting you. If you're not careful, the facade you have erected will crack apart and the real you will escape and begin to live for the first time."

Ronald sneered at her. "I'm sure that this room is not only bugged but that if I searched I'd probably find video eyes carefully monitoring us. Youman would like nothing better than to send my wife and Ralph Thiemost a video cassette of you and I fucking."

Marge refused to respond to his anger.

"It could be the best thing that ever happened to you, but there are no video cameras in our Love Rooms," she assured him, "and remember, Ronald Coldaxe, I didn't ask you to have sex with me, I asked if you'd like to lie down and talk. If you prefer to keep your clothes on, it's all right with me. Or perhaps we should return to my office. But I think you should understand one thing. Sexual pleasure with members of the Byrdwhistle family is something we don't ordinarily share with the outside world. Byrdwhistlers don't rush to orgasms. Sex is not work or a chore. It's a consummation of shared intimacy. We come to the Love Rooms to enjoy long preludes and to discover our ability or inability to complete our bodily surrender to a specific other person. No one can achieve that kind of surrender indiscriminantly, but when we discover empathy with another person we often experience the joy of total escape for an hour or so. The mental and physical stress that is created by one's ego disappears, and we capture a few delicious moments that make it possible to flow with the universal currents of all life. H.H. will assure you that this kind of lovemaking is equivalent to the aesthetics and the philosophy of a Japanese ceremony called *ma,* which is designed to foster the experience of oblivion."

Feeling awkward standing over her, Ronald finally sat nervously on the edge of the air mattress. He didn't understand what she was saying, but he knew that he was restraining a compulsive need to take Marge in his arms and bury his face in her breasts. In some inexpressible way, her naked vulnerability and her now tear-filled eyes aroused his protective instinct as well as a need to share his own doubts and accept her mothering.

"I don't know why the hell I like you, Ron. You really are a Coldaxe." Marge was now talking to him with her eyes closed, but a tiny tear trickled down her cheek. "If before you go back to California H.H. invites you to spend an evening in his commune in Merry Mount or even at his townhouse on Beacon Hill, don't refuse. I'm sure it would be a great learning experience for you. If nothing else, you should see his circular bed, which rotates like a merry-go-round but much more slowly." Marge was silent a moment and then she continued. "You're right about one thing. H.H. has brainwashed all of us with his charisma. He is probably what Plato had in mind when he referred to philosopher-kings. He's a very different kind of businessman. Many years ago he taught philosophy at Boston University."

"Are you in love with him?"

Marge reached up and patted Ronald's cheek. Her eyes were still half closed. "What you really mean is do I have sex with him. Of course I do, and with Fred, too, and Elmer, and a few other Byrdwhistlers. But I don't live with H.H. Fred and I have an apartment overlooking Boston Harbor." Laughing, she passed her hand lightly over the bulge in Ronald's trousers. "Your poor dear schlong," she said, giving his penis a separate existence. "It's going to feel just awful later on. Since you don't dare release him, for your own sanity I think we better get out of here."

14

Amused by Ronald's total confusion and uncertain whether she really wanted to spend the whole night with him even if he finally relented, and even if it would save Byrdwhistle, Marge decided that she had enticed him enough for the moment. She led him back to her office on the fifth floor, where she quickly slipped into a tight-fitting princess-style dress that clung erotically to her body. Assuming the impersonal role of businesswoman, she continued to spar with this intruder into her normal daily activities.

"In two hours there will be a Symp meeting that we can attend if you like. H.H. told me that I must give you access to any corporate information you wish. Other than our operating figures, I have no idea what a vice president of acquisitions may be looking for in a case like this."

Ronald shrugged. Now that Marge was dressed, she seemed to be even more feminine and seductive than she had been naked. He had a perverse need to yank down the zipper on the back of her dress and masterfully prove that he really wasn't afraid to make love to her. Instead, he said, "If it were my decision, I'd thank you for your trouble, and I'd catch the 7:30 plane back to Los Angeles. Unfortunately, Thornton Byrd seems to have led Ralph Thiemost astray. It's my responsibility to correct any false impressions he may have about Byrdwhistle. If you could give me your operating figures and balance sheets for the past five or six years or for the period that H.H. and Elmer Byrd actually have been running the company, I'm sure it would help."

Reluctantly, Marge opened a drawer in a row of file cabinets that flanked one side of her office, and she handed him a thick folder. "These are copies of our consolidated figures. I hope you understand that this is a private company. These figures are not for general publication." She scowled. "We don't want Thornton Byrd to become a target for every corporate predator in the country."

Ronald flipped quickly through the reports. "You don't have to worry, I wouldn't recommend Byrdwhistle to my worst enemy. I don't see any detailed information on World Corporation here. Presumably, Byrdwhistle is a subsidiary of World."

"Other than our annual dividend payments to World, there are no other transactions."

Startled, Ronald suddenly found what he was looking for. "Jesus Christ! — you've been paying World ten million dollars a year for the past five years."

Marge laughed. "That's only a portion of our earnings."

"What the hell does World do with the money?"

Marge held up a copy of King Gillette's *World Corporation,* and Ronald told her that he had already taken one from the reception room. Laughing, she told him, "You should read it on the way home. H.H. is a practical utopianist. He believes that King Gillette was on the right track." She took what looked exactly like a slightly oversized ten-dollar bill out of her desk and handed it to Ronald. In the center was an engraved portrait of King Camp Gillette similar to the oil painting in the lobby. Beneath it were the words "Give me your labor and I will give you the results of your labor on a basis of equity." Across the bottom of the ten-dollar note was printed: "This certificate is redeemable in United States currency at the value stated thereon, and until such time as the people of the United States own all the corporations they work for. When this occurs, World Corporation and the United States government will merge and create a World Congress, which will eventually absorb all the remaining service and capital industries in the world and eliminate forever the wastefulness of competition and put an end to poverty throughout the world."

"World Corporation certificates are issued in ten-dollar, fifty-dollar, and up to ten-thousand-dollar amounts," Marge told him. She was enjoying Ronald's total disbelief. "Only fifty-dollar certificates and higher pay dividends. You can show your faith in World Corporation by buying a ten-dollar certificate and eventually work your way up to dividend-paying certificates."

"My God!" Ronald kept turning the certificate over and over. "Don't tell me that people actually buy these," he said in disgust. "It's worse than wasting ten dollars on a state lottery. It seems to me like a con game. It beats Ponzi and chain letters. Why would anyone give ten good dollars for a piece of paper not worth three cents?"

"Because they *believe*!" Marge grinned. "Faith will move mountains. At least half of the present three-hundred-and-fifty-million-dollar assets of World Corporation that have been increasing twenty-five percent annually are non-dividend paying. You see, H.H. understands human psychology. If people will buy real estate on the moon, which he is sure they would, then they will be happy to invest a little in a future dream. Give me ten bucks, Ron, and take that certificate with you. You'll get ten dollars worth of enjoyment showing it to Ralph Thiemost. Or, better still, buy two of them. If you're as good a businessman as you think you are, you can probably sell one to Ralph Thiemost for twenty dollars, and you can frame the other and hang it over your bar. Think of the fun you'll have explaining such insanity to your friends."

Ronald couldn't tell whether Marge was laughing at him or with him, but not to be outdone he fished twenty dollars out of his billfold and handed it to her. "I'll put it on my expense account," he said grimly. "Now I suppose you're going to tell me that World has sold enough of these shares to buy Byrdwhistle."

"Actually, H.H. runs an amazingly effective mail-order campaign for World. With fewer than five employees located in a downtown office in the Prudential Center, World Corporation has sold over two hundred and fifty million dollars worth of the ten-dollar certificates. None of the shareholders of ten-dollar certificates are paid dividends. But in the case of Byrdwhistle—although Thornton isn't fully aware of it—the purchase was accomplished by a stock swap."

"So unbeknownst to him, Thornton Byrd owns World Corporation?"

"Not quite. He owns one hundred and thirty-five million shares of World, or rather the Byrdwhistle Foundation owns them. H.H. wanted to straighten out Thornton's estate without getting him too involved. So, with the proxies that Thornton gave Elmer and their own shares, they voted to transfer the Byrdwhistle shares to the Byrdwhistle Foundation. World pays dividends to the Foundation."

"I really am confused. What happens when Thornton discovers the truth about the Foundation?"

Marge shook her head. "Really, Ron, it doesn't matter. World Corporation certificates always retain a par value of one dollar. They are nonspeculative and they are fully redeemable in United States currency. I do recommend that you read Gillette."

"I'm beginning to feel like Alice in Wonderland. It looks to me as though Thornton couldn't sell Byrdwhistle even if he wanted to."

Marge shrugged. "To tell you the truth, I really don't know. Other than owning a couple of thousand shares of World Corporation, and they have never missed a dividend, I have nothing to do with the company. For the moment, it's a glorified mutual investment fund that's based on King Gillette's original idea. H.H. is the president, but he only takes a dollar a year as salary. The offices in the Prudential Center are very staid and proper and not at all like Byrdwhistle."

While she was talking, Marge had gathered a pile of catalogues from one of her files and handed them to Ronald. "Before you can really comprehend Byrdwhistle's consolidated figures, I should explain these to you."

Ronald flipped through the four-color catalogues while Marge gave him a running commentary. "The first and largest is our Byrdcage catalogue. It's more generalized than the others and features perennial bestsellers and fast-moving items from our other catalogues. The rest of them, like Sleepy Byrd, are designed to appeal to particular markets or to needs that don't exist but that we go all out to create. As you can see, Sleepy Byrd is bedroom oriented, everything to enhance sex and sleeping. It has everything in it from gadgets to imitate the sounds of ocean surf and pattering rain to make you sleep easier, to masks, ear plugs, vibrators, cuddly-bear sleeping bags, erotic nightwear, and bedroom furnishings. Those pillows you are admiring are designed to resemble female buttocks and are very popular. A comparable female item is our phallic pillow.

"Our Happy Byrd catalogue specializes mainly in humorous and game items such as those ceramic hands to hold toilet tissue, hot-lip teapots, dinosaur assembly-kits, fantasy ties like that one with 'P.O.E.T.' woven respectably on it." Marge laughed. "That's a very popular item. It means 'Piss On Every Thing.' We offer ties with all kinds of symbols on them, such as dollar signs and moneybags, which women love to give to their menfriends."

Ronald whistled disparagingly. "The prices aren't humorous. For God's sakes, there's nothing in this one that costs less than twenty-five dollars."

Marge shrugged. "Most of our catalogue items carry a minimum two-hundred-percent markup. If inventory items don't turn over three times a year, we are able to sell most of them at cost to mark-down stores. The catalogue you are now looking at is our Byrd Bath catalogue. It features bath oils, soaps, shower attachments, jacuzzis—even bidets complete with plumbing instructions for home installation. Byrds of Paradise and Byrds of Prey are our only catalogues devoted to male and female clothing. We compete in this area by offering very sensuous, hard-to-find clothing and jewelry. After seeing the video-tape we made of your wife, I'm sure she's the type who would look lovely in one of our ranch-mink berets. They're only one hundred ninety-five dollars, or a mink fedora, only three hundred."

"If you don't mind, I'd appreciate seeing that tape."

"I don't have a video player in my office." It occurred to Marge that having nothing better to do tonight she might as well follow through on H.H.'s suggestion. Laughing, she asked Ronald if he'd like to go to her apartment to help her prepare dinner. "We don't like to leave guests of Byrdwhistle stranded in Boston hotel rooms," she told him. "If you come, I'll play the Coldaxe tape for you." She chuckled. "I'll even re-arrange your hair, if you wish."

Ronald heard her, but his answer was devious. "I really have to get my tape-recorder back from your receptionist and dictate some notes on this trip. He knew that, if he accepted her invitation, Marge Slick would succeed in seducing him. "Incidentally," he said, changing the subject, "I didn't see your catalogue-mailing department. How do you handle that?"

"We mail over fifty million catalogues annually. All our very special-ized lists are maintained in our Iowa plant, and we mail from there. Most of our catalogues are printed in Chicago. The Byrd Nest catalogue you are now looking at is devoted to all kinds of small prefabricated build-ings that can be shipped by truck to the buyer to be assembled. Our Byrd House catalogue offers a variety of dollhouses in modern and Victorian styles as well as an endless array of furniture to go with them. Last year, we introduced a new line of flexible two-inch-high male and female dolls together with one-inch child dolls. They are anatomically perfect, with movable penises that are stiff enough to penetrate the female vaginas." Marge grinned. "We know for a fact that even the mothers and fathers like to play with them.

"Our Byrdie catalogue is completely sports oriented. Byrd's-eye spe-cializes in photographic products and video-tapes and discs. Then, there's our Byrd Seed catalogue, which, as you can see, is a complete seed catalogue. Our Byrds-in-the-Hand catalogue is for gambling games. It has everything from roulette wheels to home slot-machines and pin-ball machines to software television games." Marge was now leaning over his shoulder as he scanned the catalogues. He was aware of the pressure of her breast against his back, and the warmth of her breath on his neck.

"H.H. is interested in all kinds of computer gadgets, so he created our Byrd Brain catalogue, which specializes in items like home-calculators, chess games, remote-control switches, and computer spellers, and language translators that now, in addition to a video screen, have a human-voice supplement. Finally, there's our Byrd-on-the-Wing catalogue, which is a travel service. We don't compete with American Express yet, but H.H. believes that anything is possible. Our fly-and-drive vacations will eventually be coordinated with Byrdwhistle-owned high-rise apartments in various European and African areas."

Marge returned to the chair behind her desk, while Ronald, shaking his head, continued to scan the catalogues. "It's incredible that Americans spend so much money on useless junk."

"Not junk," Marge said equably. "They're buying dreams, and escape from reality. Pleasing themselves by buying these things is a way of sublimating their repressed sexuality. It's an inevitable by-product of a society based on the work ethic and living by the reality principle." Marge laughed, "If H.H. gets the chance, I'm sure he'll try to convince you that your personal life, and W.I.N. itself, is based on a kind of rationalized fantasy. Only a small portion of our gross national product is based on the necessity to provide basic food, clothing, and shelter. Note my emphasis on basic—ninety percent of everything we buy or consume is a cover-up to satisfy our frustrated sexual needs. All Byrdwhistlers are aware of this. We don't particularly approve of many of the cover-ups, but we are dedicated to using the machinery of society to eventually co-opt it and change it." Marge noted Ronald's grim expression. "Oh dear, I think your wife is right. Your eyes are telling me, 'Bah, humbug!'"

"There are twelve catalogues here." Ronald was trying to overcome a sudden need to subdue Marge, to whip the cockiness out of her, pin her down, and rape her while she whimpered helplessly, "Don't stop. Don't ever stop. I love you." He often had similar feelings with M'mm but had repressed them, as he was doing now. "I assume that your catalogues are integrated with your operations in various cities."

Marge nodded. "We have four other separate divisions, and three other catalogues. I'll get them for you from our marketing department. Our Love 'n Learn Book Club distributes books we publish ourselves, and our *Club Wholesome* specializes in erotica, within the limits established by H.H."

Ronald scowled. "You mean that you sell pornography by mail? What are the limits?"

"No bondage or domination. No photographs of sadistic or masochistic sexual behavior. Only movies, tapes, pictures, and books dealing with mutually voluntary sexual behavior—hence, wholesome," Marge laughed. "Since you obviously have some typical male responses, I'm sure that you will enjoy our Club Wholesome catalogue. It's fully illustrated, and it's becoming a collector's item. I'll get you one. We don't give them away. We sold more than two hundred thousand of them last year, at five dollars apiece." She paused. "Oh, I nearly forgot. We also have our Treasures of Croesus catalogue, which we only mail to families with an income of over fifty thousand dollars a year. Finally, there's our Video and Software division which is located in New York City. V & S doesn't sell direct, but manufactures video tapes and discs. Our Love Byrd tapes and discs, which are sold through our Club Wholesome catalogue, are mostly homemade."

"Homemade?"

"We don't use professional actors. Any Byrdwhistler, with husband or wife, or with someone else's spouse, if they get their spouse's permission, can write, produce, direct, and photograph a half-hour, or an hour, full-color video Love Byrd tapes." Marge was delighted with Ronald's evident distaste. "You'd really have a ball if you made one. And the results are not only funny, but warm, humorous, loving sex. We cover every aspect of lovemaking, not in a sleazy way, but with an underlying sense of caring and wonder that you can't find in commercial pornography. Unless they're swingers, most people never get the opportunity to watch others making love, yet all of us are voyeurs at heart. Watching Love Byrd tapes in the privacy of your own home is a kind of sex education. They're very popular with women." As she was talking, Ronald's priggish expression convinced Marge that he was ripe for further needling. "I'll give you a few tapes to take home. Your wife will like them. Who knows, they could help you improve your in-bed, and out-of-bed, lovemaking."

Frowning, but knowing that Love Byrd tapes were exactly the silly kind of damned thing that M'mm would buy, Ronald was a bit intrigued. He wanted to ask Marge if she had made any Love Byrd tapes, but that would have been tantamount to asking to see them. "This isn't a business," he grumbled, "it's a cuckoo's nest. I don't see how you've all managed to stay out of jail. How much do employees get paid for making your sex films?"

Marge stared at him sadly. "Ron, you've forgotten. Marcuse's belief, which is one aspect of H.H.'s Theory Z, is that making video movies of ourselves making love isn't work, it's play! So many Byrdwhistlers want to make the tapes that we now have to compete against ourselves. We present a Love Byrd Academy Award every month. A majority vote of all Byrdwhistlers decides which is the best tape, and that one is automatically included in our mail-order offerings."

"You mean that all of your employees have seen each other making love?"

"Most of them. But remember, we aren't live. We're on tape," Marge smiled as if there was a considerable difference. "Of course the tapes do give us ideas of whom it might be fun to go to bed with—if, of course, the particular spouse gives permission."

"Fred and I made a couple of tapes," Marge said, continuing. "We didn't think they were the best, but they were chosen to prove that sex after sixty—Fred's sixty-one—can be as much fun as it ever was. Chuck and Mary Hanna, who work in inventory control, taped us. Fred isn't often impotent, but he was the night we made it. It took both Mary and me to get him up, and Chuck was laughing so hard that the camera was jumping up and down. But even Chuck wasn't any great shakes when he was being photographed with Mary. We all decided that we could never work for Masters and Johnson." Marge was bubbling with laughter as she detailed the film-making to Ron. "We finally decided to title the film "Conversation and Good Sex," which it is most of the time when we forgot or were being too oral with one another. If you'd like to see it, I'll show it to you tonight after dinner."

"Thanks, but I really can't accept your invitation to dinner," Ronald said stiffly. He was suddenly losing any desire to have sex with Marge Slick. This damned woman, and obviously most of the Byrdwhistlers— ugh, Byrdwhistle employees—would jump in the sack with anyone. He hoped that down deep M'mm was more exclusive, but it suddenly occurred to him that he wasn't at all sure that she was.

"Okay, it's your choice," Marge said just as H. H. Youman walked into her office.

"What's his choice?" H.H. asked.

"Whether he has dinner with me."

"Oh, I wouldn't miss that if I were you," H.H. said enthusiastically. "Marge is a good cook. I'd even join you, but I have to go over the World Corporation investment portfolio tonight with Sheldon Coombs. He's the whiz who does most of the investing for World Corporation. Who knows, tonight Sheldon might even decide that World should buy a few shares of W.I.N. Incorporated." H.H. grinned. "Maybe we can reverse your attempted takeover process. I'm sure that you know W.I.N. stock has dropped to twelve dollars a share in the past two weeks. Evidently, some of your acquisitions for W.I.N. aren't paying off." H.H. glanced at his watch. "I hope that you're coming to our Symp meeting. Everyone is looking forward to meeting you."

Marge shook her head. "I'm afraid I got so enthusiastic over our Love Byrd tapes that Ron is more shocked than he was already." She raised her eyebrows at H.H. in what Ron was sure was a silent conspiracy against him.

"You can both set your minds at ease," he said. "I can assure you I wouldn't want W.I.N. involved when the Byrdwhistle bubble bursts."

"I hope not," H.H. said affably, "but like it or not, you might be. Thorny is hell-bent on selling the company, even if in the process it may be necessary to put Elmer and me in jail."

Marge's mouth was open in amazement. "You've heard from Elmer? Is he all right?"

H.H. nodded. "He telephoned two hours ago from the plane. Right from the *Lady Byrd.* I taped our conversation. I'm going to have it played at Symp. Come on, let's go. Jeff O'Hara is chairing the meeting today, and I haven't even scanned the D and D cards. Anyway, I'll have to propose a change in the order of business."

15

Walking toward the elevator, H.H. told Ron, "You'll discover that we're losing a little money in our video division, but it's only temporary. We'll turn that around when we really begin to manufacture Byrdwhistle video discs. The soft-ware market potential is enormous. The big operators like RCA, CBS, and North American Phillips are vulnerable. We expect that we can even take a piece of the Japanese market and garner at least two or three hundred million dollars annually of what will be a multi-billion dollar market. It's only a matter of a few years before video-disc players are in every American home. It's not just a teen-age market either. The older population, which will dominate the American market by the year 2000, will make the present younger-generation record business look small by comparison. According to my reckoning, within five years video-discs, combined with life-size home television, will eliminate moving picture theaters. Movies will be made directly for video-discs and promoted like books. There will be video-disc best-seller lists. Buying a video-disc of a complete first-run movie to watch in your home won't be any more expensive than a ticket to the movie. When that happens, our Byrds on Broadway division will be functional. Elmer has his musical *Rum Ho!* in the bag. He has another based on the Oneida Community coming up. Better still, he has a host of ideas for others—a musical based on Miami during the reign of Leland Stanford, who tried building a rail-road through Key West to connect it with gambling in Havana. That was during the 1920s. Another, called *Summer by the Sea,* is a musical built around old-style summer vacationing in the 1900s, when people went to places like Bar Harbor and Old Orchard Beach and stayed in one place for several weeks."

H.H. punched the down button on the elevator. "Too bad you couldn't meet Elmer. He should have been born in another era, but he compensates by turning nostalgia into art. And that is a very marketable commodity to Americans who like to sentimentalize the past."

"But that's not the whole story on video-discs," H.H. continued. They were walking off the elevator onto the fourth floor, a portion of which had now been transformed into a small theater, which was rapidly filling up with Byrdwhistle employees. "Just as the supermarket revolutionized grocery shopping and paved the way for self-service stores and shopping plazas, so will multiple-channel cable TV and video-discs turn shopping plazas into warehouse areas with very few employees and no direct customers. Instead of driving to a shopping plaza and walking endless miles through store after store searching for some particular item, within the next ten years you'll go shopping on your television channels. You'll be able to order for same-day delivery to your home. It will be less costly in the long run to centralize deliveries, as United Parcel does, than to have hundreds of thousands of individual automobiles burning up energy to get to shopping centers."

H.H. smiled. "By then, people will discover more enjoyable ways to while away their time than by buying things." He didn't elaborate, but Ronald guessed what he meant. "Our Byrdwhistle video-disc catalogues are a good example," he continued. "Right now, we can produce video-discs of everything in these catalogues, accompanied by live demonstrations on most items. We can combine them with psychological musical backgrounds and effective and continuously repeated subliminal messages that urge certain purchases. Video-discs will be much less expensive to produce than our four-color catalogues, and, believe me, they will be much more persuasive than the printed word."

While he was talking, H.H. had led Ronald through the theater and up a small stairway to the stage. They were accompanied by scattered groans and boos. "We've already produced a trial catalogue disc, which we are testing on middle- and upper-class housewives like your wife." Amused by Ronald's "Jesus Christ! You're dangerous!" H.H. responded: "We are discovering that highly educated women like Meredith are more vulnerable and more easily hypnotized by video-disc selling than the average high school graduate is."

Ronald didn't have time to be horrified. His attention was elsewhere. The rows of faces staring at him didn't seem too friendly, and to his surprise he suddenly realized that no one in the theater was totally naked. They had come partially dressed for the Symp meeting, wearing the snap-around terry-cloth towels that he had seen occasionally on his tour. In varying colors, open at one side, they revealed genitals and buttocks when the individual wearer was in motion.

"I don't know whether Marge told you," H.H. said, anticipating his question, "but we provide all Byrdwhistlers with terry-cloth snap-arounds and laundry service." H.H. grinned. "You might call them our company uniform. You see, we haven't yet resolved the problem that the skin on the gluteus maximus adheres to plastic seats and gets itchy as hell on cloth-covered ones."

Marge had left them to sit in the audience. H.H. introduced Ronald to Jeff O'Hara, who had been waiting for them on the stage. Jeff handed

H.H. a thick pile of three-by-five cards in various colors. "There are forty-six Digs and Delves today," he told H.H. "I don't think we can get through them all."

H.H. explained to Ronald that Digs and Delves were a convenient designation for a wide array of questions, plus emotional statements of fact and personal or self-directed criticisms around which the agenda of Symp meetings were oriented. "The basic purpose of large meetings isn't for direct accomplishment, but to create a sense of participation and company harmony," he told Ronald. "We also have small management groups of no more than four people who initiate most policy, but only after it has been reviewed and often revised at a Symp. The blue D & D cards are for any kind of interpersonal problem that occurs between husbands and wives, or between other Byrdwhistlers. Green cards are for new catalogue proposals, and we usually handle these first. Yellow are for suggested catalogue deletions, and they engender discussion of why certain items didn't produce expected returns. Orange are for overall policy matters that have been proposed by various management groups. Purple are for generalized philosophical discussions, and red are for gripes, inquisitions, and confessions." H.H. laughed. "There's often some crossover between the red and blue delves."

"Today we have three greens, no oranges, no yellows, five reds, twelve purples, and five blues," Jeff told H.H. "Most of the reds are directed at Mr. Coldaxe."

H.H. skimmed through the cards and waved for attention. "As you know," he said when the audience had quieted down, "I usually sit in the theater with you at Symp meetings. I don't try to direct the traffic; but today we have a guest with us who has jarred the usual Byrdwhistle family equilibrium." H.H. smiled at the enthusiastic applause. "So, I hope that you won't mind if I propose the order of business. It's now four o'clock. I must leave at quarter to five. We have three green D & D's that must be given immediate priority. One is an item that could appear in our fall Sleepy Byrd catalogue. A perfume known as an "exaltoloid." Presumably, it has sex-attractant pheromones in it that human beings are unable to smell consciously, but subconsciously these pheromones inspire stronger than usual sexual ardor. If you spray this stuff around your bedroom before making love, it presumably makes both the male and the female hornier. Buzz Spellman has proposed it. Jeff has fifty cans of it on the platform. Later on, any of you who wants to can sniff it, and those of you who try it out during the week can report your findings. My own opinion is that, if lovers dispense with all perfumes and really stick their noses into the bodies of their partners—providing that they are vegetarians and that they're not too sweaty—they will pick up the subtle accent of the other person's natural sex attractants. Of course this won't work if you're a meat eater. A meat-eater's sweat stinks, as any vegetarian will tell you." H.H. grinned at Ronald. "For the benefit of Ronald Coldaxe I'm propagandizing, but he should understand that we allow our guest the same privilege, if he's so inclined."

"We're offering a book called *Aroma Therapy* in our Club Wholesome catalogue," Buzz persisted, "I didn't know you were against perfumes and cosmetics, H.H."

"I'm not," H.H. said. "As you know Club Wholesome is also offering a book called *Sexual Secrets,* by Penny Slinger and Nik Douglas. They point out that, during the Tantric sexual ritual called the Rite of the Five Essentials, the male partner applies jasmine to his lover's hands, patchouli to her neck and cheeks, essence of amber to her breasts, spikenard of valerian to her hair, and musk to her vagina. She in turn rubs him all over with oil of sandalwood." H.H. laughed. "Mohammed once declared, 'Three things are especially dear to me. Women, perfume, and prayer.' Using perfume and cosmetics and makeup transforms love-making into play, and we hope by now Ronald Coldaxe knows how Byrdwhistlers feel about play." H.H. grinned specifically at Ronald. "Perfumes are like booze. Use them in the right amount in the right place and they help you relax and forget the work ethic."

"But we've got to move on," H.H. said. "Chuck Gill proposes, on his delve card, that if we can hold up the printing of the Byrd Brain catalogue, we should include a new calorie counter that he's just discovered; and if not we should get in fast with a full-color insert in this catalogue." H.H. waved at a man in the audience. "Chuck will you bring your prize up here and explain it. Also, will Carol and Harry Ashby bring up their liquid painting soap. After Chuck finishes, you can demonstrate it."

Ronald watched Chuck bounce up the stairway to the platform. Wearing a red terry-cloth snap-around, he was a lean, effervescent man with a captivating circus-barker manner. "Hold everything folks. Stop the presses!" he said. "This little baby is going to be a big mail-order item this fall. It's going to help make the world skinnier." He held up what seemed to be a slightly oversized pocket calculator. "I got this sample yesterday from the manufacturer, Samuelson Corporation. They've agreed to an exclusive for Byrdwhistle for this fall season only. They'll drop-ship it. But we've got to guarantee a sale of two hundred and fifty thousand of them. You probably can't see the video printout from where you are sitting. This little darling is programmed with a calorie counter of just about anything you can eat—including most nationally branded items and basic foods. You simply spell out the food on the keyboard, any item you wish. For example, I'm spelling "canned salmon." On the screen it now reads "4 ounces: 230 calories, carbohydrates 0." That means that a four-ounce can of canned salmon is 230 calories and that salmon has no carbohydrates. Now I'm dividing that 230 by 2, since I plan to eat half a can of salmon, and I'm pushing the "hold" key to keep count of what I ate in the memory system. As you can see, I'm maintaining a running total of what I eat during the day, and I can carry this little baby with me and get the total before I go to bed. I think we should call it a Skinny Byrd. It will stand a two-hundred-and-fifty-percent markup for at least a year. That would make it possible for us to sell it for ninety-six ninety-five. No handling—Sanderson will drop-ship it."

Several hands were waving at Chuck from the audience. H.H. acknowledged one of them by name. "Okay, Dorothy, what do you think?"

"I say great, but no guarantee."

"But then we get no exclusive," Chuck reminded her. "Everybody in the business will have it."

"They'll have it next year anyway," someone else said. "Samuelson needs us. We're the only company that can give them mail-order coverage this late in the year."

"They can undercut us and advertise it direct. I took that up with Samuelson, but they have agreed that their price would be ten bucks higher than ours."

H.H. intervened, "All right, within the next week, everyone take a look at Chuck's calorie counter. Hand your pros and cons sheets in before the next meeting. Thursday we'll discuss them and take a vote."

Chuck gestured at Ronald. "I see Mr. Coldaxe looks a little dubious. Let's hear his reaction."

"Personally, I wouldn't pay ninety-six cents for one," Ronald said. "But I don't intend to understand the insanity of the mail-order business."

"Never mind, your wife would probably buy you one for Christmas," a woman from the audience yelled. "You look as if you need to count a few calories."

H.H. interrupted the applause. "Byrdwhistlers are very blunt with each other," he told Ronald. "Actually, Ron, though you probably aren't aware of it, many Byrdwhistlers really empathize with your wife. But we should keep in mind," he told the audience, "that Ron has not had time to see our video interview with her. So let's not embarrass him."

A man from the audience said, "Why not? Maybe he'll go away."

A woman waving her hand indignantly said, "H.H., I want to know if you and Mr. Coldaxe are going to tell us what is really going on?"

"Yeah," someone from the back row yelled, "and also ask Coldaxe to tell us if he enjoyed our Love Room with Marge Slick."

Ronald looked out in the audience at Marge, wondering if they had been observed through a keyhole, and Marge responded, "Don't worry, Ron, no one knows what happened after we closed that door."

"You're getting out of order," H.H. said. "We'll deal with all your red delves eventually. Most of them are directed to Ron. If he wishes to respond, that is up to him. Remember, he isn't on the Byrdwhistle payroll yet, so he can ignore us. Let's move on to the liquid soap, which according to Carol and Harry is great for painting graffiti without doing any lasting damage, or for painting naked bodies if you want to have more fun."

Carol Ashby, a striking brunette in her late thirties, with long black hair, vermouth-colored brown eyes, and naked breasts with light brown aureolas and erect nipples, flung off her orange terry-cloth snap-around. Then she deliberately swayed her hips and lush pubic mound seductively at Ronald.

"If you'd like to try liquid soap on me, Mr. Coldaxe," she smiled at him teasingly, and handed him a brush, "Harry said he wouldn't object. Why don't you undress, and then we can paint each other and wash it off in one of the Love Rooms?"

Ronald retreated from the paint brush as if Carol was holding a spitting snake at him. "No thanks," he muttered, "I couldn't concentrate on painting."

"Neither can Harry," Carol laughed. "That's part of the fun. This soap is really an aphrodisiac. Harry always gets an erection when I paint his dong."

Harry flipped off his terry-cloth towel while Carol was talking and revealed his penis, which was already slightly elevated and looking slowly around the audience. He held up a large box filled with twenty-four three-ounce jars. "The manufacturer provides a total range of colors. The box comes with a four-color wrap and two paint brushes. Unlike regular soap, this stuff dries on contact, but when you wash it with warm water it turns to suds and rinses away. You can paint it on anything, but it's much more fun to be creative on human flesh. We can hold our regular markups and sell it for twelve ninety-five. In memory of that famous movie slogan and Clark Gable, we think it should be called Love That Soap."

"All right," H.H. said, "let's see what happens when you paint each other."

Harry took a brush and dipped it in one of the jars that Carol had opened. First he painted a red nose on her stomach, using her navel for one nostril. Then, while she giggled and her nipples became even more erect, he painted a blue wall-eye on each breast. The face was staring down at her pubic-hair beard. Turning her around, he painted her buttocks and back, quickly transforming them into the face of a plump-cheeked woman, which Carol set in motion—to the enthusiastic clapping of Byrdwhistlers—by flexing her rump slowly up and down.

Carol responded by painting brown eyes on Harry's stomach and then carefully transforming his penis into a blue nose which immediately rose out of the shrubbery and pointed at the ceiling.

"See what I mean?" she said enthusiastically. "Your nose looks as if it's about to sneeze at me."

"Before it does," H.H. interrupted the yells of approval, "take it to one of the Love Rooms and wash it!"

"And help blow Harry's poor nose, Carol," someone yelled as they left the stage.

H.H.'s eyes now searched the audience until he located Bruce Maitlin. "I know that you filed an orange delve for final approval on the copulating-deer layouts. I'm sorry I have to leave early. I assume that you've given them to Ray Simon." H.H. waved toward the projection room in the back of the theater. "Ray, you can project Bruce's layouts and copy after you've run the audio-tape of my conversation with Elmer. Incidentally, Bruce, go to work on Love That Soap. If we can't get it in the Dreamy Byrd catalogue, my suggestion is that we launch it through Club Wholesome. Now, to bring you all up to date, Ray will let you hear the telephone conversation that I had with Elmer earlier this afternoon."

H.H. sat down, and after a few seconds of scratchiness, Elmer's voice on the theater speakers filled the room.

"H.H.? Yeah, we landed in Athens this morning. Thorny and Adele were still in the pokey. I told Thorny to cool it, because it looked as if he was going to turn permanently purple with rage. I finally found a lawyer who could speak English. After much discussion, we resolved the terrible indecency to the Greek public and to the Acropolis. For five thousand dollars, distributed here and there, the whole episode never happened."

"Five thousand dollars! Christ, Elmer, the ancient Greeks used to admire their Gods naked. Why didn't you tell them that Thorny used to live on Mount Olympus with Jupiter? I hope you told Thorny the five thousand dollars was a damned expensive ransom for a few naked pictures—unless he's planning to have one enlarged and hung in the reception room. Or, maybe, if his prick looks alive and eager enough, we could use him for a cover on our new Club Wholesome catalogue."

"I didn't tell Thorny anything. He can't talk to me without going into his Judas routine. You and I betrayed him. After a night in a cell with half a dozen unwashed Greeks, thieves, rapists, and a couple of homos who tried to convince him that he'd really enjoy buggery, Thorny is mad as hell. What's more he's blaming you for the whole episode."

"Me?"

"Adele is *your* wife. Thorny has suddenly become old-fashioned. He thinks that if you kept Adele home and put your foot down and stopped her from running around the world like a female cat in heat, she'd forget her latest project—a book of naked photographs of horny old power-hungry capitalists. According to Adele, she already has fifty subjects, including Ralph Thiemost in his birthday suit. I saw the pictures. Thiemost is sporting a big erection in some ancient Roman temple. He looks like Bacchus in the moonlight. Adele showed the pictures to Thorny, and that's what caused the whole trouble. He wasn't to be outdone."

"Lovely! Tell Adele I want negatives of both pictures. We'll make dart-boards out of Ralph and Thorny. A Thiemost dart-board should be good for a sale of eighty thousand to W.I.N. employees."

"I'm not telling your wife anything. Adele is now vice president and secretary of Byrdwhistle Corporation."

"She can't be. Marge Slick is."

"Not any longer. When we finally all got back to the *Love Byrd,* Thorny started drinking ouzo and was hell-bent for election. Marvy tried to convince him that the best therapy for him was to do a Zorba—you know, the Greek dance. You can hear the bouzoukee music—it's still playing. But Thorny was in a very belligerent mood. He decided to call a special meeting of the stockholders."

"It's not valid. I wasn't notified."

"You can tell Thorny that. An hour ago he elected himself chairman and treasurer. Then he elected Adele vice president and secretary. Then he asked me if I wanted to remain on as president and get off my ass and stop writing fairy stories and really run the company. I told him, 'No way.' So then he elected himself president. After that, he elected Jack Sludge and Pinky Fresser directors. Then, on a majority vote of the directors, including Adele, they fired you, after which Thorny passed out and Adele put him to bed."

"Great! Is Adele there? I want to talk to her."

"Hello, Heman?" It was Adele's voice.

"Listen, Adele, cut out the funzies. You couldn't be secretary of anything. You can't type and you don't even know how to spell secretary."

"I do, too. S E C R E T A R Y."

"That's secret-ary."

"I know it. That's what a secretary's supposed to do—keep secrets."

"I'm telling you a secret, Adele, and if you don't tell it to Thorny when he wakes up, I'll spank your ass. When he gets over his big head, tell him that he can't afford to waste his remaining years screwing Byrdwhistle. There are too many other younger vaginas to explore. And note the accent on younger."

"Thorny likes comfortable old shoes like me. Heman?"

"Yes?"

"I think you'd better write your resignation before it's too late."

"Too late for what?"

"Thorny told me to telephone Ralph Thiemost and tell him that he had a deal. So I did. Ralph has agreed to buy Byrdwhistle. He's expecting one of his vice presidents, with a weird name—Coldballs, I think—to give him the green light when he returns to California Thursday. Is Mr. Coldballs there now? Ralph said he would be talking with him this week. After Coldballs clears it, there will be a team of W.I.N. auditors going through the corporation books, I have a feeling they could put you in jail. If you meet me in Portugal, they'd have to extradite you."

"Adele, *you* come home with Elmer. You need a workout on our circular bed. If I run it counterclockwise it will unwind you."

"No thanks, I always hated that bed. It makes me dizzy. You're really going to like it in Albuferia, Heman. You can write about your Theory Z and I can paint, and we can relax and enjoy our declining years together."

"Adele, I love you. You may be declining, but I'm not. Anyway, I'm sure that we couldn't make it together in retirement. You'd de-ball me and I'd de-cunt you. So cool it until you're ninety-six and I'm ninety. Then I might give it a whirl. Right now, put Elmer back on—Elmer? From now on, when Adele talks to you, hold your hands tightly over your ears. And, while the old man's out cold, show a little authority. You're the boss of Byrdwhistle and the *Love Byrd,* too. Tell Jack and Pinky to haul anchor immediately and take that crap-can on a cruise to Sveti Stefan and get those damned Love Rocks. Tell Adele that she has to help you. It was when I watched her holding one between her thighs, kissing it, and giving it to me as a potent love charm that I got the idea. All you have to do, if you're impotent with Marvy, is to have her rub one on your cock. Try it out, Elmer. And don't worry about Byrdwhistle. Coldballs—excuse me, Coldaxe—is here but we're scaring the shit out of him. W.I.N. isn't going to win this war."

H.H. grinned at the cheering Byrdwhistlers as the phones clicked off. "So that's where we are at the moment," he said. "I have to leave in a few minutes. Ron has been shuffling through your red delves, reading them in a state of shock. Perhaps, before I go he'll give us his reaction."

Bewildered, Ronald stood up and looked at the audience a little grimly. "My job is to make a thorough preliminary report on any potential acquisition that W.I.N. Incorporated is contemplating. While I shall continue for the next day or two to assemble my profile on Byrdwhistle, I can assure you," Ronald couldn't help smiling, "if W.I.N. Incorporated ever gets involved with this company it will be over my dead body!"

"That calls for a celebration!" H.H. beamed at Ronald over the enthusiastic whistles and applause from the Byrdwhistlers. He put his arm around Ronald's shoulders. "Ron Coldballs is no longer our enemy. He's our friend. Marge—Marge Slick. Tonight it's your job. Roll out the carpet for him. Welcome him to Everett and to Boston! Tomorrow, Ron, if you'd like to stay in my Louisburg apartment, you can try my circular bed and I'll toast you for a long life—no dead body—with the oldest wine that money can buy."

16

Thursday morning when Marge drove Ronald to Logan Airport and kissed him goodbye, he knew that in the past few days, for the first time in his business career, he had been thoroughly compromised, not only by Marge Slick, but by Heman Hyman Youman as well.

On top of that, Ralph Thiemost had informed him by telephone on Wednesday that, despite what seemed like his "unwarranted negativism," Ralph still was very much interested in Byrdwhistle. As he walked toward the departure gate, Ronald was sure of one thing. Even if he couldn't convince Ralph Thiemost that the Byrdwhistle plum was rotten to the core, Ron was sure that he could never return to Everett.

And the truth was that if it was at all possible he would never return to Boston. If he did, he was sure that he would be in greater trouble than Ulysses trying to sail between Scylla and Charybdis. Without a safe distance of three thousand miles between him and Marge, it would be impossible for him to resist his compulsion for her flesh. She told him that she hated the word fucking, but she was obviously a woman who never tired of "sex-making"—her word—and she certainly seemed to enjoy him and respond to him in bed more than M'mm had in the past few years. As far back as he could remember, M'mm had never told him, as Marge had, that she never wanted to stop kissing and tasting his lovely male body. She had even practically convinced him that, now, after her "operation" on him, he had become more handsome than Marlon Brando was in *Apocalypse Now* and was the most handsome, virile, alluring, and gloriously insatiable lover she had ever known.

Of course Ronald was fully aware that, unlike most women, including M'mm, Marge knew instinctively the kind of praise and admiration that convinced men that they were conquerors. Whether he could believe her or not, Ronald reveled in her frank and adoring approval of him and her insistence that he had been as compulsively attracted to her as she had been to him from the first moment they met. Whether it was some unique rapport based on common pheromones—or, as she had pointed out, that they were basically both left-brain thinkers—pragmatic as well as loving—or whether, in fact, Marge had been happily lying to him, the truth was that the ambience she created from the moment he entered her apartment had turned him into a demon lover, who, after his first minor failure, had remained esconced in her vagina for nearly one third of the last forty-eight hours. Whatever had happened to him, Ronald was well aware, as he slumped into his seat in the 747 headed for Los Angeles, that both inwardly and outwardly, and practically overnight, he had gone through a dangerous middle-life crisis. He wondered glumly how he was ever going to explain his new appearance to M'mm and their children and friends, not to mention Ralph Thiemost and his associates at W.I.N.

Marge had laughed at his fears. "Tell them you changed your name, too. You are now Baron Coldaxe, mighty leader of men! Really, Ronnie, you do look much more impressive than Lufthansa's Red Baron."

Dreamily trying to relive the hours from the moment he had reluctantly accepted Marge's invitation to her apartment when she had offered to whip up a cozy dinner of steak and salad for him, Ronald ignored the attaché case beside him in the seat. When the time came to disillusion Ralph Thiemost about Byrdwhistle he'd force himself to wake from this lovely mad dream and somehow he would return to the safety of his family and W.I.N. Incorporated.

When Marge had directed him to her Mercedes in the Byrdwhistle parking lot, he had still been deliberating whether to accept her invitation. He told her he'd appreciate it if she would drive him directly back to the Ritz, and attempting to counteract her meat-eating invitation he said, "I thought everyone who worked for Byrdwhistle was a vegetarian."

Marge had grinned happily at him as he sat next to her in the Mercedes. "We only have to be meat-eaters under the roof of Byrdwhistle. H.H. is a leader, not a dictator. Of course, if I know that I'm going to get H.H.'s sniff test, I don't eat meat for a few days before."

"I'll be happy to take you out to dinner," he told her as he realized that the expressway she was on was coming closer to downtown Boston, "but I really should shower and change my clothes. Later, I must have some time to dictate a rundown on my first day at Byrdwhistle."

"We can relax and have a drink at my apartment first. Maybe you'll change your mind." She patted his knee. "Don't worry, I'll get you to the Ritz for bedcheck. You can shower in my apartment." Shivering, she gestured at the fog hovering over the Boston skyline and capping the phallic protuberances of the John Hancock and the Prudential buildings like fluffy white condoms. "It's going to be a miserable, chilly night. You can feel the easterly blowing. Fred and I live on the thirty-fourth floor of the Harbor Towers. We overlook the ocean, but tonight you'll think that you've returned to a moist womb." She grinned at him. "It's a nice night to have a friend to snuggle with."

Certain that Marge was going to prove harder to resist than Circe herself, and fearful that she might transform him into something worse than a pig, Ronald tried to convince her that he wasn't a friend yet. As she drove into the apartment parking garage, he insisted again that he didn't want to put her to any trouble and that at around nine o'clock he really had to get a taxi back to the Ritz. "In the meantime, I still have a lot of questions about Byrdwhistle that I want to ask you."

"Ralph Thiemost isn't looking over your shoulder," she said. "You worked hard enough today. It's time to float with the tide. No Byrdwhistle questions tonight. Let's just talk about us."

Ronald wasn't so easily diverted. "I can't figure out your management setup. You're one of the directors, but you evidently outrank your husband. Is he only earning a median income, like the average Byrdwhistle employee?"

"You weren't listening to Elmer's conversation with Hyman," Marge said. "As of today, I'm no longer director or vice president. Adele Youman is."

"It sounded to me as if Thornton will change his mind tomorrow."

"Maybe. But Thorny can be very bull-headed sometimes." Marge led the way to the elevators. "Anyway, there are no average employees at Byrdwhistle. We're all geniuses! Only certain kinds of people could pass the Byrdwhistle examination. I'm glad that I never had to."

"I thought that all employees had to take the examination."

Marge shook her head. "I'm from before the Theory Z era. I'm the only employee who survived the shakeup after Thornton moved out and Hyman and Elmer took over." Marge grinned. "Haven't you noticed, I'm an old lady?"

"You're only five years older than I am," Ronald responded so promptly that it was obvious he had been thinking about it. "Actually," he said, daring to tell her the truth, "you look at least ten years younger than I am."

Laughing, she told him, "Didn't you know Byrdwhistlers can't grow old? It's against the rules. When we finally crap out, it has to be instantaneous, like the one-hoss shay. Anyway, whether I look it or not, I've been around for quite a while. My first husband, Arthur Cabot, divorced me." As they waited for the elevator, Marge said, "I was forty-five at the time. Arthur took off with a young filly. He would never have subscribed to H.H.'s "have your cake and eat it too" philosophy. Arthur wanted variety, but he could only cope with it legally, and one at a time. Our only child, Sylvia, is thirty-one. I never planned to marry again. I could always count on Hy as an occasional bedfriend. But then Hy informed me that, if I was going to work at Byrdwhistle, I had to get married. He and Adele knew a recent widower, Fred Slick. He wanted Fred at Byrdwhistle, but he, too, would have to conform to Theory Z. Fred was vice president of Shop and Save, a New England chain of supermarkets, but he was sure that they were getting ready to sack him before he was sixty-five. They were accused of trying to circumvent the retirement laws." Marge laughed, "So Fred took me for better or worse, and amazingly, he loves me *and* Byrdwhistle. Among other things, he's in charge of competition. He knows what every company in the mail-order business is going to do even before they do it."

"I'm a little confused," Ronald told her. "In the office you call Youman

'H.H.' Now, you refer to him as Hyman or Hy. His wife calls him Heman."

"Hy would answer your question by telling you that everyone should have several names to fit different aspects of their personality. As he told you this morning, Hyman is a Jewish name."

Ronald followed Marge into the elevator, and she smiled ruefully at him.

"Prepare yourself, Mr. Coldaxe. My maiden name was Marjorie Jacobs. If you haven't guessed already, I'm Jewish. I married a Wasp and got stung. You know, fools rush in. Now I'm playing with you, a German." She sighed, "My problem is that I'm a patsy for certain kinds of men. Ronald noticed that her eyes were wet with tears and wondered if she meant him, but then he realized that she was actually thinking of H.H.

"Like everybody else, I love that crazy man," she admitted when he asked her. "Hy looks as if he just walked out of the Plymouth plantation. The truth is that he's a lot like the ancestor he adopted after reading Elmer's book."

"Elmer wrote a book?"

Marge nodded. "It's called *Adopt an Ancestor.* The theory is, very simply, that billions of people have lived in this world and rather than try to find your own direct ancestry why not adopt an ancestor who appeals to you? It corrects the theory that you can choose your friends but not your relatives. Anyway, if H.H. invites you to his commune in Merry Mount, I'm sure he'll tell you that he adopted Thomas Morton. Morton was the bad boy from England who was trading with the Indians for furs and fucking around with the Indian girls, much to the horror of the Pilgrims in Plymouth." Marge shrugged. "Actually, I think that Hy should have adopted Jesus Christ. Of course it wasn't until he turned fifty and he finally got rid of Thorny that he fully revealed his messianic urges and that he was a prime candidate for crucifixion."

As she unlocked the door to her apartment, Marge asked him if he had any other personal questions.

"Well, not wholly personal, but tomorrow I'd like to look over the payroll figures. I presume that Byrdwhistle officials earn more than your regular employees."

"All of the Byrdwhistlers earn bonuses in addition to the median wage," Marge said. "But, despite some of the Oneida Community philosophy that he has incorporated into Theory Z, Hy is convinced that, until World Corporation takes over and people actually own the corporations that they work for, the time isn't ripe for complete monetary equality. Hold your breath, Ronnie, last year I earned one hundred and thirty-eight thousand dollars."

Ronald couldn't restrain a grimace. It was incredible. This damned woman made nearly fifty thousand dollars a year more than he did. And he was positive that if he asked her she would tell him that she didn't work, she played. "How much do Elmer and H.H. take out of the company?" he demanded.

"Elmer only gets one hundred and seventy-five thousand. But Hy has averaged about two hundred and sixty-five thousand a year since he took over." Marge shrugged. "He believes that he's worth at least as much as the President of the United States. But I doubt if he has much money saved. Hy has expensive tastes, and he invests most of his income in World Corporation, which I'm sure irritates his wife. Of course, all management income and employee income at Byrdwhistle can fluctuate, depending on our bonuses."

"But it doesn't."

"Not downward. Hy's magic money-touch hasn't failed us yet."

"I understand that Elmer flew to Athens. What kind of plane does the company own?"

"A Grumman II, the finest private plane in the world," Marge had turned on the lights and Ronald repressed a gasp at seeing the lavish living room. He was standing on a lush white broadloom with a pile that felt delightfully springy under his feet. The expensive modern furniture was in various shades of gold and burnt orange. Marge flipped on a stereo and the room was filled with a guitar concerto. "It's called Concerto de Aranjuez," she told him. "The music's a tribute to a palace in Spain near Madrid. I hope you like guitar music. This record is followed by Segovia and John Williams."

In response to her request, Ronald told her that he'd have a scotch and water, and she ducked behind a wetbar in the corner of the room and made them each one. Drinking it too rapidly, Ronald thought how shocked and impressed Ralph Thiemost would be by Youman's income. Last year, although Ralph may have earned more in stock options and bonuses, his income, which was reported in *Business Week,* was only about twenty thousand dollars higher than H.H.'s, and the Byrdwhistle company-plane could fly circles around W.I.N.'s Lear jet.

Marge refilled his glass. "It's only six-thirty." She opened a sliding glass-door that led onto a balcony. "We can relax before dinner." Shivering, she leaned against him. "Fog appeals to my amphibious genes. It makes me feel erotic." She smiled at him tenuously. "Here we are—you and I, practically strangers—and no one in this whole world knows where we are or gives a damn."

Ronald didn't dispute this. M'mm and Fred might not know that Ronald's rod was engorged and Marge's silky tunnel was probably more than a little moist, but they probably damned well would care if they did. They certainly would care if they could have heard Marge whisper: "Come on, Ronnie. It's time to stop being a cold-ass executive from W.I.N. Try being the young stud you know you still are."

Ronald had never received such an egalitarian proposition from a woman in his life. How could he resist? He couldn't. Although he couldn't see Marge's behind or pussy, the memory of them still waggled in his mind. He swept her into his arms and kissed her passionately, and she clung to him and kissed him back until he moaned, "God, we'd better stop. I'm sorry, Marge, but watching you naked all afternoon is enough to drive any man off his rocker."

Laughing, she slid out of his embrace. Asking him why they had to stop, she wandered back into the living room, moving her body in suggestive riposte to the music. She bent over to examine the electric fireplace, which she had switched on, and Ronald caught a glimpse of her naked behind. "It's your own damned fault, I'm not a saint," he muttered. He grabbed her from the rear and pushed her down on the floor and kissed and nibbled her ass fervently. "Damn you," he groaned, as she tumbled over on her back laughing and kissing his lips, "I've been wanting to do that all afternoon. You have the best looking behind I've ever seen."

"How many have you seen?" Marge hadn't pulled her dress down and now her stomach and pubic hair were fully exposed. Still wanting to bury his face in her flesh, Ronald didn't answer. "You really didn't have to wait, Ronnie," she whispered. "That's why I took you to a Love Room, to reduce our mutual stress." On her knees, she flipped her dress over her head and flung it on the couch. "Ronnie," she wailed, noticing his sudden indecision, "only you, God, and I will ever know. Take off your clothes." With practiced ease, she unzipped his pants, released his straining penis, and kissed it. "What a lovely schlong," she murmured. "If you'll undress, I'll make love with you."

Ronald was still temporizing. "I should take a shower."

"So should I, but we won't." Marge sniffed him. "You smell nice and erotic to me. Come on, the bed is softer." She led him into a large master bedroom. Naked, her breasts flopping, she bounced up and down on the bed as if it were a trampoline and then collapsed in a demure heap. "Hurry, hurry, Ronnie, I need to feel you inside me."

His frustrated penis had lost patience with him. He kneeled over her, wanting to taste and suck her breasts and vulva and kiss her lips all at the same time. Overwhelmed by the need to totally absorb the only other woman he had made love to since he had married M'mm, Ronald was like a man released from Devil's Island. His penis was touching the soft hairs on Marge's labia and then her vagina was nursing him while she moaned her mounting delight. Ron was upside-down on a roller-coaster to infinity. With a groan of sheer happiness he flooded her with his gyzym and collapsed on her breasts with one last violent shudder.

Melting into Marge's body, he could feel her hands patting him soothingly as he finally caught his breath. "Damn! I'm really sorry," he muttered.

"It's all right," she stroked his back, "Poor you. Are you always a premature ejaculator?"

It was the kind of question that he and M'mm never asked each other. "I don't think so," he mumbled, "I haven't made love for a few weeks. What do you want me to do?"

"Come back inside me," she grinned. "Obviously, not right away. Just lie beside me and talk to me."

"It's not fair."

Marge burst into laughter and his deflated penis was ejected out of her nest. Still laughing, Marge held it. She squeezed the remaining drips into her hand and then held up her palm. "Have you ever tasted yourself?"

Ronald shook his head vehemently. "God, no!"

Marge lapped her palm. "You taste fine." She wiped the glistening stuff over his bald head. "Maybe it'll make your hair grow." Bending over his shrunken penis, she took it in her mouth for a few moments, then she looked at him and grinned. "Does your wife like to suck your prick?"

Ronald frowned. M'mm hadn't been as interested in his genitals as Marge seemed to be for quite a few years. He didn't answer. Evidently Marge didn't expect him to. She was giggling happily.

"What's so funny?" he demanded.

"I'm glad to know that, at least in bed, you play fair."

Ronald was fumbling with her clitoris and he wondered if he should kiss her down there. Momentarily, his former need to explore her genitals had disappeared. "You don't have to do that," she told him. "I prefer to wait."

Ronald took his hand away, but he didn't know how to answer her. He wasn't at all sure that he could get an erection again—not for several hours for sure, and maybe not at all—especially if he kept thinking that he shouldn't ever have got involved sexually with the employee of a potential acquisition. The best thing to do now was to get the hell out of there. Get back to the Ritz as fast as possible, and tomorrow play it cool. He could go through the pretense of gathering some more information and catch a noon plane back to L.A.

Marge read his mind. "I think you're feeling remorseful. You're wishing that you dared to jump out of the bed, get dressed, put your money on the dresser, and say goodbye to the whorish Marge Slick."

He kissed her. "You're not whorish, you're delicious, but I should be trying to assimilate my material on Byrdwhistle."

"Go, if you want to," Marge said coolly. "But I can tell you won't assimilate Byrdwhistle until you reorder your priorities. I'll wager you've never made love to your wife twice in the same night."

Ronald wasn't going to confess that if M'mm made love with him twice a week he was lucky and that it was always on his own initiative. "I guess long-married couples settle into routines," he said, deciding that it would not be politic to leave yet. "What about you and Fred?"

"Fred is a protégé of Hyman. They both attribute their continuous well-being to daily sex-making."

"You always use that word. Why not love-making?"

Marge grinned. "If you understand the word *love* the way Byrd-whistlers do, I would; but most people say it like a tenor in an Italian opera. Very possessive. Right now, I'm sure that Fred is sex-making with Laura Whitehurst. She's a lovely southern woman of about thirty-seven. While you were talking with Hyman after the Symp meeting, Fred asked me if it was okay. We were on the video phone from Atlanta. As for Hyman, before the evening's over I'm sure he'll be in bed with my daughter."

Ronald glared at her in astonishment. "I suppose you asked Fred if it was okay to screw with me."

Marge was caressing his belly and her fingers were running through his pubic hair and ruminating with his still limp penis. "I told Fred that I didn't know whether we would make love or I would have to deball you; but he gave me permission either way." She grinned at him. Leaning on her elbow, she turned up the corners of his mouth with her finger. "Stop frowning, Ronnie. To assimilate Byrdwhistle, you've got to acquire a new frame of reference. Last night I slept with Elmer, but the poor dear was too pooped to pop. But remember that Byrdwhistlers are not like California swingers. We go to bed only with members of the Byrdwhistle family, or with people with whom we hope to achieve an ongoing friendship."

While she was talking, Marge got on her knees and straddled Ronald's body. To his surprise, he was staring into the curve of her ass and the warm puffy envelope between her legs. Once again his penis was in her mouth and to his amazement he could feel it faintly stirring again. Suddenly, he no longer wanted to leave. Delighted with his unrealized potential, he buried his face in her bush and tasted himself in the soft folds of her vagina. But then, when he was fully able to penetrate her again, bubbling with laughter, she jumped off the bed. She diddled his reincarnated rod, kissed him, and said, "No problem. Later on, you won't have any trouble being fair. First, since we've already burned up at least two hundred and seventy calories, let's make dinner.

Now, as the stewardess brought him a before-luncheon drink and he knew that he was at least a thousand miles closer to the dull security of his job and his home, Ronald remembered that wearing one of Fred's robes for about fifteen minutes he had actually been domestic and hus-bandly with Marge Slick. While she flitted around the kitchen in a big cotton housecoat, he sliced tomatoes and cucumbers and cut up radishes for the salad and she stopped occasionally to let him fish her breasts out of their cocoon for an affectionate kiss and quick suck.

"As you can see, I'm a practical nudist," she told him, shivering and refastening her robe. "But if it were warm, I'd be naked and you might even get pussy hairs on your steak. I'm glad it's a snuggly night."

She told him that she had bought a case of the Mouton Rothschild that he had seen in the Byrdwhistle inventory, and while he protested that he couldn't possibly enjoy drinking such an expensive wine she opened the bottle. They finished most of it before she put the steaks under the broiler. When Ronald admitted that it was smoother than any California wine he had ever drunk, she got another bottle and insisted that he open it. "What the hell, live it up, Ron," she told him as she sat down on his lap. Nibbling on his lips and cheeks, she took a swallow of the wine and held it in her mouth and then let it dribble through her kisses into his mouth—back and forth until it had all trickled down their throats. And, when he encouraged her to do it again and again, they both knew that they were smoochily inebriated, but they didn't care.

"I'd rather eat you than steaks," Ronald grunted at her happily. "But I really don't understand you, Marge. I know you're making a lot of money at Byrdwhistle, but, good God, you're really too smart not to know damned well that Byrdwhistle's a cross between a carny operation and some kind of weird cult." He looked at her a little dizzily. He was dimly aware that Marge's nostrils were suddenly flaring and her piercing eyes were shooting poison darts at him, but he plunged on.

"If I were you, I'd take my money and run. The whole damned thing is a fucking bubble that's going to burst." He shook his head pontifically. "What's more, I have a feeling that it's going to be Youman's wife, Adele, who sticks a pin in it."

Marge was listening to him grimly with tears in her eyes. "You really are hopeless, Coldaxe!" she said indignantly. Though he tried hard to hold her, she squirmed out of his arms. "Excuse me, but I think I have to throw up."

She disappeared, and Ronald, who was trying to put the kitchen in focus and stop it from spinning, didn't hear her come back. He sat moodily at the kitchen table saying, "Shit! Shit! What did I do now?" Then, before he fully realized it. Marge was standing silently behind him and she was calmly pouring the remains of the Mouton Rothschild over his bald pate. It dribbled down into his eyes, blinding him, while she yelled: "You're a fucking Philistine! Before Sampson Coldaxe shakes the temple down, Delilah is going to cut off his balls!"

He felt her grab his hair, which grew thickly around the wide curve of his bald spot and, before he realized what she was doing and could pull away from her, she had sliced off a four inch fistful on one side of his head. Then, before he could stagger to his feet, she had snipped off an even larger quantity on the other side. Defiantly, she flung the thick pile of hair into his face.

"Jesus Christ, you've ruined me!" he yelled, and he swung at her, ignoring the scissors that she was holding threateningly at him. Laughing at his futile gesture, she coolly stepped back. He stumbled and collapsed drunkenly on the floor. She immediately sat on his stomach, giggling and sobbing at the same time. "I couldn't help it, Ronnie. You revealed your true colors. You really are a shithead. I didn't mean to do it, but you're enough to drive a woman insane. For a moment I felt like Delilah." She tried to smooth what hair remained over the long white patches of skin, and she kissed his head and nose. "Poor Sampson, we're going to have to trim you up."

"You're a nasty little bitch," he groaned. "I'd like to cut your tits off."

She smiled at him hopefully, trying to elicit a calmer response. "Your hair was really too thick on the sides, Ronnie. I think I can trim it up. No one will ever notice. It really didn't make you look like a Coldaxe. You looked more like a burnt-out teddy bear."

Ronald staggered to his feet and stared glumly at himself in the kitchen mirror. "No one can trim this mess," he moaned. "What in hell do I do now?"

Marge stared at him speculatively, and she admitted to him later that, if she hadn't been pretty woozy, she would have been scared stiff to suggest anything because of the murderous look in his eyes. "Let me finish it," she urged him. "Completely bald, you'll look like a man from outer space. Everyone at Byrdwhistle will fall in love with you."

"I don't give a shit about Byrdwhistle," Ronald's belligerence had disappeared and now he was having a difficult time not to burst into tears. "What will I tell my wife?"

"That you went to bed with a drunken barber?" she asked him hopefully.

Ronald glared at her. "I really should beat the shit out of you."

"You'd feel better fucking me!"

"I thought you always said sex-making instead of fucking." Ronald was still grimly surveying the damage to himself in the mirror.

Marge sighed. "I just thought fucking would serve me right. It sounds more aggressive and obviously would suit your mood better."

"Raping would be better," Ronald shrugged, "but it's too late for that. Okay, I guess there's no other damn way out. You might as well finish the job."

"I think we need another bottle of wine," Marge said.

Ronald shook his head. "Scotch will do. That stuff is too expensive."

"Jesus! You really do have a Coldaxe mentality, even when someone else is paying for it." Marge located another bottle in the bar and opened it. "Come on in the bathroom, Ronnie. You might as well take off Fred's bathrobe. It's kind of damp. I'll lather you up."

Cutting off the rest of his hair while he sat naked on the toilet seat

and complained that he'd never be able to convince M'mm that he had
voluntarily scalped himself, Marge finally soaped his head and shaved
him clean with Fred's razor. She kissed his head as she worked and tried
to soothe him. "Really, if you don't like it, it will grow back in a couple
of months."

When she finished, she stood back and admired her work. "You're a
completely different person," she told him in an awed voice. "You look
like a demon: a genie—the kind that got loose from the bottle in that fairy
story and could give the owner of the bottle anything in the world that he
desired." She kissed his head reverently. "To tell you the truth, for the
first time you really look like what a vice president of acquisitions should
look like. You scare the shit right out of me. If you'd arrived looking like
this, Hy would have handed you the keys to the place and run for the
woods. But just wait a minute," she told him, "I've got the finishing
touch."

She disappeared into another room while Ronald examined his new
head in the bathroom mirror. He had to admit that there was some truth
in Marge's reaction. Once he got used to it, if he could talk as tough and
hard as he now looked, he'd erase any doubts in Ralph Thiemost's mind.
Byrdwhistle—if not Marge Slick herself—was for the birds. With his
bare head Ronald Coldaxe could speak with the authority of a Genghis
Khan.

Marge returned with the remains of the third bottle of wine and what
seemed to be a cardboard eye-patch. On it a spiral had been printed in
heavy black ink. She made him sit on the toilet while she stretched the
elastic that was attached to the mask around his head. Then she posi-
tioned it in the middle of his forehead. "Jesus Christ!" she shuddered. "If
I were Catholic, I'd hold up the cross. You look a little like a Mr. Clean
who drank Doctor Jekyll's poison. Look in the mirror, Baron Coldaxe,
and meet the sexiest devil ever to escape from the nether regions."

To Ronald's surprise, as he stared at himself the spiral on the patch
between his eyes was moving hypnotically in and out.

"It gives a visual effect we call the psi phenomenon," Marge told him.
"We sell it in a box filled with similar gadgets called Hypnotizers in our
Dreamy Byrd catalogue." She offered him a swallow of wine directly
from the bottle, and Ronald drank it, wondering if all this booze, even
though it cost a fortune a spoonful, would make him impotent. "Look at
me," she insisted. "You fascinate me. You're going to fall in love with
your new image. I'm going to lose you. There isn't a woman in the world
who wouldn't lie down before such a powerful looking master and open
up her legs for him while she wailed, "Take me! Take me!"

Ronald glowered happily at her with the most devilish look that he
could command, and then she calmly poured the rest of the bottle of
wine over his head. "I anoint thee, Beelzebub, mighty sexual master of

the female world." She couldn't help giggling at the resolute look in Ronald's eyes, but she was entranced by his lustful expression and by the spiral on his forehead, which was now revolving in and out madly. The Mouton Rothschild was still trickling down his face and chest. Roused from his self-hypnosis, Ronald shook her roughly. He didn't know where the words were coming from but he relished them as he spoke, "You really are a satanic, whorish consort of the devil," he hissed at her. "I consign you to eternal hellfire and damnation."

Marge sighed. "Ronnie, either it's your new head or that damned hypnotizer. I'm succumbing! I'm in your power. I'm going into a trance. Oh, Ronnie," she sobbed. "I'm all yours. I'm your willing slave. Command me, oh master! Do with me what you will."

Ronald's eyes frantically searched the bathroom. "I'd like to find a razor strop and whack your ass until it bleeds," he said arrogantly.

"Fred doesn't use a straight razor," Marge told him apologetically. "Don't you remember, honey, I just shaved your head with a new Gillette model that would have made King Gillette bug-eyed. Ask me something else. Anything. I'm your adoring slave!"

Ronald rubbed his wine-soaked body against hers. "I never had a willing slave," he sighed. "It's up to you. What the hell do you want me to do to you?"

"We shouldn't waste this wine," she muttered. She shook the bottle on his penis and a few more drops dribbled out. Ronald stared at himself amazed to discover that once again he was rampant. "Oh master, tell me that your wine soaked hard-on needs to be sucked." She sank to her knees before him.

"Suck my prick you miserable wretch," Ronald said cruelly and grabbed her by her hair.

"I obey you, Master Coldaxe," and then she giggled. "We really do sound better than the hero and heroine of any Gothic novel I ever read."

Five minutes later, still not having eaten dinner, they were back in bed. With her arm around him and one hand still holding his twice victorious penis, Ronald finally fell asleep on Marge's breasts. His former self, his ego and his total individuality had passed through his body like a torrent of rain seeking passage to the sea. And his thrusting penis, the amazing newborn turret between his legs, had been in perfect control led by both his right and left brain. For the first time in many, many years, a woman had totally appropriated him. Marge's enthusiasm for her bald lover, her moaning, screaming surrender, and finally her satiated sighing—"My God, Ronnie, whatever my motives might have been when I lured you here, the truth is that you really are a marvelous lover"—interspersed with their dreamy conversation, as they both exposed their lives and sexual needs to each other, only added to the fire of Ronald's lust for her. After years of frustration and a dull marriage, Ronald Coldaxe had become an awakened sexual giant.

"You owe it all to Byrdwhistle," she told him the next morning at breakfast. "Your wife is going to be proud of the new Ronald Coldaxe, and I'm going to miss him terribly."

Although the plane carrying him to Los Angeles had passed the half-way mark, Ronald continued to ignore his attaché case. Half awake, enjoying the euphoria of total sexual release, he wondered vaguely if, after two nights in a row, Baron Coldaxe would be able to perform with M'mm. If possible, all day Wednesday and Wednesday evening had been a crazier adventure in Byrdwhistle Wonderland than Tuesday had been. Assuming that the whole affair wasn't an erotic dream from which he would wake up either screaming or exploding in a groaning orgasm— Ronald couldn't help grinning at that alternative—then somehow he must try to assimilate his Boston-Everett adventure and decide how much of the truth he could tell M'mm and Ralph Thiemost.

Surprisingly, although his stomach muscles and penis felt a little numb and drained from the unaccustomed demands that Marge and Sylvia had placed on him, his mind was responding like an explorer who had finally found his way out of the foggy miasma of a shadowy jungle into an open plain with the clear blue sky stretching endlessly above him.

While they sipped a second cup of coffee in her living room and ate cinammon toast for breakfast, Marge ran the video-tape that Cathy and Steve Milner had made of M'mm. Cathy, a young blue-jeans version of M'mm, gave the impression that she was totally sympathetic with M'mm and her various confrontations with the established order of things.

During the ten-minute interview, M'mm insisted that she wasn't a radical. "I'm just a public-spirited citizen who believes that a dangerous combination of government and big business is turning America into a banana plantation. We, the serfs, have to challenge them in a thousand ways."

Then M'mm had calmly admitted that, although she was a corporation wife and although her husband's company made nuclear-bomb components in one of its factories, she was against nuclear bombs, too. "Whether Russia follows suit or not," she told Cathy, "we must lead the way and stop the arms race. It's ridiculous. The little people of the world have no control over their lives. Our leaders are spending trillions of dollars every year to manufacture weapons so that we can kill each other." M'mm had smiled provocatively into the camera, almost as if she were looking at Ronald. "I love my husband, but that doesn't mean that we have to see eye-to-eye on everything. Maybe I'm a socialist, but I'm not a communist."

"Your wife is spunky," Marge told Ronald when the tape finished. She kissed him reverently on his head. "I have a feeling that if she knew she had shared you with me she wouldn't mind. I hope that your new Mussolini image doesn't frighten her to death."

Because Ronald insisted, she ran the Love Byrd video-tape she had made with Fred and Chuck and Mary Hanna. And Ronald had the strange experience of watching a woman with whom he had just made love calmly revealing that she was capable of enjoying total intimacy not only with her husband but also with another man. Although the tape was funnier than it was lascivious, Ronald experienced a sudden unaccountable jealousy.

Marge sensed his reaction. "Both Fred and I had to relearn our conditionings," she told him. "Most people will never admit it to each other, but despite the kind of sexual surrender a husband and wife might enjoy, it's no guarantee that their basic sexuality, if it isn't repressed, won't surface and respond to another member of the opposite sex. Most men, enjoy female breasts and vaginas regardless of who owns them. But, when they discover that women can revel in the play-ethic of sex-making just as much as they themselves can, they are horrified." Marge laughed. "Like it or not, the truth is that most women enjoy holding and tasting more than one dork in their lifetime, particularly if the owner of neither the familiar one nor the new one gets too possessive."

Later, after they returned to the Ritz so that Ronald could change his clothes, Marge lay indolently on the bed waiting for him. Once again he couldn't resist his need to merge his body with hers. She took him in her arms and murmured, "Why not, honey? I want you, too." But he didn't answer when she grinned at him and said, "I suspect that somewhere under your corporate conditioning, if you ever dare to let go and fully release him, there's really a nice guy. Whoever he is and wherever he is, I love that Ronald Coldaxe."

But Ronald couldn't bring himself to tell her: "I love you, too, Marge Slick." Jesus Christ—yes, even Jesus! Jesus might turn the other cheek, but he most certainly would never condone adultery or saying "I love you" to a woman who wasn't your wife, or fucking with her into some kind of oblivion where life was no longer real and earnest, but relaxed and carefree.

When they finally arrived at the Byrdwhistle office, it was nearly two o'clock and, even though Marge continued to try to brainwash him, Ronald knew that he was still a long way from understanding love and sex Byrdwhistle-style. They found H.H. sitting at his desk in his office. He was staring out of the window, but apparently not seeing anything. Floating out of his momentary trance he grinned at them. "I wasn't meditating," he said. "But I find that a certain kind of day-dreaming, during which I consciously shut down the pathways of the pragmatic and orderly, sequential kind of thinking that flows out of my left brain, lets me open the conduits of my right brain and experience a delightfully irrational time sense. In addition, I often achieve a kind of extrasensory perception."

H.H. stared at Ronald thoughtfully for a moment. "Despite the faint hope that you really might absorb some of the Byrdwhistle philosophy, as evidenced by your shiny new head and a new aura of sexual appeasement that seems to have softened your features, I have a premonition that the day is fast approaching when you will try to fire me." H.H. sighed. "For a moment, I feel a little like Abraham Lincoln must have when, a few days before he was assassinated, he dreamed that he was attending his own funeral."

Ronald tried to reassure him, "I told you, H.H., whatever else I am, I'm not an axe man." Ronald guessed that whether H.H. had been privy to his seduction or not eventually Marge would tell him that they had slept together. "Actually, I find some of your ideas intriguing. Somewhere during the night, when Marge and I were reliving our lives from womb to the eventual tomb, she jumped out of bed to find a book called *Medusa and the Snail* and she read me an essay from it called "The Deacon's Masterpiece." Lewis Thomas encapsulates your "one-hoss shay" aging-and-dying philosophy. According to Marge, when it's the end of the game and there's no way back for you—hopefully, somewhere between the ages of ninety-six and one hundred—you expect to get into bed with some woman and ask her if that night she would mind being a surrogate mother to you. Then you'll try to convince her that since you originally found your way into this world through a vagina, that you'd enjoy dying inside hers."

Even before Ronald had finished, H.H. was laughing heartily. "My God, Marge, you did it! Ron is beginning to sound like a Byrdwhistler.

"Not at all," Ronald said: "I told Marge this morning that before I completely lost my sanity and either you or she brainwashed me into becoming one of your disciples, I'm leaving." Ronald's voice was suddenly crisp, "Tonight on the seven o'clock plane."

"I've tried to dissuade him," Marge said sadly. "I told him that we really want to make sure Ralph Thiemost learns the worst about Byrdwhistle." She squeezed Ronald's arm affectionately. "You haven't scratched the surface, yet, Ron. You really must meet H.H.'s alter-ego, Thomas Morton of Merry Mount."

"Perhaps Thiemost will change your mind," H.H. grinned. "He telephoned a few minutes before you arrived, Ron. It's only eleven-thirty in L.A. He seemed very anxious to speak to you."

"Did you talk with him?" Ronald demanded. The nervous clutching in his stomach exasperated him. Wasn't he doing his best? Damn Ralph Thiemost anyway.

H.H. nodded, "He seems rather abrupt, especially when I told him that he and I evidently had something in common."

Ronald stared at him, puzzled.

"My wife, Adele," H.H. chuckled. "Thiemost was a little disconcerted when I told him that he had better watch out. If Adele finds a publisher, he and Thorny and I, among others, may be introduced to the American public with our pants down." H.H. told Ronald that they'd wait for him in Marge's office. "The phone isn't bugged. You can speak privately with your boss."

When he picked up the phone, Ralph wasn't very happy. Where the hell had Ron been? Why hadn't he arrived at Byrdwhistle before two o'clock in the afternoon. Youman had told him that Ronald was probably still picking daisies with Marge Slick. Ralph's voice sounded frigid. "I hope that you're not fucking around with the top brass. Judging from the conversation I had with that character Youman a few hours ago, he is a libertine and a very dangerous man." Ralph warned Ronald not to pay attention to any crap that Youman might tell him about Thiemost and Youman's wife. "The Byrdwhistle deal is going forward splendidly. Adele Youman assured me that the company could be run without her husband. All I'm interested in are the Byrdwhistle profit figures. Are they holding up?"

When Ronald tried to tell him that the profit figures were probably correct but that the company was inextricably woven into H.H. Youman's crazy management philosophy, Ralph responded: "Don't give me a lot of shit, Ron. We've got plenty of people here who can run Byrd-whistle. Keep that in mind. No one is indispensable! Not this Youman character, not you, Ron, and not even me!"

Disgusted that he'd been unable to jar Ralph's dogmatic insistence that "Byrdwhistle could be a winner," or even begin to acquaint him with the total cracked-brain facts of Byrdwhistle and its management, Ronald told him he would discuss it with him the following week when he submitted his report on Byrdwhistle.

He found H.H. waiting for him in Marge's office. "While you may be a genius at making money," he told Youman grimly, "I am trying to convince Thiemost that you are a mad genius." Ronald shrugged, "I'll have to stay one more day, otherwise Ralph won't believe I've done a thorough analysis. Whatever happens, I'm still on your side. I'm damned sure that when Ralph understands how incompatible Byrdwhistle is with W.I.N. he'll back out fast."

Although Thiemost hadn't actually said it, he had implied that Adele Youman was trying to corral her pussy-chasing husband for his last roundup and get him into a safe pasture where she could superintend his declining years. "Thiemost is quite entranced with your wife," he said, feeling for H.H.'s reaction. "I think she's working against us. It really would help if you could deflect her, somehow."

H.H. only grinned. "Adele has a one-track mind. Her enthusiasms for men like Thiemost are usually short-lived. Anyway, I'm delighted that you're staying tonight. Marge has been on the phone with her daughter, Sylvia. The Thomas Morton Society, a commune in Merry Mount, of which I'm one of the members, is preparing a celebration in your honor and to commemorate our coming victory over W.I.N. You'll meet the eighteen current members of the commune and their kids. Our sole mission, beyond providing a low-cost communal-living environment for one another, is to restore laughter, ribald singing, and Maypole dancing to America."

"H.H. took Elmer's advice," Marge explained. "He adopted Thomas Morton as an ancestor. Like Morton, he calls himself 'Mine Host of Merry Mount.'"

"Morton was a most interesting figure," H.H. said. "After the Pilgrims—they were actually called Separatists—deported him back to England the first time, he wrote a book called *New English Canaan*. It has a bawdy humor that doesn't appear in any other early American literature. Morton wrote it to discredit the Pilgrims and to get their land grants revoked by King Charles. Morton accused them of rejecting the Book of Common Prayer, which was the Holy Writ of the Church of England, and he insisted that the savages in New England were more Christian than the Christians in Plymouth. A hundred years before Samuel Adams and John Hancock, he damned near started a revolution."

H.H. had flopped into one of the chairs in Marge's office, and heedless of any of the routine business problems that Ronald was sure must be occurring or pending, he calmly rambled on. "Morton landed in Quincy in 1620. It's south of Boston, about eighteen miles north of the Plymouth plantation. Morton traded with the Indians for fur, particularly beaver, which was very fashionable in England at the time. Years later, even Ben Franklin was wearing a beaver hat. Morton quickly discovered that the Indians were very easygoing sexually. The male Indians were totally enamored of brandy and beer. They didn't drink to be happy; they drank to get really drunk. They enjoyed the oblivion of passing out. In the meantime, the young women, being more sensible, enjoyed screwing. After a night in the bushes, they often discovered an English sachem growing in their bellies. Temporarily, it was a more joyous way to Nirvana than getting drunk and they didn't have the morning-after headaches. H.H. chuckled, "Their husbands didn't give a damn. There wasn't any excess population problem in America at the time.

"Morton erected a huge Maypole in Merry Mount and claimed that it was a beacon to give mariners their bearings. The Pilgrims knew damned well that it was a huge phallic symbol. But what really got their ass was that Morton traded firearms, as well as booze, for beaver, and he taught the Indians how to shoot. They quickly became crack shots, and shot up a few Englishmen as well as birds and game. According to the first governor of the Plymouth colony, William Bradford, who summed up Morton's peccadillos in his journal: 'Morton and his friends fell into utter licentiousness and led a dissolute and profane life. Morton became lord of misrule, and maintained, as it were, a school of atheism. They spent their time drinking wine and strong drinks to great excess—as some reported, ten pounds worth in a morning.'" H.H. laughed. "In those days, that was one hell of a lot of booze. According to Bradford, and Morton confirms it in his own book, 'They set up a Maypole, drinking and dancing about it for several days at a time, inviting the Indian women for their consorts, dancing and frisking together like so many fairies—or furies rather—to say nothing of worse practices. They changed the name of the place, and instead of calling it Mount Wollaston, after its discoverer, they called it Merry Mount—as if this jollity would last forever.'"

H.H. grinned fondly at Ron. "Governor Bradford was a very religious man. He even learned Hebrew in his old age. It irritated him that the Pilgrims were struggling for existence while Morton played and lived off the land like the Indians. Morton kept insisting that Massachusetts was 'a land of milk and honey,' but somehow the colony at Plymouth couldn't get enough to eat. It's obvious that Morton was a firm believer in the play-ethic. It would be a couple of hundred years before Freud restated the theme in psychological terms. The Pilgrims believed that, aided and abetted by the Indians, Morton was not only creating his own Indian army but that he would bring this new civilization to an end with one big orgasm. The same theme underlies the American experience from Benjamin Franklin and Cotton Mather," H.H. grinned, "to Heman Hyman Youman and Ralph Thiemost. Sylvia told Marge that tonight the entire commune is going to improvise a ballet to give you a new perspective on life. The confrontation of Thomas Morton and Myles Standish." H.H. stood up and clasped Ronald on the shoulder enthusiastically. "You're going to be Standish, and I'm going to be Morton."

"Don't let him jar you," Marge tried to smile the frown off Ronald's face. "It'll be great fun. You really should adopt an ancestor, too."

H.H. agreed. "It's a nice thing to do. You personally can bring back to life one of the billions of people who have lived on this planet and, except for a few musty records and long-forgotten books, has disappeared. It's amazing how much you can discover or infer about them. Eventually, if you discover a sympatico ancestor, he or she will become your *Doppelgänger*. You may even fall in love with him or her. It's an intriguing form of reincarnation."

Obviously amused by Ronald's unsympathetic expression, H.H. decided to grind a little more grist in Ronald's brain. "Be sure to give Ron a copy of Elmer's book," he told Marge. "Marge hasn't decided yet whether she's going to adopt Abigail Adams or Priscilla Mullins." He looked at Marge, "Since all we know about Priscilla is her 'Speak for yourself, John' message when Alden tried to turn his marriage proposal over to Myles Standish, you probably should adopt Abigail. She's more your style, Marge. On the other hand, since old Tom Morton spent more than one night on the Plymouth plantation before he was deported, you can let your mind roam. Those Pilgrim women weren't so sexless as you might think. Priscilla must have enjoyed love-making. If John couldn't find the words to ask her to marry him, his—or someone else's—penis bridged the gap. She had eleven kids. Maybe when John was off fighting Indians with Standish, Morton managed to sneak into her cabin."

Ronald shook his head. He was dumbfounded by the never-ending flow of H.H.'s weird imagination. "After a day at Byrdwhistle, I'm really having a difficult enough time finding out who I am," he said. "I certainly don't need to play around with someone else's ancestors." He couldn't help his curt response. H.H.'s, Marge's, and for that matter all the damn Byrdwhistlers' willingness to be sidetracked by any damned foolish idea that came along irritated him.

"I know," H.H. said reprovingly. "You have to work, you have to earn a living, and you have to keep your nose to the grindstone so that someday you can be the big boss at W.I.N. But you'd better be careful, Ron. One day a hundred or so years from now someone who's read Elmer's book—and believe me people will be reading it—may find *your* name in the archives of W.I.N. Incorporated." H.H. looked sad as he anticipated that future event. "If they ever discover that you were such a dour man, the chances are they'll decide not to adopt you, and you'll lie moldering in your grave."

"I'll be well moldered by then," Ronald said crossly, and he tried to get H.H. back on the track. "I can assure you what remains of me won't give a damn. Since I have to stay one more day, I really must use the rest of the time to get the Byrdwhistle picture into some kind of framework that Ralph Thiemost can comprehend."

"Good," H.H. beamed at him. "Working on the principle that the more Ralph knows, the more you'll scare him to death, tonight after we spend a little time acting and dancing naked around our Maypole in Merry Mount, and our communal friends have told you about their current enthusiasm for Peter Brook and his *Conference of the Birds,* then, perhaps, Sylvia and Marge and you and I can spend the night in my apartment in Louisburg Square. Four people can sleep in my revolving bed without one couple even knowing the other couple is there."

"You'll really like Sylvia," Marge told Ronald, sensing that he was trying to figure a way to reject the invitation. "She and her husband, Clint Marlow, are separated. She supports herself as a C.S.W.—certified social worker—but her real love and joy is acting and ballet." Marge didn't tell Ronald that he was an older version of Clint, a pragmatic person and one who had restrained his emotions for so long that he exuded a certain iciness. But she knew Sylvia was both bored and fascinated by the type. Like her mother, male moral rectitude was a challenge. It seemed impossible for her that some men in their arduous climb up the ladder of success were disdainful about play and were incapable of it, even in bed with a loving, playful woman.

Ronald suddenly wondered if he was going to be exposed to an evening of group sex, but he decided not to pursue his curiosity. Marge told H.H. that she had a lot of material to gather for Ronald, including detailed sales breakdowns by divisions. H.H. suggested a leisurely swim through the main office before lunch. Determined that since he was in Rome he might as well enjoy the Roman games, Ronald stripped in H.H.'s office. They swam together through the meandering pool, stopping here and there so that various Byrdwhistlers could admire Ronald's bare head.

Later, in a hot-tub, which H.H. told him was maintained at a seventy degree temperature—water which was not too hot or debilitating—a changing panorama of naked female and male employees joined them temporarily to listen and contribute to the discussion. In response to Ronald's probing, H.H. was trying to explain Theory Z to him.

"The basic concept is derived from Abraham Maslow's essay which is a further elaboration of management ideas he had proved in his book *Eupsychian Management.* Some business educators, like Dr. Willard Zangwill, have used the letter *Z* to define their own theories of management, but they don't go in the direction of Maslow." H.H. was sitting with the water up to his neck, while Ronald gingerly dangled his feet in it. "Zangwill simply melded Theory Y ideas, such as joint problem-solving and participative relationships between supervisors and employees, into the latest management techniques, such as Systems Analysis, PERT, and Management by Objectives. But you have to understand that Theory Z, as we are developing it at Byrdwhistle, is a completely new approach. It's an ongoing, transcendental process. Don't ever forget, Ron, that Byrdwhistle isn't just a highly profitable mail-order business. We are the prototype of a new kind of extended communal family. We're exploring the ways to unite human work with human companionship and a new, continuous form of personal growth and adventure.

"Theory Z proposes that the work environment can be modified to create a play environment, but we cannot do this now, or possibly ever, without a profit system that lures the donkey off his ass. But profit-making alone, without fun-making, is a world without zing. Keep in mind, too, that Byrdwhistlers by temperament enjoy an environment of expanded personal relationships and could never live a creative, self-fulfilling life in the kind of patriarchal environment that is basic to all managerial styles derived from Theory X philosophies. Companies like W.I.N. may give lip-service to interpersonal responsibility between management and employees but, in the last analysis, you and I know that W.I.N. is an authoritarian dictatorship run by Ralph Thiemost and possibly a small committee of top brass who bow to his superior wisdom."

As he spoke, H.H. occasionally interrupted his monologue to greet other Byrdwhistlers. After about ten minutes in the water he sat on the edge of the huge cedar tub with his arms around two naked females. He introduced them to Ronald, who having slid into the tub to conceal an annoying spurt of interest in his penis, discovered that he was not only smiling at the pretty faces of Barbara Grant, who played in the computer department, and Alice Tolvas, who handled customer service and complaints, but he also had an unobstructed view of the soft pink, hairy butterflies between their legs.

"I think Byrdwhistle is successful because of the husband and wife teams," Barbara grinned at Ronald, fully aware that her nether regions were silently talking to him. "Byrdwhistle creates a secure monogamous environment that opens up the possibility of both sexual and mental companionship with people other than the original spouses."

Alice complimented Ronald on his shaved head and said, "The underlying Zen philosophy of 'not two, not one' as a theory of creative management, takes some getting used to, but I find it very exciting."

Ronald frowned. "I don't know anything about Zen."

"Alice is simply using a Zen expression," H.H. told him. "Seeing the world as not two, not one, but as a continual flow of many diverse things encapsulates the reality of all experience. Organizations of any kind, Byrdwhistle and W.I.N. included, are basically continuous interacting forms of both structure and process. The structure of business and the process of its functioning cannot be viewed separately. They are one and the other, simultaneously. For that matter so are all human and non-human relationships. Not two, not one. The basic reason for our entrance examination is to discover people who have the potential for understanding this interaction, which is both microcosmic, as in Byrdwhistle, and macrocosmic, as in the universe itself. Our entrance examination is based on Maslow's study of Being Cognition versus Deficiency Cognition. Byrdwhistlers must have the potential for Being Cognition. They must have, or be capable of developing, a sense of oneness with the world. They should perceive unity in everything and every person. They must have a total fascination with life. They are the kind of people who can become so totally absorbed with all aspects of life that they can often transcend their own egos and achieve a fusion of themselves as the perceiver and the perceived. They can also become so absorbed in what they are doing that the self disappears. They are capable of letting things be whatever they may be. They enjoy things as ends in themselves and as intrinsically interesting for their own sake. They recognize total resolution and integration as a facet of all life. They discover, as they become aware of the essential being of the world, that they are concurrently closer to their own being. They have gained enough perspective to view both themselves and the world as amusing, playful, comic, funny, absurd, and laughable, but also poignant." H.H. paused to see if Ronald was still with him. "They understand, Ron, that laughter is often close to tears."

Later, both of them wearing terry-cloth snap-arounds, Ronald and H.H. were joined at lunch by Marge and a half-dozen other Byrdwhistlers whom Ronald could finally identify by their first names. H.H. told them that while he was personally convinced that all young people had an innate sense of Being Cognition, they lost it as they encountered the problems of growing up and making a living. If they could somehow be made aware of the possibilities later in life and weren't too set in their ways, they could recapture the Being approach to life. Only then would they really begin to live.

"Of course that's why we have the entrance examination," H.H. grinned at Ronald. "From the information we gathered on your wife, I think she might be a good prospect; but I wouldn't have too much hope for you, Ron. M.B.A.'s are so thoroughly indoctrinated by the system that they can never escape. They can't stand aside and look at themselves or chuckle at their own insanities. They can't even temporarily escape their own self-importance."

Ronald scowled, but in a friendly way, at the laughter around the table. "Since all of us are only ships that pass in the night," he said, trying to be congenial, and indirectly trying to tell Marge that she must survive without him, which he guessed she could do very well, "I wouldn't lose any sleep over it."

"You should. You should." H.H. said. "Your Theory X conditionings, and the paternalistic attitude toward both children and employees is a vanishing way of life. Deficiency Cognition, as described by Maslow, will vanish before the inroads of Being Cognition."

"What in hell is Deficiency Cognition?"

Lois Rather, who had joined them at the table, her breasts appetizingly naked over her luncheon plate, responded: "It's seeing all the parts as incomplete, as dependent upon other things. It's never seeing a gestalt. It's selective attention to some aspects of life and simultaneous inattention to others. For example," she said pointing at Ronald, to the complete hilarity of everyone listening, "despite your attention, my breasts are only one part of the phenomenon of Lois Rather."

Ronald wanted to argue with her that she wasn't completely right. He was reacting as a normal male. Part of his mind couldn't stop evaluating the female anatomy that was being so casually displayed. He presumed that, like most men, he was conditioned by his genes to enjoy a woman's tits, no matter on whom they were hung. But he was well aware that his open admission would expose his vulnerability and that that would have pleased all of them. Unlike Byrdwhistlers, he hadn't learned how to be open and maintain a defensive position at the same time.

A man who identified himself as Harry Fasnacht, from Inventory

Control, said, "Deficiency Cognition people tend to try to classify everything, to endow people with rubrics and thus identify them. The experiences of their lives are impoverished by repetition. Objects are seen as need-gratifiers. Their perception of the world is colored by their own ego. They are determined to reshape and reorganize the world."

"It seems to me," Ronald told H.H. triumphantly, "that's just exactly what you're trying to do with Byrdwhistle, and World Corporation."

To Ronald's surprise, H.H. partially agreed with him. "Like all visionaries, I believe that my way is a better way to live one's life. But what saves me from complete folly is that I can laugh at my pretensions. Byrdwhistle and World Corporation are not the *only way*. We are simply flowing with the larger currents in man's evolution, rather than against them. If Byrdwhistle can lay the groundwork for a new kind of work-play ethic and World evolves a new corporate style that allows the players in the game to become owners as well as players, they will point the way to a more joyous kind of human future. We may be considered mileposts in the ever evolving process of human societies' learning how to function together better than they ever have in the past. In contrast to Deficiency Cognition people, I, personally, am not striving. Trying to control one's destiny is not the only possible way of life. I prefer to meander along the path of least resistance. I may partially control the rain splashing on the top of the mountain, but my channels won't overflow and will function better if I'm in tune with, and accept, the fact that some routes to the sea are better than others."

"Deficiency Cognition creates deficiency values," Marge interjected. "People become objects. In the productive process, man becomes indistinguishable from his machines. It's easier to try to desacralize sex and religion—to make them graspable—than to be content with their ineffable mystery." She grinned at Ron. "D-value people take life too seriously. They don't laugh much, and when they do their humor is hostile. They are solemn and judgmental. They act like ancient gods. The creative person, on the other hand, as Maslow pointed out, 'is an innocent, and as an innocent can be defined as a grown person who is totally here now, one who lives without future or past; one who can still perceive, think, and act like a child.'"

Shaking his head, Ronald laughed, but without humor. "Thank God for D-value people," he said. "Without someone to get on with the practical aspects of living, I think B-value people would starve to death. All this psychological crap may work for a white-collar business like Byrdwhistle, but you can't walk around naked in a steel foundry or on an automobile assembly-line. We don't need daydreamers or creative people to do the gut work of this society. We simply need people with a limited mental capacity to follow orders, people who are happy with their television and their six-pack of beer and who don't ask questions."

"In our Western society," H.H. responded with a little grin, "that kind of person is an endangered species. Everyone who hasn't already is anxious to turn in his or her blue collar for a white collar, or preferably no collar at all. You're simply suffering from a failure of imagination, Ron. In the coming century, or sooner, we can re-engineer our factories. If we'd realize our priorities, there's no reason that, aided by computers, men and women in the next century can't make steel or assemble automobiles in a clean, noise-free environment, where they no longer are working, but *playing,* with all the ramifications of play, and doing it *together.*"

17

Later, as they were driving to Merry Mount, H.H. told Ronald that he had sailed to the Costa da Sol the previous spring in another company-owned yacht, a sailing ketch called the *Thomas Morton.* H.H. admitted that the ketch could no longer be charged off against taxes. "It's much smaller than the *Love Byrd.* It can't double as a freighter, which would create a somewhat more legitimate tax-deduction."

Marge Slick was sandwiched between them. H.H. was driving a Rolls Corniche convertible. Ronald had discovered that Byrdwhistle owned three Rolls Royces. When it came to management philosophy, or luxury living, it seemed to him that H.H. wasn't practicing what he preached. "Your World Corporation proposes a society where competition is eliminated, and it seems to me that your Being Cognition depends on a non-materialistic, saintly kind of world. Neither of them jibe with your personal life-style," Ronald told him.

H.H. laughed. "If you want to change the world, you must do it on its own terms, working from within not from without. Watch the carpenter ants, you rarely discover them until the house falls down. When you read my introduction to King Gillette's *Human Drift,* you'll discover that I agree with him only in broad details. For example, the goal of World Corporation is total ownership by the people of all the production and distribution companies in this country. But I don't expect it to be achieved in my lifetime. Nevertheless, World's monetary assets are very much like interest. They are compounding. Once the base is developed, they will grow very, very rapidly. In the meantime, as Gillette pointed out, 'People in Western societies are slowly discovering that personal ambition and human progress don't depend on competition between individuals for material wealth. To quote Gillette: 'Under our present system, nine-tenths of the population live from hand to mouth. The whole power of their minds is absorbed in the struggle to obtain the necessities of life from day to day, which leaves no time to develop the mind by the acquisition of knowledge. The result is that the world loses the natural progressive power which would develop under a system which would allow for the free expansion of mind.'"

H.H. smiled at Ronald's grunt of disapproval. "I can guess your response," he continued. "You believe that most of the population have no minds to develop, that they are simply cogs in the machinery that keeps them alive. But, I am sure that Maslow's hierarchy of values is right. Gillette anticipated him by saying: 'There is no passion so strong in man as a desire to learn, when he has reached that plane where he can appreciate the pleasure derived from the attainment of knowledge.'"

H.H. grinned at Marge, who was watching his face in the rearview mirror. "Marge isn't wholly convinced either. She understands, though, that the difference between me and other futurists is that I'm a pragmatic utopianist. Whether or not World Corporation achieves its goal of returning the means of production and distribution to the people and eliminating the vast amount of wasted human effort that is created by competition, I will succeed in at least one thing. The human drift is aiming at the same target I am. I want what the world wants—a lifetime of work that is no longer just work but also play."

"But en route you don't mind enjoying the prerogatives of leadership," Ronald said sarcastically.

"If you mean this automobile," H.H. patted the steering wheel, "this baby and the two bigger Rolls sedans back in the company garage are company cars. This one is only four years old, but you can see that it has been driven nearly a hundred thousand miles. Every Byrdwhistler has a chance to drive one of the Rollses sometime during the year. They can take them home weekends and surprise their neighbors. The same applies to our company ketch, the *Thomas Morton*. Right now it's in Bermuda. It was sailed there by three Byrdwhistlers and their kids who are on vacation. Unlike your boss, Ralph Thiemost, I don't own anything I'm not willing to share." H.H. squeezed Marge's knee affectionately. "Not even Marge."

"You don't own me, you horny old bastard!" Marge laughed. "But I do love you."

"Tell Ron about our weekly lottery."

"It's a non-cash award," Marge said. "Among other things, Byrdwhistlers can win the opportunity to spend the weekend at Louisburg Square and sleep on the roof in H.H.'s merry-go-round bed."

H.H. shook his head in mock sadness. "It's one of the reasons that Adele gets annoyed with me. When she's in Boston, which is usually during the latter half of the year, she refuses to sleep in it, especially if there's another couple in the other half. Tonight you can try the bed with Marge, or with Sylvia if she decides to change places with her mother."

Marge chuckled at Ronald's obvious distress. "My daughter may like your new head," she told him, "but not what's inside it. So don't worry." She fumbled in her purse and then handed him a tube of cream. "The sun's still pretty hot, you'd better put some of this on it, Ron. We can't stand you on your head if you get a sunburn."

"To come back to the point of your question," H.H. glanced at Ronald, who was gingerly applying the suntan oil. "The time is fast approaching when automobiles like these will be museum pieces, or driven only by heads of state or in parades to show the younger generation what life was like before World Corporation took over. And the essential point won't be that a Rolls was the ultimate extravagance but that, for its time and place in human development, it was one of the pinnacles of automobile achievement. We don't need Gothic cathedrals in order to pray. No one is likely to compose another Beethoven symphony or paint a Rembrandt, yet all of these are testaments to man's pursuit of excellence. The pursuit of never achievable perfection is what makes life exciting. We have a vast heritage of guideposts, standards of comparison for the future builders of automobiles that are better than this Rolls, autos that will consume less energy, and churches and music that will inspire new generations. Great music and books, aged wine and cheese, even a plate of Boston baked beans prepared by a loving cook, are all outstanding achievements in the arts and sciences, and they are a valid part of Being Cognition. They help us distinguish between the best and the shoddy and adulterated merchandise that floods our markets and wastes both human and fossil energy."

"You'll find that philosophy expressed in Byrdwhistle catalogues," Marge said. "Not only in our advertising copy, but in the choice of products. We avoid gadget items. H.H. believes that it's more fun to blow soap bubbles with a clay pipe than to dip a loop into liquid glycerine that makes bubbles at twice the cost but is only half the messy fun."

"Actually, I'm against items like vibrators and massagers," H.H. said, "and electric grass-clippers, and even power lawn-mowers, and electric tooth brushes, electric razors, and gadgets to cook one hamburger, or one hotdog, but we offer some of them." He grimaced, and Ronald couldn't tell whether he was serious or not. "When World Corporation has eliminated the drudgery of work, we'll have more time to keep in good physical shape. Lawn-mowers you push and fingers that knead and caress human flesh are closer to play-reality than power-mowers and vibrators and massagers."

"Aren't you planning to eliminate all your competition?" Ron asked. "If I understand Gillette's theory, you only need one company—Byrdwhistle—to supply all the mail-order buyers in the country."

"Of course," H.H. nodded affably, "but in the meantime we love our competitors. Together, we are proving that mail-order is the most efficient form of distribution, particularly when we have finally created one, and only one, people-owned company to channel the flow of what we now call Parcel Post. Since that may be a long time in the future, we don't actually compete; we simply try to be different from our competitors.

"Byrdwhistle hasn't moved into the mail-order food business yet, but I've been thinking about it. No one has really exploited the potential of delivering tree- or vine-ripened fruits and vegetables direct to the consumer. Of course you live in California, Ron, but here in the Northeast, after about six weeks in the summer, it's impossible, for example, to buy a tomato that doesn't taste like balsa wood. Visualize Byrdwhistle, with its own fleet of transport planes flying out of season from Mexico, Africa, and South America—all of the undeveloped countries, most of which have growing seasons opposite to us. Imagine huge freight airplanes arriving in central airports, delivering the produce to packaging houses who'd distribute them weekly to homes and apartments within a central city. The same cargo plane can fly back to these countries filled with manufactured goods purchased by their agricultural produce. All year round, people could buy the finest vegetables, with their vitamins still intact. Not only that, but there are hundreds of tropical fruits that never reach the temperate climates that could be sold in huge quantities. Most Americans have never tasted guavas or sapodillas, or experienced a ripe pineapple right off the vine, or eaten kiwifavit from New Zealand, or tasted hami-gua melons from China. Americans could eat fresh vegetables and fruit year-round at prices cheaper than frozen food."

"People are too lazy," Ronald said. "They'd rather eat prepared stuff."

H.H. shrugged, "People are also discovering that being healthy depends on themselves and what they eat, not on doctors trying to compensate with pills and injections when it's too late."

Ronald noticed that Marge's eyes were sparkling with merriment. "When Hy brought the subject up at a Symp meeting, Bruce Maitland suggested that vine-ripened African melons were ideal for masturbation. According to him, all the Arabs use them. With a hole dug into them, they're warmer and wetter than a female vagina, and they don't talk back. Bruce insists that we could do a huge business selling Byrdwhistle Masturbating Melons to hundreds of thousands of deprived males."

"Bruce's slogan is even better," H.H. ignored Ronald's rather grim smile. "Before you eat them, fill your Byrdwhistle Melon with protein. They'll taste even better, afterwards!"

Marge wasn't sure that Ronald got the point, but she was enjoying his prudish laughter. "Never underestimate the power of mail-order," she said. "You can even become a Doctor of Divinity. All you have to do to get your diploma is to send ten dollars to Brother Kuith L'Hommediev, of the Church of Universal Life."

"What Marge is telling you, Reverend Coldaxe," H.H. said, enjoying the game, "is that mail-order is really a unique way to satisfy the fantasy needs of millions of people. A few years ago, a very popular item was Pet Rocks. They were absolutely useless, but the fun booklet that came along with your personal Pet Rock became a conversation piece. We're going to do even better with Love Rocks from Yugoslavia, because we will endow them with a lovely sexual power that is transferable to the owner. But another good example is that guy in Iowa, Herman Richter, who created a mythical institution, the University of Okoboji. Then Richter designed an attractive university seal that looked just like the real thing. He sold hundreds of thousands of dollars worth of tee-shirts and pennants and university souvenirs by mail. Thousands of people have one thing in common. They like the idea of affiliation with an alma mater, even a fictitious one, and they enjoy the silliness of it. According to Richter, the University of Okoboji 'teaches perspective and a sense of humor.'" H.H. drove silently for a moment, then he grinned: "As we say: *Zoln nir leben un lachen.*"

Ronald looked at Marge curiously. "When Hy is relaxed, he often philosophizes in Yiddish," she explained. "It means: 'May we live and laugh.' Without laughter what is there?' *Kloybyn naches.* Gather joy! Ron, you have arrived. You're in Merry Mount, with a Jewish lord of misrule and his consort."

H.H. turned the Rolls into a circular gravel driveway of an old but beautifully maintained white Victorian-style mansion. Three stories high, it was complete with dadoes and filigrees adorning the window casements and overhanging the gutters. On the roof, a captain's walk overlooked the bay. The house was surrounded by a ten-foot cedar fence on the land side. On the front lawn, a huge varnished pole with streamers of all colors floating in the sultry August air reached at least fifty feet into the sky. From the house, from the grounds, and from a long pier extending out beyond low tide, kids and adults, some dressed as Indians, some wearing Puritan costumes, all evidently home-made, came running toward the car. They were dressed in sexy versions of seventeenth-century clothing. Women with feathered Indian headdresses were wearing mini buckskin skirts that revealed the curves of their naked behinds or gave glimpses of their triangles as they walked. And men wearing Pilgrim hats or English army helmets and knickers were joshing with Indian males with fiercely painted faces who were naked except for leather pouches covering their genitals. Most of the younger boys, flourishing bows and arrows, were dressed as Indians, and two little girls were very prettily dressed as Puritan daughters.

Before they were fully out of the car, the screaming mob was yelling,

"Grampy Heman is here! Heman Hyman Morton has arrived!" Indiscriminately they hugged Ronald as well as Marge and H.H. From the excited conversation, Ronald gathered that they had costumes for all of them. Tonight, like it or not, Ronald Coldaxe was going to be Myles Standish. Three of them, Willy, Isabel, and Sam, were going to play the necessary music on the flute, the piano, and the violin. A bare-breasted woman wearing a buckskin, who looked so much like Marge that Ronald stared open-mouthed, joined the crowd milling around them. A boy of about three who she was holding by the hand quickly jumped into H.H.'s arms. H.H. snuggled him affectionately and started singing, "I'm Heman Hyman and I don't care."

"I'm Razi," the boy responded, "and I don't care either."

"Marge told me on the phone that she had trimmed you up last night. I'm her daughter Sylvia." Laughing, Sylvia forced Ronald to bend his head so that she could kiss it.

Marge explained that the little boy, who was also entranced with Ronald, was Sylvia's son. His name is Aramic, and it means "My Secret," she said. "Sylvia won't tell us who the father is." Marge sighed. "Her former husband left her because he was sure that Razi wasn't his son. All we are sure of is that he's not a Youman. Hy had never slept with Sylvia when Razi was born."

When Ronald finally told M'mm about Byrdwhistle and his four nights in Boston, he omitted the night he had spent with Marge and the one with Sylvia. But he made the mistake of laughing in retrospect at the memory of the half-naked men and women in H.H.'s commune, dressed like Indians and Pilgrims but exposing their tits, asses, and balls.

"I'm surprised that you would ever get yourself so involved with the principals in a potential acquisition," M'mm told him. Actually, the first day or two after his return from Boston, Ronald seemed to be more relaxed, a little less judgmental about people. M'mm had tried to lead him on. "Especially in such an apparently loose environment. Was this woman, their controller Marge Slick, at the party?"

Ronald reminded her that neither H. H. Youman nor Marge Slick were the principals and that the majority owners of Byrdwhistle stock, Elmer and Thornton Byrd, were in Greece, but he often wondered if M'mm's claim that she could read his mind when it came to sexual thoughts might be true. He tried to divert her but without giving too many details. "Marge Slick is a little more 'straight arrow' than H.H. and his commune friends," he told her. "The only reason I went to Merry Mount was to gather information on H.H.'s personal life. It's a good thing I did. Once Ralph Thiemost gets the whole picture, he'll realize that acquiring Byrdwhistle would be equivalent to purchasing a nuthouse."

Actually, if Ronald had learned one thing from his trip to Boston—

even though he might still believe that the reverse of that proposition was true—it was that a husband shouldn't share everything with his wife. Dancing in a ballet, singing ribald songs as he tripped the light fantastic around the Maypole practically naked, and "sex-making"—not with Marge Slick but with her daughter—on Heman Hyman Youman's merry-go-round in Louisburg Square, obviously weren't deeds that one could brag about and still retain a happy marriage. So he censored the details of his last evening in Boston, and he kept his fingers crossed that M'mm wouldn't miss his sportcoat and tan slacks, which Marge assured him would eventually turn up in the commune. "Please don't mail them to me! Give them to the Salvation Army," he had begged her.

A few minutes after they had arrived at the Thomas Morton commune and he was being welcomed to Merry Mount, Marge and H.H. disappeared into the house.

A weathered, stringy-looking man introduced himself as Hale Brewster and offered Ronald a brandy and julep concoction that was mostly brandy. Hale told him that he was a direct descendant of the Mayflower Brewsters and led him to the beach where several men and women in Indian regalia were preparing what Ronald was told was an original-style clambake. Early evening was creeping in across Quincy Bay and a warm southerly breeze had dissipated the previous night's fog. He watched them pouring bushels of clams over hot stones and covering them with layers of seaweed, and then adding lobsters and corn and more seaweed, all of which Hale told them would be quickly fired with brush wood.

"Tonight, after we eat," one of the women told Ronald, "the commune will improvise a ballet and drama in your honor." She was joined by two other Indian maids who insisted that he get into the mood immediately. They replenished his brandy julep and led him toward the house. One of them, Isabel, told Ronald that he would play the part of Captain Shrimp—Thomas Morton's name for Myles Standish—and they had prepared a special military costume for him. When he insisted that he was no actor, Chloe—Ronald gave up trying to remember last names—told him that acting required no special talent. "All you have to do is let go, Ronnie. Remember how you felt when you were a kid. Didn't you ever pretend that you were Superman or a knight in King Arthur's court?"

Ronald shrugged. He couldn't remember ever deluding himself, or anyone else for that matter, with fairy-tales. Chloe told him that tonight they, like most historians, would rewrite history to suit themselves and that whether he captured Thomas Morton or Morton captured him didn't matter. In one of the downstairs living rooms next to the patio, which was serving as wardrobe headquarters, they divested him of his light-blue summer sportcoat and ignored his protest that he was perfectly capable of undressing himself if he thought it necessary—which he didn't.

They fawned over him, pressing their nearly naked bodies against him as they unfastened his tie, and Chloe and Isabel slid their hands erotically over his bare chest while Trudy quickly unbuttoned his shirt.

Before he could escape, Isabel flicked open his belt and Chloe unzipped his pants, which dropped to the floor, and Trudy reached in his jockey shorts and gave his penis an affectionate squeeze. All three of them, "ooh-ed" and "ah-ed" at the suddenly growing mound between his legs, and they wondered aloud if maybe it would be more interesting if Captain Shrimp danced naked. "Then he'd have two guns to shoot at Morton instead of one." Chloe chortled.

But they finally agreed that so much creative play had been expended in making Captain Shrimp's costume, like it or not, he must wear it. Ronald tried to make it very clear that he wasn't dancing—let alone dancing naked—and that they should choose a more appropriate Captain Shrimp. But they ignored him, wiping out his protests with affection. Chloe plunked an ancient-style peaked cardboard silver helmet on Captain Shrimp's head and kissed him enthusiastically. Then, Isabel and Trudy wrapped him in a felt uniform over which they had sewn wire mesh from some abandoned conveyor belt. Deciding he had no choice but to go along with them, he let Trudy glue a beard on his face. Sylvia, who had rejoined them, handed him a plastic replica of an ancient musket.

"You can carry it in the sheath the girls have sewn on the back of your uniform," she told him. "Try it, Ron. Just aim it at my breast and pull the trigger."

He stared at her a little dubiously. The brandy was slowly eliminating his inhibitions. Sylvia kept insisting, "Go ahead, Ron, it's only a squirtgun."

He pulled the trigger, and to his horror a stream of what seemed to be red blood was suddenly dripping over her nipple, and trickling down her perky breast. Staggering back, she did a quick pirouette, and then she collapsed in his arms and gasped, "Oh dear, you shot me. I'm dying!"

Momentarily bewildered, wondering if it was true, Ronald yelled in dismay.

"Beautiful," she sighed as he leaned over her, and she lay trembling in his arms. "You really can act, Ron. All you need is the inspiration." She grinned at him provocatively. "It's only V-8 juice and vodka. You can lap it off, if you want to."

Ronald discovered that all of the actors were equipped with either water pistols or water rifles. Strategically placed on the beach and on the lawns was ammunition, "pails of blood" in which their weapons could be dunked and quickly reloaded for the coming "capture" of Morton. But Ronald didn't lap Sylvia's breast. Not then. Not until later when she joined him on the merry-go-round and told him that one of the reasons she was there with him was to see if he agreed with H.H.'s theory, "Like mother, like daughter."

Clanking, at least figuratively, in his armor, with another brandy julep in his hand and his musket on his back, Ronald was led back to the beach by Hale Brewster, who explained to him that they were drinking brandy because other than wine and beer, it was the only "firewater" that had been available in Merry Mount more than three hundred years ago when Morton seduced the Indians. The clambake was just beginning, and Marge and H.H. and the rest of the commune, who hadn't witnessed his transmogrification, cheered him, "Hail the mighty warrior from Plymouth plantation, who has arrived in Merry Mount to capture the Lord of Misrule. Ronald Coldaxe is dead. Long live Captain Shrimp!"

To Ronald's astonishment, Marge, who hugged him and congratulated him as her "bald, bearded warrior" was now wearing an Indian headdress and a buckskin skirt that matched her daughter's. Neither of them were wearing anything else except a pair of thonged sandals. She and Sylvia were two squaws with succulent, saucy breasts bouncing on their chests. The lower curves of their buttocks wobbled teasingly below the slit in their miniskirts. Like provocative winks, they lured the beholder.

At first Ronald didn't recognize H.H., who had his arms around them. He had transformed himself into a swashbuckling seventeenth-century adventurer. With a neatly trimmed, slightly graying beard and a curly moustache, he looked like the proprietor of a London sex club as he leered at Ronald. "Aulde Tom probably hadde a bigge potte bellie," H.H. told him, speaking in a rolling Chaucerian-style English. "But when you adopt an ancestor, he's yours to improve." He put his arm around Ronald sympathetically. "You look just about as effective as the Tin Man in the Wizard of Oz. But don't worry, Ron, once the play begins you'll get in the mood."

In response to his questions about how one acted in a drama if he didn't know the plot, one of the men who was loading Ronald's plate with clams and corn and lobster advised him, "Just relax, Captain Shrimp. Our presentations are strictly off the cuff. We're all part-time actors with no claim to fame. In between jobs at local theaters, we work off and on for bread and wine. When our cash-flow is weak, we depend on Heman to tide us over. In the meantime, we are experimenting with Peter Brooks approaches to acting and audience interaction."

"Brooks is an English theatrical and motion-picture director," said Marge, who was cracking a lobster nearby. A few years ago he took a group of actors on a safari over a good portion of Africa. Late afternoons and evenings they performed completely spontaneous and unrehearsed dramas in African villages. Neither the actors nor the audience could understand one another's language. The name of the game was communication and rapport."

"Brooks called the journey the Conference of the Birds," H.H. said, and flopped on the beach with a group of communards who had made a circle around Captain Shrimp. "It's an old Persian legend. The birds engage in a symbolical pilgrimage. A long search is taken over many years, only to discover that what they had been looking for was there all the time, right on their own doorstep. Mecca is where you are. John Halpern, who wrote a book about Brooks's trek across Africa, posed the basic questions that Brooks and actors and directors after him will forever try to resolve. 'What is simplicity? What is a sound, a song, a movement? What is fantasy? Is is possible for actors, or anyone, to transcend cultural and racial conditioning? Does the audience have a role to play? What can be learned from children? Can actors create? Does creation happen by itself? What is the relationship between the abstract and the real? How freely can one move between the two? What is a play?' And Brooks answered: 'Anything with me in it.' He also said, 'If we wish to avoid the traditional trap of living in watertight separations between work and life outside, all antennae must be cut.'" H.H. beamed at Ronald, "Tonight, your friends are going to show you how to play, Ron—and to laugh."

A man sitting on the beach near them said, "Brooks is asking the question, "How can we make the theater absolutely and fundamentally *necessary* to people, as necessary as eating and sex? Something that is a simple organic necessity, as the theater used to be."

"The problem is that we've put a stopper on the bottle of life," H.H. laughed. "We have to shake it up, pull out the stopper, and, before it fizzes over, cap it with our mouths. 'Make believe is necessity.' We're proving it at Byrdwhistle," he gestured at Razi and several children who were playing hide and seek. "Do you remember Carol King's song about Pierre? Kids love it. They don't care. And neither did Pierre. Not until the lion ate him. When the lion finally growled up Pierre, Pierre had mastered him. He even invited him home to dinner."

A half-hour later, after eating at least two dozen clams and a baked lobster and slaking his thirst with more brandy, "Captain Shrimp" Coldaxe didn't care either. Lying a little dizzily on the grass, his head supported on Sylvia's bare thigh, he watched a group of communards spreading an oriental rug on the patio that overlooked the beach. Sylvia explained that the worn rug, an area of about twenty-by-thirty feet, was one of the stages on which part of the action would take place. The play would begin around the Maypole, but the orchestra would remain on the patio. Isabel, one of the women who had dressed him, was playing a portable piano that had been carried out of the house, and two other women, after tuning up a violin and a cello, were testing some kind of Indian ceremonial music that a man was accentuating bare-handed on his drum.

Ronald looked up at Marge, who was standing astride him. It was still light enough for him to enjoy the friendly sight of her puckery genitals. While he had only seen glimpses of Sylvia's pubis, and had no basis of comparison, in the shape of their bodies they were more like sisters than mother and daughter. The only difference was that Marge probably weighed about twenty pounds more than Sylvia.

"The play is about to begin," Sylvia told them. "But you can relax, Ron. You won't appear as Captain Shrimp until the last half. We have to establish the orgiastic revels at Merry Mount first."

"What the hell am I supposed to do in the last half?"

"Who cares?" Hale Brewster, who had heard him, winked at him, "We're both the actors and the audience. You can play two parts. You can join Morton's group of rebels and dance around the Maypole and screw with the Indian girls, and then later you can be Myles Standish. Remember, we only have to please ourselves." Hale pointed to the patio, which was about three feet higher than the ground below. A girl of about six or seven, dressed like a young Puritan maid, was now standing primly on the platform in front of a microphone. "Listen to Melissa," Hale said. "Tonight she's our mistress of ceremonies."

"Everybody please be quiet," Melissa said. "In a few minutes the play will begin. But first Grampy Heman, who has now become Thomas Morton, thought we should explain to Mr. Coldaxe, who will play the part of Captain Shrimp, that he is now standing near Passonagassett Knoll, which is approximately the site where Thomas Morton erected his Maypole and merged work into play. Wessagusset, where Captain Shrimp first captured Thomas Morton, is across the bay about two miles from here. Before the play begins, because Mr. Coldaxe has made this celebration possible by agreeing not to buy Grampy Heman's Byrdwhistle business, the Thomas Morton Commune wishes to present him with a token of their appreciation. My brother, Bobbie," Melissa frowned at a three-year-old boy who ran up to her and clung to her skirt, "has finally arrived and will make the actual presentation. But first I must read you something about it in Thomas Morton's own words."

Melissa paused, and Bobbie waved a small box at the audience and bowed in appreciation of the applause and laughter he received. Then, annoyed that the laughter didn't stop, he yelled at everybody, "Be quiet!"

Melissa read from a book in the same Old English accent that Grampy Heman had been using. "'When the savages went a-hunting turkies, they spread over such a great scope of ground that a turkie could hardly escape them. Deer they killed in great abundance, and feasted their bodies very plentifully. Beavers they killed by no allowance. The skins of these they traded at Wessagusset with my neighbors for corn and such commodities as they had need of; and my neighbors had wonderful great benefit by their being in those parts. Yet, sometimes, like genial fellows, the savages would present their merchant with a fat beaver skin, and always the tail was not diminished but presented full and whole, and is of such masculine virtue that, if some of our English ladies knew the benefit thereof, they would devise to have ships sent for the purpose of trading the tail alone.'"

Before Melissa finished, to the screams of laughter from the communards, Marge took Ronald's helmet, telling him that he wouldn't need it for a moment and that she would keep it for him. She shoved him in the direction of the patio, where Bobbie handed him the box. Even before he managed to open it, everybody was shouting, "Put it on, Ron. Put on the beaver's tail. We couldn't get the whole beaver for you, but we got you the magical tail!"

The dark-brown tail was held together in a circle with a clasp. Too far gone to care how ridiculous he looked, Ronald tried to get it over his head, but it got stuck in the middle. Hopelessly, he gave up struggling and pulled the furry ring down over his naked head and under his chin. Then he raised his hands in a victory salute.

Hale Brewster took over for Melissa. He pointed at the Maypole and said, "Thomas Morton, mine host of Merry Mount wrote the following words for which we have composed music: 'Drinke, and be merry, merry, boyes/Let all your delight be in the Hymen joyes/To Hymen now the day is come/About the merry Maypole take a roome.'"

The orchestra swung into a rock version of an ancient English country air. A few minutes later, everyone, including Ronald, who had shed his Myles Standish armor and was wearing only jockey shorts and the beaver tail around his neck, was dancing hand in hand around the Maypole, singing the chorus and verses of Morton's tippling song.

"'Make green garlons, bring the bottle out/And fill the sweet nectar freely about/Uncover thy head and feare no harme/For here's good liquor to keep it warme.'"

"Come on, Ron," H.H. yelled at him, "sing the chorus. 'Drinke and be merry, merry boyes!'"

Twenty or more of them, including all the kids in the commune, circled round and round the Maypole. Hypnotized by the firelight dancing on the breasts of the women—two or three of them had shed their skirts and were dancing naked—Ronald dizzily mumbled the verse. "'Nectar is a thing assigned/by the Dieties owne minde/to cure the heart oppressed with griefe/And of good liquor is the chiefe.'"

Marge detached him from the group and danced with him inside the circle. Her bare breasts rubbed erotically against his chest, paralyzing his mind. "'Give to that melancolly man'" she sang, "'A cup or two, t'now and then/This physick will soon revive his bloude/And make him of a merrier moude.'" She kissed Ronald full on his lips and twirled him into H.H.'s arms, who danced a jig with him and sang: "'Give to the Nymphe that free from scorne/No Irish stuffe, nor Scotch over worne/Lasses in beaver coates, come way/Yee shall be welcome night and day.'"

The singing and dancing was reaching a feverish pitch, and in the background Hale Brewster's voice reading from Morton set the mood as H.H. (Morton) and his band of bawdy English revelers—five of the communards, naked to the waist, dressed in pantaloons and doublets, which now hung to their knees—danced after the screaming, laughing Indian maids and tumbled them to the ground, kissing them and simulating passionate love-making with them.

"'The inhabitants of Passonagasset,'" Hale read on, "'having translated that ancient savage name to Mare Mount—Mountain by the Sea—and having resolved to have the new name confirmed for a memorial to after ages, did devise among themselves to have it performed in solemn manner with revels and merriment after the old English custom. They prepared to set up a Maypole upon the festival day, and therefore brewed a barrel of excellent beer. And, upon Mayday, they brought up the Maypole to the appointed place with drums, guns, and pistols, and with other fitting instruments for that purpose erected with the help of the savages a goodly pine tree about eighty feet long with a pair of buckskins nailed over the top of it as a fair-sea marker for the directions how to find the way to the Host of Mare Mount. This harmless mirthe made by the younger men (that lived to have their wives brought over to them) was much distasted by the precise Separatists in Plymouth Plantation, and from that time they sought occasion against Mine Honest Host of Mare Mount to overthrow his undertakings and destroy his plantation quite and cleane.'"

The orchestra struck up a thunderous note of doom, and a man dressed in Puritan garb danced into the grouping around the Maypole and handed a message to H.H. from Governor Bradford.

Hale continued reading, while H.H., dancing around the messenger, presumably read the note and tossed it away. Then he laughed at the Pilgrim who danced after him menacingly, threatening him with his pistol.

"'The setting up of the Maypole was a lamentable spectacle,'" Hale continued. "'The Separatists termed it an idol, yea, they called it the Calf of Horeb, and stood at defiance with the place, naming it Mount Dagon, threatening to make it a woeful mount and not a merry mount.'"

"Okay, Captain Shrimp," Sylvia suddenly snatched Ronald out of the circle of dancers, who were cheering H.H. and yelling nastily at his would-be attacker. "The stage is going to shift to the patio," Sylvia told him. "Morton has gone to Wessagusset. Shrimp captures him, but Morton escapes and travels through the woods to Merry Mount where Shrimp chases him and captures him again."

Ronald could never recall exactly what happened in that next hour. Above the turmoil, he knew that Hale was blithely reading from Morton:

" 'The Separatists, envying the prosperity and hope of the plantation at Mare Mount, made a party against Mine Host, accounting him a great monster. They set upon my honest Host at a place called Wessagusset, where by accident they found him. In brief, Mine Host must endure to be their prisoner so that they could send him back to England. Much rejoicing was made that they had got their capital enemy. Mine Host fained greife, and could not be persuaded to eate or drinke, because he knew that emptiness would be a meanes to make him watchful. Six persons were set to watch him, but he kept waking, and in the dead of night, up gets Mine Host and got to the second door that was to passe, which not withstanding the lock, he got open, and shut it with such violence that it affrighted some of the conspirators . . . This Captain Shrimp took on most furiously and tore his clothes for anger, to see the empty nest and their bird gone. The rest were eager to tear their hair from their heads, but it was so short that it would give them no hold. Now Captain Shrimp thought in the loss of his prize, which he accounted his masterpiece, all his honor would be lost forever.' "

Somewhere during this recital, Ronald remembered vaguely that he had danced mincingly and menacingly—while the audience howled their approval—onto the stage where Morton, no longer H.H., grinned evilly at him and shot him in the eyes with vodka and V-8 juice. Blood pouring down his face, blinding him temporarily, Captain Shrimp pursued Morton around the Oriental rug that was serving as a cabin at Wessagusset. Then his mesh armor slipped down over his knees and he tripped over Morton, who was now lying on his back and shooting at him with his water pistol, roaring with laughter, and yelling that it was too bad Ralph Thiemost wasn't there to enjoy Ronald's performance.

Finally, tossing his helmet at Sylvia, who was giving him stage directions from below the patio, and kicking off his armor, Ronald ran after Morton wearing only his beaver tail and jockey shorts, which were becoming a sodden "bloody" mess. The Indians and Shrimp's army of five Pilgrims kept yelling, "Shoot Shrimp in the balls." Ronald stopped occasionally, crouching to his knees, to take pot shots at the hysterical band of half-naked adults and kids who were following him and shooting. And then he caught up with H.H. under a tree. He remembered H.H. yelling, "Hold your fire, I need to piss"—which he calmly did while a giggling audience watched him. "Don't knock it," H.H. said. "Millions of Americans have never had the pleasure of pissing on the ground." Then he yelled, "Okay, the play goes on!"

Suddenly, for no reason that Ronald could figure out, H.H. switched sides. He and Marge and Sylvia were running toward the Rolls Royce with two buckets of blood for ammunition. Using the Rolls in the driveway as a fortress, they were shooting at the attackers while Hale and the orchestra droned on. A few minutes later, he heard H.H. yelling,

"Truce! Truce!" and the games of cops and robbers, which he had to admit he was really enjoying, were suddenly over and H.H. was kissing everybody goodbye: "I'm capturing Shrimp and taking him to Boston to ride on my merry-go-round."

Then, he, Ronald Coldaxe—or was he really Captain Shrimp?—was in the front seat of the Rolls, and H.H. was driving—somewhat drunkenly Ronald thought—while Marge sat between them, and Sylvia, her Indian headdress slumping over her eyes, was sitting with her warm bare ass on his thighs and occasionally rubbing herself against his groin, while she sleepily lapped his face and neck and whispered loud enough for Marge to hear that she hoped he didn't mind but she suspected that she was going to ride the carousel with him that night, and if that were the case she needed to sleep a little in his arms and be prepared for the next encounter. And he could hear Marge giggling and telling H.H.—as if Ronald had already gone back to California—that Ron was really "a good guy in a white hat." Whoever thought Coldaxe would have potential as a ballet dancer? He could compete with Baryshnikov! Whoever thought that the completely bald-headed vice president of W.I.N. Incorporated would be riding through the streets of Boston wearing nothing but his underwear, and a phallic symbol around his neck?

18

They were driving through Park Square, a half-mile from H.H.'s townhouse, and Sylvia was sitting on Ronald's lap, dozing against his neck and occasionally gently rubbing her warm, bare ass against his legs and groin. Then, to his surprise, he suddenly realized that she was inching her fingers over his belly into his shorts and, having managed to probe through his pubic hair, was exploring his penis with two fingers.

H.H. was singing, "A social glass and a social lass go well together. But a social lass with a social ass I deem a damned sight better." And Marge, sitting between them, was chorusing her own version, "Men only make passes at sassy asses."

It suddenly occurred to Ronald that he was practically naked. "Jesus Christ!" he yelled. "I left my shirt and suit at Merry Mount."

"No problem," H.H. laughed. "We'll stop at your hotel. It's just around the corner. You have another suit, don't you?"

"The key to my room is in my suit."

Still singing, not hearing him, H.H. circled Boston Common and

pulled up in front of the Ritz-Carlton. A helpful doorman jumped off
the curbing and stood by, ready to open the doors of the Rolls.

"Why don't you step out?" Marge was choking with laughter. "Give
the poor guy a surprise he'll never forget."

"I can't go into the hotel like this," Ronald said.

"Sure you can," Sylvia insisted, "I'll go with you. I want to see the
manager's face when you ask him for your key."

"For God's sake, let's get the hell out of here," Ronald groaned.
"Drive me back to Merry Mount." But he was too late. The doorman,
thinking he was asking for assistance, opened the door, and Sylvia, who
was leaning against it, still naked to the waist, her mini-skirt tucked into
her belt and well above her mound, tumbled into his arms. The doorman
staggered back and tripped on the curb, with Sylvia falling on top of
him. While drivers of automobiles tooted enthusiastically behind them,
Ronald, his beaver-tail swinging about his neck, and his shorts more than
a little bloodied by the vodka barrage, dashed after her. He tried to pick
her up fireman-style, but she was laughing hysterically and shoved her
hands into his shorts and bared his ass toward the crowd of onlookers
who had gathered. Automobiles were still honking as he staggered with
Sylvia and finally got back into the car with her. "Come on," he hissed at
H.H., "let's get the hell out of here before we're all arrested."

Laughing boisterously, H.H. circled the Common again while Ronald indignantly told Sylvia that she was the craziest bitch he had ever
met. H.H. finally turned onto Beacon Hill and pulled into a condo-
minium garage on Brimmer Street. Then, clinging half-naked to Sylvia,
Ronald followed H.H. and Marge through the narrow streets past repli-
cas of old-fashioned gas street-lights. He continued to moan about the
loss of his suit. Instead of listening to his woes, Marge and Sylvia and
H.H., bursting with laughter, kept repeating the details of his encounter
with the doorman.

"Maybe we should all go back to the Ritz with you," H.H. challenged
him. "We'll tell them that we were at a come-as-you-are party."

They finally arrived at Louisburg Square, and H.H. led them up the
front stairs of his townhouse. Feeling for the lock with his key, he grumbled over a large package that blocked a part of the doorway.

"It looks like another one of those damned Love Seats," Marge told
him. "Nate Marson must still be trying to convince you that you can't live
without one."

"I told that sleazy character on the phone last week that Byrdwhistle
wasn't interested," said H.H. as he dragged the package into the foyer.
"We get a lot of nuts who think they have the ultimate sex-machine for
Club Wholesome," he explained to Ronald.

Ronald was more concerned about his near nudity, "I don't give a
damn about Love Seats. I'm catching the five o'clock plane tomorrow.

My ticket is in my room at the hotel. I can't leave Boston in my underwear. What are you going to do about it?"

H.H. looked at his watch. "It's only eleven P.M., Ron. Stop fretting. You've got seventeen hours. I'd offer you a pair of my pants, but you've got a little bulge there." He patted Ron's belly, "I don't think you could zip them up."

"I'll telephone Hale Brewster," Sylvia said. "He'll find your suit and bring it into town in the morning." She was examining the package curiously. "What's a Love Seat? Can Big Chief Coldaxe and I see it?" She had put her Indian feathers on Ronald and was trying to encourage him to dance and yell Indian-style with his hand bobbing against his mouth.

"It's a silly contraption," Marge said. "Marson Manufacturing makes them. Nate wanted to drop-ship them for us—a selling price of $350 and our cost is $150. He sent two of them to us a month ago. Ninety-five percent of the female Byrdwhistlers gave them thumbs down. They're a male pipedream. Nate doesn't realize that Symp rules our catalogue choices. He's evidently trying to convince Hy separately."

"They're a pipedream all right." Laughing, H.H. ripped open the package, which was filled with several red pipes that fitted into one another. "Come on, help me. Sylvia won't be happy until she sees one in action."

In a few minutes they had erected a spiderlike metal gadget with three legs and several metal spirals designed to give support to a woman's or a man's arms or legs. When it was standing firmly on the slate floor in the dimly lit front room, it still wasn't immediately apparent how to use it.

H.H. pointed to the upper seat, finished in vinyl and attached to one of the pipes. "You climb up there, Syl," he told her. "You sit on this lower seat, Ron."

Ronald sat gingerly in the lower seat. Sylvia climbed over him, turned around, and lay back in the upper seat. Giggling, she inserted her legs into the metal supports. Trying to act unperturbed, Ronald discovered he was staring into her spread-eagled legs. Her parted labia, ready for kissing and tasting, revealed the tender, unprotected opening of her vagina.

"Now, according to Marson, dinner is ready," H.H. told him sarcastically. "Your woman is ready to lap or eat. When the male isn't hungry any more, he can insert his legs in these lower hooks and, when he stretches out, she can ride his prick, weightless."

Ron shook his head disgustedly. "We're living in a sick world," he said, but he couldn't help staring at Sylvia's genitals, and he was well aware that the view was making him rampant.

Since he didn't move to allow her to get off the top seat more easily, Sylvia, not the least embarrassed by her display, clasped his bare head between her thighs. Giggling, she slid her crotch slowly and deliberately over his head and landed lightly on her feet on the floor behind him. "I still think making love and kissing each other flesh to flesh is more erotic than this piece of junk."

"That's what I told Marson." H.H. was speaking to Ronald, who was still feeling the effects of the brandy juleps he had drunk and was waiting for his genitals to return to normal before he stood up from the Love Seat. Still sitting in the cockpit, he grinned dazedly while H.H. continued. "Love Seats are a power fantasy created for men who can't get it up unless the woman they are screwing is subservient. There are evidently a lot of men in the world who want vaginas and breasts attached to a loving slave who is in ecstasy while her dominating, macho lover slobbers over her."

"Ron seems to like it," Marge teased him.

"Could I borrow a raincoat?" Ron mumbled. The whole damned sexy atmosphere was discombobulating him, and he was getting increasingly nervous. Like it or not, it was becoming obvious that he was going to spend the night with Sylvia, who had obviously expropriated him and was determined to make love on some damned merry-go-round he had yet to see. The whole environment was immoral and disreputable. This was the kind of evening that, if it ever got publicized, could ruin a man's career.

H.H. tried to reassure him. "We're not going to send you home naked, Ron. I'll drive over to the Ritz tomorrow and pick up your luggage. Relax and float with the tide."

But Marge wasn't soothing him. She was wondering aloud if Ron would like to have her ship one of their sample Love Seats to Meredith. "They do have one positive feature," she giggled. "According to many of the Byrdwhistle women who tried them, they make some women feel quite lascivious. A psychological reaction of being served up 'in flagrante' to your lover. Hot pussy for my lord and master." Marge was obviously carried away by the idea. "Maybe a Love Seat would help Meredith express some of her fantasies that according to our questionnaire you have been neglecting."

Ronald jumped out of the Love Seat. "If you do anything like that, Marge Slick, I'll—I'll—" he stared at her grimly, unable to tell her what he might do to her.

Trying to comfort him, Sylvia took his arm. "Come on, Ron. Marge is only teasing you. She always did that to me when I was a kid. Tonight we're going to relax together on the merry-go-round and talk about love."

Ronald tried to tell himself that he might just as well humor these harmless maniacs. What could he really do anyway without his suit? He couldn't slam the door on this cuckoo's nest and walk the streets of Boston in his underwear. He was a victim of circumstance. Even Thiemost would agree. The better part of valor was not to act like a spy in the house of Lord Youman.

H.H. had turned on a master light switch, and revealed that most of the first floor was a totally open lounge, tiled in a beige and red interlocking Yang and Yin pattern and decorated with heavy Spanish-style furniture and Moorish lanterns. The far end of the floor had been cut back to ground level and a wide-open stairway with four risers gave access to a kidney-shaped swimming pool that flowed into the backyard of the townhouse and was surrounded by a tall privacy fence. The pool area had been connected to the main house by a clear plastic dome.

"I had the job done when we were remodeling the Byrdwhistle offices," H.H. said. "As you can see, I enjoy swimming. When my grandchildren visit us—from California or New York—they enjoy swimming in it bare-ass." H.H. ducked behind the bar on one side of the room and plunked a bottle down before them. "There she is. Lafite Rothschild, 1864. The people who fermented and bottled this wine lived in another century. Tonight is as good as any to open it."

"Don't do it for me," Ron examined the bottle nervously. "Your expensive wine got me into enough trouble last night."

But, grinning happily, H.H. was carefully removing the cork. "This wine will make your hair grow back. I have great hopes for you, Ron. Despite Adele, I expect to keep a firm hand on Byrdwhistle for quite a few years. But there's no question that Elmer and I need a younger man, a successor who can carry on and develop the company, and Theory Z, a man who might even have the vision to direct World Corporation."

Ronald couldn't help frowning as H.H., Marge, and Sylvia toasted him with the wine that H.H. had poured into glasses with six-inch stems. Ron twirled the wine around in the glass thinking the damned stuff was liquid gold. "It sure as hell isn't going to be me," he said. "If I ran Byrdwhistle, you'd have to drink two-dollar-a-bottle California wine."

Rolling the wine on his tongue, H.H. didn't answer. "It's better than a cheap California red," he said finally, "but not much. I prefer an aged cabernet sauvignon at, say, twelve dollars a bottle. On the other hand, this wine has something going for it, Ron. It's like drinking money. Buying it and drinking it destroys the money fetish. It proves that beyond a certain point, it's ridiculous to amass huge fortunes like H. L. Hunt, Howard Hughes, and Paul Getty did. Those crazy bastards didn't enjoy money or the simple eroticism of drinking a vastly overpriced bottle of wine in the company of two half-naked ladies."

Marge shrugged. "I think you have a Picasso complex. In his old age, Picasso insisted that he wanted to live like a poor man but with a great deal of money."

"I like Shelley's philosophy better," Sylvia said. " 'I love all waste / And solitary places: where we taste / The pleasure of believing what we see / Is boundless, as we wish our souls to be.' "

H.H. watched Ronald, who was sipping his wine dubiously, as if it might be poisoned or were in reality a new kind of truth serum. "I have a slightly different approach," he said. "To be poor and old in this country is to be despised. To be rich and old is to be venerated. Thus, if you can't be rich or if you spend all your money along the way, you must take care never to grow old. You must be more versatile and adaptable to change than those who are decades younger than you are, and certainly more so than most of your peers. When you've lost so many brain cells that you no longer are clicking and you spend most of your time extolling the past, you should immediately cash in your chips."

As he spoke, H.H. fixed Ronald with a hypnotic stare, which was counteracted by a smile that kept hovering around his mouth. As usual, Ronald found it impossible to tell whether he was serious or not, especially when he said, "Think it over, Ron, all you have to do is change your religion. Become a convert to Theory Z. Tomorrow, when you go back, tell Ralph Thiemost to shove W.I.N. up his ass. Tell him that you not only have more fun playing at Byrdwhistle but that you'll probably make more money."

Sylvia squeezed Ron's arm. "Tonight, if he'll snuggle with me on your merry-go-round, I'll try to convince Big Chief."

Sitting on a barstool beside her, Ronald shook his head. "If I do spend the night," he said, knowing that he sounded like a prim teen-age virgin who had had too much to drink, "I think I should sleep with your mother."

"My God, Mommy," Sylvia laughed, "you must have cast a spell on Big Chief."

Marge, who was sitting on H.H.'s side of the bar, leaned over and kissed Ronald's cheek. "Thank you, kind sir," she said. "I love you, but tonight H.H. asked me to share his body. You really don't know how fortunate you are. Not many men get the opportunity to compare mother and daughter. I think your real problem is that you're feeling guilty. Last night you told me that I was the only woman you had made love with since you married Meredith."

"That's terrible, Ron." H.H. shook his head in mock sadness.

"You'll never understand Theory Z or the Byrdwhistle play-ethic until you have surrendered to more than one woman. The great Zen master, Bhagwan Shree Rajneesh sums it up: 'Whatsoever you can be, you are. There is no goal. And we are not going anywhere. We are simply celebrating here. Existence is not a journey. It is a celebration. Think of it as a celebration! As a delight, as a joy! Don't turn it into suffering! Don't turn it into work—let it be play!'"

Sylvia patted Ron's cheek. "Not sex, honey. Love. Love on a merry-go-round."

"You may even discover that my merry-go-round is both a reality and a metaphor," said H.H. as he opened another bottle of wine, which he assured Ron cost only six dollars a bottle. "Sylvia is offering you a chance to avoid a midnight crisis and to recapture your youth. Just think, when you were twenty she was still playing with her dolls."

Ronald couldn't help smiling at Sylvia, "It's not that I don't appreciate your offer." He was afraid to tell her that being pursued by a woman made him nervous and that he was afraid that it might affect his potency. "The truth is that I'm a pawn in your game. Why the hell would a lovely young woman like Sylvia want to screw with me unless there was something in it for her?"

Sylvia laughed, "I assure you, neither Marge nor Hy put me up to it. My reasons are quite simple. First, I don't like to sleep alone. Second, you are a duplicate of the man I married, the guy who is really Razi's father but unfortunately doesn't believe it. He is sure that I made love with a mutual friend of ours at about the same time. Even if I did, I was already pregnant by Clint. That's my husband's name. Clint also believes that if he searches long enough he'll eventually find a wife who will adore him, a woman who has no particular interests of her own," Sylvia grinned, "like my ballet dancing, and especially one who isn't going to be a star."

There were tears in Sylvia's eyes. "Even worse, Clint detests 'far-out nuts' like Hy and like my friends in the Merry Mount commune. The third reason is that I'm still trying to discover what makes people like you and Clint tick." She looked shyly at Ronald. "The fourth reason will probably horrify you. I'm beginning to believe that Marge transferred certain odor compulsions to me genetically. The moment I hugged you at the commune, I had a gut need to keep inhaling you. You exude a sexone—that's a word coined by Janet Hopson, who wrote a book about sex and scent. Your odor is very similar to Hy's basic body odor. I can't pin it down. A combination of Moxie, sarsaparilla, and mud flats when the tide goes out. The smell not only opens the flood gates of my brain, teasing me with something very pleasant that occurred to me years ago, but it excites me."

"After playing Myles Standish, I need a shower," Ronald muttered. "We all do," Sylvia grinned. "But be careful you don't wash your sexy smell away."

"I don't know about Moxie and sarsaparilla," H.H. laughed, "but I'm sure glad that I smell like low tide. According to a guy named John Amoore, the primary odors are 'sweaty,' produced by bacteria on the human feet and in the vagina; 'spermous,' the odor of the male seminal fluid and pubic area; 'fishy,' the odor of women when they are menstruating; 'urinous,' the odor of both male and female urine; and 'musky,' the odor of scent-gland secretions. All of them are probably natural sex triggers."

While he was talking, H.H. was sniffing Marge, and on the other side of the bar everyone was in a happy alcoholic euphoria and sniffing one another from head to foot. Sylvia told Ronald he smelled "yummy" and she wasn't at all sure that he should shower. Marge led the way to an open communal shower on the other side of the swimming pool and a few steps lower. The bubbling conversation about natural pheromones, exaltaloids, copulins, and using perfumes in love-making was beyond Ronald, but he was mesmerized by the sensuous pale-blue pool lights and the romantic shadows created by the orange glow from the lamps.

The music, which H.H. told him was on a tape system with master controls on all of the floors of the townhouse, had taken on a distinctive flamenco beat. Barefoot and naked, H.H. was dancing like a Spanish bullfighter, clapping and shouting "Olé!" while Marge and Sylvia, who had thoroughly sniffed and nuzzled their men until they were amazingly rampant, had reluctantly decided to wash them a little. They were now playing the role of acquiescent harem girls. "After we swim in the pool and ride with our Sultans on the flying horses, we'll sniff you back to life," Sylvia told them. She suddenly turned on the cold water, but not before she and Marge gave their rods an affectionate squeeze.

Pattering from the shower across the tiles, they dove into the pool, and H.H. and Sylvia raced each other from one end to the other, while Marge and Ronald tread water and watched them. "I don't know what is motivating Hy," Marge said, "but the wheel of fortune is getting ready to stop on your number, Ron. Hy doesn't invite everyone he meets to his inner sanctum. He likes you. He's also intrigued by your wife. That's why he wants you to have a Byrd's-eye view into a saner world." Then Marge summed up the subject of pheromones. "After eighteen years of marriage, smelling Sylvia and me, who probably have a different odor from Meredith's, has restored your libido."

Jumping out of the pool and sitting beside them, dangling his legs in the water, H.H. agreed with Marge. "You've arrived at the age, Ron, where every other book you read has to do with 'passages,' or 'adaptation to life,' or 'mid-life crises,' or 'seasons in a man's life,' or 'life after youth,' or 'your second life,' or 'growing old in America,' or 'the vintage years,' or 'aging,' or 'the male menopause,' and, at your level, 'overcoming executive stress.' Alongside these self-help books in most bookstores there are books that offer instruction on the final stages — 'the art of dying,' or 'how to die happily in ten lessons.'"

H.H. pointed to Marge and Sylvia, who were now floating in the pool. Their hair was suspended around their heads, and they occasionally raised their silky mounds above the water and thrust them suggestively in the direction of their eventual penetrators. "Marge and Sylvia are giving you a vacation from stress. A psychologist, Homer Figler, created a five-act scenario that I guess would probably fit the Coldaxe situation. Act One: You've begun to work at W.I.N. A great job with a future. Meredith is raising the kids and making your home a 'wifey' retreat.

A womb in which you can escape the 'real' world. Act Two: You're having your forty-fifth birthday. You're a big shot at W.I.N. There are moments when you are pissed off that you haven't risen faster. After all, thirty-year-old guys are now running some of the billion-dollar companies. Your kids are in school and you are suddenly aware that Meredith has more freedom than you have. She joins clubs, plays bridge, or, to your horror, is always poking a stick in the spoke of what you have thought of as progress. Act Three: You are forty-seven. Your kids are either already in college or about ready to go. You wish that you and Meredith had more in common. If she joined the country club or played golf, you might find something to do together. Instead, you aren't communicating and you're both drinking a little more than you used to. If you dared to be honest, you'd say that you're both a little bored with each other. Act Four: You're getting pretty exasperated with Meredith. She doesn't seem to realize that you're busting your ass to pay college tuition for the kids. She seems to think that money grows on trees. When you make love together, it's not much fun, but she still accommodates you. Act Five: You take a female assistant to dinner and discover that she has much more in common with you than Meredith does. You think she loves W.I.N. the way you do. Or you go on a business trip and you get seduced by Marge Slick. You don't understand her, but you never had so much fun in bed. In the meantime, Meredith, who can 'smell' the other woman on you, asks for a divorce, or she takes up with the golf pro or the local activist who hasn't shaved his beard yet."

Tossing towels at them, H.H. jumped up and yelled, "Onward and upward!" and he led the way toward a small elevator near the foyer that was enclosed in iron grillwork. As they were being lifted to the second floor, Ronald, still ruminating on H.H.'s scenario, told him: "You're really full of shit, H.H. If you're such a damned expert, why can't you resolve your own marital problems? Tell your wife to stop seducing Ralph Thiemost and let old man Byrd keep his damned company. Then your problems would be over."

H.H. shrugged. "It would be a dull world if interaction were totally predictable. Adele and I passed beyond Act Five of the marital scenario quite a few years ago. Even though she is still in full sexual bloom, she thinks that time is running out. All her peers have become 'nice old ladies'—actually, castrating bitches—who gave up fucking, let alone love-making, years ago. They make her feel guilty. The whole ploy of trying to get Thorny to sell Byrdwhistle and, in the process, force me to retire is related to a scary feeling that, like it or not, we are senior citizens. According to her, we should join the American Association of Retired Persons and settle down."

"Why not?" demanded Ronald. "Everyone has to retire eventually."

Standing next to Marge, H.H. had cupped her breasts. He bent over and kissed each one reverently. Then he grinned at Ron. "Agreed. People retire from work, but *I'm playing*. When you give up playing, you're dead!"

H.H. explained that the ten rooms on the second and third floor were "Adele's world." He lived in them only a few months each year. "Longer than that would overcivilize me," he said. "While Adele thinks Elmer is a little whacked-out about ancestors, she really has adopted Louis XIV. But I have never interfered with her idea of play. This is the result."

As they wandered from room to room, Ronald saw that hundreds of thousands of dollars must have gone into purchasing seventeenth-century antiques. Adele had reconstructed the rich, mannered, and delicately carved and decorated ambience of another era. "I told Adele that she probably would have been happier married to a man like William Randolph Hearst. This is her San Simeon. If she'd put velvet curtains across the doors and charge admission, it would help pay our taxes. I even offered to stay in bed and make love with her on public-admission days. Old French custom, really. All the French madames entertained their lovers in their bedrooms."

H.H. pointed to a canopied bed in one of the bedrooms. It had curved legs with a painting of lovers in a pastoral scene on the headboard. "Tom Morton would have found it difficult to copulate on that," he laughed.

"Casanova would have felt right at home," Sylvia said.

"You'd better re-read his memoirs," H.H. advised her. "Casanova didn't care where he made love, or with whom, just so long as she was a loving woman. As you can see, Ron, Adele has created a place to entertain Boston Brahmins and politicians, men and women fully clothed in the most expensive fashions who spend sexless evenings together discussing the problems of the world. It's not an environment that you can feel happy in naked, or even in your underwear. It's certainly not conducive to twitching bare-asses, probing penises, or pulsating coyntes."

On the third floor, he led them into the library, which was lined with books from ceiling to floor. "I escape here," he said, and he pointed to a black wrought-iron staircase. "That's the way to the roof. A stairway to the stars."

Marge and Sylvia, a giggling melange of bobbling breasts and undulating behinds, dropped their towels and ran ahead of H.H. and Ronald up the spiral steps.

When Ronald emerged on the roof of the building. he was standing in a triangular area created by a semi-circular bed that was elevated about a foot above the floor and was enclosed in a hexagonal glass bubble. Above them, a late evening half-moon and starry sky lighted the room. Ten feet below were the silhouettes of neighboring buildings. H.H.'s roof was high enough to ensure complete privacy. Around them was the sweeping panorama of the Charles River, Boston harbor, the city of

Boston, and the skyline of watchful buildings of insurance companies and banks, stolidly standing guard over the flickering lights and the evidences of humanity below them.

"Now we can really make believe." Sylvia had straddled one of the two flying horses that were on the curve of the bed. "Turn on the merry-go-round, Hy. I want to ride a cock horse to Banbury Cross."

Leading Ron across the two-foot-thick, pink-sheeted, half-moon mattress, jumping up and down to show him that it was soft enough to lie comfortably on but resilient enough to act as a trampoline, H.H. kicked a path through hundreds of pillows of all shapes and sizes. "The whole bed is twenty-four feet in diameter," he told him. "It took a construction crew to get it up here, and a lot of creative thinking to transform a merry-go-round into a bed."

"What's on the other side?" Ronald asked in awe. They had walked half-way across the bed and were leaning against a thickly padded middle section that was chin high. "You could sleep an army here."

"Not an army," H.H. laughed, "but maybe a platoon. The other side is just the same. You're leaning against a four-foot-high, six-foot-wide, twenty-foot-long runway. As you will discover, it's a stage. There are stairs on either end for exits and entrances. In the middle are the controls." H.H. flipped several switches. The merry-go-round turned slowly. The entire bubble was suffused with subdued lighting that pulsated in colors to the searching notes of a pianist exploring the keyboard and conveyed emotions beyond words.

"It's Beethoven's *Appassionata*" said Sylvia, who had been hanging upside-down like a circus rider on one of the flying horses that was slowly charging forward on its pipe. Sliding easily to the mattress, she said, "Come on, Mommy, we'll dance for our lovers, and then they can dance for us."

19

When Ronald came through the tunnel into the Los Angeles airport, M'mm was waiting for him. Momentarily hiding her astonishment at his new appearance, she hugged him and was happy to feel an unaccustomed surge of love and a distinct sexual need for him. But that was normal. She had been without sex for nearly five weeks. Patting his shiny head, she giggled, "Oh, Ron, you look adorable. But you should have left a sprig or two. Then you'd look like a newborn baby. Why did you do it? I liked my old surrey with his fringe on top."

As the words tumbled out of her mouth she felt him stiffen in her arms, and she knew that she wasn't reacting correctly.

"I needed a trim," he said coldly. "A fast-talking barber convinced me to give it a try." Ronald was feeling quite jittery. He didn't want M'mm probing into details of his trip, particularly the past few days in Boston. To make matters worse, and not intending to, he was silently comparing M'mm with Marge and Sylvia. Of course comparisons with Sylvia weren't a bit fair. Unlike Marge, M'mm wasn't old enough to be Sylvia's mother, but she almost was. Surprisingly, although Marge was seven years older than M'mm, in some way that he couldn't clearly define Marge was sexier than M'mm. It occurred to him that possibly with a different man, and as intent on seduction as he knew Marge had been, M'mm might be even more of a temptress than Marge was. The romantic illusion was almost impossible to maintain over the reality of a long marriage. H.H. might have said that the difference was "ownership," which cooled passion. On the other hand, giving up ownership of a spouse was an unexplored two-way street. Seeing M'mm in a new perspective after five weeks, Ronald suddenly realized that Marge and M'mm had one thing in common. Their scatter-brained reaction to life was, in actuality, a cover-up for a pragmatic efficiency. Thiemost probably wouldn't believe it — H.H. would — but the truth was that either Marge or M'mm, or both of them together, could probably run Byrdwhistle or W.I.N. as well as any man.

As they walked toward the parking lot, the memory of his barber's breasts brushing against his face as she sliced off his hair made it difficult for him to concentrate, especially since M'mm shrugged off his questions about what she had been doing — "Nothing, same old routine" — and kept harping on his head. "You really do look like a two-gun macho, Ron."

"The idea was to give me a more forceful image," he said irritably. "Not to make me look like either a sex maniac or an adorable baby. Anyway, it's a nuisance to shave so much skin. I'll probably let it grow back."

Actually, M'mm was more uneasy than Ronald. His shaved head seemed like a safer subject than Byrdwhistle. She was afraid that if she asked him too many questions about what happened in Boston, she might inadvertently reveal that she was more up to date about the future of Byrdwhistle than he was. She certainly didn't think it politic to tell him that two days ago — Tuesday afternoon, when he had telephoned from Boston — she not only was sitting in Ralph Thiemost's penthouse office but was wondering how she was going to wiggle out of a second invitation to spend a few hours in bed with her husband's boss. Nor would Ron be happy to know that if his wife didn't finally capitulate and let Ralph Thiemost acquire her, it might have disastrous consequences for Ronald, and, for that matter, herself.

Telling Ron that he must be tired from his flight and that she'd drive to Santa Monica, M'mm was wondering if she had burned all of her bridges behind her. Ralph's cool shrugging response, "Next week, when I've wrapped up the Byrdwhistle project, I'll give you one more chance," seemed to leave his trade-off open. The problem was that Ralph had never exactly specified that if she finally acquiesced it would be a one-time pound of flesh transaction or whether he expected that her pussy would be at his beck and call forever.

As she turned on to the freeway, M'mm was conscious that Ron seemed more than a little remote. Usually, after an extended trip, he told her directly, or implied with friendly squeezes on her behind, that he couldn't wait to get to bed with her. At other times — before they finally got out of the airport, and after they had achieved the limited privacy of their car — he had lifted up her dress, stared at her crotch, and even kissed her and tasted her. If she wasn't wearing panties — which she wasn't — he'd tell her that he wasn't sure he could wait until they had negotiated the freeway. He needed her "freeway" right now. But today Ronald was slumped in the seat beside her and had lapsed into moody silence.

"I think that your head is still back in Boston," she told him. "Let me know when you finally arrive in Los Angeles."

"It was a rough trip," Ronald mumbled, "and it's not wrapped up yet. I still have a lot of ends to tie together."

"Come on, stop being so secretive. Tell me about it," M'mm tried to be jovial. "You must have had some fun. Did you meet any interesting women in Chicago? Or Buffalo? What's Elmer Byrd like? And that man Youman? Did you have dinner with him? And their comptroller, Marge Slick? God, she sounds like a slippery one." It was on the tip of M'mm's tongue to ask him why he hadn't arrived at Byrdwhistle at two o'clock on Tuesday afternoon, a point that Ralph had made a great deal of after his phone conversation with Ron, but she decided to reserve that probe until later.

"You have this delerious idea that I live in the lap of luxury when I'm traveling." Ronald sounded grim even to himself. "But it's not true. I stay close to my hotel-room every evening. I get to bed early. I'm not the play-boy type. This was an exhausting trip. It still isn't finished. I have to put in detailed reports to Thiemost on three companies." Ronald knew that he was exaggerating the overworked-executive routine, but he wasn't ready to share Byrdwhistle with M'mm yet. Maybe never. It was over and done with, and he was glad of that. He was sure that if he told M'mm about Byrdwhistle, and Youman's Theory Z, she would have been very interested, even enthusiastic, as she was with all far-out socialistic ideas. He certainly didn't need to listen to M'mm telling him that H. H. Youman might be the Jesus Christ of capitalism, or some other such nonsense.

"Have you changed your mind about Byrdwhistle?"

Ronald stared at her curiously. "I don't remember telling you that I had made up my mind."

A little flustered, M'mm tried to save herself. "Sunday, when you telephoned, you didn't seem too happy about the company."

Ronald shrugged. "I wasn't then, and I'm not now."

M'mm knew that and a whole lot more, but she couldn't tell Ron. Not now. Maybe never.

Ralph's invitation to have lunch in his office had really been a command performance. When he had telephoned her on Monday and told her that after swimming with her he knew that she was an adventurous kind of person, she wondered what was coming next.

"I can't discuss this with you on the telephone, Meredith," Ralph said. He had a way of stating a premise that made the listener fearful of responding negatively. "But it affects Ron's future as well as yours. Come down tomorrow—about eleven-thirty—to my office. That will give us time to talk before lunch."

Assuming that Ralph's office would be a much safer environment than his home, and intimidated, in spite of herself, by his peremptory manner, she arrived only a few minutes late. She had visited Ron's office several times. He had an especially nice view of the freeways and wall-to-wall broadloom, plus two watercolors by unknown artists. She knew that it was a working office. Ron's desk was covered with file folders, and In and Out baskets, dictating equipment, and all the paraphernalia of a busy executive. It was a no-nonsense place.

By contrast, Thiemost's office, which Ron had never told her about, wasn't an office at all. It was a lion's lair. In the lobby of the fifty-two-story W.I.N. skyscraper an attendant directed her to a special elevator that opened on command from his console. The door closed, and she was whisked to Thiemost's heaven in solitary confinement. When she stepped out of the elevator, she was in a replica of a French Tudor palace drawing-room, complete with Oriental rugs, luxurious sofas, wing chairs, and a fieldstone fireplace with blazing logs that never burned. Other than a telephone and a sculpture of a nude man and woman copulating, there was nothing else on the chief executive officer's huge French Provincial desk.

Ralph greeted her and opened a bottle of champagne that was cooling on a wetbar in one corner of the room. M'mm recognized it as one of the French varieties that cost about twenty dollars a bottle. Ralph poured some into a long-stemmed glass, handed it to her, and directed her to a sofa. She noticed a video-tube sitting on a coffee table in front of it.

"I refuse to be inundated with paper," he told her. "Anyone who is in command of a company the size of W.I.N.—an eminence that I'm sure, if he plays his cards carefully, your husband will achieve—must know how to penetrate the information forest and get to the specific trees.

"With this video-display unit, and the most thorough computer programming of any company in the United States, I have instant access to every imaginable aspect of W.I.N.—including its top-echelon employees and their spouses."

Sitting beside Ralph on the sofa, she watched in fascinated horror as he typed out her name. A number instantly appeared on the screen.

"That's your code name, Meredith. We have a detailed file on approximately six thousand of our eighty-eight thousand employees, and their wives or husbands. Most of the rest are transients and don't count."

As he spoke, the tube came to life, and M'mm watched the sharp white letters swiftly forming into words and flashing out a running resume of her life, from birth through college. Then her marriage to Ronald Coldaxe and the birth of Tina and Mitchell, followed by a running critique of her activities over the past eighteen years. "Meredith Coldaxe, since graduation from Stanford, has been involved with more than twenty 'counterculture' or 'subversive' groups." The letters chattered to a stop at the bottom of the screen. It cleared momentarily, and then the running commentary started again at the top, impassively chomping out hundreds of details of her life that she had long forgotten.

Before it was finished, Ralph flipped off the switch. "If I wanted a complete printout, I could have it here in five minutes." He grinned at her. "Of course that's just an overview. There're lots of things we don't know about you."

"You mean whether I moved my bowels this morning?" M'mm's initial shock had turned to dull anger.

Ralph was amused, "I hope you're not constipated."

"I was," M'mm said nastily, "but now I'm about to have diarrhea."

"I knew that our employee surveys would get your ass, Meredith." Ralph had responded with his usual coolness. "But, like it or not, you are a corporation wife." He grinned at her. "We know from sad experience that many men who reach the level that Ron has in W.I.N. have a greater allegiance to their wives than they have to their jobs. Your husband has great potential. I think he's the kind of man who can fine-tune his business and family life, but I want to be certain that you aren't greasing the track he's jogging on."

Ralph turned on the video-tube again and tapped several words into the machine. "Just to show you that we aren't completely Gestapo-oriented, here is an up-to-the-minute run-down on our Samuelson electronics division. Among other things, they manufacture nuclear power plant equipment." He pointed to the screen, which was suddenly filled with financial information. "If you could comprehend these figures, Meredith, you'd realize that twelve percent of the electrical energy used in the United States is supplied by nuclear power plants. And you'd understand my concern with your activities. Samuelson is in financial trouble. It's geared to produce equipment for nuclear power plants that may never go on the line, all because of people like you. You may not realize it, M'mm, but you are encouraging a new breed of total ignoramuses and social dropouts. You are sowing the wind." His voice was clipped and cold, but then his expression changed and he was smiling benignly at her. He flipped off the tube once again. "And that's why I invited you here today." He patted M'mm's knee in a fatherly way, but there was a lecherous look in his eye. "You're a very attractive woman, Meredith, but you need a friend to counsel you. I'm sure that if we work together I can give you new perspectives on reality—and an opportunity to see the light. When you discover who really butters your bread, I'm sure you'll mend your ways."

Ralph's eyes were penetrating her skull, and M'mm wondered if he was going to literally reach into her brain and try to remold the squishy putty that she was sure was there.

"I'm offering you a job, Meredith," he said finally. "I'd like you to be our new director of public relations. You'd get $35,000 a year to start, plus a few perks, like the company car that Ron has really never needed."

M'mm gasped, and she knew that she was momentarily hypnotized. She was an open-mouthed country mouse being lured by the sophisticated big-city rat.

"You have the style and the flair," Ralph continued. "You can do a hell of a job for W.I.N., Meredith. Next year we're going to budget at least a million bucks for institutional advertising. We want to make the general public as conscious of W.I.N. as they are of I.B.M. You can start tomorrow. Your office will be on the floor just below. There's a private staircase connecting it with mine."

M'mm was spared from giving an immediate answer by a white-jacketed waiter wearing a black tie who arrived with their lunch. Ralph led her to a window alcove where a rectangular mahogany table was girded by six gold-studded leather Chippendale chairs. The table was set with white linen, Queen Anne silverware, and blue and orange Imari china, and with delicate crystal wine-glasses for various courses. The waiter opened a bottle of pinot chardonnay, and Ralph told him, "The lady will taste it." After her approval, the waiter served them vichysoisse, followed by a small salad, and then veal chops cordon bleu, with stuffed tomato, ratatouille, and sautéed snow peas. Tasting the food, M'mm knew that, somewhere, it had been prepared by a master chef.

When the waiter temporarily disappeared, Ralph beamed at her. "Isn't this nice? When you're working for W.I.N., we can have lunch together at least once a week." Then he noticed that M'mm looked rather hesitant.

"I assume that you have decided to accept."

"Really, I'm too stunned to think about it," M'mm smiled feebly at him. She really wanted to tell Ralph to go to hell. It was obvious that he would go to any length to take over Meredith Coldaxe. And she knew damned well that the job offer was a two-edged sword. In one fell swoop, he planned to shut her mouth and also have a complacent bed companion. Wondering what would happen when she told him she wasn't interested, she tried to be diplomatic. "I really appreciate your offer, Mr. Thiemost—Ralph—but I've never worked in the corporate world. Since I'm involved with several groups that your advisors evidently consider subversive, I really don't think I'd be an asset to the company."

"Don't worry about that," Ralph filled her glass with wine for the third time. "Working as a high-level W.I.N. executive, your friends will understand quickly that Meredith Coldaxe has seen the light—they'll realize that you have been converted to a new religion." Ralph chuckled. "I'm sure that Ron will be very pleased. There's nothing like a conversion to impress the doubters—and that includes me. I'll give you a few days to think about it. Tomorrow, Bob Haley is flying to Dubrovnik with me in the company plane. I want you to come with us. The trip will give you a better understanding of me. As director of public relations, you'll eventually be creating a new image for me as well as the company in general. I want you to understand how I have nurtured W.I.N. from the time it was just an electrical shop in my garage until it became a world empire." He smiled at her reassuringly, "We'll have a nice few days together on Thornton Byrd's yacht."

As he said the words, his telephone rang. Scowling at the interruption, Ralph left the table and answered it; then holding his hand over the mouthpiece he grinned at her. "It's your husband." She listened while he coldly accused Ron of "picking daisies with Marge Slick" and she tried to conceal her anxiety. The thought flickered grimly through her mind that, while she was being faithful, Ron—good old I-am-Jesus Coldaxe—was screwing with some sultry cunt.

When Ralph rejoined her at the table, she said, "I gather that Ron isn't too happy about Byrdwhistle. Will he be going to Dubrovnik with you?"

"Dammit, No! Not this trip. Ron has a lot of work to do on this end. By the time he gets back from Boston, Bob Haley and I will have hammered out a purchase agreement with Thornton Byrd. Have you made up your mind? Are you coming with me?"

M'mm tried to respond demurely, using an I-hope-you-understand-I-want-to-but-I-can't tone of voice. "Ron will be home Thursday. I haven't seen him for a month. I always meet him at the airport."

But Ralph wasn't listening to her subliminal message. "I'm sure Ron will survive another few days without you," he said. "I'll have my driver meet him at the airport. You can leave a message. Tell him that you'll be back by next Tuesday or Wednesday. We'll celebrate the acquisition of Byrdwhistle together."

Groping for an easy letdown, M'mm told him that she had read there had been an earthquake in Yugoslavia the day before. She had skimmed the story. It was in the back pages of the *Times*. Not that she had read it very carefully. Bringing it up was a delaying tactic. She was nervous about refusing both the job offer and the trip to Yugoslavia. Ralph Thiemost might try to show that Winners could be good losers, but M'mm felt that God should help the winner when Ralph was the loser.

"I know all about the earthquake." Ralph was scowling at her. "That's the reason I'm flying to Dubrovnik. Thornton Byrd's yacht is trapped by a landslide in the Gulf of Kotor. There was no damage, but it may be a month before he gets it back in the Adriatic. He was on his way to Sveti Stefan, which is south of the Gulf, to pick up some crappy stones." Ralph shook his head disgustedly. "The character who runs Byrdwhistle, a fellow named Youman, calls them Love Rocks. Presumably he's going to sell them for ten bucks apiece to the suckers who see them advertised in one of the Byrdwhistle catalogues this fall. It's obvious that Byrdwhistle needs a firmer hand on the wheel. Love Rocks! What the hell has a rock got to do with loving?" Ralph chuckled. "How do you screw a rock? I think the truth is that Youman's wife knows that he's either ready for the nuthouse or experiencing early senility. She telephoned me yesterday. Thornton refuses to leave his yacht to come home and close the deal with W.I.N. She's afraid that if we don't move fast, his son, Elmer, or this H. H. Youman will talk him out of it."

M'mm didn't know if she should dare bring it up, but she crossed her fingers and said, "I gather that Ron isn't very happy about the company. Don't you think you should talk with him first?"

Ralph frowned at her. "I'm afraid that your husband is lost in the forest on this one. He's so overwhelmed by the day-to-day management of Byrdwhistle, which we both think is ridiculous, that he has forgotten that we've faced this kind of situation before. Once we take over, we can clean out the old guard. We can give it a completely new top-level management. We can hone the operations. We've done it before. We can do it again. I have a very good feeling about Byrdwhistle."

They had finished their dessert melon. The waiter cleared their dishes. When he finally left with the loaded tray, Ralph stood up and took a key from his pocket.

"This turns off the world," he said smiling conspiratorially at her. He unlocked a draw in his desk and showed her a control board with five buttons. Pushing them one at a time, he told her: "This one turns off my telephone, this one locks the elevator and all the entrances to this office, this advises Meg Thompson, my secretary, not to disturb me—except for a red alert—that's the fifth button, and there are other red-alert buttons in various locations in this office."

M'mm knew that she should run for her life. The luncheon had arrived at its inevitable climax. "What's a red alert?" she asked.

"It's internal, not external." Ralph looked at her, amused. "I'm sixty-six. If I should have a heart attack, a doctor would be here in minutes."

"Do you have heart trouble?"

Ralph shook his head. "Not that I know of. It's just precautionary." He grinned at her and pushed the fourth button. "This one, which I push when I have the right companion, unlocks the door to Alladin's cave."

To M'mm's astonishment, the bookcase-lined wall at the far end of the office slowly slid a few feet to the left. In the distance, M'mm could see a king-sized bed on a raised platform. Ralph took her arm. "It's my private bedroom and bath. There's also a sauna. I'm sure you'll enjoy it. We can relax for an hour or two—maybe even lie in bed and talk. It's very good for one's digestion."

"Oh dear, what a shame. I am sorry, Ralph," M'mm said, "but today I'm having my own red alert." Later M'mm would wonder how she managed to think so fast. Along with a smile of sadness, and what she hoped seemed like real regret, with her fingers crossed that Ralph would react like Ron and not some guys she'd known years ago who would have said, "So what?" she took his hand and patted his cheek.

Ralph was baffled. "I don't understand you."

She smiled at him timidly. "I got my period this morning. The first day is awful. Right now I have terrible cramps." She kissed his cheek. "Maybe next week, when you get back. Maybe I'll have my head on straight." She tried not to run to the elevator and was relieved when Ralph, shrugging, pushed the second button in his desk drawer and the door opened. Inside, and sighing at her second escape, she shivered at his last words. "Be careful, Meredith, it's a long way down."

20

Ronald was in his last year at Stanford Business School when he met M'mm. Braless, wearing a teeshirt that revealed her nipples and full breasts, she was handing out circulars inviting everyone to a lecture by Gloria Steinem and exhorting a group of male listeners to come and learn about the new American woman, with whom they were going to have to spend their lives.

Intrigued by her body, if not her message, he pretended that he was an enthusiastic supporter of women's equality. She agreed to have dinner with him if he would go to the lecture with her afterwards. That night he was dimly aware that Meredith Meta Mathews wasn't the kind of woman he should ever marry. Graduates of Stanford or Harvard with M.B.A. degrees needed wives who were feminine reflections of themselves rather than individualists.

She told him that she was working for her master's in sociology, and she warned him that the last time she had dated a boy from the business school she had found him boring. Guys who could spend their lives pouring over balance sheets and profit-and-loss statements were much too one-dimensional. She tried to convince him that businessmen didn't really believe in the free market they were always talking about, which was the basic element of a capitalist system. She could prove that, in one industry after another, from coal-mining to meat-packing, from steel-making to automobile-manufacturing, despite the anti-trust laws, there was a very carefully structured kind of price-fixing going on all the time. In particular industries every company fixed prices by following the chosen price leader. Despite the anti-trust laws, most major products were manufactured by one or two companies, and they thus maintained a market monopoly. Not only that, M'mm insisted, businessmen supposedly hated big government, but they actually created it. The really big companies wouldn't survive at all if they weren't supported by hundreds of billions of dollars of military expenditures.

M'mm spent their second evening together trying to convince Ronald that the Vietnam war, or any war, was a capitalist, big government, fascist plot to maintain the illusion of prosperity and progress. Sociologists, she told him, were needed to try to solve the problems that businessmen created. And then, after they had made passionate love, she told him, "I like you, Ron, but you want to be rich, and I don't really give a damn about money. All I want is to live a simple life with a guy who is alive and cares about the important things."

Despite their endless disagreements over the "important things," they were both convinced — even obsessed with the idea — that they could bend the other to their saner point of view. But even when Ronald didn't succeed, M'mm had been just as affectionate in the sack. For the first time in his limited sexual experience, Ronald discovered a woman who coolly took the initiative in love-making. It not only struck him as strange but excited him, too. She would often mount him. Straddling him like a bareback horsewoman, with her knees flexed, she would sit erect on his stomach, her hair swinging on her head, her breasts swaying from side to side. Occasionally as she rode him she would bend over and brush their fullness across his face. And then, while his hands were gripping her ass, she'd laugh, and she'd tell him, "I'm going to ride you to sexual oblivion. The reason that I'm on top of you, Ronald Coldaxe, is because now you are in my command! Your sperm is rising in your balls! You're totally helpless! You're in my power! Oh, I do love you! You are transformed. You look so helpless. You look so agonized. You need me so much."

Then, giggling, she'd hold him on the edge of orgasm and scowl at him. "When we make love, I forget. Sometimes you really are a big prick — figuratively as well as literally!"

Now, sitting beside her as she drove to Santa Monica, it occurred to Ronald that those days when M'mm had been the aggressor in bed were long past. She insisted that it was his fault. He had finally subdued her. Whether that was true or not, he knew that tonight, if they made love, he would have to make the overtures. And the big question was, after two nights in a row with two different women, could he do it again with his wife? And if he could get it up, would there be enough sperm left to ejaculate? Jesus! If he didn't try, M'mm would be suspicious as hell. Right now he should be acting really horny. Presumably, he hadn't had sex for five weeks. But, if he got it up and couldn't come, then what?

The only possible way to get out of making love tonight was to egg M'mm on and precipitate one of their wrangling, shouting disagreements. Then, as she often told him, it was impossible for her to capitulate sexually. And she didn't care if her anger acted like an aphrodisiac on him, especially when she ended up sobbing and telling him, "I hate you — I love you! You prickish son of a bitch."

But, surprisingly, tonight M'mm wasn't contesting him. She seemed nearly as reticent as he was. Happily, she wasn't probing too much. Instead she was playing the role of a demure and loving wife who had missed her husband and was maybe even a little proud of him. Ron decided that in the future he'd take M'mm on his acquisition trips. They could be kind of second honeymoons that would keep them both out of trouble.

After he hugged Tina and Mitchell and talked with them for half an hour about their schoolwork, he yawned deliberately. "I've had a tiring day," he told them. "I'm still on Boston time, and it's way after my bedtime. See you in the morning, kids." He hoped that M'mm would get the message, and he could kiss her fondly and say good night to her, too. But M'mm wasn't listening. When he came out of the bathroom, she was lying naked on the cool white sheets. He knew that if she were planning to sleep, she would have already been curled up facing the right side of the bed. Instead she was lying very sensuously among the pillows, her legs open, smiling at him with a sexy, open-mouthed look. "Did you miss me?" she asked.

"You can say that again." Ronald was trying to dispel a vivid picture of Marge on her knees lapping three-hundred-dollar-a-bottle wine off his penis. It was merging with an equally erotic version of Sylvia, arching beneath him in the moonlight while the merry-go-round revolved to the sensual plucking of Indian music designed for Tantric meditation.

The thought must have helped, because when he stepped out of his underwear he was greatly relieved to discover that his penis was still ready for business. "Maybe Heman Hyman is right," he muttered. And then aghast, he realized that he had said H.H.'s name aloud. He quickly nuzzled M'mm's breasts.

"Who's Heman Hyman?" M'mm asked.

"Youman." Ronald said. "The man is really quite crazy."

"What's he right about?"

Ronald was quite sure that he shouldn't discuss H.H.'s theory about daily sex-making contributing to longevity. Not now, anyway. "Oh, Youman was intrigued with your answers to their damned questionnaire," he said. "He thinks you must be a very loving woman."

M'mm giggled. "He's right, I am. Try me!"

After nearly forty-five minutes of very attentive and delicate love-making, surprised that Ron was taking much longer than he usually took, M'mm was on the verge of asking him if he'd been practicing with someone else. He was not only more interested in her pleasure than he had been for a long time, he was deliciously insatiable. Should she be angry? While she had been desperately clinging to her marriage vows, maybe Ron had been picking more than daisies with Marge Slick. But wisely she filed the thought away for exploration at a less feverish moment.

Friday morning, an hour after he arrived in his office and sorted and disposed of five weeks' accumulation of interoffice directives, piled-up trade journals, and junk mail — a description that he knew would irritate H. H. Youman — Ronald telephoned Ralph Thiemost's office expecting to gain an immediate audience with him, if not an invitation to have lunch with him and Tom Hudnut.

"I'm sorry, Mr. Coldaxe," Meg Thompson told him, "but Mr. Thiemost won't be back until next Wednesday. He's on a top-secret mission. He left a message for you. You're to deliver your report on Byrdwhistle to me Monday night. Mr. Thiemost's driver will pick it up so that it can be waiting for him at his home on Tuesday afternoon when he returns."

Ronald put the phone down glumly. It was obvious that Thiemost was enamored with Byrdwhistle. Personally, he wanted to forget the damned company, and particularly Marge Slick and Sylvia. He couldn't escape the feeling that he had been subjected to a very thorough brainwashing.

The few days that he had been in their clutches had been equivalent to living through an earthquake during which his moral foundations and his entire business and management values had received a rude jolt. The scary thing was that at times he knew he had actually been playing the Byrd-whistle game himself, and enjoying it. But H.H.'s broad hints that some-day, after careful grooming, Ron might be his successor and that, despite his disagreement with Theory Z, he was the logical chief-cook-and-bottle-washer of the future, were totally ridiculous. Daily association with people like Marge and H.H. was dangerous. It was worse than a daily intake of booze. Your blood adapted to it and gradually you could take increasing amounts. Finally you ended up drinking the whole bottle and suffering the inevitable hangover.

But what frightened Ron more than anything was the realization that M'mm might be right. Perhaps his cold, analytical, carefully balanced approach to the business world and his career goals was only a facade. Somewhere in the deep recesses of his brain and body there actually was a fun-loving libertine, a true believer in the play-ethic, waiting to escape. He shuddered. He could see himself twenty years from now, tempted by the devils he hadn't resisted, an unshaven watery-eyed bum, shuffling along Skid Row, wearing a greasy felt hat with a couple of pints of Silver Satin in the sagging pockets of the soiled pants hanging from below his waist.

Keeping grim thoughts like that uppermost in his mind most of the weekend, he finished his report on Byrdwhistle late Tuesday afternoon. It was a labor of love. H.H. would be proud of him. He reduced Byrdwhistle and Theory Z to rubble. He proved conclusively that Byrdwhistle wasn't a business but a dissolute way of life. While he was doing it, he knew uneasily that he was exorcising his own devils. He was trying to obliterate the memory of Marge and Sylvia, and the uneasy realization that at the age of forty-seven he was still a very sexy, exuberant man. And, even when he was working or lying in bed at night with M'mm — trying to make up his mind whether he should tell her about the new Ronald Coldaxe and share with her the scariness of his vague and un-defined self-discoveries — he couldn't help grinning and remembering. . . .

Although it had been close to midnight when they had climbed the circular staircase onto H.H.'s merry-go-round and Ronald had marveled at the beauty of Marge's and Sylvia's naked behinds undulating and kiss-able just ahead of him, and although he would have been willing, and most certainly was ready to grab Sylvia and tumble with her on the pil-lows and make love with her — make sex? — none of them seemed to be in any hurry. The sex tease seemed to go on forever. Marge told him later that H.H. believed that the environment for mobile, mental maithuna was created whenever any man and woman were alone together. Even if they had never met before, even though they might not dare to penetrate — burst through — centuries of religious behavior-modification, they were compelled to play the primordial mating game. With words, gestures, and subtle but inflaming body motions, men and women were pro-grammed to express their separate but interlocking gender roles. Often, without realizing it, they were sex-making with no physical contact what-ever. And ultimately, if they were unashamed of their magnetism for each other and if they dared, they could share voluptuous, even lascivious, love-play for hours. Unlike the moment of orgasm, Marge told him, sex-making was an art that could be practiced with infinite variations.

Shored up with pillows on one side of the slowly revolving merry-go-round, Ronald and H.H. watched Marge and Sylvia dance naked for them in the moonlight. At times Marge seemed to be leading Sylvia in a pas de deux that evoked the blossoming of a flower, while Sylvia, without touching her mother, fluttered about her, a lovely bee dusting herself with pollen. As they danced on the stage above the circular bed, the music flowed from the *Appassionata* into the *Moonlight Sonata,* and it was apparent that Marge was reenacting first her impregnation and then her conception of Sylvia. As the music concluded, Marge sank to her knees and gave passionate birth to her child, and Sylvia, with a lovely smile, twirled and floated away from her, while Marge waited with outstretched arms until Sylvia returned and embraced her.

Then, in a gale of laughter, they jumped off the stage and Sylvia fell into Ronald's arms, and Marge into H.H.'s.

"Wasn't that nice?" Sylvia demanded. "When I was five or six, and Marge was my age, give or take a year, we danced my birth together."

"Have you ever danced his birth with Razi?" H.H. asked.

"Sure, and we'll do it together when he's an old man and I'm an old lady."

"How old is old?" Ronald asked.

Sylvia, flopped on her stomach and, leaning on one arm, was trailing her fingers over Ronald's penis.

"Old is when you can't get it up any more,' she laughed. "I don't know about you, Ron, but it won't happen to Hy. He'll reenact the story of the man who died but still had an erection. They couldn't close the coffin because his big bamboo was sticking too high in the air."

H.H. grinned. "Every day I'm becoming younger. Pretty soon you'll have to give birth to me, Marge."

Ron laughed. "That's a nice thought. How do you get younger?"

"Picasso had the answer," H.H. said. "When he was eighty-six, he asked Janet Flanner, who was 90: 'Do you still love the human race? Especially your best friends?' When she answered that she did, he replied: 'So do I. Isn't love the greatest refreshment in life?'"

Then H.H. jumped up and grabbed Ronald's hand. "Before we all refresh ourselves, I think we should entertain Marge and Sylvia." H.H. pulled Ron toward the stage, and Ron protested that he didn't know how to dance. The truth was that he was embarrassed by his penis, which he was sure was becoming permanently hard.

H.H. flipped the switch on the tape-recorder console. Familiar music of an old folk-song filled the bubble over the merry-go-round. Standing on the stage, and bowing to his enthusiastic female audience, he told them, "I'm going to sing a song about immortality. Ron will pantomime it." He laughed at Ronald's reluctance. "If you're ever going to be a Byrd-whistler, you have to dare to tackle anything."

H.H. bowed to the cheers from Marge and Sylvia, and said: "My song is:

> I was born about ten thousand years ago
> And I'll lick the guy who says it isn't so.

I'm going to sing a verse and then repeat it. When I sing it the second time, Ron will act it out. Okay, let's go.

> I was born about ten thousand years ago
> And there's nothing in this world that I don't know.
> I saw Peter, Paul, and Moses
> Playing ring around the roses
> And I'll lick the guy who says it isn't so."

Ronald wished he could have had a video-tape of himself being Peter, Paul, and Moses. He could have used it to prove to M'mm that he wasn't as hard-nosed a businessman as she thought. His charade was even better after H.H. sang the second and third verses.

> "I saw Satan when he looked the garden o'er.
> I saw Eve and Adam driven from the door.
> When the apple they were eating
> I was around the corner peeking.
> I can prove that I'm the guy who ate the core."

In response to Marge's and Sylvia's enthusiastic applause, H.H. sang verse after verse. Finally, gasping with laughter at Ron's valiant attempts to be the various characters, he concluded:

> "I saw Absalom a-hanging by the hair.
> When they built the wall of China, I was there.
> I saved King Solomon's life, and he offered me a wife.
> I said, 'Now you're talking business, have a chair!'"

Both H.H. and Ronald took exaggerated bows for their performance. Back on the bed, H.H. grinned at Marge: "Come on. Your ten-thousand-year-old friend hasn't made love today."

And Ronald was finally alone with Sylvia. Once again he was aware of the difference in their ages. Sylvia was thirty to his forty-seven. Seventeen years. Although she had had a child, she seemed as vulnerable as a child herself. Kissing him as he lay on his back, her face and mouth and eyes had a wonderful innocence. The merry-go-round was still slowly turning, but the music had changed once again and the lighting had turned softly golden, creating a new environment. "Do you like it?" Sylvia asked. "You're listening to Indian music. Nataraj." Sylvia was lying crosswise to him, her head on his belly. She held his penis in an angel grip, straight up, and in the flickering shadows was languidly exploring it with the tip of her tongue. She smiled at Ronald, who was propped against huge pillows and feeling very much like a bald Indian rajah.

"I could dance it for you," she said, "but the music is really for 'letting go' and enjoying the utter amazement of each other's flesh."

Still incapable of believing that a stranger, a woman who looked as chaste as a virgin, could surrender herself to him for the evening, with no conditions, and no future, Ronald told her: "We don't have to make love if you don't want to, Sylvia."

"But I am making love to you," Sylvia said. "Not because I have to, but because I want to. Surrender, Ron. Let the music and my flesh be you." She turned. Kneeling over him, she presented her buttocks and vulva to his mouth while she continued her admiration of his penis. Later, in a mutual loving that seemed to turn into an infinite voyage into space, still genitally joined, she whispered: "Why did you tell me that I didn't have to make love with you."

"Maybe because I don't believe that this is possible," Ronald sighed. "I live in the real world where people don't share their minds, let alone their bodies. Not unless there is something in it for them. I like you, Sylvia. You're very lovely. Very defenseless. I guess I can't understand why you'd like me this much."

Sylvia smiled dreamily at him. "Because I enjoy hung-up men. Because Marge insists that you're a potential Byrdwhistler. But you aren't being honest. You've really been thinking that I'm much too available. Women can't pursue. They must be pursued. Marge is the madam. Tonight she's pimping her daughter!"

Ronald laughed. "Well, maybe I was thinking that. I was wondering if you go to bed with every man you meet."

"If I did, would that devalue the flesh between my legs?" Sylvia sounded scornful. "How do you know, Ron? Maybe a hundred, two hundred men have had their pricks where yours is right now. That would turn you off, wouldn't it?"

"I think there's a Gresham's law about sex. You know. Too much bad money drives out the good."

"Agreed. But isn't this good sex?"

The music had stopped momentarily, and then it started again. This time with an ethereal solo on a harp. "Hy has switched us to *The Violet Flame* by Joel Andrews. The Violet Flame purifies you, transmutes you, so that you flow into the Seventh Ray."

Ronald didn't know what she meant, but Sylvia was gently pushing him and he rolled with her. Still joined, she said: "Women to a considerable extent look upon sexual intercourse with more dread than pleasure." She grinned at him. "I didn't say that. John Humphrey Noyes did, at Oneida a hundred years ago. He also said: 'They regard it as a stab at their life, rather than an act of joyful fellowship. But let the fellowship stand by itself and . . . amative sexual intercourse will have a place among the fine arts. Indeed, it will rank above music, painting, and sculpture, for it combines the charms and benefits of them all . . . and thus the refining effects of sexual love will be increased a thousandfold when each is married to all.'" On her elbows, riding his penis in exquisite slow motion, Sylvia's wide-open blue eyes searched his. "I'm only promiscuous with Byrdwhistlers," she told him. "When you go back to California, you'd better tell your wife. You got married three times on this trip—to me, to Marge, and to H. H. Youman."

INTERLUDE

The author acknowledges that a lot of slippage occurs between knowing a winning strategy and practicing it effectively. The slippage can produce a loser.

Eugene E. Jennings
Routes to the Executive Suite

21

Thirty-six hours after the earthquake in Yugoslavia, while Ronald was preparing his meticulous, don't-get-involved-with-Byrdwhistle report for Ralph Thiemost and the executive committee of W.I.N.—and while at the same time he was trying to repress memories of Marge and Sylvia, which were interrupting good communication with M'mm—Elmer Byrd finally reached H. H. Youman on the *Love Byrd*'s radio-telephone.

"Did you get the Love Rocks?" H.H. demanded without waiting to hear the reason for Elmer's call.

"No, we haven't got to Sveti Stefan yet. Actually, we're in the Gulf of Kotor."

H.H. tried to be patient. "What the hell are you doing in the Gulf of Kotor? Sveti Stefan is south of there."

"I know it." Elmer's voice was bubbling up and down as if he were speaking through a straw in a glass of water. "But Thorny had never seen it. None of us had. It's one of the seven wonders of the world. It goes twenty miles inland from the Adriatic. It's a jewel nestled between five-thousand-foot-high mountains. Marvy and I think it equals the fjords in Norway."

"Dammit, Elmer. You're not supposed to be sight-seeing. I thought you'd be back in Athens with the Love Rocks by this time. We'll be getting orders for them in less than six weeks. I predict we're going to sell at least a hundred thousand of them. I don't feel in the mood to refund customers over a million bucks, especially when there's more than nine hundred thousand dollars of pure profit.

H.H. could hear Elmer sigh. "You should be happy that we're all alive, Hy. We lived through a rough earthquake. It's a heavy scene here. Most of the towns around the bay, from Hercegnovi to Kotor, even Buda, Bar, and Ulincj, have been badly damaged. Thousands of people have no homes. They're living in olive groves."

"What about Sveti Stefan?"

"We don't know, and we can't get out of the Gulf to find out. We're trapped. The *Love Byrd* may be here for weeks. The day before yesterday, the whole damned area began to shake and tremble. It was black as your hat, and then the *Love Byrd* was nearly engulfed in the trough of a huge wave. We dragged anchor and went aground just north of Kotor."

Elmer explained that the ferry from Kamenari to Lepetane was no longer operating. Rumors were that the narrows at Kamenari, which was the only way out of the Gulf and back into the Adriatic, were filled with mud. They would have to be dredged before any ship the size of the *Love Byrd* could get through. "We contacted Nick and Maria in Athens. They didn't come with us," Elmer said. "Nick flew the Grumman into the airport at Tivat last night. It's only a few miles from here. He and Maria are waiting there for us."

Elmer told him that all the roads had huge cracks in them or were covered with boulders from landslides. The runway at Tivat was damaged but still usable. One of the reasons that Elmer called was to tell H.H. that he and Marvy were going to Tivat the next day, by horse and buggy if necessary. Elmer sounded elated. "I forgot to tell you, Marvy and I are in love. She's going to do *Rum Ho!*"

Then Marvy was on the phone. "You got your wish, H.H., and then some!" Marvy was jubilant. "After *Rum Ho!* I'm going to play John Noyes's wife in *Let Us Go, Brothers, Go!* Elmer has finished the book and most of the music. Then he's going to write *Miami*."

Elmer interrupted her. "Right now, we've got to get back and start rehearsals on *Rum Ho!* I hope you haven't forgotten, H.H. We open at the Colonial on November fifteenth."

"Dammit, Elmer, I was counting on you." H.H. was trying to be saintly—the only practical way to deal with Elmer. "Who in hell's going to get the Love Rocks?"

Elmer chuckled. "You, I guess. But God knows how. At this point we don't even know if Sveti Stefan is still there. All the Love Rocks in Yugoslavia may have sunk back into the sea. Anyway, the main reason I've been trying to reach you is to tell you that your wife is hell-bent to screw up your life. Adele is convinced that, when Thorny sells Byrdwhistle, Thiemost will retire you." Elmer chuckled, "Then you can put all your energies into sex-making with her."

"I can run Byrdwhistle and do that too," H.H. said. "But Adele has to stop wandering and keep her ass at home."

"She was on the telephone to Thiemost yesterday. She told him that he'd better move fast or you'd be here first and mesmerize Thorny. Thiemost is on his way. He's flying here with a purchase agreement ready for Thorny to sign."

"Damn! You tell Adele that when I get my hands on her I'm going to tan her behind. You've got to stay there, Elmer, until I arrive. Don't let Thorny sign anything! Tell him to stop doing loop-the-loops. Tell him to fly level before he flies up his own asshole."

"Thorny won't listen to me, H.H. Adele told him that if he doesn't sell Byrdwhistle you'll bankrupt him with your mad schemes. She's convinced him that he will be doing both of us a favor. We should get rid of petty business problems and enjoy life. We're senior citizens, past our prime. We're getting old."

"Bullshit!" H.H. exploded. "You may be old, Elmer, but I'm not! Now listen to me carefully. I'm talking to you like your old schoolteacher, Frances Hardworthy. You and Marvy get your asses in motion right now! Don't wait until tomorrow. You and Nick fly the Grumman to London—Heathrow. I'll meet you there tomorrow afternoon. You can fly back to Boston with Marvy by commercial. Nick and Maria will fly me back to Tivat." H.H. suddenly realized that Elmer was listening to him but not affirming. "Elmer, don't screw this up. Be there. I'll paste a gold star on your forehead when I see you."

Three hours later, after getting Fred's permission to go with him Marge Slick had to promise that she wouldn't eat meat if she wanted to be his love-ass on this trip. H.H. was sitting next to her on a British Overseas flight to London. He was in rare good humor. "If we fail," he told Marge, "we can at least say we tried. Wild-goose chases are stimulating to the mind."

"I'm still a little disappointed," Marge said. "I thought Ron was on our side. He must have gone back to Los Angeles and given Thiemost a big buildup on Byrdwhistle."

"Maybe not," H.H. said. "I have a feeling that Thiemost hasn't even talked with Coldaxe." He shrugged. "Adele may get her wish. I may be out of a job in a few weeks. In which case I will have to try a new strategy."

"What will that be?"

H.H. laughed. "Call it the King Gillette route." He was silent for a moment. "If that happens, I'll need your help. I've been thinking I should adopt a new ancestor."

Marge grinned. "Is he more fun than Morton?"

"Let's say that he's in the Morton tradition, but precedes him by four centuries." H.H. had an amused twinkle in his eyes. "Actually he goes a step beyond Elmer's concept. There's no doubt that he existed in the thirteenth century, and even hundreds of years before that. He was a marshalik, but it's a generic name, not specific. In the Talmud, two Jews explain: 'We are merrymakers and we try to cheer up the sorrowful. Whenever we see two men at odds, we seek to make peace between them.'"

"In addition to marshaliks," H.H. continued, "there were shpielmen and letzes, musicians and clowns. The marshaliks and the letzes might have been one and the same, but the marshaliks were the stage managers for the play, too. They ushered the actors on and off the stage with all kinds of flourishes and humorous and nasty asides to the audience. They could also take part in the play if they were in the mood. They commented on the actors' lines and the playwright's motives." H.H. laughed. "We have a great need for marshaliks today. They were the balloon puncturers."

Marge listened patiently until Hyman, the rebbe, finished his orientation. "So you found the name of some person who was a marshalik?"

H.H. shook his head. "While there were thousands of men who assumed the role, none of them managed a personal identity, at least that I know of. So I created one, and gave him a name. Who knows? Possibly he did exist." He patted Marge's knee, raised her skirt and admired her legs. "Lord, I'm feeling very creative this morning. I prefer to tell you his name when I'm inside you."

Marge shook her head determinedly. "No way. This is British Overseas, not the Byrdwhistle jet. I don't enjoy sex standing up in the toilet."

"Okay. My new ancestor is still in the womb, but when he's finally born I'm going to name him Moses Megillah Marshalik."

Marge burst out laughing. "Megillah? Ye Gods!"

"Why not? I'll be the leader, the stage director, the whole megillah."

"Oh, Hyman," Marge caught her breath, "will we call you Mo or Moses? No, I have a better idea. Like Coldaxe's wife, we can call you M'mm!"

They found Elmer and Marvy at Heathrow in a landing sector that serviced private planes. The Grumman was parked near an operations tower. Even as they approached, they could hear boisterous singing coming from inside the plane. Elmer and Marvy were sitting at the gold piano.

Elmer waved a glass half-filled with Glenlivet at them. "Pour yourself a drink of good scotch," he told them. It was obvious that both of them were happily slushed. "Marvy and I are going to get married. I'm writing a song about it." Elmer kissed Marvy and they both sang, "You are my best love. I never knew it could be like this. You are my last love." Elmer stopped and grinned at Marvy. "What rhymes with 'this'?"

"Bliss," Marvy grinned at Marge, who introduced herself. "Elmer told me all about you. I'm sorry but he can't go to bed with you any more, Marge, and I can't sleep with H.H. again."

"That's silly," H.H. said. "You and I never slept, Marvy. We played. Anyway, Marvy and Elmer, take my advice. Give each other a leash. You'll last longer."

Marvy frowned. "Dogs on leashes get all tangled up. They could even choke to death."

"Marvy is monogamous," Elmer laughed. "She thinks that people who sleep around get dissatisfied with each other. Then you have to spin the wheel of fortune again, and the next number is no better than the one you lost."

"Everyone needs more than one playmate," H.H. was grinning at them. "The truth is that when you have several bed-friends you never spin the wheel again. You learn that the grass isn't greener in other yards, that it's just a different variety."

"Adele wants you to settle down," Marvy said. "She wants you to play in your own yard, H.H. If you don't, you'd better watch out. She might divorce you and marry Ralph Thiemost."

H.H. laughed. "Don't worry. Adele and I don't believe in divorce. It's not creative. If you had listened to me, Elmer, you would never have gotten divorced twice."

Marvy frowned at him. "I don't think I like you, H.H. If Elmer were married, I wouldn't be here."

"We really haven't time for philosophy," H.H. said impatiently. "Marge and I have to get to Yugoslavia. But in a nutshell, why shouldn't a true Byrdwhistler have several wives or husbands? Our Love Rooms are really marriage rooms. Instead of divorcing, we have followed John Noyes's philosophy. Everyone at Byrdwhistle is married to everyone else. If everyone adopted this philosophy, we'd all be married to each other. We'd be our brothers' and sisters' keepers. Isn't that what Jesus told you that you should do, Marvy?"

While he was talking, Nick and Maria emerged from the flight deck. They hugged Marge. H.H. nodded at them, "Elmer and Marvy are floating in a romantic cloud." He grinned at Maria, "Before Elmer tells you that he can't get under the covers and play with you anymore, will you and Nick get our airport clearance? I want to land at Tivat so that we can get to the *Love Byrd* before dark."

Then he turned back to Marvy, "Elmer told me yesterday that you are going to play Harriet, John Noyes's wife, in *Let Us Go, Brothers, Go!* I suppose you know that Oneida was based on the loving association of all the men and women."

Marvy shrugged, "So I'm beginning to discover." Then she smiled, "Don't worry. Elmer and I will play it as it lays. But sometimes I wonder. Maybe both of you escaped from some cuckoo house together. Elmer told me that he's planning to adopt John Humphrey Noyes as an ancestor before you do."

"I really love the old bastard," Elmer said. "He was into women — mentally as well as physically. Listen to this. I've condensed Noyes's words and modernized the Oneida Community song. It will be our theme music."

Elmer played, and Marvy and he sang together: "We'll build a dome on our beautiful plantation./We'll have one home and family relation./Let Us Go, Brothers, Go!/Now love's sunshine has begun./All the spirits and flowers are blooming./We have the feeling that we are one./All our hearts it's perfuming./Let Us Go, Brothers, Go!"

Elmer was choking with happiness. He wiped the tears from his eyes. "Isn't that nice, Hy? Imagine the curtain opening on the dining room at Oneida. On stage are a hundred or more men and women, all dressed in nineteenth-century clothing. They're singing a love song to each other before dinner. Then gradually some of them, in couples, move front and center, and the audience listens as they propose an evening of sex-making to each other in a very courtly way."

"My God," Marge snorted, "it sounds more Utopian than Byrd-whistle."

H.H. put his arms around Elmer. "It's great. I love it. But first we've got to tranquilize Thorny. Then we've got to get *Rum Ho!* on the road. And then you have to marry Marvy. After that, we'll do *Let Us Go, Brothers, Go!*"

Elmer looked at him nervously, "I don't think that you're going to be very happy with me, Hy." He frowned and kept picking out consonant chords on the piano. "Thorny is a self-sufficient son of a bitch. I got sick of his pontificating. He told Marvy that I was an ungrateful son. He thinks that, without him, you and I are nothing. He honestly thinks we're trying to screw him. I got so mad at him I gave him back his fucking proxies. I told him to shove them up his ass. I even signed a proxy so that he could vote my shares of Byrdwhistle stock if he wanted to."

Marge gasped, and H.H. sighed, "Here comes Moses Marshalik."

"What do you mean?" Elmer asked.

H.H. shrugged, "Nothing. Private joke. Why in hell did you lose your temper? The only way to play the game is to keep laughing. Whether you win or not."

"You have to be practical, too." Elmer looked crestfallen. "Thiemost told Adele that if he bought Byrdwhistle he wasn't interested in getting involved with any Broadway musicals. That was carrying speculation too far. Adele is going to tell him that he has to eliminate Byrdwhistle's investment in *Rum Ho!*. It's only on the books for a couple of hundred thousand dollars at this point. For better or worse, *Rum Ho!* will be ours."

"Dammit, Elmer, it's ours now! Without Byrdwhistle, we won't have a dime to produce it."

Elmer beamed. "Sure we will. Adele is pretty smart. She told Thorny that he should demand cash as well as a stock swap. Thiemost agreed to one hundred and fifty million. Ten percent cash, the rest in W.I.N. stock. Together, you and I would get four and a half million. I'll merge my twenty percent with your ten percent. We'll be Broadway producers."

H.H. groaned. "Elmer. Byrdwhistle is worth three hundred million. One hundred and fifty million is only ten times earnings. Besides, we need the video division. I want to put *Rum Ho!* on video-discs. Ten million people can see it in their own homes. The hell with Broadway. I told you to cool it with your father. Thorny isn't going to live forever."

Elmer scowled at H.H. "It's really all your damned fault. You, Alexi Ivanowsky, and the Center for Ageless Humans convinced Thorny that he's going to live until he's a hundred. All he has to do is keep fucking." Elmer sighed, "By the time he's one hundred, I'll be eighty. I haven't got as much faith in sex-making for longevity as you have."

H.H. embraced Elmer as if he were a wayward son, and he grinned at Marvy. "It's up to you, Sweetie. Play with Elmer every morning and every night. Restore his faith!"

22

An hour later, enjoying mobile maithuna in one of the berths of the Grumman II, Marge was lying face down on H.H. She whispered in his ear, "Couldn't we keep right on flying around the world this way—joined?"

Although H.H.'s eyes were closed and he seemed to be sleeping, he smiled affirmation at her and she arched gently back and forth to keep him alive within her. They didn't climax until Maria startled them on the plane's intercom with the announcement that, due to a series of secondary earthquake tremors in Yugoslavia, the runways at Tivat were now closed. They would have to land at Dubrovnik.

Standing naked in the cockpit, followed by Marge, who stood behind him cupping his shrunken penis in her hand, H.H. told Nick to contact the control towers, both at Tivat and Dubrovnik, to find out at which airport the W.I.N. corporate jet had landed.

"Can you speak Serbian?" Nick demanded. "What you're asking is beyond ordinary pilot-to-airport information."

"Hell, no! Be persistent, Nick. If they don't speak English, try French or Spanish. I can speak those. Maria must know some Italian."

"Try Yiddish," Marge giggled. "H.H. and I need to practice in case he decides to become Moses Marshalik; or in case we have to fly right over Yugoslavia and land in Israel."

"Unfortunately, the sabras only speak Hebrew," H.H. laughed. "Otherwise, Marge, you could offer yourself as a permanent putz holder."

Twenty minutes later, after many garbled conversations, they determined that Thiemost's plane might have been trapped in the airport at Tivat.

"Maybe we're going to be on time," H.H. exulted. "Anyway, it's a Byrd opening. Pawn-King Bishop Four."

But, when they landed at Dubrovnik, Nick pointed to a Gulfstream jet standing near the operations office. A few minutes later they located Captain Jerry Saite, the pilot, who confirmed that it was Ralph Thiemost's plane.

"We got out of Tivat when the rumbling started again," Saite told him. "Just in time, I hear. Thiemost is probably pissed. He was on his way to Tivat. Now he has to drive back here from Hercegnovi, which is at least a one-hundred-and-fifty-kilometer drive." Saite asked if H.H. and Marge were friends of Thiemost. "I'm expecting to hear from him at any moment. I don't know whether he's planning to drive up tonight or wait until tomorrow."

A car-rental agent who spoke English was trying to convince H.H. that he couldn't possibly get to Kotor. The roads beyond Hercegnovi were impassable. "In some places around the Gulf they are washed out. It's very dangerous. Rocks are tumbling off the mountains."

"If Thiemost telephones you," H.H. said, responding to Saite, "tell him that he can't get through. Tell him to stay on the *Love Byrd* and that some friends of his from Byrdwhistle will be there before sundown."

The only car the agent had available was a two-seater Fiat.

H.H. told Marge that if she preferred she could wait on the plane with Nick and Maria. "I'll be back in a couple of days."

"I'm coming with you," Marge told him. "I'm not letting my sex-making machine go picking Love Rocks by himself. You might never come back."

Two hours later, they were a few miles from Hercegnovi. H.H. had consistently ignored Marge's screams at his wild driving. She was sure that he was going to fail to make a turn on the serpentine road over Mount Orjen and that they'd go tumbling into the Bay of Kotor nearly a mile below them. "Please, H.H.," Marge yelled for the tenth time, "if you were sitting where I am, you'd shit in your pants." She pointed to the rock-strewn road ahead. "Slow down! If we hit one of those, we'll go ass over tea kettle into the bay."

H.H. was only casually looking at the road. "I see the *Love Byrd*!" he said, and he pointed over the cliff. A toy ship was in the bay, and miles ahead of them and far below the *Love Byrd* was glistening in the late sunlight.

With tires shrieking, he rounded a sharp curve. H.H. slammed on the brakes. Swerving, he missed a four-passenger Renault that was hanging in a culvert on the left-hand side of the road. One wheel had disappeared, the other was slowly turning in the air. The car was blocking two-thirds of the narrow road.

A deeply tanned, white-haired woman with huge sunglasses and a willowy figure shrieked at them. "You damned fools, you nearly hit us!" Two men in shirtsleeves climbed out of the culvert. They had been trying to lever the car out of the ditch with the limbs of a tree. They stared at the Fiat angrily.

The woman pushed her sunglasses up onto the top of her head just as H.H. exploded with laughter. "My God, Marge, look who's here!" He pointed at the woman who was glowering at them.

"It's Adele," Marge gasped. She hadn't seen Adele Youman for nearly a year, but she had to admit that the flashing, brown-eyed woman was a very sexy looking sixty-six-year-old.

Adele watched open-mouthed as H.H. approached. She was balancing for a second between joy at seeing him and sudden fright at what he might do to her. She had hoped to avoid an encounter between Heman and Ralph Thiemost.

"Oh, Heman," she screamed in loving happiness as he grabbed her and swept her into his arms. "Oh, I'm so glad to see you!" But then she suddenly realized that he wasn't holding her in an affectionate embrace. His hand squeezing her behind wasn't a bit friendly. She tried to wiggle out of his grasp, "Let me down, mechant enfant." Adele's voice was husky, and she hoped she sounded beguiling.

"I'm going to let you down," H.H. yelled at her. He was holding her over the edge of a rocky precipice that plunged thousands of feet down the mountain. Ignoring her screams, he swung her back and forth over the edge. Below them the bay glittered in the sunlight. "You're a very naughty girl, Adele," H.H. told her. "I'm going to toss you into the sea."

Then he noticed the two men approaching him. They were carrying tree branches, and they were obviously ready to capture this raving maniac or beat him to death if they had to.

"Please stop this foolishness, Heman. Let me down! You might slip." Wailing, Adele had her arms around his neck. H.H. shook his head grimly.

"Tell your ape friend Thiemost," he said, "that he'd better fuck off or I'll toss him over the cliff after you." He nuzzled Adele's face. "I'm not kissing you because I'm happy with you," he said grimly, "It's just in memory of our years together." He increased the velocity of his swinging motion. "I'm kissing you goodbye. When they find your body, I'll plead justifiable homicide."

But by this time Adele had him in a head-lock. She grinned at him, "Let me down, Heman, before you rupture yourself."

"The hell I will," H.H. said. "If you don't let go of me, Cynara, I'll jump. With you in my arms. It'll be a lovers' leap!"

But Adele only laughed. "If I'm Cynara, I hope you've been faithful to me—in your fashion."

"Stop acting like an ass, Youman," Thiemost yelled. He was perspiring, but not getting too close to H.H. He was by no means sure that Youman, who seemed to be in good physical shape, might not attack him next. But Winners can't abdicate. He couldn't let Adele think that he wouldn't protect her from a maniac—even if he was her husband. "I'm warning you, if you don't put her down we'll have to hit you."

"You pot-bellied slug. This woman is my wife!" H.H.'s voice was belligerent. He was enjoying his caveman role. Still holding Adele, he let her slide to her feet. "I'm very upset with you," he told her. "You have a hell of a nerve to play financial footsies with this turd. He doesn't know it, but I'm sure that you have hoodwinked him, too."

"Stop this insanity, Heman," Adele said calmly. She was unable to get away from H.H., who was holding her with one hand over her crotch and one on her arm. "I didn't hoodwink Ralph, or you, or Thornton. You're all big boys." She acknowledged Marge for the first time. "Good to see you, Slicky. I'm glad that you're watching out for Heman. Please tell him to let me go."

"I'm not letting you go until I find out what in hell you and this crummy conglomerator have been up to." H.H. stared at Thiemost coldly. "Whatever it is, cancel it out right now."

"It's too late, Mr. Youman. The water is over the dam." The younger man, who spoke for the first time, introduced himself. "I'm Bob Haley. One of W.I.N.'s corporate lawyers."

"Bob's right," Thiemost thrust out his hand. "I'm Ralph Thiemost. Be a good loser and congratulate the winner."

H.H., who was at least two inches taller than Thiemost, stared at him disdainfully. Then he grinned, "You'd better make sure that you've won. The game isn't over yet. Okay, what have we lost, Adele?"

Adele smiled at him nervously, "I was on my way home to tell you, Heman. Ralph was going to drop me off in Boston."

"Tell me what?"

"You're free of Byrdwhistle. Thorny signed the purchase agreement last night. But don't worry, you'll have about fourteen million dollars in W.I.N. stock and a million and a half in cash."

"Mazel tov," H.H. said sourly.

Adele smiled at Marge, "Meet your new boss. This is Ralph Thiemost. Ralph, this is Marge Slick. She's vice president and controller of Byrdwhistle."

Thiemost nodded casually at Marge, "I'm sure you realize that I don't personally own Byrdwhistle, Ms. Slick. W.I.N. does, or it will as soon as our auditors have confirmed the assets and liabilities."

"Without H. H. Youman," Marge told him coolly, "I can assure you they are all liabilities. You'd better tear up your purchase agreement, Mr. Thiemost, and forget it."

H.H. grinned at her, "Marge is warning you that only a Byrdwhistler can run Byrdwhistle. We've been trying to hatch a successor for years." He walked back to the Fiat. "I'm sorry, but we haven't time to fart around here. Come on, Marge, we've got miles to go before we sleep."

Adele ran after him, pounding his back. "You're not going to leave us here, Heman," she sobbed. "Really, I don't know what's wrong with you. Instead of being so pissed, you should be happy. If Bob Haley hadn't skidded into the culvert, we might have gone over the other side of the road. We'd all be dead."

"It would have been poetic justice," H.H. shrugged. "You just killed your husband."

"Listen, Youman. Let's stop talking nonsense. We need your help." Thiemost pointed up the craggy mountain, which towered over them on the inside of the road. "We're in a very bad spot here. There may be loose boulders up there that could fall on us any moment. Help us get out of the ditch. We'll take Marge Slick. You and Adele can follow us back to Dubrovnik."

"Sorry, old man," H.H. unfastened Adele's hand from his arm. "But Marge and I aren't going to Dubrovnik. Not until I've seen Thornton Byrd. That purchase agreement isn't effective yet, and Thorny has some freight to pick up for me in Sveti Stefan."

"Oh, good Christ," Adele said disgustedly. "Not those damn Love Rocks. Heman, you don't have to worry about them anymore. They belong to Byrdwhistle. Ralph has a dozen freighters. He'll get someone to pick them up."

"Byrdwhistle doesn't own my Love Rocks," H.H. laughed. "The deal I made was cash on the barrelhead. Byrdwhistle hasn't paid for them yet. I'm going to buy them myself. I'll keep all one hundred thousand of them in our swimming pool. You can take them to bed with you one by one, Adele. If you sleep with them between your legs, it should double their value."

"All right, let's cut the shit," Thiemost snarled. "We've got to get our car out of this ditch."

"I'm sure Adele can help you," H.H. said. "She's been such a big help so far, she shouldn't quit now."

"I love you, Heman." Adele sobbed. "I did it for you. Please don't leave us." She was suddenly convinced that that was exactly what he was planning to do. As he walked away, she shouted at him, "Damn you. We could be here all night." She looked around apprehensively. "There are probably wild animals around here."

H.H. shrugged. "That shouldn't bother you, Adele. You've been playing with a wolf for the past few months. Besides, you convinced me. You're absolutely right that I shouldn't strain myself. I'm getting old and decrepit." Groaning, H.H. staggered like an old man. "Damned if I'm not getting arthritic already. It must have happened when I was lifting you and thinking about spending my life in a rocking chair in Portugal."

Adele was jumping up and down. "You're making me so nervous, Heman, I have to pee. Please take me back to the *Love Byrd* with you."

H.H. scratched his head. "I might be willing to do that, Adele, if only to toss you overboard when I got there. But, alas, I can't. The Fiat only has two seats. There's not even room enough to hold you on my lap. If I took you with me, I'd have to leave Marge with these wolves. I'm sure you wouldn't want to do that to her. Powerful men frighten her. She's not a wolf-woman like you."

"You're talking like a god-damned fool," Thiemost said angrily. "Your problem, Youman, is that you don't appreciate how lucky you are. Adele adores you. She's made it possible for you to live a longer and, hopefully, a saner life. If she were my wife, I'd be happy to retire with her."

H.H. told Marge to get into the car. "I'll tell you what I'll do, Thiemost. Write Adele into your purchase agreement. We'll swap her back and forth, six months at a time." He waved cheerily. "I can see a truck coming up the road. If they won't help you, then all you have to do is take off your pants. I'm sure this place is more challenging than Evora. Adele will take pictures of you, and you can jack the car out with your prick."

Before they disappeared around a curve, Marge watched Adele standing forlornly in the road, yelling "Dirty couchon!" at H.H.

"Do you really think we should leave her?" Marge asked. "She really loves you."

"I know it," H.H. shrugged. "I love her, too. But we didn't make it all these years by being syrupy about it." He laughed, "Adele and I are two egos who only mesh about half the time."

23

Two days later, before he talked with Ronald, who was patiently waiting for him in his outer office, Thiemost telephoned M'mm.

"Too bad you didn't come with us," he told her. "Late August in Yugoslavia is beautiful. We spent a couple of days on Thornton Byrd's yacht. You'd have been right at home. Every afternoon we swam bare-ass in the Gulf of Kotor. Unfortunately, I didn't have a regular bed companion."

M'mm could hear him laugh. "I presume that you are no longer on a red alert," he said. "Perhaps we can spend Friday afternoon together."

"Ron is back," M'mm hedged. "He's been working very hard on his Byrdwhistle report. I know that he's anxious to talk with you."

Thiemost laughed. "He's waiting for me right now. Did you tell him that I was meeting with Thornton Byrd and that I had invited you to come along?"

"I didn't think that was a good idea," M'mm said nervously.

"Ron's waiting for me right now in my outer office, but I'm sure he'll last a few minutes longer. The reason I called is that I want to resolve a few problems with you. If you'll meet me at noon on Friday in San Pedro, we can cruise out to Catalina. We'll be back before sundown."

M'mm made a face into the phone. Thiemost was the most persistent man she'd ever encountered. He had taken a lien on her pussy, and he wasn't giving up easily. But the game was approaching showdown. If she was ever going to bed with another man besides Ron, it most certainly wasn't going to be Ralph Thiemost. "Really, Mr. Thiemost, I've been hoping that you'd understand. Ron and I might disagree on a lot of things, but we're quite monogamous. At least, I am. I like you very much, but I've never played around." Damn, she knew she shouldn't have used the past tense. It opened up possibilities.

"Don't worry," he said coolly, "I'll tell Ron that I am inviting you. I want our new director of publicity to meet some of our local politicians. It will be useful for you to know which palms need greasing most." Thiemost paused, "I presume that you have discussed your new job with Ron."

"No, I haven't," M'mm hoped she sounded emphatic. "Really, Mr. Thiemost, I'm not at all interested."

There was dead silence on the phone, and then Thiemost's voice was icy. "Don't be hasty, Meredith. I wouldn't expect too much of you."

"That's the problem. Anything is too much. I'm sorry."

"I wouldn't carry the challenge too far, Meredith. I believe in winning."

"So do I, Mr. Thiemost."

"All right, Mrs. Coldaxe. I don't beat dead horses, but I've learned how to bury them pretty quickly." Meredith could hear his acrid laugh.

"You may discover that smart winners aren't afraid to whinny occasionally. If you change your mind, try a loud whinny!"

For the rest of the day, M'mm kept wondering what Ralph Thiemost could do to make her whinny, but she didn't find out until Ronald came home.

After Thiemost talked with M'mm, he buzzed Meg Thompson and told her he was ready to talk with Coldaxe.

"Good to see you, Ron," he told Ronald cordially when he walked in. But then his expression changed to incredulity and disbelief. "What the hell's the matter with you? Did you have a shock?"

Ronald looked at him blankly.

"Your hair. It's all gone. Did it fall out? You look a little rat-eaten."

"I shaved it off—then I decided to let it grow back," Ronald was anxious to get Thiemost onto the subject of Byrdwhistle. "Did you get my report on the trip? Big Byte looks good. Sunwarm has potential. But Byrdwhistle you can forget."

Ralph picked Ronald's thick report off his desk. Motioning Ronald to sit on one of the sofas, he said, "I'm afraid that all of this superficial crap about Theory Z and the Byrdwhistle play-ethic and the World Corporation trying to take over the government has obscured your usually clear vision, Ron. Believe me, this character Youman doesn't believe this shit. Not as much as you do. He's a con artist. It's all window dressing to increase employee productivity. We've got a lot of that participative management frosting going on in our subsidiaries. I don't discourage it. But Youman is a little senile. He's let it go too far. Never mind, you can straighten him out, Ron, it's not too late. The reality is that Byrdwhistle is a highly profitable business. We're going to clean it up and make it even more so."

Ronald's smile froze on his face. He was determined to be honest. Repeating big gobs of detail from his report, he tried to convince Thiemost that Byrdwhistle would be a big mistake. Even if Ralph wasn't listening to him, he at least wanted it on the record. He didn't say it, but he knew damned well that Thiemost wouldn't hesitate to shoot down any of the W.I.N. family, and even try to fasten his own mistakes on them.

"I'm sorry I have to disagree with you so strenuously," he told Thiemost, "but over the past six years, by hiring husband-and-wife teams and simultaneously indoctrinating them with his crazy management philosophy, Youman has made it impossible for anyone to run Byrdwhistle. It's not a business, it's a commune." Ronald almost said "family," but he suddenly realized that Ralph's idea of family was much more patriarchal than H. H. Youman's. "Not only that, Ralph, but I can assure you we wouldn't know for years what we had bought. Or what traps lay in wait for us. Untangling Byrdwhistle's finances could take a lifetime."

"I'm going to give it to you straight, Ron." Thiemost tossed Ronald's report on the floor and sat down in a wing-chair, which made Ronald, sitting on one of the soft sofas, feel low-down and inferior. "Bob Haley and I have just returned from Yugoslavia. We spent two days on Thornton Byrd's yacht. With the help of Youman's wife, who knows that her husband has become a little soft-headed in the past few years, we drew up a purchase agreement. Thornton Byrd, who has the proxies to vote Elmer's stock-holding, has signed it. Right now, our auditors, Horner and Cole, are making arrangements to verify the inventories and assets of the various divisions. Within a week, a crew of their men will be in Everett at Byrdwhistle headquarters. If everything works out, within three weeks we'll own ninety percent of Byrdwhistle. I'm sure Youman will toss in his ten percent, and then Byrdwhistle will become the newest member of the W.I.N. family."

Ronald listened with a sick feeling in his intestines. He hoped he wouldn't have to excuse himself to use Thiemost's toilet. "Jesus, Ralph! I can't believe this. You sent me to Byrdwhistle to do an investigative job for W.I.N. I can't believe it was necessary for you to move so fast. You're making a big mistake. If you'd take time to get a better fix on the company, I'm sure that you'd change your mind."

"*You're* making the god-damned mistake. You'd better wake up," Thiemost was suddenly raging. "I had to move fast, especially when I discovered that you were probably working for the enemy."

"That's god-damned ridiculous!" Ronald yelled, and immediately apologized. He knew that he shouldn't contest Thiemost so strenuously, but he couldn't help it. "I told you on the telephone that I thought Byrdwhistle was a bad dream—it's a nightmare."

"After talking with you last Tuesday, Adele called me from Yugoslavia." Thiemost stared coldly down at Ronald. "I got the distinct impression from her, which I later confirmed in person, that Youman told Elmer Byrd, 'Don't worry. The Coldaxe from California is getting melted down.'" Thiemost grinned at Ronald's gaping mouth. "When Thornton Byrd got the message, and he realized that Youman was trying to prevent him from selling the company, he was furious." Thiemost stared at Ronald, who was too dumbfounded to respond. "Inadvertently, you made Thorny stop vacillating. We were able to negotiate quite realistically."

"Good God!" Ronald sighed. "You're going to find that nothing about Byrdwhistle is realistic. I thought you had to have the approval of the Executive Committee. How much have you agreed to pay?"

Thiemost shrugged, "It's a minor acquisition for us. One hundred and thirty-five million in W.I.N. stock, ten percent in cash. The Executive Committee will approve it retroactively."

"You can still get out of it." Ronald felt a dull sense of catastrophe, with the worst yet to come. "I'm damned sure that the audit will reveal severe discrepancies between whatever valuation you set on the assets and liabilities. I suppose you know that World Corporation owns Byrd-whistle?" Ronald wanted to ask Ralph if he'd buy twenty shares in World for twenty bucks, but he didn't dare.

Thiemost was smiling, "Without realizing it, Youman set this up for us. The Byrdwhistle Foundation will advise World to swap its stock for W.I.N. stock—about eleven million shares at the current market price. The balance will be paid in cash to the Foundation, except for Elmer Byrd and Youman, who will get theirs direct. I agreed to toss in the *Love Byrd,* but W.I.N. will take over the Grumman II, a sailing yacht, a few Rolls Royces, and any other assets that turn up."

"But Youman still runs World Corporation. He can vote eleven million shares of W.I.N. stock."

Thiemost laughed, "It's a drop in the bucket to our one hundred and fifty million shares outstanding. If Youman wants a seat on the board of directors, we'll arrange it. Youman is no problem. World is just a half-assed mutual fund. It belongs to the stockholders—a million of them—not to Youman."

Thiemost's unswerving belief in himself, a superego who could do no wrong, was unnerving Ronald. He wondered vaguely, and not for the first time, whether he could ever become like Thiemost, the most cock-sure rooster in the W.I.N. barnyard. Being totally bald-headed hadn't steeled his nerves. Maybe it came with age. "I still think that Youman's wife, or somebody else, has led you astray," he said. "You should meet Youman."

"I have," Thiemost said grimly. "He's a total asshole. He left his wife and me and Bob Haley on the top of a mountain in Yugoslavia while he went looking for Love Rocks with that sexy cunt Marge Slick, who handles the money at Byrdwhistle. It was really incredible. Imagine abandoning fellow Americans in a fucking Communist country. Fortunately, while we were waiting, a road crew came along and got our Renault out of the ditch we had skidded into. I can tell you, Coldaxe, it was a harrowing experience. Never let it be said that I haven't nearly busted my ass for W.I.N., and done it more than once."

"You mean both H.H. and Marge are in Yugoslavia?" Ronald couldn't believe his ears. "See, it's just like I told you, Ralph. For God's sake, who runs the place when they're not on deck?"

Thiemost was smiling again, "I can assure you that they have more than one competent person. We dropped Adele off in Boston and took a taxi over to Everett."

"Did you get up to their offices?"

Thiemost shook his head and laughed. "To tell you the truth, Ron, I admire their security. They keep their competitors' spies out of the place. We'd be better off if we were tougher in some of our plants. A guy named

Bruce Maitland came down on the elevator. He talked with us. When Bob showed him the purchase agreement and Thornton Byrd's signature, he got the message. The old regime is going bye-bye. Before we left, Bruce was kissing ass with his new masters."

"But you didn't get upstairs to the offices?"

"Ron," Thiemost said almost patiently, "it doesn't matter. We could have seen them, but we were afraid that we'd get messed up getting back here. Boston was having a hurricane warning. I saw the building. It's ridiculous. I don't give a damn if it has a mile-long swimming pool or if everyone runs around ballicky. Bob and I agree that Byrdwhistle would be more efficient if we consolidated the whole damn operation under one roof—in Des Moines or in some other good central location."

"H. H. Youman will never agree to that."

"He won't have to agree, Ron. You're going to fire him!"

Ronald gasped. "Me? Jesus Christ, Ralph. I'm not an operations man. Even if I were, I sure as hell wouldn't want to run Byrdwhistle."

Thiemost chuckled. He leaned over and patted Ronald's knee. "You and I both know that you're in a dead-end here at W.I.N. From now on, with an occasional exception like Byrdwhistle, we're going to grow internally. We don't need a full-time vice president of acquisitions. This is a great opportunity for you. After you've been vice president of Byrdwhistle Division for a few years, you can move back to Los Angeles into our top-executive suite. You might even become vice president in charge of our specialty divisions. If you do a good job, Ron, and increase Byrdwhistle's earnings, the sky is the limit."

"They're making fifteen percent profit after taxes now," Ronald said gloomily. "It will take a genius to improve that."

Thiemost was aware that Ronald was staring at him with glazed eyes. "Look, Ron, here's the schedule. I'm hoping that you'll be back in Boston by Monday." Thiemost smiled, "I'm sure that Meredith will cooperate. She's a winner, too. She can tidy up any loose ends here in California for you. When you get back to Byrdwhistle, I want you to follow our auditors closely. You can get rid of Elmer Byrd immediately, and don't procrastinate on Youman. A new broom, you know. Hang onto that Slick woman. Milk her. Find out if she's adaptable. If she isn't, dump her." Thiemost stood up in a gesture of dismissal, "It's going to be a great experience for you, Ron, and I'm sure your wife will like Boston."

"She's a California girl," Ronald said morosely. "Meredith hates the cold weather. We'll have to sell our house."

"Of course you will. Meredith can handle that. Tell her to take her time and get the best price. You'll probably have a nice capital gain. W.I.N. will lend you enough money to get a house as good or better in Boston." Thiemost smiled, "Your wife is a fine woman, Ron. You tell

Meredith that if she wants to ship your furniture on, she can always bunk in with me in Beverly Hills."

"I'm afraid she's not going to be very happy about this."

"Ron, don't look so stunned," Thiemost patted his shoulder genially. "You and Meredith talk it over. W.I.N. won't hold it against you if you whinny in a crisis. Tell her I always say good winners aren't afraid to whinny."

M'mm was in tears when Ron told her.

"Ralph Thiemost is a malodorous, one-track, cunt-happy clod," she raved. She knew Ron wouldn't understand her outburst, but she couldn't help herself. She remembered a Japanese movie where the heroine, in the very last scene, cut off her lover's prick. That was too good for Ralph Thiemost. He needed to be tortured first.

Fortunately, Ronald didn't ask her how she knew Thiemost was cunt-happy. He was too immersed in his own problem. "I really don't want to move to Boston either," he said. He sounded so despondent that M'mm tried to cheer him up, and as usual she picked the wrong tack. "I've told you for the past fifteen years that you should go into business for yourself. Get a franchise or something. So we'll starve a little, but you won't have to put up with that asshole." She hugged Ron. "It would be worth a lot to me if you told him to take his god-damned jobs and shove them up his ass."

Ronald didn't notice the plural. "Oh, sure," he said, "Sunday you can help me look through ten thousand help-wanted ads in the *L.A. Times.* Everyone's looking for a vice president with an M.B.A. who is forty-seven and insists on a starting salary of eighty thousand a year. Ralph knows damned well that if I want to stay in the same financial ballpark I'll probably have to move anyway." Ronald sighed, "He doesn't sympathize with you either — the route up the corporate executive ladder is an understanding and mobile wife."

Or one who goes to bed with Ralph Thiemost, M'mm thought. All she had to do was whinny. As the thought popped into her mind, Ronald confirmed it. "There may be another way out," he said thoughtfully. "Just before I left his office, Ralph gave me his usual philosophy. Then he said something about whining." Ronald shrugged. "Probably he wanted to see if I'd moan and groan and not meet his challenge."

"What did he say?"

"He said good winners aren't afraid to whine."

"You mean whinny?"

"Yeah," Ronald grimaced. "Sounds as if I were a horse. If I win the race for him, he'll give me a big red apple."

They were in bed and had been arguing all evening about what Ronald should do. If he capitulated, he'd have to be on a plane to Boston Sunday night. Tina and Mitchell had been adamant. They were Californians. They didn't ever want to live on the East Coast. Tina had quickly resolved her problem, "I'm going to be at Southern Cal after Labor Day. You and Daddy can come and visit us on Dad's vacations." Mitch told them the hell with Boston. He was sick of school anyway. He'd rather quit and get a job or become a beach bum.

Although Ronald was compartmentalized enough, at least momentarily, to decide that he wanted to make love with M'mm again—he was nursing her tit as she sat propped against the pillows—M'mm wasn't concentrating on sex. She had made up her mind. The only thing to do was to tell Ronald the truth.

"I'm going to tell you what your knuckle-head boss meant by whinny," she told him angrily. "And when I do, Ronald Coldaxe, if you don't agree with me, and if you don't go up to his penthouse office tomorrow and tell him that you talked with me and I told him to go fuck a female monkey, because that's the only kind of female who'd want him, then I'll lose all faith in you. I won't be able to live in the same house with you, let alone sleep in the same bed.

Ronald, who had given up trying to excite M'mm through her nipples and had kissed his way down her belly to her crotch, was amazed that M'mm's thighs, which had been casually open, suddenly snapped tight. He looked at her bewildered. Instead of appreciating his engorged penis, or even giving it a taste with her tongue, M'mm continued her diatribe.

"I'm sick of the subject," he mumbled. "Let's talk about it later."

"Dammit, Ron. You've got to face reality. I can't screw with you until I've talked this out. You may have the title of vice president, but W.I.N. has twenty or more of those at headquarters. You're not in the executive suite. Thiemost gives you stock options, but they're not worth a hoot in hell. You can buy W.I.N. stock on the market at a better rate than your options. After eighteen years of W.I.N., all we have is about thirty thousand dollars in the bank, and this house. We're not rich. You've been deluded by the system. We're upper-income peasants. You're just one of the knights in King Thiemost's court. If there are any dragons to slaughter, you can bet your ass he won't do it. You or some of his so-called fairhaired boys will have to. I don't think we should let a blood-sucking creep like Ralph Thiemost ruin our lives."

Ronald sighed. "As usual, honey, you're not being realistic. It's not only us we have to think about. We've got two kids to put through college. And it's not only that. You may want to get a job and live in some shabby tenement while we struggle along earning only about half what I'm earning now—but I don't. If in the process I have to kiss ass, then I will. That's the way of the world." Ronald tried to kiss her, but M'mm indignantly averted her lips.

"I wonder," Ronald mused, "what Ralph meant by suggesting that I could whinny?"

"He didn't mean you, stupid. He meant me! If I agree to fuck with your boss once or twice a week until he gets weary of me, I'm sure he'll work it out so that you're still vice president and we stay right here in Los Angeles. He'll even give me a job so that I can publicize both his business acumen and his magnificent prick." M'mm told him in detail about her two encounters with Thiemost and about his job offer. She was disappointed when Ron didn't respond like an injured husband. He should want to murder a man who sullied his wife's honor and tried to cuckold him. He certainly wasn't emoting with the horror and disdain that she had expected.

"That sounds like good old Ralph," he said when she finished. "Right down the line." Then he made a mistake. He laughed, "I can't say that I blame him. Really, M'mm, this isn't the nineteenth century. You have to think of it as a compliment. Thiemost is really a skinflint when it comes to money. It's really an honor that he'd offer you thirty thousand dollars a year just to make sure he had a strange piece of ass now and then."

M'mm jumped out of bed. "You can just go fuck yourself, Ronald Coldaxe! Go to Boston! I hope you enjoy picking daisies with Marge Slick. I'm staying in Los Angeles, even if I have to suck your boss's cock to pay the rent!"

24

On their second afternoon aboard the *Love Byrd,* Marge was basking in the warm Yugoslavian sun. Lying naked on the retractable platform that folded out of the stern of the yacht, she could hear the yells of Pinky Fresser and Jack Sludge, who were directing the digging of a trench around the grounded prow. Midship and aft, the ship was in deep water. Pinky told Thornton it would be at least another day before the *Love Byrd* would be completely afloat. Even then, it would still be trapped in the Gulf of Kotor until the entrance into the Adriatic was dredged. Hundreds of curious men, women, and children, some naked, some in nondescript bathing suits, were in rowboats anchored around the ship or swimming in the warm water watching the "crazy Americans." Occasionally, an approving male waved his hand enthusiastically in praise of Marge's lush but trim nude body. But most Yugoslavians enjoyed human nudity casually, as an interesting fact of life.

Sitting beside her on the edge of the platform was Breskva, a young Montenegrin woman made homeless by the earthquake. She was naked to the waist and suckled a two-year-old at her milk-laden breast. It wasn't her child. Her husband and six-month-old baby had both been killed in the collapse of their home. But Breskva seemed fatalistic, happy at the simple relief for her swollen breasts.

In the water a few yards away, Kruska, another refugee whom Thornton had welcomed aboard the crowded ship, was frolicking with Thorny. Diving between his legs, she surfaced. Sputtering happily, she confirmed by gestures that Thorny had a big tool indeed. Thorny swam past Breskva, who leaned over him. Giggling, she proffered him her free tit. Laughing, Thorny took a quick suck. "Squirt me a cupful," he told her. "I'll try it later with brandy." Whether she understood him or not was questionable.

The Bay of Kotor sparkled serenely; a huge cup of nectar squeezed between hostile, granite mountains. Four days ago, a hellish inferno of molten rock, deep in the earth below, had poured into some subterranean crevices. The mountains sitting on top had shifted uneasily. Marge suspected that a Youman earthquake was still to come.

Opening his eyes as he floated by the platform, H.H. grinned at her and flexed his buttocks. His penis rose above the surface of the water, a large curly shrimp in a drooping black nest.

"A gesunt dir in yeder eyverl," Marge said. Before he drifted away she managed to flick the quiescent little fellow with her toe.

"You and your damned Yiddish," Thorny grumbled. "What the hell does that mean?"

H.H. laughed, "A health to all your body parts."

"Including your brains," Marge grinned at H.H. "But I'm fearful of those, too." She was more than a little irritated at Hyman's sudden complacency. The last couple of days he had given her the feeling that without Byrdwhistle he might take a tailspin into senility. "I don't understand why you've forgiven Thorny," she told him. "Just keep in mind, he's really a big, nasty prick."

"I haven't forgotten," H.H. replied as he floated by her without opening his eyes, "but today I'm looking forward to senility."

Thornton was scowling at both of them. "Just because I've known you since you were pissing in your diapers, and long before either of us knew the incredible Heman Hyman Youman—and there's no doubt that I saved you from a life of sin, Marge Slick—doesn't give you the privilege of familiarity. I'm your employer."

"Former employer," Marge said sarcastically. "Ralph Thiemost owns me now."

Thornton shrugged. "You'll never know how big a prick I am until its inside you." Laughing uproariously and ignoring Marge's "Thanks just the same," he sank below the surface of the water. Then he rose, blowing water out of his mouth like a leathery old whale. "H.H. should forgive me. I've saved his life. Sixty-two-year-old crocks like him are dropping dead every day. Killing themselves, all because of some fucking business."

Marge grimaced, "Not because of a business. Because of stockholders like you. Barnacles on the ship demanding their dividends."

H.H. continued to float with a faraway look in his eyes. Thornton yanked his toe. "You should be very happy, H.H. You don't have to work anymore. If you really believe all this crap you've been preaching about playing instead of working, you could spend the rest of your life with me—playing on the *Love Byrd*. If we survived another twenty years, we'd be world-famous. We'd have proved that a man can screw his way into longevity."

"That's all you care about," Marge told Thorny, sarcastically. "Male longevity achieved by osmosis—sucking the life out of young women. What about female longevity? What about the poor old ladies your age who still enjoy warm male bodies?"

"Women my age are impenetrable from disuse," Thornton laughed. "You're no spring chicken, Marge, but I'll cuddle with you anytime. And H.H. knows how I feel about Adele, his sexy old wife. It's the quality of loving that counts, not the age of your partner. Your husband can join us. Fred's too damned old to be working. One or the other of us will sleep with you every night until you're one hundred."

"By that time all three of you will be doing just that—sleeping! When I'm an old lady, I'll want a young man. I'm going to ask Alexi Ivanowsky what he's researching in that area. A young man who can get it up with her would certainly give an old woman a new lease on life."

H.H. swam up to the platform between Marge's legs. "I can do anything a young man can do," he said. Before she could escape, he encircled her waist and slid her behind forward on the slippery deck. Her legs were waving in the air. With his face in her stomach and her legs around his neck, he blew a noisy rat-a-tat-tat. He snuggled his face sensuously in her salty vulva, coming up for air finally to tell her how nice she tasted. Then he jumped up on the platform and sat beside her. Breskva and Kruska exploded with laughter and pointed at his fully blossomed penis. Several curious Yugoslavian women, swimming even closer to the ship, nodded their approval, and Thornton clapped enthusiastically.

"My God," Marge shook her head wonderingly at H.H. "Last night you were in mourning, telling me that you'd have to sell your merry-go-round and that the million and a half you'd get for Byrdwhistle stock, even with the couple of million you already have, wouldn't let you live in the style to which you and Adele were accustomed. You told me that without the Byrdwhistle income and fringe benefits you'd have to change your life-style and hoard your money and live like an old man. Why are you so happy today? What's changed your mind?"

H.H. pointed admiringly at his still flamboyant penis. "It's this bit of tail," he said. "What a marvelous thing it is!" He flopped back on the platform and spoke to the sky with closed eyes. A little grin flickered around his mouth. "Last night I was play-acting. It's a trick all retirees must acquire. I was playing the old man's role. Getting ready for my new part in the human comedy. But later, when we were sleeping north to south, and I had my head between your legs, I became more philosophic. I realized that Adele and Thorny only did what their karma forced them to do. Whether it will accomplish anything in the long run depends on my own inevitability. William James summed it up: 'When a superior intellect and a psychopathic temperament coalesce in the same individual, it creates the best possible conditions for effective genius.'" H.H. laughed at Marge's bewildered frown. "James concluded: 'Such men do not remain critics and understanders with their intellect, they *inflict* them, for better or worse, upon their companions or their age.'"

Listening to him, Thornton hoisted himself aboard the platform. "You're full of shit," he said. "Be honest, H.H. You really don't believe all that Theory Z crap. You know damned well that it isn't the reason that Byrdwhistle has made so much money. You're a latter-day Barnum, a con man selling daydreams to the public in exchange for their money. You've been successful because you listened to me. I told you that Sears & Roebuck made more money from their catalogue business with less headaches than their present managers will ever do with their flossy stores." Thornton patted H.H.'s shoulder. "You've done a good job. You pointed the only logical direction that the capitalistic distribution system can take. Moving goods by mail, direct from factories or mail-order warehouses, is the least expensive way for the seller. It saves the ultimate buyer billions of dollars by eliminating the middleman."

H.H. shrugged. "You're only partially right, Thorny. You and Adele only hear what you want to hear. I'm not an old-style Ralph Thiemost capitalist. He's a cultural lag. Like King Gillette, I know there's a better way. When the people of the world own their corporations, men and women will stop busting their asses to compete with each other. Instead of working, because they don't know what else to do with their lives, they'll learn how to play. Theory Z only touches the tip of the iceberg. Competition is a poisonous yeast that was interjected into the productive system to keep the social dough rising. We don't need it anymore. We can produce all the necessities and all the Byrdwhistle fantasies and luxuries with half the effort."

"Sometimes I'm sure that you're a damned Commie." Thornton was disgusted. "It's probably a damned good thing for Byrdwhistle that Ronald Coldaxe is going to take over and run the company."

Marge gasped. "Coldaxe? Jesus Christ! Who told you that?"

Thornton shrugged. "Thiemost told Adele that he was considering him, but he hasn't made up his mind yet. It depends on certain conditions back at their headquarters."

Marge shook H.H.'s arm. But instead of being angry, he seemed remotely amused. "Hyman, did you hear Thorny? That bastard Ronald Coldaxe is a double agent."

"Thorny told me yesterday," H.H. said coolly. "It doesn't matter. He's nothing but a pawn in the game. If Thiemost decides that Coldaxe is going to run Byrdwhistle, it will give us time to brainwash him. In the long run, Adele and Thorny have done us a favor. I've given it considerable thought in the past few days, Marge. Byrdwhistle is a coming event that casts its shadow before. It's an achievable Utopia. But nothing is ever accomplished in this world unless someone puts his shoulder to the wheel. I've decided I must become an utter utopianist. I have to stop marking time." H.H. grinned at Thornton. "My objective is the same, but you and Adele have forced me to play a different game."

"Adele and I agree on one thing." Thornton shook his head sadly, "You've been bitten by the immortality bug. Your whole life is geared to getting your statue in the park for the birds to shit on after you've gone."

H.H. smiled. "Agreed. But I'm a Zen Buddhist, too. The rain will wash me off. You see, I'm fully aware that there's only one immortality worth the effort. I am the archer with his arrow poised, but I'm not tense. I'm amused. All targets are relative." H.H. sat up and churned the water with his feet. "It really doesn't matter if I hit the bull's eye on a target I didn't aim at. It could be just as valid as the one I was originally trying to hit."

"What the hell are you talking about?" Thorny demanded.

"That there's more than one way to skin a cat."

"Jesus, why don't you just say what you mean?" Thorny patted H.H.'s shoulder. "You've got to learn how to relax. It's Buddhist to say to hell with it, too. If the *Love Byrd* hadn't gone aground, we wouldn't all be here enjoying this afternoon. The trouble with you, H.H., is that you've got a deity complex. You think the whole fucking world is your responsibility."

H.H. grinned. "Someone asked Buddha if he were God. Buddha responded: 'No, I'm awake.'"

"Jesus!" Marge was more than a little bewildered. "Translate, please."

"Life is a game. Playing it is the only way to live. Just so long as you understand that there are no winners or losers." H.H. was smiling into the horizon. "Look at my prick. It's gone back to sleep. It's like Goso's story of the cow's tail. A reddish yellow cow passes by a window. The head and the horns and the four legs go past. Why doesn't the tail go by, too?"

"Oh, my God," Marge sighed, "now we get koans. One hand clapping I'm afraid to ask the answer."

"It's quite simple. If the cow really passes by it will fall in a ditch. If it turns back it may be slaughtered. As Goso said: 'This little bit of tail — what a marvelous thing it is.'"

"That's damned gibberish," Thornton said grimly.

"Not really. It means that we must live between the relative and the absolute at the same time. If we learn how, we can enjoy life in several aspects at once. The seagull yawking at the clam, 'I love you so much that I'm going to eat you, and then you will be me,' is the same message as Basho's haiku. 'The Rose of Sharon/at the side of the road/was eaten by my horse.'"

Marge whacked her hand across H.H.'s bare midriff. "Damn you. The real Zen message is: 'If you meet Buddha by the road, kill him.'" She rolled against H.H. and tumbled them both into the water.

When they emerged sputtering, Thornton was watching them, amused. "I still can't figure out how you ever made so much money with Byrdwhistle, H.H. Half the time you're living in another world."

"Not really." H.H. was treading water with one hand on Marge's back and one nestling in her crotch, "I simply have learned how to be something and nothing at the same time."

That night, in one of the master bedrooms on the *Love Byrd,* idly sex-making with Marge, H.H. was still enjoying his Zen euphoria. "The key to the W.I.N.-Byrdwhistle situation is Basho's haiku," he told her. "'Fleas, lice/Horse pissing/Be my pillow.'"

Marge kissed his cheek. "You be my pillow. I still don't know what the hell you're talking about."

"Simply that none of us understands the more profound meanings of anything in this life. Take Ronald Coldaxe. You and I sensed that, despite his W.I.N. indoctrination and a lifetime of capitalist brainwashing that goes back to his Stanford Business School days, we might have rehabilitated him. We both thought he might make a good Theory Z manager."

He kissed Marge's cheek, which she had snuggled against his. "World Corporation has to move into full gear. It's the key to the future. Within the next twelve months, if everything goes right, World will acquire stock control of W.I.N., Inc. In the process, to get the freedom I need to operate and to give Adele the spanking she so richly deserves, I must assume a new identity. Hopefully, in the process, Ronald Coldaxe will be converted, and Ralph Thiemost will be dissolved."

Marge groaned, "For God's sake, Hyman, I'm beginning to think you've flipped. You've gone crazy at last." She arched her behind to stare into his face, and they came apart.

"Put me back inside you, Marge," H.H. said patiently, "I always think more creatively when I'm close to the womb."

Marge fussed around a moment and finally recaptured his dispossessed penis. "World Corporation can never acquire W.I.N. W.I.N. must have a net worth of at least a billion dollars."

H.H. smiled. "The best Zen observation of all is a corruption of Dr. Pangloss's famous rallying cry: 'Nothing is impossible, in this best of all possible worlds.' I've given the problem a good deal of thought. To accomplish my objectives I must first become two aspects of myself. I'm going to adopt my logical ancestor, Moses Megillah Marshalik. I'll have to play the role by ear and off the cuff. Simultaneously, Heman Hyman Youman is going to cash in his chips—at least to most observers. At the moment, and you are the first to know, he has contracted Alzheimer's disease."

"What in the world is that?"

"Senile dementia."

Marge gasped. "Hyman, don't challenge fate!"

"I'm not. I intend to act the part to the best of my thespian ability."

"If you're intending to act like a bumbling, doddering old idiot, you'll never get away with it. You're not that old."

H.H. let his face droop and put on a vacant expression, until Marge shivered and told him to cut it out. "According to Alexi Ivanowsky," he said, "close to two million Americans suffer from Alzheimer's disease. By the first quarter of the twenty-first century, it is expected that more than four million Americans will complete their lives as senile vegetables. Many of them will begin to deteriorate in their early sixties." H.H. grinned at her, "We haven't been contributing millions of dollars to the Center for Ageless Humans with no goals in sight. In and of itself, this sad phenomenon interests me. Among other things, I'd like to prove that regular sex-making is a preventive medicine for most diseases of old age."

"What the hell are you going to accomplish when you're spending all your time acting like a demented idiot?"

"Not all my time. My dementia will be Adele's spanking. Alexi will tell her that she precipitated it. Unfortunately, Adele has forgotten the primary love lesson."

"Please," Marge sighed, "stop talking in circles."

"I'm not. Adele is Adele. I am Adele. Adele is me. You are Marge. I am Marge. Marge is me." H.H. laughed. "But I am me, Adele is Adele, and you are you. Adele has to learn that she must let the traffic flow where it's bound to go and that it will only respond to subtle direction. You see, Marge, we're all aspects of the one Player. There's nothing else. We are his fantasies. He's playing the game with himself."

"Himself?" Marge said. "Why not herself?"

"Okay. But better still, an androgyne. A male-female Player trying to reunite him/herself, trying to do what we are playing at right now— being each other."

Later, when they could no longer achieve an immersion, H.H. told her, "Tomorrow is prelude. If Thorny is right, and our friend Ronald Coldaxe is coming back to Boston, we must prepare him. We'll use Thorny's video camera and make a tape for Ron. The day after tomorrow, Nick and Maria will fly you to London and you can deliver the tape to Adele. Hopefully, they'll watch it together."

"What about the annual Byrdwhistle vacation? We've got to be back in Portugal in ten days."

"Nick and Maria will fly back to Dubrovnik to get me. I'll meet you in Portugal. In the meantime, I've got to get my Love Rocks. They could be a very handy door-opener in suburbia."

25

Four days later—Sunday—the week before Labor Day, bewildered by what he was leaving behind and uneasy about what lay ahead, Ronald was on the eleven P.M. plane—the "red-eye flight"—from Los Angeles to Boston.

M'mm drove him to the airport but the conversation was perfunctory. "Ralph Thiemost may be able to maneuver *your* life and even sacrifice you like a pawn to save Queen W.I.N.," she told him, "but he can keep his lecherous hands off me. And don't bother to look for a new home for the Coldaxe family in some Boston suburb. I'm very happy where I am in Santa Monica. I'm not moving!"

M'mm knew that she sounded more determined and positive than she felt. Eventually, she'd have to deal with reality. Their marriage might not have blown on the rocks yet, but the winds of change were howling too close for comfort.

Ronald shrugged off her nonstop diatribe against Ralph Thiemost. She was right, he told her, Ralph was a slimy operator. There was no doubt about it, but the only way to succeed in business was to be an s.o.b. "If you don't want to move to Boston," he told her, "it's all right with me. Keep the house. Stay in L.A. Hopefully, Byrdwhistle isn't forever. Once I mesh the damned company into W.I.N.'s gears, I can hold Ralph to his promise. I will have done my duty in the foreign legion. Then I can come back to headquarters." When M'mm sobbed that he didn't seem to care what happened to their marriage, he tried to soothe her. "I can even fly back and forth once a month."

"That would cost more than five thousand dollars a year." M'mm's forehead puckered into a frown as she did the multiplication.

"I'll charge it to W.I.N. Flying pay in the line of duty."

But M'mm still felt insecure. "And who will you be sleeping with the rest of the month, Marge Slick?"

"That's ridiculous," Ron scowled at her and briefly prayed that God wouldn't strike him dead. "Marge is a married woman. Besides, I may have to fire her, too."

"You're doing just what Thiemost wants," M'mm said angrily. "You won't be gone a day before he telephones me and invites me to share my lonely ass with him."

Ronald smiled at her sourly. M'mm hadn't been to bed with him since his cool reaction to Thiemost's proposal to hire her. "Maybe you should have accepted his damn job. Our combined income would be more than one hundred grand. Together we could beat inflation."

Then he was sorry. M'mm had a murderous expression on her face. "Okay," he said, "I know you think I should go up to Thiemost's office and blow his brains out because he tried to seduce you. I can't do it, M'mm. Anyway, I think you're probably overreacting."

Ronald was about to elaborate—Ralph wasn't like H. H. Youman. He'd take bets that Ralph probably couldn't do it more than once a week. Being a letch was simply a role that confirmed his macho image. But Ronald wisely refrained from such an off-the-cuff observation. Instead, he had tried to be cheerful, "It's too late to whinny now." He grinned placatingly at M'mm.

"Damn you," M'mm said angrily. "If you thought it would help you to get on the next rung of the ladder, I think you'd really share me with Thiemost. You're really just like him, Ronald Coldaxe. You're a dirty rat. The reason you always carry a pocket calculator is to figure the odds. But I'm warning you, it's not programmed to fit your wife."

At the airport, M'mm didn't park their car. She drove up in front of the departing flight entrance and nodded grimly at him.

"Aren't you going to kiss me?" Ron asked pathetically.

M'mm suddenly grinned at him lovingly and for a moment Ronald was tempted to get a later flight. He needed a lot more than a kiss.

"Sure." M'mm pushed her face at him. "I love you, you asshole! But if you're talking with Thiemost on the telephone and he tells you that all is forgiven and to come home, you'll know the reason. He not only acquired Byrdwhistle without your help, but your wife, too!"

The plane landed at Logan at seven-thirty A.M. While Ronald had had more than enough coffee on board, he ordered another cup in the airport restaurant and was impatiently watching the clock before taking a taxi to Byrdwhistle. He wanted to while away at least a half-hour. He was sure that none of the damned Love Asses would arrive until eight-thirty, and he was more than a little befogged himself. During the past five hours, slouched in his seat—still not first class—he was not worrying about M'mm. He was convinced that at forty-five, she would have to capitulate and that it was unlikely she had a better choice. When the chips were down, she'd have to move to Boston. Ronald put these thoughts aside and nervously rehearsed trying to convince H. H. Youman and Marge Slick that the acquisition of Byrdwhistle wasn't his fault.

He assumed that H.H. had by now returned from Yugoslavia. At this point H.H. must be well aware of the purchase agreement that Thornton had signed, but it was unlikely that either he or Marge ever expected to see Ronald Coldaxe again. He had made it clear to them that running W.I.N. subsidiaries at the firing-line level wasn't his function. On the other hand, by this time both H.H. and Marge must certainly know that the auditors from Horner and Cole would be there that morning. They would be bright-eyed and ready to find every flaw in Byrdwhistle accounting. Ronald was sure that by this time H.H. would have called a Symp meeting and denounced him as a traitor. Ronald Coldaxe was a slimy Judas. Marge would never believe it when he told her that Thiemost had engineered the deal himself.

And quite practically, if Marge hated him she wouldn't be much help in a power transfer. In fact, she could screw him up at every turn. And she'd know the truth. He needed her desperately. Without her he'd never absorb the basics of Byrdwhistle. Worse, now that the Marge Slick chapter of his life was unexpectedly re-opened, he had an unreasonable yen to go to bed with her again. But that was impossible! H.H. might sleep with his controller, and Thiemost might try to seduce a vice president's wife, but they were utilizing royal prerogative. The message for lesser W.I.N. management was Periclean. Intimacy and leadership do not mix.

Leaving the problem of Marge aside for the moment, the number-one nut he had to crack was H.H. himself. While Ron prayed that the Horner and Cole audit might reveal some awe-inspiring liabilities that H.H. hadn't yet revealed, and thus negate the purchase agreement, he still couldn't pussyfoot around. He had to make H.H. face reality. Within a matter of weeks, Youman would no longer be the executive vice president and chief factotum of Byrdwhistle. Somehow he had to persuade H.H. that an orderly transfer of power was to his advantage. H.H. must try to be a good loser. He must understand that whether Ronald admired him or not—and Ronald wasn't sure that he did—there couldn't be two chefs in the kitchen. Ralph Thiemost certainly didn't believe in Theory Z management, or the play-ethic, except for himself. Like it or not, H.H. was excess financial baggage. His day in the sun was over. Even H.H. had indicated that he should be grooming a successor. Ronald couldn't help scowling at that thought. Whoever, up there or down below, was dealing the damn cards had slipped the Byrdwhistle joker to him. Like it or not, Ronald Coldaxe was going to have to play it.

When he stepped out of the taxi in front of Byrdwhistle, Ronald saw four men in business suits standing indecisively near the front door of the building. One of them, shaking his head disgustedly, approached him. "I'm Joe Markson from Horner and Cole. Do you work for Byrdwhistle?"

"Unfortunately," Ronald said. He told him that he was Coldaxe, the man in charge, direct from W.I.N. "What's the matter?"

"There's a sign on the door that says they're closed until the Tuesday after Labor Day for the 'Annual Byrdwhistle Playweek Vacation.' The damned place is locked up tight. There's no one inside."

Ronald stared angrily at the printed message. Underneath it was a warning. The building was protected by a total security system. Ronald couldn't believe that H.H. had retaliated so quickly. He obviously had done this to screw up the takeover. But, in a little over a week, how had he managed to arrange a total company vacation? Who answered the telephones? Who handled the customer complaints? How could the Byrdwhistle mail-orders be delayed for a week or longer? And where the hell were Marge and H.H.? Playing with the rest of the Byrdwhistlers?

He rang the brass bell, pushing it again and again, as the other men joined him and Markson. "The owners are neurotic about security," he told them. "But there must be a janitor or someone inside. We'll find a pay station and call."

"I've tried that already," one of the men said. "I called from a gas station around the corner. All you get is a telephone playback of the same message. 'Byrdwhistle is on vacation.'"

"This is damned inconvenient and costly," Markson frowned at Ronald, obviously holding him responsible. "Our headquarters in California scheduled this week for the Byrdwhistle audit. Not only here but in all divisions. Our time is valuable, Mr. Coldaxe. W.I.N. will have to pay whether we do our work or not."

"Your bosses can take that up with our chairman, Ralph Thiemost," Ronald said coldly. "I'm sure that you'll be compensated."

He told Markson that he would be in touch with him at his office before the day was over. He would try to locate H. H. Youman. If he was able to, there would be no reason why they couldn't come back tomorrow and proceed with the inventory. But an hour later, although heavily armed with dimes and quarters in a telephone booth, Ronald still hadn't located Marge or H.H.

No one answered the phone at Marge's apartment. The operator advised him that the number for the Youman townhouse at Louisburg Square was unlisted. Despite his urging, she refused to reveal it.

He located the Thomas Morton Commune in Merry Mount. Hale Brewster answered and recognized Ronald's name.

"You left your suit here," he laughed. "Shall I mail it to you or will you come and get it?"

Ronald told him to give it to the Salvation Army and asked where he could find Sylvia.

"Damned if I know," Hale said. "Think she's in Europe on a vacation. She'll be back after Labor Day."

Ronald banged the receiver down. Then he remembered that Elmer Byrd had an apartment on Lewis Wharf. The president of the damned company must be in town. A woman answered the phone. He heard her laugh and say, "Elmer, I think it's that man from W.I.N., Mr. Coldcock."

Then Elmer got on the phone. "Hello, Coldcock. Sorry I missed you a couple of weeks ago when you were in Boston. What can I do for you?"

"My name is *Coldaxe*. I'm back in Boston. I'm at the plant in Everett right now."

"Oh really, what for?"

"I assume that you know that my company is about to acquire Byrdwhistle."

"Sure do. Very happy for you."

"We're supposed to be doing an audit this week."

"Go right ahead. The place is yours."

Ronald stared into the phone impatiently. "Damn it, Mr. Byrd. I'm not getting through to you. There's nobody in the building. I can't get inside. They're all on vacation. Where the hell is H. H. Youman?"

There was a long silence and then a burst of laughter. "Well, that's a damned shame. H.H. must have forgotten to tell you. It's the Annual Byrdwhistle Playweek. H.H. is planning to eliminate Labor Day and substitute Playday. He has a campaign lined up. The idea is to eventually have a national Playday once a month and maybe later a Playweek. To tell you the truth, I've been so busy with rehearsals for my musical that I forgot all about it."

"Everyday is playday at Byrdwhistle," said Ronald, suddenly feeling like a man in a sinking lifeboat.

"Well, that's all in how you look at it," replied Elmer cheerfully.

"I presume that you must have keys to the place, Mr. Byrd. Will you please come over to Everett and open the doors?"

Elmer chuckled, "To tell you the truth, Coldcock, I don't know how. When the security system is turned on, the good Lord himself couldn't get in without H.H. or Marge, or someone else in the know."

Ronald wanted to ask what the hell Elmer did as president, but he knew that was hopeless. "Where can I get in touch with Youman?"

"I haven't the faintest idea," Elmer said. "Last time I saw him was more than a week ago in London." Elmer wasn't even sure where the Annual Byrdwhistle Vacation was being held. He knew that H.H. had been considering Portugal. But the season wasn't really over in Europe until after Labor Day, and right now there might not be enough apartments available in the Byrdwhistle complex. Of course, if Ronald couldn't postpone the audit, he could catch the evening TAP flight to Lisbon. All he had to do then was transfer to a flight to Faro. Maybe Hy would be there after all. Still, as Elmer remembered, the Byrds-on-the-Wing Division was financially involved in a resort in Martinique, and also in one in Bahia, in Lower California. The Byrdwhistlers might be vacationing in either place. Then Elmer had an inspiration. "I think Adele is back in Boston," he told Ronald. "Why don't you telephone her?"

He gave Ronald the unlisted phone number. To Ronald's surprise Adele was waiting to hear from him. "I've been trying to reach Ralph Thiemost for the past few days," she told him. "I didn't get him until this morning. You could have postponed your trip until next week. I'm sure Heman did this deliberately. He's peeved with me. But he could have canceled that silly Byrdwhistle vacation. You can't imagine what a project it is. They flew four hundred Byrdwhistlers and their more than three hundred kids—three planeloads full—to Faro. Oh dear, I hope they got them all there safely."

"Does Ralph Thiemost know about this?" Ronald demanded. He was suddenly apprehensive that Ralph might tell him that he had to fly to Portugal to get the keys to Byrdwhistle.

"I think so," Adele said. "Eventually, of course, someone from W.I.N. should look over the three highrise apartments that Byrdwhistle owns. They overlook the North Atlantic near Portamaio. That's about forty miles from the airport at Faro." She laughed. "I still don't know how they got all those people from Faro to Portamaio. They must have had twenty busloads."

"Why didn't you stop him?" Ronald demanded. "I'm sure Ralph Thiemost isn't going to be very happy about this."

"That's why he sent you to take over," Adele said. "When Heman makes up his mind to do something, he's a hard man to stop. Anyway, the last time I saw Heman, Ralph was with me."

Ronald was getting totally exasperated. He wanted to tell Adele that since she and Thiemost had arranged the Byrdwhistle deal together, and she was so damned buddy-buddy with him, maybe she should call him back and ask him what ought to be done. But Adele was chattering merrily on and finally answered his question before he asked it. When she found out that he was in a telephone booth in Everett, she insisted that he get a taxi and come to Louisburg Square immediately. "After all," she said merrily, "you're a Byrdwhistler now. Since the audit has to be delayed, you might as well enjoy a playweek yourself."

Adele told him she'd be happy to offer her services. Her grandchildren were staying with her for a week. Like him, they were visiting from California. Together, they could take in all the museums and she'd show them Boston, where American history really began. "Since Byrdwhistle is joining the W.I.N. family, the least I can do is offer you bed and board," she told him. "We even have a merry-go-round. You can sleep on it with the children if you wish. Personally, it makes me dizzy."

Ronald's sudden vivid memory of his night on the merry-go-round made him shiver. But Adele prevented his attempted refusal by suddenly gasping, "Oh dear, Mr. Coldballs, I nearly forgot. Last Thursday, Chuck Gill, a man who works at Byrdwhistle, dropped off a video-cassette tape for you. Heman must have made it on the *Love Byrd*. Marge Slick brought it back from Yugoslavia. Mr. Gill said it has an important message for you. We can watch it together. Oh dear, I hope it isn't pornographic. Thorny was always trying to make video-tapes with me, and you never can tell what Heman might do."

26

Adele wasn't too sure that she was winning the battle of Heman's retirement. She knew that the only way to handle her mulish husband was to be as determined as he was, and she was only a little peeved with him for abandoning her on a mountaintop in Yugoslavia. That kind of ferocious silliness, which was often misjudged by their friends as marital mayhem, had been typical of their marriage. She knew that Heman enjoyed women who challenged him, or he would never have stayed married to her for thirty years. While there wasn't much they had ever agreed on, they respected each other's freedom to argue and disagree. Not that Adele had tried very hard to blend her ideas on female equality with what she believed was Heman's masculine need for power. Actually, over the years, she had often tried wooing Heman with abjection. Crouching at his knees, she would whimper, "I'm bad, Heman, but I love you. Strip me. Tie me to the bedposts. Whip me. Fuck me. I adore you." And of course she knew, even though once or twice he had attempted it, that he would end up laughing so hard the tension would vanish — but not his erection.

In a world where the average monogamous relationship didn't last more than seven years, their marriage was a monument to mental and sexual longevity. Heman loved her and she loved him. But right now she had to be patient with him while he played out the role of the big bad kid. She was sure that he wasn't furious with her because she had slept with Ralph Thiemost — and big-daddy Thorny. Heman knew that going to bed with Thorny had satisfied her father need for many years, and she hoped he realized that she most certainly hadn't been swept off her feet by Ralph Thiemost. Sex-making with Ralph had been both pragmatic — how else could she have led him down the Byrdwhistle path? — and a matter of research for her book. As an artist, she knew it was really impossible to judge your own creation with any amount of objectivity. But whether

Heman realized it or not, selling Byrdwhistle was not only a smart thing to do but, according to Dick Counselman of Marpeat, Young and Codbrand, if she brought it off it would be a kind of miracle—like selling a commune to General Motors.

Heman would have to agree that sex-making, with a laughing prelude, led to a joyous ludamus followed by an intimate postlude. Only by being naked together could two human beings completely expose their real selves to each other. And they had learned over the years how to enjoy intimacy, both sexual and mental, beyond the bonds of monogamy. So Heman really shouldn't be angry. Her little foray with Thiemost hadn't been very satisfying, in bed or out. She was sure that what really spooked Heman was that she had tried to play the male power-game. She couldn't help grinning at the thought. How to be a mediator between two gladiators was one chapter in her book, *The Ultimate Aphrodisiac*.

Adele was plopping a volleyball back and forth in the swimming pool with Jasmine and Eric, two of her five grandchildren, who she hadn't seen for six months—the other three lived in upstate New York and were more frequent visitors. Her thoughts were interrupted by the door chimes, which Heman had designed to play a few notes of Beethoven's Chorale. It must be Ronald Coldaxe. At the moment there was no maid. Heman had dismissed Anna when Adele left on her two-month junket to Paris, which had terminated in Yugoslavia.

Should she answer the door naked? By this time, Ralph's vice president must be accustomed to the Youman kind of informality. She had gathered, in her conversation with Ralph Thiemost, that Ronald was a "comer" in the W.I.N. organization. Ralph had told her that, although Ronald was prematurely bald, he had a bearing and manner that some women found compelling. Unfortunately, according to Thiemost, Ronald was rather puritanical and certainly not a risk-taker.

Enjoying a giddy feeling brought on by greeting a strange man naked, Adele pattered barefoot across the tiles to the front door. She was certain that Heman would agree that "Faire ce que vouldras" didn't apply only to his damned Byrdwhistle.

Momentarily stunned, Ronald gaped at her full breasts gently swinging on her tall, almost skinny body. He tried not to stare at the triangle of wet curly black pubic hairs that contrasted with her angel-white feather-cut coiffure. Did she dye her head or her vulva, or both? It was a question he didn't dare ask. But when Adele greeted him with "You must be Mr. Coldballs," he was tempted to assure her that hot would have been a more accurate adjective.

"I'm Ronald Coldaxe." He stood uneasily inside the door. "You must be Mrs. Youman. I hope that I'm not interrupting anything."

"Not at all," Adele was enjoying his confusion. "I was playing in the pool with my grandchildren."

He followed her bobbing behind into the familiar first floor of the Youman townhouse, and he wondered if H.H. had told Adele that less than two weeks ago he had entertained Ronald Coldaxe in the same room. "I really don't want to inconvenience you," he said. "If you would give me the video-tape that H.H. made, I'm sure that I can find someplace to play it back."

"I haven't watched it myself, Mr. Coldaxe," Adele said. "If you don't mind I would really like to hear what Heman has to tell you. He's so impulsive. And naturally I'd want to correct any false impressions or doubts that he might have given." Adele laughed. "Why don't you slip out of your business suit. Relax with us. There's nothing you can do about Byrdwhistle until after Labor Day."

"I think he's afraid to get undressed," said the pert little girl who Adele introduced as Jasmine as she climbed out of the pool. Her entire seven-year-old naked body surveyed him disdainfully.

From the pool, her brother agreed, "Give him a bathing suit, Delly. He's a prude dude."

Adele grinned. "Eric doesn't even know what that means."

"Sure I do," Eric yelled. "Grampy Heman told me. A prude dude is a stick in the mood."

"Mud not mood," Jasmine said.

Ronald knew these were the kind of children who needed a slap on their ass, but he had no choice. If he wanted to see H.H.'s video-cassette he was going to have to play Adele's game and placate her exasperating grandchildren. She was obviously as unpredictable and devious as her husband. Undressing in the room next to the pool, Ronald tried to shut out the memories of Marge and Sylvia in this very shower with him and H.H. just ten days ago. Before he took off his watch, Ronald noted the time. It was one P.M. Somehow he must escape by six and get to the Ritz. After his worrisome, sleepless night on the plane, he felt like a walking corpse.

Then, as he tried to amble casually back to the pool, he was shocked to see that Adele was aiming a camera at him. Instinctively, his hands covered his penis. "You're acting very silly, Ronald Coldaxe," Adele said. "You look like September Morn. I hope you wouldn't mind if I took your picture."

Ronald's penis did. Damned if the blood wasn't surging into it, creating happy readiness. Adele's camera was still clicking as he dove into the pool, and he heard Eric yelling, "Mr. Coldaxe has a bigger one than Daddy."

When he surfaced, Adele's brown eyes were drowning him. "Thanks for the compliment." She grinned at his water chastened penis. "I'm writing a book on powerful environments and powerful men, but I never got such an instant response before."

Adele told him that she hoped he would let her take a few more pictures. "Unlike most women," she said, "I'm very honest. I enjoy the different grace and lithesomeness of the male body." She granted that he
had a little boych but that he wasn't really paunchy—not like his boss,
Ralph Thiemost. Anyway, Adele said, she was delighted that he was
there because she was all at sixes and sevens, probably because of Byrdwhistle and Heman's dumb reaction to what she had done. She hoped
that he would relax. Fate had tossed them a few days. He was a stranger
in town and, unless he had something else to do until after Labor Day,
they might as well do what all good Byrdwhistlers were doing and play
together.

So saying, to the delight of Jasmine and Eric she returned the water-
ball so fast that it bounced off Ronald's head with a smack. Ronald stared
at her, dazed for a moment. Laughing, she swam to him. She slid against
him in the water and gave him a flitting caress. "Let Mommy kiss it and
make it better," she laughed. "If Heman were here, he'd tell you to watch
out. I'm a female dybbuk." She shrugged, "Of course that's not true. I
never put a noose around any man's neck." Then she had to explain to
Ronald that a dybbuk was a Jewish monkey on your back. "Only I'm not
Jewish," she grinned, "except by injection. If you haven't discovered what
that means, Ron," she said, lifting herself easily to the edge of the pool and
giving Ronald a nice view of her vulva, "then you have a lot to learn about
Heman Hyman's and Alexi Ivanowsky's theories of longevity."

There was one happy thing about being with Adele. There were no
embarrassing silences. At a lunch of bagels and peanut butter and salmon,
which she quickly tossed together, Ronald was captivated by her almost
embarrassing defenselessness, until it suddenly occurred to him that Adele,
with her limpid, questioning brown eyes and her husky French accent, was
milking him. By giving him confidences, she was getting many more in
return.

Later they went to dinner at a restaurant in the Fanueil Hall Market.
Ronald felt like a young father with his two children, forgetting that Adele
had admitted to being sixty-six and old enough to be his mother. In less
than four hours, he had told her more about his career goals than he had
ever revealed to M'mm, and he told her altogether too much about the ups
and downs of his sexual relationship with M'mm. He was damned near on
the verge of telling her about Marge, but he pulled up short and changed
the subject, or took a carom shot at it, anyway.

"H.H. really didn't tell me too much about the Center for Ageless
Humans," he said. He nodded at the children, who were eating their dinner
and ignoring them. "Perhaps we should talk about it later."

Adele laughed, "Later in bed—that would be nice." Ronald choked on
his wine and was certain that he was blushing. "Right now," Adele said, "I
can scratch the surface for you. Fortunately, Byrdwhistle doesn't own the

center, but as you may know it has been donating heavily to it for many years. Both Alexi and Heman have a great many theories about longevity. One of them, which appeals to Heman, has its roots in ancient China, where the proper conduct of one's life was of highest priority. Sex was looked upon as the yang and yin brought down to the personal level. If you were male and followed the rules, it was like preventive medicine. You'd not only have male heirs but you could increase your longevity and resistance to disease. Chinese men who understood this learned how to have intercourse with nine women at the same time, and they could bring all nine of them to orgasm without ejaculating until they were ready to impregnate them." Adele smiled at Ronald's concentration. "The Chinese males were very good to their wives. They enjoyed cunnilingus, but never let their wives commit fellatio. Part of the theory was that the retention of semen increased male longevity. The *Chou Li* records of sexual rites in the Chou dynasty describe the imperial nightlife. On successive nights, besides sleeping with the Empress, the Emperor spent the evening penetrating the vaginas of eighty-one attendant nymphs and twenty-seven beauties, all in groups of nine. This was the second way that he increased his longevity. He absorbed the female essence — the yin — which entered his body through his penis. This was called "drinking at the Jade fountain" and ensured both male heirs and longevity."

"I don't understand what you're talking about," Jasmine interrupted her.

"Neither does Ronald." Adele smirked at him, "But I'm sure that, like all males, he wants to live to a ripe old age in full possession of his powers. Since women live an average of eight years longer than men do, it obviously makes sense to absorb as much of their essence as possible." She giggled at Ronald's bewildered head-shaking. "Whether it works or not, Ronald, you have to admit it's better exercise for the male appendage than jogging."

Back in the townhouse, still not having seen the video cassette that H.H. had sent to him, and feeling so mentally exhausted that he was sure that he'd fall asleep even in the arms of Cleopatra, Ronald finally was badgered into climbing up to the merry-go-round with Jasmine and Eric. He read Jasmine's favorite story, *101 Dalmatians,* interrupted by numerous asides from Eric and Jasmine. Finally, following directions from Eric, he turned on the merry-go-round; otherwise, they assured him, they couldn't go to sleep.

Back downstairs, Ronald searched the bedrooms and finally located Adele in one of them. She was lying in a canopied bed, covered only by a sheet.

"Poor you," she grinned. "I'll tell Ralph that he can really count on you. You haven't failed in the line of duty."

"Could we watch H.H.'s tape now?" Ronald asked weakly.

Smiling at him, Adele held up a remote-control unit. "Heman's cassette is in the player. Come to bed, and I'll turn it on. Get a grip on yourself, Ronald. I'm not even going to try to seduce you. Actually, you've made me feel bad. You've made it clear that you think I've screwed up your life even more than Heman's."

"I'm sure that sleeping with you will compound my troubles," Ronald said, but he took off his trousers.

"Only if it becomes common knowledge," Adele said. "Don't worry, consider it an act of friendship. A woman's way of telling you that she's sorry. Whatever happens tonight is between friends."

Ronald shrugged. Neither Youman nor Byrdwhistle morality was easy to assimilate. But what the hell, wasn't going to bed with a woman nearly young enough to be his daughter, and sex-making with a woman chronologically old enough to be his mother, learning how to play the game Byrdwhistle-style? And wasn't it axiomatic that a good manager should thoroughly understand any new situation before he tried to change it?

Still wearing his jockey shorts, he quickly slid under the sheet next to Adele. Before she turned on the video-player, he could feel her hand patting his stomach reassuringly, and then, to his surprise, her hand was pushing down his underwear and she was holding his penis and balls in a comforting, nurturing grasp. The cassette-player and the television set were sitting on top of the mahogany highboy. The tube sputtered to life. When the confused pattern of angry images on Channel 3 cleared, they were looking at the aft deck of a yacht and the warm blue waters behind it. As the camera panned the distant mountains, Ronald recognized the voice-over.

"This is Marge Slick speaking. As you can see we are aboard the *Love Byrd* in the Gulf of Kotor."

Marge was evidently running the camera, which now had zoomed in on a weatherbeaten Thornton Byrd, whom Adele identified for Ronald. Thornton was grinning at a woman wearing only a peasant skirt, whose lush breasts were obviously full of milk. Marge's voice continued but her words ignored the action between Thornton and the young woman. Thornton seemed to be deliberating whether to take a suck of the mother's milk that the woman was laughingly proffering to him with upheld breasts.

Marge's voice sounded as if she had a cold or had been crying. Occasionally she stopped, and then they could hear her catch her breath and sob a little.

"Forgive me," Marge said, still behind the camera. "I'm only running this camera because Hyman insisted that I do it. Not only is the *Love Byrd* packed with fifty homeless people, mostly women, from the earthquake last week, but Breskva, the woman you are watching, lost her three-month-old baby and can't find her husband. Even worse, we are having terrible personal souris. I'm sorry to have to tell you that Hyman has had a very serious relapse."

Marge's voice cracked, and Thornton was now staring grimly into the camera. Then she continued, "If Adele Youman isn't watching this tape with you, Ron, I hope that you'll make sure she sees it—and I hope she'll understand. I really wanted to talk with her personally. I'll be back in Boston next Thursday—but getting the Byrdwhistlers off to Portugal won't leave me enough time. To be honest I simply don't know how to tell her what has happened to Hyman," Marge stopped, unable to continue for a moment. "Breskva, help me," she was sobbing. "You hold the camera on Thornton—let him talk."

The camera cut to Thornton. "It's really very sad," Thornton said gruffly. "We don't think Hyman had a stroke, but we can't find any local doctors to help us. Within the past few days H.H. has turned into an old man right before our eyes. Nick and Maria wanted him to fly home to get medical help, but he's really too weak. He insists that Marge go ahead with the Byrdwhistle vacation, but he is going to stay here on the *Love Byrd* with me for a few days until he can get up enough strength to fly home to Boston." Thornton suddenly grinned, "I keep telling him to try Breskva's milk. It might help him. But unfortunately, H.H. seems to have lost his sense of humor." Thornton paused, "Here he comes. Pinky Fresser and Jack Sludge are helping him up on deck right now."

The camera picked up H.H., who was being carried chair-style by two men who sat him down gingerly in a deck chair. Adele and Ronald gasped. H.H.'s hair was uncombed and stringy. His full face seemed to have caved in. His right hand was shaking uncontrollably. His soiled shirt hung loosely out of his trousers, which were only partially zipped. He stared blearily into the camera for a moment, and then he spoke in a quaking voice. "Hello, Ron. As you can see, I've lost my grip a little. Don't know what happened. Bottom fell out, and me with it." He stared vaguely into the camera. His lips were moving, but his mind seemed to be wandering over thoughts that he couldn't verbalize.

"Damn you, Heman," Adele yelled at the camera. "Stop this silliness right now. You're not fooling me. You're senile all right—like a sixty-year-old crocodile."

As if he could hear her responding to him, H.H. finally spoke. "I hope that Adele is watching this tape with you. I know she won't believe it." H.H.'s voice cracked, and a little spittle dribbled out of his mouth. "I'm trying to fight back, but I've got to face the truth. My time has come and gone. I've been kidding myself. I have to face reality. I'm an old man." H.H. sobbed and once again he was staring vacantly into the camera. "My days of sex-making are over." As he spoke, Breskva appeared on the tube. She dangled her breasts in his face. Then the camera zoomed back on H.H.'s face and tears were running down his cheek. "Even this lovely young woman doesn't excite me," he sighed. "I always told Adele that when I couldn't get it up it was time to bury me."

"You come home, you old cocker," Adele growled at the tube. "I'll get it up for you." And Ron had to believe her, because Adele's feathery but persistent grasp was counteracting his twenty-four hours of sleeplessness. But Ronald was shocked. H.H. really looked as if he had one foot in the grave. "God, it's unbelievable," he told Adele. "Losing Byrdwhistle shouldn't do this to him. He's only sixty-two. He could get another job."

"You bet he could," Adele said. "He could go to Hollywood and win an Oscar as a character actor."

Between pauses, H.H. was rambling on about the horrors of retirement. "I've lost my reason for being," he said. "I devoted the past thirty years to Byrdwhistle and now, just as I was on the verge . . ." H.H. stopped, forgetting what he was going to say. He grinned feebly at them. "I was on the verge of something. Oh, I know. I was going to make America a playland. I was going to show people how they could play and be productive, too. Productive where it counts. But now I'm washed up. I know the truth. Ron, I met your boss, Thiemost. He's older than I am. He probably can't keep his putz up either, but I know he'll force you to get rid of me. I'm not blaming Thorny. A few years ago, Elmer and I did the same thing to him. But he found a way to survive. He's lucky about one thing. He didn't marry Adele. She'd never let him by a happy old yentzer. Adele's a mome. Watch out for the mome's wrath. It outgrabes. It's really all Adele's fault, Ron. She's as dangerous as a black widow spider. If you don't play her game, before she's through she'll get Thiemost to fire you. She'll tell you that she loves powerful men, but it's only when she has a firm grip on their pricks."

Scowling, Adele released Ronald's penis. H.H. burbled on: "I love Adele," he said. As he spoke, his voice got fainter and wheezier. "But the thought of too much togetherness with her has unnerved me. I've got to face it. I'm a senior citizen. A member of the discarded generation. You, Ron—and Adele—have reprogrammed me. My transistors are coming up zeros. You started my biological clock racing ahead of schedule." H.H. shook his head wearily. Once again his mouth was moving but no words were coming out.

For a moment the camera moved in on Thorny, who now had two barebreasted women hovering over him. "Last night," Thorny said gruffly, "we tried to help him. Breskva, Kruska, and Marge all got in bed with him, but nothing happened."

The camera returned to H.H., who looked up, more woebegone than Father Time. "I couldn't get it up, Ron," he sobbed. "Three loving women, and I couldn't get it up."

"My God," Ron said sadly, "poor H.H. I can't believe it."

"Don't," Adele told him coldly. "Heman hasn't missed a day since he was sixteen."

"Maybe his theories have reversed themselves," Ron said wonderingly. "Maybe he's screwed himself to oblivion."

H.H. was still talking, "Thorny told me that I could move in with him on the *Love Byrd*. I really enjoy playing with women, but who wants to play with an impotent old man? As soon as I get my strength back, Nick and Maria will fly me home. They'll turn the Grumman over to you, Ron. Marge will bring this tape back to Boston. She promised to handle the Byrdwhistle vacation without me. Pray for me, Ron. Pray for me, Adele. Better that I die than I live on and on like this." As he was talking, H.H. slid down in his chair. His head was on his chest. From this basket-case position he opened his eyes. His last words were, "I forgive you, Adele. Give the merry-go-round to Ron. I know he can't have it moved, but let him use it. He needs it. Enjoy it together."

Then Marge appeared on the screen for the first time. She was wearing shorts and a halter, and she was very serious.

"I really don't think Heman has had a stroke. As you can see, although he is forgetful, and obviously in a severe depression, his mind is still working. I telephoned Alexi Ivanowsky at the Center for Ageless Humans. Alexi will set up a room to take care of Hyman and nurse him back to full health. Hyman wanted me to wish you good luck, Ron. The keys to the Rolls are in the package that Chuck Gill delivered to Adele. Enjoy them in good health. And start studying Theory Z, Ron—you can't run Byrdwhistle without it."

Shaking her head, Adele ran the tape back and turned off the sound. She got as close as she could get to it and peered into the tube. "The big faker is wearing make-up! I'm sure of it! No one could get that old in a couple of days." Finally, convincing herself that it was all a big scam, she got back in bed and snuggled against Ronald.

"Do you want to take a dip in the Jade fountain?" she asked. Her black-coffee eyes were simmery.

"I feel like Benedict Arnold," Ronald said, but her firm behind felt good in his hand.

Adele laughed. "Maybe you do, but right now you're acting like Ponce de Leon."

LUDAMUS III

If a man feels that the years have taken a toll of physical energy (biological aging) and he can no longer handle the old problems or adjust to new ones (psychological aging) and he withdraws from his usual roles (social aging) he is old whether he is 65, 75, 85 — or even 50. In the next generation the man 65, 75 or even older will feel and behave as young as the 50 year old of the past.

Morton Puner, *Vital Maturity*

Can you — yes, you who are now reading this — can you deny the possibility of the whole field of production being brought under corporate control, that corporate body being the people? If you acknowledge such a possibility and accord with the formation and success of World Corporation, give expression to your interest by subscribing for such amount of stock as you may be able to control.

King Camp Gillette, *The Human Drift*

Liberation is the affirmation of the right to build a society in which the abolition of poverty and toil terminates in a universe where the sensuous, the playful, the calm, and the beautiful become forms of existence and thereby the Form of society itself.

Herbert Marcuse, *An Essay on Liberation*

27

H.H. arrived in Portamaio, the sardine-fishing center of Portugal, two days after Marge Slick and her husband Fred and more than four hundred Byrdwhistlers and their children had settled into their kitchenette apartments on the Algarve for the ten-day Byrdwhistle Playweek Vacation. Three fifteen-story highrise apartment buildings a few miles from the bustling Portuguese town were a part of the complex that H.H. had convinced Elmer was a good investment and eventually could be tied in closely with the development of their Byrds-on-the-Wing Division. Among the buildings was an auditorium for conventions, a supermarket, a theater, two nightclubs, and three restaurants. Built on high ground, they fronted on a five-mile curve of sandy beach that extended to Cape St. Vincent, which could be seen on the horizon of the southernmost tip of Portugal.

Although H.H. had packed about a hundred Love Rocks into his suitcase, the balance of more than one hundred thousand, completely paid for with ten thousand dollars in American currency, were still piled in a shed near Sveti Stefan. Thorny had begrudgingly told him that Pinky and Jack would load his "damned rocks" aboard the *Love Byrd* just as soon as they could get the ship back into the Adriatic, but Thorny wouldn't say when he'd deliver them to the United States.

"What the hell do you need them for?" Thorny had demanded. "Let Thiemost worry about them. Byrdwhistle may not get any orders for them anyway. Why should anyone pay ten dollars for a fucking rock?"

When H.H. told Thornton that Byrdwhistle had inventoried one hundred thousand felt-lined boxes — worth nearly a dollar apiece — in Everett to "glamor" package the Love Rocks, Thorny was sure that Ralph Thiemost wasn't going to be very happy about it. "Dammit, H.H., Byrdwhistle could lose its shirt from such a damn-fool idea. God may not be watching over Thiemost the way He's been watching over you." Thorny sighed. "Thank God you're not working for Byrdwhistle anymore. You're retired. You've got to face reality. Turn the damned rocks over to Thiemost. With your luck, he'll pay you double your ten thousand dollars for them. They're certainly no good to you. What in the hell would you do with them?"

Actually, H.H. wasn't quite sure. But the less that Thorny knew about his plans the better. Whether he found a use for the Love Rocks or not, he was sure that they were helping convince Thorny, and would eventually convince Adele, that he was really quite mad and that he wasn't faking his sudden senile dementia. When H.H. was making the video-tape with Marge, Thorny had kept insisting that he knew the truth. "It's all part of your little game to deceive Adele," he had said. If Adele probed into the making of the tape, H.H. was sure of one thing — that Thorny would become garrulous — and it was better to leave him totally confused.

So the day before he had driven to Sveti Stefan to buy the Love Rocks H.H. began his campaign to prove that his mind really was getting squishy. At breakfast, he had greeted Breskva as if she were Marge, and he foggily pretended that he thought he was arriving at Byrdwhistle for a day's work. He rambled on to Thorny endlessly about Byrdwhistle's problems, and he refused to look out the window or acknowledge that the Gulf of Kotor wasn't the Atlantic Ocean lapping against the side of the *Love Byrd.* Thorny sent Pinky Fresser with H.H. to Sveti Stefan to watch out for him. But after they had returned to the *Love Byrd,* even Pinky told Thorny that H.H. "had gone nuts." Pinky couldn't believe that H.H. had actually paid cash for a hundred thousand fucking rocks. "And I think he was negotiating with a couple of native kids for a whole lot more of them." Sympathetically, Pinky told Thorny that the poor bastard "must have rocks in his head."

The day before he left Yugoslavia with Nick and Maria in the Grumman II, H.H. spent his last day with Thorny, lisping gibberish and walking around the ship bent over like a centenarian. Bemoaning his fate, he prayed that when he returned to Boston Alexi Ivanowsky might transplant some goat cells or monkey glands into his testicles and restore his youth.

When he arrived in Faro, he was carried from the plane on a stretcher by Maria and Nick, who were only partially convinced that H.H. had lost his marbles. Marge, Fred, and Sylvia were waiting for him. Fred, more concerned than Marge and Sylvia, had rented a stationwagon so that H.H. could lie down during the thirty-five-mile drive to Portamaio. Knowing that she must return to Fred's bed, at least part of the time, Marge had asked Sylvia if she would like to come along on the Byrd-whistle Playweek. She knew that Sylvia adored Hyman. Sylvia had told Marge that she could run the gamut of her emotions with H.H., from an admiring daughter going to bed with her father to a loving wife awed by his genius and to a lascivious, earthy mistress with a laughing, boyish lover.

Waiting at the airport, Sylvia had told Marge that Heman Hyman might have adopted Thomas Morton as his ancestor and that Marge might think he was a reincarnation of King Gillette, but Sylvia knew who Hyman really was: John Humphrey Noyes—walking the earth once again, a hundred years after his death. Didn't Marge know that from the age of sixty-two—Hyman's age—until he was seventy or older John Humphrey had sired at least seven children by three or four young women? It had occurred to Sylvia more than once that she could participate in his present reincarnation. It would be kind of joyous to be the bearer of Youman-Noyes's seed. Hyman had two sons and a daughter already, but they were grown up. Anyway, Hyman loved kids, and Razi needed a brother or a sister.

H.H. waved feebly at them from his stretcher, and Sylvia wasn't listening to Marge's view that Hyman was creative enough without making any more kids. Sylvia leaned over H.H., who winked surreptitiously at her and Marge when Nick and Maria put him down on a bench in the airport, and while Fred was looking for a wheelchair. She whispered: "I'm your playmate for the next week. I left my diaphragm home. I hope you've recovered sufficiently from your dementia to still get it up." She grinned. "You can fill me with Zephyr, a daughter fair, so buxom blithe and debonair."

Fortunately, Fred, Nick, and Maria didn't hear her quote from Milton, but Marge did. She scowled at both of them, but H.H. was a little irritated. "Dammit, Marge," he expostulated, "I may still be sane enough to play coitus interruptus with your daughter, but I hope you haven't told Fred. The only people who should know the truth are you, Alexi, and Sheldon Coombs."

"I promise I won't tell anybody," Sylvia assured him.

"I had to tell her," Marge laughed. "I don't know how long you intend to play this silly game, Hyman, but I don't suppose that you're going to give up screwing, too. Who else but Sylvia and I would go to bed with a demented old man?"

H.H. grinned. "You've got a point."

"Not a point." Sylvia laughed. "I hope it's a nicely rounded object that needs to be dipped in magical female juices to keep it alive and vibrant, and to keep you from really going over the hill."

Later, after they had wheeled H.H. into the elevator in one of the Byrdwhistle highrises and taken it up to the penthouse apartment, Fred hugged H.H. and said he hoped that he would be his old self by tomorrow. When Fred had left Marge and Sylvia to make H.H. comfortable, H.H. jumped out of the wheelchair and jigged around the room. "You're absolutely right. I'm going to need both of you. I need you Marge to keep me in close touch with what our friend Coldaxe is doing at Byrdwhistle, and I need you Sylvia, my favorite certified social-worker, to introduce me to the geriatric set," he chuckled. "In my spare time, while I'm undermining Ralph Thiemost and W.I.N., Incorporated, I'm going to investigate old age and make sure that I know how to avoid it."

When they pressed him for details, he shrugged and was noncommittal. "I'm going to work closely with Sheldon Coombs. He's turning into a financial wizard. He's been doing most of the investing for World Corporation." H.H. toasted them both with the Portuguese red wine that Sylvia had poured. "I'm hoping that in about six months we can prepare an interesting surprise for Ralph Thiemost. Other than that, I'm not sure. I don't like to outline the future—it leaves no room for surprise. Really, it's much more fun to live life off the cuff."

H.H. didn't tell them that, at his request, Thornton had telephoned Dick Counselman of Marpeat, Young and Codbrand and that Dick had confirmed what Marge had already told him. Ronald Coldaxe had arrived in Boston and was living in H.H.'s townhouse in Louisburg Square.

Marge was shocked and angry, "Adele really is a fink. Aren't you afraid she's going to go to bed with him?"

"Lord, I hope she is," H.H. grinned. "Without realizing it, Adele may be a more effective missionary in the conversion of Ronald Coldaxe than you or I."

Marge sighed. "I can't figure out what you're going to accomplish living at the Center for Ageless Humans and pretending that you are a doddering old idiot. You're going to be out of the action."

"Not at all," H.H. said. "Unlike Dracula or Dr. Jekyll, Heman Hyman plans to have a daytime transformation! Like Cinderella, I may be safely tucked in bed by midnight, but Moses Megillah Marshalik will walk the streets by day."

"What about Adele?" Sylvia asked. "She'll murder you when she finds out that her wandering husband isn't decomposing in his room at the center."

H.H. shook his head, "Alexi doesn't know it yet, but he's going to tell Adele that I'm recovering very, very slowly. The only time she can visit me will be early in the morning, before noon. During the rest of the day, I will be undergoing intensive treatments to combat my cranial athero-sclerosis," H.H. laughed boisterously, "and I can have no visitors. At night, I will be so exhausted from the treatments that I must be sedated."

"What are you going to be doing from noon until midnight?" Sylvia demanded.

"Putting a spoke in W.I.N.'s wheel," H.H. chuckled. "I can't tell you the details yet, because I haven't worked them through myself, but Moses Marshalik is going to introduce sex and play as the great neglected after-noon sport for retirees, senior citizens, and lonesome housewives."

H.H. grabbed them and danced around the room with them. "What America really needs is afternoon sex-clubs."

Marge groaned, "Afternoon?"

"Sure. All those allegedly senile old men who were forced to retire before their time could play with the lonesome mothers and housewives whose husbands are still working and haven't learned how to play yet. At least half the population in the United States should be playing and mak-ing love until the other half learns how."

After Marge reluctantly left them to find Fred, H.H. and Sylvia lay naked on one of the beds in the penthouse. The warm blaze of a Portu-guese sunset flooded through the open door of the balcony, toasting their bodies before it slowly disappeared in the west. H.H. had opened a bottle of red Madeira and dribbled a little of it on Sylvia's breasts and lapped it off. Laughing, she poured some on his belly and soaked his penis until it trickled between his legs. Languidly, tasting his genitals, she carried on an intermittent conversation. "I don't think you'll ever brainwash Ronald Coldaxe," she said. "He's very much like my husband, Clint. Ron doesn't know how to let go. He can't surrender. Or he won't. He's afraid to admit that there might be a warm, loving boy shipwrecked somewhere inside him. The nice Ronald Coldaxe has been underwater so long that he's en-crusted with barnacles. You'll never chip them off. On the other hand, I don't think he wants to fire you. Marge told me he's not the creative type. He can never run Byrdwhistle."

"Ron has to fire me." H.H. was watching Sylvia's tongue doing a minuet around his happy shaft, which she held straight up in the air. "He has no choice. I'm simply going to save him the trouble and embarrass-ment. You have to understand the roots of the coming showdown be-tween Byrdwhistle and W.I.N. Theory Z is what Alan Toffler would call a 'Third Wave'-style management. Another writer, Marlyn Ferguson, has called it the 'Aquarian Conspiracy.' Anyway, Theory Z is totally in conflict with the W.I.N. philosophy. When the wave that pounds on the shore recedes, it will suck the bottom out of the beach. You might say that it's really a religious war. Before Byrdwhistle and Theory Z predominates it may even become a holy war."

H.H. reached for a book he had dropped onto the bedside table when Sylvia had tumbled into bed with him. "I think you may enjoy Father Thomas Merton's ideas," he said. "He should be required reading for all business leaders. His thinking is like a searchlight in the darkness of our so-called reality. Let me read to you something he wrote."

Sylvia grabbed the paperback book out of his hand. "Jesus, if I told my husband that Heman Hyman read to me while we were screwing, he'd be convinced. You may really be in the first phase of early senility."

"Okay," H.H. grabbed her passionately, "let's fuck and get it over with."

Book in hand, Sylvia pushed him back on the bed and straddled him. "The hell we will. I like sex-making better."

"This is one step further. Love-making."

With her breasts pointing pertly in the air, Sylvia sitting on his belly smiled down at him. She read the title of the book, 'Conjectures of a Guilty Bystander.' My God! I don't feel guilty. I want to read to you and punctuate the sentences with my vaginal muscles. What page?"

H.H. told her. Happily euphoric, it occurred to him that a woman lifting her haunches so that a man could penetrate her while she was reading the words of a Catholic monk was equivalent to the celibate's final ecstasy with Christ, or to The Player playing with two aspects of himself. Heman Hyman Youman being Sylvia Jacobs Marlowe was simply a variation on a theme.

"'Businesses are, in reality, quasi-religious sects.'" Comfortably squatting on her lover, Sylvia grinned as she read, "'When you go to work in one, you embrace *a new faith*. And if they really are big businesses, you progress from faith to a kind of mystique. Belief in the product, preaching the product, in the end the product becomes the focus of the transcendental experience. Through "the product" one communes with the vast forces of life, nature and history that are expressed in business. Why not face it? Advertising treats all products with the reverence and the seriousness due to sacraments.'

"Can I stop now, Daddy Youman?" Sylvia bent over and kissed H.H. reverently.

"No. There are a few more paragraphs."

"'Harrington says (*Life in a Crystal Palace*)'" Sylvia reads on, "'The new evangelism, whether expressed in soft or hard selling, is a quasi-religious approach to business wrapped in a hoax voluntarily entered into by producers and consumers together. Its credo is that of belief-to-order. It is the truth-to-order as delivered by advertising and public relations men, believed in by them and voluntarily believed by the public.

" 'Once again it's a question of a game. Life is aimless, but one invents thousands of aimless aims and then mobilizes a whole economy around them, finally declaring them to be transcendental, mystical and absolute.

" 'Compare our monastery with the General Electric plant in Louis-ville. Which one is the more serious "religious" institution? One might be tempted to say "the monastery" out of habit. But, in fact, the religious seriousness of all the monastery is like a sandlot baseball game compared to General Electric. It may, in fact, occur to many, including the monks, to *doubt* the monastery and what it represents.

" 'But who doubts G.E.?' "

Finished, Sylvia collapsed on H.H. Still joined, she nuzzled his neck. "I think that you and Father Merton are trying to tell me something."

H.H. hugged her. "I'm hoping that Ronald Coldaxe is going to learn a new religion. Byrdwhistlers are going to teach it to him."

The morning after Labor Day, before the Byrdwhistlers and their children were bussed to the airport at Faro to return to Boston and other cities where Byrdwhistle divisions were located, H.H. had called a Symp meeting. During the week, when he had appeared at the swimming pools and at the diningrooms and had kissed and hugged most of the Byrd-whistlers and their children, he had tried to reassure them. Brushing tears from their eyes and patting male shoulders and most of the female behinds, he told them that after a few months in the Center for Ageless Humans, like MacArthur he would return. Although he had had a slight relapse, he wasn't giving up. Then at the Symp meeting, he was even more emphatic. He was going to do what John Noyes failed to do—take the Oneida theories as represented by Byrdwhistle and Theory Z into the mainstream of American life. Byrdwhistle may have been sold to corpor-ate predators, but the Byrdwhistle message wasn't going down the drain. It might take him six months, or even a year, but the next time the wheel of fortune stopped, all of them listening to him this morning would not only still be playing at Byrdwhistle, but individually and collectively they were going to climb to the next plateau. As World Corporationists they might even own their own playground.

"Have patience. Keep the faith." He told them. "King Gillette's dream isn't a pipedream. Byrdwhistle will be the first of many people's corpora-tions." H.H. knew as he watched their enthusiastic, shining faces—many glistening with tears because they thought their leader was fading away—that he had to be careful not to sound too logical. But he knew, too, that his little army couldn't surrender. They must learn how to confound the enemy.

"Long before most of you were born," he told them, "Mahatma Gandhi informed Russia and China and the aggressive nations of the world that India, now free from British domination, could live in the world without arms of any kind. India was unconquerable. A half-billion people could assimilate any invader. In less than a quarter-century the armies of any conqueror would have totally disappeared in the huge Indian sexual blender. Keep in mind, too, that long before India was invaded, the Romans tried to conquer the known earth. Look what happened to them. Their armies were pacified and eliminated in the beds of their enemies."

H.H. warned them to fight back subtly. "Use Theory Z techniques. Cooperate, or seem to cooperate, with Coldaxe and W.I.N. Don't contest. Transform. Seduce Coldaxe in our Love Rooms. Study his every move so that you can redirect his and W.I.N.'s high pressure, win-or-lose work-ethic toward a more joyous play world where everyone wins. If Coldaxe and his cohorts refuse to play the game by Theory Z rules, use passive resistance. At the same time, kiss and hug poor Ronald Coldaxe every day. Confound him. Teach him that only loving is profitable. Introduce him to the real meaning of human productivity. Show him the world of the future where work and play have merged. In the meantime, I promise you, despite this setback, I haven't given up. Long live Byrdwhistle!"

H.H. tottered back to his wheelchair where Marge and Sylvia hugged him, and the Byrdwhistlers gave him a standing ovation.

28

Conceiving an idea is usually easier than carrying it to fruition. H.H. had hinted to Marge and Sylvia that he planned to keep his finger in the Byrd-whistle pie; but he didn't tell them that Meredith Coldaxe was the plum that he expected to pull out. Nor did he tell them that it had occurred to him that, if he could meet Ron's wife and become friends with her without Ron knowing about it, he might infiltrate her mind and not only give her special insights into Byrdwhistle but also convert her to Theory Z. Then, with her help, he could recreate her husband and make him a worthy successor.

Portions of his counterattack strategy had popped into H.H.'s head while he was shaving the morning before he flew to Yugoslavia with Marge. But the hologram really began to take shape several days later on the *Love Byrd,* when it merged with the sudden conviction that he had procrastinated too long. He had to face reality. While he believed that humans should stop aging in their fortieth year — or fiftieth, maximum — and spend their remaining years at a fixed plateau of good health and beauty, H.H. knew that he wasn't going to live forever. Not that the thought of death bothered him. Fear of dying was really a fear of the uncertainty of how and when it would happen. H.H. had no doubts on that score. He knew he was going to leave the earth on his own scheduled Departure Day and that a century or so later he would return. On the other hand, even if he were right about reincarnation and that one day he would be around again to pick up the threads and complete his former missions, he knew he shouldn't wait. The world needed Theory Z now. If he could take Byrdwhistle out of the closet and infiltrate the play-ethic into the mainstream of American life, it would be a more joyous world when he returned. The Thiemosts of this world would have been diverted from their acquisitive insanities. A new breed of managers would be in charge—transcenders, men and women who knew that the cart and the horse were one and the same. No one had to push or pull. They could all play on the way to wherever they were going.

But he needed an accomplice to help set the wheels in motion. A Socrates to his Plato, an activist who really understood that love, laughter, learning, and ludamus were not only the keys to human happiness and could give America a new sense of purpose and savoir-faire but were also basic to human longevity. He had gleaned from his discussions with Ronald that the Coldaxe marriage was a sexually ho-hum affair and that Meredith and Ronald disagreed not only on the ends of living but also on the means. A month ago, when he analyzed the Byrdwhistle questionnaire that Meredith had completed for herself and Ron, he was amused by her responses; but they were simply one more example of the sad truth of American marital life. At the time, the Coldaxe information didn't catalyze. The final hologram began to take shape when he was amusing Marge with the idea of seeking a new identity and becoming Moses Megillah Marshalik. Marge told him that Coldaxe called his wife M'mm, and that did it. Beautiful. Why not? Two 3-M's were better than one.

He suspected that in some areas he and Meredith were probably on the same wavelength. It would be the pièce de résistance, the crème de la crème of his life, if he could not only get inside her mind but also establish a deep mental intimacy with her. In effect, it would be like going to bed with Ronald every night. As an invisible ombudsman, he could speak to Ronald through Meredith's mind as she made love to her husband. As an off-stage partner, he could continue to guide Byrdwhistle and, at the same time, fashion World Corporation into a juggernaut to crush Thiemost. H.H. believed, and in his opinion he had proved it at Byrdwhistle, that the feminine mind was a better soil in which to fertilize Theory Z than the masculine one. Women wanted their rewards in this life. The work-ethic and glory in the hereafter were male creations.

If he had told Marge and Sylvia, or even Adele, that he was going to try to co-opt Ronald Coldaxe by seducing his wife, a woman he had never met and who was seventeen years younger than he was, they would have howled with laughter. Or they would have been convinced that his brain was really addled. That giggly thought had triggered the laser beam in his brain and repositioned all the elements into the final three-dimensional hologram.

Meredith Coldaxe must never know who he really was. Moses Megillah Marshalik would supersede Heman Hyman Youman and become her intimate friend and secret lover. He was sure that Marge and Sylvia, and even Adele, would have understood the interlock that was necessary for complete mental intimacy. Only with a complete sexual surrender could he svengali Meredith, or any woman, and make her his alter ego.

A tall order dreamed up by an egomaniac? Was he in truth a frustrated cult leader, a Reverend Moon or a latter-day Jim Jones? These thoughts crossed H.H.'s mind, but he rejected them. While he hadn't figured out how he was going to accomplish this miracle and transform Meredith into a Byrdwhistler living under the same roof with Ronald, he had no compunctions about trying. With his guidance, Byrdwhistle could be the mitzvah that would refocus the Coldaxe marriage. After resolving the problems of Byrdwhistle, with Meredith's help, Ron and Meredith would have a strong bond of communication that they now lacked in their marriage. The day might come when Ronald, like a great many leaders, would confess that he owed his worldly success to his wife. Even H.H. would be the first to admit that, if Adele hadn't had the foresight to go to bed with Thorny, he would be preaching his play-ethic philosophy to a few students and writing about it in obscure academic journals that no one read. Instead, he was putting them into practice in a real-life situation. Even if by some misfortune Ronald discovered the truth and learned who the amanuensis of his Byrdwhistle destiny really was, H.H. was sure that one day before Ron died he'd be happy that they had both shared Meredith's mind and body.

The problem was how? During the three weeks since he had arrived in Boston with Sylvia, he still hadn't made contact with Meredith. Of course that wasn't his fault. Moving pieces on the chessboard of life took time and patience. Sylvia had driven with him in a taxi to the Center for Ageless Humans, which occupied two former townhouses on Beacon Street overlooking the Charles River. Alexi Ivanowski had welcomed them somewhat dubiously. But before H.H. conferred with Alexi and kissed Sylvia a temporary goodbye, he had told Sylvia to contact Marge and tell her that he needed the Byrdwhistle questionnaires that Meredith Coldaxe had filled out and that Marge should bring a video-player so that he could run the tape of the interview that Steven and Cathy Milner of Club Wholesome had made with Meredith in Santa Monica. H.H. knew that the most enjoyable way to seduce a woman was to dare to become the woman.

A few mornings later, on her way to Byrdwhistle, Marge brought the tape to H.H., and she caught him by surprise. He was sitting in a wheelchair in the antiseptic hospital room that he told Alexi could function as the Heman Hyman viewing room but that under no circumstances would it be where Moses Marshalik slept at night, lest his brain become sterile, too. Expecting Adele, whom Alexi had informed by telephone of H.H.'s arrival in Boston and of his sad condition, H.H. had purposely not shaved. His hair was unkempt and he was wearing a hospital johnny that hung on his lean body. Slumped over dispiritedly in this slovenly state, he looked up at Marge with glazed eyes and with his tongue protruding from his gaping mouth.

Marge burst into laughter, and Moses Marshalik scowled fiercely at her. "God dammit, Marge. I told you that only my enemies and those who are mourning the fall and decline of Heman Hyman Youman can visit me in the morning. When the nurse downstairs flashed the buzzer, I thought you were Adele coming to shed a fear tears and feel remorseful over the destruction she has wrought."

H.H. told her that from now on she must only visit him in the afternoon or evening and that they could see each other in another room on the top floor, which Moses Marshalik was in the process of furnishing for bachelor comfort.

"This place gives me a very uneasy feeling," Marge told him. "Bring me up to date. What the hell are Ivanowski and his cohorts really doing here?"

"The second and third floors are filled with old crocks," H.H. said. "There are about one hundred of them in residence, men and women all the way from sixty to ninety-five who have no relatives and no one who gives a damn about them. They are all in reasonably good health. They signed in here on their own accord. One phase of Alexi's research is to discover whether he can revitalize old people," H.H. laughed. Marge was hugging him and exploring under his hospital johnny. She gave his penis a quick, friendly shake. "Alexi wants to see if he can bring them to life the way you do me," H.H. told her happily.

"You mean they're all screwing together?"

H.H. shrugged. "Why not? My feeling is that, if they haven't done it all their lives, their male dippers are too bent and rubbery and the female fountains that used to ease the way are no longer flowing. But Alexi doesn't think so. He's happy to have me and Thorny as guinea pigs to prove my particular theories, but in the meantime he's leaving no stone unturned. He hasn't even rejected gerocomia. Like Abisag, who got in bed with King David to warm him up 'and didn't know him,' to Clodius Hermippus, who lived to be one hundred and fifty years old by breathing the breath of young women, Alexi pays young male and female students to spend a few hours a day here, sexing up the senior citizens. I'm sure that he's taking a whack at other ancient ideas, like those of Brown-Sequard, who one hundred years ago, at the age of seventy-two, claimed he restored his mental and penile powers with daily injections of the blood and semen of dogs and guinea pigs—so much so that Brown-Sequard could not only perform admirably in bed but could piss a longer and higher stream than he had been able to in his twenties. When you go through the lobby, take a look at the photograph of Serge Voronoff. Voronoff presumably restored more than two thousand old men to happy sex with transplanted monkeys' testes. Alexi isn't too sure about him, but he does think that the Swiss surgeon Paul Niehans is on the right track with cellular transplants—injecting healthy cells into particular organs of the body to replace the tired old cells. Alexi also has some of his controlled subjects on Gerovital H3—or buffered procaine. It's similar to novocaine. Since it's not legal in the United States, Alexi is not publicizing his use of it. Other controlled subjects here are getting Vitamin E and Vitamin B-15." H.H. chuckled. "In the winter time the temperature here never gets above sixty degrees. Alexi is convinced that human cells function better in cool temperatures, and of course it's well known that animals have a much lower metabolism when they are hibernating and because of this they live longer."

Before she left, H.H. told Marge that Sylvia had suggested to him that, since Byrdwhistle had given a lot of money to the center for their continuing research on aging, he should spend a little time learning the sad truth about getting old. "She wants me to visit some of the senior citizen centers and nursing homes that she keeps tabs on for the state of Massachusetts. I told her that I really wasn't interested."

Laughing, H.H. jumped out of his wheelchair, flipped off his johnny, swiveled his hips, and waved his perky penis at Marge. "I don't intend to get any older. Chronologically, okay, but not physically. That's why this place is called the Center for Ageless Humans. Alexi is going to eliminate nursing homes." He hugged Marge, "Maybe we can figure out a way to get rid of senior citizen centers. Just imagine a world where everyone lived his or her four-score years—give or take about ten—in excellent health and in possession of all his or her faculties. Then somewhere between eighty and ninety, after a nice dinner, and one final orgasm with a good friend, they could check out. See you later, alligator—next time around!"

Marge grinned at him. "It's a nice daydream. I'll buy it; but right now I'm trying to figure out what evil designs you have on Ron's wife. I'm pretty sure that his marital life is in a mess. A real-estate agent located a beautiful house for him in Lynnfield. You know the area. It's filled with two-hundred-thousand-dollar houses on acre lots. They're inhabited during the day by some of the forty percent of American wives who don't have to work because their husbands are keeping up with inflation. Most of them are dissatisfied. They send their kids to private schools. The better-looking ones sleep with the golf or tennis pro a couple of after-noons a week. The rest of them read all the current novels and daydream about going to bed with men like you."

H.H. groaned. "Damn! You should have talked Ron out of that location. I don't think Meredith fits into the suburban-housewife syndrome. She's not that kind of woman."

"You've got to face it," Marge said. "Ron is that kind of man. Anyway, he hasn't bought the house yet, and he may not have to. From what he's told me, there's considerable doubt whether Meredith will ever leave California. She's angry with him for letting Thiemost rule his life. She even told him that maybe they should get divorced." Marge shrugged. "Coldaxe may be a smart businessman, but when it comes to women he flunked out of the first grade."

"Is he still living with Adele?"

"At the moment," Marge said. "But he's afraid that Meredith will find out. And I think Adele has scared him half to death. She evidently told him a lot about the book she's writing about powerful men. She showed him more than a dozen pictures she had taken of famous American industrial leaders, including you and Ralph Thiemost, in their birthday suits. I think she has a few of Coldaxe, too. She told him that she wasn't the least bit afraid of libel. If any of the men she included in her study make a fuss when the book is published, she could scare them to death by threatening to tell the news media even more about them than she's written in the book."

It crossed H.H.'s mind as Marge was talking that he could use one of Adele's pictures of Ralph Thiemost in his coming campaign to sabotage W.I.N., but getting it from Adele might be more difficult than seducing Meredith—and, obviously, his master plan wasn't going to work if Meredith didn't move to Boston. He told Marge to get Meredith's phone number and call her in California to talk with her. "Give her some happy-talk about the East Coast and Byrdwhistle, and about how much she's going to like it here in Boston when she has new friends." He was about to say new friends like Moses Marshalik, but wisely held his tongue.

Marge shook her head. "I refuse to spend the night with Ronald, even though Fred has said it's okay," she said. "But eventually I might have to capitulate. Right now," she told him, "Ronald is spending the day sitting glumly in H.H.'s office while the auditors continue their investigations. Byrdwhistle is simply drifting along." Marge knew when the auditors gave the go sign, and when the purchase transaction was completed and W.I.N. was the new owner, changes were going to come fast and thick. "If I have to sex-make with Ronald to save my job and Fred's," she told H.H., "I don't want to be buddy-buddy with his wife, if and when she ever does arrive in Boston."

Ten minutes after Marge left the center, Adele arrived. Alerted by a nurse at the front desk in the lobby, H.H. was slumped in his wheelchair looking about ready to slide onto the floor. Alexi ushered Adele into the room. Towering over her, his pointed black beard and wide-open fiery eyes giving him a Rasputin appearance, he glared at H.H. and dragged him upright. Mumbling unintelligibly, H.H. gaped open-mouthed at Adele as if he had never seen her before.

H.H. knew that Alexi wasn't pleased that he was using the center to dupe his wife. "We appreciate Byrdwhistle money," Alexi had told him. "As you know, among other things we are studying the biological clock built into human cells that seems to trigger the aging process. But senile dementia, possibly a cellular response, is not a joke."

"I know that," H.H. had said, "but it's a convenient way for me to drop out for a few months, and I promise you that, if you provide the cover for me, one day I may be able to triple the Byrdwhistle contributions to the center." H.H. hadn't wanted to turn the screw, but when Alexi continued to demur H.H. pointed out that Alexi wasn't totally altruistic. Without Byrdwhistle, the center could never afford Alexi's seventy-five-thousand-dollar annual salary, and H.H. was sure that Alexi wouldn't want to give up his champagne and caviar.

Now Alexi was telling Adele that he could say quite positively that her husband hadn't had a stroke. "Nor are we sure that the sudden waning of his mental powers is caused by Alzheimer's disease. But, as you can see, he's exhibiting one of the symptoms — loss of memory. I don't think that he even recognizes you."

H.H. was giving a good imitation of a wall-eyed idiot whose mind had long ago left his body for greener pastures.

"Do you know this lady?" Alexi demanded.

H.H. grinned vacantly at Adele and shook his head. It crossed his mind that Adele, who he hadn't seen for nearly a month, was a woman that any man would want to go to bed with, especially when her saucer eyes were brimming over with tears of compassion. She was wearing a form-fitting deep-blue suit, a flimsy white blouse that revealed most of her breasts, which were supported by a half-bra, and a beret with a feather. The hat was perched jauntily on her white hair. Adele's biological clock had stopped ticking when she was forty. She *was* ageless.

"The brains of Alzheimer disease victims," Alexi was saying, "show two typical signs of deterioration. The first is a tiny accumulation of nerve fibers wrapped around each other. This prevents nutrients from reaching the brain cells. Another sign is plaques, or degenerative nerve terminals. During the next few months, we'll be examining your husband carefully to determine whether he's showing any of these symptoms."

"Can he be cured?" Adele was rubbing H.H.'s back, at first gently, but as she continued he realized that she was being more than affectionate.

Her long fingernails were digging into his skin. She was trying to eroticize him. He was about to yell, "Cut it out, you're making me horny."
But he gritted his teeth.

Alexi frowned at H.H. "There is no cure for Alzheimer's disease.
Some investigators believe that it is caused by a virus. You may be sure
that we'll get to the bottom of it. I think I can promise you that in the
next four or five months your husband will be much improved."

"Four or five months!" Adele exploded. "I don't believe it will take
that long." H.H. suddenly wondered what the hell he was doing that
made her doubt his non compos mentis. Then he realized that his damned
hospital johnny had slipped out of position and he was displaying an
erection. Not a big one, but rather like the ears of a sleeping dog, half
alert, telling their owner and anybody who was watching that there was a
possibility of action. Adele had momentarily stopped her sensuous skin
search. "Heman will never recover in this environment," she told Alexi
emphatically. I assume, Doctor Ivanowski, that you have had talks with
Heman and know that he has strong convictions about how to achieve
healthy longevity."

Alexi smiled. "I know that H.H. is a vegetarian, that he doesn't
smoke, that he doesn't eat salt or sugar, and that he swims and plays tennis. Even though, as he admits, he drinks too much, he seems to be in
excellent physical condition. He has the body of a man half his age."

"That's not all," Adele said. "Heman believes that regular daily sexual
activity is one of the keys to a long life."

Although H.H. tried to signal Alexi frantically with his eyes without
Adele noticing, he was too late. Alexi laughed and pointed at the bed,
"I'm happy to tell you, Mrs. Youman, on that point we're in total agreement. This room is private. If you think that it will help him, you can,
uh, sleep with your husband. Come here any morning between nine and
noontime. Of course, if his brain is really deteriorating, you will have to
face it. He may be impotent. In any event, our instructions are that, after
noon, for the rest of the day and evening he must not be disturbed."

"What do you mean by *our* instructions?" Adele demanded.

Alexi quickly covered his momentary confusion. "*Our* means myself
and the other attending physicians on the center staff. Your husband will
be undergoing extensive daily examinations. Evenings he will be tranquil-
ized. Believe me, we will do everything possible to restore him to full
health."

Adele kissed H.H.'s cheek. "Help me get him into the bed," she told
Alexi. "I think I can speed up his cure."

Grimly scolding H.H. and telling him that he wasn't so far gone that
he had to droop like a limp doll, Alexi dragged him to the bed. He flopped
H.H. against it and finally got him stretched out. Still not acknowledging
either of their existences, H.H. stared at the ceiling; but then to his

amazement, Alexi told Adele that she really should stay with her husband for a couple of hours and then tiptoed out of the room and closed the door behind him. Adele immediately stripped off her suit, blouse, bra, and pantyhose. Still wearing her beret, she climbed onto the hospital bed and squatted on top of H.H.

"Heman," she stared indignantly into his unfocusing eyes. "I want you to cut out this shit and make love to me." When Adele said shit, instead of the usual *merdre,* she pronounced it "sheet."

H.H. was ready enough to make love, and he was having a difficult time restraining himself from nibbling on Adele's breasts; but he knew that the slightest normal reaction would convince her that his mind and his penis were fully coordinated and that he was nowhere near so mush-headed as he was pretending to be. The truth was that if Adele was willing to be agent provocateur and would take full charge of sex-making, he would be happy to just lie there and enjoy her ministrations for hours.

It was rather pleasant to hear his wife say how much she had missed him and that there was no friend in bed like Heman, while at the same time her hands and lips were happily exploring his body. But he had to grit his teeth and not respond to her questions. "You're doing this because you're angry with me, aren't you, Heman? You know I love you. If you'll stop this shit and be nice, we could do this every day in Albuferia. Why can't you be happy with me? I don't think you're old. Really, you act younger and you're better-looking than Ronald Coldaxe. You've given enough of your life to that silly Byrdwhistle company." She kissed his penis enthusiastically. "Ah, what a big morceau. Je l'adore." Then she talked to it. "You know that you'd be happier at home. Wouldn't you?" She kept talking as she hovered over him. "Come home with me, Heman. I'll sleep on your merry-go-round with you. I'll ride your horses bare-ass. Going up and down, you can be inside me."

Then she became practical. "You can't do this to me, you silly man. You know I can't handle money. You have to take care of the million dollars that you are going to get from Ralph Thiemost and all that W.I.N. stock, too."

Then she spread her legs over him, and was talking to his erection again. "Epousez-moi! Epousez-moi! Tout de suite, oh, oh, je le veux, je l'adore."

Enjoying her thoroughly, H.H. was wondering if it would be inappropriate to manage a little foolish grin of happiness, especially since behind Adele, unseen and unheard by her, ten or so wispy old ladies and droopy old men in their seventies and eighties had opened the door and were tiptoeing into the room to watch them. H.H. could see them silently nodding with enthusiastic and ecstatic expressions of approval. Alexi must have told some of his patients that, if they couldn't do it themselves, they still weren't too old to watch. But then Adele heard their wheezy breathing.

Screaming, she jumped off the bed and waved angrily at them. "Allez! Allez!" She scrambled into her pantyhose. "You did this on purpose," she yelled at him. "I know you. You're crazy like a fox. You'll be sorry, Heman Youman." And H.H. *was* sorry. While their disappointed audience slithered back to their rooms, H.H. mumbled unhappily and pointed to his neglected penis; but Adele refused to get back in bed to help him achieve longevity.

29

The second week in October, five weeks after Ronald had returned to Boston, and just as H. H. Youman was beginning to wonder whether he would ever be able to become his own doppelganger, assume the role of Moses Megillah Marshalik, and try to seduce Meredith Coldaxe, Meredith finally capitulated and moved to Boston.

It hadn't been an easy decision. As she directed the transcontinental movers who had come with a huge van to pick up the Coldaxe furniture and what remained of the eighteen-year accumulation of possessions after a three-day garage sale, she was overwhelmed by a sense of transience and the impermanence of life. She hadn't decided to move because she was suddenly reconciled with Ronald or because she was any happier that his job as vice president of W.I.N.—and now president of the Byrdwhistle Division—obviously held higher priority in his life than their marriage. Actually, she had given serious thought to divorce. She wasn't passionately in love with Ronald, and he probably wasn't with her, but after so many years together, and two children, though they didn't agree on much, she believed that they basically liked each other. At least sometimes she liked him, and she still hoped that deep down Ron wasn't the cold-blooded, bottom-line, money-driven robot he pretended to be. She was sure that he cared as much as she did about making a better and a more loving world for their kids to grow up in.

But now, in one fell swoop, W.I.N. had won; and the God-damnable truth was that Ralph Thiemost probably wouldn't consider his last-minute inability to conquer her and reduce her to being his sexual slave a failure—nor would he consider his tactics abnormal. Neither would he believe that uprooting her life in Santa Monica was a victory.

Periodically tearing up one's roots—shallow as they often were—was a fact of upper-level corporate life in America. Climbing the ladder of success required both vertical and horizontal mobility. Friends and the clutter of material possessions weren't unique. They could be duplicated in the suburbs of a hundred other American lookalike cities. As for relatives, you couldn't choose them anyway. And blood got thicker when absence added the missing gel. Anyway, Mother Bell made it possible for love to grow stronger by satellite communication than it ever would in the daily so-called normal face-to-face family encounters.

Tina and Mitchell were adapting better to the breakup of their home than she was. All of a sudden, they loved Boston. They could fly East on school vacations and could spend the summer in New England with their parents. If Dad and Mom got lonesome, they could take a winter vacation in California and escape from all that cold and snow. Dad and Mom living in Boston while they continued their schooling in California was the best of all possible worlds.

Even before her "farewell" dinner with Ralph Thiemost on his yacht—which really clinched the matter—M'mm had been listening to her mother's warnings. "Ronald is a good-looking man, Meredith. Just keep in mind that it's a sexual jungle out there. There are millions of women who would be happy to latch on to him."

A few days later, when she tried to telephone Ron at the Ritz, M'mm wondered if her mother's words were prophetic. He had checked out of the hotel and left no forwarding address. It wasn't that she had anything particular to say to him, or that she was going to admit that she missed him, but Tina wanted to tell her father that she had been accepted at Berkeley and that she was thinking of majoring, as he had, in business administration. Tina knew that going to college to study business was like waving a red flag in front of her mother, But Tina was Daddy's girl.

When she hung up the phone, M'mm shrugged angrily at Tina's question. How the hell did she know where he was? A few days earlier, Ron had telephoned to tell her that he had found a beautiful house near Boston. Angrily, she had yelled at him. She wasn't interested in moving to a new suburban prison. It had taken her quite a few years to learn how to unlock the doors on their Santa Monica jail. Ron had mailed her a booklet that Byrdwhistle gave to new employees.

"You can hire me," she told him, and was at least partially serious. "Byrdwhistle sounds like just my cup of tea, and without the kids we don't need a big house. All we need is an apartment." Ronald tried to get through to her. The present Byrdwhistle policy of hiring only husband and wife teams, he told her, didn't apply to the top brass. Adele Youman didn't work at Byrdwhistle and never had. Besides, in a few weeks, when the purchase of Byrdwhistle was completed, and he was in charge, a lot of changes were going to be made. As a division of W.I.N. Incorporated, the company couldn't be run like a damned sex-commune. Ralph Thiemost wouldn't tolerate it.

M'mm wasn't sure about that, but she had to agree. The Byrdwhistle employee manual gave the impression that all you had to do to get another Byrdwhistler into the sack was to ask. If the answer was yes, and the spouse of the person you had a letch for gave his or her blessing, you could screw each other to oblivion.

M'mm didn't tell Tina the uneasy thoughts passing through her mind. Maybe since they both were top brass, and even without her husband's approval, Ron was sleeping with that woman vice president. Marge something or other. Slick. Marge Slick! My God!

A week later, with no further messages or phone calls from Ron, who hadn't been too pleased with her during their recent conversations, M'mm was building a case against him. She knew that all she had to do was to call Ralph Thiemost. He'd know where Ron was living. But telephoning Ralph was equivalent to whinnying, and she wasn't angry enough to do that. Not yet, anyway! The only other alternative was to call Byrdwhistle. She remembered that it was located in some town near Boston. Finally, with the help of a long-distance telephone operator, she got the number. A woman answered. "Good morning. I'm Susan. Byrdwhistle loves you. People who play together stay together. Can I help you?" Susan sounded altogether too cheery, especially when she responded to M'mm's request to talk to Mr. Coldaxe. "Oh, I'm sorry. Byrdwhistlers have just returned from vacation. Mr. Coldaxe is expected this week, but he hasn't arrived yet."

Ron hadn't arrived at Byrdwhistle after a week? That wasn't possible. He had telephoned from Boston three days ago. She was damned sure that he wasn't living at the YMCA. She decided to call Meg Thompson, Ralph Thiemost's secretary. Meg would know where Ron was. That way she wouldn't have to talk with Ralph. But before M'mm could stop her, Meg, properly impressed, said, "Oh, it's you, Mrs. Coldaxe," and put her right through to the Lord High Executioner.

Exasperated when she heard Ralph greeting her with a sexy hello, M'mm hung up. A few minutes later the phone rang, but it wasn't Ralph.

"Bill Lecky calling, Mrs. Coldaxe," the voice said. "You don't know me, but I'm the manager of the W.I.N. real-estate department."

"Did Ralph Thiemost tell you to call me?" M'mm demanded.

Lecky laughed, "The fact is that he did. Mr. Thiemost told me that W.I.N. was ready to take over your home in Santa Monica. Regardless of what we can sell it for, I'm authorized to pay you two hundred thousand dollars. Your husband has signed the papers. We need your signature."

"I'm not selling my house," M'mm yelled into the phone. "You can tell Ralph Thiemost to shove it. And you can do me a favor, Mr. Lecky. How can I reach my husband?"

"I haven't the faintest idea, Mrs. Coldaxe; but I can assure you, and I've checked it out very carefully, W.I.N.'s price is twenty-five to fifty thousand higher than you can get on the market, and with mortgage rates the way they are, you may have a hard time selling."

"I don't give a shit. I'm not selling my home. You can tell Ralph Thiemost and my husband that this is a joint property — they'll have to evict me."

In a few minutes, the phone rang again. M'mm picked it up as she was trying to suppress a sob of anger. It was Ralph Thiemost, jovial and cool. "You seem to be a little distraught, Meredith. First you call me and hang up. Now you've hung up on Bill Lecky. Did I detect a whinny in your voice just now?"

"No, God dammit, you didn't. I just wanted to find out where Ronald is. I want to talk to him."

Ralph was soothing, "He's trying to buy you a lovely home in Lynnfield, a suburb near Boston. That's why Bill telephoned you. Ron asked me if W.I.N. would help, and of course I agreed. We always try to make executive transfers as smooth as possible. Ron told me that, if he could sell your house in Santa Monica fast, he could buy a new one free and clear near Boston. You can't lose, Meredith. Real estate is the only investment that's keeping pace with inflation."

"I don't want a new house," M'mm said coldly. "I'm very happy with the one I have. There's no reason for me to move. You told Ron that he'd probably be in Boston only for a year."

"No, I didn't, Meredith. These things are very hard to gauge. The Byrdwhistle purchase was finalized yesterday. But the sad truth is that Byrdwhistle is a company that's been running itself. Ron tells me that it's going to take a major effort to turn it into one of our winners. Ron will stay in Boston just as long as it takes to do the kind of winning job that I know he's capable of." Ralph paused, "Unless, of course, I hear a little whinny from the distaff side of the Coldaxe family."

While M'mm was wondering if she dared tell Ralph Thiemost to go fuck himself, he continued blithely, "Why don't you come down here for lunch today? I'll bring you up to date on the good job that Ron is doing. Later on, we'll give him a ring at Adele's."

"Adele's?" Feeling an uneasy sensation in her stomach, M'mm scowled into the phone. She remembered Adele's name. She was the wife of the man who ran Byrdwhistle. She could hear Ralph laughing.

"Adele Youman. Ron is really getting his teeth into things. He's made friends with Youman's wife. Adele is a most interesting woman. She's writing a book about powerful men. Who knows, maybe she'll include a chapter about Ron in it?"

"Are you telling me that he's sleeping with her?"

"I didn't say that, Meredith," Ralph said smoothly. "The Youmans evidently have a big townhouse in downtown Boston. Ron is saving W.I.N. money by bunking there." Ralph laughed. "On the other hand, I must admit that even though Adele is about my age she's a very sexy woman. She makes no bones about it. She likes men. She told me that she was helping Ron find a new house for you. She hopes that you and she can be friends. She sent me an amusing picture she took of Ron. He's diving into their indoor pool."

In shocked silence, M'mm was trying to digest the information that Ronald Coldaxe, usually a very anti-social man, and one who she knew detested sleeping in other people's houses, was actually living with the Youmans and enjoying himself swimming in their pool. Was this her husband? The man who always told her that he hated swimming pools and had refused ever to build one in their backyard? M'mm was suddenly sure that it was true. Good old Ron. He probably was sleeping with Adele. He'd get to the top one way or the other. A carbon copy of Ralph Thiemost, Ron would screw his own grandmother if it would make him a winner. She wasn't listening to Ralph, who was trying to tell her that if Ron mixed business and pleasure he was sure that Ron would be very careful.

"You can tell Ron that if Adele's husband doesn't give a damn, neither do I," Meredith said angrily. "He can go to bed with whomever he wants, but in the future it won't be me."

"That's not reacting like a winner," Ralph said. "I have a suggestion. Tonight around six—it'll be nine P.M. Boston time—we'll call Ron. I'll introduce you to Adele over the telephone. I'll tell Billy to pick you up around five. We'll have dinner on my boat."

Ten days later, as she handed the keys to her empty house to Billy and got into the back seat of Ralph Thiemost's Rolls Royce, she wondered how much Billy knew about the evening she had spent with his boss. Billy had arrived just as the van in the driveway was finally loaded. She hadn't seen Ralph since that evening and had hung up on him every time he had called since that terrible night. But he had telephoned again that morning.

"I'm going to miss you," he said. "You're a hell of an interesting woman, Meredith."

"You have a god-damned nerve to keep bothering me," M'mm told him coldly. "You're lucky I didn't telephone the police and tell them what a pervert you are."

Ralph had only chuckled, "They wouldn't believe you, Meredith. I'd have told them it never happened and that you were simply acting out a typical female fantasy."

Scowling into the telephone, she listened to Ralph expound on his belief that the reason capitalism was in trouble was that too many feminine men were yielding to equal-rights pressure. Women, by their nature, had to be simultaneously protected and dominated. The smart female became a winner when she learned how to capture a male by yielding to his power needs. He wished she'd let him have a second chance to instruct her. If she changed her mind in the future and felt like whinnying, she could telephone him anytime. In the meantime, Billy was on his way to drive her to the airport. She might just as well leave California in style.

M'mm finally acquiesced. "I don't ever want to see you again," she said, "but I have a suggestion for you. Why don't you tie Billy up and rape him? I'm sure he'll kiss your ass while you're doing it." She hung up to Ralph's booming laughter.

M'mm knew that, less than two weeks ago, she had finally agreed to play in the Thiemost fire again only because she had been so angry with Ron. Instead of agreeing with M'mm that, without the kids and with the certainty that their stay in Boston would be a short one and that renting an apartment would be more sensible than buying a house, he had finally gone house-hunting with Adele, a sixty-six-year-old woman. "She wants to adopt you," Ron told M'mm cheerfully. "You'll like Adele, and H.H. is the kind of father figure you always go for."

"I know you always wanted a mother more than a wife," M'mm yelled at him, "but I detest dirty old men." M'mm was sure that any woman who had the cool nerve to help her lover choose a house for his wife wouldn't hesitate to mother him in bed. But even before she had that angry conversation with Ron and finally hung up on him, she had told him that since the gander was obviously philandering she was sure he wouldn't mind if the goose was loose.

Now, watching the back of his head as he drove to the airport, M'mm wondered if Billy had any idea what had happened to her after he had left her alone with Ralph. Probably. M'mm was sure that she wasn't the first woman that Ralph had trapped into playing his porno-power game. But Billy was one of the loyal W.I.N. family. He might not approve of his lord and master, but he would never rebel.

Wearing a pale-blue cowl-necked cashmere sweater, she had followed Billy into the maze of piers at Marina del Rey, where the W.I.N. yacht was docked. Threading their way past a half-mile or more of multi-thousand-dollar boats to a special dock that was isolated from the rest, M'mm knew that she was getting nervous. In this lonely part of the marina in the gathering dusk, it was apparent that there were few people, if any, around.

Ralph greeted her from the top of the boarding stairs. He was casually dressed, wearing white ducks and a faded denim navy-style workshirt. Taking her on tour of the yacht, he showed her the various bedrooms and the master stateroom with a king-sized bed. Amazingly, he seemed sedate and made no inuendoes about what might happen later. He explained that he had given the permanent captain and the young fellow who did the cooking the night off. But she was not to worry. There were plenty of steaks in the galley refrigerator, and there was an infrared oven. Ralph was sure that together they could whip up a fine dinner. Back in the ship's lounge, Ralph opened a bottle of champagne and told her that he had put in a call to Adele and Ron. He said that when he had telephoned an hour earlier there had been no answer; but he was sure they would be home very soon.

M'mm sipped her champagne slowly. She was determined not to drink too much. She wasn't even sure why she had come. Certainly not to whinny. Even if she decided to go to bed with Ralph Thiemost, and at the moment she wasn't at all sure that she would, she wanted to be in full mental control. If nothing else, she would drive a hard bargain. She might even convince him to tell Ron over the phone, while she was listening, that he wouldn't have to stay in Boston for more than a year—preferably six months—and they most certainly didn't need to buy any damned house.

Thinking these thoughts, at the same time M'mm was trying to absorb the luxurious furnishings of the lounge. A prolific spider plant suspended in a cast-iron pot hung halfway from the ceiling in one corner of the room. It was attached to a nylon rope that was threaded through a pulley in the ceiling and cleated to the wall. Somehow it wasn't in keeping with the Italian Mediterranean decor of the room. Later, M'mm was to discover that the hook and pulley had other uses; but now Ralph was entertaining her with a rambling story about H. H. Youman.

"I told Ron that we'd have to get rid of Youman sooner or later," Ralph was saying. "He is a very quirky character. He tried to stop Thornton Byrd from selling the company, but when he realized it was a fait accompli he turned around and retired. Now, according to Adele, he had a complete mental collapse. In the past few years, I'm sure there has been more than one screw loose in Youman's brain. W.I.N. came along just in time to save his skin."

"I thought that Mr. Youman had invited Ron to stay in his house," M'mm really hadn't thought about it but she had assumed that H. H. Youman would be living under the same roof with his wife.

"Lord no," Ralph said. "Youman is in some nursing home. He's gone over the hill."

Ralph picked up a large envelope from the coffee table, pulled out an eight-by-ten color photograph and handed it to M'mm. "That's Adele," he said. "A self-portrait. She's an expert photographer. Too bad she didn't send a full-length one. She has the body to go with the face."

M'mm stared uneasily at a strikingly sexy white-haired woman who was grinning in a very provocative way into the camera. Adele most certainly didn't look like the mother M'mm had imagined for Ron. And Ron was living in her house unchaperoned!

Then Ralph casually handed her another picture. M'mm gasped and threw caution to the wind. Downing her glass of champagne and then another that Ralph poured, she stared grimly at a picture of her stark-naked husband poised in mid-air for a dive into a swimming pool. Adele had obviously taken the picture, and Ron's big erection obviously wasn't caused by the two young children grinning at him.

Ralph was thoroughly amused by her obvious consternation. "You shouldn't get angry," he told her. "Adele is writing a book about power-hungry men. In a moment of insanity, I even made the mistake of letting her take a picture of me. I told Ron yesterday that, in a very smooth and easy way, he must not only recover the negatives of his picture but of mine, too. It's a top-priority assignment. I'm sure that the main reason Ron is still bunking with Adele is those damned negatives. They could get into the wrong hands. Nothing makes the losers of this world happier than to moan and groan over the sexual peccadillos of the winners. Look at the Kennedys, John and Ted. They're a good example."

M'mm was feeling grim. She knew that Ron was a patsy for smooth-talking, sophisticated women. Now she wondered just how many strange women Ron had been to bed with during the past eighteen years. It was really a lifetime, during which she had consistently refused all offers—several of them intriguing—of extramarital hanky-panky. She swallowed her fourth glass of champagne. To hell with it! The time had come for her to be a winner. "What are your sexual peccadillos?" she demanded, and she immediately bit her tongue. It was better not to know.

Ralph confirmed the thought. "Bondage," he grinned at her.

M'mm had seen pictures of women wearing leather blouses and slacks standing over men and whipping them. My God, was Ralph Thiemost a masochist? Was crawling around naked while some woman beat him the only way he could climax?

"I guess I couldn't do that," she said naively.

"Do what?" Ralph smiled at her like a protective father. "Don't worry, Meredith. You really won't have to *do* anything." He leered at her. "But it's early yet, let's make dinner first."

In the well-stocked galley, wondering if she should gather her wits and run for her life, M'mm helped cut up vegetables for a salad. The filet mignons were ready in what seemed an instant. Hoping the food would absorb the alcohol, M'mm ate her steak rather dizzily. Still feeling aggrieved with Ron, she continued drinking the champagne that Ralph kept pouring for her.

"This is very pleasant, Meredith," he told her. "I have a good feeling about tonight. You and I will play silly little bondage games together, and later we'll do some hard thinking about Ron's future. I've been thinking that W.I.N. may need Ron in California much more than in Boston. Are you agreeable to that?"

M'mm knew that her curiosity was forcing her to find out how agreeable "agreeable" was. Damn, if Ralph Thiemost only wanted her to whip his bare ass, she'd do it. She'd even tie him up. She didn't know if it was the champagne, but suddenly the idea was erotic.

Ralph led her up the gangway back to the lounge. She flopped on a sofa, and then he sat down beside her dangling a pair of handcuffs.

She almost giggled. "Do you want me to handcuff you?"

"Of course not, Meredith. Male bondage is sick." Before she could pull her arms away, he snapped a cuff on one wrist and then one on the other.

M'mm was suddenly sober. "Take these damned things off me!" she said indignantly.

He smiled soothingly at her. "Of course, but not for an hour or so. Subduing an aggressive woman like you is very exciting to me. I wanted to do this to you the first time I met you."

M'mm was suddenly frightened, but she was determined not to let this bastard know it. She held out her hands. "I know it won't do any good to scream, but if you don't take these handcuffs off me, I'll kick you in the balls."

Chuckling, Ralph crossed the lounge and unhooked the spider plant. The hook was dangling at shoulder height. Returning to M'mm, who lay back on the sofa thrashing her legs to keep him away, he grabbed one, pulled her to the floor, and encircled her body with his arms. Puffing, while she fought against him, he dragged her to the hook and pulled her arms up high enough to drop the chain between the loops of the handcuffs. Before she could extricate herself, he had unfastened the cleated rope. M'mm felt her arms being yanked taut over her head. Ignoring her screaming and cursing, he pulled her up, forcing her to stand on her tiptoes. Her fingers were only a few inches from the ceiling.

"You dirty rotten son-of-a-bitch, let me down," she snarled at him.

"You'll get down a lot faster when you shed a tear or two. Tonight you're going to learn how to whinny a little." Ralph was delighted with his coup. Then to her horror, knowing she was totally unable to stop him, she watched while he pulled off her shoes. Searching, he found the zipper on her slacks. For a moment his hands searched into her groin, and he grinned at her seductively. Then he pulled the zipper.

Ignoring her screams, he pulled off her panties and fished around under her sweater, found her bra, and unsnapped it. Except for her sweater and her dangling bra, which he pushed high over her breasts, she was stark naked. He caressed her, telling her he liked her thick black bush. He knelt in front of her and forced her thighs apart with his hands and examined her vulva. She tried to kick him, but with her body off balance, she was dangling painfully by the wrists.

"You're a fucking monster," she choked back her tears. "I'll never beg you, and I'll never whinny."

Then, while she watched, he stripped off his clothes and she saw his enormous erection. Helpless, begging him not to touch her, to keep his rotten mouth and hands off of her, she screamed while he kissed her from head to foot. Then, admiring each of her breasts appreciatively, he told her that she was entirely wrong. He was not perverted. He was simply enjoying the primitive bride-of-capture rites. A female taken in conquest belonged to her captor. Rape was an age-old phenomenon built into the male genes. "You belong to me. You're mine. I can do anything I want to you." He kissed and sucked her nipples. And then, kneeling, with his hands deep in the cleft of her behind, his mouth and tongue slobbered over her labia.

"I hope to hell you're having a good time," she gasped. "I'm not!" But to her own horror, she knew that Meredith Coldaxe, a writhing doll on a string, wasn't twisting and turning only from fear but from a growing excitement at being ravished. But now her hands and arms were becoming painful. "Please," she groaned, "fuck me and get it over with, my arms are dying." She wondered if he would try to screw her standing up, but Ralph had obviously taken this trip before. He inserted a footstool between her legs, released the rope from the cleat and slowly lowered her down to the stool. For a moment, with a sigh of relief, she was sitting on the stool, but her drooping arms were still held by the hook over her head.

"I think that you're getting ready to be cooperative," Ralph held her face and kissed her lips gently. "I'm glad you decided to be a good girl." He rubbed her arms to restore her circulation.

"The hell I am, I hate you, you bastard!" She spit at him. "Take these cuffs off me, Ralph Thiemost. You can't screw me this way."

"Don't count on it." He tugged the rope, and once again her arms were in the air. She was squatting, her legs separated by the footstool. Grasping her buttocks, he slid underneath her. Totally helpless, she could feel his engorged penis moving on the edge of her labia, along her perineum. "As you can see, it's going to be quite easy," he chuckled.

Kicking, thrashing as she dangled over his huge phallus, M'mm realized that she was wide open prey. She couldn't stop him. But then, with a moan of sheer frustration, Ralph's excitement peaked. He grabbed her, but she kept in motion and he was unable to penetrate her.

Groaning disgustedly, he wriggled out from under her and flopped on the floor, panting. "You're a little bitch," he said, but then he laughed; and he released the rope completely.

Sitting on the footstool, her arms by her side, M'mm held out her hands. "Okay, little boy. You had your fun. Take these damn things off me."

Ralph shook his head, still stunned by his furious orgasm. "I'm not sorry," he told her. "I'd do it again." But he found the key and unfastened the handcuffs.

"You're a very sick man," M'mm told him. Free at last but still feeling her own lust, she was a little bewildered herself. "Until tonight, you nearly had me convinced. I was beginning to think you really were a winner."

Shrugging, Ralph pulled his underwear over his deflated penis. While she dressed, he found his billfold and handed her two one-hundred-dollar bills. "Get the hell out of here, Meredith Coldaxe. Take a taxi home. You're a very irritating woman. Get out of my hair. Go to Boston and drive your husband crazy. But keep it in mind that you didn't win either. You know damn well that, all the time you were fighting me, way down inside you wanted me to win. You wanted to be fucked senseless."

Thanking Billy for the drive to the airport, knowing that Ronald was waiting in Boston on the other curve of the continent, it occurred to M'mm that Ralph might be right. But she hadn't met the winner yet who could make her lose her mind, even for a minute.

30

Adele didn't give up easily. Every morning she arrived promptly at the Center for Ageless Humans. But she made no attempt to get in bed with Heman. Instead, if he was sitting in his wheelchair or lying on the bed, she would whisper erotically to him, "Come on, honey, I know that you're not that far gone." While she breathed huskily around his face, her hands were searching his body. "You've got to make love to me. If you don't, I'll grow old and dry up, and I won't be pretty anymore."

She told him in extended detail how much more fun he was in bed than men like Ralph Thiemost, who couldn't make love for more than fifteen minutes, or poor old Thorny, who had a perpetual hard on but often couldn't reach a climax; and she revealed details of her sex-life with other "power-hungry men" who H.H. had never met but who Adele claimed were stupid. They didn't realize that the source of male power was loving women, not money.

"Most men are not like you," she told him. "They're not laughing lovers. They only have two bottom lines in their lives—profits and a woman's ass, and they think that both can be manipulated.

Even though he had bedded with either Sylvia or Marge practically every night in October, H.H. knew that he would have been perfectly able to enjoy a little sex-making with Adele. Adele's insistence, and her taking the initiative in the sex chase, was something he hadn't counted on. Not to react but just to lie there and stare idiotically at the ceiling while he was enjoying Adele's caresses wasn't easy. But he was pleased with his continuing enjoyment of the female mind. One day when he was sure Adele had learned her lesson, he promised himself that he would spend a week in bed with her and tell her about his exciting discovery. He had found the missing link for extended healthy human longevity.

Transformed as Moses Megillah Marshalik, he had already discussed it with Sylvia, who had been taking him on afternoon tours of various nursing homes and senior-citizen centers that she inspected for the state. "Paul Niehans, who lived to be eighty-nine," he told her, "treated Konrad Adenauer, W. Somerset Maugham, Charlie Chaplin, Bernard Baruch, Charles de Gaulle, and God knows how many other males with injections of male testicular cells. Niehans believed 'that the sex glands are not merely glands where spermatazoa and ova are formed, but their internal secretions are a rich source of vital fluids which give physical strength, intellectual freshness, and also improve physical qualities. They revitalize the aging organism. With their drying up, old age begins.'"

He and Sylvia were visiting the Pleasantview Nursing Home. While the view of a superhighway a few hundred feet away was no better or worse than the views of other homes they had visited, most of the inmates never looked out the window. Many of them apathetically remained in their rooms all day. The more mobile ones, cajoled by the attendants to gather in the main lounge for dinner, talked dully with each other, and others tried to respond enthusiastically to the bustling chatter of the nurses and attempted to play the little games the nurses invented for them to pass the time. Living dead, isolated from the mainstream of life, contemplating their navels, whatever their illness or their age they all had one thing in common. They were waiting in Death Row, guilty of getting old, condemned to die not only by society but by themselves. There would be no last-minute reprieve from the governor.

"This is only the beginning," Sylvia told him. "Stick around another twenty years. By then, there will be twenty-five million people over sixty-five. By the year 2020, there will be forty-two million of them." She shivered. "It scares the hell out of me. I'll be one of them. By that time, there will be no family structure at all. We'll be wards of the state. Billions of dollars will be spent assuaging consciences, trying to keep the aged from becoming totally depressed or paranoid, or trying to stop them from drinking themselves to death." Sylvia laughed grimly, "By that time, the drug of choice in these nursing homes will be marijuana. The older generation will become euphoric potheads. It would be better to offer them the choice of a fast exit."

H.H. disagreed with her. "It would be better to recreate the world that you are going to live in," he told her. "Why can't we make life creative from birth to death? That's the missing link. Niehans believed in mechanical means—cellular transplants. I'm positive that there's a close link between healthy longevity and creativity. Asa Aslan, the woman who has tried to slow up the biological clock with Gerovital H3, is convinced that creativity is 'one aspect of the will to live.' She claims that 'it produces vital brain impulses that stimulate the pituitary gland, which triggers effects on the pineal gland and the whole endocrine system.' Norman Cousins asked if it were possible that placebos might have key roles in the longevity process; but in his *Anatomy of an Illness,* he didn't explore the interface between human sexuality and creativity."

Sylvia laughed. "Seems to me that sex-making is the most basic creativity impulse there is."

"Agreed." Grinning at some of the senior citizens who watched him enviously as he patted her ass, he told her: "I'm convinced that active genitals and active brain cells are a product of each other. It's pretty well established that sex-making is beneficial physiologically and psychologically for arthritis sufferers. Sexual activity stimulates the adrenal glands and releases natural cortisones. Recently it has been established that the semen of many animals contains a substance called 'seminal plasm,' which may be just as potent as penicillin. In a woman's vagina, it protects her from the micro-organisms that cause vaginal infections. In addition, the female body absorbs semen. A few minutes after intercourse, the faint odor of male semen will appear on a woman's breath. Isn't it possible that the male is similarly absorbing life-giving chemicals from the female body?"

Listening to him, Sylvia was well aware that Moses Marshalik's room at the center was overflowing with books. Either H.H. or his doppelgänger had been avidly reading all the current theories about cellular growth and degeneration. In bed, while he was playing the happy satyr and enjoying her body and finally immersed in her vagina, he never stopped being the enthusiastic teacher, dragging his devoted pupil along with him in mind-boggling mental gymnastics.

"Thiemost doesn't know it, yet," he told her. "Actually, neither did I until a few weeks ago; but he and Adele have done the world a favor. I'm going to prove to both of them that power is not creative and never can be. Exercising power in any form is ultimately destructive. Adele may be on the right track, but she has to learn that it isn't powerful environments, but loving environments, that release male sexual power; and that's the only kind of power that can be benign and creative." H.H grinned at Sylvia. "Instead of rotting in Albuferia, I'm going to spend my inclining years making sure that my wife and Sylvia—my daughter, mistress, and lover—will enjoy the better part of their lives on this earth as sexy grandmothers."

Sylvia stared at him, puzzled. "You said 'inclining.' Don't you mean 'declining'?"

"The hell I do," H.H. told her. "Creativity is never a by-product of rolling downhill. You have to spend your life climbing even higher, sometimes running, sometimes walking, sometimes doggedly crawling and pulling yourself up the jagged mountainside, knowing god-damned well that, if you could only get to the top, all the answers would be there waiting for you."

"What if you never get to the top?"

H.H. was kissing her slowly from her eyes to her toes. "That's the secret. No one can ever get to the top. But it doesn't matter. But just trying to keeps you healthy. Creativity begets creativity. My penis is alive and throbbing, your vagina is slippery and pulsating, not just because we love each other, but because we have millions of things to do in this world before we finally check out."

When H.H. decided to counterattack under the cover of a doddering old man, he knew that his children might be both curious and concerned, especially his oldest son, Haskell Heman, who was a surgeon in New York City. But H.H. and Adele had never depended on any of them for money or companionship. Their Louisburg Square house could accommodate the entire family, including the grandchildren; and over the years, in the process of pursuing their own destinies, they had wandered in and out of the Youman commune at will. But they often acted as if their parents were visitors from some other planet. Both H.H. and Adele were well aware that at this early stage in their lives — only Haskell was past thirty — they were shocked by their parents seeming lack of sexual morality.

One by one, evidently egged on by Adele, they arrived to survey the wreck of Heman Hyman. They hugged their poor afflicted father and commiserated with Adele; but after a while they got edgy, and H.H. saw them glancing surreptitiously at their watches. After all, senile dementia is a scary disease, especially when it is being performed by an enthusiastic actor who enjoyed answering their many questions with endless gibberish and non sequiturs. While H.H. experienced a few pangs of remorse over their sorrow for him, he couldn't help being amused, particularly because his rapidly garbled responses often made sense to anyone listening carefully.

Hanan Hyman, their youngest son, an engineer with Boeing, had flown to Boston from Oregon to see him, and Yovela, their last child and only daughter, had arrived from New York City. They were dutifully sympathetic. They stared at Daddy Heman tearfully and tried to convince Adele that he would most certainly get well and be his old self again, even without his baby — Byrdwhistle. But Haskell had been more suspicious. After his first visit, he came back again.

"I had a long talk with Alexi," he told his father when they were alone one morning. "He's a good friend of yours. He insists that you are experiencing a typical past-sixty crisis. Sudden retirement and the realization that the world doesn't need you anymore has knocked you off balance." Haskell looked at him speculatively for a moment, and then said, "You can cut out the crap with me. I won't tell Adele. I'm positive that you haven't got Alzheimer's disease."

H.H. stared blearily at him and sighed. "Zol ikh, nor derleben tsu zen aza zakh." Lately, secure in the belief that neither Adele nor his children could understand the language, H.H. had been speaking rapidly in Yiddish to his morning visitors. Raving on, he continued, "Es iz a sakonedike krenk, nor az der eybershter volt gebn, ikh zol a bisl shitsun, volt ikh nokh gekunt gezunt vern."

But somehow he had miscalculated. To his amazement, Haskell suddenly jumped in bed on top of him. Straddling his father, he began to tickle him. "You're a sly old bastard," Haskell yelled at him triumphantly, and he prodded his father's body relentlessly until H.H. gasped with laughter. "You always did this to me when I was a kid, particularly when I got in one of my dropout moods. You told me that laughing would make my troubles go away."

"Stop it, for God's sake," H.H. caught his breath for a moment, "I surrender. How in hell did you figure it out, Hasky?"

Laughing, and well pleased with himself, Haskell slid off the bed and hugged H.H. "Remember, you always told us how sad it was that your kids didn't know Yiddish. Our Wasp mother didn't know it. Adele only knows words that she learned from you. You insisted that knowing Yiddish would expand our horizons." Haskell chuckled, "So a year ago I bought tapes and started to learn it. You should have stuck to the gibberish you were spouting yesterday. Just now you said, 'May I only live to see such a thing. It's a dangerous illness, but if God grant that I could sweat a little, I could get well.'"

H.H. shook his head, pleased with him but nervous that Haskell might pull the rug out from under him. "Okay, now you've got me sweating. If you tell your mother, I may never recover." He grabbed Haskell's hand and shoved it against Haskell's groin. "Like the old Romans, you must swear on your testicles. It's our secret. I need the next few months to reorganize my life." Haskell agreed not to tell Adele, but set a time limit of three months.

Then, on Haskell's last visit before returning to New York, he tried to probe his father's plans. But H.H. told him they were still too amorphous. How could he tell his son that right now business cards were being printed for Moses M. Marshalik, Vice President of Marsha Lovett Cosmetics, or that within a week he was going to ring Meredith Coldaxe's doorbell and begin the seduction of the wife of his successor?

Instead, he tried to divert Hasky with an extended discussion of the importance of Theory Z. "Anyone who can pass the Byrdwhistle entrance examination," he told him, "must be a transcender. I'm convinced that the transcender's approach to life ensures his or her longevity. Transcenders, by definition, must be creative. They know instinctively how to play. They are totally comfortable with their sexuality, and they aren't the least bit hesitant about revealing their sexual motivations in their daily lives. Thus they create an excellent mental and physical environment for healthy cell chemistry." H.H., who was still wearing his hospital johnny and was enthroned in his wheelchair, stared at Haskell for a moment. "Your medical education cost me a pile of money, Hasky. I'd appreciate your confirmation of Theory Z."

Haskell frowned at him dubiously. "It's probably a good approach, but the first requirement for longevity is that you inherit good genes. You obviously did, since Grandpops and Grandma lived to be more than ninety. But I never realized that you were so concerned about dying."

"God-dammit, Haskell, I'm not afraid of dying. I just want to straighten out your generation. It is constantly wondering what to do about senior citizens and insisting that they be put out to pasture and that the government provide peace and dignity for their golden years. In plain words, that's bullshit. The hell with peace and dignity. I want to create a world where everybody is concerned about living and millions of people enjoy playing the game; and even when they're finally drawing their last breath, but not earlier than four-score and ten years, they literally die laughing."

Haskell shrugged. "You can't escape your biological clock. No one has disproved Hayflick's theories yet. Except for cancer cells, which kill you anyway, all cells in your body divide about fifty times and then quit."

"I know that, but the process in humans should take about a hundred and fifteen years. The trouble is that most people are dead, or half-dead, long before they should be."

"Now you're asking the million-dollar question. What causes normal cells to run out of gas? Maybe it's the biochemical reactions of oxidation, or cross linkage, or hormone secretions," Haskell laughed. "I love you, Heman, but neither you nor I will live long enough to see if someone finds the answers. Maybe someday, a few hundred years from now, we will really understand DNA. Who knows? We may be able to splice cells from turtles or carp, or even redwood trees, into human cells. Then we could all live forever."

H.H. shook his head. "Dammit, Haskell, that's not what I'm after. Living forever would be a bore. I'd rather show people how to live a healthy life right to the end of those fifty cell-divisions. Then instead of a bitter end, they could say goodbye with their pricks in the air and their clitorises happily waggling."

Before Haskell left, he told H.H. he would try to reassure Adele. "I'll tell Mother that she shouldn't be alarmed, that you've had a minor nervous breakdown—really a power failure caused by the sudden realization that you weren't going to live long enough to remake the world. But I'll tell her not to worry, that your dynamos are still turning and you will get started again."

H.H. beamed at him. "Good boy! You've hit it on the nose. Give me three months, and then watch the dawn come up like thunder."

Sheldon Coombs wasn't so sure. At H.H.'s request, he had made a thorough analysis of W.I.N.'s operating figures and balance sheets. "W.I.N. only issues a consolidated report," he told H.H. "There's no specific information on their thirty-three divisions, except what you can glean from their annual reports. But we're pretty sure that only half of the recent acquisitions they've made are returning a profit. Five or six of them should have been spun off years ago. A good example is the Lovett Corporation. Like Tupperware, they've had outstanding success in the home-party direct-selling field, but they bombed when they tried the formula with Marsha Lovett Cosmetics. They haven't been able to get a toe in the door where Avon and others have done so well." Sheldon shrugged. "But Marsha Lovett is only one of the companies they should phase out."

To Sheldon's surprise, instead of being concerned that the W.I.N. purchase agreement for Byrdwhistle would force World Corporation, based on World's redeemable certificate sales agreements, to redeem Byrdwhistle stock for W.I.N. stock—thus leaving World with what in Sheldon's opinion was a very poor investment—H.H. was suddenly much more interested in Marsha Lovett Cosmetics.

"Dig out complete information for me," H.H. told him. "Put in a blind call through our lawyers. Find out if Marsha Lovett Cosmetics is for sale. Get a detailed report of how they are functioning in the east— particularly the metropolitan Boston area." He grinned at Sheldon, "Who knows? I may buy it for a hobby. After a lifetime of direct-mail selling, maybe I'll try direct personal selling."

By the middle of October, H.H. was secure. His cover was working. Elmer Byrd and Marvy had visited him and left sobbing, overwhelmed at the crumbled wreck of a friend and mentor. Even Ronald Coldaxe had dropped in, accompanied by Marge, and H.H. was sure that he had detected a tear of regret in Ron's eye at the disintegration and ruined sack of flesh and bones that was formerly Heman Hyman Youman. By ten A.M., when he was no longer available for morning inspection, H.H. hotfooted it to his upstairs room and quickly transformed himself into an astute, handsome, well-groomed con-man, Moses Megillah Marshalik.

Before Meredith Coldaxe arrived in Boston, and before he had learned through Marge that she was finally settled in her new home in Lynnfield, H.H. had been visiting nursing homes with Sylvia to cheer up real-life derelicts and had spent at least one afternoon a week with Sheldon Coombs in the offices of World Corporation, high in the Prudential Tower overlooking Boston.

Both Sheldon Coombs, a tall, lean offshoot of Cabot-Lowell-Salton-stall genes with all the important Harvard credentials — a law degree and an M.B.A. — and the offices of World Corporation exuded a much more sedate appearance than Byrdwhistle. Six years ago, when H.H. had launched World Corporation, he and his secretary had handled all the investments. But, as World expanded, like King Gillette, H.H. knew that he must be careful not to mix his huckster salesman image with the less oxygenated world of high finance. As front man, Sheldon was particularly good at impressing the Boston Brahmins and the bluebloods of the money world with World's investment sagacity.

World Corporation now had five full-time employees. With its mahogany-paneled walls, Oriental rugs, and tapestried Louis XIV chairs, and a distinguished oil portrait of King Gillette in the small waiting room, World reflected a Mellon or Rothschild kind of probity. Neither Sheldon nor his two assistants, Carleton Hill and Spencer Barlow, dressed in the casual way that H.H. did. Rather, they oozed what Adele would call the pinstriped-power look of conservative but successful young executives. And H.H. was sure that the two female secretaries in their late fifties, who exuded a kind of cool disdain associated with moral rectitude, could never be sexually rehabilitated by Alexi Ivanowsky or even himself.

But appearances are often deceiving. While Sheldon and his assistants would probably never be transcenders, or believers in Theory Z-type management or the play-ethic, they were serious world corporationists and missionaries in the service of King Gillette. Actually, H.H. had made it a condition of their employment. In addition, he had agreed with Sheldon that they could only work together successfully if they lay their disagreements on the line with each other. This gave Sheldon the opportunity to blow his top, as he often did when he disapproved of a particularly Youman-type insanity.

"We've always been honest with each other," Sheldon told H.H. when he handed him his new business card. "If you're going to play the role of some Jewish messiah while the real Heman Hyman is pretending he's senile in the Center for Ageless Humans, I really think you are being side-tracked. You're not moving in the King Gillette direction. I'm afraid that you've lost the World Corporation takeover perspective. I don't understand why you've suddenly developed this mad enthusiasm for the direct-selling cosmetic business." Sheldon grimaced. He wondered if H.H. really might be getting a little soft in the head, but he didn't say it. "Before you disappear and resurface in the hinterlands as Moses Marshalik, bring me up to date. What do you intend to do with the eleven million shares of W.I.N. stock that we've had shoved down our throats by Thornton Byrd and W.I.N.'s lawyers?"

Moses Marshalik's feet were perched on the World Corporation director's table. "Keep cool, Sheldon," he said. "We've got an important

week ahead of us. I want you very gradually to buy up about thirty million more shares of W.I.N." Moses flipped the pages of the four-color
glossy W.I.N. annual report and shook his head sorrowfully at a photograph of Ralph Thiemost on the second page. He read Thiemost's upbeat
annual message: "Despite a troublesome year and a small drop in profits,
I can assure W.I.N. stockholders that the W.I.N. management are still
winners."

Moses laughed and spit on the page. "It says here in this report that
the W.I.N. winners have about ninety-five million shares of stock outstanding. A few months ago they bought back five million of their own
shares."

Sheldon shrugged. "They're trying to make a silk purse out of a sow's
ear. But W.I.N. stock is still selling for twelve dollars and fifty cents a
share." Sheldon shoved a page of the typewritten analysis in front of
Moses. "It boils down to this: W.I.N. may still be in *Fortune*'s list of the
top one hundred companies in the United States, but it's a very sick company. Last year it had sales of two point seven billion. W.I.N. lists assets
of one and a half billion, but they're probably overstated. Their profit
after taxes this year will be less than eighty million. W.I.N. stock has
moved from a high of sixty-two to a shaky twelve dollars and fifty cents.
They could only pay a dividend of fifty cents a share this year. At current
market prices, that's less than a four percent return on investment."

"What's your estimate of what's wrong with the company?" Moses
asked, becoming H.H. for a moment.

"Top management is too damned busy acquiring new companies.
Instead of trying to improve their profits by taking over companies like
Byrdwhistle, they should have concentrated on their internal operations
and consolidated the managements of the companies they had and made
them more efficient, and got rid of some of the unprofitable ones. With a
sale of less than three billion, and their current profitability, they
shouldn't have more than sixty thousand employees. Instead they have
about eighty-eight thousand people. Everything I find indicates that
Ralph Thiemost, their chief exec, should step down." Sheldon shrugged.
"Younger management might be able to tighten the ship, but I personally
doubt it. In my opinion, we should unload the W.I.N. shares that World
has suddenly acquired. If we do it slowly, and pray, maybe we can get
out before the stock drops lower."

H.H. laughed, "You're having a failure of imagination, Sheldon.
Those eighty-eight thousand employees are going to help us buy W.I.N.
Incorporated. I have a hunch that a great many of the present investors
would be happy to take ten dollars a share and run for the woods. You
can start the ball rolling. As a ten percent stockholder in W.I.N., World
will take an advertisement in the *Wall Street Journal*. You can insist that
W.I.N. be totally liquidated, and that's the only way that the stockholders

may finally realize as much as twelve dollars a share. In a few weeks, when you've made the public very uneasy, World will offer to buy up fifty-one percent of the outstanding stock at ten dollars a share."

H.H. had begun ignoring Sheldon's devious astonishment. Finally, Sheldon couldn't control himself, "For God's sake, H.H., that would take over five hundred million dollars! Where in hell are we going to get it? World's entire assets are only about four hundred and twenty-five million, and they're in damned good investments. They shouldn't be liquidated. If you go after Ralph Thiemost's scalp, you may lose your own."

H.H. grinned at him, "Have a little faith, Sheldon. I don't want Thiemost's scalp. I'm going to de-ball him. But until de-ball day arrives, I want to explore the direct-selling business. In the meantime, I'll guide you. If you work fast, by the end of November World can launch a million-dollar mail-campaign. I have worked out some exciting approaches. I'm sure that we can sell five hundred million dollars worth of World Corporation nondividend-bearing certificates at ten dollars a share. We're going to give every American the best Christmas present they can buy themselves. For ten dollars, or more, they can make a personal statement about their faith in America."

As he was speaking, H.H. got carried away with his enthusiasm and was skipping merrily around the director's room. "Among other things, I want to make sure you get a complete mailing list of W.I.N. stockholders, and also of employees. You're going to show all of them the real Ralph Thiemost." H.H. hugged Sheldon, "Just wait until they see their leader naked as a newborn babe, and twice as cocky."

"Why do you keep saying 'You're'?" Sheldon demanded. "What are *you* going to be doing?"

"Playing." H.H. chuckled. "What the hell else?"

LUDAMUS IV

It comes to this: that to be "viable," liveable, or merely practical, life must be lived as a game—and the "must" here expresses a condition, not a commandment. It must be lived in a spirit of play rather than work.

Alan Watts
*The Book: On the Taboo
Against Knowing Who You Are*

Moses was a hundred and twenty years old when he died: his eyes were not dim, nor his natural force abated.

Deuteronomy 34:7

Do not go gently into that good night!

Dylan Thomas

31

Three weeks after she arrived in Lynnfield, M'mm still hadn't met Adele Youman. Ronald tried to convince her that she was being very silly when she referred to her new home as "Adele Youman's house." He told her he had personally chosen the New England fieldstone ranch house on the turn-around cul-de-sac called Cabot Lane. Sure, Adele had driven out with him from Boston to take a look at the house and give him a woman's opinion of it. She thought it was lovely, but it wasn't her style. Adele was much too cosmopolitan for suburban living. Besides, during the winter she was usually traveling, and most of the time H. H. Youman lived in their Louisburg Square townhouse, especially during the summer months when Adele was home.

But M'mm wasn't happy. "I may not be a sophisticated French woman who screws all over the world with men like Ralph Thiemost and is partial to bald-headed middle-aged executives," she stormed at him. "But you'd better know it. This house isn't my style either." M'mm had been unable to make Ronald confess that he had gone to bed with Adele Youman, but she was sure that he had and kept telling him with a sour grin that her real problem was that she had married a motherfucker. "Screw with her all you want to," she told him angrily. "She's probably just your style, a woman who pats her big boy on the po-po and soothes his ego. The real reason that you haven't introduced me to her is that you're too damned embarrassed to have us meet. You're afraid I'll tell her what a dud you are most of the time. But keep in mind, Ronald Cold-axe, that I'm not the Boston Brahmin type either. I'm too plebian for your Harvard-Radcliffe-Wellesley neighbors. I wasn't bosom buddies with any of the W.I.N. wives in California, and I'm not going to be bosom buddies with the wives of the people who live in these smug, yucky two- and three-hundred-thousand dollar houses on Cabot Lane."

Already, she told him, she'd been invaded by all of them. A welcoming committee had been led by Mary Hawthorne, whose husband was the president of a local insurance company. "She's the sixty-five-year-old bitch who's queen of Cabot Lane," M'mm told him. "Then there's Priscilla Forbes. She's in her fifties. She's the wife of the big boss at H.C.G., the Harvard Consulting Group. According to her, Jim can't wait to tell you how to reorganize Byrdwhistle. And last but not least is Tippy Osgood, whose husband owns a Cadillac agency. She thinks she's a sexpot, but her husband doesn't. Tippy says he's a bore in bed. He's off and on her before she's even missed him. She's searching for Mister Right, but she hasn't found him so she occasionally drinks herself into fantasyland."

M'mm scowled at Ronald. "Tippy will probably go for you. I'm sure that you'll fall in love with all these Cabot Lane women and their husbands. They're winners. They read *Time* and the *Wall Street Journal*, and all the Book-of-the-Month selections. In the summer, they go sailing together or play golf together. In the winter, they ski. The Hawthornes have a chalet near Woodstock, New Hampshire." M'mm was exasperated at Ronald's refusal to be drawn into a discussion. "Of course," she concluded abruptly, "they're not as rich as Ralph Thiemost, your chief and mentor, or as rich as you plan to be."

It wasn't just her neighbors or the rambling one-story house and the acre of manicured lawn, and it wasn't the obvious ennui of her female neighbors who spoke with flat-tongued superiority and had welcomed her to Cabot Lane as if the letter "R" had been eliminated from the alphabet. Rather it was Ron's total preoccupation with Byrdwhistle that was the source of her anger. Although he kept promising that he would take her on a tour of Byrdwhistle when the time was right, she had yet to meet any Byrdwhistlers, not even Marge Slick, who seemed to be the chief-cook-and-bottle-washer of the company.

The first week, waiting for her furniture to arrive, and despite her disgust at such luxury—although she did enjoy the Byrdwhistle Corniche Rolls Royce that Ron had borrowed from the company—they had stayed at the Ritz-Carlton. Having nothing better to do, bored by the women's boutiques on Newbury Street, M'mm wanted to go to work with Ron at Byrdwhistle. She told him that she'd be very happy to putter around the place and get acquainted. If she could get a feel for the company, then she might be able to offer him some worthwhile suggestions. At least she could listen to his problems and respond more intelligently. But Ronald was adamant. It was too soon to introduce relatives into the place, and "No, god-dammit!" he told her, "I don't run around naked or swim in H.H.'s crazy swimming pool everyday." He frowned at her. "And you're not going to swim bare-ass there either."

Ronald was certain that if M'mm ever got in the Byrdwhistle offices, despite his warnings, she'd probably shed her clothes and insist that Byrdwhistlers were really "her kind of people" and that they should all be friends. Ronald was also afraid of what Marge Slick might tell her. So, when M'mm implied that since she had nothing better to do and since, unlike Ralph Thiemost, Ron didn't seem to be interested in her potential business abilities, she might just contact her old friends at the Clamshell Alliance, Ron had only shrugged. As far as he was concerned, if M'mm got arrested at Seabrook protesting nuclear energy, she'd be safer in jail than wandering around Byrdwhistle.

"Anyway," he told her, "when the Christmas season is over, we're going to shake the whole place up. Byrdwhistle is due for a total reorganization. H. H. Youman's Theory Z and the concept of a husband and wife working together is ridiculous. Adele Youman never worked at Byrdwhistle."

"When are you going to introduce me to Adele?" M'mm asked for the tenth time.

Ronald mumbled that Adele was visiting her daughter in New York. It wasn't exactly the truth, but he hoped that it would be before the end of the week. He was trying to convince Adele that she still had some responsibility for the damned Byrdwhistle merger. At the very least she could fly on from New York to Yugoslavia and find Heman Hyman's damned Love Rocks. But during the past two weeks, though he had consistently harped on the subject, she didn't seem to understand the absolute necessity of that mission. If Adele didn't give him ulcers, Ralph Thiemost most certainly would. Ralph telephoned him once a day to ask if Adele had given him the negatives of the pictures she had taken of both of them. Thiemost was rather belligerent on the subject. Ron better get them, by God, before they appeared in Adele's book, or it would be his ass. But whenever Ron brought the subject up, Adele was devious. She told him she would be delighted to show him her darkroom, but it was always someday in the future when they would have more time together. But even though Ronald accepted Adele's invitation, and he had been having lunch with her practically every day, she still hadn't shown him either Ralph's pictures or his own, nor had he persuaded her to go to Yugoslavia without him. Ronald had no choice. Two and sometimes three hours every day, he played with Adele on H.H.'s merry-go-round.

Dalliance with Adele was becoming addictive, and H.H.'s theory of daily sex-making might be just fine, but Ronald was sure that even H.H. couldn't have managed it every day with two women. Having to edit out his problems with Adele made it difficult for him to convey to M'mm the real mess Byrdwhistle was in. "During the past week, we received cash orders for more than one hundred and seventy-five thousand Love Rocks," he told M'mm. "American consumer behavior beats the hell out of me. Can you imagine that? Two million dollars for god-damn rocks and no end in sight."

"I thought that Thornton Byrd was going to load them onto his yacht," M'mm responded. "You told me that, if necessary, to get them here on time Byrdwhistle might even air-freight them from Dubrovnik."

"That's what I thought originally," Ronald said, "but before he flaked out, H.H. got his final revenge on Thiemost. Byrdwhistle never owned the damn rocks. They weren't included in the W.I.N. purchase agreement.

According to Adele, Youman told Thiemost and her, when they all met on the road to the Gulf of Kotor, that he wasn't going to sell the rocks to Byrdwhistle. He wanted them himself. Of course no one realized that they had been offered in three different Byrdwhistle catalogues and that more than a million separate flyers extolling their merits had been distributed."

"It seems simple enough to me," M'mm told him. "Since Youman's mind is gone and he is unable to function, Adele becomes his legal guardian. She can resell the rocks to Byrdwhistle."

Ronald shook his head. "It's not that simple. I've tried to telephone Thornton Byrd's yacht for the past two days. I finally reached him by radio-phone. The *Love Byrd* is no longer trapped in the Gulf of Kotor. Thornton is cruising somewhere in the Adriatic. He told me that just before Youman lost his mind, he drove to Sveti Stefan with one of the crew, a guy named Pinky Fresser. Pinky actually saw Youman pay some native a lot of American dollars for the rocks. Pinky told Thornton that Youman may have bought more than the one hundred thousand dollars' worth that he had originally contracted for, but Pinky didn't know where they were stored. To complicate matters, before they left Yugoslavia Pinky ran off to Bled or Belgrade or some damn place with a woman named Breskva. No one knows where the hell he is."

"What about H. H. Youman?"

Ronald repressed a shudder. "I went to see him yesterday. The poor bastard is going downhill rapidly. He's much worse than the first time I visited him three weeks ago. When I asked him about the Love Rocks, he started to mutter endlessly about the roosters. He's got rocks mixed up with cocks. I think he was trying to tell me that cocks live longer when they have a home in a friendly henyard." Ronald grinned at M'mm sheepishly. The minute the words tumbled out of his mouth he knew that he shouldn't have said them.

"There's nothing unfriendly about the henyard you live in," M'mm said sourly, "but after I arrived the rooster stopped crowing. Anyway, it all seems very silly to me. The beaches in Massachusetts are covered with rocks. Why don't you hire some kid to pick them up for you?"

In an attempt to divert M'mm from his lack of sexual attention, Ronald pulled a Love Rock circular out of his attaché case. "We can't make a substitution. The Rocks must come from Yugoslavia," he said. "Just read that damned crap. Youman wrote it himself, and note that, while he doesn't exactly tell you that a Love Rock will improve your love life, he states categorically that they were discovered on a beach in Yugoslavia and he implies that they have all kinds of magical qualities."

M'mm had to admit that if she had received a Love Rock circular she would have been tempted to buy one. It was reproduced in full color with a carefully retouched photograph of a lonely beach covered with small oval, or round, pure white rocks. A young man and a young woman were embracing romantically at the edge of the pale greenish-blue water. Cut into the photograph was an insert of a picture of a Love Rock, half its actual size, sitting on royal-purple velour in a partially open lucite box. The copy suggested that the owner of a Love Rock would acquire mysterious, aphrodisiacal vibrations previously known only to the ancient Greeks who had landed on these Adriatic beaches centuries ago. How to accomplish this and transform a member of the other sex, either into a laughing satyr or a nymph, was explained in a ten-page booklet that accompanied each Love Rock. In addition, it would give the purchaser the actual startling story of what happened to H. H. Youman and his wife the night they discovered the Love Rocks at Sveti Stefan.

"I'd like to read that booklet," M'mm said enthusiastically. "What did happen?"

"Nothing." Ronald wanted to get off the ticklish subject of sex, "It's a pile of crap."

Love Rocks weren't Ronald's only problem. Women Against Pornography had sued Club Wholesome for twenty million dollars in damages. According to their lawyers, they have proved that Club Wholesome had shipped "adult" video-tapes to some boys in their early teens — one boy in Atlanta, and one in Fort Worth. Both had religious parents. Unknown to their mothers and fathers, the boys had run the video-tapes for their teen-age girlfriends before they were discovered. Worse, the tapes in question were actually made by Byrdwhistle employees. Ronald didn't tell M'mm that Marge Slick appeared in the one that was now in the hands of the police in Fort Worth.

As if that wasn't bad enough, W.I.N.'s auditors had revealed that Club Wholesome contributed more than five million dollars annually to Byrdwhistle profits — more than any other Byrdwhistle subsidiary. Even worse, a young woman from one of the Boston weekly newspapers was hot on the trail of the story, which would be all the juicier if she ever discovered that Ralph Thiemost personally contributed about ten thousand dollars a year to Morality in Media. Since Ralph Thiemost was now the owner of a highly profitable pornographic mail-order company, this obviously would make an intriguing story. Ralph Thiemost was probably still unaware of Club Wholesome's existence or that Byrdwhistle owned it. If the story broke, it wasn't going to improve W.I.N.'s image or Ralph Thiemost's. W.I.N.'s stock was at an all-time low, and Wall Street brokers kept intimating that W.I.N. might be ripe for a takeover. In the middle of all this, Ralph Thiemost kept checking with Ron, demanding to know whether he had recovered the photos. How could he explain to M'mm or Ralph that the only route to Adele's darkroom, and the negatives, was via H. H. Youman's merry-go-round and that thus far he hadn't got any farther than that.

After their furniture arrived and had been moved into the house on

Cabot Lane, and feeling a little embarrassed about his dual life, Ron made the mistake of trying to convince M'mm that Adele Youman was really a nice person and it was too bad that H.H. had flaked out. He suggested that, despite the age differential, the Youmans and the Coldaxes might have been good friends, but that only further uncorked M'mm's wrath. "You might need a mother, but I don't," she yelled at him. "When Adele Youman gets back from Yugoslavia, I'll tell her so myself. I just have a feeling, Ronald Coldaxe, that something very weird is going on. You aren't really worrying how I'll act if you take me into Byrdwhistle. You're afraid that I'll find out the truth. You've probably been playing footsies with Marge Slick, too. She may be five years older than you are and Adele Youman may be old enough to be your mother, but I know you. All any woman has to do is wiggle her ass at you and you jump up and down like a starving puppy. Adele probably told you that, since you drove her husband to the loony-bin, you're obligated to service her a couple of times a week."

M'mm knew she was exaggerating, but at least her anger jarred Ronald out of his Byrdwhistle lethargy. Anyway, he seemed completely oblivious to the fact that she was cold—literally freezing to death. The gray New England weather didn't seem to bother Ron at all. Despite the humming oil-burner, she was chilled to the bone. Ron seemed to have completely forgotten the easy indoor-outdoor existence provided by their hacienda-style California house. Here, you couldn't enjoy the sun until spring. Their Spanish-style furniture was an awkward contrast to the New England scenes on the bedroom wallpaper and the colonial knotty pine that the previous owner had lavished on the house.

"You should have been here yesterday!" M'mm had already implied that if she didn't find something interesting to do—such as a full-time job—she'd become a drinking companion with her inescapable new neighbor, Tippy Osgood. "The dear ladies of Cabot Lane keep insisting that my mixed decor is so charming. They told me yesterday that I had transplanted a little of Mexico right into old New England." She scowled at Ronald. She really didn't give a damn that the eclectic interior of their new home would never entice a photographer from *Architectural Digest,* but she needed to jar Ron. "Mary Hawthorne is sending us an invitation to join the Lynnfield Country Club, and she wants me to attend the lecture series at the library. I'm going to need about fifty thousand dollars, so that I can toss out this Spanish junk and redecorate the house."

Ronald suddenly came out of his Byrdwhistle trance. "You must be crazy. That would take everything we've got."

"You've got to change your image, Ron," she said sarcastically. "Myles Standish is your new ancestor, not Cortez. If we're going to stay in New England, El Rancho Grande has got to go."

Ronald had made the mistake of telling M'mm that he had played the role of Myles Standish opposite H.H.'s Thomas Morton, but he didn't think her remark was very funny. "Don't go doing anything drastic." He tried to sound patient. "I don't expect to be here for more than two years."

Actually, M'mm had more interesting ventures in mind than furnishing the house, or joining posh country clubs, or sitting around libraries with a lot of bored women trying to improve her mind. She had already telephoned Jeff Staller, and Jeff had told her that there was a problem equal to Seabrook right in her own back yard. Less than a mile from the Byrdwhistle home office, LNG—liquified natural gas—was being stored in huge quantities. It had been pumped from the tankers that arrived periodically in Boston Harbor from Algeria. The stuff was so dangerous that, if it escaped into the atmosphere, just one spark could blow the entire city of Boston to kingdom come. Worse, it was being moved in trucks through the streets of Everett and then onto the highways around Boston.

M'mm didn't tell Ron that Byrdwhistle was sitting next to a time bomb. He would just have put her down and insisted that she stop pretending that she was Barbra Streisand in *The Way We Were.* He would have told her that without nuclear power and liquified natural gas the United States would screech to a halt. Maybe Ron was right, she thought, and maybe he wasn't. But she wasn't going to sit on her ass all day and read novels or play golf or spend her life in beauty shops. It was her world, too, and there were too many thugs like Ralph Thiemost screwing around with it. Someone had to play policeman.

32

M'mm tried to convince Ron that just staying happily married, and continuing to like each other for a lifetime, was a greater problem than Love Rocks, or Club Wholesome being sued, or trying to stop Byrdwhistlers from sex-making in the Love Rooms, or rehearsing *Let Us Go, Brothers, Go!* during working hours. But in the past few weeks, Ron was wrestling with an even more serious problem. In spite of himself, he had an uneasy feeling that he was slowly being entrapped by the Byrdwhistle play ethic. He most certainly didn't dare tell M'mm, but he kept trying to convince Joe Taylor and Bill Redman, the young M.B.A.'s from Stanford who Ralph Thiemost had sent from Los Angeles to assist in reorganizing Byrdwhistle, that they should move slowly. His own feeling was that they probably never could remodel Byrdwhistle in the W.I.N. image, and certainly shouldn't try until after Christmas. If they screwed around with

Theory Z during the rush season, Byrdwhistle's profit wasn't going to equal last year's. During the next seven weeks, Byrdwhistle would do nearly one-half of its annual sales and, like it or not, the ghost of H. H. Youman was still running the company. But Bill and Joe did not agree with him. They were young, hot-headed new brooms and were determined to impress Thiemost with their abilities. They didn't hesitate to tell Ron that "older men needed young axe-men to clear away the debris in a take-over like this," and they kept insisting that they had to clear out some of the old guard, after which they could quickly make Byrdwhistle conform to the W.I.N. image.

In the meantime, Marge Slick kept warning him that the reason for Byrdwhistle's exceptional profits was that in Everett, and in all its subsidiaries, when the need arose, Byrdwhistlers worked their asses off. They would put in fifteen or more hours a day. In the Christmas season, they processed all the orders with no increase in payrolls. Marge tried to tell Ron that the reason they did this was that they weren't really working. They were playing. If playing included interludes, swimming around the offices, or happily lying naked together in one of the Love Rooms, or rehearsing *Let Us Go, Brothers, Go!*—or arguing with Ronald tooth and nail that transcending problems was better than wrestling with them—then unless Ronald was planning to wreck the place, he should relax and play with them.

And Marge told him that she didn't give a damn whether Elmer Byrd's musical was owned by Byrdwhistle any longer or not. H.H. had promised all Byrdwhistlers that on the opening night of *Rum Ho!,* which Elmer had postponed until December 1, the entire Colonial Theater would be occupied by Byrdwhistlers and their friends. What's more, Byrdwhistle would pay for all the seats and invite all the important New York and Boston critics. Ralph Thiemost might not be very happy about the twenty or thirty thousand dollars or more it would cost, but Ronald Coldaxe had better include this in current Byrdwhistle operating expenses or Byrdwhistlers would most certainly slow down and put in only eight-hour days through December. If that happened, customers wouldn't get their Christmas orders until Easter, and Marge assured him by that time they would be in deep trouble with the Federal Trade Commission.

Although Ron would never admit it to Marge Slick, he wished that he could talk with H.H. If H.H. weren't so fuzzy-brained, Ron might have even tried to discuss Theory Z with him. Maybe there was some compromise position, some course that he could sail between Scylla and Charybdis that would make both Ralph Thiemost and all the Byrdwhistlers happy. But, alas, whatever remained of H.H.'s brains were wandering in never-never-land. Ron's only hope was Marge Slick. But, when he had implied that a few hours a day with her in one of the Love Rooms might be very helpful—he would even discuss Herbert Marcuse and Wilhelm Reich with her if she wished—Marge had only grinned at him.

"Fred doesn't exactly approve of you," she told him, "but he doesn't object. Unfortunately, Fred is only one side of the equation."

Ron looked at her, puzzled, and she chuckled. "Tell your wife to call me and tell me it's okay with her. Remember, it's a Byrdwhistle rule that neither spouse objects."

Ron gave up. It would be as likely as a cold day in hell that he could convince M'mm that he could conference with Marge in a Love Room without experiencing Marge's vagina. M'mm had already remarked that his preoccupation with Byrdwhistle was making him forget his work at home. Damn, that really was the problem. It should be play. The passive way that M'mm responded to him proved that neither of them had learned how to play with each other in bed. But he didn't dare tell her that. She'd be sure that he was becoming a Byrdwhistler in spite of himself.

Yesterday, after his daily hegira from Everett to Beacon Hill in a taxi, he told Adele, who was waiting for him on the merry-go-round, that she had really let him down. "You were on the beach where H.H. supposedly found the rocks. If you had listened to me, you could be there right now looking for them." He sighed and kissed her remarkably well-preserved breasts. "You're a very nice person," he said, "and I won't deny that I'm very comfortable making love with you—but in the last analysis, you and your crazy husband are ruining my life."

"Honey boy," Adele said, "you've asked me to fly to the Gulf of Kotor alone to look for Heman's rocks. You forget that Yugoslavian men wouldn't be very cooperative with an aggressive American woman, and Thorny's no damned help." Adele hugged him, "But of course, if you're flying to Yugoslavia, I'll be happy to fly with you." Ronald suddenly realized that, like a naive little rabbit, he'd nibbled his way right into her trap. She was kissing him enthusiastically. "We'll have a lovely little vacation together. Nick and Maria will be delighted. I know we'll all get along famously."

That morning Byrdwhistle had received a letter from the Federal Trade Commission advising the company that they were in violation of the FTC thirty-day mail-order shipping rule. Ron had not yet summoned up the courage to tell M'mm that, if he didn't personally fly to Yugoslavia to help find the Love Rocks, he might end up in jail. Now he reminded himself that, according to the story he had previously told M'mm—that Adele was already in Yugoslavia—under no circumstance could he tell her that he was about to fly to Yugoslavia with Adele. M'mm might call Adele his loving mother, but loving sons past thirty didn't go vacationing with mothers who looked like Adele.

M'mm had listened to his story silently, but he noticed that she had looked even more unhappy when he told her that Adele had telephoned him from Yugoslavia. "She couldn't find the shed where H.H. supposedly stashed the Love Rocks," he said. "According to Adele, H.H. originally found the rocks on some beach near Sveti Stefan. Sometime later when he got the mad idea of selling them as a mail-order item he must have had someone clear the beach. All Adele has been able to find out is that they are probably volcanic rocks. Over the centuries they were polished into pure white ovals by the Adriatic. She hasn't been able to find another beach with similar rocks. She said the rocks never seemed very sexy to her, and when you walked on them barefoot they hurt like hell." Ronald sighed, "There's no way out. I'm going to have to take the Byrdwhistle jet to Yugoslavia to help her locate them. Just pray that the government, or whoever owns the beachfront, hasn't cleared all the beaches and dumped the rocks out at sea."

M'mm noticed that Ron stammered while he was telling this story. It occurred to her that, since he was finding such happiness with his newly acquired mother, perhaps she should have stayed in California and played I'll-tie-you-then-you-can-tie-me games with Daddy Thiemost.

She decided to test Ron. "If you're flying on the Byrdwhistle jet, there's no reason why I can't come with you. Just a month ago Ralph Thiemost asked me to go with him, but I was faithful to you. I've never been to Yugoslavia. We haven't had a vacation in over a year. You owe it to me."

Ronald tried not to gulp. "This isn't a fun trip," he protested. "If I go, I'll have to take a few male Byrdwhistlers along with me." Actually, he had been hoping to take Marge Slick with him in order to create a stalemate in his continuing extramarital sex-making. What he really needed was to live like a monk for at least a week.

"I'm going to need a few guys to help me load the rocks," he said. "I hope you understand, M'mm, that we've got to bring back all we can find. On the way back, there'll be standing room only."

He knew that M'mm wasn't pleased with his answer, but he hadn't told her all the details of his problems with the Federal Trade Commission. Even though Christmas was still four weeks away, Byrdwhistle had already received a dozen or more complaints from various Better Business Bureaus who had been notified by local residents of the nondelivery of their orders for Love Rocks. In the meantime, what had happened was so incredible that he couldn't believe it himself, and he sure as hell didn't want to talk about it when he got home at night. Later, he'd tell M'mm that if he didn't fly to Yugoslavia and find the damned rocks he might well end up in a federal penitentiary.

The previous day, when he finally got back to the office after his luncheon session with Adele on H.H.'s merry-go-round, Marge was waiting for him.

"Victor Watchman is waiting for you downstairs in the reception room," she told him. He's from the Federal Trade Commission, but he looks like a clone of a Nazi Gestapo agent. I wouldn't have let him come upstairs, but he wouldn't have signed our release anyway."

"Your company is in very serious trouble," Watchman said as Ron stepped out of the elevator on the main floor. Watchman was a pot-bellied man with the self-righteous attitude of a man who had worked for the government too long. He had memorized every regulation and enjoyed making mountains out of molehills. "We want immediate access to all your records," he said. "We're going to examine every single Byrdwhistle mail-order transaction for the past six months, with special attention on those for Love Rocks."

Sniffing disgustedly, Watchman pulled a Love Rock circular from his briefcase and waved it at Ron. "Not only do we have three hundred spe-cific complaints of nondelivery of this item but the product you are sell-ing is obviously worthless. In addition to nondelivery it looks to me like a case of mail fraud. We've already notified you that Byrdwhistle is not complying with FTC regulations. Now we must assess a one-hundred-thousand-dollar penalty. In addition, you must immediately return all the checks and money orders that you've received for Love Rocks. Believe me, if you don't comply you personally can end up in even more serious trouble."

Ron knew that Marge was waiting for his response and hoping that he would play it cool. A week earlier, she'd given him a booklet called, "Blow Your Kneecaps Off" written by Joseph Sugarman, President of J.S. and A products. Sugarman had exposed the length to which the Fed-eral Trade Commission would go to prosecute even an innocent com-pany if it was suspected of violating mail-order shipping rules. Marge had warned him from the beginning that they shouldn't have deposited customer checks for Love Rocks—not until they were sure they could ship them. But Joe Taylor and Bill Redman, the eager beavers from Stanford, who Ronald was sure were secretly reporting directly to Ralph Thiemost, had insisted that the only way they could control the orders was to put them through the computer and bank the money.

Ronald tried to reassure Watchman. "We'll be out of the woods on this within the week," he told him. "You have to understand that this is the height of our Christmas season. It would cost us a fortune to stop everything and get the documents that you are asking for, and it would only delay hundreds of other shipments." Ronald could be cold and brusque when the occasion demanded. Knowing full well that Watchman would be in a state of shock if he actually knew how many Love Rock orders Byrdwhistle was holding, Ronald refused to discuss it further.

"I can assure you," he said, "that we'll be shipping Love Rocks within the three-week time-limit. If anything happens and we can't, the Federal Trade Commission doesn't have to worry. We'll immediately refund every penny that our customers have paid us for Love Rocks."

"But you've already caused very serious damages," Watchman replied belligerently. "You will have prevented thousands of people from using their Christmas money for gifts they can purchase elsewhere. They have been persuaded by your flagrant advertising to order what are nothing but ordinary rocks. Our job is to protect the public from pie-in-the-sky operators like Byrdwhistle. Not only are we holding you personally responsible, Mr. Coldaxe, but the law permits us to fine your company ten thousand dollars for *each* violation of our thirty-day shipping rule."

The following day on the merry-go-round, Ronald reported this conversation to Adele. Her brown eyes were liquid with sympathy. "Poor Ronnie, you're just going to have to take me to Yugoslavia with you."

Even before he had shed his clothes, she was naked and was snuggling against him. "Poor Ralph, too," she said. "Do you really have orders for two hundred thousand of Heman's silly rocks? If Byrdwhistle is fined ten thousand dollars for each rock that hasn't been shipped, that comes to billions of dollars. I'm sure Ralph hasn't got that kind of money."

In many ways, Adele was a fey copy of H. H. Youman. Even after some twenty sex-making engagements with her, Ronald still couldn't jar her happy complacency or make her face reality. She told him that he took life too seriously and lacked the courage to deal with the potentially possible. "You not only worry about Love Rocks," she told him, "but you worry about our luncheon meetings. I'm sure that if Meredith knew the truth she wouldn't be upset about our happy hours together from time to time. When you finally get up the courage to introduce us to each other, I'll tell her that I'm no threat to her and that all I'm doing is helping to make you a better lover and showing you how to live longer and laugh more. If Heman's brains weren't so jumbled, I'm sure he'd approve. He'd be delighted that we've been enjoying each other's minds and genitals occasionally."

Ronald didn't agree with her. The truth was that in the past two weeks he had been seeing her a lot more than occasionally. Between eleven A.M. and two P.M. every damned day for the past ten days he had gone to bed with Adele. Not bed really. He had been in Adele's arms and between her legs. "Remember," she told him gaily, "Heman put it on video-tape that he wanted you to have his merry-go-round. I'm sure he'd be very pleased to know that we're enjoying it together."

Everyday that he opened the front door of the Louisburg Square townhouse with the key that Adele had insisted he have for access to the house when she wasn't there, she had been waiting for him. Naked, they romped together around the huge circular playground, drank a little wine, ate a sandwich, and kissed each other from head to toe, while the cumulous November sky revolved above their heads. But he had not gotten any closer to discovering whether Adele had included him in her book or seeing the pictures she had taken of him and Ralph. He did get her to admit that she had taken a whole roll of film of Ralph in Evora. He knew that she must have at least twenty negatives on thirty-five millimeter film. At least he was sure that she only had five pictures of him "flying in mid-air" into her swimming pool. But when he brought the subject up, once again she diverted him. "There's nothing to see in my darkroom," she said. "But if you'd pose for me, I'm sure I could get much better pictures of you. Then we could develop and print them together."

Ronald had looked at her in dismay. He was determined that he wasn't deliberately going to let Adele take pictures of him naked. He mumbled that he was sure she could find many better-looking men, but she only laughed and said, "Maybe, but I'd rather photograph a body that I have enjoyed."

Three weeks earlier, before M'mm had arrived, Ron had decided to take the bull by the horns. He knew that, even if he managed to persuade Adele to show him her darkroom, there would be no easy way to ask her for Thiemost's pictures and negatives, or even to find out where she kept them. So, late one night, with a flashlight in his pocket, he had walked to Louisburg Square from the Ritz-Carlton. Passing by the Center for Ageless Humans, he gave a sigh for H. H. Youman. Poor H.H. If he hadn't lost his marbles, Ronald Coldaxe wouldn't be in this predicament.

When he arrived in front of the townhouse, the downstairs lights were off but there was a light on in the third-floor bedroom. He hoped that it meant that Adele was reading in bed and wasn't on the merry-go-round. No one could see it from the street, but Adele had insisted that unless he rode on it with her it made her dizzy.

Cautiously unlocking the front door with his key, avoiding the swimming pool that sparkled in the moonlight shining through the glass arch above it, Ronald had the strange feeling that he was not alone on the first floor of the house. Someone was quietly moving toward him from the kitchen area. Obscured by black shadows, someone was watching him. Except for his pounding heart, there was dead silence. Was it Adele? He murmured her name, wondering how he would explain his nocturnal visit. Then a black figure leaped out of the darkness at him. Momentarily, in the glare of his flashlight, Ronald saw that it was a man wearing a ski mask. Ron stumbled back, yelling—certain that the burglar was going to murder him—and he crashed into the swimming pool and sank to the bottom. Within seconds the entire downstairs was brilliantly lighted, and Adele, in her nightgown, was laughing at him as she helped him climb out of the pool. "I thought you were a burglar after my silver," she giggled at his water-soaked suit. "There have been several robberies on Beacon Hill recently." Adele was happy that he had frightened away the real burglar, especially after he confessed—even though it wasn't true—that the reason he was there was to spend the night with her. Adele was delighted. After that, there had been no escape.

Ronald tried to convince himself that he wasn't really being unfaithful to M'mm. At least now he was home with her every night. Over and above sex-making, the short afternoon séances he had with Adele were critical to the future of Byrdwhistle and to his career with W.I.N. But despite all his forays into the subject, Adele still had those damn photographs. Ron was certain that both the negatives and the prints were in her darkroom. She assured him that in the past few years she had become quite skilled in photography and had developed and printed the color pictures of all "the darling, power-hungry men" who would appear in her book *The Ultimate Aphrodisiac.* "If I sent my films to Eastman Kodak, they probably would have censored them," she told him. But every time he told her that he'd really like to see the pictures she had taken of him and Ralph Thiemost, or that he'd like to read the manuscript of her book, she had responded: "I want you to read it, Ron honey. I really want you to. But not now. Not until you can stay with me all night again. Right now we have so little time together."

She finally told him that when they flew to Yugoslavia she'd bring a copy of the manuscript and they could read it together on the plane. "I sent the original off to the publisher a few weeks ago," she said, and she was amused when his mouth dropped open. "Don't worry, Ronnie, Ralph Thiemost is in the book, but I haven't decided whether to include my chapter on you. Adele explained that she hadn't made up her mind whether Ronald could be poured into her power-hungry-male mold. "In some ways," she told him, "You're really the Paddington-type. Power-hungry men don't usually respond the way you do to a woman like me."

She explained that Heman had once been the Pooh-bear Paddington type but had caught the King Gillette disease and that now his dream was to save the world from its own insanity. "Don't let it happen to you, Ronnie. It's better to be a happy Pooh-bear than a bewildered old man who used to be a genius." She told him that in her book she had contrasted Heman's masochistic power needs with the sadistic drive of a man like Ralph Thiemost. "You have much the same hangups as Heman. You need to be a hero. A sadistic man like Thiemost never has that kind of motivation."

Adele told him all this while they were sitting on one of the horses on the carousel. She had climbed on the horse facing him and he had slid under her legs so that she was sitting on his thighs. As the merry-go-round turned Adele rode up and down on him. Her pubic arch was warm and prickly against his belly and her vagina was a glistening grotto for a glowing gladiator.

While the merry-go-round turned, Adele assured him that Heman's consuming need to be a hero was typical of masochists from Jesus Christ to Joan of Arc to Albert Schweitzer.

"I never did understand what H.H. was trying to accomplish with World Corporation," Ronald told her. He wondered how in hell he could carry on a conversation with Adele when he was trying to control himself from a premature eruption inside her.

"Heman is ancestor-crazy," Adele said. "He's convinced that if Thomas Morton and King Gillette had met they would have been good friends. Heman even made me read Gillette's *Human Drift*. Gillette believed that competition for wealth was 'the devil's most ingenious invention for filling hell!' Heman believed that Gillette would have approved of Theory Z. Nearly a hundred years ago, when he wrote his little daydream and paid to have it published, Gillette insisted that ninety percent of the people in the world lived hand to mouth." Adele stopped talking and was kissing Ron passionately. "My, you feel very nice going up and down inside me," she laughed. "And that's really the point. Who knows, Gillette might have agreed with Heman? No one can enjoy playing like this if they're wasting their strength everyday just to be able to afford the necessities of food and shelter. But Heman is obsessed with the Gillette dream. He's tried to make World Corporation into a gigantic joint stock, money market, and Mutual fund—or something like that—which eventually would take over all the world's production and distribution of goods."

"Obviously, it's a Utopian daydream," Ronald said, and Adele smiled at him. "Some people would say that what we're doing right now is a daydream, too. Can you survive one more turn?" Her vulva was clasping his penis on the down cycle and her breasts were massaging his chest. Ronald wasn't sure, but he nodded bravely. "I have to. I want to catch the brass ring the next time around."

33

Wandering disconsolately around the empty house wearing an ivory and geranium warmup suit, M'mm was trying to decide if she should drive to New Hampshire in the new Ford Ron had bought her—Ron was still driving one of the Byrdwhistle Rollses. She wanted to see what was going on in Seabrook. It was ten-thirty. She could be there by noon and maybe she could locate some of the people she had met two years ago. She didn't hear the doorbell chime until it rang the second time. Sure that it would be Tippy Osgood, who seemed determined to be her best friend, M'mm was surprised to see, through one of the side windows near the door, a tall man with a silvery gray Prince Valiant haircut. Thinking it must be Mary Hawthorne's husband, the only male spouse on Cabot Lane she and Ron had not yet met, M'mm opened the front door cautiously.

"Good morning, Mrs. Coldaxe." The man was handsome. His laughing brown eyes instantly owned her. M'mm shivered. He handed her his business card. Frowning, she read it. "Moses Megillah Marshalik, Vice President of Marsha Lovett Cosmetics."

"I'm sorry," she smiled, "I'm not really Pharaoh's daughter." She knew she wasn't being very bright to jest with a stranger, but Holy Moses! Moses was really a weird name—especially for a man who looked as if he should be a Hollywood actor.

"My brother Aaron isn't with me today." The man was still imbibing her. "You don't have to worry about his rod. Actually I don't pay too much attention to the Lord—one way or the other. I hope you don't mind my calling on you, but I'm traveling around the country doing a survey on the cosmetics business. I'm looking for women who will give me honest reactions. I'm trying to find how Marsha Lovett stacks up against companies like Avon, Vanda, Mary Kay, and other companies who sell direct to the consumer."

"I'm sorry," M'mm was suddenly aware that she shouldn't have been so friendly. "I can't understand why you picked this house. I can't help you anyway. I'm not a New Englander. I'm from California." Moses Marshalik stared at her as if he could see right through her velour running suit. She tried to edge the door shut without actually slamming it in his face.

"Believe me," Mrs. Coldaxe, "we chose Cabot Lane because it is typical of a certain class of upper-income customers and because of its geography."

"If it's so random, how come you know my name?" M'mm demanded. "I've lived here only three weeks."

Moses had prepared for this. "The wife of the previous owner of this house, Mrs. Matthew Cobb, was a Marsha Lovett customer." Moses prayed silently. He knew the Cobb name was right. Marge Slick had checked it out for him. But only the Lord and Mrs. Cobb knew whether she had ever used Marsha Lovett cosmetics. He gestured at a van parked in the road at the far end of the flagstone path. M'mm could see that it was inscribed with a Marsha Lovett logo. H. H. Youman had carefully supervised the lettering on the rented van. The Marsha Lovett sample case he was carrying was the real thing. Sylvia had borrowed it from a friend of a friend of hers who had run out of friends to whom she could show Marsha Lovett cosmetics.

"Really, Mr. Marshalik," M'mm was agitated, "I'm not at all interested. Commercial cosmetics are a fraud perpetrated on American women by big business. They are vastly overpriced. The chemicals used to color them and to keep them from spoiling can be dangerous.

For a moment, Moses was certain that he had taken the wrong approach to seduce Meredith Coldaxe. But then, touched by his evident bewilderment, M'mm said, "Actually, when I'm in the mood, I often make my own cosmetics. They are better than anything you can buy."

Moses was beaming enthusiastically at her. Unknown to M'mm, she was offering him an approach that might be better than anything he had dreamed of. "That's really very exciting. Can you actually make your own face creams and moisturizers and deodorants? Good lord, I am in luck! You may be just the person I'm looking for. I'm sure that, if I could just sit down and talk with you a few minutes, you could give me some very valuable pointers."

Moses had a sudden compulsion to hug this woman who was staring at him so dubiously.

In reality, Meredith Coldaxe was a much more vibrant woman than he had anticipated. She projected a carefully restrained sexuality that hadn't been revealed on the video-tape that Steve and Cathy Milner had made of her. But, unfortunately, she was slowly closing the door on him. Moses knew from long experience that women who argue with men often capitulate faster than the remote kind who hide behind the facade of their own ignorance. Breaching the bastions of women like M'mm, who needed to be accepted as equals or even as more powerful than their male seducers, often turned them into very loving bed companions. "Please wait a moment," he said, smiling hypnotically at her. "I'm totally fascinated by your hobby. Good fortune is smiling on me today. You may be just the person to give new direction to Marsha Lovett. We've even been considering a new name for the company."

But M'mm was adamant, "I'm sorry Mr. Marshalik. I'm trying to be polite to you, but if you don't leave I'm going to slam the door in your face. I'm very busy. I'm on my way to New Hampshire."

"It's only fifty miles from here," Moses was fighting for his life. "I'll be happy to drive you there. We could even stop at the Mountain View Steak House for lunch."

"Good-bye, Mr. Marshalik." M'mm was now talking to him through about two inches of open doorway."

"Please, wait a minute," Moses begged to her. He was smiling, but just as determined as she was. "At least you can answer one question that's always bothered me. What if right now I passed out on your doorstep? What if I were having a heart attack? Would you leave me out here to die?"

M'mm frowned. She was suddenly frightened. Moses Marshalik might look like the answer to a bored suburban housewife's prayers, but she had a feeling that if he ever got inside the door he'd probably want to play crazier sex games than Ralph Thiemost. What the hell was there about her that at forty-five she was suddenly so irresistible to horny old men? Maybe it was because they thought that she was a horny old lady. Maybe way deep down she was. She hoped that it didn't show on her face.

"If you're having a heart attack, sit down. I'll call the police," M'mm closed the door on him firmly.

A second later, the doorbell chimed again. She could see through the side window that he was grinning. "Please go away!" she yelled. "I don't want to cause you any trouble, but if you don't go I really will call the police."

Then, to her surprise, he was talking to her through the mail slot, which he had pushed open. "If you call the police, they'll think you're being very silly, Mrs. Coldaxe. Please look at this check that I'm passing through to you." Moses was playing his trump card.

Trembling, she saw a slip of paper come through the slot and float to the floor. M'mm kneeled to pick it up and was almost eyeball-to-eyeball with him through the slot. She was utterly amazed to see that it was a certified check for two thousand dollars, drawn on the Lynnfield Trust Company and made out to Meredith Coldaxe. In the bottom corner was typed "Consultation fee for Marsha Lovett Cosmetics."

"You can telephone the bank," he assured her. On his hands and knees on her doorstep, Moses was still looking through the mail slot at her and laughing. M'mm prayed that her neighbors couldn't see him.

"The bank will assure you that its negotiable," he said.

"What can I tell you that's worth two thousand dollars?" M'mm demanded suspiciously.

"What would you have said if I told you I was your 'Love Me' representative." Moses had already decided that "Love Me" wasn't a bad name for a line of cosmetics.

"Love Me?" M'mm was still on her hands and knees. Moses was chuckling, and she could see his eyes twinkling. "That wouldn't be difficult, Mrs. Coldaxe," he said. "But, seriously, we've been thinking of changing the name of our company to Love Me."

M'mm groaned. "You mean that you're going to call Marsha Lovett Cosmetics 'Love Me Cosmetics'?" Moses was still staring at her through the mail slot. "That name stinks, too!"

"It sound sexier than Marsha Lovett."

"Not 'Love *Me*'!" M'mm knew that she was conversing with a maniac, but she didn't know enough to stop. He was making her laugh and that's more than Tippy Osgood would ever do. "I think 'Love *You*' would be better. If you buy them, the cosmetics love you."

"Great, I love you! I mean I love 'Love You.' It's a great name. May I come in? Already you've given me an idea that could make millions of dollars. I'm sure that you could earn your fee."

Actually, M'mm didn't think that Love You was that great either, but it occurred to her that, if Moses Marshalik raped her, unlike Ralph Thiemost, he'd probably be laughing when he did it. Anyway, there was no question that Moses Marshalik was making her dull day more interesting.

Still nervous but overcome by the combination of curiosity and the release from boredom, M'mm grabbed a brass candlestick and slowly opened the door. If Moses Marshalik tried anything funny, she'd conk him on the head. "You can come in," she told him, "but keep your distance." Then, as he ambled confidently into her living room, she was sure that she'd made a mistake. Putting down the sample case he was carrying, Moses flopped onto the sofa and looked at her as if he was already master of the establishment. "Good lord, Mrs. Coldaxe," he sighed, "you're a very hard woman to convince. This is my first experience in direct selling. It takes more initiative than I realized."

Still clutching the candlestick and standing behind a wing-chair, M'mm stared at him suspiciously. "I'm sorry," she said, "but you make me nervous. I'm sure that you're not telling me the truth. Why in hell would you make out a cashier's check to me?"

Moses chuckled and opened his sample case, which was filled with bottles and jars with Marsha Lovett labels. A large book, easily ten-by-fifteen inches, slid out onto the rug, but Moses ignored it. M'mm read the title *Sexual Secrets,* and began to tremble. Then Moses took three checks out of one of the compartments in the case. He handed them to her. "Read the names," he told her. "They're made out to your neighbors." To M'mm's surprise, each check was for two thousand dollars. The names Mary Hawthorne, Tippy Osgood, and Priscilla Forbes were typed on the respective payee lines.

Moses beamed at her. "By sheer luck," he said, "I picked you first. Of course, if you prefer, you can telephone your neighbors. If you invite them over, I'm sure that we could do the survey questionnaire together."

"Never mind," M'mm was beginning to feel more confident and was reluctant to share Moses Marshalik with her neighbors. Moreover, the book now intrigued her. What the hell did Marsha Lovett Cosmetics have to do with *Sexual Secrets*? She sat down in the wing-chair and put the candlestick on an end-table within easy reach. "How long will this take?" she demanded.

"Less than an hour," Moses said, "unless I can persuade you to join me for lunch. I'd really like to show you the cocktail lounge at the Mountain View Steak House. It's only a few miles from here. The owners don't publicize it, but like many other places it's become a gathering place for the geriatric set." He laughed, "Actually, the cocktail lounge functions as an afternoon sex-club for older executives who are escaping business routines with their secretaries and for retirees who are entertaining younger housewives, like yourself, who have slipped away for an afternoon of fun and laughter. All this ties in with an idea I had for Marsha Lovett Cosmetics and I'd like to get your reaction to it."

M'mm was getting uneasy again. Moses Marshalik not only sounded slippery but was obviously completely batty. To make it worse, while he was talking to her on one level he was literally inhaling her on another. And she knew she was responding telepathically to him. Moses Marshalik might be sitting quite casually on her sofa, but they both were imagining his hands roaming all over her body as she moaned, "Oh God, don't stop. I love it!" M'mm quickly erased that fantasy. One thing was sure, under no circumstances was she leaving the house with him, and Mr. Marshalik was going to get the hell out just as quickly as she dared show him the door.

"I'm on a diet, Mr. Marshalik," she said and hoped she sounded more determined than she felt. "I eat very little lunch. I'd like to get this over with. Then you can continue your survey with the other women on Cabot Lane. I hope this isn't just a big come-on. A slick way to get inside so that you can start showing me all your damned handcreams, lotions, powders, skin-moisturizers, and whatnot." She was pleased to see that Moses was responding to her belligerence with an air of humility. "What's more," she told him, "and I hope you will excuse the expression, you really are going at this ass-backwards. Women buy cosmetics from women, and usually only by appointment. I would never buy cosmetics from a man. What do men know about cosmetics?"

"You're forgetting Phillip Coty and Charles Revson," Moses laughed. "God rest their souls. Everything from high heels to eyeshadow, mascara, and perfume were invented by men to make women look sexier than they really are."

M'mm snorted indignantly. "That's the trouble with men. They can't cope with real women. They want fantasy women right out of *Playboy*. Women who never really existed.

"You just told me you made your own cosmetics," Moses countered her. "Why would you bother doing that except to be beautiful in the eyes of some man." Moses was exhilarated. The seduction of Meredith Coldaxe was going splendidly. Even though she might disagree with him—maybe even because she disagreed with him—she was finally relaxing. Even more helpful was M'mm's rebellious, anti-establishment approach to life. It meant that she could embrace far-out ideas.

"While your mind is spinning on that thought," he told her before she could think of a reply, "try this. Why couldn't we give Love You Cosmetics a larger orientation? Maybe, we could re-employ hundreds of thousands of older men, like myself." Moses chuckled. "What if you had answered the door and I told you that I was your afternoon beauty therapist from Love You Cosmetics?"

"Afternoon beauty therapist?" M'mm tried not to gasp.

Moses grinned. "It's a double-entendre. They would be men in the afternoon of their lives. Retired. Men like me who are heading for the last roundup. Instead, Love You Cosmetics could give them a new lease on life. Playing with younger women would help them live longer and healthier lives. At the same time they could teach women that Shakti, the female principle, is the driving force behind every person—every man and woman. When women dare to come to terms with their joyous, sexual, feminine selves and create loving, laughing environments, it will help make their husbands beautiful, too. Afternoon beauty therapists could arrange beauty sessions in a customer's home. The sessions would include massage, music, dancing, and just playing." Moses picked *Sexual Secrets* up from the floor. Laughing, he handed it to M'mm. "We might even develop a training program for ABT's that would include a complete study of this book. Among other things, afternoon beauty therapists could teach women what these authors call the "alchemy of ecstasy."

M'mm flipped the pages of the book. She couldn't help herself. She was suddenly laughing from the tip of her toes to the top of her head. She'd seen many illustrated sex manuals, but this topped them all. It was filled with drawings of men and women, ancient and modern, happily sexmaking, accompanied by a text that covered every aspect of Tantric lovemaking, from correct breathing to how to achieve Kundalini, to hundreds of drawings of men and women copulating in various positions.

"Among other things," Moses said as she turned the pages, "there's an interesting chapter on the art of perfume, which afternoon beauty therapists could incorporate into their beauty programs."

"You really are crazy," M'mm caught her breath. She was still turning the pages of the book, fascinated. "In order to sell cosmetics, you're going to teach women how to make love? I think you'd better figure out how to teach their husbands first. If my husband saw this book, I'm sure he'd burn it."

Moses wanted to tell her that, while Ronald might not be fully aware of it, he was actually selling the book by mail-order through Club Wholesome, but of course he couldn't. Not yet. "Our therapists will teach women how to seduce their husbands." Moses was enjoying the game. "Just imagine your husband coming home tonight exhausted from a nonfulfilling day and your asking him to dance nude for you, what would happen?"

"Nude?" M'mm was laughing again. "You mean without any clothes on?"

"Why not? Our afternoon beauty therapists could offer Beauty Parties in the privacy of their customers' homes. A particular woman could invite a few of her female friends. Our ABTs would show women erotic dance techniques, which they in turn could teach their husbands or lovers. Learning the art of sexual dancing would liberate both women and men." Moses was enjoying M'mm's growing astonishment. "Or our ABTs might teach their customers laughing games, such as nude bridge and others that we could devise. Happy laughter makes a person beautiful, too."

Moses noticed a video-tape recorder near the television set. "Here's another thought. Millions of people have video-tape players in their homes. Our ABTs could bring along a video camera and tape the therapy sessions so their customers could show them to their spouses later." Moses grinned at her, "The idea is to help people to live more loving, playful lives."

Listening to him open-mouthed, M'mm was damned sure that this was no kind of conversation to have with a strange man whom she had met less than half an hour ago. Moreover, it was a conversation she could never report to Ron. The thought suddenly occurred to her that Moses Marshalik might be an escapee from the state mental hospital that wasn't far away. "Really, Mr. Marshalik, you're beginning to sound a little silly," she said. "Please let's get on with your survey." She handed him back his check, "And I really don't want to be paid."

Moses crossed his fingers. The time had come to see if he could put wings on Meredith's feet and help her fly out of her mundane world into a laughing land of "what ifs," but he knew he'd have to be careful. After years of marriage to Ronald Coldaxe, she probably had absorbed much of his dogged practicality. Dancing around in the bright sunlight of unrestrained creative thinking, she might be temporarily blinded and frightened. He decided that he must first enlist her sympathy with the hope that eventually he could transform it into angry empathy.

"I must be honest with you, Mrs. Coldaxe. There really is no formal survey." He sighed, "The truth is that until two months ago I was the vice president of Marsha Lovett. After thirty years of service, at the age of sixty-two they decided I was too old." He grinned. "They were totally unaware that I take after one of my relatives who lived to the age of one hundred and twenty. Compared with him I'm almost a teen-ager. Unfortunately, it's an unwritten policy of W.I.N. Incorporated, who owns Lovett Plastics, who in turn own Marsha Lovett, to get rid of their older executives before they're sixty-five, because otherwise they might have to employ them until they're seventy."

As Moses anticipated, M'mm exploded. "W.I.N. Incorporated! My God! My husband is a vice president of that company. That's why we had to move to Boston."

Smiling now, knowing that he had struck pure gold, Moses looked properly shocked. He snapped his sample case together. "Damn! Fate seems to be conspiring against me. I wish I had known that."

M'mm was bewildered, "I don't understand."

Moses smiled at her uneasily. He was now playing his role off the cuff. If he were going to succeed, it was absolutely necessary that Meredith Coldaxe be able to compartmentalize and live in two worlds. If she mentioned him to her husband, Ron would quickly discover that he had his hand in the Coldaxe cookie jar. Moses was sure that if he could get Meredith to bed she'd never tell Ron—but that might take a few days.

"To tell the truth, Mrs. Coldaxe, the reason that I'm here is that I'm not taking this lying down. I'm a fighter. A sixty-year-old man is as good as a forty-year-old one any day." Moses paused to see if Meredith was getting the full impact of this thought. He was happy to see that she was nodding affirmatively. Now he had to establish that he was a free agent. "Before my poor wife died," he said, trying to look pathetic and properly contrite, "just three months ago, knowing that I would be sacked and she and I would be forced to live on Social Security and a very inadequate pension, I promised her that I would fight back. Moses squeezed out a few tears and let them trickle down his cheek unheeded. "That's the reason that I'm in Boston. I've been talking with several wealthy investors. If I could devise a new profit-making approach to the direct-selling of cosmetics I'm sure that they might be interested in buying Marsha Lovett from W.I.N. They might even make me president of the new company." Moses paused, hoping that Meredith was getting the message, and wondering if she was convinced by his acting, which he wished had been captured on video-tape. But he still had to draw the knot a little tighter, "I'm sure that as the wife of one of the top executives of W.I.N. Incorporated you can understand my position, Mrs. Coldaxe. If any W.I.N. official thought that Marsha Lovett Cosmetics could be raised from the dead, so to speak, and could really make a profit, the price of the company would go up, or they might not want to sell it at all."

Even before he finished, M'mm was nodding enthusiastically, and Moses was happy to see tears of anger in her eyes. "I know what you're thinking," she said. "But you really don't have to worry. My husband doesn't know anything about what's going on in W.I.N. either. Anyway, he rarely discusses W.I.N.'s subsidiaries with me." It occurred to M'mm that Moses Marshalik was about Ralph Thiemost's age, but he was certainly a much more gentle and loving man. "Have you ever met Ralph Thiemost?" she asked.

Moses tried not to grin triumphantly, "I met him many years ago. Thiemost is a ruthless man. Your husband should be careful in his dealings with him."

"He's worse than that!" M'mm was about to tell Moses that Ralph Thiemost was an unmitigated filthy, dirty son of a bitch, and a smelly rat to boot, but she was confused by the sudden desire to put her arms around this handsome, temporarily ruined man. She was sure that Moses Marshalik was much too much of a gentleman to play wargames with men like Ralph Thiemost, or even with Ronald Coldaxe. Helping Moses beat them both at their own game would be the greatest revenge she could think of. Instead of being director of publicity at W.I.N., Incorporated, with Moses Marshalik's help, who could tell? She might end up a hundred-thousand-dollar-a-year vice president of a new and vitalized Marsha Lovett—earning more money than Ronald Coldaxe. But even if nothing ever came of it, matching wits with Moses Marshalik would be more interesting than listening to a lot of crappy afternoon lecturers at the Lynnfield Library tell bored housewives how to realize their potential, or hypnotizing them and regressing them to previous lives.

"I really don't know very much about selling," she said, suddenly convinced she had been predetermined by the stars to meet Moses Marshalik, "but I'm very interested in cosmetics. Years ago, when I was first married, I read everything I could about the ancient Egyptians and the Jews. Frankincense and myrrh were more valuable then than gold is today. America might never have been discovered if explorers hadn't been searching for new routes to the Orient to get perfumes and oils and spices."

Moses shook his head sadly, "To tell you the truth I'm still a bit nervous about your husband."

"Ron doesn't really need to know," M'mm assured him. "Just so long as I'm here at night to soothe his shattered ego, he doesn't really give a damn what I do." She paused and tried not to seem too starry-eyed, "I guess that you'll just have to trust me."

Moses smiled, "We have to trust each other."

For almost the first time in her life M'mm had found a sympathetic ear. During the next two hours, interrupted only by Bloody Marys and tunafish sandwiches she fixed for them, she assured Moses that she would be happy to have lunch with him some other day at the Mountain View Steak House. She didn't even blink when he suggested they might stop to see an afternoon show of nude male dancers, which he insisted might be relevant to a new image for Marsha Lovett. She told him everything she knew about W.I.N., Incorporated, including Ralph Thiemost's infamous job offer to her, but not about her "hanging" and the attempted rape.

At one point, feeling the effects of the drinks, she felt she was laughing too much, but she couldn't help it. "I'm really turned off by men who think they are winners," she said. "They're really shitheads. They don't care who they pollute." Then she told him about Byrdwhistle and how Ron really hadn't wanted W.I.N. to buy the company and about what had happened to poor H. H. Youman. "It's all part of the same nasty picture," she told him. "The decline of the West. The whole world is being ransacked by power-hungry men."

Sitting at her kitchen table and listening to her while she had prepared lunch, Moses had felt very much at home. It occurred to him that afternoon beauty therapists could certainly perform a worthwhile function. Friendly, caring companions for lonesome women, they could share the burden of shopping for food and driving the kids to school. They might even learn how to prepare a nice dinner for a hard-working spouse and teach him how to play, too.

"Some people think the power drive is basic to the male psyche," Moses said, "but I don't. Much of the need for victory and conquest is a learned response. In the so-called successful nations, it is culturally induced by sexual frustration. We must learn how to create a new kind of environment for young men and women, where sex-making with each other is a natural part of their development and growth. Unfortunately, even though they aren't aware of it, most winners in the business world are losers in the bedroom."

Moses looked at M'mm querulously, wondering if she would provide chapter and verse, but when she just frowned he changed the subject. "I'm sorry to hear about this poor fellow H. H. Youman. He was a brilliant man. I've read several articles he wrote for business magazines. Theory Z and the play-ethic are the only sane approach to a full life."

To make sure that Meredith understood Theory Z, he outlined it in depth and was pleased to see that she was listening attentively and nodding enthusiastically. "Maybe this move to Boston will prove very valuable for your husband," he told her. "Running a company on Theory Z principles could be the turning point in his life."

"I doubt it," M'mm said, but she was intrigued by the perspective Moses Marshalik had given her. Maybe Ron could turn into a laughing man like Moses. She knew that Ron wouldn't be home until after six and she would have enjoyed talking to Moses for another few hours, but he suddenly pointed at the kitchen clock.

"I'm so sorry," he said, "I've been taking advantage of your generosity. It's two o'clock and we haven't talked much about the cosmetic business. Before I tackle your neighbors, I hope we can brainstorm this together, Mrs. Coldaxe. Perhaps I could come back tomorrow."

"We seem to have the same initials, Mr. Marshalik," M'mm said impulsively. "My friends call me M'mm."

Moses shook her hand enthusiastically. "Thus far no one ever thought I was 'm'mm-y,'" he laughed. "But maybe I can convince *you*!"

34

The next morning when Moses Marshalik rang the doorbell, M'mm was more sanguine. "I'm really not interested in seeing male strippers today," she said, "and you don't have to take me to lunch, but if you're really interested in the new approach to selling cosmetics, drive me to Boston. We're going shopping." She laughed mysteriously at his obvious surprise. "You won't have to spend any more money. I'll use the check you gave me."

"All two thousand of it?" Moses asked.

M'mm shrugged. "Call it research. I have an idea for Marsha Lovett Cosmetics, but first we have to find the best ingredients." She shivered happily when Moses didn't question her or hem and haw over the project the way Ronald might have. Instead he simply said, "Why not?" and guided her down the path to his van.

Sitting beside him, she said, "You amaze me. You're willing to come with me without asking where we're going or why, or wondering if I'm going to take you on a wild-goose chase."

"Spontaneous women excite me," Moses grinned at her, "especially if they're a little daft, too."

Once in the van she said, "Last night I couldn't sleep because I was thinking about my idea. It's probably pretty silly." M'mm still didn't want to give him details. She preferred to see his reaction to her day-dream as she went along. Nor did she tell him that she had got so hopped up on her idea for Marsha Lovett that she had even hugged Ronald last night and asked him if he was going to make love to her. It was a question she rarely asked Ron, but Moses Marshalik had made her feel lovable, and God knows she would never ask him, a total stranger, to make love to her. Ridiculous. Just thinking such a mad thought must have been induced by tearing up her California roots. Ever since that weird business with Ralph Thiemost, realizing that she had actually been aroused, she had wondered if her brain was getting mushy. Maybe deep down she was some kind of a sex nut. Certainly no woman in her right mind would get sexually turned on by being tied up.

She didn't dare tell Ronald about Moses Marshalik, at least not directly, but she did tell him that a sales representative from Marsha Lovett — without identifying which sex — had called on her. It made her feel considerably safer when Ron confirmed what Moses had told her.

"Marsha Lovett is a sick division of Lovett Plastics," he said. "They never got anywhere against Avon and Mary Kay. Don't buy their junk. It's probably crap. Even if it's any good, you may never be able to get any more. I told Ralph months ago that we should sell the company or close it down before it drains Lovett's profits any further."

After his orgasm, Ronald had kissed her absent-mindedly and thanked her for being such a nice wife. But even before he put out the lights he had sunk back into a gloomy Byrdwhistle reverie. His final thought was, "I hope to hell Ralph does sell Marsha Lovett before he gets some mad idea that it should be a subsidiary of Byrdwhistle."

M'mm had agreed with him that selling cosmetics by mail, even the nonallergic Marsha Lovett products, didn't seem practical. "Only old ladies would buy cosmetics sight unseen," she told him. "But it gives me a good idea. Remember that when we were first married I fooled around making my own cosmetics? I think I'll try it again. It will give me something to do. I could even make shaving cream and after-shave lotion for you. It will be fun and will save money. I might even try making perfume. Enfleurage is very interesting." Ronald was sure that making cosmetics wouldn't save them much money, but if M'mm kept herself occupied, at least until Christmas when the kids arrived on vacation—and, even more important, if she didn't get mixed up in Massachusetts Fair Share or the Clamshell Alliance or that outfit Blast that was trying to regulate the movement of LNG—it would be a great help. He told her that making cosmetics was a great idea, even if she did stink up the place. She could even give them away as Christmas gifts.

Now, sitting beside Moses in the van, she noted that the rear of the van was empty, except for a mattress, which carpeted the van from wall to wall, and a few cartons. M'mm showed him several books that she was carrying in her satchel handbag. "These were my cosmetic cookbooks," she told him, and she then called out the titles: *Back to Basics: The Natural Beauty Handbook,* by Alexandra York; *Fragrance: How to Make Natural Soaps, Scents and Sundries,* by Beverly Plummer, and *Cosmetics from the Kitchen,* by Marcia Donnan. I haven't looked at them for years, but if you like the idea we might eventually write our own cookbook." She grinned at him happily, but he was concentrating on driving and couldn't see how excited she was. "Maybe we could call it *The Love Yourself Cosmetic Cookbook and Guide to Sexual Fulfillment.* It could be a hardcover book with full-color illustrations. Then when your afternoon beauty therapist telephoned for an appointment he could tell the lady of the house that he had a gift for her. I've been thinking that maybe we should call them 'love mentors' or 'love therapists,'" she said. "That's quicker and more to the point. Anyway, they could give the book to customers as a potential get-acquainted offer."

"Give it?" Moses was delighted to lead her on. "That sounds expensive."

M'mm giggled. "It's a cheaper way to get in the door than passing two-thousand-dollar checks through the mail slot." He turned to look at her face and almost hit a passing car. He made an obscene gesture at the other driver. He suddenly thought of pulling over and taking M'mm in the back of the van to make love to her right then. Whether she realized it or not, her eyes were flashing sex signals at him. But once again he cautioned himself. If he was patient, she would reach out for him.

"The book could really be a come-on," M'mm was still bubbling with enthusiasm. "It's a good title. People love self-help books. I grew up reading *The Art of Thinking.* Ron used to love *How to Win Friends and Influence People,* and he read *Your Erroneous Zones.* And just think about that man Robert Ringer who wrote *Looking Out for Number One*; and then there's *Power and Success* by Michael Korda. And *The Power of Positive Thinking* and *How to Be Your Own Best Friend.* They all tell you that you have to love yourself first." M'mm grinned at him with a challenging look. "So does Theory Z if you come right down to it. Anyway, when the average woman reads our *Love Yourself Cosmetic Cookbook and Guide to Sexual Fulfillment,* she'll be hooked." She'll want to start making her cosmetics immediately. She won't only have a lot of fun but can save hundreds of dollars too!" Especially, M'mm thought, if the Love You therapists or mentors were all as handsome as Moses Marshalik.

Moses was puzzled. "What do we sell them? A pound of lard and some olive oil?"

M'mm laughed. "No way. Our customers can buy the cheap ingredients like powdered milk and yogurt themselves. We're going to sell them a cosmetic starter for a couple of hundred bucks, including a special Love Yourself blender and maybe an eggbeater. You get it? Love You Cosmetics will supply all the chemicals and all the crap. Whenever a buyer runs out, they'll order more from their love mentors." She frowned at Moses's laughter. "I know that you're not taking this seriously but you'll have to admit it's an interesting variation on your own insanities. Anyway, I'll bet that millions of women will love the idea." She grinned at him, "Of course it has to be part of a larger package. And that should make you happy because I'm really telling you that maybe your afternoon-beauty-therapists idea isn't as balmy as it sounds." M'mm knew that she was treading on dangerous ground, but she continued anyway. "If horny old men are going to sell this stuff to frustrated housewives, maybe we ought to call them 'love therapists.'" She really hoped she was challenging Moses. She wanted to prove to him that she could play silly mind-bending games, too. Her problem was that she was married to a man who never could jump out of his skin and dance around in his bones.

"It's a good beginning," Moses told her. "But there's one serious problem. More than half the wives in America are working wives. When women work, you can't reach them during the day, and that screws up the home-selling business." This was a Byrdwhistle axiom and, according to H. H. Youman, the key to the future growth of the mail-order business. Of course Moses didn't mention this to M'mm. "Anyway," Moses said, "after a woman has worked all day, she's probably as pooped as her old man and not too interested in making cosmetics."

"Women are never tired when it comes to being beautiful," M'mm said.

"But a male love-therapist couldn't arrive after supper to teach the wife how to love herself if the husband was looking at the tube and the kids were hanging around."

M'mm agreed. "But a couple of male love-therapists working together could offer cosmetic cooking parties. If the husband is going bowling, all the loving wife has to do is call up her girlfriends and Daddy Moses and another love-therapist could entertain them and sell all of them their cosmetics starter kits."

M'mm knew that she was running wild, but it was too much fun to stop. "Love therapists could even offer cosmetic cooking classes in the basement of the local church or synagogue. Or they could rent a local motel showroom and cook on hotplates."

"My God," Moses whistled. "I hope your husband appreciates you. You're fantastic." He meant it. M'mm was proving one of the key elements in Theory Z. Stimulating the whole brain with mental gymnastics was an aphrodisiac. The process slowed down the evaluating left brain and released the right brain so that it could go to work. Then, when a man and woman learned how to do this together, they could catalyze each other, and inevitably they would join their penis and vagina, which would help them complete the creative circuit. Finally, like God himself, after six days of play and sex-making, the lovers could rest and enjoy the wonder of the world that existed in their own minds.

But Moses didn't verbalize this fantasy to M'mm. Not yet. It was obvious that eventually M'mm would talk her way into bed with him.

By noon, after they had visited a half-dozen chemical-supply and drug houses whose addresses M'mm had copied from the telephone book, and had made several stops at supermarkets and regular drug stores, M'mm had collected nearly a hundred bottles of chemicals and oils and other essential ingredients for perfume-making. As she checked the list, she assured Moses that all of these things were necessary for good cosmetic cookery and she tried to explain their various uses.

"Many of them are emollients. They lubricate the skin and prevent it from drying out, and of course they help make a person feel sensuous and erotic," she grinned at him. "Keep in mind that some of this stuff is just wax or other things that give bulk to the creams and moisturizers that we're going to make."

"And this is only a beginning," she told him. "We need all kinds of other stuff, too, and this is where Love You Cosmetics comes into the picture. We'll make it easy to get the ingredients by selling them in one big package. In addition, we'll show women how to make cosmetics that don't need a lot of chemical stabilizers that they may be allergic to, and if necessary you can refrigerate them so you don't need a lot of the chemicals that are used to retard spoilage."

Amused by her conviction that she had discovered a unique new way to sell cosmetics, and half-convinced in spite of himself, Moses listened while she told him that they would need cetyl alcohol—although for home purposes vodka was a good substitute—and astringents and antiseptics and solvents and a humectant, like ethylene glycol—which would reduce the evaporation on skin surfaces—and emulsifiers, which would act as stabilizers.

Laughing and totally delighted with his amazement, she bought oil of wintergreen, which she told him was a safe preservative. "And we've got to have oleic acid, potassium carbonate and triethanolamine, because we're going to make soap." And she bought pigments, making sure they weren't coal-tar derivatives, to color the creams and soaps and make them look appetizing. "And we need baking soda. Love You Cosmetics could even sell its own brand and make a lot of money. It's very good as a soothing bath and for sunburns." And she bought talcs and zinc sterates and kaolin. "We'll need them for face powders and face masks and we need thymol, which is a germicide, and titanium oxide to make skin whiter."

And that wasn't all. After they had the van loaded with a dozen cartons, M'mm said, "Now we've got to make our concoctions smell better. We need perfume-oil concentrates and ambergris and musk oil and cinnamon oil and frankincense and myrrh and angelica, and flower waters, like rose water and orange water, and artificial jasmine." Knowing that she was being totally silly for the first time in her married life, but not giving a damn, she even dared to tell Moses, "We really should investigate the aphrodisiac qualities of various natural perfumes. I read somewhere that just inhaling the scent of white jasmine flowers and tuberose can turn a woman into a nymphomaniac."

Driving back toward Lynnfield and the Mountain View Steak House, M'mm gave him an extended lecture on perfumes. "Love You mentors, or love therapists, or whatever we're going to call them must become aroma therapists, too. They must be able to tell the customers about the healing and beautifying properties of essential oils and flowers and herbs. The ancient Egyptians and Jews were well aware of the aphrodisiac qualities of various scents. Perfumes were even used in religious ceremonies and on sacred occasions. In Exodus, the Lord told Moses how to make certain kinds of perfumes. They weren't to be used except in worship. When he discovered that many people were covering themselves with frankincense just for sexual attraction, Moses was very angry." Actually M'mm was testing to see if this Moses would acknowledge being Jewish, but he didn't get her message. "You probably know all this," she told him. "In biblical days Hebrew women had to be purified with myrrh before they were married."

Moses laughed. "In the good old days Jewish princesses probably never took a bath. That's why they needed perfume."

"That's silly," M'mm scowled. "Of course, they did. Because of the arid climate, they used natural oils to clean their bodies and to keep their skin silky. And, don't forget, Mary washed Jesus' feet in spikenard and olive oil, and Judas Iscariot was angry with her because it was expensive stuff even then."

"I'm only having one problem with all this," Moses said, forgetting that his complaint didn't sound quite logical coming from a former vice president of Marsha Lovett Cosmetics. "When a woman splashes all these chemicals and oils over her body, won't she cover up the odor of her natural hormones? There are subtle body odors that most men and women are totally unconscious of, but they can be strong sexual attractants," Moses stared into her eyes. "Unlike most men I've trained my mind to interpret even the most fleeting and evanescent scents. I find your odor very erotic."

M'mm moved away from him to a safer position near the right door of the van. She wasn't entirely sure whether he was teasing her or not. "Maybe you're proving a point. You're not smelling just me, I'm wearing a musk concoction that I whipped up this morning."

35

M'mm knew that feeling "safe" with Moses Marshalik, as she now did, was probably quite dangerous. His eyes often seemed to engulf her, and he gave her the feeling that she was the lone player in an orchestra that he was conducting. As she turned the pages of the musical score, there were new surprises on every page. But Moses made no attempt to touch her, and even though their conversation continued to break the barriers of normal sexual restraint between strangers, nothing he had said to her seemed to have any personal overtones. But now, a few miles from the Mountain View Steak House, and not too far from Lynnfield, he suddenly turned off the expressway and drove into a parking lot filled with automobiles and several empty buses. Girding one edge of the parking lot was a one-story brick-faced building that covered nearly an acre. There were no signs on the building, but even before they got out of the van they could hear disco music thumping through the walls and now it seemed to be vibrating in the asphalt they were walking on.

"This building used to be a furniture store," Moses told her. "Now it's called "The Big Bamboo and Jumping Banana." The new owners don't have to advertise because women tell each other about the place. Practically all the women's clubs in the area have afternoon and evening excursions here. I think we're just in time for the first afternoon floor show."

M'mm had never been in a place like the Big Bamboo, but she knew without asking that this must be the floor show that Moses had mentioned yesterday, where male strippers danced for an all-female audience. She was now very self-conscious. Somehow, the thought of watching naked men with Moses Marshalik embarrassed her. Their sexual discussions had been silly and generalized, but they were now becoming more specific. She enjoyed Moses Marshalik. Even though she fantasized about his embracing her and enjoying a long lingering kiss, she knew that much of the charm he had for her was due to the secure feeling he gave her. She certainly had no desire to see him or any man dance around naked. Before they got to the door, she tried to convey this to him. "I can imagine what it's like! Really, I would prefer to have lunch at the Mountain View Steak House and see the cocktail lounge there."

"We're only going to stay a few minutes," Moses said. "I want you to see the women as well as the men. They are part of a new and growing social phenomenon. Women are reversing roles in more ways than one. For the first time in history, women dare to enjoy men as sex objects." He laughed, "Since we are enjoying a playful 'excursion into the absurd' and trying to see if we can merge it into a new reality for Marsha Lovett, we shouldn't overlook any possibilities."

In the lobby they were stopped by a frowzy blonde woman. "Sorry," she shouted over the music, "this show is for women only. The only men inside are the male strippers. Even the bartender and the waiters are women. If your friend wants to go in, the admission price is five dollars. You can have a drink in the bar over there while you wait for her." She pointed to a bar completely detached from the rest of the building.

Moses beamed at her. "I'll be more than happy to strip for your customers—no charge. Actually, we're here to write a feature story for the *Boston Globe*. I'm sure your customers won't mind."

The woman shrugged and eyed him up and down with a lustful grin, "Okay, I'll make an exception for you. You don't have to dance, but you'll have to leave your clothes here. We don't want to make any of the women inside feel uncomfortable, and they most certainly would with a man dressed in a shirt and tie watching them."

"Let's go," M'mm said nervously. She had already guessed that Moses would rise to the challenge. Even before she could protest, Moses had pulled off his coat, tie, shirt, and pants. Slipping out of his jockey shorts he stood naked in his shoes and stockings and smirked at both of them.

The blonde woman looked at him approvingly and asked him how old he was. When Moses told her he was sixty-two, she grinned at M'mm, "Your boyfriend is in pretty good shape for an old crock. Watch out for him. There're a lot of girls—young and old—in there who might like to take him home with them."

Fortunately, inside the open-raftered barnlike room, the house-lights were dimmed. Feeling jittery but entranced by Moses's naked behind, and amazed at his casual wave to the women who oohed and aahed at him as they threaded past crowded tables, M'mm prayed that none of her Cabot Lane neighbors were in the audience. Actually, most of the almost four hundred women there were too busy cheering and screaming "Take it off! Take it off!" at the strippers to notice anything else. They were now yelling at a young man who had stripped down to his jewelled jock-strap. Sitting behind a table that the blonde woman had led them to, Moses was no longer so visible. But M'mm knew that several women near them were nudging each other enthusiastically and gesturing at Moses. They were much more intrigued by him than by the man on the floor who was bumping and grinding and flipping his very big—but not erect—penis at the women sitting at the tables ringing the dancefloor. One woman managed to grab the dancer's bouncing rod for a second, but it slid out of her hand. Unperturbed, the dancer blithely announced to the audience that, if any woman wanted to hold his prick for a few minutes, she could. "It will only cost you fifty bucks," he yelled, and was immediately greeted with enthusiastic screams of approval. "Bring it over here," one woman yelled, "We'll raise fifty bucks. I can't wait to squeeze it." But the stripper just laughed, took his bows, and was immediately replaced by a performer dressed like a young executive. Circling the floor haughtily in a pin-striped suit and homburg, he stopped to smile at two women in the audience and invited them to come forward and undress him.

By this time the Big Bamboo was so noisy it was impossible to talk, but as M'mm was wondering how Moses was going to get out of the place without being mobbed, she couldn't help staring at the continuous display of naked penises, balls, and behinds. And as the show continued, she smiled at the enthusiasm the women showed for the erotic bumping and grinding. After centuries of being sex objects themselves, these women were rebelling. Years ago, before Ron had turned so prudish, she had often dragged him to nude beaches in California. After a few minutes on the beach, most men and women stopped staring and simply enjoyed each other's naked vulnerability. But here the women were not only staring but fantasizing. M'mm wondered if they were as vocal in their approval of male genitals in the privacy of their own bedrooms. And the thought crossed her mind that, unlike Ron, who usually wasn't very comfortable with his naked body, Moses Marshalik was obviously a man whose mind and body were totally unified. But, although M'mm knew she was titillated sitting next to a strange naked male, she was positive that she would never admit it to him.

As he leaned close to her, his mouth near her ear so that he could be heard above the noise, she found that she was looking down at his nested penis. It seemed to be sleeping very happily against his thighs. "Had enough?" Moses asked. "I think you've got the picture. Shall we move on?" He stood up before she did, and she was uncomfortably aware that his penis was now nodding happily a few inches from her face.

Then, while she was praying that they could get back to the lobby and that he could get dressed before the show was over, the house-lights went on. They were squeezing by a row of tables filled with twenty or more older women with white hair piled high in lookalike beehives. They were all more than seventy, but they greeted Moses with cheers of approval as he tried to wriggle past their table. Several patted his naked behind. One of them, who was at least eighty, stood up and grabbed him. "You're a beautiful man," she murmured, and she hugged Moses and caressed his back. "You look just like my husband did many years ago."

Before he could extricate himself, a much younger woman screamed happily at him. "Hyman is it you?" She slithered into a three-way hug with the old lady. "Am I seeing things? Is it really you—bare-assed and ready for action?"

M'mm intercepted a split-second of surprise across Moses's face, but it swiftly merged into a huge grin, and he returned the young woman's hug. "Sylvia! Sylvia Marlow! Are all these lovely ladies friends of yours?" He turned toward M'mm. Meet my friend Meredith Coldaxe. When you see your mother tell her that Meredith has come up with an exciting new approach for Marsha Lovett Cosmetics." Realizing that she had put Moses on thin ice, Sylvia tried to mend her fences. "Good lord, forgive me, I even forgot your name. It's Moses isn't it, not Hyman?" She smiled at Meredith. "I can't imagine anything more interesting than a naked male cosmetics-salesman. Moses told my mother that you'd just moved from California. Your husband works for Byrdwhistle, doesn't he?" Sylvia laughed. "If you're lucky enough to get a job there, you don't have to come to the Big Bamboo. You'll get your fill of naked men every day of the week."

While trying to divert the attention of the old ladies, Moses prayed that Sylvia wasn't about to tell Meredith how much she had enjoyed her husband in bed. "Who are your friends?" he asked her.

"They all live in Somerville at the Act Three Nursing Home," she said. "The owner is very prudish. There's no place they can crawl in the sack with any of the male patients." Sylvia shrugged. "The women outnumber the men three to one anyway. If the old geezers weren't so damned wary they could achieve what they always wanted in life—two or three women in bed with them at the same time." Sylvia laughed. "Of course they have to be careful. If they get caught playing Doctor it will be curtains for all of them. I thought I'd give the ladies a little treat today."

Moses smiled and waved good-bye to the women. "Don't give up," he told them. "Fight for the right to snuggle a man."

With Moses fully dressed, they were back in the van. M'mm was a little aggrieved and very suspicious of Moses Marshalik, who obviously magnetized females, young and old. "I think you'd better take me home," she told him coldly.

Moses looked rueful. "You're angry with me. I'm really sorry. I wasn't trying to be an exhibitionist. The Mountain View Steak House is just up the road. I want you to see one more missing piece of the Love You Cosmetics puzzle."

M'mm frowned, "Really, I scarcely know you. I know that I've been acting pretty silly. The way you behave in public is none of my business, but you must understand I'd rather not be introduced to your friends."

"Sylvia's mother is the New England distributor for Marsha Lovett," Moses said, grinning inwardly. "The truth is that I met Sylvia just a week ago at her mother's house. You heard her. She didn't even remember my name."

"She's a very vivacious woman," M'mm was suddenly feeling possessive about Moses Marshalik and she knew that she was being ridiculous. She sighed, "I still don't get the connection between love therapists and male strippers." She noticed that Moses had turned into the driveway of a two-story building that sat high on a hill. A billboard-sized sign overlooking the thousand-car parking-lot announced that this was the Mountain View Steak House. She shrugged, "All right, I'll have lunch with you. Promise me that we won't be conspicuous."

Moses squeezed her hand, "Don't worry. Everyone will think you're a loving daughter having lunch with her father."

Passing by hundreds of people waiting in line on the veranda, Moses told her the restaurant could seat more than sixteen hundred people but that it would still probably be an hour before they could get a table. The number on the ticket he had been given would eventually be called and they would be assigned a table or a booth in the Wild Bill Hickok Room, the Billy the Kid Room, or the Jesse James Room. All of the dining areas in the building had been named after Western badmen. While they were waiting, he would show her the cocktail lounge.

"The reason I wanted you to see this place at this time of day," Moses told her as they sipped Martinis, "is that, like the Big Bamboo, it reveals a totally new phenomenon in American society."

M'mm shrugged. "I'm still a little bewildered. I don't know what love therapists and making cosmetics at home have to do with male strippers and a restaurant cocktail lounge." She didn't know whether it was the gin or Moses but once again she was feeling happy, sexy, and silly.

Moses smiled at her with a tender, loving expression that instantly transformed M'mm into a little girl whose father was about to read her a fairy story before he tucked her into bed. "You have to fantasize a little," he told her. "Instead of working in a brash commercial atmosphere, like the Big Bamboo's, why couldn't our love therapists offer intimate at-home strip-parties for select groups of customers?"

"Really, Moses, you're being quite silly."

"Maybe not. But, whether or not we decide to blend nude-male dancing with cosmetic cookery, you'll have to admit that successful love therapists could function as harmless, undemanding male friends to their female customers. Unlike average husbands, they could offer an escape from whatever the woman's day-to-day reality might be. Not only would they be friends to lean on in a way that the average woman's husband can never be, but as a part of the beautifying process they could help a woman find herself. They would create a warm, secure sexual ambience that would help a female customer create a new image for herself."

Moses was enjoying M'mm's dubious frown. "Let's stir another ingredient into the broth," he told her. "I hope you have noticed that Mountain View caters to three kinds of senior citizens. Practically all of the diners are either widows and widowers, older husbands and wives who are still surviving together and haven't yet checked into a senior-citizen center, or philandering older men with younger women. These men have older wives at home who have given up the ghost."

Moses gestured toward the tables around them, "This cocktail lounge is a potential recruiting office for our love therapists." He grinned at M'mm, "We could check it out if you wish. Just circulate at the bar or stop by any of these tables and you'll discover that you're in a poor man's club. The men here who are in their sixties are probably not married to their luncheon companions. And note that these younger women aren't children. They're housewives or working women in their forties. On a low-key sexual level, older men—our future love therapists—are offering the women something they can't get at home. The owners of this place, and thousands like them throughout the country, have discovered that there are millions of older Americans who live on social security or pensions who are learning for the first time in their lives that they might just as well play a little before they check into the cemetery. Mountain View provides one necessary escape environment. Love You Cosmetics and love therapists could offer the same kind of ambience."

"My God," M'mm gasped. "You are a dreamer. I'll go along with you that older men might make good Love You Cosmetics dealers, but they certainly can't compete with young studs as strippers."

Moses laughed heartily, "That's really open to dispute." He pointed to a gray-haired man with a protruding stomach. "Obviously, we would have to reject him. But look around you. There're plenty of fifty- and sixty-year-olds here who have flat stomachs and nice time-weathered, craggy faces. Unlike the strippers at the Big Bamboo, they could give their customers a unique blend of sex and security. Younger women, like you would have a unique opportunity to relive their incestuous childhood fantasies. A dancing nude daddy—still in reasonably good physical condition—would breach their subconscious dreams and make them more erotic with their husbands."

Giggling and shaking her head at this madness, M'mm wanted to ask Moses how in hell the Love You customers could keep love therapists out of their bedrooms. But she decided that it was too dangerous to carry this insane kind of thinking any further.

"You may be right," she said, "And I agree with you that half of

America works so that the other half can play, but you're working at the wrong end of the stick. A lot of these women who are still housewives are married to 'corporate bigamists.' There's a very good book on the subject that I could recommend to you. Unlike you, men like my husband are realists. They don't know how to play the silly word-games we've been playing." Without realizing what she was doing, M'mm touched his hand, and there were tears in her eyes. "I know it's all play – but it's been fun and I know we're not really going anywhere. I've enjoyed it."

To her surprise, when they finally got a table, Moses ordered a vege-table plate. "Anyone who makes their own cosmetics shouldn't eat meat," he told her, laughing. "Feeding grain to the cattle is an expensive way to get proteins. Our love therapists won't make an issue of it, but they should explain that the perspiration of vegetarians is odorless."

"What about hormonal odor?"

"Ha! That's another story," Moses said. "You see, M'mm, we can't quit now. We've really got to write a loving cosmetic cookbook together. It doesn't matter if we ever use it. Now that you've accepted me as a naked daddy, we could also work out a guidebook for love therapists." He smiled affectionately at her. "And we mustn't give up on Ron. If we learn how to play together, eventually we can teach the rest of the world *and* your husband."

36

Tossing in her bed that night beside Ron, M'mm kept trying to convince herself that her adventure with Moses wasn't hurting anyone. But both her left brain and her right brain had abdicated. Of all the god-damned impossible things that shouldn't happen to her at this stage in her life – when she was practically on the verge of menopause – was to be attracted to a sixty-year-old lecher who was probably so financially impoverished that he would be better off with a job as a bank guard than being a love therapist. God, a love therapist! She was happy that Ron, tossing uneasily beside her and probably dreaming about Byrdwhistle, couldn't read her mind. After her day with Moses, she had to put on a straight face and stop laughing. If Ron could have seen her today and yesterday, and no doubt tomorrow – and according to the digital clock on the dresser it was already today – Good lord, Moses would be here again in less than ten hours. If Ron could have seen his wife as a totally laughing, unpremeditating woman, he wouldn't have recognized her. Was Moses right? With her help and Byrdwhistle's, could Ron learn how to play?

When she told Moses that Ron was a workaholic, she launched him into a laughing discussion of the meaning of play and work. "Look in your *Webster's International*," he told her. "There's nearly a full page devoted to the meaning of play, and almost as much space defining work. It reveals an age old confusion. The word *play* derives from the Middle English *pleien,* to frolic, or the Anglo Saxon *plega,* which has overtones of 'caring for'! But the basic meaning 'moving swiftly, gamboling, frisking, frolicking or even dallying amorously in sexual intercourse' has been corrupted. Man has tacked nasty adverbs onto play so that it automatically becomes work or some other nefarious activity. So people play around, play tricks, play away, play both ends in the middle, play dead, play up, play down, play with, play fair, play havoc with, play false, play fast and loose, play for splits, play hooky, play first, play into a person's hand, play opposite, play out, play politics," Moses shook his head and sighed.

"That's not all," M'mm said, enjoying the game. "People play the market, play the horses, play to score, play possum, play one's cards, and play second fiddle." M'mm grinned at him, "Or they play hooky. Isn't that essentially what you're advocating?"

Moses laughed, "I think we should play hooky from a national insanity—the belief that work can't be play or fun, that it must be serious. If you look at the definition of work, it means 'to exert oneself physically or mentally *for a purpose.*' Unfortunately, we can't define play either without giving it an ulterior purpose," he laughed. "If we tell someone that they're not playing fair, we really mean that they aren't playing at all. Play by definition should mean with no purpose—no gain."

Driving back to Lynnfield, Moses told her that Margaret Mead had put her finger on the problem. "Margaret said that if you want to get financial support to study play, you must call it recreation—'a label that identifies its role in recreating human beings for the serious and proper business of life'—which is work!"

M'mm was aware that for the first time in her life she was experiencing amorphous, unfocused anger. She lived in a world that no longer knew how to play. People bought expensive sportsclothes in which to play or watch others play. They cheered and pretended that they were actually playing themselves. "It bugs me," she told him. "Ron has always wanted me to learn to play golf with him. But he doesn't play golf. He worries about how many strokes he takes on each hole and he curses when he slices and hooks. I played golf with him once, and it wasn't play. I had a score of one twenty-five and didn't give a damn. He insisted that I should take lessons, and he moaned about his eighty-eight because he still hadn't made par."

"The only sane purpose for work, as well as for play, is to have fun," Moses told her. "Our love therapists should teach their customers that two naked people tossing a frisbee at each other, walking along the sea barefoot, rolling in the grass or in the leaves, making love outdoors naked, dancing because the music on their hi-fi makes them *have* to dance, making cosmetics in the kitchen, or adorning each other with them, is really the only way to live." The day before, Moses's parting words had been: "If we're going to convert your husband, you've got to understand that to the workaholic work is really play, but with one missing ingredient—he doesn't know he's playing. He's usually so overwhelmed with the responsibility for his work that he's not having any fun."

M'mm was a little frazzled from lack of sleep on the third morning. Was it really Wednesday? Was Thanksgiving Day only a week away? Before Moses arrived, M'mm was nibbling nervously on a piece of toast and, although Ronald seemed remote and preoccupied, she tried to concentrate on his problems.

Before they had gone to bed the night before, she had timidly brought up the subject of Theory Z, which Moses had recommended she study carefully.

"I was reading Abraham Maslow's comparisons of Theory Z organizations with Theory X and Y companies," she had told him. She knew that he had been trying to concentrate on a Bruins–Islanders hockey game on the tube and hadn't really heard her, but she had wanted to reach out to him somehow. "You and Ralph think you're running W.I.N. on a Theory Y—participation management—basis, but you know damn well that fundamentally W.I.N. is an autocratic, big-white-father company. Thiemost doesn't recognize the difference between people and his machinery. He uses them interchangeably to profit the stockholders."

Then she had realized that Ronald wasn't listening to her and became incensed. "Why don't you admit it? Ralph's a throwback to another generation. W.I.N. is a slave plantation and, if they could, Father God Thiemost and his management committee would even decide who the male slaves should mate with. All of you are simply trying to give the impression that you're benevolent and loving and care for your employees, but the truth is that all you're interested in is extracting the last buck out of them."

"M'mm please. If you must talk don't shout, whisper." Ronald had told her patiently, but he didn't turn away from the hockey game. When she kept on raving he finally had said, "Damn it, I can't figure out why you persist in biting the hand that feeds you."

Or even rejecting the prick that rapes me, M'mm had thought grimly. She had tossed *The Corporate Bigamist,* which she had been reading, onto his side of the bed. "You better read it, honey," she had said. "The author describes you and Ralph Thiemost. You're the monster type who is truly wedded to his corporation. In all aspects of his life, the monster type is an Adolf Hitler, a frustrated dictator. Wives and families are just facades, and the monster tries to protect himself from their minor annoyances. They better be happy and be loving facades or he'll get rid of them fast." M'mm had tried to snuggle against Ron and she had even given his penis a tentative, affectionate squeeze. "You really better be careful, honey. You're traveling that road. I think you should give some thought to Theory Z and Byrdwhistle—maybe they are coming events. Maybe Theory Z is the only sane way to run a business. It seems to me that Byrdwhistle may be a new kind of big family that really incorporates the old-style monogamous one and gives it a sound and healthy environment with Mommy and Daddy working in the same place and everybody loving each other."

Ronald had not answered and had continued to look at the hockey game. "It really irks me," she cried, pounding his back, "that you haven't let me spend even one day with you at work. I'd really like to know what you're trying to hide."

"Jesus Christ!" Ronald's attention had been finally diverted from the tube. "Tonight I'm trying not to think about Byrdwhistle. I knew if I let you read that Byrdwhistle crap you'd fall for it hook, line, and sinker. I'm lucky that H. H. Youman isn't around to seduce you in person. Let him be a warning to you. It's a ruthless, cut-throat world out there. Look what happened to Youman when the rug was pulled out from under him. He turned into a babbling idiot.'

He had turned to face the television screen again, but M'mm wouldn't let him concentrate. "You call that playing hockey?" she demanded, pointing at the tube. "I call that a substitute for aggression, or murder."

Ronald had glowered at her, "You're spouting Byrdwhistle shit." But during the commercial he had made an attempt to arouse M'mm's sympathy. "You really have to help me. I can't come home every night and rehash Byrdwhistle insanity with you. If I don't compartmentalize, I'll end up in worse shape than Youman. No one can run a business in the United States in the twentieth century and treat it like a big, loving family. And it isn't going to change in the next century. Someone has to crack the whip. Someone has to be willing to be the fall guy. Maslow's belief that all we have to do is become Being People and adopt Theory Z and that then everyone will become a generalist—the idea that while they're playing together people can solve all their day-to-day problems in a happy state of anarchy—is a ridiculous daydream."

Ronald had cheered as one of the Bruins slipped a puck past the goalie. "Honestly, M'mm, be a good guy and let me watch the game for an hour without talking will you?"

M'mm had slid back to her side of the bed. Whether she enticed him or not, Ronald wasn't going to try to escape from Byrdwhistle tonight by nuzzling and playing with her body. Ronald was a time-study man. He made love with her the night before. If she anticipated his schedule correctly, the next time would be Friday night at ten o'clock — efficiently finishing in time to watch the eleven o'clock news.

At breakfast now, trying not to feel jittery about Moses, who she knew would arrive by eleven, M'mm tried once more to promote Theory Z. "I really think Abe Maslow was on the right track," she told Ronald, who was trying to read the morning *Globe.* "He believed that social indicators should be included in the accounting system. Isn't that basically what's being done at Byrdwhistle? See, for the first time I am really interested in your work. From everything that I've read, H. H. Youman made Byrdwhistle a kind of people-loving-people place. Really, Ron, you'd be much happier if you could absorb a little of Theory Z. Maybe if you did the company would make more money than W.I.N. does. And living in a world of Being Values would make you warmer and more loving and you might even learn how to transcend your ego. Maybe that's more important than monetary rewards." M'mm could tell by Ronald's expression that she should have stopped when she was ahead, but it was too late.

"Jesus Christ, M'mm, that's pure shit! Get off my back." During their eighteen years of marriage, Ronald had refused to let himself be ensnared by M'mm's Polyanna — Dr. Pangloss — all's-right-with-the-world-if-you'd-only-wake-up-and-realize-it philosophy. But sometimes, like now, she pushed too hard.

"The plain truth," he told her, "is that for some unaccountable reason Byrdwhistle already makes more money and has a greater return on investment than W.I.N. does. But, believe me, it's a sheer god-damned fluke. It won't last. If a business is going to make money year after year, the guys running it can't turn it into some kind of transcendental heaven, or kiss every employee's ass." Ronald shrugged, "You haven't even been listening to what I've been telling you. Within the next ten days, if I don't put my hands on two hundred thousand of H. H. Youman's fucking Love Rocks, I may end up in jail."

Knowing that the time had come to make his Yugoslavian trip definite, Ronald tried to explain his encounter with Victor Watchman. "If the people running the Federal Trade Commission are in the mood, and the damned assholes who run these bureaus are always in the mood to create trouble, they could bankrupt Byrdwhistle, and W.I.N. along with it. I have no choice. Monday morning I'm going to fly to Yugoslavia. I'll be back in a week. I'd leave today if I could, but I've already told you that on top of everything else we still haven't resolved the mess with those Club Wholesome sex-tapes. Somehow I've got to straighten that one out before I leave."

"What if you can't find those Love Rocks?"

"I may never come back," Ronald said grimly. "But, don't worry, you can become an expatriate with me. There's enough money in the checking account for an airline ticket to Dubrovnik."

Ordinarily, M'mm would have protested. Wasn't Ron aware that Monday was just three days before Thanksgiving? Was he actually going to leave her, still a stranger in New England, alone for Thanksgiving? But she censored these complaints because a vagrant thought was loitering in her brain—Moses Marshalik had told her that he was staying at the YMCA in Boston. She knew she shouldn't suddenly recover her good disposition and not show displeasure that Ron was leaving, but the thought did occur to her that, if Ronald was going to spend Thanksgiving with his new-found lover, she'd cook a turkey anyway and invite a love therapist to dinner.

"What am I supposed to do," she demanded. "Pretend that I'm Priscilla Alden and eat Thanksgiving dinner all alone?"

"Aren't the kids coming home?"

"You seem to have forgotten. We're not living in Santa Monica. Since you're always crabbing about money I told Mitchell and Tina they couldn't fly here for Thanksgiving and then come for Christmas, too, because it would cost too much."

Ronald was sipping his coffee with one eye on the kitchen clock. It was eight-fifteen. There really was no rush. True Byrdwhistlers drifted in and out of the office at all hours of the day and night. They had recovered long ago from the nine-to-five syndrome.

But he was postponing his departure because he hadn't yet dropped his real bomb. Now he inched open the bomb-bay doors. "Are you sure that none of our Santa Monica mail has been forwarded yet?"

"What's so important? It's only junk mail—and catalogues like Byrdwhistle's—which you never look at." She shrugged at Ronald's frown. "We've received only one batch. And you saw that last week."

So far so good, Ronald thought. He hoped to be in Yugoslavia before M'mm saw the mailing from World Corporation to W.I.N. employees. "I really hope that I can count on you, M'mm," he said. "You keep insisting that I should be a laughing man. Now, I hope that you're going to be a laughing woman." Ron stood up, ready to escape from the verbal devastation that he was sure would follow his revelation. "Thiemost telephoned me yesterday. He expects to be in Boston next week. Since I'll be in Yugoslavia, maybe it would be a nice gesture if you invited him to dinner."

"Ronald Coldaxe!" M'mm tried to stonewall her anger, but her fury blew through the cracks. "I think you must be as crazy as H. H. Youman. So that's why you were so miserable to me last night? Don't you ever listen to me? I told you that your god-damned boss propositioned me. He hasn't given up. He wants to go to bed with your wife. He wants to make you a cuckold!" M'mm hadn't even told Ronald about her worst encounter with Thiemost, but now she doubted if even the knowledge of her "hanging" would have deterred her husband. Ronald grinned weakly.

"Do you want me to invite him to stay here?" M'mm demanded. "That would save W.I.N. one hundred dollars a night at the Ritz. Why not? Your boss could sleep with me in your bed. It would be all in the W.I.N. family." M'mm banged the breakfast dishes into the dishwasher. "It may be Thanksgiving, Ronald Coldaxe, but don't think I'm your turkey!"

Ronald shook his head patiently. "I know Ralph's a cocksman. But, in this day and age, when a man like Ralph Thiemost asks a modern woman to go to bed with him, she just smiles and considers it a compliment. That doesn't mean that I approve of him either, or that I want you to go to bed with him—or any other man. But you've got to admit it, M'mm, you've aged well." Ronald bent over and kissed her cheek. "You're very attractive to older men. Anyway, I wouldn't worry about Ralph. From what I hear, since his last divorce he goes for younger stuff than you."

"To hell with you, Ronald Coldaxe," M'mm was ready to pour her second cup of coffee on his head. You'd better watch out. I'm not going to sit here like a Mickey Mouse wife. Not while Adele Youman is trying to convince you that your balls are really Love Rocks in disguise."

Ronald groaned, "Okay, let's get back to reality. Ralph isn't flying to Boston only because of the Love Rocks. I'm hoping he hasn't heard about the Club Wholesome fiasco and that, with a fast payment of twenty-five thousand dollars to the aggrieved parents of the disappointed teen-agers, we can cool their outraged morality. But something else is afoot. I'm not sure what it is. About ten days ago some Bostonian character named Sheldon Coombs, who runs World Corporation, which H. H. Youman was mixed up in, informed the *Wall Street Journal* that World is recommending that W.I.N. stockholders toss its directors out on their asses and let World liquidate W.I.N. Can you imagine that? Liquidate a billion dollar company and put eighty thousand people out of work? Coombs insists that the stockholders can make more money that way than they will from dividends for the next ten years. Thiemost is furious. Coombs telephoned him and demanded at least two seats on the board of directors of W.I.N. because of the stock that World now controls."

Ronald kissed M'mm good-bye. "I'm telling you this so you can see that it's a tough world out there and that no one is playing for fun. If W.I.N. is liquidated, I'll be out on my ass. You don't have to like Thiemost but don't forget that he's our bread and butter."

Ronald still didn't dare tell M'mm the whole story. Another reason that Thiemost was coming to Boston was those damned photographs that Adele had taken.

When he had called, Thiemost really hadn't needed a telephone. His voice was like a missile launched from California, which seconds later pierced Ronald's eardrums in Massachusetts and made his intestines tremble. "Coldaxe, you goofed! Irretrievably this time, I'm afraid." Thiemost was sounding the Coldaxe death knell. "Some asshole employee of World Corporation—a cancerous excrescence created by that madman Heman Hyman Youman—has sent a letter to all our eighty-eight thousand employees. World is offering them stock certificates worth one dollar each and telling them to buy themselves a Christmas present now. Using their money, World is going to buy W.I.N. Incorporated and give it to them—lock, stock, and barrel. It says in the circular: 'Put W.I.N. under your Christmas tree.' World Corporation is offering not only W.I.N. employees but any interested participant a plan whereby the employees will finally own the company and elect their own directors."

"Ralph are you sure?" Ron had finally interrupted Thiemost's diatribe against H. H. Youman.

"He's crazy all right, crazy like a fox," Thiemost kept repeating. "I'm a W.I.N. employee," Ronald had said. "I haven't seen any stock-purchase offer. Maybe it's a flash in the pan."

"It's no flash in the pan. It's a total eruption," Thiemost had begun to yell. "The letter from World was probably mailed to your Santa Monica address." Thiemost had laughed nastily. "You'd better have a damned good excuse ready when your loving wife sees it. Along with me, you're flying bare-ass over a map of the United States."

Thiemost had explained that along with the letter there was a four-color brochure. "And you're in it, Ron, and I'm in it. We're stark naked in a composite that has you flying over the country while I'm bleeding it and gobbling up corpses like a naked Dracula. It looks as if we're getting ready to fuck everyone to a fare-thee-well." Thiemost had then growled, "I'm glad I don't have a wife to see it."

Before he hung up, Thiemost had reiterated that it was all Ronald's fault. Ronald never should have let him buy Byrdwhistle. Ronald should have hog-tied him if necessary. "That's why I hire guys like you," he snarled. "You're paid god-damned well to keep me on the straight and narrow. You've really screwed me up, Coldaxe. I warned you that we had to watch out for Adele Youman. She's nuttier than her husband. I'm going to give you one last chance. I know for a fact that Adele has proxies to act in her husband's behalf. I haven't been able to reach her. But you can tell her for me that she'd better move in right away. She can pull the plug on this weird little rat, Sheldon Coombs. You and Adele find Coombs, wherever he is, and shut him up. Get a contract on him if necessary. Have him eliminated. Our lawyers are working on this end." Before he had finally hung up, Thiemost had yelled, "And hear this, you tell Adele that, if she puts my picture or a story about me in her book, there'll be a leather-bound copy of it that she won't be able to read. It'll be made out of her skin."

37

After she was sure that Ron had backed the Rolls out of the driveway and driven off to Byrdwhistle, M'mm quickly reorganized the kitchen. In a few minutes, she had transformed it into a cosmetics laboratory. In addition to a chemistry beaker, a lab thermometer, measuring cups, a mortar and pestle, and a thick piece of plate glass, all of which she had bought the day before, she added her own eggbeater, a few stainless-steel pots, mixing bowls, and a blender. On one counter she segregated chemicals and perfumes, and on another, the jars and bottles that she had bought. She made a mental note that in the future she would hang onto pretty bottles, especially if she and Moses decided to write a Love You Cosmetics Cookbook. Before they could include the recipes, they would have to make hundreds of different concoctions.

Thinking about it now, her mind raced. She wanted to tell Moses about her idea to include attractive labels in the Love You Cosmetics Starter Kit. They would feature the Love You Cosmetics logo and, for a fee, the kits could be imprinted with the customer's name. "Personally made by Meredith Coldaxe!" Thousands of women would be fascinated. They could prove to their spouses that they weren't squandering money. They could give their husbands and friends birthday presents and Christmas presents of soaps and perfumes and creams and astringents that they had made themselves.

Today, M'mm decided that she and Moses would concentrate on face creams, face masks, hand creams, and lotions and powders. She would show Moses how easy it was to make them. Next week they could move on to make-up, mascara, eye-shadow, and lipstick, and later perfumes, bath oils, and massage oils. Maybe, she should make bath oils and massage oils first. As she sat in the bathtub, wondering what she was going to wear, she remembered that she had read in one of her do-it-yourself cosmetics books that a cosmetics enthusiast could even turn the bathroom into a spa, or better still a love room! Moses would like that. A place where a man and woman could bathe together. A bathroom hung with erotic paintings, and hanging plants, and full-length mirrors, and big thick terry-cloth towels to lie on with one's spouse—or even one's love therapist. M'mm immediately tried to erase a fleeting picture from her mind. She was lying naked on a towel with Moses Marshalik. Oh God! She quickly censored that thought. Getting amorous with Moses would be disastrous. Better to stay away from bath oils and massage oils and their provocative overtones.

One thing she liked about the bathroom in her new home was the big square tub. Although Ronald hadn't used it—he preferred a shower—it was big enough for two people to sit in, maybe even to make love in. If it did prove too small, the floor could easily be covered with towels, and the bathroom was quite big enough.

M'mm wondered if she dared tell Moses that, in the future, he could come at ten, and he could stay until five if he wanted to. Seven hours with Moses and seven hours with Ron still left time for sleeping and would most certainly give a lift to her life. But she blushed at the thought. M'mm was dimly aware that beneath her rapidly shifting thoughts about cosmetics making, some strange sexual fantasies were taking shape. It would be better not to explore them. She had to be realistic. She had known this crazy Moses Marshalik for only two days, but already they talked as if they had known each other for a lifetime. They couldn't make cosmetics all day every day. It could wear thin. What then? What could a man and woman do together all day? No man would want to make love for six hours day after day. But they could talk. That was what was really great about Moses. He was like a woman friend of her own age. Even better, his mind was a weird kind of distillery — a huge vat in which ideas and daydreams were bubbling in a seething broth, and she was the yeast. Whatever the brew, it was more stimulating than booze or pot. She was living on a Moses high.

During their first ten hours together they had never been at loss for conversation. Even though Moses was continually playing with sexual ideas, she wasn't tense. Rather, she was intrigued. He was a laughing man. If he finally overreached himself and made a pass at her, she was sure that she could control him. And she most certainly would! If sex and passion got in the way, they could no longer be friends. Ronald might be fooling around with Adele Youman but M'mm wasn't going to give him any excuse for his behavior, and she didn't need Moses Marshalik as a father image.

Changing her dress for the third time, she finally decided that her white culottes and a frilly pink blouse would look best under her apron. The culottes fit almost too snugly around her hips and well-rounded behind, but then she shouldn't dress like a prim and proper suburbanite. She had to be herself. And even if she was only a middle-class housewife, Moses kept coming back.

Knowing that M'mm would be waiting for him, H. H. Youman bounced out of his wheelchair, relieved that visiting hours were over at last. Today no one, not even Adele, had come to survey the wreck of Heman Hyman. For this he was grateful, because ever since he had awakened at seven he had been looking forward to his transformation. Moses Marshalik was quite certain that either today or tomorrow Meredith Coldaxe was going to take him into her bed.

Just as he was about to leave the room for his private quarters upstairs in the center, Marge Slick burst in on him. "Damn," he surveyed her angrily, "I'm going to have to talk to Alexi Ivanowski. You shouldn't be here. Visiting hours are over. I can't talk with you now."

"You're rushing things," Marge grinned patiently at him. "And I'm mad at you. You've been neglecting me. You haven't come into my jade fountain for ten days." She pointed to her watch. "It's only five minutes to ten. Before you go to play with Meredith Coldaxe in her rose garden, I think you should hear the storm warnings. A swirling pile of shit from Los Angeles is gathering eastward momentum. It's expected to engulf Byrdwhistle and World Corporation next Monday morning. In anticipation, Sheldon Coombs has left town. He's gone skiing until after Christmas—address unknown." Marge nuzzled him. "A certain Ralph Thiemost is very, very angry with you."

"Zol im shinken fun kop," H.H. laughed. "I love you, Marge. Who else can I speak Yiddish to? I presume that Thiemost has received our little mailing from World Corporation. Has Ron got his yet?"

Marge shook her head. "Poor Ron, he's bewildered. Byrdwhistle is collapsing on his head. Thiemost telephoned him yesterday, but evidently Sheldon's letter hasn't caught up with him yet. He knows his picture is in it. Thiemost told him, and believe me Thiemost is ready to murder Adele Youman. You told me that you weren't going to use those pictures."

"I changed my mind. I had to give Thiemost a good shafting, and Ron is going to need several big jolts before he learns how to play Zorba." H.H. hugged her, "The Zorba philosophy is the only way to live. Laugh, dance and love, because what else is there?"

"You'd better stop being so cocky," Marge warned him. "Eventually, Adele will put two and two together. She'll realize that it was you who stole her negatives and pushed Ron into the swimming pool."

"She's already pretty suspicious." H.H. shrugged, "Yesterday she put me through an inquisition. The only way I could get rid of her was to start sobbing and yelling hysterically. A nurse finally alerted Alexi, who told Adele very sadly that in the past few weeks there was no way I could have left the center. Among other things, he told her that I have severe locomotor ataxia."

Listening to him, Marge's face was a study in wonder. "I'm beginning to feel sorry for Ron and anyone else who tackles you," she sighed. "But watch out, there's another storm brewing and this one's right here in Boston. By the time Thiemost arrives, it's going to burst all over the place. It's name is Victor Watchman. I told you about him. He'd like to knock off Byrdwhistle with a two-million-dollar damage suit."

"Watchman is a little prick," H.H. said. "He's making mountains out of molehills. You told me that the bulk of the Love Rock orders arrived within the past ten days. So we're not really behind schedule. We've got at least another ten days to get them into the mail. I hope you kept Watchman out of the Byrdwhistle offices. I'm going to have to talk with him."

"How in hell can you do that? You're senile, remember?" Marge shook her head, "Fortunately, Watchman refused to sign the Byrdwhistle visitor's release and Ron has been adamant. He knows that if Watchman saw the offices, the jig would really be up. So far, Ron has managed to keep Watchman in the downstairs reception room."

H.H. laughed. "Wouldn't it be interesting if Watchman arrested Thiemost and put him in the clinker for a few days?"

"What for? Hyman, you really worry me. Watchman is a nasty little man. You may be sure he won't risk his own ass. If you're not careful, you're the one who will end up in jail."

H.H. shrugged. "Remember I don't run Byrdwhistle anymore. Love Rocks aren't really my problem."

"Poor Ron," Marge couldn't help smiling. "Are you really going to let him fly to Yugoslavia with Adele? If his wife ever finds out—and she still doesn't know about the naked pictures Adele took—Ronald Coldaxe is going to have a very unhappy homelife."

"Don't worry. Eventually we'll put Humpty Dumpty together again. He'll be better than ever."

"What if Ron pulls a Vesco? He's distraught enough to. If he can't find the Love Rocks in Yugoslavia, he may never come back."

H.H. grinned at her. "The Love Rocks aren't there. But don't tell him that. Anyway, Ron needs a little vacation."

"Where the hell are the Love Rocks?" Marge demanded. "Remember that Byrdwhistle is my life too. Let's get the Federal Trade Commission off our backs."

H.H. hugged her, "Damn it, Marge, I really do love you, and Sylvia too, and Adele some of the time. I just wish I were three or four men. Then I could play with all my lovely ladyfriends every day. But right now I'm late. I've got to go. All I can tell you is that the Love Rocks are safe. Exactly where they are at this moment, even I don't know. Don't worry, the good Lord is watching over us. A little over a week from now— after Thanksgiving, and before *Rum Ho!* opens at the Colonial—the Love Rocks will be in Boston. Thorny promised me. Just be sure that you're ready to ship them."

A few minutes before Moses was due to arrive it occurred to M'mm that leaving the Marsha Lovett van in the street would be like waving a red flag at her neighbors. It told them that something far beyond selling cosmetics was going on in the Coldaxe house. M'mm had made no attempt to pursue her neighbors' proffered friendship, and she knew she had reacted rather shiftily to their various invitations: "Ron is so tired," and "He's working very hard," she had told them. "But as soon as things settle down, I know that he will want to meet all of you, and especially your husbands."

She knew that Tippy Osgood and Priscilla Forbes would wonder why it took four or five hours every day for a cosmetics salesman to make a sale to Meredith Coldaxe. But as she was deciding whether to open up Ron's side of the garage and tell Moses to get the van out of sight—which she knew was tantamount to telling Moses that their relationship had become something more than advisory, the doorbell rang. Moses had parked the van in the driveway and was unloading several pot-shaped aluminum reflectors. They were all at least eighteen inches in diameter and mounted on tripods. When she opened the door, he said, "I noticed the other day that your husband had a video-tape recorder." Moses seemed bubbly, and once again he was making her feel shivery. "I rented a video-camera. I can hook it up to your TV and video-tape machine in a couple of minutes."

M'mm was bewildered. "What for?"

"Yesterday you told me you were going to show me how easy it is to make cosmetics in the kitchen. If we're going to get financing, we've got to do it dramatically. The video-tapes will help convince investors that we have a new slant." Moses grinned at her, "To tell you the truth, even though I have actually watched Marsha Lovett cosmetics being made, it was all very impersonal. Actually I never gave a damn about it, so I never learned much about the chemical processes."

He lugged the tripods and cables and a home video-camera into the living room, together with a portable monitor. He was thinking of more interesting things to tape than their cosmetics cooking. He knew that he could teach M'mm how to use the camera in a couple of minutes. She'd be fascinated watching herself on television, but the camera might help uncover the well of curiosity and laughter that she had kept buried for years. Moses was sure that as their relationship progressed he would be able to convince her that they could make tapes of themselves practicing "sexual secrets." And it had occurred to him that if video-taping and cosmetics-making were combined by love therapists, it might improve the quality of Love You Cosmetics sessions.

M'mm was trying to convince herself that exploring new ways to sell cosmetics and actually blending and cooking them with handsome but fatherly Moses Marshalik, despite what some people might think, wasn't really going to be some kind of sexual orgy. But she wasn't sure that their moments together should be immortalized on video-tape. And though they were having a lot of fun together, she didn't really believe that Moses Marshalik could actually convince anyone that do-it-yourself cosmetics was a viable and interesting twist for cosmetics merchandising. God, if it ever did become a reality, how could she explain such a daydream to Ronald?

Moses was delighted with her kitchen laboratory. "Wait until you see it on the tube," he told her. He had hooked up a cable from the recorder in the living room into the kitchen, where he fastened the camera on a tripod overlooking her kitchen laboratory. While he was puttering with the equipment, she rattled on, giving him a history of cosmetics.

"The ancient Chinese, and later the arid Middle-Eastern countries, were the first people to discover that natural oils like olive oil and castor oil protected their skins against the harsh climate," she told him, enjoying her schoolteacher role. "Everyone tends to lump together cosmetics like skin conditioners, face creams, moisturizers, and perfumes with makeup, but eyeshadow, mascara, and lipstick don't help the skin. Some people think that these things make women more sexually exciting. Ancient women whitened their faces with chalk and put kohl on their eyelids and red ocher on their cheeks. In a way it was equivalent to men putting on their battle armor. Uniforms, clothing, and makeup allow us to play different roles and pretend to be someone else."

She was happy to note Moses's smile when she emphasized the word *play*. Then he told her to look at the television monitor that he had put on the kitchen counter. He snapped on the camera, which was pointing at her. She gasped. She could see almost half of her kitchen and her cosmetics bottles, her hands, and herself in full-color on the screen.

"Okay, now, just relax," Moses said. "Keep talking. Do whatever you were going to do. If we stay in this general area the camera will record everything we do." For a moment, he zoomed in on M'mm's face. "As you can see it's possible to vary the picture. Watching one scene without a camera shift can get monotonous." He grinned at her and showed her how to move the lens in and out. He grinned at her. "I'm sure you're going to make it interesting, but once in a while I'll close in on you."

M'mm laughed, "Not just me. I'm not going to make cosmetics by myself. You've got to help me. Then I'll change the lens and get closeups of you."

"There's one thing about this that worries me," Moses walked into the camera range beside her. "Will making cosmetics at home strip away the glamour?" He handed her an Estee Lauder circular that he had taken out of his Marsha Lovett case. "A friend of mine asked my reaction to it?" Moses smiled at the thought of Sylvia. She had given it to him the night before and told him that he was a womanizer—a seducer of nonvirgins.

M'mm read it disdainfully, "'Clinique—Three steps to skin care. First, there's Clinique soap and then there's a lotion to deflake and polish your skin, and then a moisturizer to replenish skin liquids.'" M'mm raised her eyes hopelessly. "Good God, and that's only the beginning. Listen, they have twenty-nine other products, including color rub, a seven-day scrub-cream, a touch stick for cover-up problems, an exfoliating lotion, a body-smoothing lotion, sloughing creams, which they call sweepers and smoothers, not to mention solid-milk cleansing grains, Swiss performing extracts, whipped cleansing creams—"

M'mm was choking with laughter. She made a face at her image on the television tube and then opened her refrigerator. She tossed a can at Moses. "Crisco isn't glamorous either, but it's a natural hydrogenated cottonseed oil and it works just fine."

Moses looked at her dubiously. "Don't worry," she said. "Love therapists will teach women how to upgrade it and give it a new image." She grinned at him tantalizingly, noting out of the corner of her eye and with some satisfaction that she might be past forty but on the tube she still looked pretty good.

"How?" Moses demanded, happy to play end-man.

M'mm shoved a mixing bowl at him. She scooped a huge tablespoon of Crisco into it. In the refrigerator, she found a pitcher of orange juice and poured a few ounces of it on top of the Crisco. Then she searched among her bottles and found some white powder. "This is borax." She dumped in a portion of a teaspoon. "Whip it up," she told Moses. "We could add a little perfume, but that won't make it work any better. It will clean your face just as well as the Estee Lauder cleanser."

"But women can buy Crisco in the supermarket, and why not ordinary soap? Who needs all this stuff to clean her face?"

M'mm shook her head. "I'm beginning to understand why Marsha Lovett fired you. You don't really understand cosmetics. If you have an oily skin, you can use a soap—but make sure that it doesn't contain a germicide. And only use soap after you've used a cleansing cream. The real point is not what the stuff will do for your skin, that's only one side of the coin." M'mm smiled, "It feels nice to rub a cream on your face and give yourself a facial massage." She chuckled, "Of course it would be even nicer if someone who calls himself a love therapist was doing it for you. That combination would give all of your cosmetics competitors something to think about."

She handed him a pot. "After you've whipped that stuff together, I'll stick it in a jar for future use. Now I'll show you how to make a more exotic cleansing cream." She pointed to the array of bottles on one counter. "I'm going to read the directions, you measure the ingredients and toss them in the pot. First you need beeswax—four teaspoons. It's in that jar. Now turn on the stove—that burner—and melt it over low heat."

Moses was torn between watching the pot and watching M'mm fiddling with the camera and closing in on him while he stirred the mess. She was unaware that her culottes were deeply outlining the cleft in her behind and the curve of her ass. He was finding it difficult to concentrate. "Now you have to beat in a few teaspoons of safflower oil," she told him, and she handed him a bottle of it.

"You have a fascinating pelvic structure," Moses knew it was an irrelevant thought, but he couldn't help himself.

M'mm heard him and tried not to appear startled. "I really don't think you're listening to me."

Moses smiled. "Don't worry, I can often manage two or three thoughts at the same time. I wouldn't be an effective love therapist if I weren't pleasantly aware of your hips and behind. You're a woman who is perfectly designed for having children."

"I've already done my share," M'mm said curtly. "Ron and I have two." Moses smiled. "I guess it's not too late. You're obviously young enough to have one more."

"I'm sure as hell not going to. Here, concentrate on cooking. You've got to add some almond oil and keep beating that stuff."

"I have a theory about good male lovers," Moses was industriously whipping the concoction together and for a moment he didn't continue the thought.

M'mm couldn't help herself. She asked him what his theory was.

"During the act of love, which should ideally take place over several hours, most males—especially if they care for the woman—have a subconscious need to impregnate her. The female obviously has a parallel need. Her genes are telling her she must get pregnant. Being unable to face that fundamental fact of human existence has screwed up an entire generation."

M'mm couldn't help laughing. "Fortunately, millions of us have learned to repress our biological urges."

"Wanting to have a baby with you doesn't mean either of us would preside over the conception," Moses said. "But if we ever made love, that need and realizing it would give a nice ambience to our lovemaking."

M'mm was unable to repress a little shiver. Moses was suddenly moving too fast. Worse, their silly conversation made her want to pull his head down and kiss him.

"You might as well understand one thing very clearly," she said. "I'm monogamous." She picked up a beaker, saying, "I'm going to mix a little borax and a teaspoon of witch hazel, and then you can take your choice of one of the perfume essences over there. It will give this cleansing cream a nice odor. What will you have?" She pointed at a row of bottles.

Moses shrugged, "Like some of my biblical ancestors I choose myrrh. Why not?"

M'mm poured a teaspoon of myrrh into the beaker and then handed it to him. "Okay, now pour it into your pot and beat the whole mess together until it cools. When it's ready, we'll add some zinc oxide to it and put it in a jar and refrigerate it. Later, if you want, I'll show you how to use it."

"You mean that a love therapist could show his customer how to apply the product?"

M'mm grinned at him. "Why not? You can give me a facial massage.'

While she was speaking, Moses had been looking over her shoulder reading one of her cosmetics cookbooks as she flipped through it. "What about bath oils and massage oils?" he asked.

Laughing, she pointed out various recipes to him, but guessing what was on his mind she said, "We'll try those some other day. Today I think we should concentrate on skin cleansers and moisturizers and skin lotions. There are all kinds. We could make oatmeal cleansing creams, crème de menthe cleansers, strawberry cleansers, cucumber protection creams, protein protection creams, and lotions beyond belief. Any enterprising woman can add rose water, witch hazel, lavender, bergemot, lime, lemon, clove, or rose marie to a pint of vodka, and it works just fine." She turned, and Moses's arms were suddenly around her.

"Of course you can't drink them," she murmured, "but they feel nice on your skin."

"M'mm," he whispered. "M'mm, M'mm, M'mm." Then he was kissing her lips and her eyes and her nose and cupping her face and telling her that she was lovely. And she knew she couldn't resist. From the first day that Moses had talked to her through the mail slot, she had known there would be no escape. She was totally involved with this mad and lovable man.

His hands were slipping inside her culottes, and now, still kissing her, he was gently clasping her behind. His fingers were tracing the contours of her ass, and they were searching deep within her cleft. She could feel him inching her culottes below her hips. Although he was still fully dressed, she could feel his penis pressing hard against her stomach.

For one last moment she shook her head, "No— no! You mustn't!" and she tried to ease out of his arms. She looked at him beseechingly, "Moses, please. I don't want to. I'm afraid."

But he didn't release her. His voice was warm and reassuring. "Sweet one, it's all right. You and I are inevitable." Her culottes had dropped over her ankles. Moses was kneeling in front of her. Kissing her knees, nibbling them at the same time he was feathering the inside of her thighs with his tongue. Slowly he lowered her panties, and then while he fingered her anus and perineum, his tongue had parted her labia and was skimming her clitoris and she was shuddering with joy. "Oh my god—my god! Please! Please!" she begged him. "You've got to stop, Moses, you're going to ruin everything. We really can't do this."

"Why can't we?" Moses had slowly risen. He was kissing her navel, and his nimble hands had unfastened her bra and he was kissing her nipples, as if he were tasting an incredible delicacy. She couldn't help herself. Her hands were kneading his head and the hair grazing the top of her breasts. She lifted his head to her face, and then once again he was kneeling before her vulva. No man had ever adored her in this way. Sobbing and kissing his head, she kept repeating, "Oh yes, yes! Please make love to me. Don't stop!"

Then she opened her eyes—to her horror she could see both of them in miniature on the television screen. "My God! You rat! No. Stop. Are you taping us?" She pulled away from him indignantly. "I suppose you're going to show this to your investors."

Laughing he grabbed her and turned her around, and she could see herself clearly on the tube. "Of course not. These are our own personal training exercises." He kissed her. "Believe me, video is a great way to get acquainted with your body. Let's move the camera into the living room where we can watch ourselves better."

"You must really be crazy," M'mm couldn't help grinning at him. "If I make love with you, I'm certainly not leaving any record for posterity."

And then the doorbell rang.

"Oh, my God! Hide that damned camera." M'mm grabbed for her panties and yanked them around her middle.

"Is it Ron?" Moses was grinning, but in spite of himself he felt a nervous pang. Moses Marshalik needed another ten days before H. H. Youman bid a reluctant good-bye to this particular ancestor.

M'mm shook her head. "Ron wouldn't ring. I didn't put the night latch on. He'd just unlock the door and walk in." M'mm was relieved to note that, although her vagina felt as if Moses's penis had already penetrated her, except for having taken off his suit coat, he was still fully dressed. His turtle-necked sportshirt and dark-blue slacks were unruffled.

The doorbell rang again. "Stay right here," she told him. "I've got to answer it. Your damned van is out in front, and it's probably one of my neighbors. Maybe they want to buy Marsha Lovett Cosmetics."

Moses laughed. "Let them in. We'll test our new approaches to selling cosmetics on them."

M'mm scowled at him, "Don't get any mad ideas. You can't be a love therapist to the entire female population of Cabot Lane."

38

Tippy Osgood and Priscilla Forbes were standing on the front doorstep. For a moment the transmitters in M'mm's brain froze. What could she say? All she could think of was "You guessed it. You caught me sex making. And I don't give a shit. Just go away please while I finish the job."

She grinned. A quick inspiration skipped through her mind. If she had to introduce Moses, and she knew it was inevitable, why couldn't he be her father's brother? Uncle Moses. Uncle Moses lived in New Hampshire— Portsmouth. Why not? Uncle Moses was a Marsha Lovett distributor. He was thinking of starting a do-it-yourself cosmetics company. He had heard that Meredith was moving east, and he remembered that she had once made her own cosmetics. So he had dropped in today. M'mm was telling him all she knew about making cosmetics.

Somehow she managed to open the front door and blurt all this out while Tippy and Priscilla, only half-listening to her, calmly walked into the front hall and moved toward the living room.

"God. What are you cooking Meredith?" Tippy demanded. "The place smells like a whorehouse." It was past noon and M'mm was sure that Tippy had already had her first shot of juice and maybe even her second.

"I can't imagine why anyone would want to make cosmetics," Priscilla was sniffing a little haughtily. "It sounds so messy. We were going over to the Burlington Mall and thought you might like to come with us." M'mm knew that was a coverup. They really wanted to find out why the Marsha Lovett van had become a fixture on Cabot Lane.

"What are you cooking now?" Tippy asked. "Can we watch you?"

It was Uncle Moses's cue. He came out of the kitchen beaming. M'mm reluctantly introduced them to her uncle, "Mr. Marshalik." To M'mm's astonishment, he said, "Meredith and I were just about to make ylang-ylang water-softener," and to M'mm, "I'm so happy that your friends dropped in on us. It's just what we need, the opportunity to test our new cosmetics idea on the kind of women we hope will become our customers."

Standing behind them, M'mm was shaking her head at Moses vehemently. One thing she didn't need was to involve these upper-class nitwits— her new neighbors, God help her—in a discussion about Love You Cosmetics and love therapists. Besides, she was more than a little bewildered. Her knees were shaking from trying to make the transition from a lustful woman having her vulva deliciously kissed by an adoring male to the role of a prim and proper housewife entertaining her father's brother and her next door neighbors.

But Moses was paying no attention to her, and unfortunately Tippy and Priscilla seemed to be as magnetized by Moses as she was. Tippy turned toward M'mm, and her lips were forming the unspoken words, "I like him. I like him. He's yummy, yummy!"

M'mm tried to give Moses a steely warning look. Uncle Moses has to be in Portsmouth by two o'clock," she said, but he only shrugged at her.

"My appointment is not urgent." He looked at his watch. "It's only one-thirty. If I leave by three, that'll give Meredith time to clean up the kitchen before Ron comes home. In the meantime, we'd be happy to show you how easy it is to make skin softeners, the kind that would cost five or six dollars at Lord & Taylor or Bonwit's." He grinned apologetically at M'mm, "I was just reading about how to make them in one of your books."

M'mm gave him a sour smile and led Priscilla and Tippy into the kitchen. She was thankful at least that the video-camera had disappeared.

"What's ylang ylang softener?" Tippy asked.

"It's very simple to make," M'mm ignored Tippy's and Priscilla's astonishment at the array of at least a hundred bottles and jars sitting on the counter and table. "You simply add the essence of ylang ylang blossoms to glycerine. Then you add a few tablespoons of water, three drops of oil of orange, and shake it up. Then you have to let it marinate for about twenty-four hours."

"If you'd like to make it," Moses said, "we can marinate it in the blender and use it right away. It makes a nice massaging oil."

Rolling her eyes and tilting her head at him, Tippy was sending sex signals to Moses so fast that M'mm wanted to sock her. "Are you offering to massage us, Mr. Marshalik?" Tippy stared at him provocatively."

Moses bowed his head happily. "I'd be delighted. You see, Ms. Osgood, Love You Cosmetics, as Meredith and I plan to call them, will be sold door to door by men about my age, men in their late fifties and sixties who can pass our stringent physical requirements, men who really enjoy women and want to keep them loving and beautiful long past their four score and ten years. Our plan is that love therapists will offer not only the ingredients for home cosmetics-making but an entire do-it-yourself-at-home program to beautify both a woman's mind and her body."

"Hear, hear!" Priscilla was beaming. "I'm fifty-five. Can you keep me beautiful for the next twenty-five years?"

M'mm was sadly aware that time was running out. There was no way that she was going to be able to boot these women out and try to recapture her tryst with Moses that day. Not tomorrow either. Moses was calmly telling them that without Meredith, his loving brother's daughter, he never would have believed that this daydream was possible. And M'mm was promising herself that Moses Marshalik, this seducer of women—Prissy and Tippy were following him with rapt attention—wasn't going to get a second chance alone with her in the kitchen, or anywhere else for that matter.

"Meredith and I are trying to visualize a whole new approach," Moses said, still ignoring M'mm's silent nasty look, which was telling him he should shut up and get rid of the two women. "Not only do we plan to show women how to enhance their natural beauty, but we hope to convince women, young and old, to stop denying their innate sexuality and not to be afraid to incorporate it into their total lives."

It was past lunchtime. Prissy and Tippy obviously had no place to go. Aided by gins and tonic and nibbling on the cheese hors d'oeuvres that M'mm reluctantly provided, they were listening to Moses entranced. Tippy was glassy-eyed from vodka and from listening to a massage idea that Moses was claiming Meredith had catalyzed in his mind just a few minutes before they arrived.

"Meredith told me that the basic purpose of skin cleansers was to clean your pores. But equally valid is the enjoyment any woman gets when she massages her face." Moses was nodding enthusiastically at M'mm. "Think about that. Self-massage. A woman strips completely. Then, free from the restriction of her clothing, she turns on her hi-fi. She puts some sensuous, erotic music on the turntable. Belly-dancing music would be ideal, and while she is dancing to it she massages herself with ylang ylang or some other skin softener." Moses chuckled happily, "We could call it a self-love exercise. It permits a woman to get acquainted with her body so that she can offer it as the ultimate gift to her lover."

"Uncles Moses sounds as if he expects love therapists to show the women how," M'mm said sarcastically. She wasn't quite so hypnotized by Moses as Tippy and Priscilla were. "Uncle Moses is intrigued by male strip-teasers. Maybe he'll show us how."

She was delighted that, for a moment at least, Moses seemed at a loss for words. But he quickly recovered. "Actually, I'd prefer to dance with one of you lovely ladies."

"Naked?" Tippy demanded. She was obviously titillated but still in control. She giggled at Moses, who held out his hand to help her out of her chair. "I couldn't do that, I'd be too embarrassed dancing naked." She grinned at him, and her expression said that she really could, if they were alone. "But if you'd like to massage me, Uncle Moses, while I'm lying down, you're welcome to do it."

M'mm knew things were getting out of hand.

Frowning, she said, "Really, this is silly. You and Prissy have to understand that we are only brainstorming. Both Uncle Moses and I know that the world is not ready for love therapists yet."

"I am!" Prissy, who had drunk two gins and tonic, suddenly came to life. She was staring at Moses happily. "I've been having strange aches all over and lower back pains," she laughed. "I've never been massaged by a man. If you'd like to come over to my house, I'll be happy to pay you."

M'mm decided the only way to put a stop to such madness was to shock Priscilla Forbes back to reality. "All right," she said gaily. "Why don't we go upstairs and let Uncle Moses massage us all." She smirked at Moses, who seemed a little startled.

Tippy clapped. "That's a great idea!"

For a moment, Priscilla seemed ready to call it quits, then she smiled, "Why not?" Even if we are all naked, it's three against one. What could a sixty-year-old man do against three women?"

"Keep that in mind," Moses laughed at Meredith's dismay. "Obviously, a cardinal rule for love therapists will be that they look fatherly, and when they run afternoon beauty parties they should be sure that the women outnumber them by at least two to one. Women will knock down the doors to come to Love You Cosmetics parties where a handsome father-figure plays with them all."

A few minutes later, Meredith had thrown a sheet across her bed, and Prissy and Tippy were in the bathroom happily undressing. M'mm knew that whatever happened she wasn't going to leave Uncle Moses alone with these predatory women. Tippy and Prissy were acting like young girls who were about to play doctor with the boy next door. When Tippy and Prissy finally emerged from the bathroom, Moses applauded the large square tub and told M'mm what a really sexy bathroom it was. Then he discovered that the former owner had equipped all the rooms with built-in hi-fi speakers. "I'll be back in a minute," he said, as he disappeared downstairs, leaving the women sitting on M'mm's bed in their slips and bras and pantics. In a few minutes he reappeared wearing only jockey shorts. Prissy and Tippy "oohed" at him and clapped enthusiastically.

"I noticed that Ron has a tape-recorder in the library and I fortunately have some very interesting musical tapes. I've put them on. I thought I'd test them. They could be part of the love therapist's repertoire." He smiled approvingly at M'mm, who had no choice. She had joined the other women and was now sitting on the bed in her bra and slip. He flipped on the bedroom speakers and the room was filled with the yearning sound of a flute.

"Now," he told them coolly, "If you will all take off your various garments and stretch out on your stomachs, I will massage you one at a time for about three minutes. While I'm doing this, I will tell you about the composer of the music you're listening to. It was written and is being played by a young man named Steven Halpern."

"Aren't you going to take your shorts off?" Tippy interrupted. She was already lying naked on the bed on her stomach.

"Not today," Moses said, laughing. "Love Therapists have to draw the line somewhere. Prissy has already mentioned that in union there is strength. I'm outnumbered, but I must admit I've never seen or felt such a lovely array of female bottoms. This is an exquisite pleasure in and of itself."

As he moved from one to the other of them, massaging their backs and buttocks, Moses explained that Halpern's music, played by an electric piano, an organ, a violin, and a flute, brought the listener into a total mind-body harmony that helped her be "in tune" with her biological birthright. In addition to composing color music, and making the seven colors of the visual spectrum aural, Halpern had composed the *Zodiac Suite* in which the gentle sound of a violin, a flute, and wind chimes expressed the signs of the zodiac, and the *Star-born Suite* that evoked images and moods of the heavens and the constellations. Right now they were listening to a live performance called "Halpern in Concert," which was essentially a trance dance.

"Oh, it's beautiful," Tippy sighed. "I'm really relaxing for the first time in my life. Your fingers feel so good, Mr. Marshalik."

And M'mm, whose treatment he had just finished, knew why. Moses's touch was erotic and he hadn't hesitated to probe his fingers deeply into her behind and run his fingers insidiously around her anus. Damn him, if he was doing that to Tippy Osgood and Priscilla Forbes, she'd kill him.

39

Four days later, still trying to suppress an occasional feeling of guilt, M'mm was sleepily entwined with Moses Marshalik. He was dozing between her thighs, lying in Ron's place, in the same bed he had used for massaging the three women. M'mm was smiling at the memory. Instead of responding to their overt sexuality, Moses had treated them all as women who had temporarily reverted to their innocent girlhood. When he had finished, he had approvingly kissed three behinds, six breasts, and three vulvas and pronounced them all unique. Tippy and Prissy had floated home in a state of ecstasy.

But right now, Moses wasn't playing a father role. He was murmuring to M'mm's backside, telling her that she smelled warm and sexy and better than any perfume and that her upside-down ass was just as pretty as it was right-side up. He promised to prove it to her the next day by showing her the video-tape.

In the past week, a time-span of slightly over a hundred and eighty hours, she had been alone with Moses Marshalik, if she included today and tonight—their first night together—a total of thirty-five hours. She wished that she had kept a journal of this dizzy week of wonder. Moses had made love to her almost continuously since Thursday. An equivalent amount of sex-making with Ron would have taken two months. When she implied to Moses that, after eighteen years of marriage, sex-making with Ron was not a way of life and estimated how long their own sexual marathon had gone on, Moses had simply wiggled his penis deeper inside her. He told her that he had been making love to her longer than thirty-five hours. He had been making love when he first talked with her through her mail slot. In case she wasn't aware of it, a mail box was a useful symbol for a vagina. And he enjoyed talking to both of her mouths, even though right now the lower one could only pout and was at a loss for words.

Inside her, and between orgasms that neither of them were ever in a hurry to reach, and while he balanced her on the edge of a precipice,

Moses reached inside her brain too. "One of the sexual secrets that love therapists must share with their customers is that loving is playing," he told her. "Unfortunately most men never really learn how to play. Or, if they do, they quickly forget when they get married. It's a woman's job to re-teach them. If men and women want to be handsome and beautiful and live a long life, then women must show men how to make playful loving not just part of their lives but their whole lives."

M'mm told him that sometimes he sounded as if he were quoting from one of H. H. Youman's essays on Theory Z, which Ron had finally brought home a few days before for her to read. "Youman's been my mentor for years," Moses told her. "I believe in him completely. The man is a genius."

Thinking back to last week, M'mm remembered that Thursday morning, the day after the crazy massage episode with Tippy and Priscilla, Moses had been on her doorstep a half-hour earlier than usual. Still a little angry with him because he had encouraged Tippy and Prissy and seemed to be totally charmed by their dim-witted conversation, she had made one valiant attempt to get rid of him before he became a more serious problem than drug addiction.

"You can get your damned van to hell out of my driveway," she had told him bluntly. "Tippy and Prissy are probably glued to their windows waiting for you to arrive. In case you have forgotten, among other things you promised to teach them how to play nude bridge. Go over to their houses. I'm sure both of them will be happy to jump in bed with you. They might even invite Mary Hawthorne over, and you can take on all three of them."

"But I don't love them," Moses was smiling at her and M'mm knew that she sounded like a jealous wife. She tried to extricate her eyes from the deep wells of caring in his gaze.

"That's crap. You told us yesterday that you loved all women."

"Of course, I do. But I don't want to be intimate with every woman I meet, only a very few special ones like yourself."

M'mm handed him the video-cassette he had brought the day before. "Here, you forgot this. I erased it." A few minutes before he arrived, she had actually run the tape of the kitchen scene and had been shocked to see that she had responded to Moses's kisses so passionately that her naked behind had been trembling. "It's a good thing Tippy and Priscilla broke up that insanity," she said. "God must have been watching over me. He prevented me from making a complete ass of myself."

She tried to close the door, but Moses moved quickly into the front hall. "You can't say goodbye when you're not liking yourself," he said.

"I like myself, I don't like you." Then before she could pull away, he cupped her face in his hands, tilted her lips toward his, and smiled ruefully at her. Her anger drained away into a sigh. "You don't mean it, M'mm," he said. "You don't want me to leave. After a few days together we both have discovered the basic key to each other and how to release each other. It takes many people a lifetime to learn that. Even better, we have learned how to recreate each other. I'm your alter ego. You're mine."

Anticipating the end of the affair even before it began, M'mm was unhappy. "You're being too romantic. All this cosmetic silliness won't last. When we run out of things to do, we will be bored with each other."

Wanting him, wanting his hands on her body, wanting him to kiss her wildly, passionately, she had suddenly capitulated. "Oh, what the hell. But no sex, today! We're going to make cosmetics. And before we do, put your damned van in the garage." She grinned at him, "I'm not going to share you with Tippy and Prissy again."

Ten minutes later, agreeing that they couldn't make cosmetics until they talked, and that it was more comfortable talking lying down than sitting up, they were upstairs in bed together and M'mm was feeling guiltier than ever. "This really is ridiculous," she told him with tears in her eyes. "Two hours ago I was lying here with my husband."

Moses had grinned at her. "I hope you were making love."

"You really are crazy! Wouldn't that bother you?" Actually she hadn't made love with Ron—not even the night before—and if she had she most certainly wouldn't be in bed with Moses. M'mm was quite sure that she couldn't have negotiated two such different men in the same day. The transition would have unnerved her.

"I love you," Moses told her, "and Ron loves you. That gives us something in common." Although he was kissing her face, he hadn't yet touched her body. "Someday after Ron has learned how to play, you can tell him that I've adopted you and your kids, and him too. I'm your father-lover. I'm not in competition with Ron, I'm in addition to him."

Lying fully dressed in his arms, she had a strange feeling that for this moment in time they were encapsulated. The world had ceased to exist. He told her to stop worrying about who he was and how many thousands of women he had seduced. "In the past sixty-two years only a dozen or so women have played with me." He grinned at her, "Playing together is the greatest gift a woman and a man can give to each other."

Leaning on her elbow, she looked into his face. "What do you actually want from me?"

"The opportunity to be you," he chuckled at her bemused expression. "There is really no greater joy in the world than daring to become someone else. Exploring each other's mind and body, finding out where we meld, and where we don't, will be a great adventure. At the same time," he told her, "we can work out the basic approaches to Love You Cosmetics. You think that I'm not serious, but I am. Together we're going to revolutionize the cosmetics industry." Then he undressed her, slowly, like a teen-ager on a first date, exploring her body under her clothing, unsnapping her bra and touching the curve of her breasts reverentially while he feathered the sudden hardness of her nipples with his hand. Then his hand was under her skirt and slowly edging under her panties. And her hands slipped inside his trousers, teasing the top of his penis and scooping it up together with his balls. Pushing her sweater and bra over her breasts he finally exposed them, sucked each nipple tenderly and grinned at her. "In disarray, with your clothes askew and your hair messed up, you are very beautiful."

That Thursday they didn't make cosmetics. They didn't even have time for lunch. Four hours later they were still in bed and M'mm had floated beyond orgasm into a complete state of body rapture. Moses's penis belonged to her and her vulva to him, and they had proved it to each other over and over again. Laughing happily when he seemed to have run out of gas, she sucked him back to life, and with his tongue he re-energized her body from her ears to her feet into one continuous current, snapping and bursting through her clitoris and vagina, and her nipples and anus, none of which could get enough of his fingers or his mouth.

Then she reluctantly told him that he must go before Ron came home. She was sure that she'd never learn how to play with Moses only one day at a time. And though she had only known this deliciously crazy man for a few days, she couldn't help being despondent. "I need you," she admitted to him. "Not just for sex but for laughter." She told him that she felt like Cinderella at midnight. In less than an hour, once again she must return to her role of a dreary corporate wife with an uncommunicative husband. She prayed that Moses would come back tomorrow and had not been frightened by her sudden melancholy. She had become insatiable. She admitted it. But tomorrow, she promised, they would make cosmetics. She would be calmer and more practical. "I guess I need you to be my life companion," she grinned, "in addition to Ron, of course."

"That's easy," Moses told her. "As long as you help keep me alive, I promise I'll be your playmate."

"My God, how can I keep you alive?"

"By playing with me every day."

"You said that loving is playing."

Moses hugged her, "Of course, that's the idea."

M'mm was dubious, "If Ron ever finds out that I've been playing with another man, he'll kill me and you too."

"Maybe not," Moses's eyes were always dancing to unevoked ideas. "Maybe we'll teach him to play, too."

Now M'mm hugged Moses. "I'm sure glad that I'm sleeping with you all night," she whispered, and she was happily aware that, even without opening his eyes, his penis had slipped back inside her again.

It had been snowing heavily since noon. When she told Moses that Ron had flown to Yugoslavia that morning, he immediately suggested that there was really no need for him to drive back and forth to Boston, especially in the bad weather. "Your husband can't possibly get to Yugoslavia and back to Boston before next Monday," he said with a provocative smile. "I was in Dubrovnik many years ago. Sveti Stefan is fifty miles south. It will take Ron two days just to get back and forth." Then he proposed all kinds of intriguing ways they could pass the time together. In the morning, like good Norwegians, they could turn the bathroom into a sauna, and after a good steaming they could play Frisbee naked in the snow. M'mm's neighbors couldn't see them. The backyard was shielded from the other houses by a row of arbor vitae. Later, in the afternoon, while she continued to teach him cosmetics cookery, they could stop occasionally and make video-tapes of themselves making love.

M'mm knew that it was completely insane to have agreed with him, and she was more than a little uncertain. "I suppose you want to invite Tippy and Priscilla over to join us," she said.

Moses grinned at her. "They really don't look like the outdoor type to me." Seeing that she wasn't entirely convinced he took another tack. "We could try out some new recipes, like making soap or bubble bath or perfume. Then we could have all Thanksgiving Day together. At night we could turn down the thermostat and bundle together. Years ago, all good Pilgrims bundled. It saved energy—not to mention firewood."

"Bundling was a premarital custom," M'mm informed him. "I'm sure the Pilgrims didn't bundle with their neighbor's wife. Besides I don't have a turkey, and I'm a lousy cook anyway."

"That's because you never made love and cooked dinner at the same time," Moses said. "And I'm sure you never made love in front of a crackling fireplace. In California, the fireplaces have artificial logs. Tomorrow I'll go shopping. There are snowtires on the van, and while I'm gone you can make your own self-love video-tape. It's an idea for love therapists that occurred to me yesterday when Tippy insisted that she couldn't massage herself."

M'mm didn't ask him to elaborate on that. To make sure Ronald didn't walk in and find her in bed with Moses, she telephoned Byrdwhistle and learned that the Grumman was kept at Butler Aviation. An obliging flight-controller there told her that Mr. Coldaxe and several others had taken off on schedule at 9:00 A.M. for Yugoslavia. He told her that they would be happy to keep her informed so that she could meet her husband at the airport when he returned. When she hung up, she grimaced at Moses. "Damned if I'll meet Ron. He's sure to bring his mother back with him."

That surprised Moses. "Is Adele Youman the motherly type?" he asked.

M'mm shrugged. "She's past sixty, but unfortunately she doesn't look it." M'mm patted Moses's cheek. "Neither do you. Ron and I must have a thing about surrogate parents."

"Are you sure that Ron sleeps with her?" Moses asked. He wished he could tell her that knowing Adele and going to bed with her would be a mind-expanding experience for Ron. "How do you know that she's so attractive?"

"I saw a picture of her—and some she took of Ron."

Before she could stop herself, M'mm had blurted out the whole story of her first encounter with Ralph Thiemost and her final evening with him. "Ron doesn't know. I never told him," she said. Tears were rolling down her cheeks and she grinned at Moses weakly, "You can count on it, the bastard will telephone me when he arrives and expect me to entertain him." Then she admitted something else. "You might as well know the worst—when I was hanging there on his boat, maybe because I was so helpless, I was turned on. Isn't that disgusting?"

Moses told her that he didn't think so. "Obviously, Ralph Thiemost takes out his frustrated need for power on women. But I have a feeling that one of these days someone is going to cut off his balls." He had kissed her and rolled her on top of him and grinned at her. "Okay, now you play conqueror. Pretend that I'm your slave."

Delighted, she asked him if she could tie his arms and legs to the bedpost. "You don't have to actually do it—pretend that they are tied," he said. "Now you can do anything to me that you wish."

"Later, can we reverse the roles?"

"Sure—but you have to be a good actress. We don't need ropes. All you have to do is cry and beg me not to hurt you. I'll show you," and he did—thrashing under her, as if he was trying to escape her sexual gluttony—until she was convulsed with laughter.

Reviewing her hours with Moses, she held his head against her breast. His tongue was indolently trilling her nipple. With one hand between her legs, he cupped her ass affectionately.

Remembering last Friday, she couldn't help smiling. Before Ron had left for Byrdwhistle, he had asked her if she was going to make cosmetics again that day. "The whole damn place smells like a funeral home," but Ron was smiling a little when he added, "I have a feeling there must be a corpse somewhere, buried under a few thousand roses." Then he had hugged her and admitted that during the past few days she had been nicer to live with and that they were getting along better than they had for a long time. He was delighted that she had found something to do that kept her occupied. He wasn't even upset when she told him that the Byrdwhistle employment manual intrigued her and that when he got back from Yugoslavia she would very much like to take the Byrdwhistle entrance exam. He even gave her another article that Youman had written on Theory Z management.

"Not that I'm being converted," he warned her. "I just think that you should understand what I'm up against. It's not just Love Rocks—and, believe me, I don't want to go to Yugoslavia—it's that every damned Byrdwhistler is thoroughly indoctrinated. It doesn't matter what they do. Whether it is dealing with angry customers, doing monotonous data-processing work, answering correspondence, or assembling idiotic items, or working together half-naked shipping orders, or even sweeping the place or waxing the floors, they insist that any damn thing they do is really not work. They're all playing! According to them, if you mix a little cre-ative fantasizing with laughter, there is no such thing as work. Except for me and Joe Taylor and Bill Redman, no one at Byrdwhistle takes their job seriously."

Ronald shook his head, and it was obvious that he was still unable to comprehend such irresponsibility. "When I get back from Yugoslavia, if you promise not to get carried away I'll bring you in so that you can audit one of our Symp meetings. But you have to promise to keep your mouth shut." He rubbed his bald head reflectively, and M'mm wondered why he continued to shave it and not let the hair grow back on the sides.

"Here's the kind of nonsense I have to put up with," he told her. "Yes-terday Lois Rather and a half-dozen Byrdwhistlers cornered me for more than an hour. They insisted that the reason for Byrdwhistle's success is that every item in every catalogue must meet a final test. Basically, it must trigger human playing. If it doesn't, it would have been rejected by the Symp committee. Then Lois gave me an extended lecture on the origins of work. She insisted that the idea of work didn't really exist before Luther and Calvin. They screwed up the whole Western world by calling anything you had to do work, whether it was filling your belly or screw-ing your wife. According to Lois, the early Protestants even got God and religion into the act. You didn't love God and God couldn't love you unless you were working and praying your ass off from sunrise to sunset."

M'mm listened to him happily. For the first time in a long time, she and Ronald were carrying on a reasonably intelligent conversation. "What do you think is the real purpose of living?" she asked him.

"Enjoying yourself," Ron answered gloomily. "Gathering rosebuds while you may. Wine, women, and song. Byrdwhistlers refuse to accept that civilization came about because everyone was discontented. They haven't learned that the reason we have flush toilets is because human beings were very unhappy when they slid around in their own shit."

When Moses arrived that Friday morning and suggested it would be more interesting if they made cosmetics in their birthday suits, M'mm said that she really had no qualms about nudity. In California she had often run around the house naked, but this was New England and it was damned cold. But she finally told him that, since they were cooking up a storm in the kitchen, and thereby keeping it pretty snuggy, she would be willing, and she undressed and made cosmetics with him.

"The reason for this experiment," Moses told her when they were both pattering around the kitchen without clothes, "is that it occurred to me that it might be a good idea to introduce a video-camera into the business of cosmetic cookery.

"When you drop some hot wax on your penis, you won't think so," M'mm told him, and she groaned when he set up the camera. "Do we really have to record this?"

"Of course," Moses assured her. "Think of the possibilities. After our Love You Cosmetics dealer leaves, the video-tape will give the customer the opportunity to see herself as others see her. Our love therapists could tape all the ladies at afternoon beauty parties, showing them how to reveal their best profile and best physical features. In addition to beauty tips, he would also offer them sexual secrets that his customers and their friends could listen to again and again."

M'mm grinned at him and squeezed his penis. "Your prick is always pointing at me. I hope you don't mind, but I think there'll be a problem if love therapists all look like you. Their customers won't give a damn whether they make cosmetics or not. Love therapists won't dare to cook cosmetics naked. Like me, the ladies might like to kiss it or take a quick suck or two."

"Love therapists will have to tell them that they can look but not touch," Moses said happily. She was surprised at his concentration as he listened to her instructions for making cleansing milk. He added an eighth of a teaspoon of cetyl alcohol to several tablespoons of mineral oil, and followed them with stearic acid triethanolamine, distilled water, and a dash of oil of bergamot. Then, swiping his hand across her behind and at the same time bending so he could nuzzle her breast, he took a quick lap on her nipple and said, "When this concoction is ready, maybe we should go a little beyond love therapy. We should relax and rub it on each other."

But despite occasional interruptions for total blending, with her legs draped around his hips so that he could penetrate her, M'mm managed to keep him working until lunchtime. They played their way through several cosmetics books, choosing recipes here and there. Moses was especially entranced with *Fragrance,* a book by Betty Plummer, who in a chapter called "The Sensuous Household" told her readers about plants and flowers that could be home grown and could be used for fragrances, and gave instructions for making organic jewelry that could be made from lemons, limes, and apples impregnated with cloves, cinnamon, and orris roots, and which Moses was sure when left to dry would eventually give off erotic odors that would heighten the ecstasy of sex-making.

And they made rose beads, and myrrh beads, and pomanders made from sandalwood and rosemary and patchouli and frankincense. And M'mm discovered recipes for herbal baths. They filled a cheesecloth bag with quarter-cup portions of woodruff, cicely, angelica leaves, hysop leaves, and patchouli leaves and hung it on the bathtub faucet. The hot water passing through it made the bathroom smell like new-mown hay, while they dawdled together in the big square tub and smoothed the brew over each other's skin.

Without Moses, Saturday and Sunday had been a wasteland, even though she made love with Ronald Saturday night. Ron refused for the second time to get involved with their Cabot Lane neighbors. Tippy Osgood had telephoned and told M'mm that with such charming relatives as Uncle Moses, she couldn't wait to meet Ronald. But Ronald insisted that he was temporarily anti-social, especially this weekend. "I'm really not in the mood for socializing," he told her. "Not until things settle down at Byrdwhistle. I don't know whether I'm coming or going."

And now, lying in bed beside Moses, who was in Ronald's place, M'mm could testify to that. How was it possible that a man fifteen years older than Ronald could know so confidently when he was coming — not once but several times a day — and seemingly was ever ready to come again and again? If this was play-making, then it was time the whole world learned how to play.

40

Moses was awake before M'mm. He watched her sleeping in a curled up foetus position, her left hand was between his legs and her index finger was intermittently inquisitive in the cleft of his buttocks. It was like being plugged into an electric cord. He had taught M'mm that maintaining flesh contact would keep her ready at the flick of a switch to light up again. Her right hand was poised on the curve of her lips and she seemed to be smiling pensively, enjoying her dreams.

Moses knew that, if Ralph Thiemost had arrived in Boston on schedule, today both Byrdwhistle and World Corporation would be steaming and whistling. Before the day was over he must check in with Marge Slick. But he couldn't telephone Marge from here — not while M'mm might be listening. Outside it was a blustery, snowy day. Ten or more inches of snow had redecorated Lynnfield. M'mm and he were virtually trapped in the house. The night before, laying the groundwork for his temporary absence, he had told her that he could easily get the van out of Cabot Lane onto the turnpike. He must drive into the YMCA and pick up a change of clothing and let people know that he was alive. He didn't identify the people. But on the way back he'd buy all the groceries for a splendid Thanksgiving dinner, enough food to last for the rest of the week, and wine and booze.

He anticipated that M'mm might want to drive to Boston with him and he had to deflect her. But right now Moses's digital watch was flicking to seven-thirty-two. There was no hurry. If he waited until nine-thirty, the early-morning traffic would have thinned and the roads would be plowed.

Watching M'mm, he knew that he loved her. Like Adele, Marge, and Sylvia, she was a thoroughly pragmatic woman, but wonderously feminine, too! Unfortunately, they lived in a world that believed that men and women could only love one person at a time. Moses knew that it might be difficult to convince M'mm that he could be in love with four women at once. But of course each of them was mentally and physically a uniquely different person. Why couldn't men and women learn how to savor and care for more than one person of the other sex and interweave them all into their lives? Heman Hyman Youman, sometimes known as Moses Megillah Marshalik, didn't doubt that it was possible. Not for a minute. It was the key to Byrdwhistle and Theory Z. Adele and he had done it for years. Men and women could play together, reveling in one another's flesh, caring for one another's frailties. Men and women creatively loving and sex-making were the highest priorities of human existence.

M'mm's closed eyes, which he couldn't help kissing, her lips, which were open so that her tongue could touch his, her serene breasts with placid pink aureolae and soft nipples silently asking him to touch them and kiss them, her ears, too, and her shoulders and the sheer loveliness of her clavicle pressing against her flesh and supporting her neck and head, all of her body manifested this basic human need. Please, please, merge your island existence with my island existence so that I'm not so alone in this world.

Amused by his thoughts and M'mm's sleepy fingers, which were now holding his penis, he hoped that one day, when he had finally merged this love lark with M'mm with his search for a Byrdwhistle successor, she would understand. He loved her, and together they were officiating at the tribal magic rites that Sir James Frazer had described in *The Golden Bough*. When the leader showed signs that his powers were beginning to wane, the man-god must be killed. His soul must be transferred to a vigorous successor. Unknown to her, but guiding the succession, was Meredith Coldaxe, the new man-god's wife! Why not? The idea made Moses feel chuckly right down to his toenails. It was a splendid insight. Most males twirling on their merry-go-rounds—some of their carousels gaudy, some decrepit—were forced to play the man-god game.

Men faced more difficult rites of passage than their female counterparts. But in the process of catalyzing each other with their Love You Cosmetics daydream, he and M'mm were mapping their way into a new kind of world. If he could put the reins of W.I.N. and Byrdwhistle safely in Ron's hands, then Ron's wife and Moses Marshalik/King Gillette/Thomas Morton/Heman Hyman—did it matter who he was?—might lay the groundwork for a new kind of senior citizen, and a new kind of America—a singing, dancing society where the third of the population that were living into their sixties and beyond would have discovered that loving and longevity, laughing and learning and ludamus, were the only reasons for living in the first place.

Like World Corporation, Love You Cosmetics would become the launching pad. He and M'mm would show millions of people how to combine cosmetics-making, sex-making, and Theory Z into a new way of life. And they would show the younger generation how to accomplish a magical transfer of power from one generation to another. Love therapists would become the vanguard of a new age, a new era with an older generation that was laughingly unashamed of human sexuality. An older generation who, before they said goodbye to this planet, would be hailed as senior sex gurus. A new SSS—"Senior-Sex-Sitizens"—male and female, would teach the younger generations how to enjoy the ecstasy of escape into one another's flesh.

M'mm opened her eyes and smiled at him. "I think I'm beginning to like New England," she said, and she burrowed beneath the covers and snuggled his stomach with her face. "My God! You are certainly very big so early in the morning. Come inside me."

She wiggled back in his arms and he grinned at her. "While you were sleeping, I was trying to absorb you. That's a better word than adore or worship. One who absorbs is thoughtful, engrossed, rapt, buried in, sunken in, deep within, lost within, fascinated, assimilated, immersed, fused, blended. An absorber is captivated, thrilled, inspired, soul-stirred by the absorbee." Moses had a faraway look in his eyes. "You can see that this is a much more mind-expanding experience than simply coming inside you and ejaculating. Before I do that—an hour or two from now— I need to absorb your flesh and merge with the warmth of the blood flowing under your skin. I want to taste you, sniff you with my nose, experience you by eating you, literally and figuratively, until finally I am no longer me. I will have become you."

M'mm hugged him, "I want to do that to you, too. Will you teach me how?"

"First, we must make a warm tent out of the blankets and sheets so so that we don't freeze to death." With M'mm's enthusiastic help, a few seconds later they were safely ensconced in their bed-womb. "Now," he told her, "close your eyes. Stretch out on your back and float while I absorb you."

A few hours later, at nine o'clock in the morning, wearing a terry-cloth bathrobe, M'mm served toast, coffee, and oranges in the living room. Moses was fully dressed. He had built a roaring fire in the fieldstone fireplace. He told her that he must drive to Boston but would be back in a couple of hours. Lying on the floor of the living room, watching the hot flames transform the early morning shadows and dispel the coldness, M'mm said, "I really don't want to let you go. You're making me feel like a teen-ager. A few minutes ago, I loved you so much I knew what you meant when you said I would want you to impregnate me." She laughed, "Not to have a squalling infant in my arms sucking on my breasts but, like Minerva, to give birth to you right out of my head." She snuggled against him. "Then I'd have two Moseses. One of you could go to Boston and the other could stay here and make love to me forever." Plaintively she asked, "What am I going to do while you're gone? Why can't I come with you?"

"It's a cold, shivery day outside," Moses told her, "and I'll be back before you know it. You can try the little experiment that popped into my mind last week when your friend Tippy told us that she couldn't massage herself." While she watched, he connected a thirty-foot extension cable to the video-tape recorder and attached an antenna and leads to the television set in one corner of the living room. Then he turned on a reflector lamp with a 500-watt bulb that he had brought with him and aimed it at the ceiling. The living room immediately was as bright as a sunny day. Unfastening the camera from the tripod he connected it to the recorder, aimed it at M'mm, and told her to watch her television set. "This tube is much bigger than the monitor I used in the kitchen. You're not Minerva, but there is another you. She's watching you."

M'mm stared at herself on the screen. She stuck her tongue out and laughed at herself. "I think you're trying to turn me into a vidiot," she told him. "Everyone in the world is becoming a voyeur. We're all spying on each other. People spend half their lives watching people on television. Ron told me that H. H. Youman had television cameras all over the place at Byrdwhistle. Evidently, Byrdwhistlers tape all their meetings and enjoy watching themselves later."

For a moment, Moses had the uneasy feeling that M'mm would suddenly bridge the gap and would look at him accusingly and say, "Oh, my God! I know who you really are." When he had adopted Moses Megillah Marshalik as an ancestor he had forgotten how difficult it would be to shake his Youman identity. "Your husband must have known H. H. Youman before he had the relapse," he said, trying to divert her. "I wish I had met him. Did Ron tell you much about him?"

M'mm shook her head, "He was in Boston with Youman for a week, but Ron wasn't very communicative. He said that Youman lived in a commune, in some place called Merry Mount. One night Youman invited him there. I guess they were having a costume party. I think Ron was a little afraid of him. He told me that Youman was charismatic and very ego-oriented." She laughed, "He probably upstaged Ron, who is also very ego-oriented. Not everyone is like you, Moses. If Ron or Ralph Thiemost wanted to absorb a woman, it wouldn't be because they wanted to be her, it would be because they wanted her to be them."

While she was talking, Moses had kept the camera on her, and she was fully aware that she was talking to herself as much as to him. "Are you recording me?"

"No. When I leave, you are going to do that." He aimed the camera at her face and body and moved the zoom lens in and out. "As you play with this camera, I think you'll discover that it can give you much more than a mirror reflection of yourself. A mirror simply reflects you on one plane. A video camera can capture you looking at yourself or looking down at your body or looking straight at yourself. It can make you seem taller; it can make you seem diminutive; it can make you seem beautiful and ugly—all within seconds of each other. It can give you hundreds of perspectives on yourself that neither you nor anyone else has ever seen." Moses took a couple of books off the coffee table, and placed them so that they supported the camera at a thirty-degree angle with the floor. "Now, open your bathrobe," he commanded her, "and walk toward the camera. Look at yourself on the tube."

M'mm moved hypnotically, opening her robe. First, she could see herself partially naked. Then her slightly elongated headless body and finally her stomach and vulva filled the screen.

"Spread your legs," Moses told her. He moved the reflector slightly so that her thighs were clearly lighted.

"My God," M'mm stared at herself, astonished. "I never saw my labia like that. Not even when I bent over and looked in a mirror."

"Neither has anyone else," Moses smiled. "Are you getting the idea? A video-camera can go far beyond the simple act of revealing yourself as other people see you. It can really introduce your body to yourself for the first time. It can help you get acquainted with a new physical you and help you blend it with a totally new mental perception of yourself. Do you see the possibilities?"

M'mm shook her head, "I'm not sure."

"To activate the camera and record yourself, all you have to do is turn on the recorder and snap this button on the camera," Moses said. "But before you do, play with the zoom lens and use your imagination."

"Then what?"

Moses laughed, "Go through your record collection, or try some of the Steven Halpern or environmental tapes. They're in my Marsha Lovett bag. Find some music you'd really like to dance to. While I'm gone, turn on your hi-fi. You're going to give yourself an erotic self-love dance-massage. And you're going to have the joy of watching yourself while you do it." Moses was grinning at her triumphantly. "Among other things, Love You Cosmetics distributors will be happy to show their customers how to do a video striptease, ending with a massage and using the cosmetics they have made. In the privacy of her own home, all by herself, a woman will not only enjoy a fascinating afternoon of physical self-discovery, but if she wishes she can show the video-tapes to her husband or lover later, and eroticize him for an evening encounter. The video-camera is a unique aphrodisiac. Love therapists will rent them to their Love You Cosmetics clients and encourage them to experiment with endless variations on a theme."

"What about vice-versa?" Can't men do an exotic self-love dance-massage?" M'mm demanded.

"Absolutely. Why not?"

"Will you do a sex-dance for me?"

"Sure, when I get back from Boston, and you can be the camera-person."

"Good, I'll wait for you and we can be camera-persons for each other."

"Not at first," Moses said. "My theory is that any woman would be much less inhibited if no one was watching her. I want to see if you dare to let yourself go and at the same time watch yourself doing it."

M'mm stared at him, astonished. "And you'd expect me to show you the tapes when you come back?"

"Only if you'd want to. You, or any Love You Cosmetics customer, may not dare to. The tapes may be too revealing. If they are, in your case you can decide to erase them."

"It sounds as if you're telling me to watch myself masturbating," M'mm grinned at him. "After yesterday and this morning I don't need to."

Moses hugged her, "What I'm telling you is that how far a Love You Cosmetics client lets herself go on her own erotic self-love trip really depends on her." He laughed, "But please don't get any massage oil on the camera lens."

An hour later at the Center for Ageless Humans, Alexi Ivanowsky was warning Moses that he absolutely couldn't guarantee that he could continue to cover for him. His senility game had gone too far. Yesterday, a blustery, red-faced man, who identified himself as Ralph Thiemost, the new owner of Byrdwhistle, together with his lawyer, Bob Haley, had arrived and demanded to see H. H. Youman.

"They agreed that you may be senile, or even insane," Alexi sounded uneasy, as if the idea had occurred to him, too, "but they insist that on some level you probably know what you are doing. They're sure that you are trying to sabotage Byrdwhistle. In addition, you have severely damaged the reputation of two of their officers and caused a multi-million-dollar drop in the value of W.I.N. stock. They are going to sue your estate and Adele for millions of dollars."

Alexi told H.H. that he had insisted that they could not see H.H. Youman, not today and maybe not tomorrow, and that he was undergoing intensive electric-shock treatments. "I told them that no one could see you—not without Adele's permission." Alexi frowned at him, "But I'm not going to continue to risk the center's reputation much longer. Thiemost told me that he was trying to contact Adele in Yugoslavia and get her permission by radiogram. His lawyer said that they would be back by Friday, or sooner, with the police if necessary. They're determined to talk to you."

Moses patted Alexi's shoulder reassuringly, "Stop worrying, Alexi, when I finish with Ralph Thiemost he'll need the room next to mine at the center. And he won't be pretending!" Moses asked Alexi to get Marge Slick on the telephone for him. "I can't telephone her myself," he said. "The Byrdwhistlers would recognize my voice."

When Marge heard Moses's cheery "Good morning, sweetheart, this is your best friend and occasional lover," she replied grimly. "You'd better talk fast, chum. This phone may be bugged. While you've been playing in the meadow with another cow, a great big bull arrived from Los Angeles with several lesser bulls, and they are all getting ready to ram their great big pricks into Byrdwhistle."

Marge spoke in a whisper and told H.H. that if she had to hang up suddenly it would be because Ralph Thiemost or one of his cohorts had appeared in her office. She told him that Thiemost had arrived Monday morning and announced at a Symp meeting that the W.I.N.-Byrdwhistle marriage wasn't going well. Ronald Coldaxe had crumbled in a crisis. When the tough should have got going, he had run for the woods, and now he was hiding behind a woman's skirt. Instead of romping in the daisies with Adele Youman in Yugoslavia, he should have sued her. He should have started legal proceedings against both of the Youmans for using his photographs in a nefarious scheme to undermine W.I.N. He was going to sue Heman Hyman Youman for stealing Byrdwhistle inventory. Whether those fucking Love Rocks were included in the purchase agreement or not, they belonged to W.I.N. Inc. Not only had Youman jeopardized the future of Byrdwhistle, but he had invalidated the Byrdwhistle purchase agreement.

"Thiemost has been trying to reach Adele all morning by telephone," Marge told him. "He's going to demand that she give him permission to have you examined by a competent team of psychiatrists. He thinks that Alexi Ivanowsky is a charlatan and a bird-brain to boot. He's insisting that Coldaxe has probably stolen the Byrdwhistle jet. He's sure that Adele and Ronald have absconded not only with your personal money but probably with Byrdwhistle money too. He believes that Ron should have stayed here and sent somebody else to Yugoslavia. In his words 'any nitwit' could have done the job. As far as Thiemost is concerned, Yugoslavia is 'nothing but a god-damned communist rock-pile anyway.' After that earthquake, Love Rocks are everywhere, sliding down all the mountains."

Moses could hear Marge sigh. "Poor Ronald," she said. "I'm afraid that he's expendable. Thiemost has put Joe Taylor and Bill Redman, his wonder boys from Stanford, in charge. Redman told me this morning that when the Christmas season is over they're going to drain the swimming pool and board it over. The Love Rooms will be torn down, and the regular nine-to-five working hours will be restored. Everyone will have to wear clothes on every floor." Marge was sobbing a little. "And that's not all. He told me that *Rum Ho!* was not included in the purchase agreement and that under no circumstances would Byrdwhistle finance the opening night. Notices have already been put up to that effect. I called Elmer," Marge said, "and I told him that he better delay opening night until he's sure that he's sold out to the general public."

Listening to her, Moses was frowning. He had been planning to delay his counterattack until next Monday morning and announce his reappearance as H. H. Youman at the opening of *Rum Ho!* Monday night. Before he took off for New Hampshire, Sheldon Coombs had told him that the response to World's mailing to W.I.N. employees had been very good. The anticipated news story hadn't yet appeared in the *Wall Street Journal* or any Boston newspapers, but Sheldon was positive that eventually World, for better or worse, would be in W.I.N.'s driver's seat. However, it would be several weeks before Thiemost was the official loser.

Moses knew that right now he had to slow Thiemost down and give him a good kick in the ass. "Listen carefully, Marge," he told her. "First, *Rum Ho!* Call Elmer immediately and tell him to give the Colonial Theater his personal check for thirty-five thousand dollars or whatever it costs to guarantee all the seats. Whatever it takes, Elmer and I will cover opening night. If we can't get it out of Byrdwhistle, eventually we'll split it between us. I want that opening to be fully attended by all Byrdwhistlers and all the Boston and New York City theater critics. Second, do you know whether Thiemost has heard about the Club Wholesome problem and the video-tapes?"

"Not yet," Marge said. "But it will probably jump out of the woodwork today or tomorrow. A young woman who works for the Boston *Phoenix* has sniffed out the whole story."

"Good. We're going to give her a story to top that one." Moses laughed, "If you really want to get rid of Thiemost and will go all out with me, Marge, with a little bit of luck I think we can get him tossed in the clinker for a couple of days, both on a morals charge and for trying to screw the public with Love Rocks."

"Hyman, I hope you're not getting any insane ideas. I'm not going to try to seduce Ralph Thiemost."

"Sane people are very boring, Marge," Moses said. "Just listen to me for a minute. I need to know three things. First, where can I find Victor Watchman? Second, what ever happened to that woman who was president of SUCKS? The one who picketed Byrdwhistle a year ago with a dozen or so of her SUCKERS?"

Marge sighed. "Watchman's office is in the Federal Building." She gave Moses his phone number. "The group of very religious women who were determined to shut down Byrdwhistle on a morals charge is not 'SUCKS.' It's 'SUGS'—the Save Us, God, Society. The woman in charge is Regina Goodbody. She's really a fat-assed busybody."

Moses was grinning happily now. "All right, I'm going to tackle Watchman. I want you to call Meredith Coldaxe and introduce yourself. Tell her all the gory details about Thiemost and Byrdwhistle. Tell her that you're going to save Byrdwhistle. Convince her that she might be able to help you get rid of Ralph Thiemost and even put him behind bars. And, Marge, while you're talking to her, assure her that Ronald is slowly becoming a good Byrdwhistler. And that he doesn't really play with female Byrdwhistlers."

"What the hell is all this going to accomplish?" Marge demanded.

Moses chuckled, "I'm not sure, but I'm living with Meredith in Lynn-field for the next few days. If she knows what's going on, it's going to be easier to communicate with her. And she knows some things about Thie-most that will give you confidence in our little scam. I've only got today and tomorrow to convince Watchman. Thursday is Thanksgiving. If I succeed, Friday will be 'Get Thiemost Day.' I'll be in touch with you, Marge, by tomorrow night or sooner, either via Meredith Coldaxe or, if necessary, I'll talk to you directly. In the meantime be sure you make contact with Regina Goodbody. Don't identify yourself. Tell her that you are a disgruntled, former Byrdwhistler who was fired because you wouldn't swim naked in the company pool or use the Love Rooms. Tell her that, even worse, the new boss has arrived from California and that you're sure he's some kind of bizarre sex-pervert."

Marge groaned, "I hate to ask you, Hyman, but what was your third question?"

"Damn, I nearly forgot. Are you naked right now?"

"No way! When Ralph Thiemost strolls into this office and gives me his drooling lascivious look, I prefer to have my ass well covered. By the

way, Thiemost has a suite at the Hyatt, and just before you called he told
me that he had contacted Meredith Coldaxe and expected to have a long
fatherly talk with her. You'd better watch out. Ralph Thiemost is a lecherous libertine. Your new friend may lose her virginity. I think Thiemost
is determined to seduce her."

Moses laughed, "Big Chief W.I.N. is not going to seduce Meredith,
Marge," he said. "He's going to seduce you. If all goes well, Friday at
about noontime you are going to play the greatest dramatic role of your
life. You can do it right in your office. Ask Fred to help you. You'll need
handcuffs, whips, chains, ropes, and maybe some leather clothing to
strew around the place. Tell Fred to take the TV camera off that wall-
bracket in the corner of your office and to make sure that it can support
a lot of weight."

"Forget it!" Marge was no longer whispering to him. "I know what
you want me to do. You want me to tie Thiemost up and put on leather
clothing and whip his ass. I'm not going to do it. Anyway, you're on the
wrong track. Thiemost is a sadist, not a masochist."

"Marge, you don't understand," Moses told her patiently. "Regina
Goodbody isn't going to catch you whipping Thiemost's ass. She's going
to pop in when Thiemost is whipping yours."

41

Before Moses left, M'mm had bundled up in a heavy sweater and ski
pants and helped him shovel snow away from the garage doors. Then,
waving goodbye, she watched the van plow through the snow in
reverse. Skidding and sliding down unplowed Cabot Lane, he disappeared. Across the street, Tippy was standing on her front doorstep.
She yelled "Hi!" to M'mm, and M'mm grimaced and nodded silently.
Now all her damned nosy neighbors would know the truth. Uncle Moses
had spent the night with her.

Back in her living room, which was now cozy with the acrid odor of
burning wood, she tossed another oak log on the fire and looked speculatively at the video-camera. Should she do it? Should she flip the switches
on the television set, the video-tape recorder, and the camera. The tube
would come to life with her reflection. "The question, Meredith Coldaxe,"
she told herself aloud, "is not should you do it but do you dare do it?"

Wondering what kind of music one should use for erotic dancing, she
flipped through Ron's and her record collection. She rejected Abba and

Neil Diamond, thought for a moment about the Village People, and then decided her first record should be "Tuxedo Junction," and then, for a change of pace, some belly-dancing music. Putting two records on the turntable, she swayed to the disco music. The beat seemed just right. "What the hell?" she thought. "If nothing else, it would be amusing to try a striptease."

After some fiddling with the camera lens she decided to leave the camera on the floor where Moses had put it. It was pointing slightly up at her. Then she snapped down the "record" button on the camera and flipped her hips suggestively at the lens. How could she ever strip off a ski suit glamorously? That was a challenge. Keeping in motion to the throbbing music, she weaved herself out of her heavy wool sweater and got it over her head. Then she unsnapped her bra and waved it triumphantly at the camera. Amazed as she watched the undercurve of her breasts bouncing against her chest on the television screen, she decided that viewed from this angle they seemed pert and seductive. She moved closer to the lens, and her bobbing breasts filled the screen. She couldn't help laughing. They really weren't bad for a forty-five-year-old woman.

Kneeling even closer to the camera until she was only a few inches from the lens, she adjusted the magnification. One breast, at first diffused, came into sharp focus. As she stared at her aureolae, one nipple was magnified so that it nearly filled the twenty-six-inch screen. She had never seen her nipple in such interesting detail. She rubbed it gently and it quickly assumed a personality all its own. It was staring proudly at her from the tube. Changing the lens perspective, she swayed her breasts in slow motion to the now quieter music and caressed them with a gentle upward stroke and admired her long fingers, which seemed to belong to someone else who was enjoying her breasts as much as she was.

Feeling a little flushed, knowing that impossibly—certainly not after her long idyllic morning of love-making with Moses—but yes, inescapably, unavoidably, once again her body was sexually aroused. She backed away from the camera, admiring a full-length view of her undulating hips. Then she twisted to the music so that the tape could record the full length of her body. She was now swinging her behind tantalizingly to the music. Delighted with the effect, she let her hands glide over her hips. Should she go the whole way? Why not? Her fingers inched slowly inside her panties. Panting, noting that her mouth was open and the microphone was picking up her agitated breathing, she danced herself out of them, and when they fell to the floor she kicked them high in the air with a happy scream. Should she continue? She knew that she was slowly being hypnotized by the lovely woman dancing on the tube. In some strange way she had separated her body from herself. A giggly thought occurred to her. What was "herself" anyway? And she couldn't stop. Her hands were sweeping her body, pausing for a moment on her breasts, and then while her hips were swaying her hands were exploring her vulva in a long, caressing movement. Turning, she watched her hands, which were now slowly massaging her behind.

Laughing, she finally snapped the camera off for a moment and ran into the kitchen. She found a jar of creamy skin softener that she and Moses had made the day before. Back in the living room, still dancing to the music, she arranged the camera so that the fireplace became a glowing backdrop for her ass and hips. The disco record was now being followed by bouzouki and drum music. She suddenly realized that she was completely entranced with the project. Watching herself, she had become a naked Egyptian belly-dancer, offering her body to an appreciative caliph. Moses was right. Knowing that she was recording herself, knowing that she could run the tape back and then view herself as if she were another person, a woman who was brazenly exposing her driving sexuality, enjoying herself as a totally erotic female for the first time in her life, she was getting acquainted with a physical Meredith Coldaxe she had never known. Momentarily, she had obliterated her mental self and revealed this woman in a strange bird's-eye and worm's-eye perspective that no one had ever seen before.

And now this independent person, massaging herself with skin-softener, her hands, caressing her ass while she was laughing uncontrollably, were spreading her buttocks. Her rosy asshole and her entire behind filled the screen. Watching this unique phenomenon, almost doubled over with laughter, she dilated her anus and made it wink a little on the tube. And then, suddenly, it was no longer Meredith Coldaxe dancing on the screen. It was a totally aroused stranger, teasing her vulva with her hands, spreading her legs so that she could see her labia and clitoris and vaginal opening in full magnification. And from head to foot, as she varied the picture from full length to awe-inspiring closeup, she watched a glistening, sinuous harem dancer who was moaning a little and inviting an unseen male to come and take her.

Then, while she interspersed teasing and provocative closeups of her ass with equally lascivious pictures of her face with her dreamy eyes and her mouth open, the top blew off. The telephone rang! Shocked, as if she had been surprised by a live intruder, she snapped off the recorder. Still panting a little, she answered the phone.

"Meredith, I've missed you." The familiar, sardonic voice was followed by an insincere laugh. "I've been keeping my ear close to the ground, but I haven't heard you whinny yet."

Meredith frowned into the telephone. Noticing that she hadn't turned off the camera and was still appearing on the tube, she continued to smoothe the last vestige of the skin-softener into her belly. She watched herself in full length as she answered. "I told you, Mr. Thiemost, I never whinny."

"Good Lord, Meredith, I had hoped by this time you would have forgotten me," Ralph sounded like a wounded lover. "I told you that the next time we played games together I'd ask your permission. If you want to, you can tie me up." Ralph was chuckling, "Admit it, Meredith, you know you were a little turned on."

Then there was silence as M'mm kept him waiting for her to answer. Finally, she said coldly, "You're not very amusing, Mr. Thiemost. You are obviously quite deluded." As she spoke the word, she couldn't help smiling. She'd have to tell Moses that delusion was the opposite of play, and Ralph Thiemost was most definitely *deludo*. "I suppose you know that Ron is in Yugoslavia," she said, and she wondered what Ron might have told Thiemost about her availability while he was gone. She certainly wasn't going to invite Ralph Thiemost to dinner.

"One of the reasons I telephoned you," Thiemost said, and his voice suddenly sounded curt and demanding, "was that I wanted you to know I am very unhappy with Ron. He's deserted a sinking ship. As a matter of fact, you may be his last hope. I'm counting on you, Meredith. Remember, you're still a member of the W.I.N. family. Don't forget that."

M'mm listened silently while Ralph lamented. Byrdwhistle was a sick, immoral company. Sex was rampant. Employees ran around the place naked. They came and went when they wanted to and spent hours in the Love Rooms with one another's spouses. Finally he got to the point. "By this time I presume you are aware that Ron has exposed me and himself, not only figuratively but stark naked to all W.I.N. employees and to the whole damned world. I warned him to straighten out Adele Youman and get those negatives, but Ron wasn't paying attention to me. Now, it's too late."

As Ralph raved on, M'mm slowly assembled the missing pieces. Adele had apparently taken pictures of Thiemost, which he hadn't shown her that night on his boat, and she had evidently given the picture of Ron that Thiemost had shown her to World Corporation. Sheldon Coombs, who Thiemost insisted was inspired by H. H. Youman, had printed it in a four-color brochure and had sent it to all W.I.N. employees. M'mm didn't tell Ralph that she had not seen the mailing that he was shouting about. It didn't matter anyway, she was terribly angry at Ronald Coldaxe. It suddenly occurred to her why Ronald had kept asking her whether their mail had been forwarded. Even worse, her sneaky, rat-fink husband never had admitted to her that he had been swimming naked in Adele Youman's swimming pool, or that she had taken pictures of him. Ron must have known that Adele, the little bitch, had taken such pictures of Thiemost, too, and that she was planning to include both his and Ralph's pictures in a book she was writing.

M'mm couldn't help agreeing with Thiemost. "Ron should have stopped her," he told her. "I told him to get those god-damned pictures. Now, instead of suing her and her crack-brained husband, he has stolen the Byrdwhistle jet. He and Adele flew to Yugoslavia yesterday before I could get my hands on them."

That revelation really stunned M'mm. "I thought Adele Youman was already in Yugoslavia."

"She took off with him yesterday. It's a damned wild-goose chase," Thiemost said angrily. "Ron could have contacted one of our European subsidiaries. He could have sent someone on the spot to Sveti Stefan. If they couldn't find Youman's fucking Love Rocks, they could have found a substitute and had them here in Boston weeks ago." Ralph sounded grim, "I don't know whether you realize it or not but Adele Youman is a very dangerous woman. I think she's trying to seduce your husband."

"It looks as if she's succeeded," M'mm held her hand over the mouthpiece. She couldn't control herself. She was sobbing.

"I really want to talk with you, Meredith," Ralph suddenly sounded fatherly. "Ron told me that you'd be alone this week. I'd like to drive out to your house tonight. I have a lot of things I want to discuss with you, and I can't do it over the telephone."

"I'm sorry. I'm busy."

"What about tomorrow night? You can come into the Hyatt and stay over to have Thanksgiving dinner with me. I've been trying to reach Adele and Ron by phone. The Byrdwhistle jet arrived at the Dubrovnik airport, but I haven't been able to get in touch with them. I need Adele's permission before I can talk with Youman. When I get it, whether he's crazy or not I'll find out where that bastard is keeping the Love Rocks. I'm going to confront him personally at the center and I want you to come with me. You could appeal to Youman's better instincts. You could give him a good sob story and you don't have to fake it. If we don't find those Love Rocks damned quick and start shipping them, it could be Ron's ass."

M'mm was dredging her mind for excuses. She wasn't very happy with Ronald Coldaxe. He was running true to form. Just like Ralph Thiemost, Ron was sure that most women couldn't wait to jump into bed with a corporate bigwig. She wanted to tell Thiemost to go to hell and take Ron with him. She hoped that an avalanche of Love Rocks would fall on both their heads. But she knew it was inevitable that she would have to see Ralph. If she wasn't careful, he might appear on her doorstep and discover Moses Marshalik running around the house naked. The silly thought crossed her mind that she could invite him to Thanksgiving dinner. She could tell him that Uncle Moses, a relative of hers, would be the other guest and that Moses had been a vice president of Marsha Lovett, which was a W.I.N. subsidiary. It would be like old friends meeting. It would be a good chance for Moses to find out if Ralph would really like to sell Marsha Lovett or let Moses and her play with it.

If she was going to stay in New England and be Moses's playmate and help him develop Love You Cosmetics, he had to understand that she had to help Ron, too. If Ralph came to dinner with Moses, she was sure she wouldn't have to worry about a hanging. But M'mm knew that she really should wait until she could ask Moses's approval, but even if he did agree she wasn't sure she really wanted to share him with Ralph or anybody.

"I'm really sorry, Ralph," she said, finally using his first name. "I've been invited up to Seabrook, New Hampshire, for Thanksgiving to have dinner with some old friends." She knew that would churn Ralph up, and it did.

"Damn it, Meredith," Ralph's voice was no longer friendly. "I want to give you one last chance. Stay away from those anti-nuclear idiots. You be here at Byrdwhistle Friday morning at nine o'clock. I want to have a serious discussion with you about your general attitudes, and Ron's future, and then we'll drive over to the center and have a talk with H. H. Youman."

He hung up. M'mm looked at her naked self sorrowfully on the television screen. Suddenly she didn't want an erotic self-love massage anymore. But before she could get dressed the telephone rang again. For a moment, she thought it was Thiemost calling back. Tired of standing, she flopped on a nest of pillows in front of the hearth. She was still visible on the tube and she raised her behind and did a quick bicycle ride. At the same time, she picked up the phone. Listening she was suddenly reminded of one of Moses's Yiddish expressions, "My ears don't believe what your mouth is telling me."

"This is Marge Slick, I'm a vice president at Byrdwhistle, Mrs. Coldaxe. We've never met, but I've read the questionnaire you filled out for us several months ago and I feel that we may be sympatico. Your husband speaks very enthusiastically about your activities, and he obviously cares very much about you. In this day and age that's nearly as good as equal rights."

Wondering whether Marge Slick's phone call had been inspired by Ralph Thiemost, M'mm listened suspiciously. Marge continued, "The reason I'm calling, Mrs. Coldaxe—may I call you Meredith?—is that many of us here at Byrdwhistle really admire your husband. We have had high hopes that he may continue the Byrdwhistle approaches, and even become a Byrdwhistler and a Theory Z enthusiast. But right now we're in serious trouble. Ralph Thiemost arrived here yesterday with Bob Haley, his lawyer. The two younger men that Thiemost sent along with Ronald to complete the merger are now in complete charge. It looks as if they are about to dismantle the place. I'll be very honest with you, Meredith, Ron's job may be at stake—not to mention my own, of course."

Marge's voice on the telephone was low and whispery and she sounded as if she were playing the part of Mata Hari in a movie. "What can I do?" M'mm asked cautiously.

"It's not easy to explain," Marge said. "While Thiemost puts on a very moral, puritanical front, we've heard rumors that he has some very devious sexual ideas. To be blunt, we understand that he's a bondage-and-whipping enthusiast." Marge laughed, but it wasn't a cheery laugh. It sounded more like the bells tolling for Ralph Thiemost. "I'll be honest with you. I've been chosen as the sacrificial lamb."

"I still don't understand how I can help you."

"Ron intimated to me that you had tangled with the bastard."

M'mm stared at the phone astounded. "Oh, he did, did he? What the hell else has he told you about our private life?" M'mm hadn't told Ron about her hanging, but Marge evidently knew that Thiemost had propositioned her. Maybe Marge Slick was leading her on. Maybe Ralph had told her that Meredith Coldaxe really liked to be tied up. Maybe Marge was trying in a roundabout way to get her to join in a threesome with Ralph Thiemost.

Marge's reply dispelled that thought. "Look. Just understand one thing. I may be a Byrdwhistler, but Byrdwhistlers don't screw around with the whole world. I love my husband, too."

M'mm wanted to interrupt her and ask if "too" meant that she loved Ron and that she had been to bed with him, but she restrained herself. Marge continued, "Friday at about noon we're going to pull out all the stops. My job is to lead Thiemost on. If he responds, we're hoping to catch him in the act. Sex perverts aren't very popular in Massachusetts. We've got some other things on him, and with a little luck we may be able to get him tossed into the jug. That should slow him down until Ron gets back."

M'mm couldn't help laughing, "Do you mean that you're actually going to let him tie you up?"

"That's the general idea. The real question is, do you think he'll try?"

"How do I know?" M'mm demanded. She wanted to tell Marge that it probably would depend on how physically attractive she was. Then she remembered that Byrdwhistlers ran around naked. Given a reasonable female body, that should be provocation enough for Thiemost. "What if he doesn't try?"

Marge laughed. "Who knows? But cross your fingers. If our timing is right, a woman named Regina Goodbody with a dozen or more cohorts from SUGS—the Save Us, God, Society—along with the police and other possible reinforcements, will arrive and drag Thiemost off to the slammer."

"My God," M'mm wondered if Marge was joking. "I guess Ron is right," she said. "Byrdwhistlers are more far-out than I thought. Even if you do get rid of Thiemost for a while, I don't see what Ron can do." She hadn't decided whether she should tell Marge her own experience with Thiemost. The only other person who knew was Moses Marshalik.

The she gasped. The thought of Moses had brought him to life. He was standing at the entrance of the living room grinning at her. She covered the phone with her hand. "How the hell did you get in?" she demanded. "I latched the front door." Then she spoke into the phone. "Hang on a minute. My doorbell is ringing." She stuck the phone under one of the pillows she had been lying on. "You make me feel like Susan being watched by the Elders," she told Moses crossly. "I don't like being stared at bare ass. Did you break the door down?"

"I got in through the garage," Moses was kneeling over her kissing her belly and breasts. "Who are you talking to?"

"She says that she's Marge Slick, a vice president of Byrdwhistle." M'mm shrugged, "Maybe she is, and maybe she isn't." She tried to push Moses away. "Jesus, stop a minute. You're driving me crazy. I want to talk to you. She thinks that Thiemost may be a sex maniac. Should I tell her that he's probably no worse than my Uncle Moses?"

"Sure. Tell her what your Uncle Moses is doing right now." Moses had spread her legs. Stretched out between her thighs perpendicular to her, he was making it impossible for her. She could feel her nether lips being parted with his tongue, and he was murmuring, "M'mm! M'mm, m'mm!"

M'mm retrieved the phone. "Sorry," she gasped into it. "Where are we? Oh yes, Thiemost. All I can tell you is that you'd better not encourage him. Not unless you're absolutely certain that your Regina Goodbody is standing by with an axe, ready to chop off his you know what."

Peering up at her through the crinkly hairs of her bush, Moses gave M'mm's vulva a quick lap and said in a very loud voice, "Tell your friend that all is well. Uncle Moses is very happy, too!"

"Sorry, that's all I can tell you," M'mm said, and then she hung up. She yanked Moses by his hair away from her pussy. "Damn! You're crazy, too. I'm sure that she heard you. When Ron gets back she'll probably ask him who in hell my Uncle Moses is."

Laughing, Moses was stripping off his clothes. "The van is filled with groceries, a turkey, vegetables, a liter of vodka and a case of white Bordeaux. But we can unload it later. God's in his heaven, and all's well with the world. You are the virgin whore and goddess. I am the boy, lover, hero, and god. My lingam needs to disappear in your yoni."

Moses really wanted to tell M'mm the reason for his exuberance. "You're turning me into a nymphomaniac," she sighed as she guided his penis into her vagina. But totally captured by her expression of sheer ecstasy and surrender, he knew that he couldn't tell her about his meeting with Victor Watchman. If he retired Moses Megillah today, Heman Hyman might not get a chance to enjoy this merger or any other with M'mm, this week or next! It wasn't going to be easy to convince her that H. H. Youman loved her as much or more than Moses Marshalik or to persuade Ronald Coldaxe that his wife needed a love therapist to play with a few afternoons a week.

But, no matter what happened, the die was cast. Less than an hour before, after he met Watchman in a dimly lit restaurant near the Government Center, he had telephoned Marge that Watchman was in the bag and he promised that she could stop worrying. The happy ending was coming. H. H. Youman would be at opening night of *Rum Ho!* with a lot of happy surprises for Byrdwhistlers.

Watchman had been cautious and suspicious with the do-gooder called Moses Marshalik who wanted to pull the rug out from under Byrdwhistle Corporation. But after three Jack Daniels—Victor Watchman's favorite drink—followed by a filet mignon, the greasy little guardian of the people's mail-order rights belched and told Moses, "I don't like this guy Ronald Coldaxe much, but if you're right and he's just a fall guy for Ralph Thiemost, who sounds like a dangerous pervert to me, then, okay, tell Regina Goodbody to contact me. We will knock off Thiemost together Friday morning." He had grinned slyly at Moses. "And please note that I'm not questioning your interest in the matter beyond your statement that you're a private citizen interested in upholding human decency and Christian morals. But you better be here at eight-thirty Friday morning with the five grand that you're willing to spend. It will make it possible to refuse bail and keep this crummy Thiemost character in jail for a few days until he's undergone psychiatric treatment."

But Moses couldn't worry about Victor Watchman now, not with M'mm rolling her rump so voluptuously underneath him. He whispered, "Roll over on top of me. It's all right, honey. Go ahead, take off into space. I'll join you later." And he clasped her ass and glided with her until she collapsed on him, sobbing and laughing at her trajectory. Her chest still heaving, she giggled. "You bastard. You tricked me with that videocamera. I've been doing my own foreplay for hours."

"Wonderful. I can't wait to see the tapes you've made."

M'mm shook her head. "Not until you've danced for me, too. Remember you promised."

"Before or after?"

M'mm laughed. "Before, while you still have a big banana."

Watching him flip through records in the library, she turned on the television set and aimed the camera at his buttocks. He put on the same belly-dance record that she had used. The insistent feverish drumming and twanging bouzouki music filled the room. Brushing his fiery penis across her face, Moses grinned at her and insisted that a male could be just as seductive as any nautch girl. Amazed that he was using his body as erotically as a woman, M'mm followed his movements through the camera lens, gliding from his face, which claimed her with a lustful expression, to his penis, which was flopping wildly up and down to the beat and then was slowly swaying from side to side as he rolled his buttocks to the slower tempo of the music.

Lying on the floor with the camera pointing up at Moses, she could see that he, too, was watching his genitals on the screen. His head had disappeared. The full length of his body was on the tube. Twisting and turning and stroking himself, he offered his penis to her, which she had magnified so that it nearly filled the twenty-six-inch screen. Then he bent over, and his dangling scrotum reappeared between his legs. Laughing hysterically, she captured the deep cleft of his separated buttocks and his anus, a wide open tunnel, on the tube. Then, to her complete amazement, he was talking to her from his rosy asshole for a moment. It no longer seemed to belong to Moses but had assumed a life of its own. It was a detached mouth, opening and closing and smiling at her.

Then he twisted and faced the camera once again, and his red-knobbed glans was pointing at her from a curly brown nest of hair, and its tiny vertical mouth was actually grinning at her. Moses was controlling his penis without his hands. With motionless hips he was making the silly thing bob up and down, and now it was singing to her: "Cock-a-doodle-doo. My dame has lost her shoe. My master loves his fiddling stick. I hope you love it too."

"I do!" she yelled happily. "I do. The damned thing looks like a dragon. Wait a minute. I've got an idea." She dashed upstairs and returned with sunglasses and mascara. Holding his penis, telling him it looked dangerously ready to spout, she daubed eyes on each side of it, and balanced her sunglasses on top of it. "It looks like a big-nosed gangster," she told him.

"It's on the lam," he agreed. "Before it's shot down, I hope you'll let it hide out in your pussy."

Then the telephone rang.

M'mm looked at it in dismay. "It's probably Ralph Thiemost," she said disgustedly. "I'm not going to answer it."

She quickly told Moses that Thiemost had called and wanted her to have Thanksgiving dinner with him and that the thought had occurred to her to invite him here to meet Moses. "Ron didn't seem to know much about Marsha Lovett," she said. "Maybe we could find out ourselves what's going on—right from the horse's mouth."

Moses was appalled, and he shook his head vigorously. "No, we don't need him. We don't want to alert Thiemost to Love You Cosmetics. If he thought we could save the company, the price would go up."

The phone kept ringing.

M'mm shrugged. "It was just a mad idea. Anyway, I promised. I have to meet him at Byrdwhistle Friday morning."

"Why in hell did you agree to that?" Moses was shocked. He was afraid that if M'mm was at Byrdwhistle when Watchman and Goodbody arrived, Thiemost might not be in a mood to play games with Marge Slick. He frowned, wondering how he was going to keep his well-laid plans on track.

"I didn't want to. You ought to know that," M'mm said. She wondered if Moses was suddenly jealous of her. He certainly didn't seem to be very happy about Thiemost.

The telephone kept ringing.

"He's not going to give up," she sighed. "I'd better answer it." She picked up the phone.

"Meredith are you all right?" It was Tippy Osgood. "Prissy and I could see Uncle Moses's van in the driveway. We knew that he must have come back."

M'mm knew that Tippy had seen the van early that morning, too, and that she was well aware that Uncle Moses had stayed overnight. "We're making soap," she said coldly. "It's very tricky. It's cooking on the stove and I couldn't answer the phone. I didn't want it to boil over."

"Last Thursday, Uncle Moses offered to teach us how to play nude bridge, Tippy said. "Prissy and I were wondering if you'd like to bring him over here? We could all play together."

Exasperated, M'mm covered the phone. "Now what do I do?" she asked Moses. "Your admirers want a piece of the action."

Grinning, Moses took the phone. "Tippy, look at your clock. It's four-thirty. I'm sure your husband will be home soon. It's really too late. I told you and Prissy that nude bridge is a game that a love therapist could use to help customers get in touch with themselves. Later they might even teach their spouses how to play, but we can't begin playing at four-thirty. I'm sure you understand."

M'mm could hear Tippy laughing. "What you really mean is that, if Jack and Harry found Prissy and me playing, they wouldn't be very happy with us—or with Uncle Moses."

"Precisely."

"Could we play tomorrow?"

Dismayed, Moses raised his eyebrows at M'mm, who could hear both parts of the conversation. She took the phone.

"All right," M'mm said. "Tomorrow afternoon at one. We'll have a Love You Cosmetics party."

She hung up. "Why did you tell her that?" Moses demanded.

"I had to tell her something," M'mm frowned. "I'm not happy about it. But it was your silly idea in the first place. Why did you encourage her?"

Moses shrugged. "I suppose we have to test our ideas on the world." He pulled her down on the floor with him and his big nose with two eyes on it was looking at her pathetically.

Laughing, she kissed it. "Just keep one thing in mind. No damned massage tomorrow. They can play bridge and then they can go home, bare-ass for all I care." She scowled at him. "Just how in the hell do you play nude bridge?"

"Damned if I know," Moses grinned at her, "I never played it. I'll have to figure it out."

42

At nine o'clock on their third night together—Thanksgiving eve—with her eyes heavy-lidded and her body feeling as if she had run the Boston marathon, M'mm collapsed in Moses's arms. "Take me to bed," she sighed. "But not for loving, for sleeping. I should share you with Tippy and Prissy. You're really too much for me."

A few minutes later, snuggling peacefully in bed with Moses, wondering vaguely where Ron might be at the moment and suppressing the flickers of guilt that kept upbraiding her serenity, M'mm laid with her head on Moses's thigh. It was a position they had discovered in *Sexual Secrets*. The Hindus called it the Posture of the Crow. Playing with his flute, she told Moses, "I agree with you. Old crocks like you, and millions of grandfathers who don't think they are really old enough to be grandfathers, need to be liberated. If they were properly trained, they could offer women past forty afternoon vacations from their spouses." She sighed, "If you can persuade Ron that it's okay, and that you're not disturbing his marital equilibrium—which I doubt—I'll be happy to run seminars with you. We could teach selected senior citizens how to be love therapists. But you'd better not let me catch you lapping Cool Whip off of Tippy's or Prissy's pussy again." She bit his cock to emphasize her words. "I mean it, not unless I'm around to keep such insanity under control." She couldn't help giggling, "I still think that you had them in mind and not me when you bought that damned Cool Whip."

"You're absolutely right," Moses said, enjoying the female heat between her legs. "Love therapists must use discretion. Basically, in addition to selling Love You Cosmetics ingredients, they must become ombudsmen. They will teach women not only how to continue to be sexual creatures, regardless of their age, but how to create an ongoing environment for their lovers and spouses to bask in."

M'mm could feel Moses's warm breath. His laughter was making little erotic puffs against her labia, teasing it, as he rambled on. "On the other hand, we've proved that Cool Whip is a valuable resource. It probably should be included in every love therapist's sales kit."

"Damn you, I still think that you are a chauvinist," M'mm said. "Why do women have to take the initiative? You definitely approach Love You Cosmetics from a male point of view."

"Unfortunately," Moses said, "most men don't realize that Shakti—the female principle—existing in equal balance with the male principle throughout the cosmos, is the key to happiness. Women must teach men how to reach Kundalini, and the most fulfilling way is for a man and a woman to take the trip together."

Moses had moved out of her octopus clutch and was straddling her body. He kissed his way through her pubic hair to her belly and breasts. Smiling, she sleepily admired his penis dangling over her face, and thought how well acquainted she was with it. She was sure that she could recognize it even if Moses weren't attached to it.

Unlike Ronald, Moses could talk as he made love. Now he was kneeling at the back of her head and kissing her eyes and nose and lips upside-down. "Love You Cosmetics will become a launching pad into a new world," he told her. "We're going to show both men and women the only way to live. Young or old, they will learn to play at love and they will dare to be the warm, purring, sexual animals they really are." He kissed his way back to her vulva. Snuggling between her thighs in a position which he assured her was popular in Samoa and other Pacific islands, he whispered, "Good night, sweet lady, if you wake before me and your vagina is lonely, play on my flute a little. I'm sure it will quickly respond to your loving song."

Not really wanting to go to sleep, because then she would be totally unaware of the body bliss she was experiencing, she entwined herself deeper between Moses's thighs. Their hands were clasping each other's behinds. It occurred to M'mm that in the past few days she had been walking the razor's edge. What she was doing was against the rules. At the very best it would end unhappily. This was adultery, an affair, an extramarital relationship. She could end up in a divorce court. And that would be really painful, because she hadn't stopped loving Ron. She had merely found a new friend, and loved him too. Of course she still was uneasy about Moses. She had surrendered her mind and body to him more completely than she ever had with Ron, or any man before him. But she couldn't believe that Moses had ever been a vice president of Marsha Lovett Cosmetics. Any company that depended on women to buy its products would never have fired a man who could hypnotize such a variety of women as herself and Tippy and Prissy. What was there about Moses Marshalik that he could make a woman feel so deliciously feminine? Or so laughably happy? Even American Gothic types like Prissy Forbes seemed to be completely unafraid to let go and become a totally sexual woman with this man? M'mm guessed that one reason was that, in addition to being suave and sophisticated, Moses was overwhelmingly cuddly. He might think that she had been reacting to him as she would to a father, but the truth was that quite often she wanted only to mother him.

That afternoon, before Tippy and Prissy arrived, she had told him that she had underestimated how easy it was for him to appeal to so many different kinds of women, herself included. "Fortunately, I'm pragmatic," she said, but there were tears in her eyes. "I know that I've been acting like a romantic teen-ager with you, and I know it can't last. Any day now, you may disappear. Even if you don't, it may be months or years before I get a chance to sleep with you all night again. Even worse, probably one day soon you won't appear on my doorstep at ten-thirty in the morning. Your mad passion for my body will have dissipated. My love therapist will have moved on to greener pastures." She hugged him. "I love you. But I do understand that I don't own you."

"But you do own me," Moses told her with a playful smile. "If you ever get angry with me, remember that between us it's a two-way need. Actually, when I tried to interview you through your mail slot, I never expected that you would trap me or that you would fuse your mind and body into mine. You're not just my lover, you're my friend." Moses laughed, "Unfortunately, sometimes even my best friends get peeved with me and give me up. But I never give up my friends." Totally naked, they had been sitting on pillows near the hearth. On one side the fire was warming their bodies, on the other, a few feet away, the video-camera fastened to a tripod was watching them.

Moses had convinced her that Penny Slinger's *Sexual Secrets* was a perfect adjunct to cosmetics cookery and should be included with every Love You Cosmetics Starter Kit. They had been gradually reading their way through the entire book. M'mm was particularly intrigued with the joyous Hindu and Chinese names for the male and female genitals. Facing each other, their legs and thighs wrapped around each other's body, they had moved their rumps so that they were sitting belly to belly. M'mm told Moses that she really needed his jade stalk in her yoni, and she smiled at him blissfully. "Is this the kind of fusion you mean?" She wiggled herself even tighter against him. Amazingly, Moses was able to keep his erection and read to her at the same time. He was deep into the subject of magic numbers, particularly seven and the yang number nine, which according to the text was the key to therapeutic love-making. Listening to him, she was experiencing a weird kind of ecstasy.

M'mm had told him that she wasn't much in favor of video-taping themselves sex-making, but when she watched herself doing the erotic self-love and dance-massage, she agreed with Moses. She had revealed aspects of her sexuality that she had been totally unaware of and that never had been revealed to anyone, not even Ron, and it had been hysterically funny to watch the tapes of herself and Moses later, when they were in calmer moods. When he told her that their tapes could be used to train love therapists, it had made her nervous. More than a little shocked, she told him, "No way!" But he only laughed and told her she might change her mind. Even if she didn't, she wasn't to worry. The tapes belonged to her. It wouldn't bother him if she wanted to share their happy lovemaking with others, and she should never be embarrassed by them. In the act of love, they had moved from sex-making to lovemaking and to an extended transcendental I-am-you merger as they searched for Kundalini together.

He said, "*Kundalini* means pool. It's the fiery pool of all the primordial elements at the core of the earth. In the process of sexual contacts, human beings can experience the Kundalini that lies within each person. Merging their bodies and their vital breaths they can experience 'the inner thrill, a liquid fire,' simultaneously hot and cold, almost paralyzing, but opening their entire being, lightening and liberating themselves and transforming each other so that they become the ecstatic dancing god of the universe." Moses smiled at her, "Experiencing that is achievement enough for anyone's lifetime."

But M'mm told him that she believed that eventually he would get bored with the intense mental and sexual intimacy that had become a way of life for her during the past few days.

"Why should I get bored?" he demanded. "Especially since you are implying that you won't."

"Women are different, I guess," M'mm said shyly. "After your jade stalk has been inside me for an hour or two every day, my mind is clearer. You're right. I become a romping, laughing, playful, dancing goddess."

While they were talking, Moses's body had been in wave-like motion against her own gentle weaving. With each thrust, his penis had been searching inside her in subtly different ways. "Those are just a few of the nine styles of exploration that are possible when the jade stalk is in the female crucible," he grinned at her. "When a man learns how to become an explorer of Shakti, he will never be bored. I'm not working. I'm playing. I'm absorbing your essence. You're absorbing mine. Playing like this not only increases longevity, but makes it worthwhile. We'll teach Love You Cosmetics customers that, after they've learned the meaning of the magic sex-numbers, especially *nine* and *seven,* they will no longer be working at sex but they and their partners will be recreating each other."

They had been so engrossed in the dual problem of making love and changing the lens position on the video-camera that they had almost forgotten the scheduled Love You Cosmetics party. Studying the drawings in *Sexual Secrets* they tried the positions of soaring sea-gulls, reeling off the silk, turning dragon, pair-eyed fish, fluttering and soaring butterfly, feet in the air, remembrance wheel, splitting the bamboo, the crab, and the lotus. Finally, still on the floor in the tortoise position, M'mm squatted on Moses's lap with his legs under her while he read to her, "'This position helps circulate and exchange energy. It holds one of the secrets of longevity.'" Moses chuckled, "The Chinese knew the basic facts of life." M'mm had been rocking on top of him. Kissing him enthusiastically, she told him that the time had come. If he really believed what they had been reading, they must immediately exchange fluids. She would absorb his semen while he was inhaling her breath and drinking her saliva.

With ten minutes to spare, they were dressed before the front doorbell chimed. Prissy and Tippy had arrived. Dressed somewhat formally in a shirt and a tie. M'mm asked him who he was trying to impress.

"I just noticed while you were dressing," he said, "that you put on seven pieces of clothing. I needed the tie to have an equal number. I'm assuming that most females wear about the same amount. If I'm right, Tippy and Prissy will be ready for action."

But when M'mm asked him why in hell anyone would want to play nude bridge and that it didn't seem half as much fun as continuing their own experiments, Moses told her to be patient. "Have faith. Love therapists never will supervise at an orgy. It's going to be an experiment in naked laughter."

Helping Prissy and Tippy shed their minks and their boots, Moses temporarily avoided any questions. He entertained them with a nonstop carnival-barker's spiel: "Good morning, lovely ladies. Your Uncle Moses is happy to see you again. I am your Love You Cosmetics therapist. Meredith and I have been developing our afternoon love therapy program in great detail. During our program this afternoon, which we hope will eventually become one segment of a continuing weekly series that we hope to offer to Love You Cosmetics customers, all four of us are going to play nude bridge. This will be followed by a snake-dance through the house, which, depending on your imagination, may culminate in a refreshing surprise. Then we will return to the living room for ten minutes of sexercising, followed by Love You Cosmetics cooking in the kitchen, where Meredith has promised to show us how to make lettuce soap and Love You vodka cologne. Promptly at four o'clock, our afternoon festivities will cease. With an affectionate kiss, we will bid each other goodbye, and you'll be home in time to relax with your children and your husbands before dinner."

Moses ushered them into the living room. M'mm was smiling and setting up a card table. She agreed with Prissy. It wasn't easy to turn the Moses faucet off. Tippy suggested that after last week's massage, playing nude bridge would be an anti-climax. "We've all seen each other bollicky, except for Uncle Moses's genitals, which he managed to keep concealed. I brought a jug of vodka with me. Why don't we just drink and get down to business?"

"I'm afraid, Tippy, that you don't really understand love therapy," Moses said patiently. "A love therapist will teach his ladyfriends how to

348 The Byrdwhistle Option

give and enjoy happy, laughing foreplay. Getting down to business sounds like work. Love therapists don't believe in work. We're happy to help all our female friends tow their toboggans up the hill. When they get to the top, we'll even give them a big downhill push." Moses laughed, "Tonight, when you are in bed with your spouse, before you zoom down the slope you can show him how to relax and enjoy the trip. And later the joy of afterplay, too!"

Laughing happily, Prissy thought that was very amusing. But Tippy seemed a little disappointed. "I'm not a bridge enthusiast," she said.

"Nude bridge is different," Moses assured her. "It will put some spark and excitement into your future bridge games. This afternoon, M'mm and I will play partners against you and Prissy. Actually, it is not so important who are partners in a nude bridge game. It's the question of who is losing their clothing that is interesting. You should keep in mind that the game can be structured with infinite variations to suit particular conditions. Actually, it has much more intriguing consequences when the sex of the players is equally divided. But you must understand that your love therapist is really the boy next door who finally grew up to discover that playing with girls the way he did when he was young is more reward-ing than battering himself against his peers in the business world." Moses smiled benignly at all of them. "Before we begin, we must even up on the clothing we are wearing. I'm wearing seven pieces. Watches and jewelry cannot be included, unless we need them to make a balance. Meredith is wearing seven garments, too."

"How do you know what Meredith is wearing?" Tippy demanded. She had kept trying to lead the conversation into a discussion of Mere-dith's extramarital life. She grinned at Meredith, "You know damned well that Uncle Moses isn't your uncle."

M'mm smiled coolly at her. "Uncle Moses told me that I should wear seven pieces, so I did. For your information, he stayed over last night and slept in the guestroom. It was snowing so hard and the driving was so bad that he couldn't go home."

Shrugging, Tippy told them that she was wearing a dress, panty hose, panties, shoes and a bra. Penny was wearing the same but she had dressed in a sweater and skirt so that she had the requisite seven pieces. Moses told Tippy that she could count her bracelet as one piece.

"Now we're ready to begin," Moses told them. "Because we have lim-ited time, we will confine the stripping to fourteen deals. When you play nude bridge later with your spouse and friends, you can prolong the game to twenty-eight deals, or you can shorten it by increasing the number of strip cards. This afternoon the strip cards will be one-eyed jacks."

"You mean if I'm dealt a one-eyed jack I have to take something off?" Prissy, finishing the lime juice and vodka that M'mm had made for her, was smiling timidly.

"Possibly," Moses said. "But not unless you take a trick that has a one-eyed jack in it. Whoever does, must divest herself of one item of clothing."

"Himself too," Tippy said. "Including your jockey shorts this time, and afterwards you're going to dance for us. You promised," she warned him.

"We're all going to dance," Moses told her. "Please keep in mind that between us we are wearing twenty-eight pieces of clothing. After each hand, two of us will have lost one piece of clothing each. If one of us is really unlucky and takes two tricks with one-eyed jacks, then that person will shed two pieces. After about twenty or so hands, three of us will be naked. The fourth, who may still be wearing a few pieces of clothing, must immediately strip and take his or her penalty."

"Penalty?" Knowing that Moses was probably inventing the game as he went along, M'mm was listening to him open-mouthed. "What kind of penalty?"

"The game wouldn't be any fun if you just stripped and sat there," Moses said. "The one who keeps their clothes on the longest and can be a voyeur, examining the others, should end up with the worst penalty." He grinned happily at them. "The first one naked must do a mime dance or charade of three nursery rhymes without music. Each of the others must identify these nursery rhymes in turn, or they will lose a piece of clothing. The second one to lose all their clothes must mime three additional nursery rhymes. If the other players fail to identify rhymes, they must lap a glob of Cool Whip off of any part of the second player's anatomy he or she may wish to place it. The third player to be naked must fantasize his or her favorite movie star, making love to him or her in a charade. The fourth player, who probably won't be totally naked, must now undress. If he or she can't identify the movie star, he or she must lap a gob of Cool Whip off the third player's genitals."

Moses roared with laughter at their shocked expressions and Prissy suddenly looked nervous. "It sounds like a silly game to me, especially the Cool Whip."

"Don't worry," Moses told her. "You can count on it, I personally am not going to be the third player naked—even if I have to lose a trick."

"But I can't remember any nursery rhymes," Tippy wailed.

"Okay," Moses said, "if you women don't like the penalties dream up your own."

"You can forget the Cool Whip," M'mm said. "I don't have any."

"Yes you do," Moses said, "I bought it yesterday and put it in the freezer."

Remembering their conversation now, as she was falling asleep between Moses's legs, M'mm couldn't help grinning. The first Love You Cosmetics afternoon had been a total success. At four o'clock, still wiping hysterical tears of laughter from their eyes, Tippy and Prissy were finally safely back in their clothing. They kissed Uncle Moses goodbye for the third time and thanked him for the zaniest afternoon they had spent in their lives. They promised that as soon as Love You Cosmetics was in business, they'd spread the word. Uncle Moses would be busy every afternoon for the rest of his life.

The silly game had ended with all three women naked and Moses still wearing his shirt and jockey shorts. Prissy was the third loser. After she had entertained them with an erotic charade, first of Little Miss Muffet sitting on her tuffet, followed by the Little Old Woman Who Lived in a Shoe and then Jack Spratt, which they all identified, she told them that was as far as she was going to go. Tippy, who was the first one naked and, to her chagrin, didn't have to lap Cool Whip off anyone, offered to substitute for Prissy.

Holding the open container, still deliberating with a huge tablespoon of Cool Whip that she'd scooped out of it, Prissy finally told them she'd stick it on herself but only if Moses would tell them why or how, with all these naked women staring at him, he hadn't had an erection. "Maybe that's part of your Love You program," she said with a challenging look at Moses. "You could keep everything safe and respectable with impotent love therapists."

Moses grinned at M'mm. "That may be a good idea," he said. But when Prissy stood naked in front of him and calmly spread the Cool Whip on her lush breasts and delta, Moses delighted them all by lapping it off and rising to the occasion.

Ignoring their screams of approval, he turned on the hi-fi and put a jumping rock-record on the turntable. Then he led them all through the house laughing and yelling and kicking in a happy snake-dance. They didn't even break the chain when he opened the door to the back patio and led them into three feet of new snow. Before they could retreat, he swept his arms around them and tumbled all of them, screaming, into a snowdrift.

"Time for a snow massage," he yelled. "Grab any handy flesh and rub snow on it. Very good for your skin." Slipping and sliding, M'mm, who was massaging and being massaged, caught a glimpse of Tippy. She was rubbing snow on Moses's balls and penis. To save himself, he picked up a huge handful of it and gave her ass a deep freeze.

A few minutes later, they were all back in the living room and Moses was showing them how to do knee/ankle rolls, thigh tightening dances, buttock tighteners, breast lifters, and hip swings. It occurred to M'mm as she followed his instructions that exercising naked with a naked male leader was much more interesting than being organized for body-conditioning or weight-watching by a dominant female in leotards. Watching Moses's bouncing genitals made the exercises much more exhilarating. Moses evidently felt the same way, because he complimented them all on their pretty behinds and their smiling vulvas.

In the kitchen, still naked, they watched M'mm whip up a batch of lettuce soap. While that was cooking Moses poured a cup of vodka to which he added oil of bergamot, oil of lavender, oil of lemon, verbena and three drops of tincture of ambergris and three of musk. Shaking it well, announcing that it was Love You cologne, he patted it on their breasts and behinds and told them that the Love You Cosmetics session was over and that they should now get dressed, and he wished Tippy and Prissy a happy Thanksgiving and hoped that they would find time to play with their spouses that night.

Thanksgiving night, drifting in and out of sleep, remembering that before she had put the turkey on the dining-room table that afternoon she had been so aroused video-taping Moses's flute that she had told him: "It's your turn, my Lord. Eat my essence. Drink the waters of release. Oh, be my son! Be my slave! Be my father as well as my lover!" She had read it in *Sexual Secrets*.

Smiling at the memory, almost asleep for a moment, she thought she was dreaming. The front doorbell was chiming insistently. Someone was at the front door!

She leaped out of the tangle of Moses's legs. Whoever it was, was now pounding and ringing the bell at the same time. The digital clock on the dresser clicked eleven-forty-one. It couldn't be Tippy or Prissy. Moses beat her to the front window. A Rolls Royce convertible, headlights still on, was in the driveway. He almost yelled, "Jesus, it's the Byrdwhistle Rolls!" but even in extremity his mind censored the name Byrdwhistle.

"Oh, my God," M'mm gasped. "What are we going to do? It's Ron." How can he be back from Yugoslavia so soon? Why didn't those morons at the airport telephone me?"

Paralyzed with fear, she watched Moses scooting around the bedroom and bathroom. "I feel like the lover in Chaucer's *Miller's Tale*," he said. M'mm couldn't believe it. She was terrified, and Moses was grinning at her, "Too bad I didn't lean a ladder against the back of the house." He gathered his clothing and shaving kit. Somehow, M'mm found her nightgown and pulled it over her head. "Give Ron a hug for me," Moses told her. "I'll leave by the garage."

Downstairs they could hear Ron yelling.

"Wait a minute, Ron," M'mm yelled back. "Have patience, don't wake the whole damned neighborhood. I'm coming." She had a grim vision of Tippy watching the scene from her bedroom window across the street.

"You can't get the van out of the garage," M'mm was trembling. She tried to get a grip on herself. "Ron parked the Rolls in front of the garage door."

Moses paused on the landing. Clutching him she whispered, "What if Ron insists on putting his damned car in the garage?"

Moses shrugged. "You either talk him out of it, or you'll have to introduce him to your lover." By this time Moses had reached the kitchen and the inside door to the garage. He kissed her nose. "Stop worrying—there's a mattress in the van. I'll sieep in the garage."

"You can't. You'll freeze to death."

"Better than dying at the hands of an irate husband. I'll see you in the morning after Ron's gone to work."

"I'll have to go with him," M'mm wailed.

"Why?"

"I promised Ralph Thiemost."

"Don't go. You'll get in worse trouble."

"I have to. He's going to fire Ron if I don't talk with him."

Ron was still pounding on the front door. M'mm had almost made up her mind. She'd have to let Ron in and face the consequences. "Maybe I should brave it out," she told Moses. "I'll introduce you to each other. 'Ron, meet my Uncle Moses.'"

"Not tonight," Moses told her. Shivering, she followed him into the garage. He pushed her back into the kitchen. "Let Ron in. But for God's sake keep him out of the living room until you hide the camera and video tapes. After he's in bed bring me some blankets. I'll sleep in the garage and leave tomorrow after you've gone."

By the time she removed the night latch and let Ron in, M'mm resembled a victim of St. Vitus' dance. "I'm sorry," she stuttered, "I wasn't expecting you. I was on the toilet. I have diarrhea." And that was no lie. If her intestines didn't fall on the floor right now, she was sure they would before she got upstairs.

"What the hell is going on?" Ron demanded. "I tried to come in through the garage, and through the patio. You've got the place locked up like San Quentin."

"I was alone and I was afraid. You scared the hell out of me."

Ron dropped his suitcase in the front hall. "I'm sorry. I expected to be home this afternoon and have Thanksgiving dinner with you—but we ran into bad weather. We had to fly in via Goose Bay. I'm pooped."

"You better go right up to bed," M'mm was mentally reciting Hail Marys. "I'll fix you a turkey sandwich."

"I'm not hungry. I've got to put the Rolls in the garage."

M'mm took his arm firmly. "No you don't. Let the Rolls stay out. It's a nice night."

To M'mm's relief, he went out and turned off the headlights and got his suitcase from the front hall. She followed him upstairs. While he undressed she visually checked the much rumpled bed and spotted Moses's tie on the floor. She caught it with her toe and pushed it under the bed. Wondering about the bathroom, M'mm followed Ron in and noticed while he was brushing his teeth that a can of Moses's shaving cream—very definitely not the kind Ronald used—was sitting near the basin. But Ron hadn't seen it, and when he left she tossed it into the clothes hamper.

"You certainly had a fast trip," she said, wondering what excuse she could muster to spend a few minutes downstairs. Poor Moses, he must be freezing! But worse, those damned video-tapes were strewn all over the living room, together with the camera and the lights. Lessening her guilt was the sudden thought of Adele Youman. Fighting fire with fire might be her only salvation. "I understand that you flew to Yugoslavia with Adele."

Ronald looked at her blankly.

"Before you left, you told me that Adele was already in Dubrovnik."

Flopping on the bed, Ronald muttered. "Obviously, you've been talking with Ralph Thiemost. Did you invite him to dinner?"

"No—God-dammit. He wanted to come, but I didn't invite him."

"All right," Ronald said wearily. "I lied to you. You were being such a pain in the ass telling me that I was sleeping with my mother, I thought it would be simpler if I told you that Adele wasn't around. Anyway, you can restrain your imagination. We weren't alone. We were chaperoned. Three Byrdwhistlers, plus the pilot and his wife were on the plane." Ron knew that he was weaving a tangled web, but how could he tell her that it wasn't easy keeping Adele out of his bed, especially when she had really tried to help him find the Love Rocks and was as worried about his problems with Byrdwhistle as he was. If he hadn't been such a good husband, instead of coming home tonight he could have been sleeping on her merry-go-round.

"So you have been to bed with Adele Youman?" M'mm was suddenly feeling very much happier about her competition. If Ron should discover Moses sleeping in the garage, at least it was tit for tat.

"I didn't say that," Ronald said. "For God's sake M'mm, I'm not like most men you know, including Ralph Thiemost. I can be friends and work with a woman without wanting to go to bed with her. Please, let's talk about it tomorrow. I just took a valium. I'm half-asleep."

"What about the Love Rocks? Did you get them?" M'mm was feeling more confident. Somehow, she'd get upstairs to Moses in the garage.

"No," Ronald groaned. "A Yugoslavian beach-boy at Sveti Stefan told us that Thornton Byrd had arrived in the *Love Byrd.* He evidently found where Youman had stashed them. Several local Slavs confirmed that Thornton had them. He hired a dozen or more people. They cleaned all the beaches in the vicinity and they picked up every rock that was either circular or oval and measured at least two inches in diameter. There is not a damned thing left on any beaches that matches the Love Rocks in the Byrdwhistle catalogue. Nothing you could sell to anybody for ten bucks." Ronald stared at M'mm, "Christ Almighty, I'm getting as nutty as the rest of them. No damned rock is worth ten dollars, not unless it's got gold in it."

M'mm was a little bewildered. "Where are the Love Rocks now?"

"I told you, Thornton Byrd's got them. They're on the *Love Byrd*. He must have at least a half-million of them."

"Where's Thornton?"

"Only God and H. H. Youman know."

M'mm frowned. "How could Youman know? I thought he was senile."

"That doesn't mean that he doesn't know. Thiemost told us via radiophone that he's convinced that Youman is faking, or if Youman is really over the hill then Ralph wants you and Adele to go to work on him and convince him to tell us where the Rocks are and that he must turn them over to Byrdwhistle or the purchase agreement is invalid."

"Me and Adele!" For a moment M'mm completely forgot that Moses was waiting for her in the garage. "You must be crazy. I'm not kissing Adele Youman's ass for you or anyone!"

"M'mm—you don't even know her," Ronald said.

"I sure as hell don't want to know her," M'mm said. "And I can't understand why you're so happy with her either. She screwed you and Ralph Thiemost with her damned photographs. And what's more Ronald Coldaxe, it's very damn peculiar to me that you didn't dare tell me that you had been naked with her."

Ronald sighed, "Believe it or not, I didn't pose for those pictures. But you're getting to the point. As you no doubt have discovered, Ralph is very pissed off with me. It's his contention that you may be my last hope. You can save my ass and Adele's at the same time."

"How can I save your ass? Why would Youman want to talk with me? I never met him."

Ronald grinned feebly at her. "Marge Slick told Ralph that before H.H. cracked up he had said he had a soft spot in his heart for me. He actually told Adele that he had willed me his merry-go-round. He thought that I was the best one to succeed him. He thought that I was a potential Byrdwhistler."

"Are you?"

Ronald sighed. "The decision may not be mine. If Thiemost fires me, who the hell is going to hire me? I might just as well give up and play." Ronald gave a little snore. "Please, M'mm I'm falling asleep."

Before she ran downstairs, to make sure that he was asleep M'mm patted Ron's cheek gently. She felt like slapping it good and hard instead, and would have if Moses weren't in the garage. Ron's eyes didn't open. "I'm going to make some hot milk," she whispered to him. "It's supposed to be good for diarrhea—and a nervous stomach."

43

A few minutes later, carrying blankets, stumbling over the lawnmower and garden tools left by the former owner of the house, M'mm found a path through the unlighted garage and crawled into the van. Moses was sitting on the mattress wearing an overcoat.

"Nice to see you again," he grabbed her and hugged her enthusiastically. "It's been a long time."

"I'm not sure that Ron's really asleep." She was suddenly afraid that he might have followed her downstairs. But Moses was oblivious to her fears. He was exploring her body under her bathrobe and nightgown. With one hand on her vulva, he was happily kissing her breasts.

Shivering both from jittery nerves and the cold, damp garage, M'mm tried to pull away from him. "For God's sake, stop it! You really are a sex maniac. How can you keep kissing me when you don't even know how you're going to get out of here?"

Moses laughed, "I didn't get a chance to say goodbye to you properly." He knew that he couldn't sleep in the van all night. He'd promised Victor Watchman that he would meet him at eight-thirty in the morning with five thousand dollars worth of grease to put in the Thiemost frying pan. Even if M'mm managed to get Ron out of the house and on his way to work without finding the van in the garage—and that was a long-shot—he would have to leave Lynnfield at about the same time or even earlier. Earlier was obviously impossible, since the Rolls was parked on the other side of the garage door. To complicate the problem, he hadn't expected that Ronald would be back from Yugoslavia when Watchman and Goodbody raided Byrdwhistle and dragged Thiemost off to the jug. If both Coldaxe and his wife were in the Byrdwhistle office tomorrow, Marge might not be able to entice Thiemost into a juicy whipping scene or coordinate it for the arrival of the police.

He gave M'mm's breasts an affectionate goodnight kiss and told her not to worry. "Go back to bed," he told her. "And in the morning just make sure that you keep Ron out of the garage. If you insist on going to Byrdwhistle with him, tell him that after you've talked with Thiemost— and get it over with as quickly as possible—you're going shopping. Meet me in the lobby of the Sheraton Hotel at noon."

"Is the Sheraton near the Center for Ageless Humans?"

Moses was happy that M'mm couldn't see his mouth gaping in surprise at her question. "Just a few blocks," he said. Why?"

"Ron told me that I'm supposed to meet Adele Youman at the center at about ten o'clock tomorrow morning. I'm supposed to give Youman a sob story and find out where he's keeping those silly Love Rocks." She kissed Moses goodnight and grinned at him, "I've been thinking about Rabbenu Gershom. Maybe I will marry you."

Twenty minutes after she left, Moses felt his way through the garage into the kitchen. It was obvious that, if he wanted to postpone the demise and quick burial of Moses Marshalik the next morning, he had to make a spectacular end-run around the combined onslaught of Adele and Meredith.

Hoping that M'mm was finally in bed with Ronald, he located the kitchen telephone and dialed his only possible rescue team.

"Tell Fred to climb off your lovely body," he said in a hushed voice in response to Marge Slick's sleepy hello. Get your sled out. Harness up the dogs. Yell mush! I'm trapped in a snowdrift a few miles north of Boston, and the wolves are howling and ready to eat me." He laughed softly, "I'm sorry to interrupt your sex-making."

"Fred dreams about it more than he does it," Marge sounded indignant. "Right now he's happily snoring beside me. Where the hell are you? Did Ronald Coldaxe catch the two M'mm's together in the sack?

"Why didn't you telephone me when you found out that he had come back?" Moses demanded. "You should have warned me."

"How could I? What would I have told your new bed-friend? Am I supposed to know that M'mm is sleeping with a meshugna cosmetic peddler?"

Moses was sure that he heard someone moving around upstairs.

"Listen, if I keep talking, Ronald Coldaxe will be arrested tomorrow morning for the murder of Moses Marshalik. Get out your Boston street directory. Tell Fred I hate to disturb his sleep, but if you don't pick me up in forty-five minutes I'll be frozen stiff under a streetlight at the beginning of Cabot Lane in Lynnfield. It's not far from the turnpike exit. Don't miss it. We've got a lot of decisions to make. I don't want to postpone your behind-whipping, but I didn't expect Coldaxe would be in the middle of it."

An hour later, after waking Fred and telling him that she was going down to Byrdwhistle to catch up on some important work she had left, she warned him that, if he noticed Thiemost going into her office the next day and the lady from SUGS didn't appear in the next five minutes, he should break the door down.

Marge turned off a narrow suburban street in Lynnfield and stopped her Mercedes next to a forlorn night-prowler huddled in an overcoat under a flickering streetlamp.

Moses waved at her feebly and got into the car. "God, it took you long enough," he grumbled. "Where's Fred?"

"You seem to have forgotten. Fred thinks you are a vegetable rotting in the Center for Ageless Humans," Marge laughed. "If he thought about it, he'd have guessed the truth. Old goats never quit."

"That's how they get to be old goats," Moses hugged her. "I thought that by this time you would have finally told Fred the truth."

"You made me promise not to tell anyone," Marge patted his cheek. "I'm faithful to you even if you're not to me."

"Marge," Moses sighed, "you know I love you, too."

"Good," Marge turned the car around. "I'm tired. Where are we sleeping for the rest of the night?" She grinned, "It's all right. If Fred knew that I was going to be with you, I'm sure he'd give me his permission."

Moses couldn't help grinning. He never expected to plunge into two jade fountains in one night. But it was Thanksgiving. "In the center, where else? And I really have to sleep. By tomorrow morning, we've got to figure out how H. H. Youman is going to tell Meredith Coldaxe where his Love Rocks are without her meeting Moses Marshalik."

"Why don't you give up and confess?" Marge demanded. "If she bought all your love therapist nonsense, she'll still love you anyway."

Marge slowed the car down for a moment. "Did I hear you say you were going to tell her where your Love Rocks are?"

Moses laughed, "I'm going to keep mumbling horny, horny."

"You mean Thorny?"

"Same thing!"

"Where is Thorny? Damn you, Hyman. Why are you being so secretive with me?"

Moses shrugged, "Thorny is somewhere on the high seas sleeping with the Love Rocks. Keep in mind that I told all the Byrdwhistlers when we were in Portamaio not to panic, that Youman would return. But I want him to do it dramatically on Monday night at the Colonial Theater, and hopefully without Ralph Thiemost."

Spooned into Ronald's back, her arm around his stomach, M'mm tried to get readjusted to the feel of her husband. Moses was bonier, and it was unlikely that Ron would ever sleep with her all night, Samoan style, in the posture of the crow. But that wasn't really bothering her. Her brain was searching madly through her limited marital programming for a longtime solution, a way of life that would let her have her cake and eat it too. Ronald for breakfast, Moses for lunch, Ronald for dinner. She sighed, the only print-out her brain could muster was "Insufficient data" or "Try Rabbenu Gershom."

Moses had told her that the Jewish side of his ancestry extended back to the Ashkenazy Jews. In the year 985, Rabbenu Gershom, a very wise rabbi, called a Rabbinical synod in the town of Worms. An edict was issued ordering that for the next thousand years Jewish males must give up polygamy and have only one wife. This would keep the envious Christian males off their backs and help stop Jewish persecution. The thousand years were nearly over, and soon there wouldn't be any religious restraint. Polygamy would be back in style.

"I suppose," M'mm had told him a little sourly, "that you're planning on having two wives. Sorry, chum, I refuse to be number two."

Moses grinned, "Women have come a long way since Gershom. Now there's an alternative. You can marry me and have two husbands."

The digital clock had flicked from five-fifty-nine to six o'clock, and M'mm knew that she could delay no longer. If Ron woke up, she'd never get a chance to see if husband number two had made it through the night.

When she opened the van, Moses wasn't there. He had left a note, which said, "See you at the Sheraton. Leave the garage door unlocked. I'll have some elves rescue the van."

Two hours later, driving to Byrdwhistle in the Rolls, M'mm congratulated herself. Ron hadn't shown any interest in the garage or in any of the subtle disarray that was so apparent in the kitchen, which overflowed with cosmetic bottles and jars. He hadn't seen all the pillows out of place in the living room or the records strewn around, nor the Steven Halpern cassette that was still in the tape deck. Last night, afraid to go back in the garage with Moses, she had hidden the video equipment and the two tapes in the front-hall closet. If Tippy and Prissy would only keep their mouths shut, and after the way they had carried on with Moses that should be no problem, she could still be a happily innocent housewife going to work to help her husband soothe his irate boss.

But that was a problem. She decided that she shouldn't report her conversation with Marge Slick to Ron. If she did, it might mean belatedly telling him about her disastrous meeting with Ralph Thiemost—and, worse, coming up with a reason for not telling him sooner. Whatever was going to happen at Byrdwhistle that afternoon was Ron's problem. She didn't have to stay there all day and listen to Thiemost. Moses would be waiting for her at the Sheraton. After four days with Moses, her only concern was how they would adjust to the simple act of eating together before kissing and tasting each other as hors d'oeuvres.

Interrupting her thoughts, Ronald was trying to explain to her that Adele was positive that Sheldon Coombs had stolen the negatives of the pictures she had taken of Thiemost from her darkroom. "We've got to find Coombs and stop him," Ronald said. "I haven't seen that mailing he sent out to W.I.N. employees yet, but he's determined to give Ralph and me a bad reputation. He's trying to make us look like the bad guys who are wrecking both Byrdwhistle and W.I.N. Incorporated."

Ronald gestured at an ivy-covered building before he turned the Rolls into the Byrdwhistle garage. "This is it," he said. "We're here. I know you hate Thiemost and I agree with you. He's a bastard, but please don't shoot your mouth off. If you want to continue to live like a princess, be sweet and talk nice to him."

"I'm married to you," M'mm told him. "I'm not a princess, I'm an old bitch queen. What if he still wants me to be his director of publicity? What if he offers me a special perk—the pleasure of his company in bed occasionally?"

"All I'm asking is that you palaver him a little," Ronald said patiently. "You can stop all this crap. I'm not trying to sell your body to anyone."

A man ran up to them as they got out of the Rolls. "Glad to see you back, Mr. Coldaxe. Thiemost is upstairs already. Marge wants to talk with you. She says to use the elevator in the lobby. She's waiting there for you."

"How did she know I was back?" Ronald demanded.

The man shrugged, "Don't know. Maybe Nick or Maria told her."

M'mm gasped when she saw Marge. Naked to the waist, wearing only a dark blue skirt that matched her eyes, Marge's natural blond hair was piled high on her head. Her full breasts seemed to be living a happy life of their own and smiling at Ron. But her eyes, even bluer than M'mm's, seemed friendly. "Welcome to Byrdwhistle," she greeted M'mm, with a quick kiss on her cheek, "or what's left of it since Thiemost arrived." M'mm sensed that Marge wasn't going to mention their phone conversation, but she quickly realized that Marge wasn't too happy that Ron had returned so soon.

"I wish you could have stayed in Yugoslavia until Monday," Marge said. "Maybe by then things would have cooled down a little. Thiemost is in a rage. When he telephoned the airport, they told him that you got back last night. He expected you to telephone him."

"It was too damned late. Anyway, I haven't got the Love Rocks."

"The Love Rocks are the least of his problems," Marge said. "I knew you wouldn't have time to catch up on your *Wall Street Journal,* so I thought I'd fill you in. You and Thiemost are national celebrities. The whole story of the World Corporation take-over attempt was in the *Journal* on Tuesday. They even included line drawings of you and Ralph bare-assed. Of course your genitals aren't showing, as they are in the brochure that World sent out."

"I haven't seen that damned mailing yet." Ronald frowned at M'mm, "You're not hiding it from me, are you?"

M'mm shrugged. "Your genitals belong to you. You can flash them on whomever you please. But if I were you I wouldn't be too happy with Mother Adele."

Marge grinned a sympatico grin at M'mm. "Thiemost most certainly isn't. He was on the phone with her for half an hour. But that's not all," she said. "W.I.N. stock has dropped to nine-fifty a share. Rumors are that World is going to get the necessary financing and is going to be able to gobble up enough stock to take over the company."

"What happens to W.I.N. is not my fault," Ronald said emphatically. "I told Ralph that he should never have got involved with Youman. Youman was a god-damned maniac before he went crazy."

Ron pointed at the portrait of King Gillette hanging on the wall and said to M'mm, "There's one of the ancestors that Youman adopted." Ronald scowled, "Before he cracked up, Youman even looked a little like Gillette."

M'mm had already been staring at the painting, wondering why it looked so familiar. Then it dawned on her that Gillette looked a little like Moses Marshalik, too!

In the elevator, Marge told Ronald that Thiemost was waiting for him in Youman's old office. "You might as well know the rest. The lawyers haven't been able to settle the lawsuit against Club Wholesome. Thiemost saw the video-tapes yesterday. The same one the Texas police have. And he's not very happy with me either. It's the same tape that Fred and I made with a couple of other Byrdwhistlers."

Ronald whistled, "That's one of Club Wholesome's best-selling tapes."

"Thiemost doesn't give a damn. He's ready to shut down Club Wholesome."

"Is it a sex tape?" M'mm asked. Then she asked Ron why he hadn't brought it home.

"I didn't think that you liked that kind of stuff." Ronald grinned at Marge, "Actually it's kind of harmless—no ins and outs—just Marge and Fred naked and another woman and her husband hugging each other."

Marge thought that M'mm was a bit distressed, and so she changed the subject. "One other thing you should know is that, even though Elmer is subsidizing the entire cost of tickets for the opening of *Rum Ho!,* there's a slowdown. No one is working the way they used to. Redman and Taylor put up notices yesterday that, effective Monday, Byrdwhistle is going to operate on a strict nine-to-five schedule. Timeclocks are going to be installed. Nudity is no longer permitted. Anyone who swims in the pool must wear a bathing suit."

"You don't seem to be obeying the rules," Ronald said.

Marge laughed, "Neither is anybody else. Even Byrdwhistlers who never undressed before are running around naked. It's a kind of rebellion."

They found Ralph sitting grimly behind Youman's desk. Ronald noticed that Adele's self-portrait was no longer hanging on the wall. "God dammit, Ron," Thiemost said angrily, "I told you yesterday to call me when you arrived. I still can't figure out what in hell possessed you to take off on a vacation with Adele Youman in the middle of a total crisis."

Ronald's face turned red. "I wasn't on a vacation with Adele, and you know it." And then, trying to keep his voice calm, he said, "It was very late when we got home. Have you got any marine information on the *Love Byrd*?"

"Fuck the *Love Byrd*!" Thiemost shouted. "Trying to find a ship in the Atlantic is like looking for a needle in a haystack. We don't even know if Thornton Byrd is headed this way or not. At the moment, he's the least of my worries."

Ralph frowned at M'mm and said to Ron, "Your wife has been too busy to talk with me." He grinned nastily at Meredith. "She was very evasive on the telephone the other day. You better keep an eye on her. I think she may have other male friends beside you and me."

M'mm wanted to sock him, but now Thiemost turned to Marge, who had followed them into his office. Thiemost was staring at Marge's breasts. "God dammit, Mrs. Slick, do me a favor and put a bra over your tits. Get dressed. And stop playing footsies with these Byrdwhistlers." He looked at his watch. "It's nine-fifteen. Call a cab for Mrs. Coldaxe. Adele Youman will be waiting for her at the center. After you've got her in the cab, come back here. We've got a lot of problems to settle and I want to brief you both on how to handle Victor Watchman if he shows up today."

Thiemost's parting words to M'mm were, "I just talked to Adele and to that asshole Alexi Ivanowski who runs the center. They both know that those missing rocks are a serious problem. Ivanowski agrees with me. Youman might respond to a woman in distress. Believe me, Mrs. Coldaxe, you are in distress! Put on a good tearful act and find out where he's hiding those stinking Love Rocks. I'll expect you to report back here by noontime, and I've got some personal things I want to discuss with you and Ron."

Marge led M'mm into her office. Grinning at her, she phoned for a cab and said, "With a little luck, our nasty friend Thiemost is going to get his goose cooked this afternoon. Take my advice, don't come back here today. And this is important, when you get to the center, telephone Ron. Tell him to meet you for lunch. He's going to be a hell of a lot happier if he's not around here when the bomb bursts."

"I'm not planning to come back," M'mm said. "I can't meet Ron for lunch either. I have another engagement. And Ron knows damned well that I'm not very happy with him or Thiemost. I'll go to the center because I want to meet this bitch Adele Youman, but I'm not going to help her con her poor, sick husband. And I'm not going to shed any tears over a doddering idiot either, or try to seduce him. According to Ron, the damned rocks belong to Youman anyway." M'mm shook her head, "I don't see why you put up with this insanity."

Marge laughed, "As Ron would say, 'It's a living.' Anyway, we all like your husband. We don't want him to get hurt. We have great hopes for Ron. Many of us here think he's married to a potential Byrdwhistler." She took M'mm's arm affectionately, "The cab will be waiting downstairs. I really wanted to take you on a tour of the place, Meredith. Come back next week when things have calmed down. Who knows, one day Ron might even offer you a job. I'm sure you could pass the entrance exam."

"Ron's a long way from letting his wife run around bare-ass in mixed company." M'mm looked at Marge speculatively, "You're a very attractive woman. Do you mind if I ask you a personal question?"

Marge shook her head.

"Have you slept with Ron in one of your Love Rooms?"

Marge chuckled. "No one sleeps in the Byrdwhistle Love Rooms," she said. And then she decided she'd better be honest. "Before W.I.N. bought Byrdwhistle, I purposely tried to seduce your husband. But now, if Ron asked me to spend a few hours in one of the Love Rooms, he'd have to ask your permission. It's a Byrdwhistle rule."

Walking out of Byrdwhistle to the waiting cab, it occurred to M'mm that, after her last week with Moses Marshalik, giving Ron permission to snuggle on Marge Slick's big tits didn't seem quite so horrendous an idea as she might have once thought.

Adele and Alexi Ivanowski were waiting for her in the lobby of the center. Before M'mm could retreat from this willowy woman, whose wind-ruffled white hair framed a lean, tanned face unmarked by time, Adele embraced and kissed her lovingly on both cheeks. "I didn't even have to ask," she bubbled, and M'mm noticed that her eyes were tear-filled. "Ron has told me so much about you. I love you, too." With her arm around M'mm she introduced her to Alexi. "Oh dear, I don't know whether to be happy or sad. Heman is cured! He's well! He's got his mind back! But poor Ron may be in serious trouble."

Aided by Alexi, trying to adjust herself to the good news that she wouldn't have to put on an act for H. H. Youman and that Adele didn't seem to be either an ogre or a femme fatale, M'mm pieced the story together.

"It really is a miracle," Alexi was smiling jubilantly. "Just an hour ago, poor H.H. was in such bad shape that I thought we might have to transfer him to a sanitarium where he could receive intensive care. He was literally banging his head against the wall. We were so afraid that he might hurt himself that we had to cover his head with a sponge rubber mask, and we bandaged him up like an Egyptian mummy. When Adele told me that you were coming to talk with him, I didn't think we could let you see him. You never would have recognized him."

"I never met him," M'mm said, "I haven't the faintest idea what he looks like."

"Oh, you'll just love Heman," Adele said. "All the women do. He's very handsome. Right now, I'm ecstatic. Heman is well again! Before I flew to Yugoslavia with Ron, my son Haskell—Hasky, who is a surgeon

in New York City—told me there might be one cure that would work."
Adele smiled brightly at M'mm. "Even though we didn't find the rocks,
you were so nice to let Ron go with me. I couldn't have done it alone."

M'mm frowned and tried to get Adele back on the track. "You said
your son cured H. H. Youman?"

"Not exactly," Alexi broke in. "Haskell suggested that some kind of
personal shock might jar H.H. back to reality. If a patient suffering
from this kind of mental deterioration hears something that really pene-
trates his brain cells, figuratively of course, it has often proved more
effective than electric-shock therapy. In some cases a complete and
immediate remission occurs." Alexi was so happy to be rid of Youman
that he would have sworn to the medical truth of his statements. "The
problem was to find the key to turn the lock."

"Haskell told me that I should tell Heman that I was going to divorce
him and marry Ralph Thiemost," Adele laughed. "But I was afraid that
Heman would just give me his blessings. A week ago, I told him that I
was going to have a baby!" Adele's brown eyes were dancing merrily,
"But instead of getting upset he seemed happy. I'm sure he thought that
he was the father. Then I told him I couldn't have the baby because I
might have leprosy, but he only smiled."

"You should have told him that Ronald Coldaxe was the father,"
M'mm said to herself grimly.

"And then, early this morning, Thornton Byrd radio-phoned from
the *Love Byrd*. Poor Thornton, he shocked me so much I hoped it might
have the same effect on Heman." Tears were gathering once again in
Adele's eyes. "Oh honey, I don't know what Ron is going to do. When
that dreadful Victor Watchman finds out what's happening he'll most
certainly put Ron in jail. It's incredible. All the time that Ronnie was
searching for Love Rocks in Yugoslavia, Thorny had them on board the
Love Byrd and was sailing to Boston with them."

"Right now the *Love Byrd* is caught in a very bad storm somewhere
north of Cape Hatteras," Alexi added.

"But it's leaking badly," Adele wailed. "Thorny has put out a Mayday. A
tanker nearly two hundred miles away has responded, but Thorny thinks
they may have to abandon ship before it arrives. If they don't get assistance,
the *Love Byrd* will sink to the bottom of the Atlantic with a half-million
Love Rocks aboard," Adele giggled through her tears. "Dear God! What am
I laughing at? But Heman was so funny. A half-hour ago when I told him,
he jumped right out of his wheelchair. He ripped off his bandages and his
hospital johnny. Jumping up and down, he yelled, "For God's sake Adele,
get me some clothes. I've got to save my Love Rocks. If I don't, Byrdwhistle
will go down the drain and Ronald Coldaxe will end up behind bars."

M'mm was suddenly frightened. "Ron hasn't done anything illegal.
He just inherited this Byrdwhistle mess. If your husband talks to that

man from the Federal Trade Commission, he'll set him straight. Where is Heman?"

"He took a taxi to the airport." Adele nodded at a nurse who was summoning her to the telephone. "Maybe that's Heman. He told me that he was going to rent a helicopter and fly out to the *Love Byrd*. Poor Thorny, if it's a choice between him and the Love Rocks, I'm afraid Thorny's about to meet his maker."

M'mm followed her to the telephone.

Adele listened a moment and then stared at M'mm. "Oh mon Dieu! Yes, I did, Marge. I did! I begged Ronnie to have lunch with me today. He usually does, but he told me last night that with Thiemost in town he couldn't possibly get away. Yes, Meredith is here." Adele looked at her watch. "It's eleven-thirty. I really don't think we can make it in time. In the noon traffic it will take us at least forty-five minutes." Adele handed the phone to M'mm. "It's Marge Slick. She wants to talk with you."

Not at all pleased to learn that Ron had been having lunch regularly with Adele Youman, M'mm took the phone. "Ever since you left, I've been trying to get Ron to leave the building," Marge said. She sounded really jittery. "But he won't listen to me. He's in conference with Thiemost and the W.I.N. lawyers. Meredith, please trust me. In the next half-hour, the top is going to blow off. I'm going to transfer this call to Ron. Tell him anything. Tell him to tell Thiemost that he has to go to the men's room. Instead he should run, not walk, to the front door and get the hell out of here."

Ronald picked up the phone, and M'mm could hear him say, grimly, "I told you Marge, no calls. We're trying to resolve this damned World Corporation take-over crisis."

"You've got a bigger crisis," M'mm yelled. "The *Love Byrd* is sinking somewhere in the Atlantic, and all your Love Rocks are on board. You better take a taxi to the airport immediately and help H. H. Youman. He's trying to save them."

"M'mm," Ronald said coldly, "I never should have let you talk with H.H. Don't listen to him, He's telling you some kind of cock-and-bull story. Go shopping. Be back here about five. I'm sorry. I can't talk with you now." Ronald hung up.

M'mm was sobbing now, "He wouldn't listen to me. Did Marge tell you what's going to happen?"

Adele shook her head.

"I think she's going to try to seduce Thiemost and get him arrested on a morals charge, and she's afraid that Ron will get mixed up in the scene when the police arrive."

"Come on," said Adele, dragging M'mm toward the door. "We've got to save our baby!"

44

But they were too late. Automobiles were honking impatiently as they inched through Boston. The taxi driver threw up his hands and told Adele to get off his back, the cab didn't have wings. On Charles Street, M'mm spotted a clock on a building. It said twelve noon, and she remembered Moses Marshalik with a hollow feeling in her stomach. Would Moses think that she had decided to call it quits? She wanted to tell him telepathically that, although she had been scared silly when Ron arrived, without her love therapist life in Lynnfield would be dullsville. And she wondered if Moses had rescued the Marsha Lovett van from her garage. Unless she tried to contact him in the YMCA—and she really didn't believe he lived there, the YWCA would have been more appropriate—it would be two more days until she saw him again. What would she do if he didn't appear on her doorstep Monday morning? God! What was she going to do about Moses Marshalik and herself anyway? Maybe it would be better if he never came back. Adele Youman might be married to a man who didn't care if she had a few playmates in her life, but Ronald Coldaxe wasn't that kind of man. If he had discovered Moses in her bed, he would have murdered them both.

But now, listening to Adele, who was sitting beside her in the taxi, blithely telling her that she had encouraged Ronnie to keep his head shaved because it made him look so masculine, it occurred to M'mm that having a wife hadn't deterred Ron from enjoying a little extracurricular loving. Why shouldn't she? As Moses had told her, what else in life was important anyway?

And Adele, harassing the cabdriver and telling him how to maneuver in the traffic, didn't look as motherly as M'mm had expected. She couldn't suppress a grin. For a moment she wanted to tell Adele about Moses and his idea of employing older men as love therapists. Adele might not look like Ron's mother, but Moses was the best-looking daddy she'd seen in a long time. Even though she wasn't quite so angry or jealous of Adele as she had been and was somewhat entranced by the dumb-bunny sophistication of this woman—who was probably smarter than most men she tangled with—M'mm knew that it was too soon to be completely honest with her.

"Poor Ralph," Adele said, confirming M'mm's suspicion that, despite Thiemost's irritation with her, when push came to shove "poor Ralph" would tumble back into bed with Adele and forgive her. "Deep down he's really not a bad person," Adele chuckled. "But I do hope the Byrd-whistlers cook his goose a little. He telephoned me at six this morning and used the most awful language to me. He told me I was a tricky little

cunt and that I had given Sheldon Coombs the pictures of him and Ron."
Adele looked at M'mm beseechingly, "Oh honey, I hope you know I never
would do anything like that. And please don't be angry with me, but Ronnie looked so sweet in his birthday suit that I just had to immortalize him."

M'mm raised her eyebrows in amazement. "I lived in California all
my life," she said. "Half the population out there screws around with the
other half, but after a while they get mad at each other and get divorced.
You and your husband evidently go to bed with whomever you wish."
She paused, and then decided to grab the cow by its tail, "Including my
husband, but you and your husband stay married and don't get angry or
jealous of each other."

"I can assure you that Heman hasn't gone to bed with Ronnie." Laughing Adele hugged her, and M'mm didn't pull away. Resisting Adele was
like trying to lie flat on a water bed. "Both of us are totally heterosexual.
But we're not really promiscuous. In the past year, Heman has probably
been intimate with a couple of other women. I either know them already
and like them, or when Heman eventually introduces me to them, I like
them. Heman knows that I've loved Thorny for years and years. At
the moment, he doesn't approve of Ralph Thiemost and neither do I. But
sometimes, when Ralph isn't trying to be a winner, he can be very nice."

M'mm didn't want to contest Adele's vacillating appraisal of
Thiemost, but she was exasperated with her devious answer. "What
about Ron?" she demanded.

"Of course I love Ronnie." Adele sounded as if the word *love* ab-
solved her from any guilt, and M'mm wasn't able to contest that. If she
did, how could she justify Moses Marshalik?

"Before you came east, Ronnie spent a few nights with me, and we
slept together in Yugoslavia. But Ronnie really loves you, Meredith,"
Adele smiled at her. "I prefer to wake up in the morning with a friend
I've made love with, but I'm really no threat to you. Since the day you
arrived in Lynnfield, I've made sure that Ronnie was home at night. And
you should understand that I'm useful to Ron. A young man can relax
with an older woman. It's a rare marriage when spouses can be perfectly
honest with each other or reveal themselves completely. After a few years
of marriage, most spouses become too judgmental and too critical of the
person they live with day in and day out. Most of us who have been married for a long time don't dare admit that we're really quite childish and
never want to grow up. We're even afraid to play with each other. And
we'd be very nervous sharing the strange ideas that dash around in our
brains. I'm teaching Ronnie how to do this, how to let go. Eventually he
will dare to try with you. Ronnie knows that I adore Heman. But often I
need to escape from him, especially when he's adopted some crazy ancestor and tries to behave like him." Adele grinned, "People need occasional
changes of human scenery in order to survive."

The cabdriver was now bumping the cab over potholes on the side streets of Everett. With brakes screeching, he turned abruptly into a narrow street and was waved down by a policeman.

"Who the hell do you think you are?" the cop demanded. "Barney Oldfield?"

"Blame these broads. They said it was a matter of life and death," the driver pointed to an ivy-covered building flanking one side of the street. "That's Byrdwhistle, isn't it? What the hell is going on?"

Stepping out of the cab, Adele handed the driver twenty dollars.

They could see that the entire street was jammed with police cars, paddy wagons, and hundreds of people milling about and shouting. A siren was still blasting and blue lights were flashing ominously.

"Shut the fucking place down!" someone yelled.

"It's a disgrace to the city."

"Aw, I like Byrdwhistle. Don't encourage the fuzz. They're a pain in the poopic."

"Why don't they arrest the crooks and politicians and get off our backs?"

M'mm, followed by Adele, wiggled and squirmed through the crowds. It looked as though most of the people in the streets had run out of adjoining buildings to see what was happening.

"What's your hurry, lady?" someone yelled at her. "Are you a Byrdwhistler?"

M'mm said that she was, and the guy laughed at her. "You better not admit it. No more screwing while you work, honey. Regina Goodbody says it ain't nice. She's in there right now arresting everybody."

"Regina says this is Mass-no-ass-achusetts!"

But then, as they approached the Gothic arch of the front door, which was surrounded by police, it slid open and Byrdwhistlers came out dancing, skipping, laughing, singing "Let Us Go, Brothers, Go!" Most of them were bare-legged and wrapped in overcoats. A few of the women opened their coats and shook bare breasts and naked pelvises at the astonished policemen.

One woman threw herself around a young cop and said seductively, "If you take me back upstairs, I'll swim naked with you in our pool."

Another yelled, "Regina Goodbody is a dried up old prune. Go upstairs and squeeze her ass and see if there's any juice left."

"Yeah, ask Thiemost, he'll help you!"

A burly Irishman stared pop-eyed at a dozen or more men and women dancing in the streets, swirling with their coats wide open and exposing their naked or half-dressed bodies. "You better watch out," he yelled at them. "It's against the law to show yourself bare-ass in Everett, Massachusetts."

"Oh, go arrest the mayor!" a bystander yelled.

"They can't," another retorted. "They'd never catch him with his pants down."

"I'm the wife of the man who runs this company," M'mm told the policeman who was guarding the open door. "Let me through. I want to go up to the Byrdwhistle offices."

"Sorry lady. This isn't just Regina and her SUGS group doing a sex-bust. It's a federal raid, too. If your husband is Ronald Coldaxe, he's in big trouble." He pushed M'mm and Adele into the arms of a Byrd-whistler. "You wait here, your old man will be coming out."

One of the Byrdwhistlers recognized Adele. "Too bad that H.H. can't be here," she shouted. "He'd be tickled silly. That big time winner Ralph Thiemost is going to get shafted."

"What's happening?" Adele demanded.

"We're eliminating a few winners. We called the police and Regina caught Thiemost in the act, beating Marge Slick bare-ass!"

As he spoke, a half-dozen policemen came out of the building and broke through the cheering and booing crowd. Between two of them was Ralph Thiemost, handcuffed, blustering, and red-faced.

"Damn you!" he yelled at the laughing Byrdwhistlers. "I'll get you for this." He tried to shake loose from the determined cops who were leading him to the paddy wagon. "Can't you see these bastards framed me? The Governor of Massachusetts will hear about this."

Behind him, Bill Haley, his lawyer, was trying to soothe him. "We'll have you out within an hour, Ralph. Just keep cool."

Behind Thiemost, two more policemen were dragging a reluctant Ronald, who was cursing them all. He saw M'mm and yelled. "For God's sake, get me a lawyer. I don't want to get mixed up with Ralph. I'm not being arrested on a morals charge."

"Let him go," M'mm screamed, and she pounded the chest of one of the cops. "You can't arrest him. He's my husband."

"Get out of our way, ma'am. This man is a crook. He's being arrested for swindling Byrdwhistle customers out of millions of dollars. Take his advice. Get him a good lawyer."

Following them, escorted by two policemen but wearing only a mink coat, which she coolly flashed at M'mm and Adele, Marge Slick was waving her hands triumphantly at the cheering crowd.

"The police wouldn't let me get dressed," Marge was laughing so hard tears were running down her cheeks. "I've got to go down to the police station and swear out an assault and battery and attempted rape complaint against Thiemost. Ralph the winner is a dirty old sinner." She bussed Meredith's cheek. "When Regina and I get through with him, he'll swear off women for life."

M'mm and Adele followed her to the police cruiser. "What's going to happen to Ron?" they asked in unison.

Marge shook her head sorrowfully, "I told you to get him out of here. But don't worry. The only morals charge they have against Ron is playing fast and loose with Love Rocks."

Fred Slick followed Marge into the back seat of the cruiser. "I'll call Jack Siddley, the company lawyer," he told Adele. "You know him. He'll get Ron out right away. See you down at the station."

Marge hung out of the window of the car. "Take the Rolls, Meredith. With Thiemost and Ron gone, you're in charge. Don't let Redman and Taylor give you any bullshit."

The cruising car disappeared, wailing through the streets, just as Regina Goodbody appeared at the front door. She ignored the boos of the Byrdwhistlers. Buxom, blonde, and taller than Brunhilde, she towered over Victor Watchman, who was standing next to her. Standing at military attention like a concentration camp commander, Regina waved the Byrdwhistlers into silence. "Go back to work. SUGS isn't preferring any charges against any individuals of this depraved company except for Ralph Thiemost and Ronald Coldaxe." Regina sounded like a determined schoolteacher admonishing her naughty children. "From now on you don't have to work in this lewd, vile, immoral environment. You won't have to sell your bodies for a paycheck. These whore-masters who have been running this company, destroying morality, and ruining the family, are going to be behind bars. You won't have to go to Love Rooms and have orgies with your bosses or swim naked in the swimming pool." Regina ignored the boos and yells of the Byrdwhistlers. "You may not appreciate us now, but the Save Us, God, Society is on your side. Go back to work. Put on your clothes. God loves you. Byrdwhistle is no longer a sexual playpen."

While Regina was speaking, Adele had inched her way through the crowd toward Victor Watchman. He was nodding and clapping enthusiastically at Regina's words of wisdom. Adele grabbed Watchman by his coat and shook him. "Ronald Coldaxe is an innocent victim. My husband, Heman Hyman Youman, created Byrdwhistle. If you want to arrest someone arrest him. He'd scrunch a little worm like you."

Angrily, Watchman twisted out of her grasp. "Someone has to pay the piper," he yelled. "I don't give a damn about Youman. He sold this company to W.I.N. When they bought it they knew what was going on. I warned Coldaxe two weeks ago. He shouldn't have messed around with the Federal Trade Commission." Watchman grinned at her nastily. "We've been watching both of you for some time. We know that Coldaxe visits you every day. You should have told your boyfriend to give you back the money." Watchman patted her shoulder patronizingly. "I'm sorry, sister. Coldaxe may have balls for some things, but right now he needs rocks. Love Rocks."

Twenty minutes later, M'mm calmly drove one of the Rollses out of the Byrdwhistle garage. Adele insisted that it was theirs to use, and neither

Bill Redman nor Joe Taylor tried to stop them. Then she double-parked in front of the Everett police station. Adele assured her that no policeman would tag a Rolls Royce. They found Marge and Fred inside the station arguing with Victor Watchman, Regina Goodbody, and numerous Suggers. They were all being refereed by a policeman whose desk marker identified him as Captain Tim Flaherty.

Flaherty was trying to calm Fred Slick. "I told you, Mr. Slick, Ralph Thiemost and Ronald Coldaxe are not here. We have no facility to detain criminals. They've been taken directly to a state prison. If you want to arrange bail, you can call your lawyers." He waved at Marge, "Thank you for signing the complaints. We don't need you anymore." He kept assuring Regina and Watchman that neither Thiemost nor Coldaxe could carry out threats they had made against them.

Marge slipped away and embraced M'mm and Adele. She turned so that the Suggers who were watching them couldn't hear her or see her conspiratorial smile. "Watchman is a slimy crook," she smiled apologetically at M'mm. "He's a double agent. He and Regina were supposed to arrest Thiemost—not Ronald. I'm really sorry. But we weren't expecting Ron back today. Fred is telephoning Jack Siddley. I'm sure Jack will bail him out."

"Did you actually plan this?" Adele asked incredulously. "Does Heman know about this?"

"Not exactly," Marge said cautiously. "I tried to talk with Heman yesterday. But as usual he was a little foggy."

"He's not foggy anymore." Adele told her about Heman's miraculous cure. Marge was elated. She hugged Adele. "Oh, I'm so happy. I adore Heman." Then she grinned at M'mm. "It's all right, Adele knows I love him."

M'mm noticed the see-what-I-mean look in Adele's eyes. "Poor Thorny," Marge continued. "I'm worried about him. He needs the *Love Byrd*. It gives him a romantic image. I think we should go right to the airport. Maybe we can help Heman save the Love Rocks."

"What about Ron?" M'mm demanded as Fred Slick joined them.

Fred shrugged, "Watchman and Regina have convinced the police that both Ron and Thiemost are dangerous criminals. I telephoned Jack Siddley. He's in court. His assistant doesn't think we can arrange bail until tomorrow."

M'mm wanted to drive to the state prison and assure Ron that they were going to get him out on bail. "God, if they put him and Ralph in the same cell together they'll kill each other." M'mm wondered if Ralph might try to implicate her. It was a curious coincidence that Marge had tricked Ralph with a sexual obsession that only she knew about. Or had she told Marge Wednesday when she telephoned? How could she remember what happened when Moses Marshalik's head was between her legs?

But Fred, Marge, and Adele insisted that the first order of business was to help Heman Hyman. "Drive me back to the office so I can get my dress. Then we can all go to the airport," Marge told M'mm. "If Heman gets the Love Rocks to Boston safely, Ron's troubles are over."

Before they left the police station, Adele suddenly shifted ground and tried to placate Victor Watchman. "I'd really like to include you in my new book," she smiled at him seductively. "It's called *The Ultimate Aphrodisiac*. It's about power-seeking men like you. They fascinate me."

Watchman backed away from her suspiciously, but he was obviously intrigued. He shrugged, "Maybe I could grease the path a little for Cold-axe. I'll telephone you or I'll drop by tomorrow. I know where you live," he said with an oily smile.

"Come for lunch," Adele told him. "We can have a little swim in my pool."

In the Rolls, M'mm was still shuddering. "He'll grease Ron's path all right. Right to the electric chair. I'd be nervous if I were you. I wouldn't want to be alone with him. What are you going to do with him?"

Adele's eyes were dancing. "Not just me, honey—you and I together. We'll convince him that he hasn't lived until he's swum naked with us."

"I'm sorry," M'mm said, "I really have to go home. I'm not sure I locked up the house properly." Actually, she wanted to make sure that Moses had rescued his van and maybe even left her a little love note, and she wasn't at all sure that she wanted to be so chummy with Ron's mother-lover.

"Don't worry," Adele said merrily. "After we find Heman, the three of us will drive to Lynnfield together. Then we'll drive back to Boston. You can stay with us until we get Ron out of jail. Tonight, if you like, you can sleep on Ronnie's merry-go-round. I'm sure Ron must have told you that Heman gave it to him, and Heman's not an Indian-giver."

On the way to the airport, after Marge had recovered her dress and was sitting in the back seat of the Rolls with Fred, she told M'mm how to get to the Sumner Tunnel. Adele asked Marge how she had trapped Ralph Thiemost. "In case Watchman gets obstreperous with Meredith and me," Adele said, "you might be able to give us some good ideas on how to handle him."

"I couldn't have done it without Fred's help," Marge said. "Ron and Ralph were in Heman's office all morning with Bill Haley and those klutzes that Thiemost saddled us with from Stanford. I telephoned Ralph from my inside line, and I whispered to him in a very seductive voice that he should take a few minutes off, that he needed to relax, and that I was waiting for him in my office with lunch. To further tempt him, I told him I had a good idea how he might stop Sheldon Coombs and the World take-over." Marge laughed, "You have to understand, I was pretty sure that my invitation would work. The minute Ralph arrived on Monday, he had made it obvious that he couldn't wait to get his hands on me. Yesterday and this morning he practically made it a command performance. I was supposed to join him tonight in his suite at the Hyatt and have a drink with him, and later dinner—presumably to discuss Byrdwhistle. I no sooner hung up and was flinging whips and bondage crap all over my office than Fred called and told me that Regina had arrived ten minutes early. She was in the reception room howling for blood. Praying that Ralph would get his ass in motion, I handcuffed myself and was hanging by my wrists when Ralph opened the door. The poor sap looked as if his lower jaw had become detached. But he no sooner caught his breath and started yelling at me, demanding to know what was going on, when Regina and her Suggers charged in, followed by the police. It was perfect timing," Marge chuckled. "But for a moment it was touch and go. I was scared to death that Regina would arrive before Ralph. She looks like a dyke, and I think she would have used the whips on me if Ralph hadn't been there."

At the airport, they finally located the charter service from whom H.H. had rented a helicopter. The pilot, Jerry Carver, who had flown Youman out to the *Love Byrd* had just returned. H.H. wasn't with him. "He's aboard the yacht," Carver told them, and he sounded shaky. "It's about one hundred and fifty miles out in the Atlantic. It's blowing like hell out there, the remnants of the Thanksgiving storm."

Carver told them that before he lowered H.H. onto the *Love Byrd* they had been in radio contact with a tanker, the *Yankee Dreamer,* a liquified natural gas carrier headed for Boston Harbor and the Distrigas Company in Everett, where it would unload its cargo. "Youman tried to convince Captain Gregory Kakas that he had been a business neighbor of Distrigas and often watched the tankers unloading from his office. But Kakas wasn't very friendly. He told Youman that under no circumstances could he tow the *Love Byrd* into Boston harbor. He said it was against the law. He was carrying a very dangerous and explosive cargo." Carver shrugged. "He evidently thought that Youman might be an Arab terrorist. He didn't believe that the *Love Byrd* was really sinking and thought it might be a trap to hijack his ship. He kept asking Youman what the trouble was with the *Love Byrd,* and Youman told him that he wasn't sure but that possibly it had been overloaded. Youman told him that the *Love Byrd* was carrying rocks, a half-million of them that by a rough estimate weighed about thirty tons."

Carver paused and looked at them dubiously. "Maybe you know what's going on, but it sounded pretty fishy to me. Kakas told them that the best thing they could do was to abandon ship. If they did it immediately, he'd pick them up from the lifeboats, but for his own protection he would have to put them under guard. Youman told him that was impossible. Finally, he insisted that I lower him onto the *Love Byrd.*

It wasn't easy in that wind and the rough seas. I made a half-dozen passes before I got him aboard. After that I left. My gas was running low."

All they could do was wait and pray. M'mm drove back to Boston and dropped Marge and Fred off at the Harbor Apartments. She finally agreed with Adele. Like it or not, Adele was her only friend in the city. Driving with her to Lynnfield, M'mm was still a bit uneasy about Adele's cool assumption that her fornication with Ron—M'mm knew that Moses preferred the word *playing*—was really nothing for her to be upset about. They both loved Ronnie didn't they? Ronnie was twice blessed. And maybe, M'mm thought, as she turned into her driveway in Lynnfield, maybe she was too. Maybe, unknown to her, Ron had handed her a carte blanche to enjoy Moses. But when she opened the garage and discovered that the van was gone and that there was no trace of Moses, she was both relieved and apprehensive.

"I think I should drive you home and come back here," she told Adele. "Ron may try to get in touch with me."

"Please," Adele begged her, "I'm all alone too. If Ronnie can't reach you, he'll telephone me. You don't have to sleep on the merry-go-round. We have two guest rooms. When Hyman gets back and Ron is out of jail, we can all celebrate together. And, don't forget, Monday night is Elmer Byrd's opening of *Rum Ho!* Channel 5 is televising it. You're a Byrd-whistler. You have to go!"

45

Even after she'd packed a suitcase with some changes of clothing and a special dress for opening night, M'mm still was worried. What would happen when Ron got out on bail? Would she, Ron, and Adele sleep together on the merry-go-round? It irked her that Adele was so sure that Ron would call her, but she couldn't also believe that Ron would have the nerve to ask her to sleep in the same house, let alone the same bed, with his wife. On the other hand, Adele was a pretty loose goose. If that happened, Ron would have just what every man wanted—two adoring women. But Meredith Coldaxe wasn't going to be one of them. And what if Heman got back and all four of them were in the Youman house together? What then?

"I'll stay tonight," she told Adele, "but tomorrow when Ron gets out on bail we have to go home." One thing M'mm was sure of was that on Monday morning, whether Ronald was still in prison or not, she was going to be waiting in Lynnfield for Moses Marshalik.

Driving back to Boston, during a momentary lull in Adele's tale of her happily insane life with Heman, the music on the car radio gave way to the six o'clock news. "There's a wild and woolly story in the making," the news reporter said. "Full details are missing, but somewhere off the coast of Massachusetts a million-dollar luxury yacht, the *Love Byrd,* is sinking. Owned by the former Bostonian millionaire Thornton Byrd, the ship is rumored to be carrying a valuable and dangerous cargo—possibly radioactive rocks filled with uranium. The LNG tanker *Yankee Dreamer,* piloted by Captain Gregory Kakas, is in the area. Kakas has notified the Coast Guard and the Navy that he suspects the floundering vessel isn't in trouble at all and it may be an elaborate plot to hijack the tanker. At this moment, the Navy and the Coast Guard are on their way to the area, which is a few hundred miles out in the Atlantic. A security silence is being maintained. No further information is being released by the Navy." The announcer concluded with a warning, "A few years ago, in a book called *Time Bomb,* the author fantasized how a terrorist group could easily take over an LNG tanker and blow up New York City with an explosion that would make the bombing of Hiroshima look like the Fourth of July."

M'mm told Adele that she had read the book and that she had been thinking of joining a protest group against the storage of liquified gas in urban areas. "I told Ron that there were storage tanks only a few miles from Byrdwhistle and that the stuff was damned near as dangerous as a nuclear-plant blowoff. But Ron wouldn't pay any attention to me."

Adele only smiled at M'mm. "Heman's philosophy is that a life without risks would be a very dull life. But, don't worry, I'm sure that Heman won't blow himself up. He's not the hari-kari type."

Following Adele's instructions, M'mm parked the Rolls in the Brimmer Street garage, and they walked to Louisburg Square. Even before Adele unlocked the front door of the townhouse, M'mm was impressed. The narrow cobblestone streets, the gas lamps, and the ivy-covered brick buildings were more to her liking than the upper-income suburbs. But Moses probably wouldn't agree. It wouldn't be a likely prospecting area for Love You Cosmetics or for love therapists.

The telephone was ringing and Adele urged the unseen caller to be patient and not hang up. She finally got the lights on and answered the phone. "Ayatollah Heman Hyman Youman is telephoning you from the yacht *Love Byrd,*" the marine operator was laughing. "He told me to say that," she said. Then Heman's voice was on the phone. "Whatever you may read, hear, or see in the newspapers or on radio or television, discount it," he said. "This is your loving husband, Heman, and not an Arab terrorist. The *Love Byrd* hasn't sunk yet, but it's pretty wet down below. Unfortunately, the radio operator on the *Yankee Dreamer* is hysterical. Before we calmed him down, he advised the Navy that pirates had taken over the *Yankee Dreamer*." Adele could hear Heman chuckling, and she heard him talking with someone else. "Thorny sends you his love," H.H. said. "He's a little afraid of me. Up to now, he was afraid I had really lost my mind. I told him it was all his fault and that, if he hadn't sold his private gold mine to Ralph Thiemost, we wouldn't be in this predicament."

"What's happening out there?" Adele demanded.

"I can't hear you very well, Adele," H.H. said. "I'm sorry that I didn't get a chance to talk to you this morning, but I presume that, since you got back safely from Yugoslavia, Ron is once again in command."

"He's not in command. He's in jail," Adele was shouting as the maritime connection faded in and out. "Meredith Coldaxe and I are running things. Did you hear me, Heman? Meredith—"

"I heard you. Where is she now?"

"Right here, standing next to me."

Adele shook the phone and looked at it. "Heman isn't answering. It's a bad connection. I can't hear him. Ah, there he is!"

"Take good care of her, Adele. And, Adele, call Victor Watchman. Tell him to get off Ron's back. If the Navy keeps their hands off me, we'll have the Love Rocks in Boston by Sunday afternoon. Then Ron can sue the Federal Trade Commission for damaging Byrdwhistle's reputation."

"Are you being towed to Boston?" Adele could hear Heman chuckling.

"The caca Captain of the *Yankee Dreamer,* a nutty character named Kakas, refused to tow us. An hour ago I convinced him to come aboard the *Love Byrd*. He arrived in a lifeboat with a couple of crewmen. One of them was carrying a machine gun. When Kakas saw the Love Rocks, he told us that if we put everyone to work shoveling them overboard we'd be all right. He offered us a couple of pumps and insisted that we could make it to Boston without his help. I told Jack Sludge that there was no way out. This bastard was going to let us all drown. It was a case of survival. Sludge slugged the kid with the machine gun, Fresser jumped on Kakas, and we were wrestling all over the deck. But Thorny got the machine gun. He told them that this was Custer's last stand, and this Custer wasn't going down with the ship even if he had to pull the trigger and knock off Kakas and his crew."

Adele could hear Heman laughing, but once again his voice was fading in and out. "I can't hear you, did you say Sludge was piloting the tanker? Heman, he's an ex-convict! Where's Kakas?"

"I told you he was going to let us drown. We had no choice. We've got him locked up on the *Love Byrd*. I can't hear you, Adele. Goodbye. See you Sunday. Thorny and I will be home for the grand finale."

But seventy-two hours later, when M'mm and Adele arrived at the Colonial Theatre for the opening of *Rum Ho!,* no one was quite sure where H. H. Youman and Thornton Byrd were, or whether the *Love Byrd* had sunk. Late Monday afternoon, Ronald had finally been released on bail. He told Marge Slick that he hadn't forgiven her and would take his revenge on her later, but first he had to find H.H. and Thorny. A half-hour before showtime, neither Marge nor Ron had returned.

Rumors were that H.H. was either still on board the *Love Byrd* or was helping Jack Sludge pilot the *Yankee Dreamer,* and that both ships were being escorted to Boston by Navy cruisers and armed Coast Guard vessels.

Jack Siddley called Adele to tell her that he had heard that Youman had threatened to blow up the *Yankee Dreamer* if the Navy attempted to board either ship. The Navy was determined not to let him bring a cargo of radioactive rocks into Boston harbor. Other rumors were that the *Love Byrd,* floundering in heavy seas, had broken loose at the entrance to the harbor and smashed into the *Yankee Dreamer.* If that had happened, the tanker might be leaking liquified natural gas, which would asphyxiate or deep-freeze anybody or anything it came in contact with. One spark and low lying gas vapors would ignite. The *Love Byrd* and the *Yankee Dreamer,* along with the city of Boston, would be blown to kingdom come. The city was in a state of siege. The only thing that was certain was a terse announcement from Navy headquarters. The entire harbor was to be cleared of any moving vessels and all incoming aircraft to Logan had been diverted elsewhere. Low flying private aircraft must keep out of the harbor or they would be shot down by the Navy.

Adele had not heard anything further from Heman Hyman. M'mm had discovered that nothing discombobulated Adele. She was a cool, unflappable woman, equal to any emergency or circumstance. At times she seemed almost naive and disarmed women as well as men. Adele might be Ron's mother, but M'mm decided that twenty years from now when she was Adele's age she wanted to be the same kind of woman—a laughing, totally feminine, totally loving, totally capable woman, who could challenge a man with both her ass and her brains. A woman who wasn't worried about equal rights because she knew, without using them, she had superior rights. She could not only seduce a man but organize him, too.

Saturday morning, after drinking two bottles of champagne on Heman's merry-go-round and a sleepy talk that extended into early morning, she and Adele finally got to see Ronald in the prison visiting-room. Ron was furious. He blamed them for not getting him released and accused them of knowing about the police raid and not warning him. Both he and Ralph Thiemost (who hadn't been bailed out either and was in the cell next to his) were personally going to whip Marge Slick's ass. When they got through with her, she wouldn't be able to sit down for a year.

"What in hell did Marge or any of the other crazy Byrdwhistlers accomplish?" he demanded. "Thiemost told Bill Haley that he doesn't care if he goes broke. Monday morning he is to fire everyone and replace them with new people!" Ron stared grimly at M'mm. "Thiemost keeps mumbling that he's sure that you're involved in this. You and Marge cooked up that whipping scam between you to get even with him." Ronald sighed, "I tried to get them to move me to another cell. I finally got so fed up with his bullshit that I told him he didn't have to fire me because I quit."

Adele hugged him. Looking uneasily at M'mm, Ron tried to pull away from her. "It's all right, Ronnie," Adele told him. "Meredith knows that I love you, too. And I'm very sorry. I know now that I made a terrible mistake. I should never have encouraged Thorny to sell the company or try to get Heman to retire. But never mind," she kissed his cheek enthusiastically, "everything's going to be all right."

She told Ronald about Heman's remarkable recovery, but he only shook his head sadly. He had heard about H.H. on the radio already. It was all over the prison that they should get another cell ready because one more Byrdwhistler would be arriving soon. Ronald was sure that H.H. had really flipped. "It's one thing to fool around with the Federal Trade Commission, but even if H.H. does save the Love Rocks he's going to be in real trouble. No one takes on the United States Navy. I heard on the radio that he had taken over the tanker and wouldn't let the Navy or the Coast Guard aboard."

"At least it isn't a government ship," M'mm said. "The *Yankee Dreamer* is a private tanker. I warned you that liquified gas was very dangerous."

But Ron was even more shocked when M'mm coolly told him that she knew that he and Adele had played on Heman's—now *his*—merry-go-round together. "And I know that you've played in other places, too!" she added flatly. "But you can stop worrying. I'm not angry or jealous. I've discovered that Adele and I are kindred spirits. Adele's even asked me if we'd come to live with her and Heman in Louisburg Square." M'mm laughed at Ronald's astonishment. "I told her that I wasn't too sure about that. I might have other fish to fry. But she is my friend, and while you're working at Byrdwhistle—or somewhere else—Adele may help me with some projects I'm interested in, and I can travel with her occasionally and help her write a sequel to her book. I want to discover what motivates power-hungry men, too." M'mm knew that was a subtle way of jumping on Ronald when he was down, but she couldn't help it and he deserved it.

Ron was positive that Watchman was paying the police and that was why Jack Siddley had been unable to bail him out. Before they left, Adele assured him that she would find out why he hadn't been released.

"You'll be out of this nasty place by Monday morning, I promise you."

Saturday afternoon, when Watchman arrived, M'mm couldn't believe how easy it had been to subdue him. He'd obviously come out of curiosity, but Adele told M'mm before he arrived that that wasn't the only reason he would show up. "He's Boston bred," Adele said. "Our local politicians and those who work for the government here are all alike. They want to live in a style to which proper Bostonians are accustomed."

During the first few minutes, while his eyes were surveying the affluence of the Youman home and its huge indoor swimming pool, Victor had been pugnacious. He wasn't giving an inch. He was sorry. He agreed with Adele that the police might be blocking any attempt to bail Coldaxe out, but facts were facts. The FTC had received more than five hundred complaints of nondelivery of Love Rocks. And he knew this was only the tip of the iceberg. Ronald had compounded the problem by refusing access to Byrdwhistle files.

While he was talking, Adele had surreptitiously pressed something into M'mm's hand, and when M'mm saw that it was a miniature camera she closed her hand over it quickly. Watchman agreed to have a drink with them, and Adele asked M'mm to help her make them. At the bar she whispered, "When the time comes, click it at Victor and me. But not until his little rod comes up. Then keep clicking it. It advances automatically."

M'mm wondered how Adele was going to get Victor undressed. Adele sat with him near the pool and insisted that it was all her husband's fault. But poor Ronnie! She knew Victor didn't really want him to stay in jail with common criminals until Heman could straighten things out. Victor wasn't a vindictive man, was he? She knew he wasn't. Three Jack Daniels later, and much more mellow, Victor was listening to Adele tell him how she really enjoyed men, especially men who were forceful and, like Victor, knew that their virility and power needs were closely interwoven. Adele wished that he had brought his bathing suit. They could have all had a swim together. Then, giggling, she confessed that M'mm and she were really Byrdwhistlers at heart and enjoyed swimming naked. She hoped that Victor wasn't like Regina Goodbody, who most certainly didn't appreciate good bodies.

Grinning a little lasciviously, Victor told her not to identify him with Regina. "She had her job to do," he said. "I had mine. The fact is that after seeing the Byrdwhistle environment, I realized that it could be a very pleasant place to work—especially if you could enjoy one of those Love Rooms with a good friend." His smile indicated that Adele was fast becoming a good friend. "If your husband manages to get those damned rocks of his ashore, I'm sure that he and I can work things out. I'm on the board of a charitable organization that could use a new endowment fund."

Adele assured him that Heman was a very charitable man. Then she suggested that, since they were all so relaxed, if Victor wanted to he could swim in the pool in his underwear. She said she hoped he wouldn't mind if she and Meredith swam naked—it was so much more sensuous feeling the water against one's entire body. Beaming, Victor told her that he didn't mind. In fact he was something of a naturist himself.

M'mm had never used such a small camera and was afraid that Watchman might see her. But Adele kept him occupied. Cheerfully massaging his back, she clapped her hands delightedly when his "teeny-weeny" got bigger. She told him that he shouldn't be embarrassed and that she considered it a compliment. An hour later, telling Victor that they were both delighted to become good friends with such a real man, Adele cheerily kissed him goodbye. Victor was both hypnotized and a little drunk. He gave her his phone number. "I'm married, you know," he giggled. "But so are you. If my wife answers the phone, tell her it's government business."

"I will! I will!" Adele told him. But Sunday morning, before M'mm had awakened, she dropped prints of the pictures on her bed. "Wake up, honey, and take a look at the nice job you did. I'm going to discuss some government business with Victor." She dialed the telephone. "It's Adele, Victor. Didn't we have fun? I've got a surprise for you. Meredith took some nice nudie pictures of you and me. Poor Ronnie. We keep thinking about him in jail on a nice Sunday like this when we could all be swimming together." Adele grinned at M'mm. "Yes, Victor. Of course I want you to have your pictures, and the negatives too. You can come and get them or I'll mail them to you just as soon as Ronnie is out of jail. You'll just love them. These pictures will keep much longer than any endowment."

Now, walking into the crowded, brightly lighted lobby of the Colonial Theater and waving at the television cameras, which they could see zooming in on them, Adele told a program director, "Yes, Meredith and I will talk with you. But later, please." They were immediately surrounded by supercharged, cheering Byrdwhistlers. Half of the people in Boston might have left the city, they told Adele and M'mm, but Byrdwhistlers were unafraid. If Heman Hyman blew up Boston, they'd go to their maker together singing songs from Elmer's musical. Opening night of *Rum Ho!* had come at last. No one had heard anything yet from Ronald or Marge. Elmer had left the theater an hour before and promised that, even if it took all night and he had to row out into the harbor himself, he'd get H.H. and Thorny and bring them back. This was H.H.'s big night too. From now on, Heman Hyman Youman and Elmer Byrd would produce musicals, and Byrdwhistlers would take them on the road all over the country.

Inside the theater, the orchestra was tuning up. An usher led M'mm and Adele to front-row seats and told them that Marvy Upjohn would like to see them in her dressing room. As they wended their way backstage, they marveled at the scenery—an interior of a Provincetown sea-captain's home, a nightclub in Nassau, and masts and sails and the railings of a large ship, which when lowered would give the audience the illusion that they were watching the action on a ship at sea. They found Marvy in her crowded dressing room, where television cameramen were just finishing taping. "Elmer just telephoned," she said, hugging them both. "He's on his way back. We're going to hold the curtain until he arrives. H.H. and Thorny are both under arrest—charged with kidnapping and attempted sabotage. But it's all right, the governor and the mayor just made statements on television. They assured everyone that there was no danger to the city or to the harbor of Boston. The *Yankee Dreamer* is in the Mystic River discharging its cargo into storage tanks. The *Love Byrd* has run aground. It's off George's Island in the outer harbor, but it isn't sinking."

Marvy was laughing and crying, tears streaming down her cheeks, "God, Adele, I adore that man of yours. You know what he just did. I heard him on the radio. He announced to the press that the bad guy is not Thorny or himself, but Captain Kakas. He told the reporters that Kakas ignored their Mayday signal. He would have let everyone aboard the *Love Byrd* drown. 'I'm not a criminal,' H.H. told them," and Marvy did a surprising imitation of his voice. " 'Unintentionally, I've simply done a job that needed to be done. I've alerted the good citizens of Boston, and I hope the whole country, that whoever we are, and wherever we live, we can't escape. Life in this century is equivalent to sitting on a time bomb. Being blasted by liquified gas or radiated by a nuclear plant are only a few of the risks we must take so that we can all live and play in this world.' " Marvy chuckled, "H.H. said it much better, and then he told the reporters that he was going to spend the rest of his life showing people how to really play with each other."

Marvy told them that she would hold the curtain until ten minutes past eight. "I told Chris Williams, the orchestra leader, to get the audience singing. He's going to play the theme song from *Let Us Go, Brothers, Go!* She hugged Adele and M'mm and told them that she would see them after the performance.

Back in the theater, standing beside their seats and listening to the orchestra, M'mm could see all three balconies overflowing with people. In the back of the orchestra, people were standing. And they were singing: "Now love's sunshine has begun. / All the spirits and flowers are blooming./We have the feeling we're one./Let Us Go, Brothers, Go!"

Then the house lights dimmed and floodlights and a spotlight lighted the stage. M'mm and Adele sat down. Between them were the only unoccupied seats in the house—for Ronald, Marge, and Fred, and for H.H. and Thorny. The curtain parted, and Elmer appeared at center stage just as Ronald slid into the seat beside her. He was followed by Marge and Fred.

"We got them," Ron whispered to her. "H.H. and Thorny were released by the police on their own recognizance. The good Lord must love them."

In the center of the stage, grinning and waving his hands, Elmer was trying to quiet the bedlam. "A few months ago in Portamaio when you were all together for the Annual Byrdwhistle Vacation, H. H. Youman told you that he would return. And now he has—together with another friend of yours and mine, my old man, good old unsinkable Horny-Thorny.

Two men stepped past the curtain, and the cheering and screaming were deafening. No President of the United States and no hero moving down the streets of any city had ever received a greater ovation. The taller, a gray-haired man was nodding and waving, but his eyes were staring down at M'mm and his lips were forming the words "Moses loves you too!"

"You rat-fink-prick! You bastard!" she moaned softly, and Ronald, standing next to her, not hearing her over the noise, asked what she had said. She shook her head, tears pouring down her cheeks, and then, when the cheering finally died away, before H.H. could speak, she stood up, pointed her finger at him, and shrieked, "You're not Heman Hyman Youman. You're Moses Megillah Marshalik, my love therapist!"

And then she collapsed in Ronald's arms.

APPENDIX

AN EXTRACT FROM THE FIRST-QUARTER
FINANCIAL REPORT OF W.I.N. INCORPORATED

. . . In addition to the foregoing detailed financial information, which reveals the surging profit potential of our new company—a family of playful winners not yet three-months old—and the more detailed social audit, which appears in another section of this report (and will be a continuing feature of future reports), as your new President I want to share with you the background and some of the more intimate details of what has occurred between Meredith and me, Adele and H. H. Youman, and Ralph Thiemost since last January, when it became apparent that W.I.N. employees had made it possible for World Corporation to appoint a new board of directors for W.I.N. Incorporated. Together, we have moved a few steps forward toward the realization of King Gillette's dream. But even more important, now, and in the immediate future, we can show how Theory Z and our new approach to work will create a new kind of capitalistic America and how it can transform your life as it has mine.

For those reading this report who may not be as fully informed as our nearly one hundred thousand employee stockholders, let me fill in the missing gaps briefly. The employees of W.I.N. Incorporated, through their shareholding in World Corporation, are now in full control of the management of W.I.N. and all its subsidiaries, including Byrdwhistle, the newly acquired Sunwarm Corporation, and Byte Corporation, and our new Love You Cosmetics division, which was formerly the Marsha Lovett Division of Lovett Plastics Corporation.

Marsha Lovett is now headquartered in Boston. Before the end of the year, operating under its new name, Love You Cosmetics, we'll have branches in all the states in the nation. The Love You message, and the sale of home cosmetics-making kits will be carried to every village, town, and city in America by more than one hundred and fifty thousand certified love therapists.

I'm happy to tell you that my wife, Meredith, was unanimously elected President of Love You Cosmetics by our new board of directors. She hasn't yet met our thousands of new friends and winners personally, but I'm sure that most of you have become acquainted with her through our internal video-cassette exchange system that is now operating between all W.I.N. locations. When you get to know M'mm personally, she may challenge you a little; but I know that you will come to love her as I and her friends have. In addition to selling Love You Cosmetics, Meredith believes that our future army of love therapists can give millions of Americans the Byrdwhistle experience and acquaint them with Theory Z. She is sure that thousands of our female employee/stockholders will soon be making cosmetics in their homes guided by local love therapists.

In passing, I would also like to mention that Thornton Byrd is back in the Mediterranean with the *Love Byrd* and that over a period of time we are developing plans so that thousands of Winners may enjoy a short cruise aboard the *Love Byrd* with Thorny, as well as vacations at Portamaio and at other Byrds-on-the-Wing locations.

As most of you know, Byrdwhistle is now being run by Marge Slick. Marge is being ably assisted by Bill Redman, who, to our surprise, passed the Byrdwhistle entrance examination with flying colors. Unfortunately, Joe Taylor has left the company. He explained to Marge that he was unable to adjust to Theory Z techniques.

While we all believed that H. H. Youman would be the logical chairman of W.I.N. Incorporated, and the directors would have unanimously elected him, Sheldon Coombs has taken over the post of chairman of the board. H.H. explained that after devoting most of his adult life to Byrdwhistle and World Corporation, he was too busy playing with Love You Cosmetics to continue to play at Byrdwhistle or function as chairman of W.I.N. Working with Meredith, he is now developing a nationwide training program for love therapists that is being designed to release men in their late fifties and sixties from their work-ethic hangups. This is essentially a retraining program, and H.H. is certain that it will eventually be federally funded and adopted by thousands of companies as a part of their retirement programs. The three-month rehabilitation will include longevity training, weight reduction and control, and a revitalized sexuality seminar that will teach these older citizens how to merge sex, play, laughter, music, and dance with creative brainstorming for fun. Anyone who finishes the complete course can take the final examination. If they pass, they automatically become certified as love therapists.

During the past few months, many Winners and Byrdwhistlers have asked me how I personally managed to incorporate a totally new approach like Theory Z into my life and whether I really believe "all this Theory Z foolishness," or is it true that I have been seduced by the hypnotic Heman Hyman Youman? I must admit that at the beginning, without realizing it, I was deliberately brainwashed by certain Byrdwhistlers. But keep in mind that, like millions of you, I was raised with strong religious conditioning that was literally bred into my bones. Presumably our country became powerful and you and I became strong because of our hard work and self-denial. I was raised in the belief that everyone must sacrifice and save for the future and never, never depend on government handouts. I grew up believing that Adam Smith's idea of "self-love and self-interest" and earning profits for oneself ultimately benefited everyone. In such a world, even the poor were winners.

But, like millions of Americans, I've seen this philosophy develop into what Daniel Bell has called "the cultural contradiction of capitalism." On the one hand, we embrace "the nominal ethos of work, delayed gratification, career orientation, devotion to the enterprise," but in our everyday life when we are not working we presumably play in a world of continuous consumption spurred on with "glossy images of glamor and sex and promises of voluptuous gratification." And this is basically what makes the system work. It's a world where "people are straight by day and swingers by night." Even worse, underlying this reality is another, more sinister one. The system survives in a world that must have winners and losers. And it creates an environment where men and women are so busy competing with each other and hating each other that they don't dare reveal the laughing, loving, joyous people they really are.

The truth is that down deep I've always believed that there must be a better way. I married a woman who has spent most of our married life trying to convince me that this is so. But not until I met Heman Hyman and began to embrace bits and pieces of the Byrdwhistle play-ethic was I sure that there was a better way. A way *beyond winning.*

Last January, after the new board of directors had elected me President, and the dust of recriminations from past directors and executives had settled, to my astonishment Ralph Thiemost invited Meredith and me and the Youmans for a weekend at his Beverly Hills estate. He thought it would be a more friendly environment than a hotel. During that weekend, I discovered that I was not alone. Even old unreconstructed Winners like Ralph Thiemost have a soft core of doubt. Knowing that we had sold our home in Lynnfield and had moved into the Youmans' townhouse in Louisburg Square, where we happily play together as a two-generation family when we are in Boston, to my amazement (but evidently not to H.H.'s—he had been having long private conversations with Ralph) Ralph suggested that, since the Coldaxes and the Youmans would be leading very mobile lives in the future, he hoped we would consider his home our home whenever we were in California. Even more astonishing, Adele convinced Ralph that he had great potential as a love therapist, and H.H. and Meredith agreed with her. Ralph is now busily studying many of the basic books being made available to the entire W.I.N. family through their divisional and subsidiary libraries.

A selected list of these books from W.I.N. libraries has been included in this report. The annotations in this bibliography have been made by the Coldaxes and the Youmans. We hope that you enjoy reading or skimming many of them in the coming years. I'm sure they will give you, as they have me, a greater understanding of our company and of a new world where there is no lack of human growth and productivity because everyone is *playing* for a living.

As the man who wrote "The Purple Cow" said: "Not the quarry, but the chase / not the laurel, but the race / not the hazard, but the play / make me, Lord, enjoy alway."

Ronald Coldaxe
President

BIBLIOGRAPHY

Playing with John Humphrey Noyes and King Gillette

Adams, Russell. *King Gillette: The Man and His Wonderful Shaving Device.* Boston: Little, Brown, 1978. This is the first complete biography of Gillette. Unfortunately, it has the aura of a company-sponsored promotion book and skips rapidly over Gillette, the Utopian dreamer.

Carden, M. L. *Oneida: Utopian Community to Modern Corporation.* New York: Harper Torchbook, 1971. If you want to understand the parallels between Byrdwhistle and Oneida, read this excellent study that reveals many of the financial details of Oneida.

Gillette, King C. *The Human Drift.* Delmar, N.Y.: Scholars' Facsimiles & Reprints, 1974. This is a reprint of Gillette's first proposal for a new society, which he wrote in 1894. Gillette proposed that all corporations eventually be consolidated into one giant corporation owned by the people. The book gives a complete prospectus for the United Company, which later became World Corporation. Absolutely fascinating reading. If current Gillette officials, instead of being embarrassed by their founder's anti-establishment ideas, had a sense of humor, they'd proudly publish this and other Gillette books themselves as corporate giveaways and extol the life and thought of a most unusual American businessman. This edition comes with an excellent introduction by Kenneth Roemer, who teaches Utopian studies at the University of Texas at Arlington.

Gillette, King C. *World Corporation.* Boston: New England News Co., 1910. Gillette was obsessed with the ideas first promulgated in *The Human Drift* and refined them in this book, which he paid to have published at the time he set up the offices of World Corporation on Beacon Street in Boston.

Gillette, King C. *The People's Corporation.* New York: Boni & Liveright, 1924. Continuing his enthusiasm, Gillette enlisted Upton Sinclair, who collaborated (or helped him) write this final book. Unfortunately, both *World Corporation* and *The People's Corporation* are out of print and not easy to obtain.

Noyes, John Humphrey. *History of American Socialisms.* New York: Dover, 1976. This is one of the few books by John Humphrey Noyes that is readily available. Unfortunately, Noyes devotes most of the book to other communal groups and gives only a few pages of details about Oneida.

Noyes, John Humphrey. *Male Continence.* New York: AMS Press. A reprint of the first edition published by the Oneida Community. Absolutely fascinating reading by a man, who, one hundred years ago, understood more about human sexuality and loving than most writers today. Order a copy, together with Noyes's *Bible Communism.*

Parker, Robert Allerton. *A Yankee Saint: John Humphrey Noyes and the Oneida Community.* New York: Putnam, 1935. This is the best, most thorough biography of Noyes. It should be in a quality paperback. Anyone in the musical theater who hasn't read it, should! They would immediately want to invest in Elmer Byrd's production of *Let Us Go, Brothers, Go!* Noyes's story is high sexual-drama.

Robertson, Constance Noyes, ed. *Oneida Community: An Autobiography, 1851–1876.* Syracuse: Syracuse University Press, 1981. You'll never really appreciate Oneida and John Humphrey Noyes unless you read this book by his granddaughter, which is based entirely on actual writings of the people who lived in Oneida and who made it so successful.

Roemer, Kenneth, ed. *America as Utopia: Collected Essays.* Burt Franklin, 1980 (American Cultural Heritage Series, distr. by Lenox Hill Publ. & Distr. Corp., 235 E. 44th St., New York, NY 10017).

Talese, Gay. *Thy Neighbor's Wife.* New York: Doubleday, 1980. If you want a short survey of John Humphrey Noyes's life, Talese has written it in this book. Surprisingly, he was evidently unaware of the original group marriage of John and Harriet with George and Mary Cragin, which has more interesting ramifications than many of the people Talese has reported on.

Playing, Mostly, with Marcuse, Maslow, and Zen

Fry, John. *Marcuse—Dilemma and Liberation.* Atlantic Highlands, N.J.: Humanities Press, 1974. An excellent study of Marcuse, paralleled against "reality." You'll either agree or violently disagree.

Goble, Frank. *The Third Force: The Psychology of Abraham Maslow.* New

York: Grossman, 1970. A good survey of Maslow's thinking.

Hoffmann, Yoel, transl. *The Sound of One Hand Clapping: 281 Zen Koans and Answers.* New York: Basic Books, 1975. Wonderful paradoxes to try during laughing sex-making or when you dare to abandon rationality. When you know what the sound is, you'll have transcended yourself!

Koestler, Arthur. *The Ghost in the Machine.* New York: Macmillan, 1968. "No man is an island—he is a holon." If you are managing any organization, or looking forward to Byrdwhistle, you must understand holons.

Linssen, Robert. *Living Zen.* New York: Grove Press, 1960. How to detach yourself from the world and live in it at the same time. Good reading.

Low, Albert. *Zen and Creative Management.* New York: Anchor Press, 1976. Absolute required reading for Byrdwhistlers and anyone who is managing or being managed in any kind of people-structured work environment. Fundamental to learning how to play.

Marcuse, Herbert. *Eros and Civilization: A Philosophical Inquiry into Freud.* Boston: Beacon Press, 1955. If you read this book carefully, you'll begin to appreciate the potential of a society based on the play-ethic.

Marcuse, Herbert. *One Dimensional Man: Studies in the Ideology of an Industrial Society.* Boston: Beacon Press, 1964. Further perspectives on the play-ethic and Byrdwhistle!

Marcuse, Herbert. *An Essay on Liberation.* Boston: Beacon Press, 1969. This, and all of the following books, further expands and illuminates Marcuse's philosophy and proposals for a new understanding of man and work.

Marcuse, Herbert. *Counterrevolution and Revolt.* Boston: Beacon Press, 1972. If capitalism is organizing to meet the threat of revolution, it may end up with an H. H. Youman-King Gillette solution.

Marcuse, Herbert. *Five Lectures.* Boston: Beacon Press, 1970. Other perspectives on Freud and the work-ethic.

Marcuse, Herbert. *Soviet-Marxism.* New York: Vintage, 1961. If you believe that Marcuse was a communist, this book will change your mind.

Marks, Robert W. *The Meaning of Marcuse.* New York: Ballantine Books, 1976. Read this book before you read Marcuse. A good searchlight in the dark.

Maslow, Abraham. *Eupsychian Management.* Homewood, Ill.: Dorsey Irwin, 1965. An autographed copy of this book reads: "To Bob Rimmer, worker in the same vineyard." Much of Byrdwhistle Theory Z thinking was evolved by Abe Maslow in the summer of 1962, which he spent in a business management situation.

Maslow, Abraham. *The Farther Reaches of Human Nature.* New York: Viking, 1971. A complete collection of Maslow's writings, which include his essay "Theory Z" and a four-column comparison of other organizational styles with Theory Z. Absolutely necessary to understand Theory Z. If you can't locate it, drop a line to Bob Rimmer, Quincy, MA 02169.

Maslow, Abraham. *Motivation and Personality.* New York: Harper & Row, 1954. Abe Maslow's first book, basic to understanding his theories and further development.

Merton, Thomas. *Conjectures of a Guilty Bystander.* New York: Doubleday, 1968. He probably wouldn't—but Heman Hyman keeps thinking that Father Thomas might approve of Byrdwhistle.

Sohl, Robert, and Audrey Carr. *Games Zen Masters Play: The Writings of R. H.*

Blyth. New York: New American Library, 1976. The only way to understand Zen is to jump in and play.

Suzuki, Daisetz T. *The Essentials of Zen Buddhism.* New York: Dutton, 1962. All you ever need to know about a way of life that is not a religion, but may have more humor and laughter, even among the various disciplines, than most religions.

Watts, Alan. *The Way of Zen.* New York: Pantheon, 1957. If you have never read any book by Alan Watts, start here. You'll become addicted!

Watts, Alan. *The Book: On the Taboo About Knowing Who You Are.* New York: Collier Books, 1966. More Vedanta than Zen, but, like all of Alan Watts's books, essential for learning how to let go and play.

Wheelis, Allen. *The Moralist.* New York: Basic Books, 1973. "The path of moral progress is one of increasing awareness and creating an ever widening field of empathy within which we take the part of the other." Good reading.

Zurcher, Louis A. *The Mutable Self: A Self Concept for Social Change.* Beverly Hills: Sage Publications, 1977. An interesting new perspective for understanding yourself in four different ways: the Mutable Self, the Social Self. the Reflective Self, and the Oceanic Self. After you read it, perhaps you can detach yourself and laugh at yourself.

Playing — Sex-making

Archer, W. G. *The Hill of Flutes: Life, Love and Poetry in Tribal India.* University of Pittsburgh Press, 1974. Nearly a million Santals living in Bihar, India, have merged sex and love into a total life-style.

Bahr, Robert. *The Virility Factor.* New York: Putnam, 1976. Everything you wanted to know about testosterone. But this is after the fact. H.H.'s theories for ageless humans are much more fun.

Baxandall, Lee, ed. *Wilhelm Reich — Sex-Pol: Essays 1929-1934.* New York: Random House, 1972. Reich's interweaving of sex and sexual morality with the realities of Western life is basic to understanding the need for a Byrdwhistle approach to work. Among other things, Lee Baxandall is chief factotum of Free Beaches, Oshkosh, Wisconsin. If you need some place to run around bare-ass, write him.

Block, William. *Dr. Block's Do-It-Yourself Illustrated Home Sexuality Book for Kids.* Prep Publications, 1575 Parkway, Trenton, N.J. 08628. Order direct $15.95. Meredith Coldaxe insisted that this book be in the libraries and day-care facilities of all W.I.N. subsidiaries, including Byrdwhistle. The best book on the subject. If you have kids, buy it. Joyously, laughingly, lovingly illustrated by a man who knows how to play.

Bubba Free John. *Love of the Two-Armed Form.* Order direct, $9.95, from the Dawn Horse Press, Middleton, CA. Bubba Free John was born Franklin Albert Jones and is an American. He has thousands of followers, but is not a Reverend Jones! Byrdwhistlers love him. The subtitle of this book sums up why. "The free and regenerative function of sexuality in ordinary life and the transcendence of sexuality in true religious or spiritual practice."

Butler, Robert N., and Lewis, Myrna. *Love and Sex After Sixty.* New York: Perennial Library, 1977. One of many books recognizing that the human sexual drive never ceases. But none yet has appeared that explores the life extension and modified aging effect of a daily dip of the jade stalk in the jade fountain.

Chang, Jolan. *The Tao of Love and Sex.* New York, E. P. Dutton, 1977. H. H. Youman is convinced that this is the best sex-book for men ever written! Among other things it tells you how to enjoy a thousand or more playful thrusts in the jade fountain, daily—not only for longevity, but to make your woman happier.

Chesser, Eustace. *Salvation Through Sex.* New York: William Morrow, 1973. A good survey of the life of Wilhelm Reich, whose sexual philosophy is embodied in Byrdwhistle approaches.

Cummings, Anne. *The Love Habit: The Sexual Confessions of an Older Woman.* New York: Bobbs Merrill, 1978. Anne Cummings is sixty-four. Her lovers are all much younger because most men her age have quit the habit. Love therapists take notice!

Dallas, Pat. *Dallas in Wonderland.* Reed Books, 1979. Like Adele Youman, Pat Dallas enjoys photographing naked men—and she loves them, too! This is the laughing, playful story of a *Playgirl* photographer.

Douglas, Nik, and Slinger, Penny. *Sexual Secrets.* New York: Destiny Books, 377 Park Avenue, 10016. If you can't find this book in your bookstore, send a check for $12.95 to Destiny and tell them that Moses Marshalik and your love therapist insisted that you read it. The best book on Tantric Sex and other ancient sexual approaches for lovers everywhere. Penny has provided hundreds of line drawings, which shows she really understands the relationship between loving, laughter, learning, ludamus, and joyous living!

Douglas, Nik, and Slinger, Penny. *Mountain Ecstasy.* New York: A&W Publishers, 1978. The Tantric experience. "Where there is ecstasy there is creation." A four-color book that will set you dreaming.

Dunkell, Samuel, M.D. *Love Lives: How We Make Love.* New York: Signet, 1978. A lovingly written how-to-enjoy-it book that, together with humorous line drawings, treats sex as play.

Evans, Mary and Tom. *Shunger—The Art of Love in Japan.* New York: Paddington, 1979. Shunger "spring drawings" of Japanese men and women were produced by all major Japanese artists in the seventeenth and eighteenth centuries. They reflect a society where sex-making, Byrdwhistle-style, was done with joy and laughter and was nothing to be ashamed of. This is a good collection with explanatory text.

Ewing, Elizabeth. *Dress and Undress: History of Women's Underwear.* New York: Drama Book Specialists, 1979. All Byrdwhistlers must read this book to understand the sexual-playful aspect of female underclothing.

Foucault, Michel. *The History of Sexuality.* New York: Pantheon, 1979. Is confessing, analyzing, and studying human sexuality simply a part of man's desire to control his fellow men? Foucault thinks so.

Giele, Janet Zollinger. *Women and the Future: Changing Sex Roles in America.* New York: Free Press, 1978. Includes an interesting chapter on women and work and the realization that 40 percent of the labor force is now female. But the book offers no logical Byrdwhistle solution for a national strategy for employing men and women in the same workplace.

Gray, Mitchell, and Kennedy, Mary. *The Lingerie Book.* New York: St. Martin's

Press, 1980. Lingerie as an expression of women's sexuality may not appeal to many feminists, but it does to female Byrdwhistlers who enjoy working naked, too! This book has almost as many sexual photographs as the *New York Times Sunday Magazine*!

Gulik, R. H. van, *Sexual Life in Ancient China*. Atlantic Highlands, N.J.: Humanities Press, 1974. Fully illustrated bedside reading for H. H. Youman and all Byrdwhistlers. Unfortunately, at $50 a copy, you'll have to convince your library to buy it!

Halpern, James, and Sherman, Mark. *Afterplay*. New York: Stein & Day, 1978. What do you and your lover do after the orgasm? Continue to play? If you don't, you need this book and a love therapist!

Hofer, Jack. *Sexercise: How to Exercise Your Way to Sexual Fitness*. New York: A & W Publishers, 1979. The key to long sexual life is keeping in shape physically. There're a lot of other ways besides sexercising to accomplish this, but love therapists recommend afternoon sexercising to their customers.

Holroyd, Stuart and Season. *Sexual Loving: An Illustrated Guide*. New York: Bookthrift, Inc., Exeter Books, 1980. A very delightful book with the most loving and best sexual drawings of sex-making in any book that has been published so far, including *The Joy of Sex*.

Horson, Janet. *Scent Signals: The Silent Language of Sex*. New York: William Morrow, 1979. What are the links between odor, memory, emotion, sexual arousal? Can your nose get an erection that is transmitted to your penis or clitoris? This book is must reading for love therapists.

Katchadourian, Herbert A. *Human Sexuality: A Comparative Development Perspective*. University of California Press, 1979. Good reading for future Byrdwhistlers.

Kelly, Gary. *Sexuality: The Human Perspective*. Woodbury, N.Y.: Barrons, 1980. Excellent coverage of human sexuality and required reading for Byrdwhistlers.

Khanna, Madhu. *Yantra : The Tantric Symbol of Cosmic Unity*. London: Thames and Hudson, 1979. Yantras exemplify the fundamental unity of the male and female principle. To attempt to achieve the "ninth chakra" through meditation on Yantras can be a "fun" part of sex-making.

Kiell, Norman. *Varieties of Sexual Experience: Psychosexuality in Literature*. New York: International Universities Press, 1976. Selections from world literature depicting every conceivable kind of sexual experience, including group marriage as described by Bob Rimmer in *Proposition 31*. An interesting college or high school course in human sexuality could be organized around this book.

Lips, Hilary M., and Colwell, Nina Lee. *The Psychology of Sex Differences*. Englewood Cliffs, N.J.: Prentice-Hall, 1978. Psychological sexual differences are largely man-made. This book is an antidote for Freudian thinking.

Martino, Manfred F. *Sex and the Intelligent Woman*. New York: Springer, 1974. Here's a book that proves that the Meredith Coldaxes may be hard to live with—if you're the establishment type—but they're much more fun in bed.

Nagera, Humberto, M.D. *Female Sexuality and the Oedipus Complex*. New York: Aronson, 1975. At Symp meetings, books like this come up for discussion and H. H. Youman goes to war with Freud.

Nundell, Adele. *For the Woman Over Fifty.* New York: Avon Books, 1978. Books like this are vanguards of a new age, when women past fifty will enjoy their sexuality as much as any teen-ager.

Raimy, Eric. *Shared Houses, Shared Lives.* Los Angeles: J. P. Tarcher, 1979. Inevitably we are moving toward a more communal world. Good reading for Byrdwhistlers.

Rajneesh, Bhagwan Shree. *The Tantra Vision.* One of many, many books by Rajneesh that will have you walking on air and searching for a company employing productive players who believe in Theory Z. All Rajneesh books, video-tapes, and audio-tapes are available at very reasonable prices from Rajneesh Meditation Center, P.O. Box 12A, Antelope, OR 97001, where Rajneesh himself resides and where the new World headquarters is located.

Reich, Wilhelm. *Genitality in the Theory and Therapy of Neurosis.* New York: Farrar, Straus and Giroux, 1979. A revised edition, previously not available in the United States, amplifies *the function of the orgasm.*

Robertson, James. *Power, Money and Sex.* London: Marion Boyars, Ltd., 1976. If you don't think that the drive for power and money eliminates play from sex, read this book. Also Jim's latest book, *Sane Alternatives,* is a prophetic proposal for a new kind of society that is required reading for all Byrdwhistlers.

Rimmer, Robert H. *A New Moral Minority.* A one-hour video-tape in full color recorded May 29, 1981, in which Bob Rimmer lectures to members of Cleveland's City Club (the oldest public forum in America) and proposes many of the sexual approaches mentioned in Byrdwhistle. Price $25, VHS only. It also has a provocative half-hour question segment from the audience. Order from Cuyahoga Community College, Video Dept., 2900 Community College Avenue, Cleveland, OH 44115.

Rosenman, Martin. *Loving Styles: A Guide for Increasing Intimacy.* Englewood Cliffs, N.J.: Prentice-Hall, 1979. Includes Marcia Laswell's and Thomas Laswell's *Styles of Loving Test.* This book and Marcia's *Styles of Loving,* Doubleday, New York, 1980, will orient you for employment at Byrdwhistle!

Rinder, Walter. *Love Is My Reason.* Milbrae, Calif.: Celestial Arts, 1975. Walter's various books of poems, including *Love Is an Attitude, Spectrum of Love, Aura of Love* and many others, evoke love as play. Order direct, 231 Adrian Ave. $4.95 each.

Smelser, Neil, and Erikson, Eric. *Themes of Work and Love in Adulthood.* Cambridge: Harvard University Press, 1980. An exasperating collection of essays, such as "Adulthood as Transcendence of Age and Sex" and "Work and Love in Anglo-American Society," which makes the point that a playboy spends his life playing and does not work.

Smith, Bradley. *The American Way of Sex: An Informal Illustrated History.* New York: Two Continent, 1979. To understand the inevitability of sex and play becoming synonymous, a historical perspective is necessary. Fully illustrated. Good reading.

Stoehr, Taylor. *Free Love in America.* New York: AMS Press, 1979. A must reading book for twentieth-century lovers who have moved beyond monogamy to make them aware they are in a long tradition. An excellent introduction by Stoehr and five hundred pages of writings by people like John Humphrey Noyes that are unattainable elsewhere.

Stoller, Robert J., M.D. *Sexual Excitement: The Dynamics of Erotic Life.* New York: Pantheon, 1979. An interesting study but mostly of aberrant sexual arousal. Why doesn't someone take the Youman (Maslow) approach and study healthy, laughing sexuality?

Symons, Donald. *The Evolution of Human Sexuality.* New York: Oxford University Press, 1979. Is human sexuality a unifying or divisive force in society? Byrdwhistlers wouldn't agree with Symons's sociobiological answers.

Tannahill, Reay. *Sex in History.* New York: Stein & Day, 1980. A story of human sexuality that is bound to make you more playful.

Tennov, Dorothy. *Love and Limerence: The Experience of Being in Love.* New York: Stein & Day, 1980. If a Byrdwhistler joins you in a Love Room with his/her spouse's permission, it's not for limerence—it's for a new kind of being-you-is-fun love!

Tweedie, Jill. *In the Name of Love: Love in Theory and Practice Throughout the Ages.* New York: Pantheon, 1978. A look at love past and love future in a world where women are no longer dependent on the male for survival.

Walters, Margaret. *The Nude Male: A New Perspective.* New York: Paddington Press, 1978. Good reading for love therapists who offer their customers erotic dancing. Note that it was written by a woman and is fully illustrated.

Playing with Passages and Longevity

Abbo, M. D. *Steps to a Longer Life.* Mountain View, Calif.: World Publications, 1979. A good guidebook with a lot of things you know already but keep forgetting.

Chew, Peter. *The Inner World of the Middle-Aged Man.* New York: Macmillan, 1976. The publisher's blurb "a concrete guide for maturing with dignity, intelligence and flair in a society geared to youth" does not express Heman Hyman Youman philosophy.

Cousins, Norman. *Anatomy of an Illness.* New York: Norton, 1979. Long life through laughter and learning. Must reading.

Blythe, Ronald. *The View in Winter.* New York: Harcourt, Brace, Jovanovich, 1979. A beautifully written book about middle and old age in an English village. But with a tear in your eye, you may prefer *The Byrdwhistle Option.*

Dunton, Loren. *The Vintage Years.* Berkeley, Calif.: Ten Speed Press, 1978. If you think that past-sixty are the vintage years and *Modern Maturity* and the American Association of Retired Persons your cup of tea, you'll like this book. Old Byrdwhistlers are too busy sex-making to bother to read it.

Elrick, Harold, M.D., et al. *Living, Longer and Better.* Mountain View, Calif.: World Publications, 1978. Everything from good exercising to good eating for a long life.

Estes, Caroll L. *The Aging Enterprise.* San Francisco: Jossey-Bass, 1979. An excellent examination of the failures of public policy on aging and a new vision of the possibilities, including greater intergenerational bonding.

Figler, Homer. *Overcoming Executive Mid-Life Crisis.* New York: Wiley-Interscience, 1978. After you read this book, try sex-making on a merry-go-round. Ronald Coldaxe did when he was 47, and look what happened to him!

Fisher, David Hackett. *Growing Old in America.* Oxford University Press, 1977. In 1790 only 20 percent of Americans lived to age 70. Today 80 percent do. *But* being old and really living is something else again. This book will make you want to contribute to the Center for Ageless Humans.

Fontana, Andrea. *The Last Frontier: The Social Meaning of Growing Old.* Beverly Hills, Calif.: Sage Publications, 1977. A good chapter on the meaning of leisure—but, alas, nothing on play in all its manifestations.

Galton, Lawrence. *The Truth about Senility and How to Avoid It.* New York: Crowell, 1979. H. H. Youman bought this book before he read the index. There's no reference to sex, let alone sex-making; so he ordered it for the Byrd-whistle library—as a warning!

Hewitt, William F. *Geri-Sex Repressed.* Society for the Study of Alternative Life Style, 2742 W. Orangethorpe, Suite A, Fullerton, CA 92633. This article in the SAL journal surveys the negative sexual ambience of nursing homes. It will scare you to death. If you write the Society, Bob McGinley, one of the founders, will tell you about his Lifestyle Conventions and probably send you a copy of his swingers' newsletter, *Wide World.*

Hravchovec, Josef P. *Keeping Young and Living Longer: How to Stay Active and Healthy Past One Hundred.* Los Angeles: Sherbourne Press, 1972. An excellent book that covers all the aging theories and gives sound advice that will keep you sex-making at one hundred! Some publisher should re-issue it in a paperback.

Jacobs, Ruth Harriet. *Life After Youth: Female, Forty, What Next?* Boston: Beacon Press, 1979. Good reading for women who want to take the bull by the horns, but not by his penis.

Kent, Saul. *The Life-Extension Revolution.* New York: William Morrow, 1980. A complete survey of everything from aphrodisiacs to transplantation, regeneration, and cryonics. But the fundamental question remains—Without loving and learning as priorities what's the purpose of living at all?

Langone, John. *Long Life.* Boston: Little, Brown, 1978. An excellent survey for the general reader that covers all theories of the aging process, including Gerocomy, Gerovital and daily sex-making!

Lawton, M. Powell. *Planning and Managing Housing for the Elderly.* New York: Wiley-Interscience, 1975. Senior-citizen centers and nursing homes with little or no intergenerational contact are simply way-stations on the path to the cemetery. "Longevity with souris," H. H. Youman would say. Read this book and weep.

Leaf, Alexander, M.D. *Youth in Old Age.* New York: McGraw-Hill, 1975. A fascinating study of the Hunzas in Pakistan, and groups in the Caucasus in Russia and the Vilcabamba in Ecuador where many men and women live into their ninetieth years and some well over a hundred—many still sex-making. Basically, they have in common great physical activity, a daily drink of home-made wine, and a lot of play and laughter.

Levinson, Daniel J. *The Seasons of a Man's Life.* New York: Alfred Knopf, 1978. Here are the theories that Gail Sheehy popularized in *Passages.* Does every man (women are not covered in this book) pass through a series of specific age-linked phases? H. H. Youman says no, not if you live a life filled with loving, learning, and ludamus!

Livesey, Herbert B. *Second Chance: How to Change Your Career in Mid-Life.*

New York: Signet, 1977. Boredom with your work will inevitably decrease your life-span. Changing horses in midstream is dangerous playing, but may keep you alive.

Long Life Magazine, Box 490, Chicago, IL 60690. Annual subscription is $12.00. Can you live forever? Do you want to? Whether you believe in immortality or not (or freezing or hibernation to prolong life, see Bob Rimmer's *Love Me Tomorrow*) this magazine is really human playing carried to its ultimate.

Luce, Gay Gaer. *Your Second Life: Vitality in Growth in Middle Years*. New York: Delacorte, 1979. "A good person of sixty can grow as much as a child of six." Sound advice for Byrdwhistlers everywhere.

McQuade, Walter, and Aikman, Ann. *The Longevity Factor: A Revolutionary System for Prolonging Your Life*. New York: Simon & Schuster, 1979. Some things you may not have thought of, but the authors never consider living and learning and ludamus as the most necessary ingredient.

Mandell, Arnold J., M.D. *Coming of Middle Age*. New York: Summit Books, 1977. Mandell is a psychiatrist who had a heart attack. He thinks open marriage "violates the brain system" and "penis behavior in men and women is a piece of naked brain sticking out for all to see." If, like H.H., you'd like to play polymorphously sexually, you won't like this book.

Mayer, Nancy. *The Male Mid-Life Crisis: Fresh Starts After Forty*. New York: Doubleday, 1978. Nancy includes a chapter called "Penis Angst and the Balm of Nubile Girls." There isn't much she hasn't missed in this book, including "reinventing marriage."

Puner, Morton. *Vital Maturity: Living Longer and Better*. New York: Universe Books, 1979. This book is the best one you can read on the subject. Originally titled "For the Good Long Life"—it is required Byrdwhistle reading.

Research on Aging, A Quarterly of Social Gerontology, Sage Publications, Beverly Hills, CA 90212. The basic reason we have a new science of gerontology is that we didn't teach people how to live, love, and enjoy ludamus, and thus never grow old. Until we do this, here is a journal that covers the battlefield.

Still, Henry. *Surviving the Mid-Life Crisis*. New York: Crowell, 1977. Still another book about the new American discovery of passages. This one has a chapter on sexual transactions for the 4,000 or more Americans who become sixty-five every day.

Tyson, Wynne and Jon. *Food for the Future: The Complete Case for Vegetarianism*. New York: Universe Books, 1979. Can you live to ninety on a vegetable diet supplemented with proteins from nuts and other sources? Bertrand Russell and George Bernard Shaw did! If you really want to pursue vegetarianism, subscribe to the *Vegetarian Times*, 41 East 42nd Street, Suite 921, N.Y.C., 10017. $12.00 for 8 issues.

Uris, Auren. *Over Fifty: The Definitive Guide to Retirement*. Radnor, Pa.: Chilton Books, 1979. A very good book to own and read before you are fifty. Either you'll appreciate the advice or it will provide you with ammunition to fight back!

Uselin, Gene, ed. *Aging: The Process and the People*. New York: Bruner/Mazel, 1978. If you're going to lick it, you've got to know your enemy. A good guidebook.

Weitzman, Hyman G. *The Retirement Day Book*. Radnor, Pa.: Chilton Books,

1978. Believe it or not, this is a large-sized paperback with inspirational messages and blank spaces (a journal) for your first year of retirement. The guidelines to journal keeping also give sexual advice, including romance. But, alas, not Thornton Byrd's, Heman Hyman's, or Adele Youman's style!

Playing with Achievable Utopias
and
Corporate Management Theories from A to Z

Baramash, Isadore. *For the Good of the Company: Work and Interplay in a Major American Corporation.* New York: Grossett & Dunlap, 1976. A fascinating story of two warriors, Meshulam Riklis and Samuel Neaman, playing wargames with Rapid American Corporation and McCory Stores.

Battalia, O., and Tarrant, John J. *The Corporate Eunuch.* New York: Crowell, 1973. How to survive in a modern corporation, even if you get your balls cut off . . . with or without help from the corporate wife.

Best, Fred, ed. *The Future of Work.* Englewood Cliffs, N.J.: Prentice-Hall, 1973. A good collection of essays exploring a world where work and joyous living might coincide, before Byrdwhistle!

Blake, Robert R., and Mouton, Jane. *Managerial Grid.* Houston, Tex.: Gulf Publications, 1972. An invaluable study that puts all the theories of management on a grid where they can be evaluated numerically. Must reading for Byrdwhistlers.

Briggs, Bruce, B., ed. *The New Class.* New Brunswick, N.J.: Transaction Books, 1979. Excellent essays in search of the armchair professionals who decry capitalism and, unlike Byrdwhistlers, put their chips on expanded government. Which are you?

Brown, Stanley H. *Ling.* New York: Bantam Books, 1972. James Joseph Ling and Ralph Thiemost have a lot in common and can be pretty scary fellows.

Brown, Stanley H. *H. L. Hunt: A Biography.* Chicago: Playboy Press, 1976. H.L. and H.H. have nothing in common, except their love of women. But Heman Hyman is much more loving and H.L. never played!

Coleman, Richard C., and Rainwater, Lee. *Social Standing in America.* New York: Basic Books, 1978. Are you upper-class or lower-class and why? Read this book and find out.

D'Aprix, Roger M. *Struggle for Identity.* Homewood, Ill.: Dow Jones-Irwin, 1972. The search for meaning in corporate life, with an interesting chapter titled "The Changing Organization from X to Y."

Davis, Stanley M., and Lawrence, Paul R. *Matrix.* Reading, Mass.: Addison-Wesley, 1977. Ronald Coldaxe is using the "multiple command system" of matrix management and project teams combined with Theory Z to unify W.I.N. This controlled form of decentralization could help humanize any organization.

Dickson, Paul. *The Future of the Work Place.* New York: Weybright & Talley, 1975. Coming events cast their shadows before. This book foreshadows Byrdwhistle, but it doesn't offer Love Rooms!

Drucker, Peter F. *Management: Tasks, Responsibilities, Practices.* New York: Harper & Row, 1974. This huge volume is required reading for all Byrdwhistlers.

Drucker, Peter F. *The Practice of Management: A Study of the Most Important Function in American Society*. New York: Harper, 1954. Note the subtitle. Drucker's most recent book, *Managing in Turbulent Times*, projects the future but overlooks the Byrdwhistle Option.

Edwards, Richard, *Contested Terrain: The Transformation of the Work Place in the Twentieth Century*. New York: Basic Books, 1979. The past structure of work in America and the palace revolution that is now taking place. Illuminating.

Ewing, David. *Technological Change and Management*. Boston: Harvard University Press, 1970. Interesting lectures on management by top administrators.

Feinberg, Mortimer R. *Corporate Bigamy*. New York: Morrow, 1980. A guidebook to understanding Ralph Thiemost and pre-Byrdwhistle Ronald Coldaxe.

Ferguson, Mildred. *The Aquarian Conspiracy*. Los Angeles: J. P. Tarcher, 1980. Whether there is a "conspiracy" or a "third wave," Byrdwhistle is playing its part. This book is upbeat reading for pessimistic times.

Fischer, John. *Vital Signs*. New York: Harper & Row, 1975. Experiments in community planning that parallel the Byrdwhistle Option.

Gilbert, James. *Designing the Industrial State: The Intellectual Pursuit of Collectivism in America, 1840-1940*. Chicago: Quadrangle, 1972. A good survey of socialistic thinking including King Gillette.

Golde, Roger A. *Muddling Through: The Art of Properly Unbusinesslike Management*. New York: Anacon, 1979. A pointed, laughing, H.H. Youman-like look at the pretensions of management theories, particularly Management by Objectives.

Hareven, Tamara K., and Langebach, Randolph. *Amoskeag: Life and Work in an American Factory*. New York: Pantheon, 1979. In the early years of the century, family life was totally organized around the factory. Working wives (and children) were taken for granted. Byrdwhistle is a twenty-first century approach to merging the family as a playing (working?) unit.

Harvard Business Review: On Human Relations. New York: Harper & Row, 1979. A good reading collection of articles on interpersonal managing, including another look at *Zen and the Art of Management* by Richard Pascale, who teaches management at Ronald Coldaxe's alma mater, Stanford.

Harvard Business Review: On Management. New York: Harper & Row, 1975. Essays on all aspects of management, including one by Morse and Lorsch (business school professors) titled "Beyond Theory Y," which offers a contingent theory but, alas, not Theory Z.

Hennig, Margaret, and Jardin, Anne. *The Managerial Woman*. New York: Pocket Books, 1977. Only 12,500 women (in 1977) earned $25,000 or more a year. A how-to-get-there-and-survive book.

Huizinga, Johan. *Homo Ludens: A Study of the Play Element in Culture*. Beacon Press, 1950. Absolutely must reading for potential Byrdwhistlers. This book could change your entire philosophy of life. Huizinga proves to you that in most cases — when you are working, praying, or even at war — essentially you are playing. Martin Buber called the book "one of the few informed works about the problems of man.

Jay, Antony. *Corporation Man*. New York: Random House, 1971. The subtitle

"Who He Is, What He Does, Why His Ancient Tribal Impulses Dominate the Life of the Modern Corporation" gives you a clue. Scary.

Jennings, Eugene E. *Routes to the Executive Suite.* New York: McGraw-Hill, 1971. This book was Ronald Coldaxe's bible before he became president of W.I.N. Inc.

Klein, Howard J. *Other People's Business: A Primer on Management Consultants.* New York: Mason/Charter, 1977. Would you hire Heman Hyman as a management consultant? This book gives you a look at top consulting firms who don't play around.

Kurtz, Paul. *Exuberance: A Philosophy of Happiness.* Prometheus Books, Buffalo, N.Y., 1977. Paul Kurtz offers delightful insights on how to live with your feet in the air in all areas of life, including "creative work," "love and friendship," "eroticism" — all combined into an exuberant, "playful" philosophy of life.

Lamb, Edward. *The Sharing Society.* New York: Lyle Stuart, 1979. Lamb is a multi-millionaire who believes capitalism won't survive in its present form. Reflects some overtones of King Gillette's thinking. Good reading.

Lasch, Christopher. *The Culture of Narcissism: American Life in an Age of Diminishing Expectations.* New York: Norton, 1978. Christopher wouldn't like Byrdwhistle, but Byrdwhistlers read him to understand why the naysayers have a one-dimensional perspective.

Lefkowitz, Bernard. *Breaktime: Living Without Work in a Nine-to-Five World.* New York: Hawthorne, 1979. A fascinating survey of hundreds of people who have stopped working and are playing, but not strictly Byrdwhistle-style.

Levinson, Harry. *The Exceptional Executive.* New York: New American Library, 1968. Harry runs the Levinson Institute and is a management consultant. A thought-provoking book.

Maccoby, Michael. *The Gamesman.* New York: Bantam Books, 1976. How to play games that will make you a corporate winner!

MacPherson, Myra. *The Power Lovers: An Intimate Look at Politicians and Their Marriages.* New York: Putnam, 1975. Must reading for women who are married to Coldaxes or Thiemosts.

Manuel, Frank E., and Manuel, Fritzie P. *Utopian Thought in the Western World.* Cambridge: Harvard University Press, 1979. Neither John Humphrey Noyes, Heman Hyman Youman, or Bob Rimmer are in this book — perhaps because they deal in achievable Utopias. Nevertheless, it is the most fascinating book available on the subject. Required reading for managers who at present don't have an Utopian outlook.

Margolis, Diane Rothbard. *The Managers: Corporate Life in America.* New York: William Morrow, 1979. A devastating view of the Ronald Coldaxes in operation.

McClelland, David C. *Power: The Inner Experience.* New York: Irvington Publishers, 1975. Adele likes to read this book to her friends on Ronnie's merry-go-round. A classic study of human and national motivations to achieve power.

McGregor, Douglas. *The Human Side of Enterprise.* New York: McGraw-Hill, 1960. McGregor discovered Theory Y and distinguished it from Theory X. Must reading to put Theory Z in perspective.

McLuhan, Marshall, and Nevitt, Barrington. *Take Today: The Executive as*

Dropout. New York: Harcourt, Brace, Jovanovich, 1972. A McLuhan mind-blower. "The winner is one who knows when to drop out in order to get in touch."

McMurry, Robert. *The Maverick Executive.* New York: Anacom, 1974. "He is a benevolent autocrat mainly by instinct." Heman Hyman chuckled when he read this book.

Mintz, Morton, and Cohen, Jerry. *Power, Inc.: Public and Private Rulers and How to Make Them Accountable.* New York: Viking, 1976. One of Adele Youman's guidebooks to understanding the ultimate aphrodisiac.

Musashi, Miamoto. *Rings of Passion.* New York: Overlook Press, 1974. A translation of a Japanese Samurai classic, this book presents the Japanese approach to success—"slash swiftly and without warning"—and puts business management in the same category as warfare. It skyrocketed in sales in late 1981 when it was "discovered" in the business community by most leaders who believe in work, not play.

Odiorne, George S. *MBO II: A New Approach to Management by Objectives for the 1980s.* Belmont, Calif.: Fearon, Pittman, 1980. Odiorne's law, "Things that do not change will remain the same," is good Byrdwhistle philosophy.

Ouchi, William. *Theory Z.* Reading, Mass.: Addison-Wesley, 1981. Surprisingly, since Theory Z is an extension of Douglas MacGregor's Theory X and Theory Y principles, Ouchi makes no reference to Abraham Maslow's Theory Z, which preceded Ouchi's concepts by ten years. Ouchi's Theory Z proposes a strong company philosophy within the environment of a distinct corporate culture—plus long-range staff development and consensus decision-making. Which at first glance makes it seem like the Byrdwhistle approach, but alas no one plays here either!

Pascale, Richard Tanner, and Athos, Anthony G. *The Art of Japanese Management.* New York: Simon & Schuster, 1981. According to the authors, Western companies have tended to favor *Strategy, Structure* and *Systems* in operating their businesses "which produces an arid world in which nothing is alive." The Japanese, on the other hand, pay attention to the soft esses—*Staff, Skill, Style* and *Subordinate Goals.* The 7 esses are a little pat and Harvard Business School-style, which doesn't teach M.B.A.s how to play.

Peterson, Rodney. *The Philosophy of a Peasant.* Order direct: Inter-Action Books, Heber Springs, AR 72543, $12.95. Rod is not quite a King Gillette, but almost. A former president of Hertz Corporation, the only way he could write and promulgate his total economic and political philosophy was to resign from Hertz and do it. Fascinating reading.

Pfeffer, Richard. *Working for Capitalism.* New York: Columbia University Press, 1979. A day-by-day account of work at its lowest level in a large piston-ring factory whose management doesn't play.

Rapoport, Rhona and Robert, eds. *Working Couples.* New York: Harper & Row, 1978. In the 1960s no futurist predicted that 60 percent of the wives in the United States would be working. Want to speculate what will happen in the future? Perhaps thousands of companies will be offering variations from the Byrdwhistle Option. This book will give you perspective on why it has to happen.

Rodgers, William H. *Corporate Country.* Emmaus, Pa.: Rodale Press, 1973.

Scary reading! From the cover: "When the crunch comes it's not how you play the game, it's whether you win or lose."

Sayles, R. Leonard. *Managing Large Systems: Organizations in the Future.* New York: Harper & Row, 1971. Good reading for World Corporationists who have other approaches.

Schumacher, E. F. *A Guide for the Perplexed.* New York: Harper & Row, 1977. More interesting philosophy by the author of *Small Is Beautiful,* who might not have understood that Youman and Gillette were aiming in the same direction he was.

Scott, William G., and Hunt, David K. *Organizational America: Can Individual Freedom Survive within the Security of Its Promises?* Boston: Houghton, Mifflin, 1979. Good reading but a not too hopeful view of the future.

Theobald, Robert, ed. *The Guaranteed Income.* New York: Doubleday/Anchor, 1967. An outdated book that will give you perspective on the Byrdwhistle policy of hiring husband-and-wife teams.

Toffler, Alvin. *The Third Wave.* New York: William Morrow, 1980. Alvin goes "Utopian" in a lot of his conclusions, which he synthesizes to produce some kind of rationality out of the irrational events we are living through. Byrdwhistle, couple-style employment is much more likely than his expanded family working in an electronic cottage. But Alvin's worth reading because he's always optimistic.

Vaillant, George. *Adaptation to Life.* New York: Little, Brown, 1977. A report on the study of 268 male graduates of private northeastern colleges and how they coped through most of their adult lives. A quote from Leo Tolstoy sets the tone: "One can live magnificently in this world if one knows how to work and how to love, to work for the person one loves, and love one's work." Alas, Tolstoy didn't know how to play either.

Vandervelde, Mary Anne. *The Changing Life of the Corporate Wife.* New York: Mecox Publishing, 1972. Meredith Coldaxe read this book and realized that she wasn't alone. If you are a corporate wife, don't miss it!

Why S.O.B.'s Succeed and Nice Guys Fail in Small Business. Financial Management Associates, 3824 East Indian School Road, Phoenix, AZ 85018. Order direct, $16.00. A guidebook for Ralph Thiemosts and other would-be winners.

Woodmansee, John. *The World of the Giant Corporation.* North County Press, P.O. Box 12,223, Seattle, WA 98112. $3.50. Order direct. A mind-boggling look into the operations of the General Electric Corporation.

Youman, Adele. *The Ultimate Aphrodisiac.* New York: Provocation Press, 1985. Adele finally put Ralph Thiemost's picture in her book. But after completing Heman Hyman's course in love therapy, Ralph has forgiven her and he no longer needs to hang unsuspecting women to enjoy his playful penis. Ronnie, of course, has long since posed for Adele on his merry-go-round.

Playing with Cosmetics and Aroma Therapy

All of the following books are offered by Love You Cosmetics, Inc., and may be ordered from your love therapist or obtained in most libraries.

American Medical Association. *Book of Skin and Hair Care.* New York: Avon

Books, 1976.

Donnan, Marcia. *Cosmetics from the Kitchen*. New York: Holt, Rinehart & Winston, 1972.

Genders, Roy. *Perfume Through the Ages*. New York: Putnam, 1972.

Plummer, Beverly. *Fragrance: How to Make Natural Soaps, Scents, and Sundries*. New York: Atheneum, 1975.

Rinzler, Carol. *Cosmetics: What the Ads Don't Tell You*. New York: Thomas Crowell, 1977.

Sagarin, Edward. *The Science and Art of Perfumery*. Greenberg, 1945.

Tisserand, Robert B. *The Art of Aroma Therapy: The Healing and Beautifying Properties of Essential Oils of Flowers and Herbs*. New York: Inner Traditions International, 1977.

Traven, Beatrice. *Here's an Egg on Your Face, or How to Make Your Own Cosmetics*. Old Tappan, N.J., Hewitt House, 1977.

Traven, Beatrice. *A Book of Natural Cosmetics*. New York: Simon & Schuster, 1974.

Wageman, Dolly Reed. *Six-Week Make-Yourself-Over Plan*. New York: Signet 1977.

York, Alexandra. *Back to Basics: Natural Beauty Handbook for Making Your Own Cosmetics*. New York: Harcourt, Brace, Jovanovich, 1978.

Zizmore, Jonathan. *Dr. Zizmore's Brand-Name Guide to Beauty Aids*. New York: Harper & Row, 1978.

Just Playing with Music and Drama, and Playing with Fire, Too!

American Musicals. A veritable gold mine for American musicals lies untapped in the nostalgia and actualities of the period 1830 to 1930. *Rum Ho!*, of which a libretto exists, is only one example. The possibilities of *Let Us Go, Brothers, Go!* and a musical based on Miami in the 1920s, or *Summer by the Sea*, are only a few of the possibilities.

Bruner, Jerome S., et al., eds. *Play: Its Role, Development and Evolution*. New York: Basic Books, 1976. Required reading for all Byrdwhistlers and Winners!

Byrd, Elmer. *Adopt an Ancestor*. Boston: Love-n-Learn Books, 1985. On the theory that King Gillette or John Humphrey Noyes are two of the many ancestors worth adopting, Elmer's book is included in this bibliography.

Caldicott, Helen, M.D. *Nuclear Madness*. Autumn Press Inc., 25 Dwight Street, Brookline, MA 02146. Order direct, $3.95. M'mm is on Helen's side. Heman Hyman and Moses Marshalik believe that without risks there is no adventure. Can we dare not to take the nuclear risk—short term, anyway?

Dally, Peter. *The Fantasy Game: How Male and Female Sexual Fantasies Affect Our Lives*. New York: Stein & Day, 1975. Complete the questionnaire at the end of this book to determine whether you are basically a sadist or a masochist; and when you do, you'll be playing at a new level in your life. Required Byrdwhistle reading.

Davis, Lee Niedringhaus. *Frozen Fire*. Friends of the Earth, 124 Spear Street, San Francisco. $6.95. Meredith Coldaxe recommends that you read this book. Liquified natural gas explodes on contact with water and an LNG tanker could conceivably explode with an energy equivalent of fifty-five Hiroshima bombs!

Environments: A Totally New Concept in Sound. Syntonic Research Inc., 175 Fifth Avenue, New York 10010. Sounds of the Pacific Ocean, a Caribbean lagoon, and Alpine blizzard, a country thunderstorm, and the ultimate heartbeat. The final record, which plays 27 minutes with all the varying subtleties of an actual heartbeat, is great for a lot of erotic lovemaking on a merry-go-round, or elsewhere.

Gowan, Suzanne, and Eakey, George, et al. *Moving Toward a New Society.* Movement for a New Society, 4722 Baltimore Avenue, Philadelphia, 19143. Order direct, $4.50. If you feel M'mm-y—get acquainted with people who have a lot more to offer than a 1960 hangover.

Halpern, Steven. *Tuning the Human Instrument.* Spectrum Research Institute, 620 Taylor Way #14, Belmont, CA 94002. Order direct, $6.00. A study of Halpern's musical philosophy. His various LP records "The Antic Frantic Alternative"—a revolutionary approach to "sound health"—are also available from Spectrum at $8.95 each. In Halpern's words: My approach to sexuality is based on sensuality. My music reflects this. It does not depend on lyric or heavy beat, but rather on an entire body massage that is provided by music." And, of course, love therapists!

Heilpern, John. *Conference of the Birds.* Indianapolis, Ind.: Bobbs-Merrill, 1978. An 8,500-mile journey across Africa with a community of actors guided by Peter Brook to produce spontaneous drama for African villagers. Don't miss this book. It anticipates Byrdwhistlers performing Elmer Byrd's musical in the workplace.

Inter-Dimensional Music Thru Isasos. Beautiful music for merry-go-rounds or your own bedroom. Order direct from Unity Records, Box 12, Coste Madera, Calif. 94925.

Jennings, Lane. *Future Fun.* Washington, D.C.: Futurist Magazine, December 1979, World Future Society, P.O. Box 30369, 20014. An excellent article on the future of play, which even considers sex-making in zero-gravity.

Lesse, Stanley. *Anxiety: Its Components and Treatment.* New York: Grune & Stratton, 1970. You won't find "play" or "laughter" or even "sex" in the index of this book. Byrdwhistlers read it as if they are visitors from another planet.

Linde, Peter. *Time Bomb.* New York: Doubleday, 1978. Do we have to play with fire in order to survive? Heman Hyman says yes, M'mm says no. But it stimulates their sex-making!

Machlowitz, Marilyn. *Workaholics: Living with Them—Working with Them.* Addison-Wesley, 1980. Many workaholics are really playing and refuse to admit it. H.H. would distinguish the play-nuts from the paranoid workers.

McCullagh, James, ed. *Ways to Play.* Emmaus, Pa.: Rodale Press, 1978. Required reading for Byrdwhistlers, both for the running philosophy as well as the examination of various how-to's.

Panken, Shirley. *The Joy of Suffering: Psychoanalytic Theory and Therapy of Masochism.* New York: Aronson, 1973. If the title doesn't shake you, it shocks Byrdwhistlers. Read it and beware!

Roszak, Theodore. *Person Planet: The Creative Disintegration of an Industrial Society.* New York: Anchor Press, 1978. A brilliant analysis, but offering ephemeral rather than positive solutions.

Shipee, Nathan. *Becoming.* Prudential Press, P.O. Box 747, Old Lyme, Conn., 1979. Order direct, $9.95. A book that makes you glad you're alive to be-coming!

The Violet Flame. Original music on an LP by Joel Andrews. The Group Inc., Route #9, Brooksville, FL. Order direct, $8.00. For loving sex-making and to transport you in a world of I-am-thou.

Varrell, William. *Summer by the Sea: The Golden Era of Victorian Beach Resorts.* Portsmouth, N.H.: Strawberry Bank Printshop, 1972. Inspiration for an Elmer Byrd musical.

Yiddish. Heman Hyman believes that everyone should learn some Yiddish, if only to express laughing souris (sorrow). Here are some guides: Feinsilver, Lillian. *The Taste of Yiddish,* Thomas Yosaloff, 1970; Marcus, Martin, *The Power of Yiddish Thinking,* Doubleday, New York, 1971; Matisoff, James, *Blessings, Curses, Hopes and Fears: Psycho-Ostensive Expressions in Yiddish,* Ishi, Philadelphia, 1979.

Zukav, Gary. *The Dancing Wu-Li Masters, An Overview of the New Physics.* New York: Morrow and Quill Paperbacks, New York, 1979. On the theory that the more they know the more Byrdwhistlers can improve their transcendence. This book is required reading.

Playing in Merry Mount

William Bradford, landing in Plymouth with his Pilgrims in 1620, and Thomas Morton, seven years later setting up his Maypole in Merrymount and dancing and fornicating with the Indian women, epitomize and symbolize the continuous American conflict between work and play. If you are adopting Thomas Morton as an ancestor, you're going to have to make up your mind who was right about what kind of man he really was.

Adams, C. F. *Three Episodes in Massachusetts History.* New York: Russell and Russell, 1965 (originally published in 1892). Written nearly one hundred years ago by one of the original Adams descendants, this book (available in most libraries) gives a detailed study of Thomas Morton. Amazingly Adams had a twinkle in his eye when he wrote about Morton.

Bradford, William. *History of Plymouth Plantation.* Available in many different editions. After you've read Martin's account of the doings at Merrymount, you should compare them with Bradford's.

Benet, Stephen. *Western Star.* New York: Farrar and Rinehart, 1943. Benet describes Morton as a man who loved his country: "The one man with a sense of humor in all New England."

Childs, Lydia. *Hobomok.* Boston: Cummings and Hilliard Co., 1824. This is a novel that depicts Morton as inciting the Indians to massacre the Pilgrims using the rifles Morton traded with them for the beaver hides.

Davidson, L. S. *The Disturber.* New York: Macmillan, 1964. A novel that attempts to recreate the complete story of Thomas Morton at Merrymount.

Hanson, Howard, and Stokes, Richard. *Merrymount, An Opera.* Harms Inc., 1933. This opera, which has been performed by the San Antonio Opera Company, is based on Richard Stokes's narrative poem of the same name and depicts Bradford (Morton's persecutor) as tormented by his detested longing for "fair lascivious concubines of Hell / with dewy flanks and honey scented breasts / who tug away the covers, prick my flesh / with hands of fire.

Hawthorne, Nathaniel. *The Maypole at Merrymount*, from the collection of *Twice-Told Tales*, available in many editions. Hawthorne contrasts jollity versus gloom, hedonism versus asceticism, and he mourns that gloom wins out over the vibrancy and gaiety of Merrymount.

Longfellow, Henry W. *Tales of a Wayside Inn*. Boston: Houghton Mifflin, 1922. Henry describes poor Thomas as "roystering Morton of Merrymount / that petti fogger from Furnival's Inn / Lord of Misrule and riot and sin."

Lowell, Robert. *Endicott and the Red Cross*. A collection of three one-act plays in the book *Old Glory*. Farrar, Straus. New York, 1965. Lowell makes Morton a much more complex character in this play, which covers the May Day Celebration at Merrymount and the conflict between Morton and the Pilgrims at Plymouth.

McWilliams, John P. *Fictions of Merry Mount*. Spring 1977, *American Quarterly*, Van Peit Library, 3420 Walnut Street, Philadelphia, PA 19174. A fascinating, detailed essay covering the literary history of Merrymount. If Morton intrigues you, start here. Order direct, $3.00.

Motley, John Lothrup. *Merry Mount: A Romance of Massachusetts Colony*. James Munroe, Boston, 1849. According to Motley "Morton was eloquent, adroit, bold, good humored, and his appetite for money, liquor and women are not lustful or depraved." Obviously, Heman Hyman respects this opinion.

Sedgwick, Catherine. *Hope Leslie* (original edition, 1827). Reprinted by Garrett Press, 1969. A historical novel in which Sedgwick depicts Morton as a "maniac who leaps upon everyone who enters his cell."

Williams, William Carlos. *In the American Grain*. New York: New Directions, 1956. This book contains an essay, "The Maypole at Merry Mount," which depicts Morton as the victim of the Puritans' repressed sexual energy.

Willison, George F. *Saints and Strangers*. New York: Reynal Hitchcock, 1945. All sides in the Bradford-Morton-Standish feud are presented in a well-written history.

Playing with Mail Order

Consumer Mail-Order Industry Estimates. Maxwell Sroge Company, Inc., P.O. Box 11031, Chicago, IL 60611. Price $37.50. If the mail-order business intrigues you, this complete survey will fill you in on the financial details.

Direct-Mail Advertising Association, 6 East 43rd Street, New York, NY 10017. While Byrdwhistle isn't listed *yet*, this association, the biggest one in the industry, publishes *The Great Catalogue Guide*. Price $2.00. It's really worth owning. The 1982 edition lists and categorizes 630 companies selling by mail and gives their leading items and their addresses. With this guide you can get on hundreds of mailing lists.

Horchow, Roger. *Elephants in Your Mailbox: How I Learned the Secrets of Mail-Order Marketing Despite Having Made 25 Horrendous Mistakes*. New York: Times Books, 1980. The fascinating thing about men who have made it in the mail-order business is their compulsion to write their autobiographies and tell everyone how they did it. Roger's book is a homey and down-to-earth story of his purchase of the Kenton Collection, a money-losing subsidiary of Rapid American Corp., for $1 million from Meshulam Riklis, after which it became the Horchow Collection. Roger Horchow is a mail-order operator who thinks like H. H. Youman. Good reading for entrepreneurs, from a man who tells in detail how he built one of the top companies in the mail-order business.

Joffe, Gerado. *How You Can Make at Least $1 Million Dollars in the Mail-Order Business.* New York: Harper & Row, 1980. Joffe is a president of a mail-order business. If you follow his advice and make a million, do it Byrdwhistle-style — playing!

Lovin' Distributors, Box RIM, 9117 Airdrome Street, Los Angeles, CA 90035. The chief factotum of this mail-order company is Pat Fischer, a Byrdwhistle-style lady. Her motto is, "We manufacture and distribute anything for loving." Among their products are packages called "The Act of Love," and "The Taste of Love," massage oils flavored with almond, musk, lemon grass, sandal-wood, tangerine, patchouli, cinnamon, honey spice, and various vanilla and chocolate concoctions that you can taste! "The Shade of Love" painting kit for joyous body-painting is approved by Byrdwhistle and sold by Love You Cosmetics therapists.

Marcus, Stanley. *The Quest for the Best.* New York: Viking, 1979. While Nieman Marcus doesn't depend on mail-order for their existence, they are among the most sophisticated in the field. Stanley, a former chairman, doesn't know Heman Hyman, but H.H. loves him.

National Mail-Order Association, 5818 Venice Blvd., Los Angeles, CA 90019. An interesting rallying point for the novitiate mail-order operator. The big boys have several of these associations of their own.

Sugarman, Joseph. *Blow Your Kneecaps Off.* JS & A National Sales, JS & A Plaza, Northbrook, IL 60062. Price $1.50. This is the booklet Marge Slick told Ronald Coldaxe he should read. The story of a mail-order man's continual rebellion against not only the Federal Trade Commission but bureaucracy in general.

Sugarman, Joseph. *Success Forces.* Chicago: Contemporary Books, 1980. Joe Sugarman is a laughing man — when he isn't angry with Uncle Sam and the Federal Trade Commission. His biography proves that the real secret to any success is an ability to bounce back from failure and persist. You can buy it for $10 from JS & A.

The Unusual By Mail Catalogue. St. Martin's Press, 175 Fifth Ave., New York, NY 10010. Order direct, $7.95. Everything hard to find or exotic from 150 mail-order sources.

The Wholesale By Mail Catalogue. St. Martin's Press, 175 Fifth Ave., New York, NY 10010. A detailed list of 350 mail-order companies offering all kinds of merchandise at substantial discounts.

TWENTY-SIX GOLDEN NUGGETS
FROM ONEIDA COMMUNITY CIRCULARS
FOR BYRDWHISTLE EMPLOYEES

1. *From the First Annual Report of the Oneida Association, January 1, 1849*

Dividing the sexual relation into two branches, the amative and the propagative, the amative or love relation is first in order of importance. God made women because "he saw it was *not* good for man to be alone" (Gen. 2:18), i.e., [he made woman] for social not primarily propagative purposes . . . How can the benefits of amativeness be increased and the expenses of propagation be reduced to such limits as life can afford? A satisfactory solution of this grand problem must propose a method that can be shown to be natural and healthy for both sexes, and effectual in its control of propagation. We insist that the amative function — that which consists of a simple union of persons making "twain of one flesh" and giving a medium of magnetic and spiritual interchange — is a distinct and independent function.

2. *From the Circular, Brooklyn, N.Y., November 30, 1851*

We tell each other plainly and kindly our thoughts about each other in various ways. Sometimes the whole Association criticizes a member in meeting. Sometimes it is done privately by committees, and sometimes by individuals. In some cases criticism is directed to general character, and in others to special faults and offences. It is well understood that the moral health of the Association depends on the freest circulation of this plainness of speech; and all are ambitious to balance the accounts in this way as often as possible . . .

We believe that all systems of property getting in this world are vulgarly called the "grab game," i.e., the game in which the prizes are not distributed by any rule of justice, but are seized by the strongest and craftiest; and the laws of the world simply give rules, more or less civilized, for the conduct of this game . . .

Members of the Association, as fast as they become intelligent, come to regard the whole Association as one family and all children are children of the family. The care of the children, after the period of nursing, is committed to those who have the best talent and the most taste for the business, so parents are made free for other avocations . . .

3. *From the Circular, December 11, 1852*

Our views for a fair view of the millennium: Abandonment of the entire fashion of the world, including marriage and involuntary propagation . . . cultivation of universal love . . . and dwelling together in Association of Complex Families.

4. *From the Circular, October 8, 1853*

We feel roused to new earnestness to favor the *mingling of sexes* in *labor*. We find that the spirit of the world is deadly opposed to this innovation, and would make it very easy to slip back into the old routine of separate employments for men and women . . . We believe that the great secret of securing enthusiasm in labor and producing a free, healthy, social equilibrium is contained in the proposition "loving companionship and labor, and especially the mingling of sexes makes labor attractive."

5. *From the Circular, August 12, 1854*

The plan is founded on the simple proposition to substitute the family relation for the system of hiring . . . in other words let every distinct form of business which employs a number of workmen be the gathering point of a family sufficient to man the business . . . Let the employer, whatever his line of business, *live* with his men (and women) and make them interested partners instead of holding them by the mere bond of wages.

The material advantages of this condensation would be in part as follows: (1) Opportunity of acquaintance and constant consultation between workmen. (2) Enthusiasm, induced by aggregation and an entire community of interest . . .

The educational . . . advantages of this plan would be manifold. Every important business would be the gathering point of an extensive family. (3) That family embracing of course persons qualified to instruct, in constant opportunity for meeting in mutual help, would become a school.

6. *From the Circular, July 23, 1857*

Two spheres of activity are open to man: one is outward and from himself upon the material world, the other is inward and towards himself . . . Every man is naturally more biased toward one of these spheres than to the other. If he follows the first bias, he becomes the simple worker and man of enterprise; if he follows the second, he becomes a man of culture—poet and musician, and lover of general literature. The former becomes rich in all material and outward results, but poor in himself. The latter becomes rich in himself but deficient in all acquirements of the former. Both of these men are one-sided—distorted, even positively weak . . . Accordingly any undue preponderance of one bias over the other is soon felt by the body, and promptly regulated by our system of criticism.

7. *From the Circular, April 29, 1958*

I have had many thoughts . . . upon the subject of old age in connection with our victory over death . . . Old age is insidious, underhanded—steals upon all alike constantly, and by imperceptible degrees . . . The thought occurred to me whether we could not create an opposite atmosphere—one which would resist and repel the advances of old age and make it more easy to *grow youthful* than to grow old and infirm. Can we not by our combined faith generate an element which will reverse the process and make it difficult to lose our youth?

8. *From the Circular, July 15, 1858*

It is better that things remain as they are, partially disorganized, than that we should come into a legal cramped . . . kind of order. The *law of love* among us is to take the place of legality and forced restraint.

9. *From the Circular, January 20, 1859*

To many people . . . suppleness of the will in small matters looks like the loss of individuality—a sort of death: in reality, it is found to be no such thing. What better index to the inborn nobleness of a person's character, or the reverse, than to know in what sphere he uses his will. If he is obstinate about small things, you are tempted to mark him as a man who takes a pin-hole view of the universe.

10. *From the Circular, June 14, 1860*

Those amusements in which the greatest number can join which are not restricted to the young, or to one sex, and which best promote universal fellowship, are superior to those games which are limited and which excite antagonism and rivalry. In this view dancing is superior to ball playing . . . and should be most cultivated.

11. *From the Circular, March 26, 1863*

Mrs. R. is a kind-hearted, friendly woman . . . She seems very desirous that others should love her—thinks it very desirable to be loved—which is true enough—but she does not sufficiently appreciate the profound blessedness of simply *loving*, whether she is loved in return or not . . . It is a good thing to be loved; it is better to *dwell* in love and love for love's sake only.

12. *From the Circular, April 25, 1864*

It is a point of belief with us that, when one keeps constantly in the same rut, he is especially exposed to the attacks of evil—the devil knows where to find him; but inspiration will continually lead us into new channels by which we shall dodge the adversary.

13. *From the Circular, August 1, 1864*

The Community was not born to fortune, and we have worked heartily through our narrow circumstances; but are fast growing into circumstances of ease and leisure. If we do work, we are comparatively without care in consequence of the division of responsibility which our system affords, and we average less hours than the industrious classes in the world. We don't have to work; that is, one has the same chance to be lazy as members of any common family have.

14. *From the Circular, August 8, 1864*

Our breakfast is ready at six, to be sure, and those whose business makes it more convenient or whose taste inclines them to be up with the sun can sit down at that time; but the breakfast lasts until half-past seven. The waiters are assiduous until then, and the loiterers after that, though they have to wait on themselves, find breakfast without too much trouble.

15. *From the Circular, February 6, 1865*

In respects to these points of difference between marriage and whoredom, *we stand with marriage*. Free love with us does not mean freedom to love today and leave tomorrow; or freedom to take a woman's person and keep our property to

ourselves; or freedom to freight a woman with our offspring and send her down-
stream without care or help . . . We are not "free lovers" in any sense that makes
love less binding or responsible than it is in marriage.

16. *From the Circular, August 7, 1865*

In ordinary society the family is one thing and the church is another . . . but here
the church is the family, and the family is the church, and the child that is born
into the family is born into the church.

17. *From the Circular, August 14, 1865*

In order to keep your spirits bright, in order to maintain a spirit of ripe vivacity,
you must be just as busy with great purpose of heroic accomplishment as you
were at 22 . . . You must measure and judge your spirit by this test: If you are
saying to yourself "Well, I cannot accomplish anything for I shall not live but a
little while; I am getting old — my best days are gone, great purposes are for the
young, and I have got by them." If that is the way you are talking you are surren-
dering to old age and the devil. The way you should talk is "I am 22 years old now
and never shall be any older . . . my heart is as open to great plans as it ever was.
The idea that I have seen my best days come to their end is all humbug.

18. *From the Daily Journal, January 3, 1867*

Money in one sense is like blood in the body . . . I am not very much a physiol-
ogist; but I believe the blood is mainly manufactured by the stomach. I don't
think that it is God's purpose to make us immensely rich in the sense that many
men and companies are in the world. It seems to me that individuals and corporations when they amass property that does not play an important part in their
business, and in moral influence on society, are like persons who are getting a big,
overgrown belly. Now, a man does not want to carry around a larger belly than
is necessary . . . I like to be in good condition and see others so and . . . to see the
community grow strong, but I don't believe that it is God's purpose to have us
become pot-bellied.

19. *From the Circular, August 2, 1869*

Among the many advantages arising from the Association is the opportunity we
find of frequently changing employments. Such an advantage not only relieves
the hardship of following an occupation after the taste for it has ceased, but gives
a freshness to every department that facilitates progress and opens the way for
inspiration. To many it may seem a waste of talent for a machinist to be looking
after milk, a carpenter to work in the kitchen, or a mechanic to pare potatoes, but
experience proves that such talent carries improvement where they would scarcely
reach if this department were exclusively the province of women. A first-class
joiner who worked in our kitchen invented a mop-wringer . . . he also introduced a system of washing potatoes by means of a circular cage revolving in
water, and now a young mechanic from the trap-shop has conceived that potatoes
may be rid of their jackets on the same principle that we "tom" the rust from iron.

20. *From the Circular, March 21, 1870*

Our theory is equal rights of women and men and the freedom of both from habitual and legal obligations to personal fellowship. It is the theory that love *after* marriage, and always and forever, should be what it is *before* marriage—a glowing attraction on both sides and not the odious obligation of one party and the sensual recklessness of the other.

21. *From the Circular, July 10, 1871*

The kinds of men and women who are likely to make Communities grow spiritually and financially are scarce, and have to be sifted out slowly and cautiously. It should be distinctly understood that these Communities are not asylums for pleasure seekers or persons who merely want a home and a living.

22. *From the Circular, November 20, 1871*

We do not think . . . that our minds should all run in the same groove or our souls be all cut after the same pattern any more than you should dress in the same uniform or have the same colored hair or eyes. No, indeed! The more complex you get your unit, the more varied its component parts will be.

23. *From the Circular, October 28, 1872*

Medical men say that eating three meals a day is a habit not a natural instinct, and that it has been conclusively proved that better digestion, better assimilation, better sleep, and brighter faculties are the rewards of those who limit themselves to two meals . . . Habit is a tyrant, and it is good to rebel from it from time to time . . . We have a notion that it is possible to really hoodwink the devil when he thinks he has got you started on some track, where he will be sure to find you all the time, by suddenly switching off and making him lose scent.

24. *From the Circular, November 17, 1873*

We aver that intercourse between the sexes . . . is open to criticism and controlled by the good sense of the entire body instead of being left as it is in marriage to the mercy of each man's passion, dealing with woman in single-handed and irresponsible privacy. We aver that intercourse of the sexes is next to religion . . . that intercourse of the sexes is restricted by voice and heart of all to entire abstinence from the propagative act.

25. *From the Circular, March 23, 1874*

I judge that about six hours labor is as much as anyone ought to do on hygienic principles. My impression is that about six hours continuous labor is enough for anybody. Labor reformers talk about eight hours, but I would reduce the working hours to six, and have them come between eight o'clock and three, or between breakfast and dinner, and give the rest of the time to study and recreation.

26. *From the Circular, December 13, 1875*

There are great businessmen here who are engaged in great enterprises, but there is danger in losing sight of the idea that the object of business is *education* and instead taking up the idea of the world that the object of business is money . . . We start in business under inspiration and with objects that are pure and true, perhaps, but the spirit of the world broods over us and about us . . . turning our attention to the object of making money; to the external objective result instead of the subjective, which is education and development.